How to Not Fall in Love: A Close-Door Romantic Comedy Complete Series

Interior Design by Mountain Heights Publishing

Author website: www.megeaston.com

Nestled Hollow Romance

Coming Home to the Top of Main Street

Second Chance on the Corner of Main Street

Christmas at the End of Main Street

More than Friends in the Middle of Main Street

Love Again at the Heart of Main Street

More than Enemies on the Bridge of Main Street

———

Love Started romances

It Started with a Sunset

It Started with a Note

It Started with a Glance

———

Silver Leaf Falls romance

Coming Home to Silver Leaf Falls

HOW TO NOT FALL IN LOVE

A 4-book romantic comedy collection

HOW TO NOT FALL IN LOVE

USA Today Bestselling Author

MEG EASTON

Contents

VOLUME 2

VOLUME 3

VOLUME 4

VOLUME

One

HOW TO NOT FALL for the GUY NEXT DOOR

CHAPTER 1

Addison

I TURN my car into the parking lot of Gateway Groceries in Quicksand, Oregon, and then pull into a stall before calling my sister. Just like every time I've talked to her over the past three days, I can hear her concern just from the breath she takes in. Before she can even say, "Hello?" I say, "I didn't die."

Chloe squeals. "So you're home, then?"

Home. It feels weird to call Quicksand "home." I spent my summers from ages ten to thirteen here, but that hadn't made it "home" any more than playing Barbie Dreamhouse meant I was married to Ken. Amarillo is home. Quicksand was always temporary. An exciting game of dress-up. I wonder how long it'll take before calling this place *home* won't seem weird.

"I'm in Quicksand, but not at the inn. The moving truck is forty-five minutes behind me, so I'm stopping at the grocery store." My stomach is growling almost as loudly as my radio was playing, so getting food is essential.

Chloe lets out a relieved breath. "Oh, I'm so glad you made it safely."

"I told you I could make it sixteen hundred miles across six states on my own. See? You should leave the worrying to the older sister. I'm better at it anyway."

I grab my purse and get out of my car as my sister laughs. Then I take in a long, deep breath of air I haven't smelled in over thirteen years. It's fresh, like trees and rich soil, both of which are currently wet from a recent rainstorm. The air itself feels wet, actually. Maybe because there are so many trees here, all with moss-covered trunks. Trees and blackberry bushes.

I shake out my legs and stretch my back before I start walking toward the building. Spending twenty-five hours in a car, six of them this morning, really did a number on my muscles.

"Speaking of worrying," I say, "I still feel awful that I left a week before you move out of the freaking country. Do you need me to fly back to make sure you get off okay?"

"Nope. Dustin and I have everything under control. *You stay there.*" Each word is a punch. A hammer on a nail to hold me firmly in Quicksand. "I didn't make your website and ads for you to miss your first clients."

"You're so bossy."

I hear Chloe's grin through the phone. "I learned from the best. Now, go grab that fresh start by the horns and show it who's boss!"

"Yes, ma'am!"

"And then call me after the movers leave."

"I will."

I push the phone into my purse, take a deep breath, and walk through the automatic front doors of Gateway Groceries. Packing up everything I own, saying goodbye to the city where I've lived my entire life, leaving the sister I've never lived more than a five-minute drive from, and moving halfway across the country to a place where I know exactly zero people is fine. I am fine. Everything is fine.

Piece of cake.

As I wander aimlessly up and down the aisles with no plan, I realize I probably should've spent less time on the drive jamming out to the radio, playing the license plate game solo, and trying to distract myself from thoughts of Matthew, my old job, my hometown, and everything I left behind, and more time coming up with a grocery list. I have no idea what food is at the inn if there is anything at all. For the past four years, my Aunt Helen hadn't used the property as an inn—she lived there with her nurse like it was just a big house. And for the past three months since she passed away, no one has lived there at all.

So there could be things like spices, flour, sugar, coffee, and maybe even some food in the freezer. Or there could be nothing —I have no idea if anyone packed anything up at all. It's a mystery. And mysteries are fun, right? I mean, it's what I spent two years trying to convince Matthew of. This would probably drive him nuts, all the not knowing. But things between us are over, so I am going to relish every single mystery that he would've hated.

I change my mind about shopping for staples before checking out the inn, and instead, I decide the best plan is to get some fresh fruits and vegetables and maybe soup I can easily warm up. With only a few things in my cart from my meandering trip through the store, I turn toward the produce area.

The deli faces the produce section, and as the older man behind the counter finishes up with a customer, he turns his attention my way, studying me. Against his olive skin, his white eyebrows stand out, looking rather judgy as they come together over his curious eyes. At a population of ten thousand, Quicksand isn't exactly small-town-ish enough for everyone to know everyone, so I must have an *I'm new here* look about me. Maybe he's trying to figure out if I am just visiting or putting down roots.

He has pretty keen eyes, too. Maybe he's seeing me deeply enough to notice that under the surface, I have a panicked *my life was recently planned out, perfect, and organized and is now a big mess of uncertainty and chaos* look about me.

I give him a little smile and shift my eyes to his case of hot food, hoping he'll do the same. My stomach rumbles again at seeing the food. It's been too many hours since I grabbed that muffin and orange juice from my hotel back in Boise. Maybe I should forget the microwaveable soup and go up to the man and get some fried chicken, or a burrito, or some potato wedges. It isn't what my body is begging me for, but it's some-thing I can eat in the car on my way to the inn, and right now, my body is saying that the speed at which I get food in my belly matters.

After I get produce. I turn away from the warm, fried foods and aim my cart's trajectory toward the apples.

Before long, I have a cart full of enough fruits and vegeta-bles of differing colors that my Aunt Helen would've been proud. They say you shouldn't go grocery shopping while hungry. But maybe going when you're ravenous after having just spent two and a half days in a car while eating nothing but junk food is the absolute best time to go if you want a cart full of healthy stuff.

The fruit aisle has a few other shoppers in it, so I leave my cart at the end of the aisle and make my way down it. Blueber-ries! That's exactly what my body needs. I pick up a few of the plastic cases, inspecting them closely to find the freshest ones. Two containers are perfect enough that my mouth starts water-ing. I have got to finish this shopping trip quickly so I can gobble up at least one of the containers. I spin toward my cart, a container of blueberries in each hand, and smack right into a man's very firm chest.

I yelp as we collide, and several nearby customers leap back as the flimsy plastic containers burst open, sending blueberries flying like soda from a shaken can, hitting the laminate floor with dozens of the softest pings, followed by the only slightly louder sounds of the two plastic containers making their landing on the floor.

"Oh no. I am so sorry." My face flames and I quickly brush at the bluish-purple spots that a few of the more aggressive blueberries left on the man's light blue t-shirt, as if a few swipes of my fingers will make the stains disappear.

"It's okay." The man gently moves my frantic hands away from his shirt. Probably because he's a little uncomfortable with having them all over his chest. "It's not a big deal. Really. I don't even like this shirt."

The man's voice is deep and rumbly, like summer thunder on the beach. I finally look up to meet his eyes and blush even more at seeing that his face is even nicer than his considerably nice chest. And his stunning blue eyes, which definitely look like his shirt should get a medal for what they do for them, aren't angry or irritated or frustrated—they are amused.

Amused is good. It isn't *good* good, but on a scale of one to thoroughly embarrassed at the grocery store, I'll take being the source of someone's amusement over being the source of someone's anger or frustration.

"Cleanup in produce," sounds over the intercom, and I look over at the very unimpressed man at the deli who now has one white eyebrow raised in an *I knew you'd be trouble* arc.

I force myself to breathe. Then I clear my throat and crouch, pick up one of the fallen plastic containers, and start putting blueberries back into it. The man crouches, too, which puts us in very close proximity especially since we can't exactly take a single step in any direction without squashing blueberries.

It takes several fast heartbeats before I steal another glance at him. I'd been so distracted by his eyes before that I hadn't noticed his beautifully strong jawline or the way that, when relaxed and in their natural state, the muscles of his face show that they spend a good portion of their time smiling.

And there's something about him that's familiar. I'm about to ask him if we've met before, but then a gangly teenage boy comes over with a broom and a dustpan and says he'll finish cleaning up the mess. As I carefully tiptoe away from ground zero and toward safety, I decide against asking the man. Mainly because I don't want to do anything else that might make me more memorable to him or anyone else right now. And besides, I know absolutely no one in this town, so just because he has a familiarity about him doesn't mean I know him.

The man steps to the edge of the fallen blueberries and reaches across the strawberries and blackberries to grab two more containers of blueberries. Then he hands them to me and says, "It looks like we both survived the Great Blueberry Explosion. Congratulations."

"You, too." I carefully add them to my cart so I don't accidentally bump one of the lids and make it pop open. "But I am sorry that we didn't all make it. If you would like me to say any words at the funeral of your shirt, let me know."

He chuckles. "Are you visiting?"

"Just moving in," I say, then in a panic, I glance at my watch. I somehow completely forgot that I don't have all the time in the world. "I've got to run. I'm supposed to meet the moving truck at the inn in ten minutes."

This time when he gives me that amused expression, I notice the smile that came with it. A smile that could melt the snow on Mount Hood. "I'll see you around, then."

"And next time," I call out as I hurry toward the checkout lines, "I promise not to be armed with blueberries."

I'm back in my car and trying to somehow magically get to the inn more quickly—without speeding—when the embarrassment hits me again. I wasn't even in my new city for thirty minutes before making a fool of myself. It isn't exactly the stellar start I'd been hoping for.

But embarrassing or not, I smile when I think back on how our interaction ended. Those last few comments I made could probably be considered flirting. I, Addison Sparks, had actually flirted with a very cute man. I am pretty proud of myself. Matthew and I had been together for more than two years, and we were long past our days of flirting with each other. And since our breakup, I've been mourning the loss of the future I thought I'd have with him, which made me not exactly feel like flirting. Honestly, I wasn't even sure I remembered how to flirt.

Today feels like progress. I kind of wish Matthew had witnessed it.

Not that I'm likely to ever again see the man I inadvertently attacked with blueberries. I went to my neighborhood grocery store back in Amarillo all the time for years, and I rarely bumped into people I knew, so I know that chances are small that I'll see him again. But it was nice flirting with him because it made me realize that one day I'll eventually want a relationship again, even if I don't want one now. And I'm glad the man will stay a stranger. I prefer first interactions to not involve ruining a man's shirt and then accidentally putting my hands all over his chest.

My face flushes again at the memory, so I try to focus on the road. I haven't stayed the summer at the inn with my aunt since I was thirteen, but I can still make my way to the inn on autopilot while scarfing down a protein bar that I picked up at the grocery checkout. And the scenery here easily grabs my attention. Amarillo doesn't have these tree-lined streets, and there's some bucket in me—I'm not sure what—that gets filled by driving in an area where the trees aren't just along the streets but seem to crowd in everywhere, only willing to pull back a bit for the homes and businesses around.

Coming to this place as a kid feels like a lifetime ago. So much so that during the two years Matthew and I dated, I never once told him about it. It feels weird to be in a place he knew nothing about. I wonder how he's doing back in his scheduled, predictable life while mine is in such new territory.

I somehow manage to arrive at the inn before the moving truck and pull into one of the eight spots in the small parking lot on the side, leaving the curving driveway in front open for the truck. After unlocking the front door, I walk back out to the edge of the road and stand next to the *Hidden Inn* sign so I can flag down the truck.

The sign that used to make my stomach leap in excitement as a girl now makes my heart palpitate and my muscles twitch. I wasn't at the reading of Aunt Helen's will, and I'd been unable to even form words when I first found out my aunt wanted me to have Hidden Inn. I added the inability to stand on my own two feet to the speechlessness once I found out my aunt said it was because "Addison will know what to do with it."

Some of my favorite childhood memories are of staying at the Hidden Inn, with my aunt treating me like I was an adult living in my own place. I spent many days there dreaming of the time when I'd be a strong, independent businesswoman in a power suit, living on my own.

I *never* dreamed of one day running the inn. Not even for a teeny tiny second. Why my aunt thought I'd know what to do with this place is beyond me. My parents were fairly absent when I was a kid, and the moment Chloe and I became adults, they moved to Florida. With their absence most of my life, I've craved family. And running an inn where I'd always be spending time with strangers doesn't sound appealing in the least. It wasn't until Chloe suggested that I run it as an apartment instead of as an inn that moving here felt right.

But *is* it right? Can a girl who's never lived more than five miles from her childhood home—and never more than two miles from her sister—make it in a new city by herself?

As I stand at the edge of the road, looking at the inn that I'm now responsible for, I'm not so sure. Yes, the building is paid for, but I've done the math, and for utilities, property taxes, taking care of the grounds, repairs, and a million other little costs that came to me one night at three a.m., I'll need roommates in at least three of the five bedrooms in the inn. Where am I going to find three roommates in a city where I know zero people?

My heart rate multiplies as I see the moving truck in the distance, lumbering its way toward me.

Then I remember reading that the only difference between nervousness and excitement is breathing. If you hold your breath, your body assumes you're nervous. If you breathe through it, it assumes excitement.

So I breathe. As the truck nears and then turns into the curved drive of the inn, the excitement builds.

And then the truck runs over one of the shrubs lining the driveway, squashing it completely flat. The driver rolls down the window and calls toward me, "Sorry 'bout that!"

I breathe. Only excitement here. Nothing else to see.

I direct the movers to the three rooms my furniture and boxes need to go in—the kitchen with its big dining table and half a dozen breakfast tables, the gathering room that will be my family room, and my bedroom. The one Aunt Helen saved for me every summer for four years straight. The one that still makes me giddy as an adult every time I think of it. Then I head back outside to help bring in the boxes. I make it exactly one step from the house onto the wraparound porch before I freeze mid-step.

The man from the grocery store is standing near the back of the moving truck, wearing a dark gray shirt now, which is probably a smart choice if he's going to risk being around me and a moving truck. And, surprisingly, his eyes look even bluer than they did when he was wearing the blue shirt. Maybe it's just the Oregon sun working in his favor.

But what is he doing here? And how did he know this was where I was meeting the moving truck? The memory of smacking into him with the blueberries and sending them flying is admittedly a stronger memory than every little thing I might've said in my flustered state, but I'm pretty sure I didn't give him my address or any other location clues.

My shock at seeing him must last a second too long because that amused smile plays on his face again. He jumps out of the back of the truck, walks to the bottom of my porch stairs, and holds out his hand. I make myself remember how to use my legs again and walk forward, take the three steps down from my porch, and hold out my hand. He shakes it and says, "Hi again. Neighbor."

Neighbor? My eyes flash to the left—at the fancy wrought iron gate in the middle of a hedgerow that leads to a neighbor's house. And suddenly I realize why the man had looked familiar.

No, no, no. I can't be next-door neighbors with a guy I just embarrassed myself in front of at the grocery store. A guy who I was instantly attracted to, even while still getting over my ex.

And definitely not Ian Kendrick, the guy I had my very first crush on.

"You're looking good, Addi."

"Addison."

"What's it been? A dozen years?" He walks up the ramp of the moving truck, pausing to look back at what is surely a bewildered expression on my face.

"Thirteen. Did you recognize me at the grocery store?"

"Not until you said you had to meet the moving truck at the inn. Then I pieced it together." He disappears into the moving truck just as one of the movers comes out of my house.

I guess I did mention a location clue after all. "Why didn't you say anything?"

Ian emerges from the truck a moment later carrying one of my boxes and shrugs. "I thought this would be more fun."

I glance at the box he's holding. In the upper left corner, nicely printed on a label, are the words "Label collection." Yes, I like using labels. Yes, I like collecting labels. And not just labels —half the boxes filling the moving truck are empty organization containers of every size. Yes, I know from living in this world that most people think my obsession is weird. Ian already experienced blueberries with the adult version of his childhood friend. I don't need his second experience with me to be finding out this detail.

I'll just offer to take the box from him before he notices what it is. I rush down the stairs and toward the truck as he walks down the ramp with the box. My foot catches on the rock border at the edge of the curved driveway, and I lunge forward just as Ian steps off the side of the ramp, knocking us into each other.

Which, honestly, wouldn't be awful if he weren't holding the box. But the pressure of us crushing the cardboard box between us changes its shape just enough to pry the bottom flaps free from the packing tape and it flies open, dumping all of my labels of every size and shape, along with half a dozen different types of label makers, all over the driveway. And it happens just as one mover steps out of the truck and the other steps out of my house.

Ian and I both freeze, looking down at the contents of the box. Then he meets my eyes. "Do you always crush random containers between you and nearby men, or is it just me?"

"It's just you, Ian. Only you." Maybe I should just get in my trusty Camry and head back to Amarillo right now.

CHAPTER 2

Ian

I'VE SPENT the last several hours in the shop in my backyard, doing all the saw cuts, sanding, and pre-building I can on a massive built-in fireplace mantle, entertainment center, and bookshelves that will span an entire wall in the home I'm contracted to do the woodwork in.

As I run the piece across the belt sander, I look out the window and smile when I see Addi and one of her roommates talking in her backyard. She crouches down and runs her fingers across the top of the cut grass, seeming confused as to how it's freshly mowed when she hasn't done it. Sometime soon, I'll have to tell her that I'm still taking care of the inn's grounds, just like I did every summer growing up and like I've done for the last year and a half since I bought my grandparents' home.

I didn't actually recognize Addi when we had our rather explosive first meeting at the grocery store. It wasn't until she was at the registers that I placed where I'd last seen the adventurous gleam in her golden-green eyes or the familiar blush on her cheeks. She'd been pressing a flat rock into my palm that she'd painted with a scene of the two of us jumping into Quicksand River and telling me that she'd see me next summer. Then, while I was looking at the rock, she darted forward and kissed me on the cheek. It surprised me so much that I just stood there like an idiot who'd lost all ability to think or move.

And then she'd run off to get into her Aunt Helen's car, and they drove away to the airport. I was fourteen, so she must've been thirteen. I came back to spend the month of July with my grandparents the next summer, but she wasn't at the inn. Not that summer or any summer after.

I want to ask her about that and to catch up on where life has taken her in the past thirteen years. But when my now ex, Cara, stomped on my heart four weeks ago by calling off our wedding, she'd kind of stomped on my confidence, too, and now I'm questioning everything. So I've been keeping my distance from Addi, but because it's the right thing to do, I've still gone over to the inn to help every time I've seen one of her new roommates moving in during the past couple of weeks. I've discovered that I'm not the only one keeping my distance— Addi has pretty expertly avoided me every time, too.

I should probably just go tell Addi right now that I'm taking care of the yard because I doubt her aunt put it in writing anywhere. Yet, I hesitate. It's a busy season at work, so I have limited time to take care of the inn's grounds during daylight hours. But since Addi's avoiding me, part of me wants to see how long I can keep mowing at times when she's not home, just to keep her guessing.

———

When I get all the boards cut for the built-in, it's well past the time I usually stop for lunch and my stomach is growling louder than a table saw hitting a nail in a board. Since I have to spend the afternoon cutting and installing trim at one of my sites, I close up the shop and head toward the house. I smile as the sounds of laughter from the ladies in my grandma's origami club reach me before I even get to the door. I'm so glad she didn't have to move away from her friends.

As soon as I step through the kitchen door, a chorus of "Ian!" greets me. I smile as all the ladies seated around the table tell me how good it is to see me and how glad they are I'm here during their club.

"You all sure know how to make a guy feel like a rock star when he walks into a room."

"Honey," the white-haired Frances says, "if you ditched the flannel and donned a t-shirt and leather jacket, you'd have adoring groupies following you around wherever you went."

Brenda nods. "Especially with that perfectly mussed hair."

The hair is more a product of the air displacement from the saws and sanders than any actual styling, and I have to keep myself from reaching up and brushing some of the sawdust out of it. Instead, I wash my hands, then pull open the fridge and start pulling out lunch meat, cheese, mayo, mustard, and lettuce.

"I like the flannel," Grandma's longtime friend, Carol, says. "It's what attracted me to my dear Henry. I tell you, it was quite the trick to follow that boy around everywhere and make it seem like he was the one following me around for long enough to get him to propose." She sighs. "I would've followed him anywhere."

I chuckle as I pull a hoagie bun out of the bag and slice it open. The fact that Henry and Grandpa let me into their conversations in the work shed when I was a kid spending my summers here is a big part of why I went into carpentry. I like to imagine the two of them hanging around a band saw in heaven, still telling stories about the good old days.

"I agree about the flannel shirt," Meera says. "And with that face of yours, you could be in one of those sexy calendars filled with men in flannel." She turns back to the ladies around the table. "Don't you think he could be in a calendar, posing with that shirt?"

I smile at their conversation while I spread the mayo on my sandwich, very pointedly trying not to glance in the direction of the table but feeling every pair of eyes on me.

"Definitely," Frances says. "Especially if he posed with the sawdust still on him."

When cheers sound around the table, I'm sure my cheeks redden.

"I like to call that 'man glitter,'" Meera says, and all the ladies laugh even more.

I shoot Grandma a look, but she just shrugs, like she can't do anything about the conversation. She probably could. But she tells me every night what a "beautiful young man" I am, inside and out, and she seems to get that I think she's only saying it because she sees me through the lens of a loving grandma. Right now, she's wearing a look of triumph—one that tells me she's loving not only having her opinion validated but having it serve as proof to me that she's right.

Of course, all these ladies are wearing grandma lenses, too. I've known all of them from spending every summer here as a kid, and I've known all but one of them over the past year and a half that I've lived in Quicksand because of their bi-weekly club meetings. Brenda is the only one of Grandma's friends I haven't known as an adult—she'd moved in with her grand-daughter in Phoenix to help her through cancer treatments around the same time I moved to Quicksand. This is her first club meeting back.

"You've always been such an adorable boy," Brenda says. "I'm surprised that no one has snatched you up yet."

Grandma might not shut down a conversation about my looks, but she's always quick to shut down conversations about my love life—or lack of it—and for that, I'm eternally grateful. I just need to keep stacking meats and cheeses on my sandwich while she does, then give a quick goodbye and head back out of the house, sandwich in hand.

"Do you know who would be perfect for him?" Brenda asks. "Emily Erickson. Don't you think? I was excited to see that she still lives here, and she's such an adorable girl. It's hard to believe that she's still available, too. And she could use a man as helpful and thoughtful as you. But you better act quickly, because I bet it won't take long for someone to come along and sweep her off her feet."

I can tell by the way Brenda's voice changes for that last sentence that she's directing it at me instead of the group, so I glance at the ladies as I put the top bun on my hoagie. Frances's, Carol's, and Meera's eyes are all fixed on their scattered colored paper and the intricate pieces they're folding, but Brenda's are on me. I really don't need the reminder that even though I'd been in love with Cara, I hadn't been a great catch for her in the end. I gather up the meats, cheese, and condiments and start putting them back in the fridge as quickly as possible, the familiar guilt already eating away at me.

Brenda continues on. "Have you met Lauren Pearson? She's Linda's granddaughter, and she's delightful. Oh, and speaking of granddaughters, I have one moving to Quicksand in just over a month! If you've had trouble meeting eligible women since you've been back, I'm sure that between the five of us, we could set you up with quite a few just like that." Brenda snaps her fingers.

I put my sandwich on a paper towel and quickly clean up

the mess of crumbs I've made. Then I wrap the paper towel around the sandwich and hold it in one hand so I can make a quick escape. I stop by the table, though, and wrap my hand around Brenda's papery one, giving it a squeeze. "Thank you, truly, for thinking so highly of me and being willing to set me up on dates with people you respect. But I'm going to have to decline."

"Oh! Are you not single? I thought you were single." I almost pull my hand away, but she grabs hold of my forearm and turns to the other ladies around the table. "Is he not single?"

"I am," I say, then set my sandwich on the table and pat the woman's hand that still grips my arm. "It's not that. But thank you for being willing to set me up."

Brenda lets go of my arm and turns back to the table, so I grab my sandwich.

"Why would he not want to date if he's single?"

Grandma opens her mouth to answer. But before she can say anything, Meera says, "Because he got his heart ripped out 'bout a month ago. Their wedding was supposed to be a couple weekends ago, and he's still a bit broken."

I freeze where I stand.

"What?" Meera says. "It's the truth, right?"

"It's—" Grandma turns her gaze from Meera to me, her eyes clearly asking for forgiveness.

She's my grandma. I know she tells her friends everything —I wouldn't be upset with her in a million years just because Meera stated my reason in such a succinct, yet blunt, fashion. She tends to say everything with facts and force.

"Thank you for explaining for me, Meera. Now if you'll excuse me, ladies, I need to get back to work."

As I'm opening the kitchen door and escaping outside, I hear Carol say, "Don't you just love how polite he is? If anyone deserves love, it's that boy. If I had a grandson like him, I wouldn't be in the predicament I'm in now with my house."

I shake my head as I bite into my sandwich and walk toward my truck. Every once in a while, I wish I could put on a pair of grandma lenses and look at myself in the mirror to see the perfection they see.

CHAPTER 3

Addison

I PULL into a parking space at the Oregon Trail Drugstore, turn off the ignition, and slump back in my seat. Rain has been drizzling on and off all day, and the lack of sunshine for days on end is getting to me. I wonder what Matthew is doing back in Amarillo and grab my phone to pull him up on social media.

Then I stop myself. This isn't what I want—he's in my head only because of habit.

What I really want to do right now is curl up on the couch with a mug of hot chocolate and an episode of *Organize My Space*. Or even better, haul my tired bones up the stairs, pretend I don't know it's barely six p.m., collapse into bed, and sleep until morning. And not just tomorrow morning—Thursday of next week sounds nice. With the dark clouds overhead, I could probably convince myself it's night.

But as nice as that plan sounds, I have another life goal, and that's to not stink. Since I used the last of my deodorant this morning, a drugstore visit it is. I sit up straight, put my shoulders back, pull down the visor, and slide the cover so I can see the mirror. My hair and makeup look as bedraggled as I feel, so

I remove my ponytail band, run my fingers through my curls, pull my hair back into a ponytail, and put the band back on. It doesn't help much, but it's something.

I run my hands over my face, hoping to make it feel more awake, and I smile the biggest, happiest smile I can make and hold it until I feel it.

Then I force myself to say, out loud, good things that have happened to me in the past week. My rules are that the list can only contain good things, no buts allowed, and can't include anything I should've done but haven't.

"I went from having zero roommates to having three," I say. "*Me.* The girl who knew no one found three people who wanted to move into the inn with me. Girl, you are so phenomenally impressive that you even impress yourself."

And, amazingly enough, all four of us have really clicked. I hadn't had the first idea how to even go about finding roommates. Then, I happened to see a flier on the bulletin board at Gateway Groceries about a creative women entrepreneurs seminar that was taking place in two days. Since I was new at not only living in this city, living away from my sister, being single, and owning the inn but also running my own business for the first time ever, I decided to go.

And then imposter syndrome hit hard and I decided not to go.

Then, the morning of the seminar, I must've had an extra dose of confidence because I changed my mind again and went. For one part, they put us in brainstorming groups, and my group had only women with home-based businesses. Of the eight other women, three were not only single but talked about the struggles of running a business while living in cramped quarters. I told them about the inn and *bam*! I had the three roommates I needed to cover the costs of the inn.

And to think that I almost didn't go.

Okay, that happened a few weeks ago, so I can't claim it in this week's wins, but I still give myself a literal pat on the back again for that one.

Then I chuckle at myself and then continue. "You are going to have your third weekly roommate dinner tonight, and it isn't your turn to cook." Hallelujah for that one. With as busy as my last week has been, if I had been in charge of the meal tonight, the four of us probably would've had to eat peanut butter and jelly sandwiches.

"You finished your first client home organization jobs of your brand-spankin' new business and survived." Even though one of them wanted four rooms organized, including their jewelry-making supplies. Organizing the thousands of beads ranks right up there with finding roommates.

Surviving the first few weeks felt huge. I had no idea how exhausting running my own business would be when I first decided it was my plan.

"Okay, one more." I drum my fingers on the steering wheel, thinking, and then a big smile spreads across my face. "And you successfully managed to avoid Ian Kendrick for a full four weeks." I made a fool of myself the last time I saw him when I was thirteen, and twice the very first day I saw him at twenty-six. The amount of potential embarrassment I've saved myself by avoiding him over twenty-eight days is probably astronomical.

"Nice work," I say out loud, and I feel it. Between smiling at myself and saying out loud awesome things that have happened, it's the "Give me energy, quick!" trick that works for me every single time.

I even manage to have a spring in my step as I swing my purse over my shoulder and race into the drugstore, and it's only partially because the drizzle has turned to actual rain and probably made my curls even crazier. But I find my favorite brand of deodorant, which I wasn't sure they'd have in Quicksand at all, and I toss it into my basket. Life is good.

I don't really need to buy anything else, but those bins at the back of the store are calling my name. Maybe I'll find something fun I can give to each of my new roommates.

There are other people in the store, browsing, and I manage to not pay attention to any of them. But somehow, even though I barely spot a fellow shopper at the edge of my periphery, my eyes still go to the head I can see over the top of an aisle on the far side of the store. The guy's back is to me, and as I look at the thick, dark hair with the perfect amount of wave that makes me want to run my fingers through it, I whisper, "Please don't be Ian. Please don't be Ian."

And then the man must find what he was looking for on that aisle because he turns and starts walking toward the back of the store. It's definitely Ian. And from what I can tell, the big bins at the back aisle of the store have drawn his attention, too. I glance around frantically, looking for an escape route. None of the aisles are high enough to hide me. If I dart down one, crouch to look at something, and he miraculously doesn't happen to walk down that same aisle to go to the registers, he'll still see me from the registers.

So I do the only thing I can—I crouch where I stand, which puts one of the giant bins between Ian and me. Hopefully, he didn't see me before my disappearing act. Now, all I have to do is wait for him to finish looking at whatever has drawn his attention, cross my fingers, toes, and anything else crossable, and hope he doesn't decide to wander to the bin of fuzzy socks I'm hiding behind.

I glance down the aisle I'm completely exposed to and see the teen behind the register at the other end of the store watching me with an eyebrow raised. I give him a pained smile that probably looks more like a grimace. Holding my breath so

I can hear better, I strain my ears to catch any footsteps nearing over the sound of Kelly Clarkson's *Catch My Breath* coming from the speakers. Ironic.

No footsteps. Only the sound of nothing holding Kelly back. I wish something would hold Ian back.

I spent the summers here when I was ten, eleven, twelve, and thirteen. Ian didn't spend the full summer visiting his grandparents like I did, but he was here all of July. Four full months together over four years, spending a good chunk of our days playing together. It gave me plenty of opportunities to embarrass myself around him. And every time I wanted to run and hide under a rock, he would just keep putting himself right in front of me until I had to look at him, and within moments, we'd both be laughing.

I cross my fingers with more force. If he's seen me, he isn't the kind of guy who would quietly exit the store, leaving me with dignity. And let's be honest: my dignity is in short supply at the moment. Running off to hide from embarrassment is one thing when you're ten. It's something else entirely when you're a grown woman.

Why does he have to be so good-looking now? As ridiculous as it is, I know that if he was completely unattractive, I wouldn't be hiding right now.

Hiding is stupid. I don't get embarrassed this easily normally, and I pretty much never deal with embarrassment by hiding. It's like my childhood self took over the moment I saw Ian walking toward my aisle. We're neighbors, after all. It's not like I can just avoid him forever. The awkwardness between us will eventually go away. Maybe I should just stand up with my keys in my hand, like I dropped them and was picking them up, and then face him like the adult that I am.

Or maybe I could've done that when I first crouched here,

but it doesn't exactly take a full two minutes to pick up keys. Nope. At some point, I'd committed to this winner of a plan.

Was that a noise? A footstep? I hold my breath again and strain my ears. Nothing but Kelly Clarkson.

Two loud crashes sound, followed immediately by hundreds of smaller pinging crashes. The shock of it makes me shoot up from my hiding spot, whipping toward the source of the noise in alarm.

Ian is standing only a handful of feet away, next to an endcap of five shelves of Secret deodorant. The top two shelves are now lying precariously on the third shelf, and the floor around him is a sea of baby blue deodorant, a few of them still skittering to their final resting spots.

Ian meets my eyes, looks down at the sticks of deodorant covering the floor, and then glances at the employees and other customers all being pulled toward the train wreck at his feet. Then he looks at the shelves, like they've somehow betrayed him, and says, "So much for leaning here, looking all nonchalant, waiting for you to finally stand up."

He meets my eyes again, and there's something about the shocked and sheepish expression on his face that is so adorable I actually burst out with an uncontrolled laugh. Then I quickly try to stifle it. If our roles were reversed and I was in the middle of a sea of *Va Va Vanilla*-scented Secret, I wouldn't want to be laughed at. But oh, how sweet it is to finally have the roles reversed. And inexplicably, it makes it feel like I'm on even footing with Ian again.

Ian chuckles. Then he puts his fists on his hips like he's looking down at a puppy who just tore his favorite novel to shreds and says, "You're not living up to your name. Thanks a bunch, Secret."

Then he looks at me, those blue eyes sparkling. For a moment, he glances toward the registers and his confidence seems to falter, which is so unlike the Ian I remember. Then he meets my eyes again. "It's great to see you again, Addi. What do you say we get together for coffee sometime and reminisce?"

Back when we were kids, he always called me Addi. Never Addison. Hearing him say the name I've only ever been called by him instantly takes me back to our childhood and the rush of feelings of independence, excitement, and adventure. Reminiscing with the only person who lived it with me actually sounds quite nice.

It's not a date.

It's just two long-ago friends chatting about the past. That, I can do.

CHAPTER 4

Addison

I RACE from my car to the inn, holding my bag over my head to block some of the rain, then shake it off after I get under the cover of the wraparound porch and go inside. From the giant lobby where guests used to check in—a space I haven't figured out what to do with yet—I hear voices coming from the right. So I head into the kitchen and dining area where my aunt used to serve breakfast to the guests.

All three of my roommates—Bex, Peyton, and Timini—are gathered around the island, snacking on veggies and hummus.

"Addison," Peyton says, her blond ponytail bouncing as she hurries to meet me halfway to hug me. "I'm so glad you made it!"

"But you're late," Bex says with a hand on her hip, somehow looking both relaxed and fierce. Fierce, but not angry. More like she's just stating a fact.

Timini swishes her hand like she's brushing away my lateness. "Fifteen minutes isn't even late enough to be called 'late.'" Then she brushes off an errant piece of thread from her shirt.

"I'm sorry," I say as we all sit down at the main table and

Peyton goes to the oven to pull out dinner. "I got distracted by fuzzy socks at the drugstore, and then I got waylaid trying to hide from Ian."

"Listen up, Adds," Bex says, putting both hands on the table like she's about to push herself out of her seat but doesn't. Instead, it just makes her look intense. It's amazing how intimidating she can appear for as slight as her figure is. "That man is way too fine to hide from. Who cares if you embarrassed yourself in front of him once or twice?"

"I didn't only embarrass myself at the grocery store and with the movers a month ago. The summer I was here at age thirteen, I experienced my first crush ever—and it was on Ian."

"See?" Timini says, turning to Bex and Peyton. "I told you there was crushing going on."

I shake my head and just continue my story so they'll get it. "We spent a lot of time at Quicksand River that summer—and I found a great rock on the shore. It was five or six inches wide and very flat, so I painted a picture on it of the two of us holding hands and jumping into the river. I daydreamed for hours about how I was going to give it to him and how he was going to keep it by his pillow every night and think about me even after we both went back home.

"And, okay, I may have thought about it a bit too much, because when it came time to say goodbye, nerves got the best of me, and I just said, 'Here!' and shoved it into his hands. Then, instead of waiting for him to be touched by my thoughtful gift and reach for my hand and tell me how he could never forget me and that he would always treasure it, just like I had planned, I panicked and kissed him."

Bex hoots. "And what did he do?"

I shrug. "I don't know. It was a quick kiss—our lips barely had time to touch. I saw the shocked look on his face for about half a second, then I turned and ran. I hopped into my aunt's car, we drove to the airport, and I didn't see him again until four weeks ago at the grocery store. And that,"—I say, spreading my arms like I'm presenting an artifact for all to see —"was the beginning of the awkward phase of our relationship. Thirteen years later, it's still going strong."

"You know," Bex says as she leans forward and grabs from the basket a roll that looks freshly baked, "if you see him enough, it'll dilute your percentage of embarrassing moments with him."

"I mean, you'd *hope* it would," Timini says, a teasing gleam in her eye. "Unless your percentage is unnaturally high to begin with."

"No one's is *that* high," Peyton says as she nests a pan of Mushroom Florentine pasta between the rolls and a dish of asparagus.

"Or," I say, dragging out the word, "I could see him, hide behind a bin of fuzzy socks like I'm five, and in his attempt to catch me in the embarrassing moment, he could accidentally send crashing to the ground and spilling across the back of The Oregon Trail Drugstore hundreds of sticks of deodorant. And I pop up out of hiding just in time to see him standing sheepishly in a sea of Secret blue."

The laughter that erupts over the incident makes my heart do a happy dance all over again.

Bex shakes her head. "That is one effective way of lowering the percentage, girl. So are you going to stop hiding from him?"

I nod as I dish myself up some pasta. "Yeah. I am now officially fine with us being neighbors who were friends once upon a time."

"Nothing more?" Peyton asks, a look on her face like she's a kid asking for a cookie but knowing the answer is going to be no.

"Nothing more. We made a pact not to fall in love that night we decided to be roommates, remember?"

"I remember we all came here after the seminar to check the place out," Timini says.

Peyton nods. "I remember eating way too much caramel popcorn."

"Way too much," Bex says. "And I remember Timini's story about how her boyfriend sent her a breakup text saying, *It's not you, it's me. Well, me and my new girlfriend.*"

Timini chuckles. "Which I thought was pretty bad until Peyton told the story about how her ex 'mis-scheduled' a social media post that announced their breakup before he actually broke up with her."

I nod. "We all told our stories, and then we all made a pact…"

Peyton freezes in the middle of dishing up her pasta. "Only because we were all coming off bad breakups. But oh my lands, we aren't actually sticking to that pact, are we?"

"I am," Timini says as she grabs the dish of asparagus. "But Bex isn't."

"The pact is to not 'fall in love,'" Bex says. "We said nothing about dating. I'm as dedicated to the pact now as I was then. I can date all I want—I just don't plan to fall in love."

I stab a bite of the pasta dish, getting pasta, mushroom, and spinach all together in one bite, and put it in my mouth. It's so creamy without being heavy, the flavors all perfectly combining. "Oh my, Peyton. No wonder you're so successful at your business!"

"Truth," Bex says. "I would hire you to be my personal chef any day, Pey."

Peyton looks both annoyed at the nickname Bex has been calling her since the day she moved in and pleased at the compliments. "How about your business, Addison? You've been pretty busy this past week!"

I swallow the bite I've been relishing. "I am already booked out for the next few weeks! I tell you, my sister is a genius at websites and branding and marketing."

It's such a relief. I've never really pictured myself running my own business, and I couldn't understand why people would turn down a steady paycheck from a good employer. Starting this business took almost as big of a leap of faith as moving across the country by myself did. I still can't believe Chloe managed to talk me into chasing a dream so big and uncertain, especially when she isn't even in the country to help me run it.

"Speaking of branding," Timini says, pointing her fork at each of us, "who decided to brand themselves the Post-it Queen?"

I chuckle. I've run into more than a few Post-it notes in the past five days.

Bex points her fork back at Timini, a bite of Florentine already on it. "We only have these dinners once a week. Sticky notes are a good way to communicate issues in between. Like letting someone know it's annoying when people leave stacks of fabric and sewing machines on the tables in here."

"We only use this big one," Timini says. "The other six? They can be used to run our businesses."

I should probably weigh in on the conversation since they're working out things that pertain to all of us, but I hear the faint sound of the text tone I set for only one person—my ex. I wish I'd left my phone on the check-in counter in the lobby with my purse and bag from the drugstore. But since it's right here in my pocket and I know the text came in, I can't *not* read it. It's the first time he's texted since we broke up six weeks ago.

I pull the phone from my pocket and stare at it, unable to process the words.

"Addison!" Peyton and Bex both shout my name at the same time and when I look up, I realize they must've said it several times. I don't know what look is on my face right now, and I don't know how to explain my zoning out other than just telling the truth.

"My ex, Matthew, just texted."

"Oh, no," Bex says, shaking her head.

Timini leans forward. "Does he text often?"

"What did he say?" Peyton asks.

I shake my head. "He doesn't. Not since we broke up." I look back at the text, my thumbs hovering over the keyboard. "He said he heard that I moved here, and he's asking how I like it. How should I respond?"

All three women shout that I shouldn't, and just as I look back up, a question on my face, Bex leans forward and yanks the phone from my hands.

"Seriously, don't do it," Peyton says. "It's a trap."

I look at where Bex set my phone on the table, screen side down, and then at each woman's face, confused. "How is saying something like 'I'm doing great. Thank you for asking' a trap?"

"Because, honey," Bex says, "then you'll start thinking about him again."

Peyton nods. "And wondering how he's doing."

"Before you know it," Timini says, throwing her arms up in the air, "you're wondering if you made a mistake and if you should try to work things out."

"I'm not going to—"

"Do you know what she needs?" Bex asks. "A rebound guy."

"Definitely," Timini says, then turns to me. "Our neighbor would be perfect for it. You're clearly attracted to him."

"No." I can't deny that I'm attracted to Ian. He is sweet and fun and so totally, absolutely *not* what I need right now. Even if the thought of dating him causes a happy fluttering in my stomach and spontaneous daydreams of what it would be like to be wrapped in his arms.

Yeah. Rebound dating him is the worst idea ever.

"Did you know that rebound relationships are actually healthy?" Peyton says.

I raise an eyebrow. "I'm pretty sure they're the opposite of 'healthy.'"

"No, they are!" Peyton ticks off items on her fingers as she says them. "They help you to move on and recover faster, they improve self-esteem and well-being, and they combat loneliness."

Bex puts her hand on my phone. "And they prevent unhealthy reunions with exes."

"Plus," Timini says, "they help you figure out what kind of guy complements you. Super helpful."

I stab a mushroom with my fork. "You all forgot to mention that rebound dating can keep you from properly dealing with the breakup. That's why rebound relationships rarely work out." And Matthew still crosses my mind way too much for me to believe I'm ready for a new relationship.

All three women open their mouths like they're about to say something to counter it, so I head them off with a hand like a stop sign held by a very insistent crossing guard. "Rebound relationships tend to be short. My interactions with Ian have been awkward and embarrassing enough—do you really think it's a good idea to get into a short relationship with a guy who is our next-door neighbor, and who, after our breakup, I'll still have to see practically every day?"

The thought of how awful it'd be to have a quick relationship with Ian and then to bump into him everywhere makes the tingling at the back of my neck and the tightening in my chest even stronger than when I kissed his cheek and ran off after putting the painted stone in his hand as a kid. And thoughts of dating Ian are just as exciting now as they were when I was thirteen. But it's not any more possible now than it was back then. Sure, I'm older now, but dating takes a desire to date from both people.

"I agree," Peyton says. "It definitely shouldn't be our neighbor. How about some random guy?"

I cock my head, trying to figure out why Peyton seemed like she was trying to hide something when she said that. "What aren't you saying?"

She lifts a shoulder in a shrug and keeps her eyes on her fork that's moving around mushrooms on her plate as she says, "I just think you should date anyone other than Ian."

"Why?" Timini asks. "We already know she's attracted to him."

Peyton sets her fork down and lets out a huff of a breath. "Okay. I'll say this and then nothing more because I don't even know enough to tell anything more. At the restaurant where I used to work, one of my coworkers was roommates with this girl Cara, and Cara dated Ian. They were pretty serious. I think they might have even gotten engaged.

"I saw my friend at the gym a couple of weeks ago. We were chatting and just catching up, and I asked how her roommate was doing. She said they just broke up. Anyway, it sounds like he took the breakup pretty much a thousand times harder than you are taking your breakup with Matthew, and I'm pretty sure that two people both having rebound relationships with each other isn't the best idea ever. Especially when one of them probably isn't even close to being ready."

"Oh," I say.

That explains why he seemed skittish earlier. I already don't think rebound dating is a good idea for me at all. And now I definitely don't think it sounds like a good idea for Ian. Add in the fact that being neighbors would make everything worse, and it's obvious that dating or any form of crushing on, flirting with, daydreaming about, or falling in love with is the worst idea ever.

"Well," I say, "I guess that settles it. Let's make this official: my entire goal while living in Quicksand is to *not* fall for the guy next door."

CHAPTER 5

Ian

THE DEAFENING SOUND of my portable air tank shuts off, and I use my finish nailer to put the last couple of nails into this part of the built-in. I run my hand along the section, feeling to make sure it's as smooth as it looks.

Someone whistles behind me, and I turn to see my friend and most frequent general contractor I work with, Garrett, walking into the room. "She's a beaut!"

I brush a bit of sawdust off a shelf. "Wait until you see how pretty it'll be when I finish."

Garrett comes closer to get a better look at it. "I feel bad that it's always me and not you who gets to hear homeowners praise your craftsmanship."

"Well, you do have to take all the blame for anything that goes wrong, so it seems fair."

Garrett nods. "It's true. And every time you're available to do the woodwork in a house I'm building, I figure it's the universe's way of trying to counter the complaints. I owe you, buddy. Oh, hey, guess what? Ellie just finished reading her first book by herself last night. We made a big deal about it and asked what she wanted to do to celebrate, and she said she wanted to get a pedicure at a real salon. So, of course, Emmie wants to as well, and because Ellie is Ellie, she said having her little sister there would make it more special."

"Isn't Emmie three?"

Garrett chuckles. "Yeah, so she'll probably sit on the chair for a full sixty seconds before getting down. I hope the person painting her toenails is fast. Anyway, so Paige is taking them, which leaves me free tonight. I was thinking of getting the guys together to go axe-throwing. Are you in?"

I shake my head as I root around in my bag for my putty knife and the wood filler. "I'd love to, but no can do. I've got Junior Woodworkers tonight."

"Oh, that's right. Instead of hanging out with a bunch of adult men destroying a block of wood, you'll be hanging out with a bunch of seven- to nine-year-olds destroying a block of wood."

I laugh out loud. "We've definitely destroyed some wood along the way. You'd be impressed at how good they're getting, though."

"You know, one of these days you might want to get a junior woodworker of your own."

I'm surprised it's not Cara who comes to mind immediately, as usual—it's Addi. But maybe I shouldn't be surprised. Addi is taking up more and more of my headspace all the time, and I really need to stop thinking about her. I can't face that kind of pain again anytime soon, if ever. The damage that Cara's words inflicted when she broke off our wedding isn't the kind of thing that just goes away. It made me question everything about myself. "It's not in the cards for me, and you know it."

Garrett holds up his hands. "All I'm saying is you've got, what, four single women living in the inn next to you now?

And regardless of what Cara said or what you tell yourself, you're a good man, Ian."

"I'm not interested." It's mostly the truth. I'm not interested in going through what I had with Cara ever again, and the best way to do that is to stay away from all relationships. With my elbows resting on my crouched knees, a putty knife in one hand, I let out a breath. "It looks like my wood filler isn't here. I'll have to run into town to get some." I stand up and toss the putty knife back into my bag.

"You mean this wood filler?" Garrett nudges the jar of it with his foot.

I stare down at the container. How did that get there? And why didn't I see it? But more importantly, why does it disappoint me to realize it's here?

I shake my head as it dawns on me that I was hoping to see Addi when I was in town. Like she would just appear nearby when I thought of her, like a well-timed ad on social media just when I thought of an item. I obviously need to step up my not-thinking-about-her efforts.

———

Many of the kids in Junior Woodworkers are also in Cub Scouts. Since they have their pinewood derby coming up, we spend the hour in my shop working on their cars instead of building stools, like we've been doing. Normally, I choose projects where I can teach them how to build furniture correctly and use tools properly and safely—all things my grandpa taught me—but it's fun to see their more creative sides come out in their car designs.

When we finish and the last kid is picked up by their parents, I blow most of the sawdust off myself with the air hose, then close up the shop and head into the house through the kitchen door. Grandma loves to cook, and although she doesn't cook every night, she usually does on Junior Wood-worker days, knowing I'll be coming in late. And sure enough, she's got beef stew in the crock pot, and it smells great. Usually, she's in the room when I come in. I kick off my boots and head down the hall at the back of the kitchen toward the family room.

As I near, I hear voices and move closer to say hi, but I pause when I hear Addi's voice. I'm a little surprised she's in the house, considering how much she's been avoiding me. And having her here isn't exactly the best way to move forward with my not-thinking-about-her plan.

I take a few steps closer, trying to hear what they're talking about so I can guess if this will be quick or not. If it's going to be quick, maybe I'll slip back outside and clean my shop for a bit.

As I near, I can start to make out Grandma's words. "...told me how easy it was to move your things into the inn because of how organized you are. I want to be like that. And, as you can tell from all of this, I've got a long way to go."

"How long have you lived here?"

"Fifty-four years. Since I was eight months pregnant with Ian's dad. I thought I'd have to move when my dear Sheldon passed just over a year ago because this place is too much for me to care for on my own. But Ian is so sweet. He barely hesitated before packing up his stuff in Salem, buying this house, and moving in so I could stay. He's such a good boy.

"Anyway, a year ago, I started to go through everything, and all it taught me was that it's too big a job to handle on my own. So when Ian told me that you help people get organized for a living and I looked you up online..."

Their voices fade as I walk back toward the kitchen. It's sweet that Grandma is saying good things about me. It's not so sweet that I'm standing here eavesdropping. I can't tell how long they'll be—Grandma might be asking for advice, and that could take a while. I should probably head back outside to my shop.

But then I hear Grandma more clearly, so she must be close to the family room doorway. "But this isn't all of it—I need to show you my office and bedroom."

Oh no. My bedroom door is open, and I know for a fact that I didn't make my bed this morning. I'm not sure, but I might possibly have a dirty shirt or two on the floor. My room isn't too messy, but it's not something someone like Addi would call "organized."

When we were kids, it wasn't weird at all to have her in my room. When we visited here each summer, my brothers and I shared the room I live in now, and it's where we kept the Legos. But now that Addi and I are adults and don't know each other as well as we once did, it feels strange having her in my house. And it would feel even stranger to have her seeing my things. And if Grandma is showing Addi her office, they'll need to walk right past my room.

I can't go toward the family room and get to my bedroom hall from that direction, since that's where they are. So I race into the living room and head into the hall from the opposite way. I come at my room a little too fast and bang my arm, from shoulder down to elbow, into the doorframe, making a loud thud. But I manage to pull my door shut just before Grandma and Addi round the corner.

"Oh my goodness," Grandma says, looking around, "what was that bang?"

I shrug and then wrap an arm around Grandma's shoulders, giving her a hug. Then I turn to Addi. "Hello, Addi. I wasn't expecting to see you here. How are you?"

Once upon a time, I was good at talking to girls. Somewhere

along the way, probably after ending things with Cara, I must've forgotten how. Seriously, "I wasn't expecting to see you here" is the best I can do?

"Oh, hi, Ian. Your grandma didn't think you'd be back so soon."

I glance at Grandma and catch the hint of a smile before she hides it. I always come in at the same time on Junior Woodworkers days.

"Addison is every bit as amazing as you said she was."

Addi ducks her head, but I think I catch a bit of a blush before she does. To tell the truth, I'm feeling a little warm around the ears, too. I told Grandma that Addi was good at what she does—I didn't think she'd make it sound like I talk about Addi nonstop. That's only partly true.

"I asked her to come over to see what she could do for me and all the stuff I've collected over the years. That way, when I die, all that work won't be left to family. Now don't worry, I don't plan on dying anytime soon. But I tell you what—this girl here is in high demand. Probably because everyone figured out how good she is. I thought I wouldn't have a chance swaying her to help me, but she says she's going to stop by in the evenings and on weekends, just to help an old woman out."

Then Grandma winks at me, and she's not exactly subtle about it.

"Your grandma was pretty hard to say no to when we were kids," Addi says, then shrugs, "and she's just as hard to say no to now. And of course, I'm happy to help a neighbor out."

Addi's golden brown hair is pulled into a loose bun, and with the mass of curls she has, it's beautiful. I especially like how a few curls have escaped and fallen next to her slender neck. A lot about her has changed over the years. Not those mischievous green eyes I remember so well from our childhood, though.

Grandma beams at her. "Isn't she the best?"

I realize I'm gazing at her. I clear my throat and say, "So, you're going to be here a lot after work, huh?"

She eyes me, and I can't read the expression on her face. Is she happy about that? Sad? Wary? I'm not even sure what expression is on my own face. Part of me is smiling just thinking about how she won't be able to easily duck out or hide when I'm around. The much bigger part of me is terrified to have someone I'm attracted to—and thinking about way too much to be healthy—be so close.

"Just two or three times a week."

Okay, then. Two or three times a week, I need to silence the part of me that wants to see her and give the terrified part free rein to find reasons why I suddenly have to be away from home.

CHAPTER 6

Addison

I miss Chloe. I'm used to talking to my sister daily and texting dozens of times a day. When I walk through the door of the inn and drop my purse and keys on the reservation counter, I glance at the clock on my phone. It's been an incredibly long day organizing a shoe and jewelry hoarder's bedroom all the way over in Lake Oswego, and I'm beat. But I do the math, and it's after 3 a.m. in Paris, so a phone call is out of the question.

Instead, I send a text. *Call me when you're free to talk business strategy?* My business started out with a bang, mostly because of Chloe's genius, but my openings further out aren't being filled as quickly as I'd like, and it's making me a bit nervous. I hesitate a moment, phone still in hand, then send a second text. *And maybe chat a bit about my neighbor.*

There. I sent it. Chloe will grill me about it, but she'll also let me talk through things without too much judgment. It's not that I *want* to be thinking about Ian. But my subconscious doesn't seem to get that memo, so my mind keeps wandering to him without my permission.

I glance at the stairs, thinking about how nice it would be to go up, flop on my bed, and stream a TV show until I get some energy back. But my body is already turning toward the kitchen, and I'm mentally going through what food is in the fridge and how much effort it would take to put something in my grumbling stomach.

My stomach growls even louder just thinking about my options. Food it is. Maybe that will replenish my energy. I head into the kitchen and find Bex at her laptop, with a smile on her face that says she's either editing one of her YouTube videos or replying to comments from her fans. She glances at me but keeps working, so I go to the fridge. Yes! Peyton made enchiladas and put an *Anyone can eat* sticky note on the top.

I'm just putting a plate with two enchiladas on it into the microwave when Bex must've finished what she was working on, shuts her laptop, and turns toward me. "So... I saw our neighbor today."

"Yeah?" I try to make the word sound uninterested. I might even succeed.

"He'd just walked out of his shed and was brushing sawdust off those muscled arms and chest."

I turn around to face her. "Bex."

"I'm just saying that maybe you should reconsider dating him."

"You're still pushing that? Even after hearing that he's just coming off a hard breakup?"

"You moved in, what, five weeks ago? And his relationship ended sometime before then. Maybe he needs a little rebound dating, too."

As the microwave does its thing, I lean against the counter behind me, arms folded, shaking my head at Bex's tenacity. "Even if you took away all the problems of rebound dating for each of us, it's not like dating someone is all my choice. It takes two people."

"And?"

"And," I let out a frustrated breath, dropping my arms, "I've never had guys lining up at my door. I've had plenty of crushes before—guys I really would've liked to have dated—but that didn't mean they felt the same way." It was probably a big chunk of the reason why I stayed with Matthew for as long as I did. The whole time, a part of me knew that if we broke up, I might go a very long time before dating someone new, whether I liked it or not.

Bex looks at me like she's confused or like I'm crazy. Bex has probably never experienced being interested in dating someone and not having him feel the same. "But you're gorgeous."

I shake my head and then run my fingers through my long curls, looking at them as I do. "I know the hair attracts men. Enough that we start chatting and texting and getting to know each other. And then, before we ever get to 'We should go out sometime,' they're coming to me for dating advice. I'm the friend, never the girlfriend. Even if I did want to date Ian—*which I don't.* I just got out of a two-year relationship, after all—it doesn't mean the choice is all up to me. And I can tell that Ian's just not interested in going out with me."

Before Bex can respond, we both stand up straighter and cock our heads toward the sound of a lawnmower starting.

"Is that in our yard?"

Instead of answering, I race back out into the front lobby and then into the gathering room, Bex on my heels as we run by the couches and chairs in the large area. At first, we can't see any sign of the lawnmower in the backyard. Then, a few seconds later, it appears from behind some shrubs that hide the maintenance shed, being pushed by none other than our neighbor, Ian.

"Ian's been the one mowing?" Bex asks.

Maybe I should've guessed—it was Ian and his brothers

who took care of the yard as kids when they were here for the summers. But who would've guessed he'd still be doing it now?

"You should go talk to him. Your car is parked on the side by his house, so he has to know you're home. It'd be rude if you saw it was him and didn't thank him. I mean, *I* could thank him, but I don't own the building, so it wouldn't carry as much weight coming from me. I think it has to be you."

I take a deep breath. "You're right. It's the neighborly thing to do."

I stop by the downstairs bathroom to make sure my hair isn't too crazy, and then I head out the back door. Ian has just turned to mow the next strip, so his back is to me as he mows the length of the yard. I wait. I tell myself it's not so I can watch him—it would simply be rude to walk behind him when he can't hear me coming.

Seeing him mow now is nothing like seeing him push the mower when he was eleven or even fourteen. The last thirteen years have definitely treated him well. Especially in his shoulders and the top of his back, where his muscles are showing very clearly through the fabric of his t-shirt. He doesn't know I'm watching, though, so I start feeling like a stalker and walk out to meet him instead.

I'm still a good fifteen feet away when he reaches the end of the yard and turns the mower so he's facing me again. He shuts it off as soon as he sees me. He glances at the part of the lawn he's already cut, then scratches the back of his neck. "Looks like I'm busted."

I laugh as I take the last few steps toward him. "Have you been mowing all this time? Why didn't you tell me?"

"I have. I've never stayed next door and not taken care of this yard, so it feels wrong not to. As far as why I haven't told you…" He lifts one of those strong shoulders in a shrug. "Everyone loves a mystery, right? I was just giving you one."

That makes me smile. Of course, he did. "Did my aunt line up payment with you before she died? Do I owe you past lawn mowing fees?"

"She used to pay us when we were kids. But growing up, my brothers and I did a lot of yard care for others in Salem, and my dad's rule was that we had to mow at least one yard a week for someone who needed it and not charge them. When I moved back here more than a year ago, the inn became my one yard a week."

That is so sweet. And to still be doing it now, when he's no longer mowing lawns as a kid for money and therefore obligated to mow one for free. Maybe that's why his eyes look so kind—because he genuinely is.

I realize I'm looking into those eyes a little too deeply and shake myself out of my stupor. "I want to do something to thank you. I'm not much of a baker, but I'm pretty good at buying baked goods. Maybe I could get a pie, or cupcakes, or… ice cream! Not that ice cream is a baked good."

"How about coffee?"

He's smiling that adorable amused smile, and it suddenly makes me forget what we're talking about. "You want me to bake you coffee?" My brow crinkles. "Oh! We had plans to go get coffee and catch up. Right."

"Tomorrow after work?"

I nod. "Tomorrow it is."

As I walk back to the inn, knowing he's watching me, I'm hyper-aware of how I'm walking and suddenly can't remember how to walk normally. But it's definitely not whatever I'm doing right now. I can't even talk to him normally. What is wrong with me?

It's probably his eyes.

Yeah, it's definitely those eyes that are throwing me off. The eyes that are the same blue as the sky I painted on that rock back when I first forgot how to talk around him. All I have to do is avoid the eyes, and I'll be just fine.

————

After I grab the enchiladas I nearly forgot about from the microwave, I head up to my room and sit at my desk with my laptop. As it boots, I take a bite of the dish that makes me, once again, so grateful Peyton is a roommate. Then I open a browser and type in the search bar, *How to stay away from a rebound relationship*.

The results show links to several articles about how to tell if you're in a rebound relationship, but I have to scroll quite a bit to find one about how to keep from getting into one. Unfortunately, there isn't one titled *How to keep from falling a little more for your neighbor every time you see him*.

So I remind myself that rebound dating = bad. Bad for me, bad for Ian. Even if his eyes are kind and beautiful. Even if his jawline is pretty near perfect. Even if he looks incredible mowing the lawn or covered in sawdust as he tries to surreptitiously close his bedroom door before I can see inside. Even if he does things like buy a house so he can help his grandma, mow people's lawns to be nice, or volunteer to teach kids woodworking skills. None of that matters, because *rebound dating = bad*.

Maybe I should write it in giant letters on my arm with a marker so I can't forget.

I'm only partway through the article when I grab a notebook and start writing down things I need to remember to keep myself from being attracted to Ian. I write in all caps across the top of the page, *HOW TO NOT FALL FOR THE*

GUY NEXT DOOR. Then I make my list of things from the article.

> *—If you want to date someone just to make your ex jealous, you're not ready to date.*
> *—If you hope your ex will call and let you know how he's doing, you're not ready to date.*
> *—If you think of your ex constantly, you're not ready to date.*
> *—If you struggle to delete photos of your ex, you're not ready to date.*
> *—If you have a hard time deleting your ex's phone number, you're not ready to date.*
> *—If you're still pining over your ex, you're not ready to date.*
> *—If you're still looking at your ex's social media, you're not ready to date.*
> *—If you're rushing a new relationship because of a sense of urgency, you're not ready to date.*

Then I add one more that the article doesn't mention but is important for me to remember.

> *—If your neighbor experiences any of the above, then he's not ready to date, either.*

I look over what I've written. Matthew lives seventeen hundred miles away, so it's not like he'll ever see if I date anyone else. So I'm pretty safe with that first one. I still think about Matthew too much and often wonder how he's doing, but I've been fairly good at the other things. Mostly. More than how much I'm thinking of Matthew, I should probably be concerned about how often I'm thinking of Ian.

I'm making progress on all the items, though, and that's what matters. It's a good list to keep in mind. If I ever catch myself doing any of those things, I'll know I'm not ready to move on.

Just like writing *I won't run in the halls* a hundred times when I broke the rule in fourth grade, writing *You're not ready to date* so many times, underlining it each time, has actually helped my mindset.

Actually, two of the things don't need to be on the list at all. I open my phone, go to the photos app, and delete the entire folder with pictures of Matthew and me together. Then I go into my contacts and delete his number. It feels good! Healthy. Wise. Powerful.

Grinning widely, I cross both items off my list with as much glee as my high school English Lit teacher marked up my *Hamlet* essay.

Not that I'm aiming to just cross all the items off the list. I'm in Quicksand for a fresh start, and that means figuring out what I want out of life without a boyfriend affecting the plan.

No, this isn't a list of things to accomplish so I can move on to something new. This is a list to help keep myself from falling for Ian.

CHAPTER 7
Ian

I SIT on a bench at the trailhead park, smiling as Addi pulls into the parking lot slowly. Then she looks down, probably at her phone. She looks back at the road she just turned off before she glances toward the trail and spots me. She smiles and pulls into a parking space.

I hope she's up for walking the trail. Sitting across from each other in a coffee shop where all we can do is stare into each other's eyes while we talk feels too much like a date and not like old friends catching up. I remind myself, once again, that's all this is. I stand as she opens her door and steps out of her car.

"It's a good thing you were sitting where I could see you—I thought I got the address wrong. This isn't exactly a coffee shop."

She's come straight from work and is wearing dark jeans that are fitted and make her legs look incredible. She has on a flowy pink blouse, which is a little dressy for a walk in the woods, but at least she's wearing flats. If I were spending the day organizing someone's house, I'd probably show up in a t-shirt, jeans, and athletic shoes. I assumed Addi would be dressed similarly, so I didn't anticipate that changing up the plan would be an issue.

"No, but since we've had a few rain-free days, I thought a walk along Chipper Creek Trail might be more fun than a stuffy coffee shop. Plus," I turn to grab the two cups of coffee I already picked up from Doug's Donuts and hold one out to her, "I've got coffee."

Addi looks at the cup for a long moment before taking it. "I was supposed to pay for coffee, remember?"

"But then I changed up what we're doing without warning you or giving you a chance to dress for it. Let's consider us even."

"We're even, then," she says and bumps her cup into mine. I'm loving this sunny day even more as I gaze at how it lights up Addi's face and hair. It gives both a golden glow that is breathtaking on her. And those mischievous eyes I love are looking more golden than hazel.

Okay, I've got to stop noticing every detail about her.

Addi's gaze shifts over my shoulder to the trailhead. "I haven't even thought about this place in so long. I used to love coming here as a kid."

"If you'd rather not in those shoes—"

"No, I'm good." She starts walking toward the trailhead purposely like she's afraid I'll change my mind. We've only walked on the trail for maybe a dozen feet before she says, "It still blows my mind how green everything is here."

I've lived in Oregon my entire life, so this trail is nothing new. But Addi only spent four summers here half her lifetime ago, and I imagine the surroundings are a bit different than in Amarillo. I try to look at the thick forest filled with green things growing at all different heights through her eyes. It's beautiful as always, but I haven't really paid attention to exactly how green everything is until I picture how it must look to a girl who grew up in an area with wide, open spaces and rainstorms that don't occur every few days.

"In Amarillo, everything is so brown. I mean, not in town so much—people have grassy yards—but if you get out of town at all, there are so many shades of brown. There's no brown here."

I haven't ever thought about it, but she's right. Even the tree trunks are green here with all the moss that grows on them.

The trail isn't crowded, but there are people ahead of us, and a few pass by walking in the opposite direction every few minutes. Mostly, it's just the sound of our feet on the crushed gravel trail as I ask her about how work is going, and she asks me the same as we sip our coffees.

As much as I like talking to her about what's going on with us now, I'm dying to ask her about what happened thirteen years ago. As soon as the conversation moves past enough pleasantries to be polite, I say, "When you were last here, you said you'd see me the next summer, but you never came back."

Smooth, Ian. Could you be any more blunt?

"It wasn't my fault, I swear. My little sister, Chloe, never came with me to Aunt Helen's because she was into fashion marketing from pretty much the day she was born, so she always went to Fashion Designer Camp. The year I was thirteen and she was eleven, she came home from camp with a portfolio of her work." She glances over at me. "I know. Overachiever, right?"

I chuckle.

"Anyway, it made my parents decide that it was time I stopped spending my summers playing and started spending them developing skills. I went on a bunch of week-long camps every summer until I was sixteen and had a job. So, I went to," she says, ticking each item off on her fingers as she says them, "soccer camp, young explorers camp, drama camp, young novelists camp, leadership camp, space camp—you name the camp, I probably did it."

For years, I'd wondered if she never came back because my reaction to her gift and kiss was to freeze and not say a thing. I didn't realize it was still weighing on me until her explanation lifted the weight. "No Organizer's Anonymous Camp?"

I soak in the sound of her laughter as we walk onto one of the five bridges that cross the meandering stream. "No, surprisingly, based on the variety of ones I went to. And even though one probably didn't exist, I didn't have every second of my future planned out at age fourteen enough to know I even wanted that. I still don't let Chloe forget how she ruined my summers with her unnaturally young career planning."

She stops to lean over the bridge's railing and look at the water, so I do, too. After a moment, Addi says, "I miss Aunt Helen."

I nod. "I do, too. She was a phenomenal woman."

"She was, wasn't she? I'm lucky I got to spend so many summers with her. I wouldn't be who I am without her."

We are both silent for a long moment as we just watch the water pass by below us. Then Addi says, "Remember when we were kids and your grandma taught us how to make origami boats out of waxed paper, and we'd drop them off at one bridge, and then race down the trail and try to beat them to the next bridge?"

I laugh at the memory. "And the boats always won, except at the very end of summer when there wasn't as much water flowing. And then, half the time, it was because they got stuck along the way."

She turns to me. "Let's go down by the stream." Her smile

lights up her face and makes me smile. It had when we were kids, too, but somewhere along the way, her smile became even more beautiful. Mesmerizing.

We walk to the end of the bridge, toss our coffee cups in the garbage can at the bridge's edge, and head down to the water. I should've known—water always draws Addi to it. It was why we spent so many of our summer days either here by Chipper Creek or in our favorite cove at Quicksand River.

I'm glad to know she didn't stop coming to spend her summers with her aunt because of me. But I'm still curious about that kiss she shocked me with. I step up next to her, and we both watch a squirrel race to the water's edge, then scurry back, then to the creek again, each time getting closer and closer to us. "So, you know that painted stone you gave me? I still have it."

Addi's attention flies right to me, a surprised look on her face. "You kept it all these years?"

"I was hoping to one day ask you about it again." Her eyes search mine, and I work up the courage—and try to come up with the wording—to ask if she kissed me because she liked me, or if it was just a friendly goodbye, but every sentence I think of sounds awful. It's not like I need to know so I can sleep better at night or anything. Well, okay, that knowledge prob-ably would've helped me sleep better back when I was four-teen. But I hadn't thought about it for years before seeing her again in Gateway Groceries.

Maybe just letting it go again is the best thing. But I feel like I owe it to the fourteen-year-old me to just spit the question out, no matter how awful it sounds, so I don't have to wonder.

I'm just opening my mouth to ask when a dog's barking gets rapidly closer, right along with shouts from the dog's owner. Both Addi and I turn in time to see a large dog racing toward us—or, more likely, the squirrel that had been very near us—with its leash bouncing behind it as it hits rocks and tufts of weeds, its owner chasing after it. Neither of us has time to react before the dog plows into Addi, knocking her backward.

I grab her arm as she falls, and between the efforts of both of us, she manages to stay upright, even though she has to take a giant step into the stream to stop her fall. The dog takes off in the direction of the squirrel just as quickly as it came, leaving both of us breathing heavily from the adrenaline of it all.

"Are you okay?"

She nods, and I pull her toward me and out of the stream. As soon as she lifts the foot that had been deepest in the water, though, the rushing stream grabs hold of her shoe, which, as a slip-on, has only about two inches holding it to the top of her foot, and sends it downstream.

"No!" Addi shouts, lunging for it.

"I've got it," I yell, racing after the shoe. Within moments, though, it reaches the next bridge and passes beneath it. The bridge is too low to duck under, so I race around the structure that suddenly seems overly massive for the size of the stream, and then I dash alongside the water's edge. The shoe is ahead of me by a couple hundred feet. I leap over rocks and tree stumps and fallen branches as I run after it. But no matter how fast I go, it keeps getting further and further away.

Finally, I realize what a lost cause it is, and how my chasing it down the river has left Addi balancing on one foot upstream. I jog back to where I abandoned her to find her making her way back up to the trail, doing a mix of hopping and touching just the ball of her foot down on the most rock-free parts of the ground. I race to her side, and she puts an arm around my back to steady herself.

"I'm so sorry, Addi. I swear it took your shoe downstream

even faster than it took our boats." I glance at the foot that still wears a shoe. "They looked new, too."

"Today was my first time wearing them."

I cringe.

"But they've been killing my feet all day. They aren't nearly as comfortable as the website made them look."

"Your feet have been hurting all day in those shoes, and yet you still agreed to walk the trail?"

She shrugs. "It's not much different from wearing heels on a date." Her eyes go wide, clearly shocked at what she just said. "Not that this is a date! I didn't mean that. I just meant… Friends. Catching up. This is a 'friends catching up' get-together."

"I've missed you, Addi." I'd forgotten how much being around her ratchets my happiness level up. Or how much I love the blush that frequently lights up her face.

We both look at the trail. Sure, down by the water there are rocky areas as much as there are patches of grassy weeds and dirt. But the trail itself is crushed gravel—the kind you definitely don't want to walk on barefoot.

She's right. We're just old friends catching up. This isn't a date. But still, I've been feeling an attraction to Addi pulling me the entire time. So, I know how much what I'm about to do will take me to very dangerous territory, but I offer anyway. "Well, I guess there's only one solution: I'll have to carry you back."

"What? No. That's like half a mile, Ian. You can't do that. Your arms will want to fall off if you carry me that far."

"You have that little faith in my muscles?" She checks out my muscles, and she blushes again. I have to admit, it makes me feel pretty great. "All right, then. Ready?"

She nods, and I pick her up, one arm around her back and one under her knees. She wraps an arm around my neck to hold on. With her in my arms, her arm around me, her face so close to mine, all my reminders to myself that we're nothing more than old friends fly away faster than her shoe going down the river.

Right now is the point when I should very emphatically remind myself that I never want to date again, and even if I miraculously did, it's too soon, so I should keep my distance. But that voice just as quickly fades away in the breeze. Apparently, too big a part of me wants to just let myself be in the moment.

And that's all it is. A moment. Nothing serious. Just old friends.

"Do you know what else I kept?" I'm so close to her, all I have to do is whisper.

She barely shakes her head no, like nothing more is needed while we're in such close proximity.

"Those cheesy rhymes you used to write whenever we got on each other's nerves and you wanted to lead me to where you were hiding so we could make up."

"No," she says, dragging out the word. "You didn't."

"I so did. Every last one."

Her ears turn pink, and she looks out at the woods for a moment before meeting my eyes again. "Seriously. Tell me you didn't."

"They were pretty catchy rhymes. Let me think—I might still have my favorite one from when you were ten or eleven memorized." I gaze up at the sky. It's been a long time since I thought of it, but I still have the preamble to the Constitution in my brain from memorizing it in eighth grade. So that has to mean that I have her rhyme in my head, too, because I cared a lot more about memorizing it than I did the preamble.

I clear my throat. "'You said my Lego door was dumb, which made me mad!'"

"Stop it."

"'You told me sorry, but I wasn't done being sad.'"

"Ian."

"'I am now, so go where I stuck my gum on that tree stump. Walk fifteen steps until you come to the grass clump.'"

She's laughing now.

"'Then go left and run forty big, giant paces. Turn around and you'll see where my hiding place is.'"

The pink is all across her cheeks now, and I can feel her laughing against my chest. "I cannot believe you remember that. That was the time I sat in my hiding place for thirty minutes, and you never came."

"Only because you never said in your rhyme in which direction I should walk the fifteen steps, and I chose the wrong direction because that entire field was covered in grass clumps. And then Mrs. Walters got mad at me for running twenty-two of the forty big, giant paces through her garden."

She laughs again, and the sound feels like home out here. Like birds singing in the trees.

"I took a poetry class in college. I think my professor would tell you that my skill in writing poetry hasn't improved since I was a kid."

"Suddenly, I want nothing more than to read your poetry written as an adult." No, that's wrong. There is something I want more.

A smile spreads across my face as I realize I'm much more likely to get an answer with her in my arms than while she's in the path of a dog on a mission. "But first, a question." A genuine smile crosses my face as I watch her expression. "When you left your aunt's inn to head back to the airport that last summer and you kissed me, was that a new way of saying goodbye that you were trying out, or did you kiss me because you liked me?"

Addi laughs and looks up at the sky, shaking her head. I'm

not sure she's going to answer, but then she meets my eyes again. "I had a crush on you, okay? It was my first one ever, and I obviously wasn't very good at it. The painted stone was so that you'd think of me often while I was in another state."

I smile doubly—for the fourteen-year-old me and the twenty-seven-year-old me—as I look at the path ahead. "Well, I have to say that your plan worked."

CHAPTER 8

Addison

I've been helping Ian's grandmother organize her origami supplies in their family room for a grand total of about eight minutes when Ian gets home from work. Based on the feigned surprise on Shirley's face at him being home and Ian's confusion at her surprise, I get the distinct impression she's playing matchmaker. Too bad she didn't have me come over early enough that I could've told her about my recent breakup and how I'm not ready for anything new yet.

And especially not with a guy who's recovering from his own breakup and happens to be my next-door neighbor.

Two weeks ago, when Ian carried me—minus one shoe— back to my car, something changed. Maybe it was from having our faces so close together that we could feel each other's breath as we talked. Or maybe it was because of how perfect it felt to be held by him. Or because I had my arm around his shoulders, holding tight.

Or the fact that he offered to carry me in the first place. He could've just been a support, walking next to me as I hopped back to my car. Or he could've left me at the side of the river while he drove to get another shoe from my apartment. But he didn't—he *carried* me.

Maybe the change I'm sure we both felt two weeks ago was simply a product of proximity. Like when two magnets stick together when they are near each other. But it's not like we search each other out from across the room when we aren't close. We don't feel the pull unless we're near. It's nothing but proximity.

Because if it were more than proximity, it would've pulled him to me before now. During the last two weeks, he's been avoiding me as expertly as I avoided him before the big deodorant debacle in the drugstore. Several times, we've accidentally run into each other, as neighbors do. But each time, his small talk feels forced, like I'm a long-winded neighbor with a differing political opinion or endless cat stories and he's trying to get away to avoid hearing them.

Whether we acted like magnets for that half mile two weeks ago or not, it's not that way now. I tell myself it's a relief because I'm not ready for a relationship. I don't know how long ago he and his fiancée broke up, but it's obvious he isn't looking for a relationship either. I can tell because I've been at his house several times over the past few weeks, helping his grandma, and each time he's suddenly had things he needed to do that have kept him away.

He underestimates his grandma's ability to get him to help with this project, though.

I brought several storage pieces that will work together to organize all Shirley's colored paper squares and rectangles and her origami books. The biggest issue with organizing her hobby is what to do with all the unique origami creations she's made that are currently living in cardboard boxes stacked on top of each other.

"Ian?" Shirley calls out. "Can you come here for a minute?"

When Ian walks into the family room at the back of the house, she says, "Addison came up with a plan to showcase my origami pieces, and since it'll change the look of the room, I want to know what you think about it."

"Grandma, you know I'll be okay with it. This is your home, too. You can display your things however you'd like."

"And it's also your home. So zip it and listen to Addison's plan."

I hide a smile and explain to Ian that I suggested we hang each of the paper creations from the ceiling using fishing line so it wouldn't be seen. "We'll do it at all different heights just in front of this blank wall, so it'll be an art installation—a masterpiece people can spend a while looking at."

"I love it."

"Wonderful!" Shirley claps her hands. "Because we're going to need help installing it. You're free tonight, right?"

My eyes flash to Shirley as my chest tightens. I definitely didn't say anything about needing help. Ian's expression is every bit as alarmed as mine.

"What?" Shirley says to me, trying to look innocent. "We *do* need help. Getting on a ladder without someone supporting it isn't wise, and these arms aren't as supportive as they once were."

So, as Shirley lays out each of her creations along the floor, adjusting which ones are where and changing up the heights on all of them until she likes the way they look, Ian and I sit on the floor, cutting lengths of fishing line and tying them to each piece. Actually, it doesn't feel so different from when we were kids, sitting side by side, making Lego villages. It's kind of fun.

I imagine doing this same thing with Matthew. Unplanned. And on a Thursday night. I nearly laugh out loud. If I had somehow gotten him to do a crazy project like this, there's no way I would've gotten him to sit on the floor to do it.

And there I go, accidentally thinking about my ex again. Obviously, I should squash any feelings I have toward Ian right now before my heart thinks it can get invested any more than it already is.

Except Ian is so sweet to his grandma, and he's so patient. Every time he talks to her while sitting on the floor and tying fishing line to a folded piece of paper with his big hands that somehow don't hinder his ability to work with something so delicate, it makes him that much more attractive. It makes those eyes of his even more beautiful.

Those eyes are going to be my undoing.

Seriously, Addison. Squash those feelings!

It takes a while, but we eventually get the line tied to all four dozen origami pieces and bring out the ladder to start attaching them to the ceiling. While Shirley chats about how the summers weren't the same once I stopped coming to Hidden Inn and how sad it was for Ian, especially that first summer I wasn't here, I put the ladder in place and hang the first couple. Ian dutifully holds onto the side of the ladder, just as his grandma requested, even though it feels completely unnecessary.

Each time I step onto the ladder, I'm acutely aware of how close we are to each other. So is my stomach, apparently, because it fills with butterflies. We're not holding onto each other like we did at Chipper Creek, yet I swear the butterflies are flapping even stronger—like maybe they drank caffeine instead of nectar.

The same as when we were kids, I can sense Ian's emotions just by looking at him. He's feeling something, too, like he was when he was carrying me.

When I finish hanging a cute little origami frog, Ian hands me the next one so I don't have to get off the ladder. And when I take it from him, our hands brush, and it sends a thrill across my skin. It's like Shirley picked up those magnets from opposite sides of the room and put them next to each other again.

And we've got some pretty strong magnets. I so need to get some distance from this man!

Especially because after I move the ladder to the next spot—and the next four spots after that—Ian conveniently turns to say something to his grandma every time I'm climbing the ladder at the moment when our faces would've been so close if he hadn't turned. And when he hands me the fishing line for the next one, he holds it in a way that I can grab it without touching his hand. He clearly doesn't want our magnetic selves to be so close, either.

When we've hung the colorful creations about two-thirds of the way across the long wall, I hear the faint sound of my sister's ringtone, so I quickly pull out my phone to see if it's really her.

Still looking at the phone, my eyebrows crease. "This is my sister, and it's the middle of the night where she is. Do you mind if I take this?"

"You go right ahead," Shirley says.

I answer as I'm walking through the kitchen to the back door. "Chloe! Is everything okay?"

"Everything's so good!"

I step outside and shut the door behind me. "Isn't it after two in Paris?"

"Yep. Dustin and I went to the most amazing fashion show and after-party tonight. I got to meet so many of my idols! When we got home, Dustin crashed in about four seconds flat, but I'm still too wired to sleep, so I thought I'd call."

"I love that you're getting so many opportunities to do what you love! Even if it does mean that you're not in my city. Or state. Or country."

"Yeah, that's definitely been the worst part. So how are things going with you? Have you seen Ian much since you went on that not-a-date coffee walk with him through the woods?"

I glance back toward the house, almost like I'm checking to make sure he can't hear from where he is, which is ridiculous. "I'm at his house right now, actually. Just helping his grandma."

"Interesting. Also, I still think you lost your shoe in the creek on purpose. If you'll admit it, then I'll admit it was a brilliant plan."

"It wasn't on purpose—they were really cute shoes, even. Uncomfortable as could be, but super cute. And brand new. Also, I'm not brilliant, or I wouldn't be over here at his house, reminiscing about the creek with every glance or accidental touch. Especially when I know it's going nowhere."

"No. Don't you be talking like that's the most that's ever going to happen between you two. He was your first crush, and it took fate to bring you together again. It's practically meant to happen."

"Chloe, he doesn't want it to. He's making it very clear that whatever we shared on that walk was a fluke. He's not interested, and neither am I. I'm just not ready to date again yet."

Chloe lets out a long sigh, like she doesn't really agree with me but is humoring me. "How will you know when you are ready?"

"The websites I saw said it usually takes a good three months before dating again won't be a rebound. Matthew and I broke up nine weeks ago, so I've got about a month to go. By the time I'm ready, Ian will have forgotten all about our walk in the woods."

"Okay."

"Chloe," I say cautiously, "why were you smiling when you said 'Okay'? Tell me."

My sister chuckles quietly. "I just can't wait to see if fate agrees with your timeline."

CHAPTER 9

Ian

I WALK into the bowling alley later than I'd planned and look around for the guys. I wish I'd been free on axe-throwing night—I enjoy that more than bowling. But I'm really just here to see the guys.

Garrett stands and waves, and I wave back before stopping at the counter to pay and get shoes. When I head over to the lane the guys are already at, I see Garrett's wife, Andre's girlfriend, and a woman with Isaac that I haven't seen before. When I get to the bench, Garrett sits next to me.

"Is the Williamson house still giving you troubles? I was beginning to think you wouldn't make it."

"It's been putting up a good fight, that's for sure. I didn't want to leave before I finished the trim. Was it date night tonight?"

"Sorry about that. It wasn't going to be, but Paige's mom asked if she could take our kids tonight, so I didn't want to come without her. I didn't know that Andre was bringing Rose, and the woman with Isaac is someone he met here. I should've texted you."

"No, it's fine," I say, and it is. Because I also know that if Garrett had texted, I likely wouldn't have shown up at all. I dated Cara for long enough that I got used to constantly having a date for things. I'm still not used to being the only dateless one in a group.

Since there are seven of us, we've got both of the lanes that share the seating area, and the other two guys and their dates are already playing in their lane, which leaves Garrett, Paige, and me in ours. Paige finishes putting our names on the screen, and the three of us start bowling.

Work today was frustrating. It took a long time to get everything perfect in some really unusual and intricate areas, and it feels good to relax with the guys. They're a fun group, even if I often feel the pain of being alone. They're quick to laugh and joke around, and Addi would probably love hanging out with them.

The thought surprises me. I need to get her out of my head better than I've been doing.

On the third frame, I get a strike and high-five everyone as I walk back to the bench and sit by Paige while Garrett gets up to bowl his frame.

"So, what's new, Ian?" she asks.

"Not much. How about you?" I assume the question is basic small talk until she shifts on the bench to look at me as she talks.

"No, I meant for real, what is new? There's something about you that's... different."

My first thought is Addi. Which is stupid because it's not like I'm around her that much.

"Um, I got a haircut last week."

Paige raises an eyebrow and her lips quirk up in a smile. "Yeah. Haircut. I'm sure that's it." She gives her husband a double high-five as he walks back after getting nine pins down and waits for his ball to come back up through the chute.

The waiting gets ridiculously long, though, so Garrett's eyebrows come together, and he looks toward the shoe rental counter. "I think my ball got stuck. I'm going to go let them know."

Paige turns back to me. "Are you dating anyone?"

I scratch the back of my neck, looking away, embarrassed. Paige knows my whole sorry story—I dated Cara for years, and we double-dated with Garrett and Paige through the whole thing. She saw everything practically firsthand. Me falling hopelessly in love. My proposal. The wedding plans. The invitations going out. Cara breaking up with me just two weeks before the I do's.

The fact that Paige can see something different in me— enough to suspect I have feelings for someone new—feels like she can see how foolish I'm being. Like I'm just setting myself up for another fall that she and Garrett will witness. I really have to get Addi out of my mind. Cara is a good person. If she found me unworthy of marrying, it's probably wise for me to stay far away from any future relationships.

I turn as Garrett comes walking over, the Lewis & Clark Lanes employee at his side. As they pass by us, Garrett looks at Paige, motions to the back of the furthest lane, and says, "We're going to go behind and get it!" with as much excitement as a ten-year-old about to go on his first rollercoaster.

I think Paige is going to press me for more information, but instead, she changes the subject. "Do you remember when Emmie was born, and I was trying to figure out life with a baby who cried nonstop and a toddler whose entire mission was to destroy the house?"

I chuckle. "I remember when Garrett would come to a site,

he had new stories daily of things like finding the milk in the pantry and the cereal in the fridge."

Paige laughs, too. "I swear I couldn't even have told you what six plus three was for those first couple of months. With the amount of sleep I got with a baby like Emmie, my maternity leave was over way too soon."

"I bet."

"So one day, I was back at the hospital, working a twelve-hour shift, and I went into a patient's room to do all the discharge teaching. I told him he needed to be on a liquid diet for the next week, the name of the doctor he'd need to follow up with, what medications to take—all of it. The guy was just so happy the whole time, which is my favorite thing to see when I'm discharging a patient. Thirty minutes after I sent the man on his way, I found out that I had gone into the wrong patient's room."

"You sent the wrong guy home?"

Paige nods. "He'd been so happy because he thought that meant he didn't have to do the MRI he was dreading. All the information I'd given him—diet, doctor, medication, everything—was wrong."

She shakes her head at the memory, and we both chuckle.

"It was funny, sure, and we all had a laugh, including the patient I accidentally sent home and the one I was supposed to discharge. But as I went home that night, I just kept thinking about what could've happened if it had been a patient who had needed a lifesaving medication. Or one of a million other scenarios that could've been just as devastating. The list of ways it could've gone so wrong kept piling up in my head, keeping me awake all night long.

"The truth was, my sleep-deprived brain very well could have caused a major catastrophe. The thought sickened me. The next morning, I called my supervisor and let her know that I needed a longer leave, and I didn't go back for another five weeks."

"I never knew that was the reason why you decided to stay home longer. I figured it was because of Emmie."

She nods slowly. "I felt very damaged. I questioned whether I even deserved to be a nurse. I was embarrassed, and I asked Garrett not to say anything to anyone."

"I'm sorry."

She looks over my shoulder and smiles, so I turn to see Garrett coming out from the door leading behind the pin deck, holding his bowling ball over his head like it's a trophy and he just won the Super Bowl.

Then she meets my eyes again. "Do you think I should've quit after that? That it was too big a mistake for me to ever be a nurse again?"

"No!" Is she thinking about quitting? That feels so wrong. Being a nurse is so much of who Paige is. "You're amazing at what you do. Garrett tells me all the time about how much your patients and the entire hospital staff love you. It would be a tragedy if you let that one mistake define your entire career and choose to quit."

She meets my eyes for a long moment, and then says, "Right. Just like it would be a tragedy if you let one failed relationship define the rest of your life and keep you from developing a meaningful relationship with someone else."

Then she stands up to go congratulate her husband on his successful bowling ball retrieval, leaving me on the bench feeling like I just got hit with a semi-truck of truth that I'm not sure I'm ready to accept.

CHAPTER 10

Addison

I JUST FINISHED a four-hour walk-in pantry job at a client's house and head back to the inn. The big jobs are the most satisfying, but the quick ones like this here and there are fun and give me the boost I need to tackle the big things.

And I have a massively huge job starting tomorrow. A client in a mansion in Lake Oswego wants me to organize both the husband's and wife's office spaces, a craft room, four bedroom closets, a toy room, and a family room. I plan to spend a full eight days at their house. I've already met with the client to assess and make a list of all the organization products we'll need to accomplish the monumental task. I ordered them from my favorite supplier, but the shipment was delayed, and I've been worried it won't arrive in time.

But I got a text that all the boxes were delivered to the inn just before I left my client's house. I can't wait to open them and get everything organized to start on the house tomorrow morning.

Not only is organizing the supplies one of my favorite parts but getting everything ready before starting is essential to the job going as smoothly as a job that large can go. I even grab lunch at a drive-through in Gresham so I can get started the moment I step foot into the inn. With as much as I ordered, it'll probably take every table in the dining room to get it all sorted.

I spot Ian's truck in his driveway even before I'm around the bend in the road enough to see the inn's sign, and I smile. Sure, the truck means he's home, which means he's close to my place, but it's not like I'm going to see him. So I'm really just grinning over seeing his truck. Ridiculous. I shake my head as I turn off the road and onto the inn's long driveway.

The fact that I can't find a parking space in my own eight-car parking lot is my first clue that a lot is going on at the inn. Still, I'm not quite prepared for the chaos I find when I open the front door.

All the boxes of supplies—all twenty-eight of them—are stacked in the lobby. Two little kids dressed like monkeys, who look like they're probably three or four, are pounding their plastic dinosaurs on the terrain of the multi-level box tower. I have no idea who the kids are, so I just wave and say hi. The loudest sounds are coming from the gathering room, so I walk to the left and poke my head in the double-wide doorway.

Bex must be filming her *Sterling Sisters* segment because she and all four of her sisters are seated in a semi-circle, each one talking before the previous one quite finishes. All of her sisters' kids who aren't old enough to go to school are running around the room, laughing and squealing and screaming, like they're trying to prove that their mom and aunts can stay cool amid chaos.

Interestingly enough, it doesn't explain who the kids playing dinosaur on my boxes are. Movement from the opposite side of the lobby—beyond the doorway to the kitchen and dining area—catches my attention. I leave the chaos of the gathering room, step over all the boxes and little kids dressed as monkeys in the lobby, and head to, hopefully, a more serene kitchen.

The room is so full of people and things that it takes a moment to make sense of what I'm seeing. Every single table in the room is filled with something, and four kids and half a dozen adults are all moving nonstop at the end of the room opposite the kitchen area. From the kitchen, Peyton waves, flashes her bright smile, and calls out, "I can't stop stirring, but come over."

Bewildered, I head back to the kitchen end of the room. Peyton holds her arm out—the one that isn't currently whisking some kind of sauce on the stove—and gives me a hug. "A little crazy in here, huh? I am making a week's worth of meals for a family of six because tomorrow morning the mom is going into the hospital to have a baby—child number five, if you can believe it. And if anyone needs a week's worth of meals already prepared, it's them, for sure."

A week's worth of food for six people. With the kinds of meals Peyton prepares, it makes sense that every burner on the stove has a pot on it, and every bit of counter space is taken up with food, cutting boards, and bowls of things in progress. The big dining table we eat on is filled with food containers, all with their lids neatly next to them, all of them labeled, some of them filled.

"And Timini?" I ask, motioning to the other end of the room.

"Oh, remember that client who was doing the extravagant production of *The Wizard of Oz* for preschoolers? They wanted a photo shoot of the kids wearing the costumes Timini made. And, of course, there are a ton of last-minute alterations. She's even had to sew an emergency lion's tail. She's so fast, it's unbelievable.

"Anyway, that's why her sewing machines and fabric are

everywhere. The woman in the yellow shirt is the client, and the one in navy is the photographer. Obviously, I mean she's the one with the camera. The other three are moms of the kiddos."

Timini is helping to get four kids and a dog—Dorothy, Tin Man, Scarecrow, the Cowardly Lion, and Toto—looking perfect, while the photographer and the client are attempting to pose them and the moms are trying to get them to stay put and not be distracted by the dog that's yapping like it's trying to narrate a high-speed car chase. Timini definitely has her hands full. With how introverted she is, when this is all over, she's going to crash like a toddler on the car ride home from a playground after being hopped up on sugar, sunshine, and friends for too long.

"What about you?" Peyton asks as she moves the sauce off the burner and starts cutting some vegetables. "What's on your schedule for the rest of the day?"

I glance toward the lobby, then race forward and catch Dorothy's basket that one of the kids from the photo shoot threw, saving the container of mashed potatoes on the table it's heading for. I toss it back to Timini, who seems to notice me for the first time and calls out, "Thank you!"

Then I turn back to Peyton. "I need to open all those boxes in the lobby and get everything organized. Some pieces will need to be put together, and then they all need to be grouped by which day I'll need them."

Peyton grimaces. "Well, at least the lobby's still available."

I nod. There's a free room upstairs where I plan to put everything, but it isn't big enough to open and assemble all twenty-eight boxes of supplies and still have room to organize. So really, the lobby is my only option.

When I get back to the boxes, the two monkeys are climbing on them like, well, monkeys, and the boxes probably aren't strong enough to hold them. So I convince them that empty boxes are more fun for their dinosaurs and hand them the cardboard boxes as I open them. And I'm right—the cardboard boxes *are* more fun. Fun enough that the half-dozen I've handed over to the kids have drawn in the six kids from Bex's family and the other four kids from the photo shoot.

Apparently, the lobby is also the "staging area" for the photo shoot, so before long, we're joined by the moms of the photo shoot kids and a whole lot of noise. Everyone is trying to direct kids and adults alike, even though no one can really hear what anyone is saying. The louder this group gets, the louder Bex and her sisters in the other room get, trying to be heard over the din.

The lobby is so full that I don't even have space to open another box. I worry that if I start carrying things upstairs, all the chaos will follow me, so I do my best to step over kids and boxes to get to the items I've already opened and move them to the top of the check-in counter.

All of it happens to the tune of kids shouting and making dinosaur, monkey, lion, scarecrow, and tin man sounds, adults directing, and cardboard boxes shuffling. Then I stack the unopened boxes in a tall, even pile, so they don't resemble a mountain terrain or steps—hopefully making them less enticing to climb on.

I cross my fingers that all the supplies in the boxes will be safe, then take the first opening in the crowd to escape down the hallway toward the back door and head outside.

As soon as the door closes behind me, most of the noise disappears, and I collapse against the stone wall of the inn, feeling like I just escaped from a stampede at the zoo. I guess I should've expected this when I found my roommates at a Creative Women Entrepreneurs seminar in a group of women who run their businesses from home.

I glance across the beautifully mowed grass to the always-open gate separating the inn's yard from Ian's, and I suddenly want nothing more than to go through that gate and see if he's in his shop. From what I've noticed, he's gone to sites three or four days a week, and on the weekdays that he's home, he's usually working in his shop.

But no. That's a very bad idea. I need to keep my distance and focus on something else. Like the weeds in the flower beds that need pulling or the blackberry bushes that are encroaching along the back fence.

Because somewhere along the way, I've realized that I'm not ready to open myself to a new relationship for more reasons than just worrying it could be a rebound. I'm also not ready for the probable rejection. To let a guy know that I like him only to be turned away. I've experienced it way too many times in the ten years I've been dating, and it's painful every time.

It hits me then that the underlying reason why I broke up with Matthew was rejection. He didn't reject dating me or even becoming an item. His rejection was more subtle, so I hadn't recognized it. But he rejected me every time I wanted to do anything that would progress our relationship into something less casual. Or do something outside of our usual takeout Tuesdays and Saturday afternoon hike or bike ride followed by a movie. He rejected my wanting to build a life with him. Or spending more time with him, talking about life goals together, or even just talking more.

Then, while eating Tuesday takeout one day, instead of talking about what we were going to do on Saturday like always, I told Matthew I needed to buy a new coffee table and asked if he wanted to go shopping with me that Thursday. A *Thursday*, of all days. Apparently, either coffee tables or Thursdays were Matthew's kryptonite, because he said we were going too fast, that he wasn't ready, and that he didn't know when he ever would be. After two years of dating, seeing me a third time in a single week to shop for a coffee table was moving things too quickly.

So, in the end, it was the constant rejection that made me break things off with him. And now, standing in my backyard, I know I'm not ready to face that again. Weeds and blackberry bushes are definitely the better option. I march right over to some nearby weeds and yank them out just to prove my point. The goal right now is to figure out what I want in life and decide if moving to Quicksand and starting my own business was the right thing to do. My goal is not to become interested in my neighbor.

But as I pull more and more weeds, I keep seeing Ian's shop from the corner of my eye, and I start to wonder what it looks like inside.

And, okay, maybe what he looks like as he works inside.

He's probably wearing a t-shirt, and those muscles I saw when he was mowing are probably straining his t-shirt as he works.

With as much care as he seems to put into everything I've witnessed him do, he's probably crafting beautiful things that are practically works of art. And his eyes are probably there, looking amazing and amused, and waiting to draw me in and make me forget how to form sentences.

Before I even realize what's happening, I'm through the gate separating our yards and halfway to his shed. Maybe it wouldn't be so bad to stop in and see him. After all, I haven't been stalking Matthew on social media, haven't thought about what he might think of me dating again, and haven't hoped he'd send me a text letting me know how he's doing. So I'm good. No rebound issues at all.

I hear the sound of a saw for a moment before it shuts off, so I raise my hand to knock on the door, imagining the moment he opens it, a smile spread across that beautiful face, and my heart practically floats.

Then I picture what his face would look like if he didn't want to see me, and my heart feels like fragile glass plummeting toward the ground, about to shatter. I change my mind. This really is a very bad idea. I turn around without knocking and head straight for the gate to escape back into my own yard.

CHAPTER 11

Ian

I SHUT off my bandsaw and am brushing the sawdust off a beautiful piece of oak when I think I hear something. A quiet knock? Just footsteps? Maybe my subconscious picked up on a shadow or something because I suddenly feel like someone's at my shop door. It's probably nothing, but I head to the door anyway.

When I open it, I see Addi walking away, and she's almost at the gate to her yard. "Addi!" She turns around, and from the blush on her cheeks, I guess she might've been at my door but left without knocking. "Want to come in?"

She glances toward her house before looking back in my direction. She's clearly still hesitating. But she walked all the way to my shed, so at least part of her wants to come in. And a big part of me really wants her to. I push the door open all the way so if that part wins out, she'll have a clear path.

She shakes her head and chuckles as she walks toward me. "You, Ian, must have supersonic hearing. I swear I didn't make a sound coming up to your door."

I shrug. "What can I say? It's my superpower." It's not my

superpower. Especially because all the noise from the saw I just ran is still making my ears ring. But claiming that is better than admitting what might've actually happened—that so much of my focus is on her at all times I can practically sense her nearness.

"Welcome to my shop," I say, motioning to it all. Addi walks slowly around the space, looking at everything as she goes, her eyes seeming to fall on each thing without missing any. I'm suddenly dying to know what thoughts are going through her head.

"It's different than your grandpa's shop. More… airy."

I nod. "I had to tear his old shop down and rebuild before I could move my equipment here—it wasn't up to code anymore. That back wall, though, is finished with all the wood from his shop, and everything hanging on it is from my grandpa." It's the best part of the space. My grandpa taught me so much every summer that the man deserves an entire wall as a shrine. By the way Addi smiles while taking in all the details, she agrees.

She asks for a tour, so I show her everything. I figure she's just asking to be polite, but when she asks more questions about everything, I start telling her about the names of every saw, sander, and tool.

"I never knew you were interested in this kind of stuff."

She lifts a shoulder in a shrug, and it makes me notice just how great her shoulders are.

"Back in Amarillo, I designed storage solutions, and I worked closely with our manufacturing plant. We mostly made our pieces out of plastics—the kinds of things you'd find at Target or Bed, Bath and Beyond, so it was basically nothing at all like what you do here. It's just interesting to see the difference between that and what you use for woodworking." She runs her fingers along the piece of wood I cut moments before she showed up at my door. "Your finished product is a million times prettier. What are you making with this?"

She jumps up to sit on the counter at the end of my shop. I figure it means she really wants to hear, so I talk about the fireplace I'm designing for a remodel and explain the parts I assemble in my shop and the parts I do during installation at the client's home.

And she listens the whole time. I try to think of the last time I've had a captive audience like this, and I can't come up with one. My grandma listens, of course, but she already knows pretty much everything there is to know about carpentry from my grandpa, so I never get to talk to her about it like this. Cara definitely never wanted to know anything about my job. Ever. She wanted me to have a good job with steady pay—she didn't want to have to hear about it. That was stuff I was supposed to chat about with my "carpentry friends." Having Addi listen is new. It's nice.

When I finish telling her all about it, she says, "Play Rapid Fire with me."

That's a game I haven't played since that summer when I was fourteen. I cock my head. "You offering anything?"

Addison looks up, like she's trying to think of anything she can offer, but then shakes her head.

"Awesome. Double Rapid Fire it is." I was hoping she didn't have anything to offer in payment for a one-sided game because I really want to hear her answers, too. I sit on the worktable across from Addi, an aisle separating us.

"One, two, three," Addi says, as we bounce our fists on our thighs. Then she makes scissors with her hand and I make paper. She's less predictable than she was as a kid. "Yes!" she says. "Okay, last serious relationship—how long ago, and how serious?"

"Wow, Addi. Just like when you were a kid, you jump into the hard questions."

"Sorry. Want to use a skip?"

"Nope. It's okay." I don't exactly want to talk about it, but I also want her to know. "Lasted just over a year, ended two weeks before you moved in. It was pretty serious. I thought we'd get married." I hold back my own flinch saying it and am surprised that Addi's face doesn't hold distaste at hearing it. In fact, all I can see is curiosity, like something just clicked into place, and something else I can't quite place. Not pity. Understanding, maybe?

"Two years for me, also ended two weeks before I moved in, went nowhere."

Interesting. We both had relationships that ended at virtually the same time. Maybe that was where the understanding came from. But now I'm the curious one. I expect her to ask a follow-up question—since she won the round, she gets to ask first. She must see my reluctance to talk about it because she doesn't ask.

Unless she doesn't want to open herself up to me asking a follow-up to hers. Fair enough.

She wins the next rock, paper, scissors battle, too, and asks, "On a scale of one to ten, how much do you love your job?"

"Eight." The point of the game is to answer fast, without giving yourself a chance to think. My answer kind of surprises me.

"Eight," she answers for herself as well. Then she says, "Huh. With as much as you light up when talking about it, I would've guessed a nine or ten."

She wins the next round. I need to switch up my rock, paper, scissors strategy. "If you could give up one aspect of your job, what would it be?"

"Trim."

"Bead collections."

I finally win a round and ask, "What's the part of your job you like the best?"

"Finding creative solutions to problems that seem impossible to solve."

"Building things."

Then I win again and ask, "What would make your job a ten?"

"Owning my own organization design business."

I'm dying to ask her about it, but I have to answer first. That's the rule. "Owning my own custom cabinet shop."

Her eyebrows shoot up and her mouth opens like she's about to ask me something, but since I asked the question, I get to ask a follow-up question first. Also the rules. "I want to hear more about this design business."

"I love helping people to organize the spaces in their homes. I really do. There are just so many times that I think of a storage solution that would be perfect—if it actually existed. If I still worked at my old job, I would've made a mockup and really pushed for it in our production meetings.

"Back then, though, I wasn't in people's homes so much, organizing their spaces, so I didn't have the practical knowledge I've gotten from being in the field. I'd love to combine both. And with my own shop, I would have that kind of freedom."

Everything about her comes alive as she talks about it. Happiness and excitement fill her expressions and her tone of voice. Her sense of adventure was what first made me want to become friends with her when I was eleven—I love that she hasn't lost that. I want to have those adventures with her again. And I want all those big dreams of hers to come true.

"Now, I want to hear about your custom cabinets because,

Ian, that's perfect! I can totally picture you doing that. Would you run it out of this shop?"

I shake my head. "It's too small. About all I can make here is one built-in at a time. I would need a shop large enough to build several sets of cabinets at the same time and have space for some employees. So it'll take time, but all the decisions I make as a subcontractor are aiming me toward that goal."

I haven't shared that dream with anyone. It feels great to say it out loud and to have someone hear it. Especially someone who seems so interested and believes I can do it. I hadn't guessed how great that would feel. Like a helium balloon in my chest.

"If you start doing custom storage cabinets for parts of the home other than kitchens—like mudrooms, storage areas, laundry rooms, things like that—let me know. I have several clients who I bet would love to have you build them some."

No words come out of my mouth. I just sit, looking at Addi. I haven't had a ton of experience with serious relationships other than Cara, and with her, support only went one way. She never would've offered to give my name to potential clients. I thought Cara and I had a pretty perfect relationship. But the more time I spend around Addi, the more I realize that maybe I'd been romanticizing our relationship. Maybe it wasn't all I'd thought it was.

I become aware that I've just been staring at Addi when she shifts her gaze to the floor. I lean forward a bit. "Thank you." I hope my words come out as heartfelt as I mean them.

She meets my eyes, a look in hers that I haven't seen before. I don't know what it is, exactly—all I know is that I want to reach out and touch that earnest, beautiful face. Then I glance at her lips and realize how badly I want to pull her close and kiss those lips.

There's a good three feet of aisle separating us, but when she leans forward, I know she must be feeling it, too.

Her shift in hand placement made her push down on the edge of a board that hung over the counter's edge. It flips it up, sending both it and the container of one-inch-long wooden dowels resting on it flying. The board clatters to the ground and the dowels scatter to the floor, rolling everywhere.

We both jump off our seats on the work surfaces pretty quickly, and Addi's hands fly to her mouth. Then she mumbles, "Oh my goodness. This is blueberries all over again."

I chuckle. "Nah. Nothing like blueberries. Which is good because I like this shirt."

Her eyes fly to my chest, and my pecs may involuntarily flex, which is closely followed by her face reddening and mine breaking into a grin. She grabs the empty container from where it has rolled right next to my drill press, and I take it from her and set it on the counter next to me. "It's okay, Addi. Not a big deal."

She grabs the container back and bends down to pick up the dowels. "There isn't a surly man in deli to call for clean-up on the front aisle, so it's the least I can do."

I smile and crouch next to her, picking up the little round pieces of wood that have spread themselves everywhere. As we work side by side, our knees, arms, and sometimes hands brushing each other, all I want to do is turn toward her, cradle her face in my hands, and kiss her until we both forget about the spilled dowels.

Addi looks over at me with her face so open and beautiful, and I nearly do just that. But then her eyes shift to how far the mess has spread behind me, and I look, too. As much as I want to kiss her, the mess tells me I can't. It's like the universe is showing me a physical representation of the mess I'd make of things with Addi if I did, and I like her way too much to do that to her.

CHAPTER 12

Addison

I HEAD HOME from a half-day job in Gresham, wishing I had a job lined up to take the other half of the day. It's still scary having my own business and knowing that a paycheck isn't going to magically appear from a company anymore, so gaps in my schedule make me nervous. I have another half day unscheduled next week and two the week after that. Sure, I might get more clients in time to fill them, but I can't guarantee it.

As soon as I open the front door, Bex comes running from the dining room, phone in hand, looking like she's simultaneously going to hold her arms up in a V while running a victory lap and pull at her hair in desperation. "Adds! I'm so glad you're home! I was literally just pressing on your contact to call you. Are you off for the rest of the day?" When I nod, she says, "Oh good. I need a giant favor from you, and I promise I will let you cash in on that favor at any moment of any day."

The sounds of kids eating, laughing, arguing, and telling jokes all at the same time are coming from the kitchen, and it's all I can do to keep my attention on Bex and not walk in there to see what's up.

"Remember how I've been dying to get an interview with Steve Stonebreaker for my channel for months? I just got a call from his publicist—he's in Portland and has an opening. Today! But there's no school today, and I already told my sister I would watch her kids, so they're here, and I can't take them with me. Adds, you have to help me. I can't pass up this chance."

"You want me to watch your sister's kids?"

"Yes. Thank you! Seriously, I owe you big time. Peyton is doing that big catering thing until late tonight, and Timini isn't back from visiting her parents until tomorrow. I already cleared it with my sister, and she's good to have you watch them instead."

"Bex, I don't know how to take care of kids! I have one sister who is two years younger than me, so it's been forever since she was a kid, and I have zero nieces and nephews. I wouldn't even know what to do!"

Bex brushes away my comment with her hand as she goes to the check-in counter and starts filling her oversized bag with things she keeps in the drawer, placing her video equipment on top. "It's seriously not hard. There are only four of them, and they're good kids. It'll be a piece of cake. It's an hour drive there and an hour back, and probably an hour for the interview, so I'll be gone three hours, tops."

She finishes packing her bag and looks at me. "Just take them to the park or something." She holds up a set of keys. "My sister traded me vehicles, and I can trade you, so you'll have her Yukon with the car seats for the younger ones. She keeps it stocked with wipes and a first aid kit and everything else you could possibly need."

Panic rises in me more and more by the second.

Bex sets the keys on the counter and says, "These are for the

Yukon," and then grabs my keys right out of my hand. She gives me a hug and a quick "You're the best!" before poking her head into the dining area. "Addison is going to watch you all until I get back. She's awesome, and I know you'll all be angels for her." Then she races out the door.

Before I've even taken a step toward the kitchen, Bex opens the front door again and pokes her head in. "Oh, and watch out for Drew. He has even less stranger danger than the rest of them." Then she's gone again.

Shock keeps me from moving a single inch from the spot where I stand for a good thirty seconds. Then, I hear shouting over whose carrot stick someone just took a bite out of was whose, and I rush into the dining area to hopefully quell whatever is going on. Four kids sit at the dining table, and two of them are having a tug-of-war over a carrot stick. The other two are using their carrot sticks for a mini sword fight. The moment they see me, all four put down their carrots and smile at me like they have actual halos over their heads.

"Hi," I say, giving a little wave. "I'm Addison, and I guess we're going to hang out today."

The oldest kid shrugs, picks up his sandwich, and takes a bite. The two youngest go back to sword-fighting, and the remaining girl just grins at me. So I take a seat facing the girl.

"Do you mind introducing me to everyone?"

"No problem." The girl points to her older brother. "That's Ash. He's eight, but just barely. He's the oldest, so he thinks he's the smartest. I'm Beth. I'm six and the one that's *actually* the smartest."

She flinches when Ash's carrot stick hits her in the arm but keeps going like nothing happened. "That's Chelle. She's five, and the one sticking the carrot up his nose is Drew. He's four." She reaches out and yanks the carrot stick from her youngest sibling's nose. "If you forget, you can just call us A, B, C, and D," she says, pointing to each of them in order.

"Clever." I try not to let the shock of being in charge of four kids who are all basically a year apart in age show on my face.

"But it's like secret cleverness," Beth says, leaning in and cupping her hand at the side of her mouth conspiratorially, "because our actual names—Dasher, Elizabeth, Michelle, and Andrew—aren't alphabetical at all. Only our nicknames are."

"Extra clever."

The younger two switch from sword-fighting and nose-sticking their carrots to throwing them, and it only takes about one-fourth of a second for the older two to join in. "Okay," I say, standing up, "it looks like maybe you're done with lunch. Want to go to the park?"

They all give their yeses in the form of fist-pumping, jumping up and down, ear-splitting shouting of words I can't even make out, and, in Chelle's case, dancing.

"Let's, um, get lunch cleaned up, and then we'll head out."

They throw all their garbage away like the trash can is a basketball hoop and they're in a slam dunk competition. They're all wearing shoes and look like they're probably ready to go. Thankfully, it occurs to me to ask if anyone needs to go to the bathroom before we leave.

Even though they were mostly ready, it still takes a full fifteen minutes to get them all outside to the Yukon and hop in. And then back in. And then back out. It's like we're playing a game of whack-a-mole where one of them keeps popping up outside of the vehicle every time I get another one in.

Eventually, all four are buckled into their correct seats, and all the doors are closed. As I go around to the driver's side of the vehicle, I stop at the back and lean against it just to catch my breath.

"Looks like you're having a party over there."

At the sound of Ian's voice, my attention flies to where his truck is parked at the end of his driveway, just twenty feet away. It's been a week and a half since we came so close to kissing, and I still think about it daily and long for a moment like it to return. But right now, I long for some help even more.

"Ian! Please tell me you have absolutely nothing going on in your life for the next little bit and have been hoping someone would come along and ask you to spend an afternoon at the park."

He smiles that amused smile he seems to have reserved just for me that's getting way too much use. "Where'd you get all the kids?"

"They're Bex's nephews and nieces, and she begged me to watch them for the afternoon. Do you have any experience with kids?"

"Sure—all my brothers have kids, and I love hanging out with them. Plus, I host my Junior Woodworkers club every week."

"Ian, please help me. I don't have any experience, and I don't know if I can survive this on my own."

I jolt in surprise as something hits the window just behind me, and I turn to see that an all-out stuffed animal war is going on in the back seats. I hadn't even seen stuffed animals in the vehicle. But Ian is walking toward me, either out of morbid curiosity or because he's willing to help. Hopefully, it's the latter.

"Bex says it'll be a piece of cake, and that they're angels."

"Clearly, she's right."

"Of course, if you gave thirty kindergartners unlimited snow cones and cotton candy and then put them in a room together and asked Bex to play a game with them, she'd emerge an hour later saying it was a piece of cake, that they were angels, and that she wants to do it again soon."

Ian glances toward his shop.

"Do you have a lot of work that has to get done today? If you do, you can tell me no. I'll survive it on my own." I mean, I'm pretty sure I will. I glance at the kids. Okay, I'm maybe five percent sure.

He looks at his shop for a long moment, and then he turns back to me. "Nothing I can't get done later tonight."

"So you'll come with me?"

He nods, and I have to stop myself from throwing my arms around him to show my overflowing, can't-contain-it, have-to-show-it gratitude. I stop fighting it and give him a quick hug before I can decide it's a bad idea, then run around to my side of the Yukon. We need to leave before the little ninjas inside the vehicle find a way to escape and I have to start the process of getting them buckled in all over again.

Once we get to the biggest park in town and all the kids run squealing in excitement toward it, I let out a huge breath of relief that I no longer have to keep them contained. But it doesn't take long before I've used a handful of wipes, half a dozen squirts of hand sanitizer, two bandages from the first aid kit, an extra pair of socks from the bag in the car, made three trips with kids to the bathroom, caught Drew trying to escape four times, and asked the kids not to show me any snails, snakes, beetles, squirrels, or slugs they find. And better yet, not to pick them up at all.

Right now, the kids are all together, huddling under one of the platforms leading up to the slides, talking with some other kids they've made friends with since we've been here. It's the first time they're all within sight at the same time and no one needs to go to the bathroom. I collapse on a bench next to Ian.

"Thank you again for coming. I don't know how I could've gotten through this without you. Seriously—I can't even imagine the shenanigans they could've gotten into each time I took one to the bathroom or went to the car for a bandage."

"You say that as though we've already gotten through it, but I'm pretty sure they're having a war council as we speak."

"As long as they let me sit here next to you for thirty seconds right now, I'm okay to let that be a problem for future me."

From where we've both flopped down on the bench, our hands are next to each other, our fingers bumping. Ian moves his pinky finger, running it along the edge of my hand. I close my eyes and let myself feel every single thrill of goose bumps that go all the way up my arm and to my heart. Maybe he really is feeling the same things I am.

Ever since Ian told me how recent his breakup was and how serious it had been, I've tried not to push him. Fear has stopped me plenty, too. But I'm falling for him—more so every single time I see him.

I'm in the middle of imagining what it would be like if he ran those fingertips of his all the way up my arm when I hear breathing next to my other ear and my eyes fly open. "I know you said no bugs, snakes, or… I can't remember what else," the five-year-old Chelle says, "but this isn't any of those. Check out this frog I found!" She plops the big-bellied thing down on my arm, and it lets out a big *Crooooak!* at the same time that I scream.

Chelle grimaces as it hops away. "So… No frogs, either?"

"Pretty please?" I beg.

"Check," Chelle says, drawing an invisible checkmark in the air with her finger. "No more frogs." She's halfway back to the slide when she turns back. "Tadpoles aren't frogs, right? Because I think there's a pond back there."

"I think we better say no to tadpoles and no to going to the pond," Ian says.

Chelle writes another invisible check, then turns to the others under the platform and shouts, "The tadpole plan is out, guys!"

I bury my face in my hands and mumble, "How much more time do we have?"

"Until Bex's three hours are up? Um, it looks like about fifteen minutes."

That's worth taking my hands off my face for. "Oh, thank heavens. So, we can head back now, right?"

Ian smiles the sweetest smile at me, and then he reaches out and gives my hand a squeeze before standing up. His hand is only on mine for a second, but it sends such a jolt of electricity through me that I think I might be able to handle the monumental task of getting all four kids back in the vehicle.

I can't help but check Ian out as he brings all of the kids together for a huddle and pulls me into it, talking to the kids like he's the quarterback explaining to the team what the next play is. Then he rallies them to grab any shoes that somehow fell off, water bottles that have been tossed aside, and anything else they left, and we all head back to the Yukon. He's so cute with them that I could watch all day. Remarkably, they all listen and head to the vehicle.

Getting them inside it is another story. I've never seen so much opening doors, running around to the other side, closing doors, opening again, and running around again. And it's coming from all the kids and in all different directions. If it were a choreographed show on Broadway, I'd still be impressed.

Ash and Beth are giggling on the opposite side of the SUV from me. I almost walk around to ask them to get in, but before I can, Drew takes off running at full speed toward the playground. No sooner does Ian run after him than Chelle takes off in the direction of the pond, so I chase her down. By the time we get them both back to the vehicle, I want to kiss Ash and Beth. They're both in their seats, seatbelts on, actually looking like angels.

And they even stay there while Ian and I get Chelle and Drew buckled in. I let out a huge breath as I get into the driver's seat and start the Yukon.

Ian motions to the clock in the console. "With as long as that took, Bex will probably beat us back to the inn."

"Music to my ears," I whisper as I pull out of the parking space.

A few minutes into the drive, I realize this is the quietest the kids have been since the moment Bex left me with them. It's quiet enough that I can even hear the radio—I hadn't even realized it had been turned on this whole time. All that's coming from them now are whispers and giggles.

Ian must notice at the same time, because he says, "You all sure are being quiet."

There's more giggling, and definitely more whispering and "*Shh*"s coming from them.

At a stop sign, I glance at Ian. "Maybe we just wore them out?"

Ian twists to look at the kids, then turns back and mumbles only loud enough for me to hear, "Or this is the calm before the storm, and they're about to carry out those plans they made in their council of war earlier."

I look at him in alarm. "No. It can't be that."

Ian looks out the window, squinting at something in the distance, not meeting my eyes. "Yeah, I'm sure it's fine." He reaches over and gives my knee a gentle squeeze, which isn't quite the comforting gesture he's probably meaning it to be. Especially when he adds, in a voice I don't believe at all, "We've got nothing to worry about."

CHAPTER 13

Ian

THE KIDS in the back seat keep up the whispering the whole ride home. That part is nice. And they've kept calm enough that I've been able to marvel at Addi. She may not have experience, and she may not have been planning on this today, but she's been such a trooper. Especially in taking care of kids as rambunctious as these. I can tell that she's exhausted, but she's still giving me the cutest smiles whenever she feels my gaze on her.

Today isn't what I had been planning on, either. But I wouldn't trade the past three hours with Addi for anything. As chaotic as it has been, it has also been… magical. It has shown me how much I like working with Addi. How much I like partnering with her.

I glance back at the kids. Whispering is fine—it's the giggling that worries me. I actually love it when my nieces and nephews giggle about some secret plans they've made. But I have a feeling these kids aren't giggling because they've drawn a smiley face on the inside bottom of my plastic cup of punch at a family party or because they've hidden their plastic insect toys like Easter eggs throughout the house.

Addi pulls into the circular drive in front of the inn. Unfortunately, her car—the one that Bex is driving—isn't parked in the lot. As all the kids unbuckle their seat belts and start climbing out, Addi turns to me. "Thank you again for coming with me. Is there anything in your shop I can do that will help you make up for the time you lost today? I could come over as soon as Bex gets here."

I glance out the window. Instead of the kids running off in all directions and having to be herded back into the house like I expected, they're all in a cluster at the back of the vehicle. "I don't think you better say goodbye to me yet. We might want to hold off on all plans until Bex is here."

Addi must catch some concern in my voice or expression because she looks at the pack of kids at the back of the vehicle, worry and wariness all over her face. When we get out of the SUV and walk around to them, they're lined up with their backs against the vehicle, hands behind them, grinning like they've never been more proud of themselves.

"Look what we brought back with us," Beth says, and all four of the kids motion like they're Vanna White, presenting a young boy who's standing in the middle of their group. He's one of the friends they'd made at the park who'd been present at their war council under the slides.

Addi's gasp is audible, and her hands fly to her mouth.

These kids are even more ingenious than I gave them credit for.

"His name is Jaxon," Drew says. "We're friends now. He wanted to come over and play."

"So we planned everything." Chelle throws her arms wide. "Aren't we the best at planning? You guys didn't even know we did it!"

"And we even got the timing perfect," Ash says, puffing his chest out. "Drew and Chelle took off running so you'd chase them, which gave us all the time we needed to get Jaxon hidden under the blanket in the back."

"And I stayed quiet the whole time!" Jaxon looks so proud of himself for that feat.

These kids pulled it off like pros. They probably have a bright future ahead of them as actors, business strategists, or criminal masterminds.

Addi starts breathing fast and pacing in a small circle. "I can't believe I just kidnapped a kid! His mom is probably running around frantic, searching for him. The police are going to come, they're going to arrest me, and I'm going to jail for kidnapping."

"It's going to be okay." I take a step toward her and place my hand gently on her shoulder.

"No, it's not. We have a kidnapped kid right here! What do we do? Do we take him back to the park and say sorry? What if they're already out searching?"

I pull out my phone and say, "Let's see what the police want us to do," as I dial 9-1-1. Because Addi's so panicked, I wrap an arm around her shoulder. She turns into me, and I hug her to my chest as well as I can while holding the phone to my ear.

"Nine-one-one. What's your emergency?"

"We want to report an accidental kidnapping. We were babysitting some kids and took them to the park. As we were packing up to leave, they very expertly snuck a new friend into the vehicle when we weren't looking and hid him under some blankets."

"Can you describe the child for me?"

"Um, yeah. He looks like he's about five."

"I'm six!"

"Correction—he's six, and his name is Jaxon. He's got brown hair and a green shirt."

"Which park was he abducted from?"

I flinch at the use of the word *abducted*. "Pioneer. Listen, I swear this was an accident. Well, accidental on our part. It was very purposeful on the kids' part."

"Pioneer Park. Okay, it sounds like another operator is talking to his very alarmed mother right now."

"Do you want us to drive him back there?" All the kids are racing around to the backyard, and Addi is chasing after them, so I follow.

"No. We have officers on their way to your location right now."

"Perfect. Thank you." I hang up, grateful that we don't have to try and get all five kids back into the vehicle, and I help Addi get them all back to the front yard. That way, when the police come, we won't have to explain how we just lost the kid we kidnapped along with the ones we were babysitting.

The first officer must've been close by because he's there in minutes. Before long, there are four police cars, all with their lights on, pulled in from both sides of the circular driveway, surrounding the Yukon. I didn't even know Quicksand had that many police officers on duty at once. Right behind them, the local news station, who must've been listening to the police scanners, pulls in and starts filming.

The officers split up, one asking me questions, one asking Addi, one asking Jaxon, and one asking the kids we're babysitting, probably checking to see if our stories match up. While my officer takes notes on what I say, I can hear Addi talking to hers.

"No—we didn't kidnap the other kids, too! They're the nieces and nephews of my roommate Bex Sterling. She was supposed to watch them today but then had an interview in Portland, and let me just call her. She can confirm."

As soon as the guy interviewing me—a balding man with

his hair cut close who looks like he's in his early thirties—starts asking more questions, I can't focus on Addi any longer. Until she grabs hold of my arm and I turn to see a horrified expression on her face, her eyes wide, her phone still up to her ear.

"Bex is still in Portland! She's not finished, so she's probably still an hour and a half from being home."

I wrap my arms around her like she's just gotten in a car accident and is going into shock. "We'll make it."

Luckily, Jaxon's mom comes speeding into the driveway not long after, skidding to a stop behind the police cars. She gets out and runs to Jaxon. He eventually manages to wiggle out of her smothering hugs long enough to introduce her to his new friends and to ask if they can play again tomorrow.

If nothing else, Jaxon's words to his mom assure the police officers and the reporter that the events of the day were unintentional by all adult parties involved. Whatever excitement the reporter thought they were going to be a part of isn't exactly national news-worthy, so they don't stick around for long.

This entire afternoon has given me a lot of time to witness how Addi handles everything. Her nerves are frayed and she's stressed and exhausted, but she never took it out on the kids. I'm impressed.

I'm even more impressed by her bravery when she suggests we go into the house and make cookies. Which, of course, makes a huge mess and leaves two adults and four kids with shirts covered in flour and one with melted chocolate chips all around his mouth and cheeks. But the kids are quiet for a solid five minutes while they scarf down their confections.

I take the moment to put an arm around Addi and let her rest her head against my chest. She smells like strawberry lemonade, and I soak it in. I soak in every bit of the feel of her against me. I may have thought I could keep myself away from

Addi before, but no longer. Not after today. Now, I want nothing more than to be near her.

Nearly five hours after she left, Bex bursts into the house with apologies and professions of undying gratitude and excitement over her incredible day. She barely sets her bags down when the kids' mom, Bex's sister, comes through the door. The kids emerge from the gathering room, where they'd been playing chase, all calm and full of smiles, looking as if they'd been angels the entire time.

While Bex is giving hugs to her nieces and nephews and saying goodbye, Addi grabs my hand and pulls me into the gathering room. Tired as I am, the feel of her hand in mine sends heat to my chest, and I know I'd follow her anywhere.

Luckily, where she leads me is to a couch, and I gladly collapse into it next to her.

"Did you ever think five hours could be so exhausting?"

I laugh and shake my head. "If you'd have asked me this morning what kinds of things were more tiring than taking care of kids for five hours, I could've easily listed a dozen. Now, though, I can't think of a single one."

Soon after we hear Bex's sister and the kids leave, Bex comes into the gathering room, holding a bag and a drink holder with two drinks. "I know that I still owe you both, big time, for watching the kids for me, and I will pay you back. But," she drags the word out as she puts the items on the table, "for now, this is an apology for taking so much longer than I thought. And for that whole thing with the police."

Addi leans forward, peeks into one of the bags, and her face lights up. "You brought us food from the Dragon's Chopstick?"

Bex nods, smiling. "And now, I'm going to leave you two in utter peace and quiet while I go upstairs. And leave you alone. With no one else home. Just the two of you."

Addi raises an annoyed eyebrow at Bex, and Bex holds up

her hands. "Okay, okay, I get it. No one said that 'overdoing it' isn't my middle name."

As the sound of Bex's footsteps on the stairs fades, Addi looks at the bags of food, not moving. "Are you ever so tired that you wish you could just teleport yourself into bed? Well, right now, I wish I could teleport this food into my belly. I'm starving, but I think I'm too exhausted to even eat."

"I don't think I could ever be too exhausted to eat food from the Dragon's Chopstick. Lean back." I give her a little nudge backward, and she lets herself sink into the backrest of the couch. Then I pull all the items out of the bag and open each of the boxes. "Do you like sesame chicken?"

She nods, so I pick up a good-looking chunk of chicken with the chopsticks and bring it to Addi's waiting mouth. She closes her eyes as she chews it, and I just smile at her, loving the way her eyes crinkle at the sides, the way her smooth skin looks almost golden in the light of the early evening sun, making her cheekbones look so touchably soft. And the way her curls shine as they frame her face. Even after a day of stress and exhaustion, she's beautiful. How did I ever think I could keep from being attracted to her?

With her eyes still closed, she opens her mouth again, so I feed her another piece of chicken. Then she smiles before opening her eyes and looking at me. "I think you just saved my life by feeding me those two bites."

"So that's twice I've saved you today."

"You'll be getting your Medal of Honor in the mail any day now."

"No ceremony?" I take a bite of beef and broccoli, grateful for some meat since all I've eaten since breakfast is cookies.

"You have to save me three times for that."

"Duly noted."

After a few minutes of silence, where all our focus is on

eating as a way to overcome our starvation and exhaustion, I say, "Do you want kids someday? Or did today ruin any chances of future Addi offspring?"

She gives a soft chuckle. "I think today would be effective birth control for anyone. But yeah. I do."

"Good. Because you're really great at it."

She gives me a look that I want to search for hours, trying to figure out what it all might mean. I only get a moment, though. It's enough to know that she appreciates the compliment.

"How about you?"

I've always wanted kids and jump at any chance I get to hang out with my nieces and nephews. But as crazy as today was, it has me thinking about how much I want kids of my own. After the way things ended with Cara, not only have I not allowed myself to think about it being a possibility, but the whole experience has left me questioning whether I'd ever be good enough.

All day long, though, as Addi and I took care of Ash, Beth, Chelle, and Drew, I haven't been able to stop imagining what life might be like with Addi. And that life has included kids of our own. Even through all the chaos of the day, I loved every moment of being with her. She's helping me heal. I don't want to be anywhere other than by her side.

I know the thoughts are dangerous, and I'll likely pay later for the hope they've raised that will be dashed, but right now, I don't care. I just want to live in that hope.

I nod. "I do, too."

Our eyes meet, and for a long moment, neither of us breaks eye contact. We just study each other, and I'd give anything to know what she's thinking. She's the one to finally break the connection. She grabs the box of Kung Pao Chicken, and while she's picking up a piece with her chopsticks, she says, "Thank you, again, for helping me through a rather memorable day."

I set down the box of beef and broccoli I'm holding. "What do you say that for our second date, we do something every bit as memorable?"

She swallows the bite she's eating a little too quickly and nearly chokes. "Second date?"

"Obviously, today was our first date."

She raises an eyebrow in challenge.

"I very distinctly remember me, looking all manly as I pulled lumber out of the bed of my truck, and you, asking me out on a date to the park. In fact, I also remember begging being involved. And," I motion at the table, "dinner."

"Well, then," Addi pauses to take a sip of her soda, "I think it's only fair for there to be begging involved when it comes to asking for a second date."

I hold up one finger and grab my soda with my other hand. I take a long drink, then clear my throat, get down on both knees on the carpet between the couch and the coffee table, and bring my hands together. "Addison Sparks, I would like to beg you to go on a date with me. Preferably one that doesn't involve the police or possible kidnapping charges."

"And no parks, frogs, snails, snakes, or insects?"

I nod. "We'll even take tadpoles out of the running. What do you say?"

Addison bites her lip, looking up at the ceiling like she's trying to decide. All I can focus on is her lips. Then she meets my eyes and says, "If it can be a spontaneous date. Not planned in advance."

I cock my head. "Interesting request. Deal."

I stand and hold out my hand to shake on it, and when she puts her hand in mine to shake, she instead tugs, pulling herself off the couch and to a standing position just inches in front of me. She's close enough that I can feel her breath on my neck. I'm not sure I'm breathing at all.

As the sun sets, throwing brilliant colors behind the woods just out from the giant bay windows in front of us, she holds my eyes, and I study hers. I get the distinct impression that a decision is being made. I desperately hope that whatever it is, it keeps her standing this close to me.

She reaches out and places a hand on my chest, right over my heart, and my pulse races, electricity buzzing through me at her touch.

Then she slowly, nervously, carefully, like she's testing whatever decision she's made, slides her hand up to my shoulder, her fingertips barely skimming the skin at the edge of my collar, sending chills up the back of my neck. I keep my eyes on hers, trying to guess exactly what she's thinking, but when her eyes flick to my lips, I can't help my gaze falling to hers.

Her eyes lock on mine once again before she rises up on her toes and presses her lips into mine. It surprises me. But at the same time, it feels inevitable—like everything since that first moment in the grocery store has been leading up to this. Maybe from the first moment when she was ten and I was eleven, and I saw her through the gate between my grandparents' backyard and her aunt's inn's grounds.

I wrap my arms around her, placing one hand on the small of her back and the other in the middle of her upper back, reveling in how it feels to hold her as her lips move against mine. After Cara called off our wedding, I hadn't imagined ever being interested in a relationship again. But everything with Addi just feels right.

She brings her other arm up, wrapping both of them around my neck, holding me just as close as I'm holding her. My heart races, beating a rapid Coryce against my chest, my fingers tingling, my head light.

When she breaks the kiss to take a few deep breaths of air, I take a long, slow breath to ground my senses, and then I place three gentle kisses in a trail from her temple down to the spot just under her earlobe, enjoying the short, quick breath she inhales.

"Wow," I say. "I am really glad that Bex insisted on leaving us alone for dinner." And then I soak in the smile that Addi gives me in return.

CHAPTER 14

Addison

I'VE HELPED a lot of people organize their clothes. Some have big walk-in closets, some have taken over closets in other rooms in the house, and one client even turned a spare bedroom into a closet. With every person, I usually find one item that they hoard. I've helped people with massive collections of shoes, sweaters, shirts, dresses, pants, humorous t-shirts, scarves, and even a client with a huge collection of every style of socks imaginable.

But this woman's Achilles hoarding heel is bras. *Bras.* Bras are the worst item of clothing to shop for—even worse than jeans. Why would someone pick that item of clothing to over buy? Apparently, this thirty-one-year-old advertising executive never buys a shirt without buying a bra to match. She says it makes her feel secretly well-organized. Like it gives her superpowers.

As I'm putting bra after bra on four hanging organizers that each hold a dozen, my mind can think of nothing except the kiss last night. Actually, it's the only thing I've been able to focus on all morning.

Well, that, and everything leading up to it. For five hours straight, I witnessed firsthand how Ian reacted to what was often a stressful situation. And every time, he helped calm things when they got out of control, paused to help one of the kids, came up with a fun game for them, calmed me when things were crazy, or comforted me when things were hard. Over and over, I fell a little more for him, somehow forgetting any reservations I had about dating someone new.

And then, as we ate, I fell even harder. I worried it might've been because of how exhausted I was and the fact that I had fallen pretty hard into that couch, but even in the light of a new day, I feel all of the butterflies constantly in my stomach and the tingles that race up my spine at every thought of him.

I haven't exactly had the best experience when it comes to guys feeling the same way about me that I feel about them, and last night, I was afraid. All through dinner, I kept hoping that he'd give a very obvious sign that he was feeling even a bit of what I was feeling. I didn't think I'd get it, but then he asked me out.

And then I gathered up every single bit of courage I could find and convinced myself that I was brave enough to be the one to go in for our first kiss.

It's not that I never kiss guys. It's that I've probably kissed fewer than anyone else who lives at the inn. Probably fewer than most twenty-six-year-olds on the verge of twenty-seven. But I know enough to know what to expect.

And that expectation is exactly why I'm still so blown away by Ian's kiss. I hadn't even imagined that kissing could be so incredible. Just remembering how his hands felt on my back, his breath on my cheek, the faint smell of wood he still had from working in the shop that morning, the softness of his lips against mine, those kisses by my ear, all while I'm pressed against his chest, is causing goosebumps to cover my arms all over again.

"Addison."

The voice of Jessie, my client, is insistent enough that I realize I've gotten a little too far into my own head. From where I sit on her closet floor, I look up at the woman, whose cleaning and organizing outfit of choice is a baggy pair of sweats and a t-shirt that says "The Office" on it. It's a very different look than the pantsuit and heels she wore at our first meeting. Jessie has her hand on a tote that sits on the bed, but I can't guess what she was just talking to me about.

"Yes?"

"You are somewhere else today, aren't you?" A smile spreads slowly across her face. "It's because of a guy, isn't it? All morning, you've had *I'm currently daydreaming about someone* face."

Based on how hot my ears suddenly are, I'm sure that face is covered in a deep pink blush.

Jessie sits down cross-legged on the closet floor in front of me. "Tell me about him."

I finish hanging up the bra I'm holding and let out a long, slow breath before meeting Jessie's eyes. "He's a guy I kissed last night. Which was probably a big mistake because he's my next-door neighbor."

"I guess that depends. On a scale of one to ten, how would you rate the kiss?"

I look down at the floor of the closet, smiling. "Ten. A ten so solid and far up there that I hadn't even known ten could be that high."

Jessie squeals like we're teenagers. "Then it's not a mistake, regardless of how it ends."

"Maybe. All I know is I've got to get my mind off him. Like right now. What's that tote you've got on the bed?"

Jessie reaches up and pulls it onto the floor next to us. "I was wondering if you have any ideas for how to organize my swimsuits. I went through them last night and narrowed it down to thirty."

My eyebrows shoot up. "Swimsuits are the only thing I can think of that's worse to shop for than bras. How are they what you collect? Do you have a trophy somewhere in here awarded for leveling up your shopping skill to the highest it goes? Maybe a medal, a ninja belt?"

Jessie laughs a tinkling little laugh, and I take the moment to force myself back into my actual job until this organization project is finished, and far away from that amazing kiss.

———

Since Jessie is an early riser, we finished her closet by noon, and as I head back to Quicksand, my brain is so jumbled from the mess of thoughts constantly swirling inside that I decide I really need to talk things out. Not with my roommates, though, because I already know what they'll say. I need my sister. So I pull over to the side of the road and send her a quick text.

> Addison: Hey, Sis! I really want to talk to you about Ian.

Her response comes quickly.

> Chloe: And I really want to listen to you talk about Ian.

> Addison: I also kind of really want you to meet him first. How would you feel if I invited him to join in on our birthday call?

Chloe: Oh my gosh. This is huge. YES PLEASE.

And then tomorrow, I better get a phone call where you talk about him.

Addison: You sound too excited. DON'T EMBARRASS ME CHLOE.

Chloe: I wouldn't dream of it.

Addison: And Chloe, guess what?

Chloe: You're smitten?

Addison: Not the point. The point is, there's a good chance Ian will say yes.

Even though I just thought of it, and will be giving him almost no notice.

Just like he said yes to helping me babysit yesterday with no notice.

And even though it's not Tuesday or Saturday!

Chloe: This is dream-come-true stuff for you right now, isn't it?

Addison: It's not that I need a guy to be spontaneous all the time. Or even most of the time. I just need to know that he can be.

Chloe: I can't wait to meet him!

Addison: Chloe, I need to hear that you won't embarrass me.

> Chloe: Aww! Dustin is lighting a birthday brownie for me. Gotta go! See you in 30 minutes!

I'm not sure if Dustin really is bringing her a brownie, or if it was just Chloe's way of getting out of making the promise. It doesn't help my nerves when it comes to texting Ian. Sure, we kissed, but I still don't really know how he feels about me. So I straighten my shoulders, slide the mirror on the visor open, and say out loud, "You can be brave. You were brave last night, and look what it got you." And of course, just thinking about it again makes me smile.

Before I know it, I'm typing a text message to him.

> Addison: Do you have a lunch break today? If so, are you free? I am having a video chat with my sister at 1:00, and I'd love to have you meet her.

I send the text then realize I probably should've included an apology. Feeling unsure, I figure I should also give him an easy way out.

> I know it's midday on a weekday and you're at work—she's nine hours ahead, so we had to plan it while she's awake. But there will be other times when you can meet her.

I pull the gearshift into drive, deciding I'm too nervous to wait around for an answer that might very well be no. But he responds before I can even take my foot off the brake.

> Ian: I will be there with bells on.

My heart soars somewhere around the top of my car the

entire drive home. I hope I'll have a couple of minutes to get inside, set up my laptop, maybe run a brush through my hair and put on some lip gloss, but as soon as I pull into a parking spot, Ian walks over from his house. He must've either been working in his shed or come home from a job for lunch.

CHAPTER 15

Addison

I can't stop staring at Ian as he strides toward me. He's so calm and confident without being cocky. The wind is even blowing the right amount to ruffle the slight wave in his hair. All I need is a video camera and the ability to watch it in slow motion, and I'd have my eyes glued to the screen for hours.

I shake myself as I realize I've frozen mid-step, gawking at him. I need to figure out what I should be doing other than mimicking a statue, but then Ian says, "Hi," as he nears, and my brain stops working.

"Hi," I say back, taking in those piercing eyes that are gazing at me, and I try not to imagine what it would be like if he walked right up to me, put his arms on my back, and dropped me into a dip, kissing me right in the driveway.

No drop kiss happens, but he does step up very close to me and tucks a curl behind my ear, then runs his fingertips down my neck, across my shoulder, and down my arm to my fingertips, sending thrills throughout my body and really not helping my ability to form words. I don't want to lose the ability to walk without falling, too, so I try to avoid looking into his eyes. In fact, turning and walking toward the door sounds like the safest course of action. So I do, pulling my keys out of my purse.

"I know you wanted our second date to be spontaneous, but I thought I was going to be the one doing the asking this time."

I glance at him as we walk up the porch steps. "This isn't a date."

"I don't know. You asked me over to meet your family. That sounds pretty date-ish."

I point at him with my keys before putting them into the lock. "Not my family—just my sister. It's so when we talk about you, she'll be able to picture you better."

He looks like he's trying to hold back a smile but isn't very successful at it. "Then I fully support this non-date."

I open the door to a lobby filled with balloons and a big sign that reads, *Happy Birthday, Addison!*

"It's your birthday?"

I duck my chin but glance at the beautiful man next to me. "Um, yeah."

"Why didn't you say anything?"

I walk to the check-in counter where a cupcake with a candle waits, along with a piece of paper that reads *Happy 27th!* in fancy handwriting—probably Peyton's doing—and *Remember that we're having a roommate dinner at 7:00 to celebrate!* below it.

"I don't know—it's awkward. How do you even bring that up? After our kiss last night, was I just supposed to say, 'Oh, by the way, my birthday is tomorrow'?" I grab my laptop off the counter and start walking up the stairs, Ian at my side.

"That might not have been the most elegant way to bring it up, but it would've been effective."

"Oh, but see, my roommates were both elegant and effective. So it worked out well that they took it into their very capable hands."

He raises an eyebrow but doesn't say anything.

I'd thought about setting up my laptop in the gathering room but I don't want any of my roommates walking in during the call. That's the thing about living in an inn full of creative women who run their own businesses—the hours are strange, sometimes ridiculously long, and it wouldn't be entirely unusual for any or all of them to walk in at 1 p.m. on a Thursday.

If it was just me and Chloe on the call, I'd set up in my room. But with Ian with me, that feels much too intimate. So I lead him to the storeroom instead. It's a bedroom we could use for another roommate, but instead, it holds all my storage supplies for clients I'll meet with in the next two weeks on one side, some of Timini's sewing supplies and equipment on the other, and a bed pushed up against the wall that Timini and I both use more as a couch or a table when we're working in here.

Once my laptop boots up, I get it situated on a container I'm going to use for wrapping paper storage for a client and go into the video chat. Chloe's call comes through about three seconds later, and when her face pops up on the screen, she's nothing but exuberant smiles. I introduce Chloe and Ian to each other, and Chloe's husband, Dustin, pokes his head in to say hello before leaving us to our call.

"Happy birthday, Addison!"

"Happy birthday, Chloe!"

"Wait," Ian says. "It's both your birthdays?"

"You didn't tell him?" Chloe asks.

"She didn't even tell me it was her birthday."

I hold in a grimace, glance at Ian, and motion to the screen.

"This is my inelegant way of telling you that we share a birthday." His hand is next to mine, and I have to ignore the fact that our shoulders are brushing together or I won't be able to think. "Except for the year Chloe was born and was in the hospital for my second birthday, we've spent every one of our shared birthdays together. This year it's just over video instead of in person."

"So you're two years apart in age, yet both of your birthdays are on the *exact same day*?"

We both nod.

"Wow. Your parents must've…"

I laugh when his comment trails off. "I know what you're thinking—I got there too when I was a kid. The very day I found out how babies were made, I Googled exactly how many days it took from conception to birth, did the math, and was one hundred percent confident that I discovered what day of the year we were both conceived."

"And from that year forward," Chloe says, "you couldn't convince Addi to stay home that night for anything."

"Come on. Do we have to tell him this story? It's embarrassing."

"Yes, we do, because you didn't tell him it was my birthday. So for the first couple of years after Addison's discovery, she'd call our grandparents and ask if we could sleep over. When we got a little older, we planned things with friends until curfew. I, of course, being the little sister, didn't understand what was going on."

"Because I, the big sister, was trying to shield you from the horror."

Chloe shoots me a look, then turns her focus to Ian. "All she told me was that we couldn't be home because that was the night of the year that our parents made babies, and you never knew when there would be another one. When I asked how they made babies, she just said, 'It's gross, and trust me: we don't want to be there for it.'

"She wouldn't tell me anything more. I remembered hearing from someone at school that their parents told them it was a 'special kind of hug.' So, that's what I had to go on. A gross, special kind of hug. Then, not long after, we had a barbeque with some family friends. My dad was out at the grill, my mom was stirring something on the stove, and Chloe and I were playing with their son Griffin.

"I went to tell my mom something and caught Griffin's parents in the hallway. They were hugging, and Griffin's dad's hands were cupping his mom's rear. Which, of course, was so gross. I thought, 'This is it. This is how babies are made.' So for three years—" Chloe shoots me a glare— "*three years*, I believed that was how babies were made."

Ian laughs so heartily that the sound practically bounces off the walls. "I think that might be the greatest story I've ever heard."

"Okay, for the record," I say, my ears getting hot, "I didn't know that was what she had assumed until much later."

"And you fully believed it?" Ian asks.

"Well, yeah," Chloe says, "because get this: when Griffin came to school on Monday, for show-and-tell, he announced that his mom was pregnant and he was getting a little brother."

"Well, obviously you believed it. Griffin practically handed you proof of your theory."

"See?" Chloe says, motioning to Ian, thrilled she's getting vindication all these years later for her misinterpretation of the facts.

Ian laughs, and I want to reach out and touch the smile lines at the edges of his eyes. Then he turns to me and says, "See? This is why, even if it's in-elegant, you should go for the effective way of telling someone something, instead of letting them figure it out on their own."

Chloe is grinning from ear to ear. Ian is so funny and charming and sweet, and I can barely keep my eyes off him. I can tell from how Chloe is reacting to him that she genuinely likes him and would totally support me being "smitten" with Ian. And who wouldn't? He's pretty great. It still feels so unreal that he's interested in me.

I smack him in the arm. "You just wait until that request comes back around to bite you."

His smile is big and beautiful. And then he picks up my hand, places the sweetest kiss on the back of it, and mumbles, "I look forward to it."

Embarrassing story after embarrassing story, the call finally ends, and I thoroughly regret having given Chloe the opportunity to tell so many. I should've called Chloe to ask about inviting Ian to the video chat instead of texting her. Then I could've made her promise on a stack of Bibles not to tell stories about our childhood.

I walk Ian to the front door and open it for him. He pauses in the doorway, then turns back to face me. "Do you want to go on a date with me?"

"Those stories didn't scare you away?"

His smile is big. "Quite the opposite. So are you free right now?"

"What? No. You can't miss work today because of me. You already took the entire afternoon off yesterday to help me babysit."

"And I'll be scrambling to make up for lost time later, but it's your birthday, and we've got five hours until you need to be back for your roommate dinner." He reaches out and takes my hand, tugging me toward him. "Come on. Let's go on a spontaneous date."

Our hands are touching and his captivating blue eyes are pulling me to him like we are, once again, magnets. I'm not sure I could tell him no to a spontaneous date with this beautiful man any easier than I could walk away from a sale on office supplies.

So I nod. "Okay, a spontaneous date it is."

CHAPTER 16

Ian

I HOLD Addi's door open as she climbs into my truck. "Where are we going on this date?"

I close her door, walk around to my side, and get in. "I don't know. You wanted spontaneity, so I think we should decide as we go." I tap my lips, thinking. "It is beautiful outside. We could go for a walk through town, or maybe even go check out the viewpoint?" I hope I've said it in a way that makes my preference for the viewpoint slightly known—enough to sway her to that choice but not enough to make it feel like it wasn't hers.

"Ooh! Let's go to the viewpoint. I haven't been there since I was about eleven."

A smile spreads across my face as I pull out of the parking lot and head in the direction of the viewpoint. "You've been here, what? Eight or nine weeks? How is it that you haven't been to the viewpoint?"

"I guess I forgot about it. Do you go there often?"

I shake my head. "Mostly when I need to think or if I want to feel… centered."

The drive to the viewpoint is only a couple of minutes long, but I enjoy every moment of the drive with Addison sharing the front seat with me. I want to reach out and hold her hand, but even though we kissed last night, the action still feels big. From the corner of my eye, I see her pinky twitch toward me, like she wants to reach out but is waiting for me.

So I reach out, sliding my hand into hers, and she curls her fingers around mine immediately. The smile on my face is probably going to be stuck there for the rest of the day.

I pull into the parking area at the viewpoint. Only one other vehicle is here—the one I expected. After I open Addi's door for her, we walk to the guardrail at the edge of the parking lot and look out across the valley filled with trees. Only a few clouds dot the sky, casting giant shadows across the valley while the sun lights up parts of it in brilliant greens and gold. Quicksand River meanders through the valley, framed in the distance by the ridge of the Devil's Backbone and the brilliant white of Mount Hood. "I forgot how beautiful it is here," Addi breathes.

I step up next to her, marveling at the valley. We move to the telescopes to see everything closer, and while she looks, I glance up the road. Cory should be here any minute.

"I don't think I've ever been here on such a clear day," Addi says. "Check it out—you can see the sun glinting off the river clear out there."

As I look through the telescope, I hear the sound of wheels on gravel behind me. It's all I can do to keep looking through the telescope until I hear a woman say, "Excuse me."

I turn to see Cory and his girlfriend, Becca, each with one foot on the flat base of an electric stand-up scooter, one hand on the handlebars, and a helmet tucked under their other arm.

"We rented these scooters at the little station on Settler's Boulevard. We were about to put them in the back of our truck to return them, but they're paid for until five. Are you two interested in taking them?"

"You're okay trusting a couple of strangers to get them back in time?" I ask.

The grin on Cory's face is going to give him away. "You two look trustworthy."

I turn to Addi and raise an eyebrow. "What do you think?"

"Sounds fun!"

Perfect. Cory and Becca drive off, so I leave my truck behind, and the two of us put on the helmets and head down the road on the scooters, the wind blowing in our faces as we ride. I keep glancing over at Addi to see if she's having fun or hating it, and the look of bliss on her face tells me I've made a good choice.

When we reach the end of the road and stop at the stop sign, I say, "What do you think? Should we head toward town?"

She nods and turns right. Each time we come to a road where we have a choice of which way to turn, I glance over at her. I can mostly tell which way she's thinking about choosing before she does it, so I only make the choice when hers would've taken us away from where I'm aiming.

We're getting closer to the middle of town when I spot the small food truck up ahead. "What do you think? Should we stop in the shade by that truck so we can decide where to go next?"

Addi nods and heads toward it.

When we pull to a stop, I take off my helmet. "What did you think of the scooters?"

"This was the funnest thing I've done in so long! I think I'm going to have to get one of these for myself sometime."

I hadn't been sure if she'd like them or not, so I'm thrilled that's her reaction.

The guy at the food truck, Rohan, pokes his head out of the window. "Hey. The lunch rush is done, so I'm packing up. I have enough fresh lemonade for a couple of cups full that I'd hate to throw out. You two interested?"

"Wow, thanks," I say. "We would love some."

After Rohan gives us our drinks and we thank him profusely, we sit at the picnic table in front of the truck.

"Does this kind of luck always follow you around?" Addi asks. "Because it doesn't for me, so I figure it must be you."

I shake my head. "Not for me, either. I think it must be the two of us together."

As we finish and get back on our scooters, I cock my ear in the general direction of the high school. "Do you hear music?"

Addi cocks her head too, concentrating. "I'm not sure."

"I swear I hear it. Want to find its source?"

The grin on her face says she's up for the adventure, which doesn't surprise me. We head off on our scooters, with me mostly choosing which direction we take until we're close enough to really hear the music. Then I let Addi lead us the rest of the way to the high school. The entire band class has their chairs, music stands, and instruments set up on the lawn just outside the band room.

"Do they always practice outside?" Addi asks as we pull to a stop at the edge of the parking lot by the grass.

I shrug. "Want to stay and listen for a bit?" I motion to a woman sitting with her two little kids on a blanket, watching the practice. "Looks like it's okay to."

Addi nods, so we get close and stand with one foot on our scooters, watching. Less than a minute later, the woman comes up to us, her toddler in her arms, the preschooler standing next to her. "Can you two do me a huge favor? My husband is the band director—we came to watch them practice. But my son needs to use the restroom, and I don't want to pack up all our stuff to take him. Do you mind sitting on my blanket until I get back so the wind won't blow it away?"

"We'd be happy to," Addi says, and we sit on the blanket,

legs outstretched, leaning back on our arms as the band plays a concert for two.

When they finish the song they'd been practicing when we arrived, they start playing Ed Sheeran's *Perfect*—a song I heard playing in Addi's room when I was helping Timini move in, so I figure there's a good chance she likes it. And I'm right. She snuggles in closer to me and whispers, "I love this song."

They play a variety of songs, and each time, the band teacher says something like, "Let's do the song we've been practicing for halftime," or, "Let's do our concert number." Then, after about fifteen minutes, he says, "Let's practice the one we do for birthdays."

Addi's eyes flash to mine, a look of wonder on her face. It's beautiful, and I try to memorize her expression and everything about the way she looks at this moment.

As they play the first few notes, I murmur in her ear, "Looks like the universe wants you to have a great birthday."

She turns and murmurs back, "I think the universe is doing a pretty amazing job of it." Her breath is warm and soft against my neck, and between her words and her breath, heat spreads through my chest.

Right after the last notes of the *Happy Birthday* song, the mom and kids come around the corner, so we stand up. With my back to Addi, I mouth, "Perfect timing" to the mom and give her a thumbs up.

We meander on the scooters through streets neither of us has been on before, just talking about random things. I find out she likes baby goats, things organized alphabetically, and cheesecake, but really doesn't like her mom's meatloaf or pens that write in black ink. Her favorite way to relax is watching home organization shows, she has an irrational fear of revolving doors, and she gets the cutest dimples on her cheeks when she's thinking about something that makes her happy.

The more time I spend around Addi, the more I realize how truly good a relationship can be. For so long, I've been hurt that Cara called off our engagement and canceled our whole future together. As Addi and I ride scooters and chat, I finally realize that, although Cara could've handled things differently, she wasn't mean or malicious. Calling off the wedding had been the right thing to do. By ending things, Cara opened the possibility for me to have a life with Addi.

And imagining what a life with Addi might be like is a million times more incredible than anything I ever imagined with Cara. My whole soul fills with a forgiveness toward Cara that I hadn't realized I'd been holding back until this moment.

Just before five o'clock, we head back toward Settler's Boulevard and return the scooters to the kiosk.

"How are we going to get back to your truck now? Maybe we should've just ridden back to the viewpoint and put them back in your truck to bring them here."

Except that would mess with the next part of my plan. So, I shrug. "It's your birthday and we're together, so I'm sure the universe will have our backs on that, too. Want to go for a walk down Settler's?"

We chat more as we walk by shops and restaurants, enjoying the rare cloud-free day. As we walk past the front of a café, a man inside knocks urgently on the bay window. When we turn to look, he holds up one finger, asking us to wait, then races around the other tables in the café to the door. He opens it at about the same time we reach it, and he says, "My wife and I just finished eating, and they've cleaned up the plates. They were about to bring us dessert, but my wife just went into labor, so we have to leave. Do you two want to come in and have the dessert? It's already paid for, and I'd hate for it to go to waste."

Addi looks blown away by how this date is turning out, and

I'm thrilled. We go inside, thank the couple, wish them the best with the delivery, and then sit down in their seats.

"What are the chances of this happening, especially after everything else magical today?" Addi asks, her voice filled with wonder.

I shrug, doing my best to keep the grin off my face.

The waitress comes over to our table, holding a dish with a slice of chocolate cake, two scoops of vanilla ice cream, and a candle sticking up out of the ice cream. Three other employees trail behind her. "What's your name, honey?" Addi looks confused. "What's going on?"

"The couple who were here before ordered this dessert with a side of birthday wishes, so I need your name for when we sing happy birthday."

"Okay," she says, eyeing me suspiciously as I do my best to look perfectly innocent and just as surprised as she is. "Addison."

The four employees sing their restaurant's version of *Happy Birthday*, and guests at a few other tables join in. After the waitress sets the dessert on the table and says, "I hope you have a wonderful birthday," Addi goes back to eyeing me as she picks up her fork and gets a bite of the cake. I scoop up a bite too, making sure to get some ice cream with it, while she continues to analyze me as we both chew.

"Did you set this up?"

"I'm pretty sure the couple who just left did that." I put another bite in my mouth, keeping my expression as neutral as possible.

"Ian. You still do that eyebrow thing you did as a kid whenever you're not telling the whole truth. Confess. You knew it was my birthday before today, didn't you?"

"Yes," I say slowly, "but I didn't know until last night."

"Bex?"

I nod. "Moments after I left the inn last night, Bex knocked on my kitchen door. When I opened it, she said, 'Remember how I said I owe you for watching my sister's kids today? I'm going to start paying you back by letting you know that Addison's birthday is tomorrow, since I know she didn't tell you.'" I give Addi a look, reminding her how I feel about the fact that she didn't tell me. "Then I started making calls."

"So you knew the couple who was here before us?"

I nod. "Caden and Danielle. Caden's a buddy of mine who does the electrical work at a lot of the same sites as me."

"His wife didn't just go into labor?"

"She still has two or three weeks. I bribed them with the meal they ate before we got here if they'd set up this," I say as I point at the dessert with my fork, then I load up another bite.

As I chew, I see her working through the date in her mind, analyzing each thing. Her expressions switch between confusion and realization. "And the couple who gave us the scooters?"

"My friend Cory and his girlfriend Becca. They took them for a ride along Ridge Street and planned it so they'd be at the viewpoint by two-thirty."

She shakes her head in disbelief, but there's amazement there too. Like she's impressed. "You set up the lemonade too, didn't you?"

I nod. "I stopped by this morning on my way to a job and ordered them, then talked Rohan into playing along, which he was way more excited about doing than you'd guess."

"Don't tell me you set up the band, too."

I smile and shrug, then I take a bite of the cake. "This really is delicious. You better have some more before I accidentally eat it all."

"How?"

"The high school band? My grandma is friends with the

band director's grandma. She asked if they'd practice outside, and his wife wanted to join in on the fun by getting the blanket there and ready for us."

"And you planned all of this today?"

"Nah. A lot of it happened last night."

"And you did all this for me?"

I want to reach out and smooth the disbelief from her face.

"Just so I could have the perfect 'spontaneous' date?"

"*And* so you could have a great birthday."

"Ian, I..." She trails off, pressing a knuckle below her bottom eyelashes. "I think it's the sweetest thing anyone has ever done for me."

Her words hit me like a warm wave, and I know I've made the right choice. She looks at me with those beautiful eyes rimmed in gold, and I can tell she's touched by the effort. It makes all the time and planning completely worth it.

"So, how were you going to get us back to your truck?" she asks.

In a move I couldn't have planned the timing on better, a man bursts into the restaurant and says, "Anyone need an Uber? I was supposed to pick someone up, but they said never mind. I can take you anywhere in Quicksand that you need to go—it's already paid for."

And then, to my surprise, Addi leans across the table, grabs my collar, pulls me closer, and kisses me on the lips.

CHAPTER 17

Addison

I DON'T STEP through my front doorway—I float through it. As soon as the door closes, I lean against the wall, breathing out the biggest happy sigh of my life. All three roommates rush into the lobby.

"How has your birthday been?" Timini asks.

"Have you had a good day?" Peyton is practically bouncing.

"I thought you were only working until lunchtime," Bex says, trying and failing to look innocent. "I'm surprised to see you just getting home."

"You all need acting classes. Bex, Ian already spilled the beans about you sneaking over to tell him it's my birthday."

Timini grins. "So how was the date? I saw you two on scooters."

"It was so amazing," I breathe. "Best date of my life."

"Oh my lands, Addison! That's so wonderful!" Peyton claps her hands together. "Isn't that so wonderful? It's what we've all been hoping for! And to have it on your birthday is just perfect."

"Come," Bex says, herding us toward the kitchen. "Talk around the table. Food's getting cold."

As soon as I step through the doorway, the oddest scents hit me. I sniff, trying to figure out what they could have possibly made for dinner, and fail. I'm not even sure if I think it smells good or not.

"My plan," Timini says, motioning to the messy kitchen, "was to make chicken scampi. I found a recipe and thought I could do it. I had the timing worked out on each part of it, too. But really, that just meant that every single part burned at exactly the same time."

"But the timing was flawless," Bex says as we all sit down at the table.

"Bex helped me clear out the smoke and get everything thrown out so we wouldn't keep smelling it. And then we— okay, mostly Bex—threw together chicken fajitas out of practically no ingredients at all."

"And I brought cake!" Peyton adds.

"This is perfect," I say. "Absolutely perfect. I started the day pretty bummed because it was going to be my first birthday without my sister. But you all made it wonderful."

"Well," Bex says, clearing her throat, "I don't think it was only us who made it wonderful."

My cheeks warm just thinking about the date. "Okay, Ian helped quite a bit, too."

"Aww, now see?" Timini says, grabbing the dish of tortillas. "I want a guy who will make me blush like that."

"Me, too," Peyton says.

Bex grabs a couple of tortillas when they come to her. "And me."

When Bex hands the dish to Peyton, Peyton says, "I don't think you can get to the blushing stage by only going on a string of first dates."

Bex picks up a cherry tomato and tosses it at her. "Or by not noticing what's right in front of your eyes."

Peyton just looks confused, which makes me laugh out loud. Someday, she might figure out that she likes her best friend. At the rate she's going, though, it might be a while.

Timini adds cheese, lettuce, and sour cream to her fajitas like she's making a work of art. "Obviously none of us have a love life worth chatting about, so tell us more about yours. We need to live a little vicariously."

"Even though you, Addison Sparks," Bex says as she piles the peppers and onions high on her fajita, "are going against our No Falling in Love pact."

"I never said I was falling in love."

Peyton laughs in a way that's very close to a snort. Her eyes go wide and her hands fly to her mouth in shock that she made the undignified sound.

"No, really," I protest. "I have just fallen in like."

"Yes," Peyton says. "Like. A very strong, can't stop daydreaming about him, thinks everything he does is perfect, notices how beautiful he is, *like*."

I nod. "Exactly. Besides, I'm not so sure this relationship will go very far, so I'm not about to let myself fall in love." *I'm not*, I say with much more convincing force in my head.

"How can you be so sure it won't go far?" Timini asks. "I saw how you two were together today—it looked pretty magical."

"Oh, it definitely was. Like 'I'm your fairy godmother and I'm here with a wand' magical. It's the future I'm unsure about."

Bex shakes her head. "I don't get you one bit."

"I'm just..." How can I even explain? I'm just going to take Ian's advice and tell it however it comes out because inelegant is still effective. "I'm just not the girl who gets the guy. Ever. I actually had a guy say to me once, 'You're not the kind of girl that guys like to date—you're the kind they like to marry.'"

"He did not," Bex says.

"I swear to you he did."

Peyton looks around the table, eyebrows drawn together. "What does that even mean?"

I shrug as I wrap my tortilla tightly and pick it up. "I don't know. That I wear mom jeans? That I'm responsible but not fun? Who knows? But it explains why the only guy I did manage to ever keep was someone who didn't want a real relationship—just one of convenience. Kind of like how you're grateful for your microwave when you need it but you don't want to have to think about it when you're not standing there holding a plate of cold chicken casserole."

I take a bite of my fajita, which is actually pretty good despite the strange smell—apparently of burned chicken scampi—still hanging around the kitchen. Talking about Matthew doesn't hurt, which surprises and pleases me. And as long as I don't think about Ian and that I will probably lose him before long, I'm just fine.

"I think you're wrong," Timini says. "I mean, I don't know about your past, but I know you pretty well in your present. I've seen you and Ian and the looks you give each other, and I think you're wrong about your future with him."

I swallow my bite. "The point is, guys like Ian don't fall for girls like me. He's amazing! So, so, so incredibly amazing. He really could have his pick of anyone.

"If he's even ready to get serious with anyone yet. One of the reasons I planned to stay away from him was because he hadn't recovered from his broken engagement yet. And then, I don't know, life just kept pushing us together and I went and fell for him when I was trying not to."

That's the biggest part. The more time we spend together,

the more I'm convinced that Ian is my happily ever after. I hope I haven't destroyed any chance I have with him—small as it might be—simply because everything between us is happening before he's ready.

I point at each of my roommates and make my words come out in a jovial tone. "So when things go wrong and I'm a blubbering mess because I let my heart get in danger, just know that I'm coming to the three people who tried to talk me into it in the first place."

"And we'll be here for you," Bex says. "We'll wrap our arms around you and tell you that you're pretty and that everything's going to be okay."

"And we'll feed you cake!" Peyton says, getting out of her seat and grabbing the layered cake from the counter behind her.

"So what I'm hearing is," I say, "that I can fall as fully for Ian as I'd like because when I fall, I have a soft spot to land."

"Exactly that," Timini says.

I take another bite and think about how easy it'd be to do exactly that. Or maybe I don't need to fall fully for him. Maybe I'm already there.

CHAPTER 18

Ian

I PULL INTO MY DRIVEWAY, turn off my truck's headlights, and get out. I never want to be the one holding any part of construction up at a site, so I stayed at the Koermer house as long as it took to finish my part, even though it meant working so late. I drag myself into the house through the kitchen door and kick off my boots.

"Grandma?"

"In my office, sweetie!"

I open the fridge and find the lasagna Grandma texted me about. I'm so hungry I could probably eat everything left in the pan, but I cut a large piece, put it on a plate, and stick it in the microwave. As it warms, I head to find her.

The sound of voices meets me as I turn the corner into the hallway, and when I enter her office, I'm rewarded with smiles from my two favorite people. Addi and Grandma are sitting across the desk from each other, going through piles of papers. After such an incredibly long day, I can't believe how great it feels to come home and see Addi's face smiling at me.

"Hi, sweetie. Did you see the lasagna?"

I nod. "It's in the microwave. Addi, have you eaten?"

She smiles as I pull her to her feet and wrap my arms around her waist. "I ate with your grandma before we got started."

I glance at Grandma, and then at the recycle bin next to her. "Are you sure you want to throw that paper on top away?"

As Grandma turns to look at the paper she tossed, I pull Addi close and kiss her, savoring the warm softness of her lips. I nudge the curls away from her ear and whisper, "It's so good to see you."

She lets out a breathy giggle as my words tickle her ear, then snuggles in a little closer, even though I'm covered in sawdust. I leave a few kisses on her neck while I'm there.

"Why would I need to keep a receipt from having our lawn aerated eight years ago? Oh! You were just trying to get me to look away. You know, I can leave the room if you want privacy."

I laugh and let my arms fall from Addi's waist so she can sit back down. "No need, Grandma. I'm going to go eat some of your lasagna."

I apparently can't stand being in the same house as Addi and not being in the same room as her, so I bring my food into the office and eat while the three of us chat. When I'm finished, I announce I'm going to take a shower and don't miss the blush that crosses Addi's cheeks. That's now officially my favorite color.

"We're working on the closet next," Addi says, "and there are a couple of boxes in there with your name on them."

"There are?" My brow furrows. I vaguely remember a few boxes I didn't unpack when I moved in after Grandpa died. I haven't thought about them since that first week.

"Yep," Grandma says, "and if you don't go through them and get your stuff organized, Addison and I are going to."

There's a teasing gleam in her eyes, but that doesn't mean she's not being serious. "Wait, really?"

She nods. "So you might want to get to them."

I look toward my room and then back at Addi and Grandma, holding out my hands like I'm trying to pause them. "Just—just leave them there. I'll take a quick shower and come right back."

I race into my room, shut the door, then go into my bathroom and shut that door, too. Hopefully, I'm quick enough. I drop the shampoo once and hit my elbow into the shower wall twice, fully aware the office is on the other side of the wall. Probably ten minutes later, I'm back in the room, wearing a clean T-shirt and jeans. If it were just Grandma and me working, I'd probably be in gym shorts, but with Addi here, I still want to look good.

They both smile as I walk in, and it's obvious they've been talking about me. I hope it's good. The closet has quite a few boxes, so I start pulling them out and organizing them based on what's written on them. I find three labeled with my name. I don't remember what's in them, but I want to be the first to look.

As I go through the first box, I remember why I didn't already unpack these. They're full of stuff that's fun and memorable but not things I need. I'm not even sure what to do with it all. I pull out some artwork from elementary school and chuckle. Maybe I should've taken Grandma's offer to go through it with Addi.

Still, it's kind of cool to relive all the memories while chatting with Addi and my Grandma. I start making a pile of things that could go into a scrapbook, a pile of objects I want to keep but don't want sitting out, and a pile of things I want to put where I can see them—a pile that currently holds two items.

I pull the third box toward me after finishing the second. As soon as I cut the packing tape, I remember exactly what it contains. It started out as a box filled with random things that I'd only halfway unpacked when I moved here. For a long time, it sat on my closet floor with the flaps open, so I'd started tossing in mementos from when Cara and I were dating and engaged—wristbands from concerts, playbills, museum fliers, and even a restaurant receipt from our first date. When Cara ended things, the box became too much to face. I sealed it up and put it on the floor of the office until I could decide what to do with it. Grandma must've moved it to the closet.

Cara broke up with me two and a half months ago. It's been long enough that I can handle dealing with this stuff now. I start tossing mementos into the "throw away" box, getting rid of quite a few things, until I come across our wedding invitation. It sits on top of everything that's still in the box, staring at me. We'd already sent them out before Cara called the wedding off. In fact, the RSVPs had come back, the seating chart was done, and presents had started arriving.

I glance at Addi. She's going through a box with my grandma, and I'm grateful she's not witnessing any expressions on my face. Especially because all the questions I'd asked myself when Cara ended things come rushing back. Was I just not good enough? Or was I so oblivious that I hadn't seen our issues? That night, Cara had said to me, "When you asked me to marry you, I thought I wanted to spend the rest of my life with you. Now I know I don't. Not because of any one specific thing—it was just…a little of everything, I guess."

I wish it had been something specific. Then I'd know. But since it wasn't, I have to assume it was everything. I was happy enough in our relationship, and at the time, I thought that was adequate. It hadn't dawned on me that Cara's expectations, dreams, and vision for our future couldn't be realized.

Sometimes I worry that I must not be husband material.

Other times, I force those doubts away and remind myself that it's not true. But when I do, the nagging thought creeps in: maybe Cara and I just weren't a good match. If that was the case, then I'd failed to see it. And that's an issue all on its own.

Cara and I worked together to undo all the wedding preparations—to cancel everything, return everything we bought for the reception, send back the gifts, and get out of the contract for the apartment we were days away from moving into. It was mentally tough and so draining. If my judgment had been solid, I would've realized our issues before it got that far.

I can't handle dealing with anything else in this box related to the wedding that never happened. I shift a big stack of memorabilia and cards to see if there's anything else underneath it that I need to go through and spot the edge of a rock. I reach in and pull out the flat stone, smiling.

The scene Addi painted is exactly as I remember it. I run my finger across the trees by the shore and the way the river curves outward in our favorite spot, making the water calmer and perfect for jumping in. Not that it was deep—most of the time, it barely reached our knees. Even though little Ian and little Addi are only about an inch high in the painting, she still managed to capture the big smiles on our faces as we held hands and jumped in.

"You really did keep it," Addi breathes.

I glance up to see her looking at the stone and smile. "Of course, I did."

Then a stabbing pain hits me. What if things go wrong with Addi? Can I handle the pain of going through with her what I went through with Cara? With Addi, I'm happy. More than happy—I'm thrilled. I am so much happier now than I was at any point in my relationship with Cara. If things go wrong with Addi and me, I'll have so much further to fall.

I put the stone back into the box and stand. "Listen, I've got to go. I'm sorry to run out on you two, but I have to..." What? I don't even know, so I can't finish my sentence. I just need to go somewhere and think.

After giving Addi a quick kiss on the forehead, I grab my keys and shoes and head out to my truck for a long drive.

CHAPTER 19

Addison

"I NEED NEWS ABOUT YOUR MAN."

That's how Chloe answers the phone when I call her on my way to the grocery store on Saturday morning. "What if you won't like the news?"

"No, Addison! *No bad news.* There can't be bad news. You two are too adorable together. What happened?"

"I don't know. Maybe nothing. Maybe something."

"Oh. That explains everything."

"It does?" Chloe has so much more experience with dating and guys and understanding what's going on.

"No, that was sarcasm. Don't they have sarcasm in Oregon? Explain."

"You know how I was worried about Ian being a rebound guy for me? Well, I realized that rebounding for me wasn't about getting past feelings for my ex, because Matthew and I never had very strong feelings for each other. What I most miss about our relationship is the security of knowing right where I stood with him."

"Please don't tell me you're thinking of going back to Matthew."

"No. Not at all. I want a relationship where the amount of love we feel for each other is at a ten. With Matthew, it never got over a three. But it was a solid three, and I really miss that it was so solid.

"When I'm with Ian, he is so sweet, and it feels like we are connecting so well, and I just *know* he really likes me. And then other times, we just…don't, and it leaves me feeling unsure about everything. Like last night. I was helping his grandma in her office and he came home from work. You should've seen his face, Chloe. It completely lit up when he saw me. Like I am his entire world. I wish I had a video of it so I could just watch it over and over."

Chloe happy sighs.

"And then we were all working on organizing the office and just chatting about random things, and he got really quiet. I looked over to see what was up, and he was holding the stone I painted for him. Remember that?"

"Oh, I remember. I swear you talked about it for a year straight."

"There was just something different about him while he was holding it. Heavy. Sad. Anxious. Regretful. I don't know—it's hard to explain. Then he just got up, said goodbye, and left."

"Huh." The line goes quiet for a few moments, and then Chloe asks, "Did his grandma say anything?"

I pull into a parking spot and turn off my car, then pick up my phone when Bluetooth switches it over from the car's speakers. "She did. She said that maybe it wasn't the rock that made him all morose—maybe it was what was under the rock. So I looked. It was a wedding invitation. *His* wedding invitation."

"Get out."

I very nearly open my door at my sister's command, then roll my eyes at myself and stay put. I'm the older sister, after all.

"He didn't get married, though, right?"

"No. I knew his last relationship had been serious. He told me he'd thought it would end in marriage. I just didn't know he thought it would end in marriage because they'd actually planned the wedding. Shirley said their wedding was supposed to happen the same weekend I moved here." I let out a deep breath. "Remember all the research I did to make sure that Ian wouldn't be a rebound guy?"

"Yeah."

"I think I probably worried about that more than I needed to. What I should've been worrying about was becoming the rebound girl."

"Oh."

"So what do I do? The same thing I've been doing? Back off and give him space? Buy myself a spinning wheel and a bunch of wool in preparation for a life of solitude?"

"Communication is the number one thing. Go out with him again soon and bring it up."

"I can do that." I pause for a moment. "Thanks, Chloe, for dating a million guys before finding Dustin so you can answer my questions. Even if half a million of them were ones I had hoped would ask me out."

"What are sisters for?"

After hanging up the phone, I send a text to Ian, not allowing myself to stop and overanalyze before I do.

Addison: Are you free tonight?

It takes long enough for his response to come in that I

almost grab my list and head into the grocery store. Finally, though, I get a text.

> Ian: I'm not. I have to install all the cabinets in a home today, and it's huge. They'll be ready for me to start at noon, and I won't be finished until late.

I almost reply with a frowny-faced emoji and prepare to spend more of the weekend feeling unsettled, but then I decide that I'm not going to quit so easily.

> Addison: You still have to eat, right? How about I bring dinner to the site? And then I can help. With a little direction, of course.

> Ian: But what if you came and all I wanted to do was kiss you? I'd never finish installing the cabinets.

I keep re-reading the text, my heart doing a little jump every single time.

> Addison: Then we'll have to turn it into a game. We install one cabinet, we get one kiss.

> Ian: I like it when you're in charge of the games.

I smile, grab my list, and get out of the car. I can make exactly two dishes well, and one of them is chicken piccata. I already have the list of things to buy because I'm making it for my roommate dinner turn later this week, so I'll just get double.

————

I pull up to the house Ian texted me the address for. It's a newer neighborhood with three houses under construction next to each other, and he wasn't kidding when he said it's huge.

Ian must sense me pulling up because he comes out quickly enough to reach me before I even get the passenger door open. He gives me a big smile and a kiss, then says, "That one didn't count—the game hasn't started yet."

But to my lips, which are still tingling from feeling his, it definitely counts.

"It isn't takeout—you cooked dinner? For me?" He picks up the dish with the hot pad, then he lifts the foil and breathes in deeply, a look of bliss spreading across his face.

"Now don't get all excited. This and enchiladas are the extent of what I can cook."

I grab the basket and a blanket and follow Ian into the house. A couple of other guys are working on different things in the house, but Ian shoos them away when their noses bring them straight to the food, and he leads me into what I assume will be a guest bedroom. The carpet hasn't been laid yet, so I spread the blanket on the plywood floor. Ian puts the chicken dish I've paired with pasta on the blanket, and I pull dishes, rolls, and a green salad from the basket and place them on the blanket, too.

Ian seems to love the food and gives me compliment after compliment. Enough that I don't even want to bring up his engagement, but I know that if I don't plow ahead with my questions, I might get cold feet.

"So, you were engaged and nearly married, huh?" Wow. When I thought through this part of the night in my head, it came out so much less blunt.

Ian ducks his chin and rubs the back of his neck. "Um, yeah. I should've told you already. It was just…"

"Awkward?"

"Yeah. I meant to tell you when we had our catch-up coffee date, but before I got a chance, I was carrying you in my arms. It seemed weird to say, 'Oh, and by the way, I was engaged, but my fiancée broke it off right before the wedding.'"

"That might not have been the most elegant way to bring it up, but it would've been effective." I smile because I'm pretty sure I quoted his words pretty close to exactly.

Ian's laugh is loud and booming, bouncing off the smooth surfaces of the empty room. He scratches his cheek. "In all fairness, you did warn me that I might not like it when my request came back around to bite me, so I shouldn't be surprised."

I chuckle. But I need more info, so I prod. "And? Tell me about it."

He starts by sharing the parts that Shirley already told me. Then he tells a little about their relationship. It doesn't sound like it was bad, but it doesn't sound like it was great, either. It's a little like my relationship with Matthew, where we weren't in each other's lives enough in all the important ways.

But my relationship with Matthew had been practically unmoving for years, so it wasn't a big deal to hop off that stalled train. Ian's relationship with Cara had plowed ahead like a freight train, so when she pulled the brakes, it jumped the tracks and injured everyone. It sounds like it was awful. And the way Ian becomes more sullen and weighed down as he tells the story confirms its awfulness.

"Wow. I really brought down the mood of the room, didn't I?"

"Luckily," I say, "I brought apple cobbler. It's guaranteed to bring it back up seven notches."

"You made apple cobbler?"

I hold the container back as he grabs for it. "No, I *bought* it. I can make two things, remember? Getting your expectations higher isn't allowed."

He's still leaning forward from trying to grab the cobbler, his face inches from mine, so I kiss him. He smiles into the kiss and says, "This one doesn't count, either."

I *really* want things with us to work out. I can already picture the marital bliss—waking up next to him, kissing him as he comes home all covered in sawdust, joining forces to accomplish his goal of opening a cabinet shop and mine of opening an organizational design business and finding all the ways we'll work together. Then finding all the ways we'll work together to raise happy little children that are running around with Ian's dark, wavy hair.

We clean up dinner and start working on the cabinets. Ian and an assistant—a kid who used to be a Junior Woodworker, apparently—have hung all the upper cabinets before I got here, which is good, because those sound more difficult, and I don't have a clue what I'm doing.

If I'd ended our date right after we ate, I probably would've walked away feeling relatively confident about our relationship. As the night goes on, though, I'm less and less confident. There are times when we laugh as we work and he very enthusiastically kisses me after each cabinet is finished. At other times, he seems to be thinking too much, and it's as if he's avoiding me as much as one can while working together to maneuver a cabinet into a tight space. My attempts to find out how he's feeling fail.

It's obvious that something is wrong—he seems to be trying to hide his emotions but not managing to. We finish with the kitchen, two of the bathrooms, and one of the washrooms when I say, "You seem to be doing a lot of thinking tonight."

"I'm sorry I've been so distracted." He wraps his arm around my waist and pulls me in close. I put my arms around his neck and soak in how right it feels to be so near him. Everything about this is right. He leans in close to my ear, his breath tickling my neck. "Coming here tonight to help me was an incredible thing to do. Thank you."

My mouth is right by his ear, too, so I breathe, "You forgot to mention dinner."

I feel his smile right next to my ear, and he pulls back enough to meet my eyes. "So was bringing me a delicious meal. And giving me kisses like they were fuel to keep going."

I drop my hands to his chest. "So what you're saying is, I saved you twice today." It's what he said to me after he helped me with Bex's nieces and nephews and fed me dinner.

He chuckles and smiles that amused smile that first pulled me in at Gateway Groceries so many weeks ago. He drops one hand to my hip and brushes a curl away from my cheek with the other. "In the who-saves-whom category, it looks like we're tied. It's anyone's guess who's going to be getting that Medal of Honor in the mail."

When we finish, he picks up the picnic basket and blanket and carries them out to my car, walking hand-in-hand with me. Which is good, because he turns the power of those beautiful blue eyes on me, and my knees are suddenly too weak for me to make it on my own.

At my car, he puts the blanket and basket inside, cupping his hand so gently at the back of my head, and gives me the sweetest kiss ever. I practically melt into a puddle right by my car. The kiss alone tells me that maybe everything will work out between us just fine.

CHAPTER 20

Addison

I'M SO glad you've been able to help me today," Peyton says as I chop the last piece of cooked chicken in the tray.

"I'm glad I had the day off—it's been fun!" I never thought that spending the day cooking could actually be fun. It's a nice change of pace from my usual. It feels good to just mindlessly chop food. And Peyton has been so grateful.

"It really has." Peyton smiles her perfect smile, her hair looking pretty even while she spends the day in the kitchen. Then she removes the empty tray and puts a full one in its spot.

"More chicken?"

"This is why I'm a personal chef and not a caterer. With catering, there's so much monotony. Seriously, thank you, Addison. It's a client I cook for all the time who's having a big luncheon, but still. I don't know what I was thinking when I took this job. I couldn't do it without you."

I get lost in the rhythm of my chopping while Peyton mixes the rest of the ingredients for the chicken salad in a giant bowl.

"How are things going with Ian?" she asks.

`I shrug. "I don't know. And I hate not knowing. All I do

know is that he's everything I ever wanted but hadn't known yet. I've fallen pretty hard for him."

Peyton smiles dreamily.

"But let's talk about something else. I've already analyzed everything more than an IRS agent analyzes a suspicious tax claim, and I've got brain exhaustion from it."

Peyton's phone dings, so she washes her hands, goes to where it rests on the counter, and touches the screen. Then she smiles at it—the kind of smile I've only seen her use with one person.

"Is that a text from Max?"

She nods. "He's a funny friend."

I shake my head, wondering if she'll ever refer to him as something other than a friend.

Timini finally comes back into the room, hugging a kid-sized dress form and taking small steps so her legs don't bang into it too much as she walks. She sets it down with a huge exhale and starts adjusting its size.

"Okay, let's switch to a new subject, then," Peyton says, pulling another tray of croissants out of the oven. "How's work?"

"I kind of imagined that most of my days would be spent blissfully organizing people's homes. There is so much more to running a business that I'm learning as I go. I'm a little stressed by how many blank spots I have in my schedule coming up since that's what's paying the bills."

The truth is, I'm a lot stressed out by it. I'm not great at marketing or advertising because I didn't have to deal with that side of the business back when I worked for a company in Amarillo instead of owning a business myself. It all comes so naturally to Chloe, and it makes me wish we lived close again. With her help, I'd have my schedule filled for sure.

"I think you should just not worry about it," Timini says.

"Clients will come in when they come in. Stressing about it won't change anything."

Bex drags herself into the room, wearing baggy sweats and a baggy t-shirt, her hair pulled into a messy bun, no makeup on, and flops into a chair at the table. "Guys, I'm sick. And I have episodes to film. Make me better. Please? I'm begging here."

"I'm pretty sure there's a sticky note somewhere that says it's against the rules to be sick," Timini says without even cracking a smile as she puts a half-finished bodice on the form. Me? I have to hold in a laugh.

"Get your germs away from the food!" Peyton screeches, making shooing motions. "Go sit on one of those tables."

Bex just looks at the other tables like she doesn't have the energy to get up and move. "Can't. They're too messy."

"Really, they are," I say. "Can we get a little more organized everywhere?" I don't mean to direct the comment at Timini, but she's definitely the one contributing the bulk of the chaos at the inn.

"If things are too organized," Timini says, her voice calm as she adjusts the mannequin, "then creativity flies right out the window. The same goes with rules." She shoots a glare at Bex.

"While we're discussing issues," Peyton says as she adds the chopped chicken to her mixture, "can we talk about adjusting the temperature? It's always freezing in here!"

"Are you kidding?" Bex says, looking like Peyton's comment gives her some life back. "It's always a furnace in here. Especially when you cook."

Peyton looks to Timini and me for support, but I don't say anything—I think the temperature is fine. "Okay, then, maybe we can talk about keeping the volume down a bit while we're all trying to work."

Bex sits up straighter. "Is this referring to when my sisters and their kids come over? Because loud is how you know they enjoy being around each other."

"Maybe we just need to change things up a bit," Timini says, glancing around. "Rearrange the rooms down here. Maybe all we need is an infusion of change to refresh everyone."

"No!" Peyton begs. "Change doesn't rejuvenate. It stresses people out."

This whole conversation is stressing me out. Normally, I love it when we're all together, whether we're working out issues or not. My parents were never around much, and Chloe and I didn't always have the same schedules, so I felt like I never really had much of a family growing up. All my roommates in a room together make this place feel like home.

But my nerves are too frayed from my worries about Ian and work. I duck out of the room and take a few deep, calming breaths once I get to the lobby, kind of missing the teeny apartment that I had all to myself back in Amarillo.

I stop breathing and cock my ear when I hear gurgling and popping sounds, almost like knocking. Then there's a loud hissing. I've heard the knocking before, but never the hissing, never this loud, and never when I could tell where the sounds are coming from. Walking carefully so I can hear the noise as I go, I head down the hall toward the back door and stop right in front of the utility closet. Yep, the hissing is definitely coming from in there.

More than a little wary, I reach for the doorknob just as a gush of hot water soaks my shoes. I fling the door open and see water pouring from a valve about two-thirds of the way up on the water heater. Water is gushing out, filling the little room and spilling out into more and more of the hallway.

I must've screamed because all three of my roommates are suddenly by me, frozen in shock, gasping at what they're seeing.

"We need something to catch the water!" I say as I race into the bathroom just down the hall and dump the hand towels out of the decorative bowl on the tank of the toilet. Then I run back to the water heater. Bex, Peyton, and Timini come running up the hallway, their footsteps splashing in the water, carrying bowls from the kitchen.

Bowl after bowl, one of us catches the water until the container is full, and then the next person catches the water while the first one runs it to the bathroom sink.

Finally, I shake my head. "We aren't getting to the end of it. More water must be filling it still." There's a hose connected to the top of it, so I search for some kind of valve to turn it off but can't see anything.

"We need to shut off power to it, too," Bex says, crowding into the small room, searching for the power while I search for the water valve and Peyton holds a bowl, with the water all around us and everything going wrong.

The power is easier to find than the valve, but we eventually manage to shut both off and dump the last of the water into the sink. Even with all our efforts, the long hallway and the lobby are covered in water.

The adrenaline of stopping the water took all the energy Bex had, so she heads upstairs to bemoan her sickness alone. Timini, Peyton, and I scoop the water off the tile floor with dustpans. Eventually, we get the water amount down enough that we just have to use towels, wringing them into a bucket constantly.

When we finally finish, Timini and Peyton head upstairs to their rooms to put on dry clothes, but I just stay downstairs. Exhausted and dreading how much a new water heater is going to cost—not to mention what a pain it will be to shower and wash dishes until it's replaced—I sit down on the second stair and let my head fall into my hands, giving into the despair.

My phone, which I forgot was in my pocket, rings. I really hope it's a miracle worker calling to solve all of my problems. "Hello?"

"Hi, Addison."

It takes me a minute to place the voice. "Matthew?" I pull the phone away from my ear long enough to look at the number to verify. It hadn't occurred to me that by deleting him from my contacts, I wouldn't know it was him if he called. Sure enough, though, it's the 806 area code. I wonder if whoever wrote that website article thought about the perils of accidentally answering a call from your ex simply because you deleted his contact information.

"It's good to hear your voice. I just wanted to see how you're doing."

I sigh. "Today isn't really the best time to ask that question. How are you?"

"Good. What's happening today that's got you down?"

I shrug, even though he can't see me. I know he's only asking because it's the thing to do—Matthew has never really been interested in day-to-day details—but I tell him because he's asking and I apparently need to get it out.

"Let's just say I'm having second thoughts about my job, I'm unsure about a lot of things, actually, and right now, a teeny apartment with a landlord who swoops in to fix any problem sounds heavenly. Oh, it's rained for twelve hours straight, and I'm talking the gloomy kind of rain, and I miss the sun. You know, the kinds of things that make you question whether moving somewhere new was a mistake."

"Well, I did see a 'now leasing' sign in front of your old apartment building."

I laugh. It's obvious he's trying to lift my spirits, and it actually works. Partly because it makes me think—just for a second

—about moving back to Amarillo, which helps me to realize that, awful day or not, I really don't want to. I want to be here.

"Thank you, Matthew. I guess I needed that. What's new with you? Are you dating anyone?"

He chuckles. "Actually, yeah. My Tuesdays and Saturdays got a little lonely."

"That's great news, Matthew. Everything's going well?"

"It really is."

Thinking back to how stagnant our relationship was makes me wonder how I ever thought we should stay together for as long as we did. But it surprises me how happy I am for him that he's found someone new. It's a little reminder that there's someone for everyone.

"So, listen," he says. "I was actually calling because I'm flying to Portland tomorrow for business. I still have a box of your things, and I was wondering if I could drop it by."

"Oh, sure. Yeah, that'd be great. I'll text you my address."

"And I'll let you get back to your crisis and re-evaluation of your life choices."

I chuckle, and Matthew does, too. "You sound good, Matthew. I'm glad."

"You do, too. I'll drop that by tomorrow night."

After hanging up and texting him my address, I slide my phone back into my pocket. Who says communicating with your ex is a bad idea? Talking to Matthew and finding out he's doing well and has moved on feels like closure. Like it marks the end of my rebound period. Like that part of my life is done and wrapped up all clean and neat with a bow on top.

Now I just need to figure out how to deal with the mess that my current life is.

CHAPTER 21

Ian

I GLANCE at the clock on the wall of my shop. The parents of my Junior Woodworkers are going to start showing up any minute, and we still haven't finished cleaning up. We spent most of the hour sanding their stepstools, and the kids managed to get covered from head to toe in sawdust. Probably because instead of being one hundred percent focused on them like I need to be, my mind keeps wandering to Addi. With as dusty as the kids are, their parents aren't going to want them to get in their vehicles.

Luckily, I turned on the air compressor before they arrived, so it's ready to go. "Okay, woodworkers—put your project in your cubby, get your safety goggles and dust mask on, and then come line up just outside the door."

Nothing gets them to clean up more quickly than needing to be blown off with the air hose. The first kid races out of the shop and waves at his mom, who's already waiting at the edge of the grass. I squeeze the trigger on the nozzle and blow the pressurized air on the kid as he turns in a circle, sawdust scattering to the wind. Then he leans forward so I can blow the dust out of his hair, then holds out one foot at a time so I can get his shoes.

He pulls off his dust mask and goggles and wipes away the last of the dust behind them. He turns to his mom, holding his arms straight out, a big grin on his face. "How do I look?" Leaving with hair that looks like he's been in a tornado seems to be his favorite part of the week. He says goodbye, I thank his mom, and then I start blowing the dust from the next Junior Woodworker in line.

By the time I get to the last kid, half the group has already left with their parents, and the rest are chasing each other around my backyard. Jella, one of the most talkative kids and the one with the longest hair, is last. As I blow the sawdust off her while she turns in a circle, she says, "It took my mom thirty-two minutes to brush all the snarls out of my hair after last time."

I immediately turn off the air. "I'm glad you told me before I used this on your hair then."

"No, do it! Make it as crazy as you can. I'm trying to set a new record."

I glance at the driveway, hoping her mom or grandma is there to tell me if they'd rather I skipped this part, but I don't see either of them. "How about we work on setting a record in the opposite direction? We'll try to get all the sawdust out and only need five minutes of brushing."

Jella shrugs, so I carefully blow air from the top of her head, keeping it directed straight down. But at the last second, too quickly for me to stop her, Jella shakes her head wildly, making the air blow her hair into a crazy mess anyway.

I turn off the air hose, and Jella, grinning at her messy hair, says, "You know that girl Cara who you were going to marry—the one who was sometimes waiting for you after Junior Wood-workers? I saw her."

"Yeah?" I start coiling the air hose.

Jella nods. "At Cascade Mini Golf. She was with some guy, and they were all loving on each other and kissing pretty much the whole time. I just wanted to march right up to her with my hands on my hips like this and say, 'You shouldn't be here as a pair like you don't even care. You should be home crying for a month straight because of how mean you were to Ian!' And I would've done it, too, but my grandma and mom told me I couldn't."

I can't help glancing across the hedgerow to Addi's home. "As much as I appreciate you looking out for me, Jella, it's okay that Cara is dating someone else. We aren't together anymore."

"That's what my mom said. But it just doesn't seem right that she's so happy." Jella glances at the other kids. "Oh—Priya is having trouble catching Ajay. I better go help her." And then she runs off to join the kids racing around my backyard, squealing and laughing.

More parents arrive to collect their kids, so I herd the remaining handful to the front yard. Jella's mom is the last to arrive, and I apologize about the state of her hair while Jella demands that her mom take a picture of the masterpiece.

As soon as they finally drive away, I pull out my phone and open Cara's social media, needing to see who this new guy is that Jella saw her with. Sure enough, there are several pictures of a smiling Cara with a man's arm—Dylan Brady, the tag says—wrapped around her.

A rush of an emotion I can't quite name floods me. "Jealousy" is the only word that comes to mind, but it's not quite right. I'm not jealous of Dylan. I don't want to be the one with my arm around Cara. I'm actually happy she's found someone.

So what is it, then?

I glance at Hidden Inn. I want Addi to be happy and fully in love, too. I want her to be happy and fully in love with *me*. I want to be the one who brings a smile to her face whenever I see her just like she brings a smile to mine. I want the best of everything for her.

Then I realize that the emotion hitting me feels like jealousy because I'm jealous of *Cara*. In the few pictures she posted, she looks like she's moved on just fine and has no worries about whether her new relationship could end and exactly how much it will crush her if it does.

Yet I'm having worries about mine.

I love every single second I spend with Addi and want her in my life more and more. Right now, I want to walk over to the inn, wrap my arms around her, kiss her senseless, and then hear about how things went with today's client and what her future plans are. I want her in my arms as we talk for hours.

Yet I'm still worried that she will see in me whatever Cara saw that caused her to cancel our wedding. I close out of the app and shove my phone back into my pocket. This is making me crazy and not helping at all. To help distract myself, I walk to the mailbox and grab today's mail.

Before I even look down at the mail, movement at Hidden Inn catches my eye, and I glance over. A car just pulled into the circular drive in the front, and a man gets out. He's pretty good-looking, and I assume he's here for Bex. She seems to date a lot, and it usually isn't the same person.

I walk my fingers along the top of the envelopes, glancing at what came as I head back toward my house. Then I glance over again and see Addi answer the door, not Bex. I can't see the guy's face, but I can see Addi's, and it's all recognition and smiles. The man hands her some kind of gift box, they hug, and he kisses her cheek. Then she invites him inside.

The only explanation I can think of is that it must be her ex from Amarillo. But here in Quicksand? Why? And why does she look so happy to see him?

————

As I clean up from work and eat dinner, my mind goes in circles, the tension weighing down my shoulders. Before Addi came back to Quicksand, my doubts and fears were probably in the high range. I was having a pretty rough time.

Then Addi moved in. And I got to know her as an adult. And then I really started to fall for her. Somewhere along the way, the unease and uncertainty just kind of floated away, like they didn't even exist. When I do consciously think about it, it isn't enough to cause any kind of action on my part. I've been too busy falling completely for Addi to pay it any attention.

Over the past week, though, my fears have kicked back into high gear. Especially since I've fallen for Addi so much more deeply than I ever fell for Cara. I thought I was ready to fully open my heart to her, but all these fears are making me less sure.

I wander around my house, hoping for peace or direction, but all I get when I wander into the kitchen is the little green-and-yellow origami frog my grandma folded and left on the table with a note in its mouth reminding me that she's gone to the Paperworks Folding Fest conference and won't be home until late.

I glance out the window—there's probably a good thirty minutes before it gets dark. Since wandering around my house aimlessly isn't helping, maybe I should go mow the inn's back-yard. The noise and the work might get my mind off things. I put on my work gloves and head out to the gate in the hedgerow that leads to Addi's yard.

I've only made it five feet onto her lawn when she walks out the back door, a bag of trash in her hand. Our eyes meet, and she gives me a small smile, tosses the garbage into the can, and then walks toward me.

She glances at my gloves. "A little late for mowing, isn't it?"

I shrug. "It's been one of those days."

"Yeah, it has." She leans against the metal archway that holds the fence between our yards, looking exhausted or sad or upset—I'm not sure which.

I immediately leave the mower behind, stepping closer to her. "Is everything okay?" I want to reach out and comfort her, to wrap her up in my arms. But the worry weighing so heavily on my shoulders stops me. Instead, I lean against the other side of the archway, facing her.

Addi rubs her fingers on her temples before dropping them to her sides. "Today and yesterday have just been the kind of days that make me question every decision I've made in the past couple of months."

My heart seems to suddenly weigh more, sinking down in my chest. Is that why her ex stopped by? Because she's rethinking her decision to break up with him? I'm already dreading the answer, but I still ask, "Like what?"

She looks up at the darkening sky. "Choosing to start my own business instead of getting another corporate job, leaving Amarillo, moving across the country, living at the inn instead of selling it—pretty much everything."

Her eyes search mine, and I try to guess what it is she's looking for, but alarm bells are going off too loudly in my head at the words "pretty much everything." She's unsure about every single thing that brought her here—that brought her into my life. I swallow down the lump in my throat. "Does that include your decision to date me, too?"

She studies my eyes, biting her lip. "Sometimes."

My mind keeps circling back to every negative thought I had about myself when Cara first broke things off with me. Is that the direction things are heading with Addi? I don't know if I'm strong enough for that.

But if we wait longer and I fall even more in love with her, I definitely won't be strong enough if things end.

"Listen, Addi. I…" I look at the ground, releasing a long breath before I meet her eyes again. "I can't do this anymore." I can't believe the words actually come out of my mouth.

Addi stands up straight, her eyebrows creasing together. "This? As in *us*? You want to break up?"

No. I don't want to break up at all. I want to hear why she's questioning her job and her move and see if I can help, and I want to hold her and comfort her if I can't. I want us to cheer each other on as we reach for our dreams. I want to marry her and have a bunch of kids with her that are hopefully less wild than Bex's nieces and nephews. Or more wild. I'd take that, too, if Addi and I could do it together. I want to be with her always.

But if Addi and I get to the same point Cara and I were at when we broke up—the thought of how infinitely more painful it would be with Addi sends panic coursing through me.

So, like a cowardly fool, I nod.

She doesn't say anything. Tears start to pool in her eyes, and I want to reach out with a knuckle and wipe them away. I want to wrap my arms around her and make everything better. But then she just turns and walks toward the inn, so I turn toward my house and close the gate separating our yards.

CHAPTER 22

Addison

I SLUMP into the kitchen where my roommates are all still chatting after washing the dinner dishes in the sink, using water we had to heat up on the stove. "Remember when you guys said that you'd be my soft place to land? I need a room full of downy feathers."

Peyton looks from me to the direction of the backyard and back again, her eyebrows drawn close together. "Just from taking out the garbage?" Then, realization seems to dawn on her, and her hands fly to her mouth. "No. No, no, no. Oh my lands, you two didn't just break up, did you?" She races forward and wraps me in a hug. "What happened?"

"I don't know. He just said he couldn't do it anymore."

Timini and Bex join the hug, and I hold the three of them tight for a long moment.

"No more of an explanation than that?" Timini asks.

I shake my head.

"And you didn't demand one?" Bex asks.

I mean, sure, I could have. I just didn't think I could handle the answer.

"Oh my goodness," Peyton says, looking around frantically. "I told you that if you ever broke up, I would provide cake, and I have no cake!"

"It's okay," Bex says, walking over to the freezer. "I think I have fudge pops in here. Yep! A full box." She sets it on the island counter that we've all gravitated toward and tears the box open. She even pulls one out for me, takes off the wrapper, and puts the stick in my hand.

I'm pretty sure I don't want a fudge pop, but I lick it anyway. "My list said not to rush a new relationship, and I swear I didn't. I actually kept myself away from him when I really wanted to see him just to slow it down. I know it's only been ten weeks that I've known him again. It just kind of went fast even without me helping it along. So that makes this my second breakup in just under three months. See? I told you rebound dating was bad."

Timini shakes her head. "Ian wasn't a rebound, and you know it."

I let out a huge sigh. "I know I know it. That's what makes it so awful." I lick my fudge pop and then run a hand across my forehead. "When I first broke up with Matthew, I think what I mourned was the loss of certainty of knowing what the future held, because I no longer knew what my life was going to be like."

I set my fudge pop down on its wrapper. I really don't want to have to keep licking it, and if I don't, it's going to melt all over my hand.

"But with Ian, nothing has been certain, and I had no idea what the future held. The only thing I knew was that I was going to wake up, he was going to be amazing, and I was going to be more in love with him than I was the day before. That was the constant I could count on."

I know that the shock of the sudden breakup isn't over, and

when it is, that's when I'm going to feel the full depth of what I've lost. I can feel the weight of it hanging around the periphery, like an actor waiting for his turn to take the stage.

Bex tosses the remainder of her own fudge pop into the garbage can and then puts an arm around me. "Come. Let's go into the gathering room. We'll all squish together on the big couch and either watch music videos of sad breakup songs on YouTube or an action flick on Netflix where the love interest dies. Your choice."

I nod and let them lead me into the gathering room. I'll watch and soak in their support and strength as long as I can until the grief and loss won't wait any longer for their turn on stage. Then I'll flee to the solitude of my bedroom.

CHAPTER 23

Ian

I'M INSTALLING the trim around a doorframe in another new house that Garrett is the general contractor for when he comes to check on everything. As soon as my friend sees my face, he jerks back in surprise. I just grab the board I've already cut for the right side of the door and line it up with one hand, finish nailer in the other.

"Bad night?" Garrett tries to act nonchalant, as if he didn't just notice how awful I look.

"You could say that."

"Have trouble sleeping?"

"Yep."

"Drank a Mountain Dew after eight p.m. again, huh?"

I don't say anything—I just keep nailing.

"Oh. *Oh.* Addison broke up with you, huh? I'm so sorry, man."

"I broke up with her." I grab the stepstool and the piece for the top of the door and start lining it up.

"*You.* The guy who is so in love with a woman that he actually started singing on the job *broke up with her.* Dude, that makes no sense whatsoever."

I just keep working and don't answer.

"It was fear, wasn't it? Ian, you can't let that stop you. It's not right."

"Of course, it's going to stop me. That's fear's entire purpose."

Garrett stays quiet for a few minutes while I grab the three pieces of trim I've cut for the next doorframe and give the air hose a shake to untangle it as I pull it to the next doorway.

"And how did Addison react?"

I lay two of the pieces of trim on the floor and position the third against the doorframe. "She didn't say a word—she just walked away. I think that means she agrees it was time." I position the finish nailer and pull the trigger, the tool making a *pshhhht* sound as it sinks the nail.

"There are a lot of reasons why she might've walked away. Don't assume you know her reason." He pauses for a moment, then asks, "So, do you think you did the right thing?"

With a hand holding the piece of trim against the frame, I close my eyes and let out a slow breath. "Right before I broke up with her? Yeah. Now? I don't know. All I know is that I feel awful."

"Okay, tell me this. How did you feel right after you and Cara broke up?"

How *did* I feel? I try to look back at those first couple of days with the lens of time I have now and really think about it. "Like the future I had planned was taken away from me, I guess." Another *pshhhht* as I sink another nail.

Garrett nods. "And how do you feel after breaking things off with Addison?"

"Like I'd held the most valuable treasure imaginable in my

hands, and I just let go. Not only did I lose it, but I left it damaged."

Garrett stays quiet as I shoot the rest of the finish nails into the piece of trim. Then he says, "That might be a clue as to whether or not you did the wrong thing last night." He thumps me twice on the shoulder and then leaves me alone with my thoughts.

CHAPTER 24

Addison

"Ian and I broke up."

Chloe gasps on the other end of the line. I pull over to the side of the road. I'm on my way to work—wishing for the first time that I didn't have my day filled—when I know I can't make it through the day without talking to my sister.

"Oh, no. I am so sorry. How are you?"

I shake my head and look out at the cars passing by me on the highway. "I feel like my heart finally found what it had been searching for all along, and then it was torn away."

"When did this happen? And why?"

"Last night. He didn't say why, and I didn't ask. It was hard enough hearing that he didn't want to date anymore—I didn't think I could handle hearing the why."

"Fear can be a powerful little monster."

"Yeah, it's not the first time it has stopped me."

"I was talking about Ian."

I pause. "Do you really think that fear was his reason?"

"Addison, I saw how much the man adores you. There's no way he broke up because of you."

My exhale of relief comes out as a sob, and I have to force my emotions down so it doesn't ruin my makeup or make me look all red and puffy right before I step into my client's home.

"What are you going to do about it?"

"What *can* I do? A relationship takes two people, and if one of them doesn't want it to continue, then there's nothing the other one can do about it."

Chloe is silent for a long moment before she speaks again. "Okay, from what I've seen, this is how you normally handle relationships. Correct me if I'm wrong with any of it. You meet a guy who you start to like. You flirt as you get to know each other.

"If you get to know him a bit and you still like him, you hope he'll ask you out. And then if you like dating him, you hope the relationship will progress. If you don't like him, you hope he'll break it off. If you do like him and he breaks it off, you hope he'll figure things out and want to get back together.

"If things continue to go wonderfully, you hope he'll propose. You hope the guy will be on the same page and make the choices you would make and feel bad when he doesn't. Does that sound about right?"

"Pretty much. I guess I'm good at hoping."

"Hope is a really important thing, Addison. But it's only half of the equation. The other half is action. To make dreams come true, you have to have both. Have you ever asked a guy out? Been the one to initiate a first kiss? Been the first to say how you feel about him? Tried to work things out after a breakup if you wanted to still be together?"

Chloe already knows the answer to most of those. But I do say in a quiet voice, "I kissed Ian first."

Chloe squeals. "Yes! I knew he was special! Do you love him?"

I nod, even though Chloe can't see me. "I think I started

falling in love with him my first day back in Quicksand, and I've fallen a bit more in love with him every single day since then. I imagine I'll keep falling more in love with him every day for the rest of my life."

Chloe lets out a sigh that sounds like a whimper. "That's so beautiful." She sighs again. "Okay, Addison, listen. You moved to Quicksand for a fresh start, right? You were determined to grab that fresh start by the horns and show it who was boss, right?"

"Right."

"You didn't say that with nearly enough conviction, Addison."

I don't hold back. I take a deep breath and shout, "Right!" Who cares if I just yelled so loudly that the dog in the distance is probably barking in response to my shout?

Chloe's smile is evident in her voice. "So, now you need to figure out what you're going to do about it. When you kissed Ian first, you proved to yourself that you can be the one to take action. And you know what you want. Are you willing to fight for it?"

I take a long, deep breath that fills me with determination and bravery. Then, in a voice Chloe could never accuse of not having enough conviction, I say, "Yes. I am."

CHAPTER 25

Ian

I GO STRAIGHT from finishing the trim at the Olson home to working in my shop, hoping the sound of the saws and sanders will drown out my thoughts. Eventually, though, my stomach is what draws me back to the house.

I walk in the back door and find Grandma and Carol sitting at the kitchen table, eating blueberry crisp and ice cream. I lean down and give Grandma a one-armed hug.

"I didn't make dinner," Grandma says, "but there's still mac and cheese casserole in the fridge. And, of course, warm crisp for dessert. Carol and I are just brainstorming options for her home."

"And offering commiseration," Carol adds.

"The place must feel pretty big with Henry gone," I say, putting some casserole on a plate and covering it.

"Yeah. A little too big. I'm not sure how long I'll be able to keep up with it."

I put the plate in the microwave and start it. "Do you need some help?"

Carol smiles and looks like she's about to get out of her seat to come over and squeeze my cheeks like she did when I was little. "You're a gem, Ian. But I need more help than you can give."

I plan to make small talk with the two of them just until my food finishes warming, then I'll escape to my room to eat and shower. But then Grandma tells me, "Sit." So I sit.

"Now," Carol says, "Shirley told me that you and Addison are no longer dating, but she says you haven't told her much about the why. She's your grandma, and since I've been your honorary grandma since you were a toddler, it's time you spill it."

I know that the combined power of Carol and Grandma is impossible to resist when they want information. I can't fight it, so I take a deep breath and let it out slowly. "It was just a bad idea to start dating her in the first place."

They share a look that makes me want to bolt for the microwave—that dings to let me know my food is ready anyway—and then escape to my room. But Grandma senses it and puts her wrinkled hand on my arm. "Stay. Please."

"You love her."

I glance at Carol. It's not a question—she said it like a fact. So I nod.

"So much more than you ever loved Cara. Or anyone before her."

She's so certain that it makes me flinch in surprise. I've talked to Grandma about Addi and she probably told Carol, but I've never talked about Addi specifically to Carol.

"Oh, don't be surprised that I know. You wore your emotions on your sleeve when you were little, and you still do now. It's clear as day how you feel about Addison."

I glance at Grandma, and she adds, "It's true."

Apparently, I don't have a future in playing poker or being a secret agent. "Okay, yes, I do. It's hard *not* to love her, Carol.

She's just amazing. She's so talented and smart and supportive. And so fun to be around. She cares about people, has such big dreams, and she is brave enough to go after them. I love being with her."

Grandma gives a single nod. "And she loves you." She also says it like a fact, not a guess.

"You think so?"

My grandma nods. "She's almost as easy to read as you are. We've talked quite a bit while she's been helping me organize, and I watch how she reacts whenever I bring up the subject of you."

The thought causes an aching in my chest that makes me long to be near her. But if she does love me now, that doesn't mean she always will, and that's the biggest problem. "She said she's questioning every decision she made that brought her here. Even dating me."

"Ian." Grandma's voice is soft, and I turn to her. "In every relationship, you'll each question whether the other person is right for you at some point. Asking yourself those questions and figuring out what the answers are is how you assess whether the relationship has staying power. It's a necessary part of the whole process. It doesn't mean that the relationship is doomed to end."

"And," Carol says, pointing a crooked finger at me, "if you're going to break things off at the first sign of trouble, then you're denying her the freedom to have any emotions that aren't positive. She deserves to feel whatever feelings she has without worrying that it will mean you'll end the relationship."

It feels like a punch to the gut that leaves my head swimming in a fog. Is that what I've done?

"You don't need to be afraid." Grandma's voice is quiet, yet powerful and certain. "Just trust her. Trust that as she asks herself those questions, she'll find the answers." She reaches out and taps me on the chest, right over my heart. "I can tell that all the love you've got for her in here is bursting full. Trust that, not your fears."

"She's right." Carol's statement is as matter-of-fact as when she stated I love Addi. "You trust those fears of yours, and you're going to miss out on the kind of relationship that me and Henry or your grandma and grandpa had. As Shirley said, trust your love."

I lean back in my chair, letting the force of their words sink into me. After a few moments, I say, "Thanks, Grandma and Carol. I really needed to hear that."

"Do you know what else I've been hearing?" Grandma says. "The microwave beeping to let you know your mac and cheese is done."

I chuckle, then get up and give both of them a hug before getting my dinner out of the microwave.

CHAPTER 26

Addison

I PACE back and forth on the grassy shore of Quicksand River, right next to the cove where Ian and I used to play as kids. I shake out my hands and glance back at the shortcut trail we used to take. By the time I got off work, I wanted to go straight to Ian's house or workshop or job site—wherever he was—and tell him how I feel.

Instead, I decide I want to tell him here. In our favorite place. And at some point today, I got the brilliant idea to ask him to come by writing him a cheesy rhyme that will lead him to me, just like I did so many years ago. It wasn't hard to mimic the style of my twelve-year-old self as a twenty-six-year-old— something Professor Rosati wouldn't be surprised by at all.

Now, though, as I wait for Ian to come—and hope it won't be like that time I forgot to mention the direction he should run, or worse, that he doesn't want to come at all—I wonder if this was a terrible idea.

I run over the poem in my head again. Apparently, they're easy to memorize after all. The first time, I wonder if I should've changed any of the wording. I go through it again, wondering if I gave good directions. And I go through it another time, imagining what Ian might be thinking as he reads it.

You said we shouldn't see each other anymore.
Which is hard, since you're my neighbor next door.
But even more impossible is trying to not love you.
Which I can't do, so I hope you'll follow each clue.
Go where we were given the "unplanned" scooter rides.
Jog 400 feet south to where the road divides.
Take the left that leads to our old animal trail.
At each fork, choose the one more traveled and you'll prevail.
Soon, you'll end up at the place I painted on that rock.
And then maybe we can have a little talk.

I shouldn't have ended it by saying we should talk. Nobody likes to hear those words—they sound ominous and bad. Why didn't I think to change that before having Peyton deliver it to Ian? I hope he doesn't think the worst and it makes him not want to come.

I pull out my phone to check the time. Peyton should've dropped off my rhyme at his house twenty-five minutes ago. If I got a note like that, I'd check my hair and makeup, maybe even change clothes. So five minutes there. The drive is about ten minutes to the quasi-trailhead. And then it's at least a fifteen-minute walk to where I am—if he doesn't take the actual trail, which is two miles down from the viewpoint. With all its meandering, it would take much longer.

And that's assuming he was home when Peyton dropped off the note. And that he even wants to come.

I pace some more.

And some more.

Maybe my directions were bad. Maybe I should've chosen a

location we've actually been to as adults, like along Chipper Creek Trail where I lost my shoe. Or the park where we watched Bex's nieces and nephews. Or the high school or that restaurant or the viewpoint or the lemonade stand.

Or maybe I should've just knocked on his front door like normal people do instead of leaving a note.

Finally, I decide I didn't give bad directions—he just isn't coming. I'm bending down to pick up my bag when I hear the sound of footsteps through the undergrowth, and I spin around.

Ian emerges from a non-existent path in the trees that isn't the animal trail shortcut or the main trail. He's a dozen feet from me, wearing dark jeans and a light blue t-shirt so similar to the one he wore when I first saw him in the grocery store, with a plaid shirt over it like a jacket. His hair is perfectly tousled, the sun is shining down on him in the clearing, and he has that amused smile on his face that I love so much.

He jerks a thumb over his shoulder. "I might have, uh, made some wrong choices on a couple of those forks in the path. It's been a while."

I smile. "You have a little…" I motion with my hand on top of my hair, and he reaches up and pulls out a twig that must've hitched a ride during one of those wrong choices.

He drops a backpack I hadn't noticed he'd been wearing to the ground and steps a few feet closer to me. It's strange, seeing this very grown-up, very beautiful man in the same space we spent so much time in as kids so long ago. Except for some minor changes, the place looks largely the same as it always has.

It's the opposite for us, though. We're the ones who've grown and changed. That crush I had on Ian when I was thirteen was a little sapling. Something I thought had withered and died from lack of water over the years but had really just been waiting for its time to grow into something more beautiful.

Or at least I hope it still has a chance to keep growing. Ian looks like he has things he wants to say just as much as I do, but we're both standing awkwardly on the bank of a river, eight feet apart, not talking.

I look at the bend in the river, where the water laps against the small rocks and dirt as it lazily turns back to join the slightly faster-moving water. Then I meet Ian's eyes. "That night, when you said you didn't think we should see each other anymore"— Ian flinches, but I press forward anyway—"I wanted to say how I really felt. But I was afraid to do it because I wasn't sure you felt the same, so I walked away. Kind of like I did when I was thirteen and I gave you that painted stone. Except this time, I didn't run, so obviously, I'm making progress."

Ian chuckles quietly.

I shake out my nervous hands again and then wipe them on my hips. Maybe I haven't made as much progress as I thought. I force myself to take a few slow breaths to calm my nerves. "But I'm ready now. I'm ready to tell you exactly how I feel."

Maybe I shouldn't have spent so much time writing the rhyme and then worrying about his reaction to it and spent more time figuring out how to say everything that's in my heart.

"You were a big part of everything magical in my summers as a kid, and you're an essential part of everything magical about my life now. I love the way you look out for everyone and the way you make me laugh. I even the way you smell. Which sounds weird, I know, but you smell *really* great. And that smile! Yep—that one right there. I really love that smile.

"I love the way you get me, and how you'll drop anything to help someone in need. Plus, you have really great eyes. Have I mentioned your eyes? Sometimes they make me forget how to think, which sounds like it'd be a bad thing, but it's somehow not. I just... I love your whole heart, Ian. I love you.

"Anyway, I just wanted you to know that I fought off some pretty big fear demons since we talked at the gate, which I'm pretty sure gave me some impressive muscles." I hold up my arm and flex muscles that are anything other than impressive. "And I guess I'm giving up some pretty big insecurities, too."

I figure it's probably time to quit rambling, so I stop talking and just make eye contact with him. Even though I feel so vulnerable after revealing so much, I fight the urge to look back down at the river. I swallow, then say, "I know you had a pretty serious relationship not too long ago, and maybe we started dating too soon. Maybe you need more time, and I'm happy to give it to you. Because I don't want to be your rebound, Ian. I want to be your forever."

Ian meets my eyes for a long moment, and then, in three strides, he's right in front of me, cupping my face in his hands like I'm the most precious thing in the world and he wants to protect me. I look into those blue eyes, made even more vibrant by the early evening sun. Then, without a word, he leans forward, and his lips meet mine with such intensity that I find myself fisting his shirt at his chest, holding him close.

Then his kiss slows, and it feels like he's pouring his whole heart into it, just like I poured out my heart in words. I slide my hands up and entwine them behind his neck, trying to return his kiss with all the words I hadn't managed to get out.

I never want this moment to end. Eventually, though, Ian breaks the kiss and smiles, leaning his forehead against mine, breathing fast.

"So," I breathe, "does this mean you want to start dating again?"

CHAPTER 27

Ian

I LAUGH, happiness from Addi's words filling every single cell in my body. "I never wanted to *stop* dating. I was just battling my own fear demons." I hold up an arm and flex it, just like she did. "Since you gave up some insecurities, I'll give up my own about the future."

"Oh yeah?"

"I was apparently holding onto them so tightly that it's amazing I didn't choke them to death."

"Fears are pretty resilient creatures."

I glance at the water in our little cove that we used to play in so much as kids, and then I look back at Addi. It's a hot day, and she's wearing shorts, which make her legs look incredible. But more importantly, she's not wearing pants. Her shoes are lace-up canvas ones that look like they can handle getting wet and have a much better chance of staying on her feet than the ones she wore at Chipper Creek. I'm wearing jeans—I hadn't thought about the water, just about all the branches and tall weeds along the animal trail we used as a shortcut so long ago.

"What do you say we recreate the scene you painted on that stone?"

"You want to jump in?"

"For old time's sake."

Addi seems like she's all in, so we go to the spot at the edge of the bank before it drops off to the river a foot and a half below, right by the big cedar tree. I wrap my hand in hers, and she looks at me with a grin so wide and so brilliant that I can't help but feel the same joy. Then, holding hands, just like in her painting, we jump into the river, laughing as we land in the water.

I wrap my arms around Addi's waist, and she slides her hands up to rest just behind my neck as the water swirls at our calves, the gurgling rushing sounds of the river moving faster downstream just beyond our cove.

"I remember the water being deeper," Addi says.

"I remember being worried I was going to step in quicksand and get trapped, and you'd have to save me."

Addi chuckles. "Me, too. And I don't remember it being this cold."

"I don't remember being this in love with you."

Her gaze turns from the river to me, and she smiles. "Is this you, admitting that when you were fourteen and I was thirteen, you were kind of in love with me?"

I try to hold back a smile, but I'm not very successful. "If how much I thought about you over the years is any indication, I'd have to admit that I was."

"You thought of me?"

"Every single summer since then, especially when July rolled around. Every family barbecue. Every time I visited my grandma. Every time I saw any directions written down, even if they didn't rhyme. And every time I saw Legos, or flat stones, or a picture of a shallow river, or an empty field, or the Hideaway Inn."

She studies me for a long moment. "And now?"

"Since the day you moved in, I don't think I've gone a whole five minutes without thinking of you."

"And if that's any indication—"

"Then it's a guarantee, Addison Sparks, that I am hopelessly, completely, more entirely in love with you than I thought it was possible to be. You are perfect exactly how you are, and being with you makes me the happiest I've ever been."

She kisses me on the lips, but she's smiling so much it only lasts half a heartbeat. She stays close enough to kiss me for several long moments, though, both of us grinning like it's time for the Fourth of July fireworks.

"Let's get dried off," I say, reaching for her hand again and leading her up to the bank. I grab my backpack from where I dropped it and pull out a blanket, spreading it on the grassy clearing. "I didn't have time to make a meal, obviously, but," I say, dragging out the word as I reach into my bag, "I brought blueberries. I figured going with what re-started all this would make an appropriate start to us dating again."

"You didn't," she says, playfully pushing my shoulder.

I pull back. "Careful. I like this shirt."

Addi laughs a beautiful laugh that comes from her belly and seems to fill my whole soul.

We sit down next to each other on the blanket, our shoulders touching, and our legs outstretched. Addi leans in close enough that I can feel the breath from her whispers. "Also in honor of new beginnings and embarrassing moments, I used Secret's *Va Va Vanilla*–scented deodorant today. What do you think of that?"

I chuckle softly. "I think," I say, looking deeply into her

hazel eyes with that rim of sunshiney gold, "that I fall more and more in love with you every single day."

Epilogue

BEX

I SET one of Ian's moving boxes down in Addison's room. As I'm heading back toward the stairs, I open my phone, hold it up with the video camera turned toward me, and push the *Record* button. "Hello, Bexlandians! As promised, today I'm bringing you the very first video in my *Hidden Inn Roomies* segment! I decided to start with the events of today—"

Timini pokes her head into the frame and cuts me off by saying, "—because she wanted to catch us in all our t-shirt and sweat pants-wearing, ponytail-sporting, box-toting glory."

I switch the camera to get a good shot of Timini. "And it is glorious. This is my roommate, Timini. You can call her Tim." Timini waves at the camera, and then I turn the camera to Peyton as she walks up the stairs. "And this is Peyton, but you can call her Pey."

Peyton comes in close to the camera and says, "No, you can't."

Laughing, I whisper to my viewers, "You totally can—it'll just make her twitchy like that. But no, the real reason we are starting this today is that we are getting a new roommate! Our other roommate is Addison, and she is getting married tomorrow."

All three of us squeal.

"As you can see, we are more than a little excited about it. Ian's a great guy, and they are so freaking adorable together. We are moving most of his stuff in today because the two of them are leaving for their honeymoon straight from their reception, and this way, when they come back from their honeymoon, they'll have a place to come home to. Peyton, what do you think about getting a new roommate?"

"I'll admit that at first, I thought it was a little weird to have a guy moving in. It's always been just the four of us girls, and Ian has always been our next-door neighbor. But then Timini pointed out that, hello, this is an inn! For decades, people—mostly couples, even—have been staying here, and the couples didn't even know each other at all. It really is different here than just a regular apartment. And Ian's great, so we're all just excited. For this and the wedding."

"So am I," I say. "They only wanted a small wedding with just family and a few friends—and they specifically said no video. So sorry, Bexlandians! You won't get to see the wedding itself. But here's a sneak peek of me in my bridesmaid dress." I'll add the picture Timini took of me wearing my dress when I edit the video. "Isn't it fabulous? It's why Adds is my new favorite person ever. I will show you a few pics of the wedding itself in my segment next week."

Addison walks from the gathering room to the lobby at the base of the stairs and opens the front door, so the three of us head down the stairs to join her. We've probably spent way too much time slacking at the top of the stairs anyway. The four of us step onto the big wrap-around porch, leaving the front door open behind us like it's been most of the day.

"And this is my roommate, Addison," I tell the camera. "If you can't tell by the glow, she's the bride-to-be."

Addison smiles, waves, and says, "Hi" to the camera. Then her eyes immediately go to the start of the hedgerow that separates the inn from Ian's house. A few seconds later, Ian and a guy I haven't seen before come into view, hefting a heavy-looking dresser.

I turn the camera to Addison just in time to catch her happy sigh. "I can't believe I get to marry that man tomorrow."

"Girl," I say, "you are so joyfully smitten it's practically bursting out of you. I wish I could bottle it and give some to all of my viewers."

"He's just so..." Addison motions to where her future husband carries the dresser down the curved drive in front of the inn, the weight of the dresser showing off his impressive back muscles. "Perfect."

I chuckle quietly. Addison is so clearly blissfully and completely in love that there's no way my viewers are going to miss it. They are going to eat this up. Especially because Ian is putting off the exact same vibes and that man's emotions show on his face as clear as day. I make sure to get a good long shot of him hefting that dresser.

I've been so focused on showing Addison and Ian and capturing how they feel about each other that I've practically missed the guy who's helping Ian with the dresser. "Hello, Mister Hot Stuff." I zoom in on the guy, who is also displaying some incredible upper body strength, along with a jawline so strong I want to put my hands on his face. The hair is pretty fabulous, too.

"So, who's the tall drink of cool water on a hot day? Please tell me he's single. And that he has an easygoing personality and a soft spot for YouTubers, puppies, and large, noisy families."

"Don't you already have a date for the wedding?" Peyton asks.

I keep the camera on the guy as they come up the front walk. "Yeah, and he's all those things. But we've already gone out twice, and I can tell you he isn't forever material."

Timini bumps her shoulder into mine. "Which makes him exactly your type."

I laugh as I film the two men hefting the dresser up the stairs and through the door.

"His name is Roman Powell," Addison says. "He's Ian's friend from college. He's in town for the wedding."

The guys set the dresser down in the lobby, and Addison immediately wraps her arms around Ian's neck and tells him how impressive it is that he hauled something that heavy over from his house. Then they kiss, even with the camera aimed right at them.

"See what I'm talking about?" I say to my viewers. "Aren't they just the sweetest couple you've ever seen? I may have to put up some sticky notes about PDA-free zones, though."

"I would think you could come up with a more organized way of making house rules than posting sticky notes everywhere," Roman Powell says.

I flip the phone's camera back to me. "Oh. So the wrong type of guy, then." I roll my eyes, knowing my viewers are probably rolling theirs right along with me. I've gotten enough footage for a bit, so I turn off the camera and slide the phone into my pocket.

"After Roman and I get this dresser upstairs," Ian says, gently brushing his knuckles back and forth along Addison's jawline, "I'm going to head back over to my house and help get some of Carol's things moved into my room. That way, when her grandson comes next week to help her move in with my grandma, they'll just have to switch out my bed for hers."

Addison smiles. "Is your grandma excited to get a new roomie?"

Ian shakes his head, chuckling. "They're like twelve-year-olds going to sleep-away camp for the first time. There has been actual squealing and jumping up and down." Then he turns to us. "You'll check in on them every day while we're on our honeymoon?"

"Of course!" I say. I love Ian's grandma. I've only met Carol a few times, but she seems like a pretty awesome lady, too.

Ian nods a thank you to us and turns back to Addison. "Then I'll get showered and meet you at the dinner tonight."

Okay, so I'll admit that I may have ogled Roman Powell as he and Ian worked to get the dresser up the stairs. He might not be the easy-going type I'm looking for, but he is one good-looking man.

Once the two men head back to Ian's house, I gather Addison, Peyton, and Timini into a circle in the lobby, and we all interlock arms. "This is it. The last night that it's just the four of us."

"Can you believe it? I get to marry Ian tomorrow! I thought this day would never get here."

"I can't believe it either," Timini says. "Especially since you were so strongly for the 'No falling in love' pact at the beginning."

"If I had to guess, I wouldn't have picked you to be the first to break it," Peyton says.

Addison smiles. "'*The first.*' So, that means you know I won't be the only one to break it." She pointedly turns her focus in my direction.

I hold up my hands in defense. "Hey, don't look at me! I am *definitely* not going to break the pact." Peyton or Timini might, but it's not going to be me. I am not going to fall in love.

———

VOLUME

Two

HOW TO NOT FALL for the WRONG GUY

CHAPTER 1

Bex

I SIT BACK as my sisters Kenna, Nikki, and Roxanna talk over one another, discussing which pet is the one they would never let into their home—a mouse, fish, or a snake. My viewers love how lively the discussions get in my *Sterling Sisters* segments on my YouTube channel. I love it because everyone talking over one another is the sound of home.

A very lively, raucous, chaotic-as-a-crate-full-of-kittens home.

I turn to my oldest sister. "Let me get this straight, Kenna. You would seriously rather have a *snake* in your house than a *fish*? A fish can't even survive out of its tank!"

Sometimes, my sisters and I discuss serious issues, like politics, relationships, or world problems, and sometimes we discuss inconsequential or un-serious subjects, like which pet we don't want, where we'd go on a dream vacation, or our favorite fast food restaurant. It doesn't matter the subject—all five Sterling sisters have reinforced-steel opinions and an even stronger need to share them.

"Yes, but," Kenna says, holding up a finger, "when I look at a snake, I'm not reminded of sixth grade, Joey Peterson, and how I accidentally killed the fish he gave me."

"Fair enough," I say. "I mean, as long as I don't have to ever have a bird in my house, I'm okay with whatever animal issues you all have."

"Asher wants a bird," Vivian says.

I throw my hands to my cheeks in horror. I'm partly playing it up for the camera but in reality, I do actually feel a bit of the horror. "You aren't going to let him, are you?"

"Are you kidding?" Vivian says. "Our house is already too much of a zoo."

"I forgot about you and birds," Nikki breathes, a mix of nostalgia and wonder in her voice. "It was because a couple of seagulls stole the bread off your sandwich at the beach that one time, right?"

"It wasn't *a couple*," I say, the hairs on my arms lifting just thinking about the terror of that moment again. Then I tell the story because my viewers love dramatic stories. Even if this one is my phobia origin story and makes me feel the drama myself. "There were *a dozen*. A dozen strong-winged, pointy-beaked, claw-footed swooping menaces. They didn't just steal my bread —it was my entire sandwich.

"And if stealing my lunch right out of my hands wasn't enough, then they attacked me! Even after I told them they could have my sandwich and ran away. They chased me down, stabbing their beaks into my pockets and squawking at me for being so rude as to not have brought more."

My sisters all give each other knowing looks, and Vivian holds up two fingers, mouthing *there were two birds* as if I can't see. I might be sporting an actual blush across my cheeks right now, but I'll take the razzing because my viewers are probably loving it.

"Whatever. You guys remember it how you want, and I'll

remember it how it actually was." There were definitely a dozen of them. Probably more.

At the sound of ten kids bursting through the back door of the inn—which means they will be in the gathering room where we're filming in about 3.5 seconds—I say, "Thank you for joining us for a rousing Sterling Sisters segment. Don't forget to like the video and subscribe and—"

"And"—Fiona cuts in—"leave memes and gifs of birds for Bex in the comment section!"

"Don't do that," I say in my sternest voice, looking straight into the camera like I'm trying to bore straight into the thoughts of every single viewer. And knowing full well that my viewers are going to do exactly what Fiona asked them to do anyway.

I click the remote on the camera to turn it off as my four-year-old nephew, Drew, shoots through the room and leaps, plowing into his mom to give her a hug. I reach out to grab hold of the back of Vivian's chair and Nikki reaches out to do the same from the other side, keeping it from falling over backward from the force of Drew's hug.

"Woah," Vivian says. "You nearly knocked me over with that one."

"My love for you is strong," Drew says, pounding a fist into his chest.

"Make sure you save some for your siblings and your dad. Now run and get on your shoes—it's time to go."

"All the rest of you, too," Kenna calls out. "Shoes on and head to the lobby."

I stand, hold out a hand to my pregnant sister, Nikki, and pull her to her feet. Then I gather my sisters into a group hug. "You all are the best. Thank you, once again, for voicing your strong opinions, even when we disagree on things like the facts of certain events."

Fiona grins. "Oh, you love that we disagree, and you know it."

"True. These segments would be boring if you all didn't have such strong opinions that you'd defend with your dying breath, no matter how inconsequential the subject."

"I don't know about you all," Kenna says, trying to usher her three kids toward the front door, "but, Bex, I'll happily tell you that you're wrong any chance I get."

"As the one who has spent my entire life as the youngest in a houseful of bossy older sisters, believe me, *I already know*."

My sisters shoo their kids toward the door while trying to gather up all their things and make sure every child has shoes on. Ten kids. And all I want to do is gather them together and surround them with hugs.

I don't know what look is on my face, but Nikki sees it. "You'll find the right guy soon. You'll add your own kids to the mix before you know it."

I let out a long breath. "I don't know—it's looking rather doubtful."

Once Kenna, Vivian, Roxanna, and all ten kids make it out the door and into their cars, Nikki and I head back into the gathering room and to the desk I have set up near the back windows for our weekly planning session.

We sit across from each other and Nikki pulls out the planner that contains the schedule of my life, down to the minute. If it weren't for that planner, my life would be like a giant box of beads that burst open, spilling everywhere. That's why I hired her as my detail person—because Nikki takes care of all the little details that often get missed when I'm focusing on the big picture.

"The biggest thing we need to discuss," Nikki says as she absently rubs her hand on her pregnant belly, "is your plans for episodes that will go live during the judging period for the Eddie Awards."

I tap my pen on my lips. "For the *Sterling Sisters* segments, we need a couple of fun and interesting debate topics. Like what one non-electronic device you'd want if you were going to be trapped inside an office building for a month, or the most effective way to talk your significant other into choosing to watch the movie you want them to choose."

"Ha! I can already imagine Kenna's answer. Maybe we could even do one about our most embarrassing moments." She glances at her phone that just lit up, then picks it up from the desk. "Aww!" She turns the phone toward me. "How sweet is this?"

I lean in to see my brother-in-law's text that reads *This is what's waiting for you when you get home,* along with a selfie of him stirring a pan of chicken tikka masala.

"Is he the greatest, or what?"

"He's a solid four point five trillion times better than your last husband." I smile at my sister's pregnant belly—the belly that holds my future nephew—and I'm so glad that Nikki divorced the jerk before having any kids. I'm happy knowing that the little guy who's going to make an appearance in a couple of months is going to get such a good guy for a dad.

"You've got that right. Okay, so do you know what you're doing for the *Hidden Inn Roomies* segments?"

I nod. "Mostly. Still working out the details, but we'll have fun with that one."

"And your interviews?"

I grab Nikki's arm. "I can't believe I haven't told you already! I put a poll out to my viewers asking who they wanted me to interview, and I set it up so anyone could add choices to the list. As you can probably guess, the list grew to roughly the length of a CVS receipt in the first couple of hours, but then favorites started rising to the top. Guess who has been on top for the past thirty-six hours? Corbin Shields!"

"Are you kidding me?! Oh, wow, Bex. If you could get him…"

"I know. I want it to be a four-part interview, and I think he'd be so perfect for that. The guy has so much charisma, so many interests, and he's always willing to put on a show for his fans. If I could get him to agree to it, I think we'd have a good chance at this award."

"You'd have it in the bag. Getting him to agree to a four-part interview might be close to impossible, though."

"Even if he's willing, I'd have to hope his publicist could fit it into the cracks of his schedule." It won't be easy, but I know the guy's fans are important to him, and so is appearing to be accessible to them. I think I can play up that angle with his publicist and talk him into it.

I grab my laptop that sits on the edge of the desk and pull it toward me, opening it and turning it on. "The last time I checked—which was over four hours ago—one hundred thirty-two thousand viewers voted to have me interview him. Voting closes in five days, and I'm hoping that he has an impressive enough number by then that he won't want to say no."

I log in and bring up the site. Then I just stare at the poll numbers, not comprehending what I'm seeing.

Nikki leans forward, squinting at the screen. "Who is Roman Powell?"

"*No.* No, no, no. How is he in first place?" I refresh the screen, hoping it's a mistake, but he's still in the number one spot. How did this happen? Corbin Shields is now in second place, a full nine thousand votes behind Roman. I run my hands over my face, but it's about as effective at reversing what happened to the votes in the past four hours as rewinding a movie in hopes that it'll end differently.

"Bex!" Nikki says. "Who is Roman Powell?"

"He's one of the groomsmen from Addison and Ian's wedding."

"Oh. The good-looking one who drove you nuts and made the flower girl chuck the flowers?"

"That's the one. Nikki, he can't win! Corbin Shields is so charismatic that not only will we be able to come up with some fun ideas for the interview, but my audience will eat it up. It'll be a win-win for both of us. Roman, though, is a cardboard cutout of a man in a tailored suit with a severe allergy to fun. His idea of an interview probably includes a desk, studio lighting, one camera angle, and zero smiles."

"But *who is he*? How do"—Nikki motions at the screen—"two hundred fourteen thousand of your viewers even know enough about him to vote for him?"

I shake my head. "I have no idea. Can we finish our planning session later? You've got chicken tikka masala and a sweet husband waiting for you at home, and I have some big questions for Ian about his groomsman."

As I say goodbye to my sister at the front door of the inn that my roommate Addison owns and runs as our apartment, sounds of chatting and smells of something delicious cooking come from the dining hall, so I head in that direction with my laptop.

All four of my roommates—Peyton, Timini, Addison, and Addison's brand-new husband, Ian—are all either behind the island counter cooking or sitting on the bar stools chatting. I breathe in deeply. "Is that shrimp scampi I smell? And here I was geared up for enchiladas or chicken piccata."

Addison grins at Ian as they stand side by side behind the stove. "It's one of Ian's specialties. And it's not the only fantastic meal he knows how to cook, so for our roommate dinners, we won't have to eat one of the only two I can make when it's my turn to cook."

I take a seat on one of the bar stools and place my laptop on the counter. "I knew it was a good idea to invite him to our roommate dinners."

"Because he *is* a roommate now," Peyton says.

"And I've enjoyed all four days of being one since we've been back from our honeymoon," Ian says and then gives Addison a kiss on her temple. "But I don't think I should come to every roommate dinner. Maybe every other time it should just be you four. The original roommates. Then on the weeks I come, it can be 'significant other' night or something."

"Except the rest of us don't have significant others," Timini says. "In fact, we made a pact not to." She raises an accusing eyebrow at Addison.

Addison holds up her hands. "In my defense, we made that pact when I had just come off a two-year relationship and before I realized that trying to resist Ian was pointless."

"And when Tim was still getting over her ex," I say, "and Pey had just stopped dating that guy who still shared an address with his mother, and I'd just gone on like my tenth date in a row with a guy who cried about his recent breakup." I lift a shoulder. "But none of us broke the pact."

"When you do, though," Addison says, "we will throw you an engagement party every bit as fun as the one you all threw for Ian and me. You're still planning on convincing Corbin Shields to let you interview him so he can fall in love with you, marry you, and be the father of your children, right?"

I can't believe I said that, regardless of how late we stayed up, or how punch-drunk we were from laughing during our roommate catch-up session last night. "That was the sleep deprivation talking. And besides, your friend," I say, jabbing a finger at Ian, "is putting my plan in jeopardy."

"*My* friend? Who? How?"

"Roman Powell." I bring my laptop back to life and then turn the screen toward Ian as everyone leans in to see it. "Any idea how in the world enough of my viewers even know who he is to have put him at the top of the list? Above Corbin Shields?"

Ian stares at the screen in confusion for a small moment, then looks up at the ceiling while whatever it is dawns on him. He chuckles, shaking his head. "Oh, wow. I can't believe that many people are voting for him." He takes a couple of steps closer and leans across the counter to get a better look at the laptop. "Whoa. He has two hundred eighteen thousand votes? What I wouldn't give to be in the room when he saw this. I wouldn't want to be the one to tell him, but man, would I love to see his face."

"*Why* is he on my list, Ian? He runs a small company that makes apps for phones. How do my viewers suddenly know who he is?"

Ian laughs, shakes his head, and then laughs again before going back to the stove to pour the shrimp scampi from the pan into a serving dish. "Before the wedding, he was hyped about an interview he'd had with *Business Success* magazine. They were going to feature ten stand-out CEOs, and they picked him.

"Then yesterday, he called. The magazine had released, and, well, it kind of pointed out that he was single and available and at the helm of a business that was going places. And they put him on the cover, looking a little..." Ian shrugs, "...like he was searching for someone to make him no longer single and available."

Addison puts her hand over her mouth like she's trying to hold back a laugh. "Oh, my goodness. Oh, I bet he was mad. Can I please be in the room with you, honey, when he finds out about this poll?"

Peyton furrows her brow. "Why would that make him mad? I mean, he must've looked good and had a great article written about him if that many people want Bex to interview him. That's exciting and fun! Why would he not think it's a good thing?"

"You've met the guy," I say. "I don't think he does 'exciting and fun.' What was I thinking when I turned the interview choice over to my viewers? If I have to interview Roman, I'm as good as forfeiting my chance at the Eddie Award."

"I wouldn't worry about it," Timini says as she reaches out with a fork that seems to materialize from out of nowhere and sneaks a piece of shrimp from the serving dish. "It's just his fifteen minutes of fame. It'll be over in less than twenty-four hours, and Corbin Shields will make his way to the top of the list again."

"I hope you're right," I say. "Because I really want to win that vlogger award, and I can't do it with the wrong guy winning that poll."

CHAPTER 2

Roman

I LOOK DOWN at my tablet as I walk from my office to the conference room to meet with my department heads. In big, bold letters at the top of my meeting agenda is my company's and my own personal motto: *Be the Best You*. I like to remind myself of it before everything I do in my company.

But it doesn't pump me up the way it normally does. Probably because of the annoyed feeling that lately seems to always hang around like gum under a middle-schooler's desk, even when I'm not thinking about the reason why.

Four of my five department heads are already in the room. I glance at the empty seat. "Has anyone seen Everly?"

"I'm here, I'm here," Everly says as she blows into the room like a force of nature and slaps her stuff down onto the table before taking her seat. "Don't worry. I'm late for a reason."

"It's a good thing you're so skilled at what you do," I say, although we all know Everly isn't late. One of the things I love about my team is that they always show up five minutes early, ready to go. That, and they're all amazing at what they do and none of them complain about the slash in their job titles that means they are doing the work of more than one department. We're barely beyond startup status, and running lean is paramount. I've managed to bring together a dynamic bunch who all have the same goal as I do—to push the company forward.

Since this meeting is about the launch of our latest app, I start by going around the table and having each department head give an update on where they're at. The development department and the design and user experience department tell how things have gone for the advance users in the final round of testing, my finance guy talks about the advertising budget, and my assistant slash human resources head, Melinda, talks about a couple of promising interns we're about to give job offers to. The whole time, Everly leans forward, elbows on the table, tapping her pen or drumming a finger.

Melinda reaches out and puts a hand on top of Everly's fidgeting one but keeps her eyes on me. "The offers will go out today. Hopefully, they'll say yes because marketing and app testing could both really use the help." Then she looks at Everly. "With as much as you've apparently wanted to go first today, it wasn't the best day to come into the meeting last, was it?"

"No—I've been dying for my turn!"

Everly looks at me, so I motion to her. "Give us your update, since it looks like you might explode if you have to wait another second."

Everly looks visibly relieved to finally be able to speak. "My team, of course, is always looking out for ways to have our products stand out in a crowded market. And an opportunity to help launch *Nudge Out* has practically dropped into our lap." She pulls a magazine from her stack and tosses it to the middle of the table, beaming.

And there it is. The source of the annoyed feeling that has followed me around since the magazine was released four days ago. I close my eyes, shaking my head, trying to keep my temperature from rising.

"Stop," Everly says. "You've got that vein by your temple popping out again. This is *Business Success* magazine! And you're on the cover! Remember how much we celebrated when you got the email saying they wanted to line up an interview and photo shoot with you because they chose you to be in their *Top Ten CEOs Under Thirty* list? And that was before they decided to put you on the cover. This is a big deal, Boss."

"It was a big deal back when I thought it would all focus on LivenUP and our products. It became considerably less outstanding when they changed the title of the feature to *Top 10 Young (and Single) CEOs* and chose a picture that makes me look like I'm smoldering at the camera."

I still don't know how they managed to snap the shot at all —I swear I didn't smolder at the camera a single time. It was probably taken at the moment when I suddenly wondered if I actually clicked send on the email I had written to Daran about setting up a meeting to discuss a new app idea. I can't help the fact that, with the right photographer, my thinking pose looks like an invitation to ogle me.

"It's a good smolder," Everly says.

"It looks more like they're advertising an episode of *The Bachelor* than spotlighting CEOs who have built successful businesses." The picture they used is a full-body shot of me in a suit, leaning against the back of a chair—a pose more suitable for a menswear model than a CEO. The second I saw it, I knew what my dad's reaction would be: embarrassment.

"But the article is good," Everly says. "They asked a lot of great questions about the company and our products, and you answered them perfectly."

I shake my head. "The article also includes a lot of personal stuff that I thought was just small talk. Off the record." It still makes me mad that I fell for it.

It doesn't matter what I say; Everly's excitement doesn't seem to dwindle. "But it shines you and this company in a great light. Pointing out that you're young and single doesn't take any of that away. What it *does* do is make people interested enough to want to find out more. And that's exactly the goal we had when you agreed to the interview. Who cares if they put you on the cover because you have a face that sells magazines? This extra exposure is golden."

"This is how I see it," Daran, my app development head, pipes in. "It's like you're going on a trip. You reserved a mid-sized car, but when you get to the car rental counter, they say they're out and they are going to upgrade you to an Aston Martin. Sure, it's only temporary. But it's an Aston Martin! Are you telling me you're just going to complain about how much gas it guzzles and not drive that beautiful piece of machinery every second you can?"

"This," I say, reaching for the magazine in the middle of the table and holding it up, "isn't an Aston Martin. It's not a gift. It makes me look like I'm not serious about this company. Or worse, that I'm not legitimate. That I only made the list because they needed someone to look good on the cover."

Sloan, my graphic designer slash user experience manager, crosses her arms and looks down, trying to hide a smile. With her looks and stature, she has probably dealt with the same thing herself more than once and is glad it's me this time.

"Whether you appreciate being on the cover or not," Everly says, "it *is* a gift. It's what got those investors you're meeting with today to be interested. They saw the 'shiny car' on the front cover and opened up the magazine to get the specs. It got their attention, just like it'll get the attention of others. It's a good thing, and we need to capitalize on it."

I fold my arms and lean back in my chair. I don't like it, but she has a point. It's enough that I should at least hear her out. "Tell me what you're thinking."

"There's a YouTuber who has a big audience, and she often does interviews with people. Six days ago, she put out a poll asking viewers who they would most like her to interview, and anyone could add a name to the list. The results were fairly predictable—various celebrities—until four days ago when *Business Success*'s latest issue came out. Shortly after it did, BuzzFeed picked up the online feature, and another YouTuber who makes videos also aimed at our target audience posted about it. Then someone wrote in your name as who they would like her to interview. Fast-forward four days and you currently have forty-two percent of *all* the votes. Nine percent more than the next most popular choice."

One of my biceps flexes involuntarily, and I raise an eyebrow. Forty-two percent. That's pretty impressive.

"My team has defined a very specific audience we believe it is vital to reach for the product launch of *Nudge Out,* and we've been brainstorming ways to reach that audience. We looked at the demographics of these viewers, and they are exactly the audience my team defined. An interview there might get people talking enough that it gives a significant boost."

"How big of an audience are we talking about?"

"She has over two million subscribers. Not all of them voted, of course, and she probably had a lot of people vote who haven't subscribed, but as of about five minutes before I walked in here, an interview with you currently has six hundred seventy-five thousand votes."

I sit up straight. That's a lot of people we could reach. "And you think we can get this interview?"

"If six hundred seventy-five thousand of my viewers

wanted me to interview you, I don't think you'd have a hard time talking me into it."

"Okay, tell me about this YouTube channel."

Everly grins, probably sensing victory. "One of the things that I think definitely swings in our favor is that the creator is a woman who lives here in Oregon, so I think we'll get some extra hometown support." She pulls a manila folder from her stack of papers and slides it across the table to me. "Her viewers are rabidly loyal. She's no stranger to interviews, but she doesn't pimp products often, even for the people she has on her show. When she does, her fans jump at whatever she suggests, so if you can get her to suggest they use our app, it'll likely make a huge difference."

I open the folder to see a picture of the YouTuber, her opening screen logo, and her YouTube stats. I immediately shut the folder and push it back across the table toward Everly. "Yeah, this isn't going to work."

"What?" Everly says, looking around at everyone else, a bewildered expression on her face. "Why? Roman, this is *perfect*."

I shake my head. "I met her a couple of weeks ago at my buddy's wedding—she's one of the bride's best friends. I know her and her channel well enough to know it's just fluff, and it's not the direction we need to go."

"Are you sure?" Wells, my finance guy, says. "It sounds like Everly found a potential advertising avenue that could have a great ROI."

Of course, Wells is focusing on the money aspects of it. One of the reasons why LivenUP is in such a great financial situation is because Wells guards our money like a mama bear guarding her cubs. Money isn't the only factor at play, though.

I hold up the magazine with my picture on it. "You want to capitalize on this, Everly? Great. There are some important things in this article. But there are also parts that are ridiculous and irrelevant. Those are exactly the same parts that Bex Sterling will try to capitalize on—*not* the important parts."

"I disagree. If she can get her Bexlandians on board, it'll be exactly the kind of boost we need."

I want to roll my eyes. *Bexlandians.* Not only would being interviewed by her embarrass my dad, but it's enough that even my brothers would get in on the ribbing.

"I think it would be a mistake to not jump on this," Everly continues. "Since you've already made a connection with Bex, it would probably be best if you reached out, but if you'd prefer, I am happy to as well."

With as happy and energetic as Everly is, she often gives the impression that she's easygoing. But she doesn't back down when she sets her mind to something. It's one of the reasons why I hired her and why she's a department head. But I'm still the boss, which means the decision rests with me.

"No. Don't contact her." I feel my phone buzz in my pocket and pull it out to see that it's my dad calling. Probably about my meeting with the potential investors. Since we've already discussed everything here that we need to discuss, I might as well answer my dad's call now instead of dealing with him later.

"But—"

"Everly, it's a firm no. Thank you all for your input this morning. Meeting adjourned."

As I walk out of the room, tablet in hand, I answer the phone. "Hello?"

"Hi, son. Today's the big day, right?"

"It is." I head down the hallway toward my office.

"And you've got a spit-shine on your business plan?"

"It's all ready to go. I meet with them in thirty minutes." Of course, it's all ready to go. These investors could mean the difference between LivenUP moving forward slowly and really becoming a major player in the app world. Everything I've been doing—everything I've helped this company to do—has been with investors in mind. Their support could mean everything.

"Okay, listen up. You may sell some apps that they might consider 'entertainment,' but you're a serious businessman. Show that to the investors. Don't fall for the same tricks that the interviewer at *Business Success* used on you. You're young and don't have a ton of experience with the media yet, so you didn't know how sneaky they could be. I don't blame you for the article turning out the way it did. But 'fool me once' and all that. Fall for it again, and it's on you."

I grind my teeth at the young and inexperienced comment but keep my mouth shut. My dad is probably sitting in his office behind his massive mahogany desk, floor-to-ceiling windows behind him. He might be leaning back in his chair, looking relaxed, but the man is a boulder the size of a house and impossible to so much as budge. This man would hate every single thing about me being interviewed by Bex Sterling.

When I get back to my office, I set the tablet on my desk and start flipping through the pages in the first of four manila folders, checking to make sure I have everything.

"Keep things professional with these investors. If they start asking personal questions, steer it away. Show them you can keep your eye on the ball. And son?"

"Yeah?"

"Land these investors, and we might just have to celebrate by going on a rafting trip down the Columbia."

I'm so speechless I can't respond. My two younger brothers have each made our dad proud enough to earn a trip down the Columbia—Drake when he was interviewed for a business magazine after landing his first Fortune 500 company as a client, and Legend when he sold his first architectural design—but it's been quite a while since I had anything on the horizon that my dad deemed worthy enough to even dangle the carrot. Nothing is going to stop me now from doing whatever it takes to get these investors on board.

"Now head into that meeting and show them what a Powell is made of!"

"I will. Thanks, Dad."

———

I successfully shake off all talk of the *Business Success* article and walk into the meeting with the investors feeling calm, confident, and ready to convince them to invest in LivenUP. My presentation is professional, precise, thorough, and concise. If my dad were a fly on the wall, he would be flying over to give me a pat on the back.

When I finish, the investors talk a lot about their vision of the company, which mirrors mine, and how they don't want to interfere with the way I run my business. If they had wanted to control how I run the company, I would've walked away. They ask lots of questions, and I field them left and right, the consummate professional. I ask them questions, too.

Then, Thomas Hayes, the investor who seems to be in charge, closes his folder and places his hands on top of it. The other two follow his lead, and then they all look at each other and shift in their seats. "You've built a good company here. I can tell you've put together a solid team of people, and that you're all working together for the same goal."

I nod. That's exactly how I feel about LivenUP, so I'm glad they see it, too. I hold my breath for the *but*, though. So far, everything is too good to be true.

"But we knew all that before coming here today. We've had

our eye on you for months exactly because of all the things you just confirmed for us. We didn't ask to meet until now, though, because we were waiting to see the spark. That extra something that would tell us that you were going to be around for a while and that you were going places. We saw that spark in your interview in *Business Success*."

I flinch in surprise. What could they have possibly read in that interview that made them want to invest more than the presentation I just gave?

The woman sitting next to him adds, "We didn't really see that spark today."

How could they have not seen a spark today? I love this company, and I know that I've spoken about it with a lot of passion. Sure, I don't let them see *all* the passion I have—that's part of being professional, after all—but they had to have sensed it.

The third guy leans forward, resting his arms on the conference table and meeting my eyes. "Too many CEOs keep their noses to the corporate grindstone and lose touch with the customers that they are creating products for. We want to see that you are keeping that connection to your users."

"Keeping in touch with the pulse of our users is something we take very seriously here," I assure him. "We have a user experience team who tries out new ideas with focus groups, works closely with beta testers, polls our audience for preferences, and implements all the feedback we get. It's one of the reasons why our apps are rated so highly in app stores."

"And that's important," the woman says. "We wouldn't be here if you didn't do all those things. But that's not the spark we're talking about. That's how you connect to your audience. We are talking about how your audience connects to *you*."

"Why does that matter? I'm the man behind the curtain. I'm supposed to be invisible."

"Once upon a time, sure. And for most types of businesses, it still very much is. But not for a company like yours, and not if you want to grow in the way that we think our investment will help you grow. It's time for you to come out from behind the curtain. Your audience needs to see you and be able to connect with you. They need to view you as a real person. Find a way to do that, and we'll have no problem investing in LivenUP."

They get up to leave, so I walk to the door to see them out, feeling baffled. I'm not sure I really understand what they expect from me. As the woman reaches the doorway, she pauses and says, "You wear your professionalism like a mask. We want to see the man behind the mask. The part of the interview where you said you eat oatmeal every morning with peanut butter and jelly in it was a nice touch. Keep up stuff like that, and you'll do great."

The part of the interview that was supposed to be off the record and had absolutely nothing at all to do with my business —*that's* the part the investors liked? How am I supposed to remain professional yet "connect" with my users like that? They've given me a proposal about what they can do for me, and I really want them to invest. But I'm not sure I can do what they're asking.

I walk them to the front door and stand there long after they leave. I couldn't have asked for investors who are more on board with the direction I'm taking my company. With their backing, I would be able to grow the company the way I've been envisioning for so long but haven't been able to do yet.

And signing with them would make my dad rafting-trip proud. But signing with them also means doing something that would make my dad the opposite of proud.

I'm not thrilled about it myself, either.

And I know that I shouldn't care what my dad thinks, but I do.

Everly comes up to me and stares out through the glass doors with me for a few moments before asking, "How did the meeting go?"

"What do you think the chances are that my dad would watch *Bexlandia*?"

Everly snickers and I look over at her.

"Sorry. What do I think the chances are that Dr. Richmond Powell IV, D.B.A. will watch *Bexlandia*? Zero, Roman. I think the chances are zero percent."

I really hope she's right. I nod, my mind made up. "I think I'll reach out to Bex Sterling."

The smile on Everly's face isn't visible from where I stand, but I know it's there.

CHAPTER 3

Bex

WHEN MY THIRTEEN-YEAR-OLD NEPHEW, Enoch, kicks the ball, I run from third base toward home. Dylan catches it, though, and quickly throws it at me. In an attempt to keep it from tagging me, I dive, landing in the grass of my parents' backyard a good foot away from home base. And the ball hits me anyway.

I don't even have time to push myself up before three of my nieces and nephews pile on top of me, pinning me to the grass.

"Guys," I say, laughing, "this isn't football!"

My seven-year-old niece, Tessa, leaps onto us, adding to our pile of bodies. "No, but our parents said we get bonus points for tackles anyway."

I manage to free my arms so I can tickle my niece. "But you're on my team!"

"And you're supposed to be on second base," Asher says. Then he pushes off me and races after the kickball.

"Dinner's ready," my dad calls out from his station in front of the barbecue, and the score and where everyone is supposed to be is forgotten.

I'm at the food tables with the rest of my sisters, brothers-in-law, parents, and everyone's kids, putting items on my plate, when my phone buzzes. I pull it out to see it's a text from Ian, my newest roommate.

> Ian: Remember how you asked about Roman Powell the other day?

> He wants to meet with you and is hoping to set up a dinner with you through me. He wants Addison and me to come, too, probably to make it less awkward.

> What should I tell him?

I turn my phone so that Nikki can see it.

"Wow. Roman is coming to *you*. I assume he's planning to ask for an interview. Are you going to say yes?"

"Of course, I'm going to try to make an interview work! Voting closes in two hours, and he's got nearly *half* of all the votes. As much as I wanted to interview Corbin Shields, Roman has two hundred thousand more than him. Roman Powell is who my viewers want to see. I was going to contact him as soon as the barbecue was over, but it looks like now I won't have to." I type out *Tell him yes* one-handed and slide my phone back into my pocket.

I'm just putting a big scoop of potato salad on my plate when my five-year-old niece Chelle tugs on my shirt. "Aunt Bex? Do you have a corner brownie? Because I called one, but Drew took the last one and then licked it."

"I do have one. And because I think you're the bee's knees, I'm giving it to you." Chelle beams as I put it on her plate.

Nikki shakes her head. "You're such a pushover."

"Nope—it's all in service of my goal. Maintaining 'Favorite Aunt' status with the kind of competition we have isn't easy, so I have to butter them up any chance I get."

"I really need to step up my game," Nikki says as she reaches across the table to grab a roll. "What's your plan if an interview with Roman doesn't work out?"

"Then we sweet-talk Corbin Shields's publicist. My readers would be sad I couldn't get Roman, but Corbin would make for a much better interview. I'm pretty sure they wouldn't mind that for a consolation prize if I at least tried to get Roman first."

"And it might just win you that Eddie Award."

———

I step into the lobby of the restaurant with Addison and Ian. Ian set everything up with Roman, and he said Roman was the one who chose to travel from Gresham to Quicksand. Okay, so maybe the guy gets a checkmark in the positive column for that one. I don't know if it was Ian or Roman who chose Buffalo Bill's Steakhouse—not that there are a ton of other choices in Quicksand.

We check in with the hostess, who says, "Oh, I've already seated the other rough rider in your group."

Wow. He's early, even. Another checkmark in the positive column. As the hostess leads us across the Western frontier-inspired decor, complete with lassos, horseshoes, wanted posters, wagon wheels, and saddles attached to the walls, Roman stands up from our table at the far end of the room. He's dressed in a suit, which seems at odds with the cowboy hat light that is hanging just above our table and the boot-shaped menu holder on the table, but to each his own.

Overdressed or not, the man looks stand-up-and-applaud fine in a suit. Like millions of others who wouldn't normally pick up an issue of *Business Success* magazine, I've seen him on the cover. They made a good choice in putting him there—I heard it skyrocketed their sales. If I can just get the guy to let his guard down a bit and stop being so stiff and serious, an interview with him might do really well on my channel.

When we reach Roman, he greets Ian and Addison, and the two take their seats at the table—thankfully across from each other—and Roman holds out a hand to shake mine. And wow, it's a good handshake. It sends zings of electricity right up my arm. I had put my arm in his as we walked up the aisle together as a bridesmaid and a groomsman, but I haven't touched his hand before.

"It's good to see you again, Bex."

"You, too," I say as we both take our seats across from each other. "Started any brawls between three-year-olds lately?" I don't know why I say it. Probably to try to crack that shell of seriousness just a bit.

But Roman's brows knit together, and I can practically see his defenses rising. "I wasn't the one who—"

"Either way," Addison interrupts, "it was a fun moment to catch on camera. Made the wedding even more memorable."

Then she shoots me a look, so I put on my best innocent yet apologetic expression.

As we each give Roman our recommendations on the menu, I study him. When I look at him through the lens of my viewers, I notice how much depth his beautiful brown eyes have. As if dark chocolate, milk chocolate, and honey all tried to see how epic they could be if they formed a team. His skin has a golden glow to it like maybe he doesn't spend all day scowling at a computer screen.

And that jawline, too. The first time I saw him, I immediately wanted to put my hands on his face and feel that perfect amount of scruff. To run my fingers through the hair just above his ears that curls slightly.

Of course, that was back then before I'd spent some time around him. But I'm sure my viewers will be noticing that fine jaw and everything else I noticed my first time seeing him.

The waiter comes over to take our order. He's probably twenty-one but looks seventeen or eighteen and introduces himself as Kenyon, which I already know from eating here so often. When I order the sirloin steak and baked sweet potato, from the corner of my eye I see Roman's flinch of surprise, so I look over at him. "What?"

"I'm impressed you got the steak."

I lift a shoulder. "This is a steakhouse. 'When in Rome' and all that."

He nods, and then also orders a sirloin steak, but unlike the rest of us, he orders a regular baked potato. I think about telling him that their sweet potatoes are to die for, but I let it go.

After the waiter leaves, Roman asks Ian and Addison how their honeymoon in San José del Cabo was, and they both light up like a grandma who was just asked to show off pictures of her grandkids.

I'm glad the two of them are sitting across the table from each other. Not only does it mean that Roman and I can discuss business face to face instead of shoulder to shoulder, but it means that Ian and Addison can only make moon eyes at each other instead of cuddling up, basking in their honeymoon glow, making things awkward for Roman and me.

But man, do I wish Roman would relax a bit. Slouch in his posture. Be a little less guarded. Maybe ditch the tie and undo the top button. I'm wearing a dress, but a casual, wear-grocery-shopping-on-a-Tuesday dress. And, because we're at Buffalo Bill's, I'm also wearing cowboy boots. Addison and Ian are both wearing jeans.

It's not that I have anything against seriousness. My dad is rather stoic, and I love him. He's a pretty cool guy. But on Roman, it feels wrong. I read people pretty well, and with

Roman, it feels like the inside doesn't match the outside. That there's more to him than meets the eye.

Kenyon returns, holding a tray with our drinks on it, and starts passing them out. "Okay, and you two also wanted water on the side, right?"

Roman and I both nod, so the waiter puts one in front of me. As he's reaching out to place Roman's water in front of him, Cassie, one of the other waiters, turns around from a table she's waiting on and bumps into Kenyon's back. As Kenyon lurches forward, the glass of water spills all over the table and onto Roman.

"Oh, no. I am so sorry, sir." He pulls some napkins out of the front of his apron and starts dabbing at the water. "I am so sorry. I didn't mean to..." He holds out a few napkins, like he's going to press them against the water that has spilled on Roman's suit, but then thinks better of it. Good choice.

"It's okay," Roman says. "We'll just go with the flow. It's all water under the table now."

Huh. It's almost like there's a real person under the exterior he always has up.

Roman didn't come into town much before the wedding, so I haven't gotten to know him too well. Mostly what I know is that he was even serious at a wedding and that he thought he knew much more about kids than me. As the outcome of the flower girls walking down the aisle showed, he clearly did not.

Something catches my eye, and I glance at one of the tables to the side of us. It's a family of four, and the two daughters, who look like they're maybe ten and twelve years old, are looking at us, giggling and trying to nudge each other out of their chairs. They both seem to get nudged enough at the same time because they stand up, shoot a glance back at their parents, and then timidly walk over to our table, bumping each other the entire way. They're probably fans. I'm not recognized everywhere I go, but things like this happen about once a week or so.

The girls don't come up to me, though—they go straight to Roman. The older one taps the younger one twice on her shoulder, but the younger one whispers, "No, you ask him."

So the older one stands taller and says, "Um, we were just wondering, are you Roman Powell?"

Roman's head cocks ever so slightly, showing his surprise that two girls he's never seen before know his name. "Yes."

Both girls giggle, but the younger one says, "We read about you."

Roman's eyebrows shoot right up. "You did?"

The older one nods. "And from the way you're sitting, your pants come up just a bit, so we saw that you're wearing fun socks, just like you said you did in your interview. We wanted to tell you that we think it's cool."

"Yeah," the younger says, "and I wanted to tell you that Emma has quoted your phrase 'Life's too serious for your socks to be' like five million times."

He doesn't say anything for a long moment—he just looks back and forth between the girls. Then, finally, he manages to get out, "You read *Business Success* magazine?"

"Well," the older one says, "it's our mom's, but I saw you on the cover—"

"*I* saw you on the cover," the younger one corrects. "And so I showed my sister, and then we read the article together."

"Well, okay, Bailey saw it first. But I made a goal to someday be on the cover of *Business Success*, too, because I'm going to start my own business."

Roman smiles a big, genuine smile. "That's a great goal. I hope you do."

The girl beams, but then her younger sister says, "I think she just wants to be on it because she has the magazine with you on it hiding in her room so she can make kissy faces at it every night. If she gets on the cover, then it can be right next to your cover and the two magazines can basically get married."

"Bailey!" the older sister hisses. "I can't believe you just told him that!"

The girl shrugs, hands upturned. "Well, Dad says to always tell the truth, so…"

Red-faced and humiliated, the older girl turns her back on her sister and stomps back to their table. Bailey shares a faux innocent smile with Roman, then whispers, "She's going to be mad at me for like a week, but it was totally worth it."

Roman looks about as horrified at the exchange as the older sister is, and I try really hard to hold in my chuckle. I'm used to conversations like that with young fans, but Roman obviously isn't. If anything, it shows that audiences can really connect to him. They don't connect with everyone—I hope he realizes what a gift that is.

"Aww," Addison says when she turns back from seeing the girls sit back down at their table. "Your fans love you."

"They weren't—" Roman says. "They aren't even *Business Success's* target audience."

Our conversation is halted as Kenyon comes over to our table, carrying a much bigger tray with our food on it, and puts the stand into place in the aisle. As he's lowering the tray to the stand, Callie bumps into him again, and exactly one plate slides off the tray and onto the floor: Roman's. The one with the regular baked potato.

A quiet, frustrated growl comes from Roman as Kenyon stands frozen for a long couple of seconds. Then Roman mutters, "Do they not teach you how to share the aisle here?"

Kenyon scrambles to the other side of the tray stand and picks up Roman's plate, putting the steak, baked potato, and steamed veggies back on it. "I can't believe this is happening. I'll get them to make you a new meal." Then he holds Roman's plate, twisting side to side like he's just realized that he has nowhere to put the plate while he serves the other three plates of food.

I feel awful for the kid. It's bad enough to deal with an issue like that without the comment Roman made. I reach out and put a hand on the server's arm. "It's okay, Kenyon. It wasn't your fault. Why don't you take that to the kitchen, and do you mind bringing back an extra plate when you come?"

As Kenyon races off, I look at Roman and take a deep breath. "Do you have siblings?"

He jerks back a little at the abrupt change in subject. "Yeah, two brothers."

"Did you do things to annoy each other growing up?"

He nods. "Like it was a sport."

"Where are you in your family?"

"Oldest."

"So when other people picked on your younger brothers, what did you do? Join in like it was a sport?"

"What? No. I stepped in and said that if they messed with my brother, they messed with me."

I nod. "This is our restaurant. It's family. Don't mess with it."

I could swear a smile tries to break its way through to Roman's face. Then he meets my eyes and says, "I want you to interview me."

Kenyon comes back and places the empty plate near me, then gives Addison, Ian, and me our food. He opens his mouth like he's going to apologize to Roman again, but Roman beats him to it.

"I apologize for what I said earlier. That was very unprofessional of me."

Unprofessional. He's not apologizing for being a jerk, but for being unprofessional.

As I cut my steak and potato both in half and move half of them and my steamed veggies to the empty plate, I say, "So, I point out that you were rude, and you respond by asking me to interview you?"

"You don't have to give me half your food. They're remaking mine."

I push the plate across the table to him. "And I expect you to share with me when it gets here." Then I keep my eyes on him, one eyebrow raised, waiting for his response.

"My last interviewer was very accommodating and would've never told me off. I didn't like that interview much." He takes in a slow breath. "So here's the thing. I saw your poll asking who your audience thought you should interview. By a strange twist of fate that I don't think either of us would've guessed a week ago, my name is at the top of that list. My company is launching a new product, and my social media manager thinks our audiences overlap. And I figure that you want to give your viewers what they want. So, if we do an interview, we both win."

I take a bite of potato and chew slowly. I have a big audience—Roman would be stupid to not want the interview. But I have imagined how this meeting would go many times over the past few days, and it always ends with him not saying yes to it. Truthfully, it surprises me to hear the words that he wants the interview actually coming out of his mouth.

"Okay, then, let's talk." My usual strategy is to ease my way into what I want, but that doesn't feel right with Roman. I sense he likes things straightforward and blunt. "I want a four-part interview."

"No. We can cover it in one."

"I don't—"

"If we're only talking about me and my company, one is sufficient."

I study him long enough that I hope I make him uncomfortable. I don't like being cut off or having someone else tell me how to run my own show. "I'm not CNN, and this isn't a news story. People go to my YouTube channel because they want to be entertained. I am successful because I know what they want, and I give it to them. If you want this interview, it'll be in four parts, and each one will be in a different location so it won't get boring."

"Do your viewers get bored easily?" I'm thinking of all the witty jabs I could make, but he must sense them coming and doesn't want to take the insults, because he adds, "If you'd like me to do demonstrations of my apps, we can do it in four."

"The interview won't be only about your company and your apps. And we aren't just going to talk about the surface stuff when we talk about you and your company. Oh, now stop looking so panicked—I'm a good interviewer. You'll have fun. It won't be nearly as uncomfortable as whatever it is that you're imagining right now."

I think I'm lightening things up, but whatever stoic wall he's built, it's strong.

He starts sawing his steak into bite-sized pieces like he's pouring all his frustration into it. Honestly, I worry about the knife. And the steak. And the plate. "How comfortable I am during the interview isn't the issue. It's that people don't need to know about the personal stuff. It's none of their business. I just want them to get interested in my business and our products."

I jab at a zucchini on my plate with my fork and meet his eyes. "You're looking at this wrong. If they get interested in *you*, they'll be interested in your business. I read your *Business Success* interview, and I can see why people are eating it up.

That pretty face on the cover got them to open the magazine to read about you. But it was things like the fact that you wear fun socks because it's the one way you can express yourself and still dress professionally that got all my readers interested in you and dying to know more about your business."

Roman narrows his eyes. "Nobody needs to know about what kinds of socks I'm wearing. Did you not see how awkward having that information out there makes things?"

"Did you not see how invested in you those two kids were? And the interviews are not going to only be about your socks. They're just not going to only be about your business or your products, either."

"It doesn't need to be about any personal things at all! I'm not looking to be a celebrity. I don't need people to get to know me or to like me—I just want them to enjoy our apps."

"And I think you're wrong." I look at Ian and Addison for help in explaining to this bull-headed man why it's beneficial for him to open up a little. It doesn't even have to be a lot—I'm not asking him to divulge his secret hopes and fears. All it has to be is a few bits for my readers to connect with him. But the two of them look all too happy to be staying out of the fight.

Why am I pushing for this so much? Just so I can win? To claim that I'm right? I don't even want to do this four-part interview with him. "Do you know what? No, you're right. If you don't want people to get to know you or like you, then my channel really isn't a good match, regardless of what my viewers think. You should be on a show that better fits with your goals—one where they only talk about businesses and products."

"And you should stick with interviewing people like...Who was in second place again? Some movie star?"

Kenyon comes over just then, holding Roman's new plate, looking like he has just stepped into a field of mines and isn't quite sure if he dares take the half-step closer to our table to set down the plate. He does, though, then quickly steps back. He opens his mouth to say something—probably to apologize again—but Roman speaks before he gets the chance.

Without taking his eyes off me, he says, "Actually, do you mind boxing this up for my table-mate here? I'm sure she's going to need a good solid meal before her next interview because her viewers are dying to know what kind of socks Corbin Shields wears."

"And I'm sure that Corbin Shields will see the value in letting them in on a minuscule part of his life."

"It sounds like it's an interview match made in heaven." Roman pulls out his wallet, opens it, takes out several bills, and then hands them to Kenyon. "This should cover all four of us. Thank you for your service—keep whatever is left as a tip." He turns to his right. "Ian, Addison, it's good to see you again. Bex, thank you for meeting with me." Then he stands up and walks away in his overly-fancy suit, looking like a dream.

I watch him until he exits the lobby doors at the other end of the building because if nothing else, he does look mighty fine in that suit. Then I pull his plate—the one that contains the other half of my meal—toward me. "On the bright side, I got dinner with two of my favorite people, and I got half of my steak cut up for me." I stab a piece of it with my fork and stick it in my mouth, enjoying every bit of the perfectly cooked morsel.

I should be mad right now. Or at least frustrated. Why do I feel so exhilarated? Probably because I actually got to defend what I do to someone who sparred back and held his ground. Even if he did duck out before the match was over.

CHAPTER 4

Roman

I'VE BEEN DREADING my eleven o'clock meeting with Everly since I came into work. I know what she's going to say, so I schedule the meeting to take place in my office instead of in the conference room or her office, just so I have home-field advantage. It's a jerk move I usually don't use on my own employees, especially on my inner team, but desperate times.

My office door is open and she blows in like the north wind, not even waiting until she's fully seated or has put her tablet down before she asks, "So, how'd your dinner with Bex Sterling go?

Unwelcome as it is, my mind fills—once again—with all the emotions from last night. The water spilling on my lap. The waiter dropping my food and my reaction. Embarrassment at the two sisters talking about my article. How amazing Bex looked in that dress and cowboy boots. How infuriating it is that the woman can't agree to do a simple interview.

"Not well. There won't be an interview. So let's go over the plans we have in place for the product launch and brainstorm ways we can get it where we need to be."

"Wait. Why? What happened? Did she just say she didn't want to? After so many of her viewers requested you?"

I let out a frustrated breath that Everly won't just let this go. Not that I thought she would, but it sure would make things easier. "We both agreed that it wasn't a good match. End of story."

"But it *is* a good match! Did she give you a hard no? Because I don't think we should let that stop us from trying again. I bet I could smooth things over with her."

"Everly. The interview—which would be four parts filmed at four different times, by the way—isn't going to work out. This meeting is about finding other options. We need to turn our focus to that."

Everly leans back in her chair—something she so rarely does that its piercing effect feels stronger. Especially because she also crosses her arms, studying me. She stays silent for a long moment before she says, "Remember shortly after you hired me when you formed your inner team? In that first meeting with Daran, Sloan, Melinda, Wells, and me—all of us together—you said that we need to respect your decisions."

"Exactly."

"But," she says, emphasizing the word in a way that tells me I won't like what comes after, "you also said that we should call you out when we thought you were making a decision based on emotion instead of logic."

I cross my arms, too. "Spit it out, Everly."

"You have issues with this interview that are emotional, not logical. You know how important it is to come out of the gate strong with the release of *Nudge Out*. And you also know that our advertising budget alone isn't going to get us where we need to be so it's important to find out-of-the-box ways to meet our goals. It's what this business was built on. You couldn't have led us to where we are now without doing exactly that."

She leans forward like she wants to make sure I'm absorbing everything she says. "This business is healthy because we all believe in that vision. It's why *Business Success* named you one of their *Top Ten CEOs Under Thirty*, and it's why those investors are thinking of forking over so much cash. This interview with Bex Sterling exactly supports that vision."

I growl and look to the side. Deep down, I know that. It's what makes me so frustrated.

"So, talk to me. Help me understand why you are resisting this so much."

I don't want to admit to Everly that I'm worried about my peers thinking I sold out, or that I'm not a real business, or that I no longer take my company seriously if I do a frivolous interview on a YouTube channel. Would they make fun of me behind my back? To my face?

And I especially worry that I'll make a fool of myself in front of a big audience. I'm not a natural in front of the camera, so chances are pretty good that I'll end up being the punch line of jokes everywhere. And doing four interviews will give me quadruple the chance to royally embarrass myself. Since the content won't belong to my company, it's not like we'll have any say over something getting edited out.

And what about the fact that I'm attracted to Bex? She isn't the type of girl I normally date, and she definitely isn't the type to fit into my family. Bex is the kind of girl who thinks she should get everything she demands. I have experienced that enough in my life to know it isn't for me.

So obviously being attracted to her is a terrible idea, and I should stay as far away from her as possible.

Being attracted to her aside, what would my dad think about the interview? I run my hands down my face. If my dad found out I did an interview that was even more casual and less professional than my one in *Business Success*, he would definitely not be proud of me. I hate that I even care. But that's the only part that I'm willing to admit to Everly, so I say, "My dad will hate it."

"Your dad doesn't have to know."

Even if he doesn't ever find out, I shouldn't be spending the kind of time a multi-part interview would require when we have an app to launch. "This is clearly a time I should be focusing on the business, not doing four interviews for the same channel."

"This *is* focusing on your business. I can set up a meeting with Bex Sterling and be there to mediate so we can come to a mutual agreement on the terms."

There are so many things about this interview that I don't like. I can't agree to it.

"The bottom line is," Everly says, "you care about the health of this company. That's obvious in every single choice you've made. Make the healthy choice here, too."

If I put all my feelings about the interview aside, I know without a doubt that Everly is right. She's right about the interview, she's right that I would do anything for this company, and she's right that saying yes to Bex is a healthy choice for my company. But is it a healthy choice for *me*?

I'm sure it isn't, but against my better judgment, I find myself giving her a nod of permission to set up the meeting.

CHAPTER 5

Bex

I SPENT the morning with Nikki, going over the edited video for our Sterling Sisters segment, updating my schedule for the next two weeks, and brainstorming all of the ways we will advertise and interact with fans during the judging period for the Eddie Award. My roommates are all out working with clients, so once Nikki leaves, the place feels empty, which doesn't happen often. It's days like this, when I have hours of administrative tasks to do, that I like to take my laptop to a crowded coffee shop or deli to work.

But before I do that, I need to get Corbin Shields's publicist emailed since the interview with Roman isn't going to work out. I bring up the email draft Nikki has written and I'm tweaking the wording when I hear the front door open. A moment later, it opens a second time, and then I hear talking coming from the front of the inn. Curious, I get up from the desk by the big back windows of the gathering room and head to the lobby and then, following the voices, to the kitchen.

It's Addison and Ian—neither of whom I expected to be

home right now—and they are mid-kiss when I walk in. Which I totally *would've* expected if I had known it was them.

"Check you two out, both home in the middle of the day."

"I only scheduled the first half of my day with clients," Addison says. "The rest of my day is here, organizing for a big job."

Ian opens the fridge and starts getting out items for sandwiches. "And since my afternoon is better with a boost of Addi, of course, I'm going to come home for lunch."

"Aww. You two are as sweet as ice cream on apple pie."

Addison joins Ian in the sandwich-making, standing shoulder to shoulder like they are magnets and can't help being stuck together when they're near. "What are you up to today?"

"About to send an email to Corbin Shields's publicist. Speaking of which, what is the deal with Roman? Other than last night and the wedding, I don't know him a ton, but he always seems guarded. Like he's trying to keep us from seeing the real him. Please tell me he wasn't like that in college, because if he was, I just can't see how you two became friends."

Ian shrugs as he piles enough meats and cheeses on a slice of bread that I am sure he'll never be able to get his mouth around it. "I don't know. Yeah, I guess I'd call it 'guarded.' It wasn't as bad in college, but he's always kind of been somewhat that way. Probably because his dad is about as intimidating as a starving mountain lion staring you down as he thinks about which part of you he's going to eat first."

I reach across the counter to grab an apple. All this food and talk of food is making me hungry. "And it makes Roman close himself off?"

Ian glances at me when he reaches for the mustard. "All I can say is that the University of Oregon was just far enough away from Lake Oswego that he could justify going home only once or twice a semester, and that we hated when he went home because he was a bit of a jerk when he came back. But I don't know. I guess I could sit down with him and have a heart-to-heart discussion where we try to really get to the root of his feelings so he can acknowledge where they are coming from."

I reach across the island counter and give Ian a playful smack on the arm. "You've leveled up your ability to deliver sarcasm. I am so proud." I take a big bite of my apple.

Ian takes a little bow, then puts the top slice of bread on his sandwich, admiring his handiwork. "All I can say is, regardless of anything else, he's a good guy. And a good friend."

Yeah. I sense that. And a part of me—the woman part—is drawn to that. And, okay, the jawline and those intriguing eyes fringed with the most amazing lashes. But the YouTuber part of me knows that if I put someone who is guarded in front of a camera, the audience won't connect with them no matter how easily they'd be able to connect with someone like Roman otherwise. It's good that he already told me no.

"And," Addison says as she puts the finishing touches on her sandwich, which, unlike Ian's, looks like a human could actually open their mouth wide enough to take a bite of, "you two look adorable together. You did at the wedding, too. I know you really just got on each other's nerves at the wedding, but I swear that there were sparks last night." She flashes me a wide smile. "You two should date!"

Luckily, I have already swallowed the bite of apple I'm chewing, or one of them would probably be wearing it. "Ha. No. No way. Any sparks that may or may not have been present are irrelevant because I don't date guys like that."

Ian's eyebrows draw together. "Guys like what?"

"You know," I say, waving my hand around like I'm trying to catch something so obvious I shouldn't need to define it. "The kind of guy who likes to be in charge, and is driven and opinionated."

"Oh," Ian says, an amused smile on his face, "so someone like you?"

"Exactly. There can only be one of us in a relationship. I grew up in a house with a mom and four sisters who all like to be in charge and are driven and opinionated. All five are happily married to guys who are easygoing, thoughtful, and willing to go along with any wild plan one of us comes up with."

Addison shakes her head. "That doesn't mean that's the only type of guy who will work out."

"Yes, it does." I punctuate it with a firm shake of my apple in Addison's direction. "Nikki married someone who also liked to be in charge, and was driven and opinionated, and their marriage was awful. I'm talking explosively awful. Thankfully, they figured out how toxic they were for each other before they had kids.

"Then she met Dylan. He's kind, thoughtful, and easygoing, and they're adorable together. Being the youngest comes with drawbacks. Like getting hand-me-down underwear. *Underwear,* y'all! So you better believe I take the perks when I can get them. And one of them is having older siblings who make all the mistakes so I don't have to. I'm not about to make the same mistake Nikki did."

I study my apple, choosing the best next bite. "Besides, I can guarantee I will never see Roman Powell again. After last night, whenever you guys get together with him, I can tell you right now that he will move heaven and earth to make sure it only happens when I'm nowhere nearby."

The moment I bite down on my apple, my phone rings. I chew quickly as I pull it from my pocket and look at the screen. It isn't a number I have in my contacts, but it says it's from Gresham, Oregon. I finish chewing, then swallow and answer it.

"Hello, this is Bex Sterling."

"Hi, Bex. This is Everly Richins. I'm the marketing and social media manager at LivenUP."

I glance at Ian, my head tilted to the side. Isn't LivenUP Roman's company?

"I was wondering if you would be willing to come to Gresham for coffee this afternoon to meet with me and Roman Powell."

I did not see that coming at all. A big part of me has been glad that I might get to interview Corbin Shields instead. But beyond all the reasons why I want him over Roman Powell, what I want most is to honor my viewers' wishes. And they want Roman. It's enough to say yes to a second chance at working things out with him.

"Um, sure. I'd be happy to. Just text me the time and location."

After Everly says goodbye, I hang up the phone and stare at it for a good ten seconds as I try to make sense of what just happened. "Well, that was unexpected."

CHAPTER 6
Roman

I SET the tray holding three coffees and an assortment of creams and sugars down on the table. Then I sit in the spot I have claimed as "mine" since the first time I walked into this coffee shop the day I signed the papers on my current office building. Not that I actually drink my coffee here often, but I do come here daily.

Being in my own territory when meeting to discuss this mutually beneficial arrangement is better. Sure, I chose the location the last time I met with Bex, but it was clearly her place enough that she called it family. This is mine.

Everly sits in the seat next to me and grabs a cup of coffee from the tray. She removes the lid off and, while dumping in an obscene amount of sugar, says, "We need to do whatever it takes to make this happen."

I notice Bex through the window the moment she steps out of her car. She is dressed in dark jeans and a baby blue v-neck shirt that looks amazing on her if I am noticing that kind of thing. I kind of wish she would dress as inappropriately for the occasion as I had when we met at Buffalo Bill's Steakhouse. But this is a coffee shop. It's not like there's a wrong way to dress.

It doesn't matter. This is my place, and I am in charge of this meeting. I have the upper hand this time, and I am going to run the meeting my way from beginning to end.

The moment she steps through the doorway, I stand, ready to give my "I mean business" handshake. But her eyes don't immediately go to mine the way mine go to hers. She starts scanning the room, but before she gets to me, her eyes land on the manager, and both their faces light up in recognition.

"Roger!" Bex says, hurrying toward him as he comes around the counter.

"Bex Sterling," Roger says, giving her a hug in greeting. "It's been a while. How are you?"

As the two of them chat, I roll my shoulders back and flex my jaw, trying to keep from clenching it. I chose *my* place, and she is a long-lost BFF with the manager.

"Relax that drum solo," Everly says, pointedly looking at the two fingers I am tapping on the tabletop. "We want her to be comfortable because then she'll be more likely to give us what we want. Her knowing the manager is a good thing."

It doesn't stop my jaw from clenching again.

"Do you remember Marco?" Roger asks Bex. Then he turns his head toward the back of the store and shouts, "Hey, Marco. Come here a minute."

Then Marco comes out, and apparently she knows him, too, and it's reunions all over again. I have never even seen Marco before. So Bex knows more people than I do at my own coffee shop?

Luckily, Bex's conversation with both men ends quickly, and her gaze shifts in my direction. She gives me a brilliant smile when she sees me, which I meet with my own hard smile as she walks to our table.

"Hello." She reaches out, shakes my hand and then Everly's, and then bangs her knee into the chair as she takes a seat. The sound is loud, and she hisses in a breath, wincing.

A smile tugs at my lips as I sit. It's not enough to make up for the fact that she has leveled out the playing field by knowing the people at my home field, but it definitely helps.

"Thank you so much for meeting with us," Everly says. "Roman and I have talked, and we decided that, even though the two of you have a difference of opinions on a few points, he would really like to do the interview. We are hoping that we can talk about a few of those differences so that we can come up with something mutually beneficial."

And this is why I hired and promoted Everly. She can take my "I hate everything Bex wants to do but still see the value in bringing in the new users" and turn it into something professional and courteous.

Bex sits straight in her chair, looking regal and professional, which is impressive, considering the critical look that is just beneath the surface. She is quiet for a moment, then says, "Interesting. Because when Roman and I talked last night, he didn't seem to think very highly of my channel."

Probably because it is a channel not meant to be thought of highly. It's just there for the sake of entertainment. I open my mouth to talk, but Everly must sense that what I am about to say won't get us the interview, so she touches my forearm to pause me.

"That was before he spent some time watching your videos. He especially liked your interview with Brooke McClellan."

By "watching your videos," Everly means that she forced me to watch five minutes of that interview.

"It's one of my personal favorites," Everly says. "I don't think I've ever laughed and sighed and cheered and cried so much in one fifteen-minute period. I've seen interviews with her before, but I never felt like I got to know her the way I did in your interview. That's actually what led me to your channel initially and got me to subscribe."

"Thank you," Bex says. "I'm so glad you connected with it."

I take a deep breath. I am being a jerk with my thoughts, and I need to stop. *This will help LivenUP,* I remind myself. And regardless of what I think of her channel, she is very good at what she does. "I would like to do the interview. But the reason I would like to is because we have a new app releasing, and I want to get the word out. That's my entire purpose."

"Roman," Bex says, and my chest lifts a little hearing my name on her lips, "I think we've had a bit of a miscommunication. I want you to get the word out. My plan all along was to help you with promoting your app. But that'll be most effective if people can connect with *you*. They aren't going to watch long enough to learn about your app if they don't."

"Fine."

"So you'll do the four-part interview and let me get personal?"

I look out across the coffee shop. This is a bad idea. I am used to running this company with my gut, and my gut is telling me to run far away from this woman and from this interview.

But, strangely, it is also telling me to stay. I don't know whether it's because of the investors, who want me to do something like this, or if it's because of Bex herself, but I can't deal with the conflicting messages. I just need to make a decision. So I give a curt nod.

Then something catches my eye—a mother and daughter who are standing in line, looking over at us as the daughter whispers to the mom. She looks like she is probably thirteen, and I do not want to relive the embarrassment of last night again when the two girls came over to our table. Not in front of one of my employees, and especially not a second time in front of Bex. Maybe they'll leave it at whispering about me from a distance.

But then the two of them break away from the line and walk over to our table. Instead of walking toward me, though, they head straight to Bex.

Bex greets them with the same big smile she gave Roger and Marco when she first walked in.

"Hi," the girl says. "You're Bex Sterling, right?"

"I am."

The girl's smile widens. "I'm a Bexlandian. I love your show! It's my favorite. I watch it, like, seriously, the second a new video comes out. And then my friends and I get together to rewatch it. My favorite episode is the one where you're bringing the happy birthday cake with the candles to your nephew, and their dog attacks your ankles, and the cake splats everywhere."

As the girl and Bex chat about how hilarious that was, what a mess it made, and how many times the girl watched it, I seriously question my choice. My target audience isn't kids who would be content watching fail videos all day long. It's adults who are looking to live their lives more fully. Adults with cash to spend on apps. And I definitely don't want myself lumped in with the birthday cake debacle.

I am turning to Everly to suggest we cut our losses while we can when the girl's mom speaks. "You're Roman Powell, right?" When I give a nod, she says, "I read your interview. I like that you admitted to wishing you could stay in bed some mornings and just laugh at funny memes, but that your responsibilities always get you out of bed early." The woman nods a few times. "I'm the same way."

I am never going to interview with *Business Success* again. And I definitely am not going to with Bex, either.

When the mother and daughter leave, I say, "Actually, the four-part personal interview isn't going to work out after all. Let's do just one, focusing only on the company and products."

Those hazel eyes of hers bore into mine. Like the golden ring around the edge of her iris has magical powers. Then, after a pause long enough that it makes me uncomfortable, she says, "Okay, I have an opening for that in a couple of months."

"Nothing sooner?" Everly asks. "Our new app releases in two weeks."

"Listen," Bex says, "between two weeks from now and six weeks from now, I am being judged for an Eddie Award. I have to put my best work forward during that time, and I'm not about to do the kind of interview that is going to get people to click away to a cat video thirty seconds in. Because that's what they will do if we have an interview like that."

"Roman," Everly says, her voice pleading.

But what am I supposed to do? Say yes to something I don't believe in? If a regular interview won't work with her audience, then my first instinct to walk away was right. It means her audience isn't mine. I am about to stand up and end the meeting, but Bex folds her arms and gives me a look that somehow keeps me in my seat.

"Did you not see what happened with that mother and daughter?" she asks.

"Yeah, I did. It was the same thing as what happened in the restaurant last night. Random strangers pulled out the insignificant facts instead of focusing on the important ones. That's not what I'm looking for."

"No. What you saw was someone who read an article about you and found a way to connect to you." She turns to see that the mother and daughter are just walking away from the counter after ordering. She calls out, "Kendall? Do you mind coming back for a second?"

I hadn't noticed that the two had given their names. When they come back to our table, Bex says, "Do you mind if I ask you a couple of questions?" The woman shakes her head, so Bex says, "You read the article about Roman, right? There were articles about nine other young CEOs. How many of those did you read?"

"All of them."

"I'm impressed that you remembered Roman's name. Do you remember the names of all of them?"

The woman lets out a breath that is equal parts laugh and snort. "Nope. None of them."

"Why do you think you remembered his?"

The woman blushes. "I don't know. I guess I just felt like I knew him more."

Bex nods. "Do you know what company Roman runs?"

"Yeah! LivenUP, right? You're the company that makes some great apps. I got the music one right in the middle of reading your article. I use it all the time."

Bex is smiling like the woman is telling her she thinks her puppy is cute. "And how many other company names do you remember?"

"I don't know. Two or three?"

Bex gives her a brilliant smile, then thanks her as she and her daughter go off to find a booth. Then Bex turns that brilliant smile on me. And she keeps it on me without saying a word.

Not that she needs to. I am a smart enough guy to get the point she is trying to make. Knowing that I wished I could shrug off responsibilities and laugh at memes got this woman to buy our app. This must be what the interviewers were calling the "spark" that they were looking for. Maybe sharing a tiny bit of me wouldn't hurt. As long as Bex keeps it to surface stuff.

"Fine. We'll let it get a little personal. Four parts."

The look of triumph on Bex's face is only there for a moment before it is replaced by a look of professionalism. "Then you'll agree to a rapid-fire interview right now? This won't be released—it's just to help me decide on interview locations."

I can feel Everly's eyes on me, hoping I'll say yes. So I nod. I am used to doing hard things for work. How hard can this be?

Bex turns on her voice recorder, then leans forward on her elbows, meeting my eyes without flinching. "Okay, give me the first answer that comes to mind. Don't stop to think about it. Ready?" I nod, so she says, "First employee's name?"

"Daran."

"Where did you grow up?"

"Lake Oswego."

"Favorite thing to do outdoors as a kid?"

"Go camping for scouts."

"Favorite childhood memory?"

"Building a blanket fort in our family room with my brothers and eating ice cream in it."

"Favorite sport to watch?"

I pause, hopefully not long enough for her to notice. "Basketball."

"Favorite sport to play?"

"Racquetball."

"Favorite color?"

"Blue."

"Why did you pause when I asked what your favorite sport to watch was?"

Because the first thing that came to mind was dance competitions, and it would be one hundred degrees on the tip of Mount Hood before I admit that. "Trying to decide between basketball and hockey."

"Fair enough." She turns off the recorder and looks between me and Everly. "Okay, I'll contact you both by tomorrow at noon with a proposed schedule and filming location for our first interview." Then she grabs her cup of coffee for the first time, nods a goodbye, and walks out the door.

I am still staring after her while completely ignoring Everly's victorious grin as I wonder what, exactly, I just got myself into.

CHAPTER 7

Bex

I PULL into the parking lot at the Mirror Lake trailhead Saturday morning, and Enoch and I get out of the car. As Enoch gets all of the camera equipment ready, I bring up my notes on my phone and start going through them.

I'm glad that Roman was willing to meet so soon to film. I had other segments originally planned for the four-week judging period, and most of them were filmed and edited already. But when I became a finalist for the Eddie, I decided I wanted something more spectacular to post during the judging period. Which means I am so much further behind than I am comfortable with.

Tires sound on gravel, and I look up to see Roman pulling into the parking lot.

"Are you sure you're good to hike with that weight?" I ask my nephew.

"Of course!" he says, flexing his biceps. Not that the kid has an abundance of muscles, but what he has, he shows proudly. I should've known he'd be just fine. At least the hike isn't long or difficult.

"Remember to keep the camera rolling the whole time."

"I know, I know. 'We always find gems in the parts when the camera normally wouldn't have been rolling.'"

"And you even quote me. See? This is why you're the best cameraman." I put on my backpack which contains a few water bottles and a small first aid kit. When Roman gets out of his vehicle and nears, I call out, "Are you ready for this?"

Roman nods and smiles up at the trail. "It's been a long time since I've been up here."

Then he sizes up Enoch, and I am suddenly seeing my nephew through Roman's eyes. Young. Skinny. He has grown enough recently that he hasn't quite figured out how to use his new height. And his hair isn't so much the signature perfectly-styled-to-appear-messy look as it is an accidentally messy look.

"You're using a, what—fourteen-year-old—kid as a cameraman?"

Enoch doesn't see it as a rude comment. In fact, he puffs out his chest in pride that Roman thinks he's older than he is.

"He's twelve—"

"—and a half," Enoch cuts in.

"—and not only is he my nephew, but he's a kid who's interested in the filming side of the business and does a mighty fine job of it. So don't look at him like he's not legit."

Roman holds up his hands in surrender. "No offense meant at all. I think it's great to know what you want to do at such a young age." He looks at the trail again. "So, how does this work?"

He seems nervous. I am used to trying to make a guest feel comfortable during an interview, but sometimes people who aren't used to having a camera on them struggle with it a bit more. Hopefully, Roman will get used to it very quickly into our hike.

"Well, it starts with you being more like yourself." I see a flash of confusion cross his face for the briefest of moments before he is back to his guarded self, so I explain. "It's like your exterior isn't aligned with your interior. If you're not being authentic, viewers will pick up on it, even if they can't say exactly what the issue is."

"Got it, Barbara Walters."

I realize that it isn't nerves I'm witnessing—it's straight-up reluctance. Of course. The guy is way too confident and in charge for nerves. This is going to take some serious interviewing skills and a whole lot of patience. "We'll chat while we're hiking, then I'll ask a few questions at the lake while we stop and admire the beauty, and then we'll chat on the way back down. Sound good?"

We've barely made it far enough along the trail to not see the parking lot anymore when Roman stops and glances at the camera. I stop, too, hoping he isn't going to call it off because whether interviewing him during the judging period is the best idea or not, I have committed to it.

"I've got one request before we go too far," he says.

I cock an ear toward him. "Oh good. I was afraid it would be a demand."

The corners of his mouth lift in not quite a smile, but something edging toward it. "Only because you're going to agree to it without it being a demand."

I raise an eyebrow, trying not to smile.

"You let me install Nudge Out on your phone, and you let it pick the location for our fourth interview."

I study him for a long moment like I am trying to decide if I should let him. Of course, I am going to say yes, because that sounds interesting and makes that fourth interview an unknown entity, which, coming from a guy who seems to like everything planned down to the last detail, makes it even more interesting. I kind of want to make him sweat a bit before I do.

Then I pull my phone from my back pocket, lift it to my face to unlock it, and hold it out toward him.

His fingers brush over my palm as he picks up my phone, and it sends a thrill straight to my heart. Again. This man is going to be the end of me. Why did I push for this interview?

I watch as the expression on his face changes from stoic to something resembling happiness as he installs the app on my phone and does whatever he is doing to make an app that isn't actually live yet work on my phone.

Then, he hands it back to me, and I look down at the blue and green Nudge Out icon that is now on my phone.

I always film an introduction to my guest separately and start the finished video with it, but I still need to lead into the interview, and I hadn't planned to do it like this. As we walk up the dirt trail, trees lining both sides of it and blocking out all sounds other than nature and the squeals of a couple of kids hiking with their family further up the trail, I fall into the rhythm of an interview.

"So you're the CEO of LivenUP, and your company has quite a few very successful apps, like Musicbound and Group Eat, but this one you just put on my phone is brand new. It releases today, even." It doesn't actually release today, but this video is going to air on the day it releases. "Tell us about it."

"People stay in their comfort zones because everything is nice and easy there." He glances up the trail as we walk, and then his eyes quickly come back to me. "There's a quote that says, 'Life begins at the end of your comfort zone.' People know that great things lie on the other side of whatever normal is for them, but most feel like it's such a huge, terrifying leap to try something new, or they don't know where to start.

"When you install this app on your phone and go about doing all the things you normally do, it'll learn what your comfort zone is. Then it'll nudge you to try something just outside of your comfort zone."

"I get it," I say as we walk, Enoch and the camera on us the whole time. "So the nudge it gives you is an easy thing since it's not too far out of what's normal for you. Nothing terrifying."

"Exactly. The more you do the things it nudges you to do, the more things you'll experience, the further you'll be stepping out of your comfort zone, and the more rich your life will become. There are great things out there for everyone, and you'll get to them if you take those little nudges."

"Wow. That sounds pretty amazing. So it's working right now on my phone?"

Roman nods. "In a week or so, after it gathers enough data, a notification will come up saying it's ready to suggest something new. When it does, you can tap the *Nudge Me Out* button, and we'll know where we'll be having our fourth interview."

My grin spreads wide, and I look right at the camera. "Usually, I try to have an interview in a location that has something to do with the person I'm interviewing—a place they know well, a place that feels at home to them, or one that has something to do with their job. Remember, Bexlandians, that Roman put the app on *my* phone, not his. Tell me in the comments if you're hoping that the fourth interview will be in a location I would've chosen for Roman, or if it'll be one that will nudge him—or shove him—right out of his own comfort zone."

Roman laughs, and the sound is magical. Partly because we are in some pretty dense woods where we can currently see no other humans and it mixes with the nature all around us. But mostly because it's something I hadn't expected from him at all.

"This entire interview series is well outside my comfort zone, so maybe if that fourth one is, too, I'll feel right at home."

This is good. He's relaxing. Letting his guard down a bit. He has a long way to go, but a teeny bit of authenticity is actually coming through.

"I'm guessing you've tested the Nudge Out app yourself. What's something the app has nudged you to try?"

"I play racquetball and lift weights. It suggested I try yoga."

"And did you?"

"Of course."

"What did you think?" I am suddenly picturing myself doing yoga next to him, the morning sun shining through the window on us, which is definitely not keeping my head in interview mode. I work to get it back.

"Six weeks later, I'm still doing it daily."

"Impressive." *Don't think about it, Bex. Stay in interview mode.* "Favorite pose?"

"Half pigeon."

"No."

"Why? What would you have guessed?"

I lift a shoulder. "One of the warrior poses, I guess."

We chat more about his company and Nudge Out as we hike the trail. It's steep in some sections, but there are handrails in places where it's especially steep. Most of the twenty-minute hike is easy, though. Easy enough that a lot of the trail, Enoch even walks backward in front of us so he can film our faces. Other times, he finds a rise or a boulder to climb onto so he can get a good location shot of us hiking.

The end of the trail opens onto the shore of Mirror Lake. The day is clear and absolutely stunning. The wind isn't blowing at all so the surface of the lake is still and is showing off exactly how it got its name. We soak in the sunshine as we walk around to the backside of the lake. From there, we can see almost the entirety of Mount Hood reflected in the waters along with the trees surrounding the lake, the blue skies, and the white puffy clouds.

We stand in silence for several long moments, enjoying the incredible display of nature around us while Enoch gets a lot of video so my viewers can experience it, too.

"I wish we had a canoe," Roman says.

I look at him in surprise. Really, I am impressed that he showed up in jeans, a t-shirt, and an athletic jacket on our hike instead of a suit. But when I picture Roman in a canoe, I have a hard time imagining him without the suit, and the mental image just looks wrong. "You like to canoe?"

"It's been a while. Since I was a kid."

"You were a Boy Scout, right?"

He nods. "This one time, we were camping by Estacada Lake, and a bunch of us were out in canoes. This kid named Justin was with me in mine, and a couple of scouts in another paddled over to us. We were all just horsing around and splashing each other, and then Justin leaped out of our canoe, nearly capsizing it."

"I got low to the base, holding onto the sides and steadying it, and Justin reached over the side and grabbed my oars. Then he swam with them to the other canoe, tossed them inside, and then climbed inside himself. As they paddled away, he laughed and told me good luck getting back in time for mess duty."

"What do you do?"

"I tried paddling with my arms which, of course, didn't work at all—I could barely touch the water. So, I stretched out in the base of the canoe, pulled my hat down low to keep the sun out of my eyes, and enjoyed the most peaceful nap of my life.

"Two hours later, the Scoutmaster showed up in a canoe, gave mine a little shake to wake me up, and I was back on the shore not long after. When I got back into camp, dinner was ready, and Justin was looking not too happy that he had to take my place making it."

We both laugh. And suddenly the mental picture of him in a canoe on the lake isn't just him in it by himself, wearing a suit, but it's the two of us in it together. In shorts and t-shirts. We're both rowing, him putting those strong shoulder muscles to good use. And I look blissful.

Then I realize that I am probably staring at him with that blissful face—on camera!—so I quickly shake myself out of it. But I don't stop marveling at the look on his face. It's like the facade he's been hiding behind has dropped at least partway, and I'm seeing him. The real him.

But then Enoch moves to the side for a different shot, his feet scuffling across the rocky dirt as he does, and it's as if the sound makes the facade shoot right back up into place. The guarded Roman is back.

As we head down the trail, Roman glances to where Enoch is walking beside us. "By the time we reach our cars, you'll probably have over an hour of footage. How long will the video be when it airs?"

"Twelve to fifteen minutes, depending on which angle we decide to take and what is going to keep the pacing moving along well."

"Then you'll be able to take out the story I told."

"Probably not."

"It's irrelevant."

"Nope."

"I want to approve the video before it goes up."

"You don't seem to have a lot of faith in what I do. Why did you say yes to the interview?"

He squints off into the woods. "I want our product to launch well."

"Okay, but why did you say yes to *me*? There are other ways to launch a product well."

"Off the record?"

I nod, but he looks at the camera. Enoch does a good job of trying to be unobtrusive and becoming invisible to most people I interview. But Roman can't seem to forget he's there. And, of course, Enoch knows to not stop the camera no matter what. I'll just edit out the stuff that shouldn't be there later.

Roman shakes his head. "I know better than to fall for that 'off the record' trick."

I don't hide my eye roll or my annoyed hand on my hip. Of course, he'd answer that way. This conversation is about how he doesn't trust me, after all.

"Let's turn the question to you instead. Why did you say yes to interviewing a guy who you knew wouldn't give you as good of a show as Corbin Shields would when you have an award on the line?"

I stop and look at him for a long time. I have to respect the fact that he will just come right out and say it like it is. "Because my fans are loyal to me, and I am loyal to them. They said they most wanted me to interview you, and since we have each other's backs, I'm interviewing you."

The tiniest bit of movement catches my eye from just off the path beside us, and I look to see a deer staring at us. I suck in a breath and mumble, barely moving my lips, "Don't make any sudden moves. A deer is watching us from your seven o'clock."

To his credit, Roman actually turns to look very slowly. The deer doesn't move. "Wow. Deer are usually afraid of people. It's unusual to see one this close without spooking it."

"I don't think she's afraid of us. I think that if it could kill us just with the power of an intense stare, we'd be goners."

"She doesn't want to kill us. Deer don't go after people."

"Are you sure? Like one hundred percent of the time they don't?" I don't dare move an inch for fear that if I move, the deer will, too.

"Ninety-nine percent of the time. My Scoutmaster told us

that sometimes when people feed deer, they can become aggressive toward humans."

My heart rate rises even more. "They're aggressive because people give them food? That's the definition of biting the hand that feeds you," I hiss.

"I don't make up the rules." He puts a hand on my shoulder, nudging me in the direction of the path. "Let's just walk back, slowly."

All three of us take a few hesitant steps, Enoch still aiming the camera at the action. But I can't keep my eyes on the trail ahead because I can't stop staring off into the woods at the doe. The look the deer is giving us tells me that it definitely woke up and stepped in coyote dung first thing this morning. "I think people have been feeding this one." I can hear the quiver in my voice.

Roman turns to look, and the deer takes that as her cue to attack. She lowers her head and comes charging at us, which is something I thought that only male deer did, but apparently, I was wrong.

The three of us take off running in the opposite direction of her—through the trees and brush and weeds and dirt and rocks. Roman grabs my hand, and we jump over a fallen tree trunk. Enoch races past us, his long legs and thin body propelling him over obstacles with no problem even while carrying the camera. He manages to get quite a distance in front of us quickly, and then he stops so he can aim the camera at the action.

After seeing him run on this uneven terrain, I know I don't need to worry about him. I need to worry about the angry deer that is still running after us like we're the embodiment of everything wrong in Deer World and chasing us away is the only path to justice.

Then the deer makes a sound that is somewhere between a

bark and a gigantic prehistoric bird squawk, and I pick up the pace. The doe is definitely looking to murder us. She doesn't have antlers, so maybe she plans to kick us or stomp on us or… I have no idea how deer typically take down humans they are inexplicably angry at. Are deer like cheetahs and can only run for a short amount of time? Or can they run indefinitely?

I look over my shoulder and see she is way too close. I scream as my feet hit a stream that runs through the undergrowth, making me slip and fall flat on my back in the water. It takes me a moment before I'm able to take another breath after the one I had was forced out of me, even though I'm panicked and feel the need to get up quickly so I can keep trying to escape. When I open my eyes, all I can see is Roman, smiling an actual smile and holding out a hand to me.

"Where's the deer? Is it about to attack?"

He shakes his head. "That scream of yours scared it off. We probably should've just started with that instead of running."

As he pulls me to my feet, I take several heaving breaths, trying to get my lungs to catch up after all the running and the terror and the fall. Then I look at Enoch, who has the camera aimed at me. "Please tell me you got that."

"Every last bit," my nephew says, grinning. "The running, the chasing, the angry deer sounds, the epic fall—all of it."

At least there's that. I try brushing myself off, but there isn't much I can do about how wet I am. The day has been decently warm, but we are in the shade now and my clothes are soaked. I wrap my arms around myself and have to work to keep my teeth from chattering.

"Here," Roman says, taking off his jacket and sliding it around my shoulders. He keeps his hands on my shoulders a moment, like he maybe wants to pull me close to warm me up, but then thinks better of it quickly. He drops his hands, but I can still feel the heat of where they've been, warming me far more than they should've been able to.

His jacket holds his scent, though. One I didn't even realize he had until now, as I am wrapped in it. It's nice—it's as warm and comforting as his jacket, yet it smells clean, too. Like maybe it's from his body wash, and it holds the scent of someone who knows what they want and isn't afraid to go after it.

He looks off in the direction of the path we're supposed to be on, and I take the moment to admire the way the part of his jaw by his ear curves down to his jawline, highlighting the dark stubble. And the way his dark hair teeters on the edge of being just short enough and styled enough to show he is a respectable businessman and long enough and just barely disheveled enough to show that there is more to him than that. It's too bad he has the same need to be in charge that I do because he is one very attractive man.

He's looking at me in a way I can't quite interpret. Enoch has the camera mostly on me right now, getting more of the backside of Roman. I wish he had it aimed right at Roman's face so I could watch it back as many times as needed to figure it out. "Um," my eyes dart to the direction we'd just come from, "do you think the deer will be waiting for us?"

He smiles at me in a way that tells me it's just for me. He's not thinking about the camera at all. It is one of the most beautiful things I've ever seen, and I'm suddenly very aware that the camera is on me and I'm staring at him with that blissful face again.

"I think you scared it enough that if it sees us, it'll run in the opposite direction now."

I don't realize how far we have traveled away from the path until we spend what feels like an hour to get back to it and then down the path to the parking lot. As I near my car and Enoch heads to the back passenger's door to lay down the camera equipment, Roman stops me.

"You asked why I was willing to do the interview with you."

My eyebrows shoot up. I didn't think I'd ever get an answer from him.

"It's because of your sense of loyalty and because you're willing to stand your ground." His mouth quirks up in a smile. "Except in the case of trying to run over a stream while being chased by a sweet deer, of course."

"I may not have stood my ground, but let's remember that I did manage to scare off the beast."

Roman seems amused that I call it a "beast." But it definitely isn't a "sweet deer." Maybe he's forgetting the sounds it made. Or the way it looked at us like it needed to avenge the deaths of every deer that ever lived.

"And it was a pretty impressive scare-off if I do say so myself. If it was impressive enough to also scare you off from another interview…"

"Nah. I didn't get to where I am by being easily scared off."

I may not have been thrilled about interviewing Roman when I first agreed to it, but it surprises me how much I want us to continue now. "Are you free during the first half of the week? The episodes will only air once a week, but I don't want to be so tight on editing, and the more time I get to promote, the better it will be for both of us."

He gives me a smile that is so adorable it makes my insides flutter. Then he says, "I'll check out my schedule and get back to you on that."

I know he is very much the wrong guy for me. But that doesn't stop me from noticing how right he looks as he walks back to his car.

CHAPTER 8
Roman

"ROMAN!" my mom says as she puts her hands on the tops of my arms and kisses both of my cheeks. "I'm so glad you could make it!"

I like that my mom is always so happy to see me. And that she acts like it's my choice to come for Sunday dinners, even when we all know it's mandatory if you're the offspring of Evelyn and Richmond Powell.

"Come in, come in! Your brothers are already here." She puts her arm in mine and walks me to the drawing room that's just off the dining room. Most families have a living room—or they would even call this space a family room—but not the Powells. We have a drawing room like it's the eighteenth century and we're nobility.

My two brothers are already in the room, standing, with drinks in their hands. The brother just younger than me, Drake, is next to his wife, Claire. They're a good match. Claire has the classy look and ability to host an event that's silently required of Powell wives. But she's also smart and has big ambitions.

Not Briza, though. She's the woman my youngest brother,

Legend, has brought to the previous two dinners. She's strictly shallow eye candy, like most women my brother dates. Which would be fine, except Legend seems to need someone who is less predictable. I don't think I'll see her at too many more family dinners.

It takes me aback when I realize that Briza is exactly like most of the women I've dated, too. *Huh*. Maybe that's why my relationships never last long.

My brothers turn to look at me as I walk in, all big smiles.

"Hey, bro." Drake claps me on the shoulder. "Why so serious?" He glances at my feet. "Don't tell me you wore serious socks today."

"Ha ha."

"Don't listen to him," Claire says. "I read the article, and I thought it was great."

Legend nods. "Top notch. I especially liked the part about how your favorite scent is the smell of chocolate chip cookies baking. I wish I could've been there to see the look on your face when the interviewer asked you if that's the scent a woman who was interested in you should wear."

I'm about to make a show of acting like I'm going to leave because of their comments, but when I turn, my dad is just walking into the room from his office. "Now don't give your brother a hard time. He's learned from his mistakes and won't be so forthcoming on personal details next time. You just wait until you have your first interview with a magazine journalist—you'll find out how wily they are."

"And when you do," Drake says, "follow my lead, not Roman's."

Surprisingly, I actually enjoyed the interview with Bex yesterday, and I've spent the rest of the day—and today—thinking about her.

But all day today, I've been second-guessing the wisdom of doing the interview in the first place. As if it isn't bad enough that my brothers are razzing me about sharing personal stuff in my *Business Success* interview—just like I shared personal things with Bex in her interview, which I will never tell any of them about—my dad has to come in and defend me, like I'm too weak to stand on my own two feet. The icing on the cake is Drake reminding everyone that his first interview made our dad proud enough that it earned him a trip down the Columbia.

Of course, I could pay for myself to take a trip down the Columbia at any time. It isn't about the money, though, or the actual trip itself. It isn't about camping or rafting or water or even spending time together. It's about my dad deeming something I do as worthy enough to warrant the trip.

And I'm not going to make my dad proud enough to earn my own trip unless I get the investors on board, which isn't going to happen if I don't do the interviews with Bex. It's a catch-22 that makes me want to leave this dinner for real.

Drake's reminder must've made my dad think about the trip as well, because he says, "Speaking of which, how are things going with the investors?"

"Good. They have some requests we're working on meeting right now. But they seem ready to get on board." I shoot my mom a glance, hoping dinner is ready so the subject can change before my dad asks more questions.

"Briza," my mom says, turning to her, "Legend mentioned that you just finished midterms for your final semester. How did that go?"

I take a relieved breath as Briza talks excitedly about a public relations class that had a simulated public image issue to resolve for a fictitious client. Both of my parents beam, probably because she's shaping up to be a perfect potential Powell daughter-in-law. A docile trophy wife who can plan parties and look pretty.

But neither Drake's wife nor my mom is docile or shallow eye candy. I haven't realized it before, but maybe all Powell men need someone strong and driven at their side. Maybe that's what I need. But for now, I'm just glad my dad isn't asking me any more questions.

Until my parents' personal chef steps into the room and says that dinner is ready to be served. As we walk toward the dining table that separates the drawing room from the open kitchen, my dad says, "It's been a while since you've brought a woman to a family dinner."

"I'm not dating anyone right now." The bigger truth is, it's been a while since I've wanted to subject anyone to our family dinners. I imagine Bex coming to dinner and talking about her YouTube channel and how she likes to get personal with guests. Then I imagine how my dad would react and how much he would despise her work and probably everything about her. And how Bex would stand strong and not let something like the intimidating presence of Dr. Richmond Powell IV, D.B.A. make her back down from her convictions.

Actually, I really like the thought of that showdown. It would definitely make Sunday dinners more interesting.

I feel a notification on my phone, so I sneak a peek. It's an email from Tarak, the guy from *Business Success* who interviewed me. He's asking me—and not for the first time—to join him on a panel about social media at the *PNW Open for Business* convention. I'm going to ignore it, just like I have the others.

At every weekly dinner, everyone gives an update on what's going on at their jobs. Drake talks about his work as a business strategist who just helped another Fortune 500 company. I update about my business, too, but keep it to how our release plans are going for Nudge Out. Legend talks about a new playground he just designed. Playground equipment isn't the direction our dad envisioned Legend using his architecture degree, but it fits him. And since he's the youngest and can do no wrong, going in an unexpected direction is exactly what earned him his trip down the Columbia.

As everyone talks, all I can think about is texting Bex. It takes me by surprise that my method of getting myself out of a family dinner is wanting to talk to the woman whose interviews have caused me so much stress. But I actually enjoyed getting to see her in action and getting to know her better. I smile just thinking about that deer chasing us and the look on her face when I offered a hand to pull her up after she slipped into the creek. Or especially when I took off my jacket and wrapped it around her.

Like every Sunday dinner right about the time the main course is served, my dad tells a story or two about something that happened in some business meeting or business get-together of his. This one is about a social gathering one of his executives hosted at their house. It sounds like they had a dozen or so guests and that the guy's adult son, Bennett, was there as well.

"Everyone was in small groups, sipping their drinks and eating refreshments, when, suddenly, the woman Bennett brought to the reception slaps him right across the face and then storms out of the place. Of course, Bennett just stands there, stunned and looking sheepish, while things get uncomfortable for everyone in the room. We didn't hear what Bennett said to cause her to react, but there were whispers that he made a joke about a gift she sent to his office after he lost a big client."

My mom shakes her head. "Why he thought that bringing up something personal between the two of them at a get-together with business associates was a good idea—and to make a joke about it, nonetheless—is beyond me."

"Bennett's parents were so ashamed," my dad continues. "I had to take Roy aside and assure him that no one looked down on him just because his kid made a poor choice that suddenly became everyone's business. But we all knew that everyone was, indeed, looking down on them."

Before I have a chance to think about what I'm doing, I find myself standing up, my phone in my hand. "If you'll please excuse me, this is a business call I have to take."

I walk back into the drawing room and keep going out the doors to the patio. I don't know why I'm out here—I haven't gotten a phone call. All I know is that I have to get out of the dining room with all the judgment, and the only acceptable reason for leaving is to take a business call. That, and I've been thinking of Bex, and hearing my dad's story makes me want to see her. To call her. To set up a time for our next interview.

Which is foolhardy and irrational. Hearing my dad all evening should've put me in a mind to call off the rest of the interviews and talk her into not airing the first one. As I think about all the things I shared with her—not just on audio or on paper, either, but on video where there will be no mistaking what I said—I know they're things that will disappoint my dad greatly.

Hah. That's an understatement. His reaction would probably be more along the lines of writing me out of his will. I can imagine the will reading right now: *And because Roman went on video with a site inelegant enough to be named "Bexlandia" and shared that he liked the Half Pigeon Pose and once got trapped on a lake in a canoe without paddles, I bequeath to him exactly one item—something I bought especially with him in mind: An outhouse by a rundown cabin in the Mount Hood National Forest.*

But instead of reacting like a sane human would in this situation, I call Bex. I'm playing with fire, and I know it. But for some inexplicable reason, those flames are drawing me to their warmth.

The phone rings twice before I hear her voice. "You've reached the voicemail of Bex Sterling. If you are calling with complaints about the previous interview or to make any more requests on what should be cut and what is allowed to be aired, please hang up and don't try again. If you are calling to schedule the next interview, please remain on the line."

I chuckle. Hearing her voice is definitely what I need to make it through the rest of this Sunday dinner.

"Oh, wow. That was close to an actual laugh. Does this mean you're calling to set up the next interview?"

"I told you I would, and I'm a man of my word."

"Spoken like a true Boy Scout."

"I'm free Wednesday and Thursday in the evenings. What do you have in mind for a location?"

"That depends. Tell me about racquetball."

"Okay. It's a sport played with a racquet and a hollow rubber ball, with two or four people, usually in an indoor court." With as into personal details as Bex is, I know that's not what she's asking for, but I can't help myself. I feel like a rebel today.

"Fascinating," Bex says, her voice monotone. "I can see why you chose it as your sport."

"The description was what sold me, too."

"It's not the sport most kids pick. Tell me why you really chose it."

"I didn't—my dad chose it for me."

"Interesting. Do you always do what your dad tells you to?"

"If I did, I'd be working at his company instead of owning my own."

"Fair enough. So tell me, what sport would you have chosen?"

"You're not recording this, are you?"

"Roman." I can practically hear her eyes rolling in that one word.

I glance toward the dining room windows where my family sits, eating dinner without me. "I played all the usual sports when I was young, and I was terrible at all of them."

This time, Bex chuckles. The sound is breathy and beautiful. "Big, strong, athletic you? I have a hard time picturing that."

"I wouldn't have called myself any of those things back then. In third grade, my mom decided that I would do better at sports if I had better awareness of my body and better coordination, so she enrolled me in dance classes. I still don't know how she talked my dad into it. I was embarrassed at first, especially because I was just as bad at it as I was at soccer, baseball, basketball, and football. But I got good at it and really liked it."

"Wow. I did not see that answer coming. Did you dance competitively?"

"Yeah."

"How long did you dance for?"

"Just until sixth grade. Then, one of my friends said something that really hurt my feelings, and I cried to my mom about it. My dad came in, said that I shouldn't have gotten my feelings hurt over something like that, and blamed my 'emotional state' on dance. He said it was time for a more manly sport, and since racquetball was his sport, that's what they signed me up for."

I can't believe I'm telling her all this. I haven't told a soul about it, ever. I rub at the tingling on the back of my neck, then pull at my shirt collar. Assuming she's going to push for more information, I start thinking of a response to shut her down. To my surprise, she backs off and goes a different direction, and I'm grateful.

"You listed it as your favorite sport, though, so I'm guessing you fell in love with it on your own at some point."

"My mom had been right about dance. By the time I started racquetball, I was significantly more athletic, and I got good at it quickly. It's easy to love a sport you can win at."

"That I have no problem picturing."

I smile just thinking of her picturing me playing racquetball. I hope she likes what she sees.

"Okay, how about we meet for the next interview on Wednesday at seven p.m.?"

"Seven it is."

"I'll text you the address by Wednesday afternoon. No showing up in a suit and tie. I suggest something more along the lines of athletic shorts, shirt, and shoes." She's silent for a long moment, then she says, "I'm glad that at the beginning of the phone call, you didn't hang up and not try again."

"Me, too."

But as I hang up and walk back into my parents' house to rejoin Sunday dinner, I wonder what in the world I've been thinking. Had it been anyone other than Bex, I actually would've hung up and not tried again. No, actually, I never would've called in the first place.

When it comes to Bex Sterling, I'm definitely playing with fire.

CHAPTER 9

Bex

ANYTIME I FILM a segment for my channel, I send all the footage to my sister, Nikki, along with a list of things I want to make sure make it into the final cut. Then Nikki does her magic, sends a draft of the video to me, and we go through it together, either in person or over FaceTime, and talk about edits.

Today, I've been working with Nikki over video chat, and I've spent the past forty-five minutes watching Roman as we go through the footage. I pause it at the spot when we're next to the lake and he's talking about canoeing, and switch the phone camera so that Nikki can see my screen. "I swear you can see the moment right *here* when he lets his guard down. Did you notice it when you were editing?"

"I did. I didn't know your lock-picking skills had reached a level capable of unlocking defenses as secure as this guy's. I'm impressed."

"I don't know. He noticed they were down like two seconds later and put them right back into place."

"But you got them down a second time, so there's hope."

They actually came down a third time when we were

talking on the phone yesterday. During our first dinner at Buffalo Bill's Steakhouse, I never would've guessed that he'd let his guard down enough to tell me that story about dance and racquetball. I would've listened to his stories about both for an hour, but I know those defenses are poised and ready to snap right back into place at the slightest misstep, so I backed away slowly. Someday, I vow, I'll get them down for more than just a small moment.

Nikki and I get to the part of the video that shows the walk back, where I had all my focus on the murderous deer and hadn't been able to give any attention to Roman. But I'm paying close attention to him now.

I see the moment that shock and worry cross his face at seeing the deer's hollow stare, but unlike mine, Roman's expression quickly turns to confidence. I see his face when we're running and he reaches for my hand. And then the look of amusement and concern as he reaches out to help me up after I scream and fall flat on my back in the stream.

I pause the video on that expression of his, mentally thanking Enoch for his camera skills and for keeping it running the whole time, even with all the chaos going on. I'm going to have to thank the kid with copious amounts of Taco Bell, Red Vines, and Mountain Dew—his three favorite things that he doesn't get often.

I realize I've been staring—possibly a little dreamily—at the video when I see from the corner of my eye Nikki shaking her head. I'd forgotten that my sister could see me, and I really hope I haven't actually reached out and touched Roman's face on the screen like I wanted to. "What? He's cute."

Nikki nods. "He really is. Before I saw this interview, all I got from you was how much he irritated you, so I didn't think you'd noticed. But girl, between what I saw while editing and what I'm seeing now, you have definitely noticed."

"It was obvious in the footage?"

"Oh, no—I'm sure it wasn't obvious at all. To blind people."

Heat rises to my cheeks, and for a second, I feel the familiar resistance that makes me want to edit it out. I learned long ago how to push past my fear of being vulnerable on camera, though. Letting my audience see the real me is how they connect with me.

"Do you know what? It's fine. I'm betting a big reason as to why they voted him as the person they most wanted me to interview was because they saw how good-looking he was and wanted to get to know him more. They'll be feeling it, too, so it's okay if they see it from me."

"Which is why I kept so much of it in there."

"There was more that you cut?" Because I've seen plenty of myself very much noticing Roman's attractiveness.

"Enough for a lengthy compilation video. Want me to put together one? I'm betting I can find a great soundtrack to go with it."

"That's a hard no. It's fine if my fans really commiserate because they're feeling the same things. It's not fine if they start making up a relationship name for us. Roman isn't the kind of guy I can fall for."

"If you say so."

"All right, Nikki. You can stop giving me the 'It's so cute you don't see the things that I, as the older sister, can see.' It doesn't matter how very attractive Roman is—he's the wrong type of guy for me, and I will not be falling for him."

Nikki makes a show of wiping the amused expression off her face and replacing it with a neutral one. As we get back to work, I make sure I don't stare dreamily at the screen even once.

I can do that later when Nikki isn't watching.

I manage to stop thinking about Roman once we finalize the

video for our first interview. Then I actually get work done on some ads, plan some future videos, reply to comments, write a few newsletters, and respond to an interview request. I haven't even realized how much time has passed until Peyton gets home. As soon as she comes into the inn, she walks into the gathering room and plops down on one of the couches. I save what I'm working on, close my laptop, and go to the end of the room where Peyton is.

"You're not your normal, peppy self. What's up?"

Peyton takes in a deep breath as she lifts her hands in an exaggerated shrug, then lets her arms fall to the couch as she exhales. "Between my biggest client telling me they 'no longer needed my services' on Friday, my crappy date on Saturday, and Max still being gone on a photography trip to the Cascades, I just can't seem to get out of my funk. You should have seen the butternut rolls I made at a client's home today. Even they were sad. Tell me I have good things going on in my life."

"Well, first of all," I say, "you have awesome clients who love you. More than you can handle. Your biggest client didn't treat you as well as the others, and now you'll be able to spend more time with the ones who do."

"True..."

"As far as dating, you are one step closer to finding the right guy, so cross that off your list." That one doesn't make Peyton perk up as much as the first, so I keep going. "I've had your butternut rolls, and I would eat a dozen regardless of how sad-looking they were. And just because one of your best friends is beyond cell reception in the Cascades doesn't mean you don't have a houseful of best friends here."

"Thanks, Bex."

"Do you know what you need? A dance party." I pull out my phone and start looking through my playlists for the perfect one.

"Bex, I'm too tired for a dance party."

"That's because there's no music playing right now. Just wait. You'll see." As I stand up, I notice Addison's car pull into the drive. Perfect. I walk to the stairs at the base of the lobby and call up, "Timini! Mandatory dance party in the gathering room!"

Within seconds, the stairs pound as Timini runs down them. "Dance party? I've needed that all day." Timini reaches the bottom of the stairs just as Addison opens the front door, so Timini loops her arm in Addison's and leads her to the gathering room, too.

As I pair my phone with the speakers, I say, "Peyton's feeling down. You two pull her off that couch and we'll all pull her out of her funk." I start playing the music loud enough that Ian's grandma, Shirley, and her friend and now roomie, Carol, could probably have their own dance party at their house next door.

Then I set my phone to start recording video and place it on the mantel. And then we all start dancing. My roommates are used to me videoing random things and trust that I'll get approval from them before ever posting anything online. Now they expect me to film things like this.

Not only are these types of situations often perfect—you never know when a three-second clip of a dance party will liven up a video or provide the perfect humor—but my roommates enjoy having this time of our lives documented. Maybe we'll get together when we're all in our eighties for roommate reunions and watch these videos of us having fun and just being there for each other.

At first, Peyton only dances half-heartedly, no matter how much energy Addison, Timini, and I put into it. It only takes a couple of songs, though, before we're all singing along to the chorus of Rachel Platten's *Fight Song* and jumping up and down like we're kids at our first middle school dance.

We're still going strong when the front door opens a couple of minutes later and a confused Ian walks into the lobby. The confusion changes to happiness soon after, and he immediately comes into the room and starts dancing alongside Addison. I love that he so easily joins in whatever wacky thing we're doing. I wish Roman was here right now to join in, too.

Whoa. I've had exactly one interview and one phone call with him that have gone decently, and suddenly I'm wishing he'd show up to a roommate dance party? Clearly, I watched too much of him on that video today. I need to find a way to stop thinking about him so often. Just as soon as I get our next interview planned.

And then have the interview.

And then plan and carry out the next two.

And edit those three.

And release them and promote them all.

Okay, new plan: I just need to not allow myself to think of him anytime I'm not doing one of those things. Because he's the wrong guy, and I'm not about to fall for him.

As the song quiets near the end, a grinning, breathing-heavy Peyton says, "Holy guacamole, this is fun. Can we make mandatory dance parties an official thing?"

I walk right out to the lobby where we keep the roommate calendar and message board and pull out a pad of sticky notes. In as big of letters as will fit, I write *Mandatory dance party every Monday night* and stick it to the board.

There. It's official.

And while I'm writing it and sticking it up, I congratulate myself on going a full twelve seconds without thinking of Roman. This is going to be no problem at all.

CHAPTER 10
Roman

I PULL into the parking lot of the address Bex texted me, fully expecting to see a recreation center or some other building that might house a racquetball court since that was the direction she had taken our phone call. Instead, there are outdoor courts similar to tennis courts, but a bit smaller. I might've thought I was in the wrong place, but Bex is on the court with one of her roommates, a guy I recognize from Ian's wedding, and her videographer nephew, Enoch.

I like sports fine. I like them a lot, actually. What I don't like is walking onto the courts for a video interview while wearing gym clothes instead of a business suit. As I step through the gates onto their court, I'm even more wary as I notice they are holding paddles instead of racquets.

From the look on Bex's face as she takes me in, she is at least appreciating my clothing choice. Maybe it's a good thing I went for the shirt that shows off my chest and shoulder muscles. And she is looking pretty amazing in her tennis skirt and tank top.

"Hey, Roman. You remember Peyton and Max?"

I say hi and shake both of their hands. I'm glad Bex

reminded me of their names because I hadn't remembered them at all. Then I say hi and shake Enoch's hand before I turn to Bex. "Couldn't get a reservation at a racquetball court?"

"Didn't even try."

I eye her. "So instead, we are going to play pickleball."

I must've made a face because her responding grin shows all of her teeth and is mischievous. And beautiful. "Yep. For two reasons. First: I didn't want to play against you in a sport you dominate at. Plus, racquetball is noisy and not conducive at all to interviewing. And second: you explaining your Nudge Out app inspired me to choose something similar to what you liked but a departure from your normal. A nudge out of your comfort zone."

So we are going to have the interview *while playing pickleball.* A sport I've never played before. One that I have never even watched before. I have a vague sense of it being something like life-sized ping pong. This is a far cry from the "across a desk from each other" interview I requested. Knowledge of this is definitely going into a vault to be kept far from my dad and brothers. And everyone else I know.

And I am never letting Everly put me in the company's social media plan again.

Luckily, Bex tells me about the rules and how the game is played and even lets me warm up a bit and try serving a few times before the camera starts rolling. Which is good, because those balls are so light that I assume it takes a lot more force to get them to where they need to go than they actually need. In fact, I really have to hold back.

I pick up the ball that has holes in it, like a whiffle ball from games when I was little, and walk to the back of the court. "Can we realistically carry on an interview while playing?"

"Yep. I find it helps calm the nerves a bit since all of the focus isn't on the interview and all its trappings. I'm hoping that it'll help you drop your guard a bit."

It definitely isn't doing that. I regret feeling so bold on Sunday when I talked about playing racquetball and am seriously rethinking the wisdom of saying yes to these interviews in general.

She walks over to me and presses down on my shoulders with her wrists, since her hand is holding a paddle, and my heart rate ramps up just having her so close. "Relax these muscles. You're wearing your seriousness like a suit of armor, and it's hiding what you've really got inside. People will connect with what you're saying about your products more if they can connect with you."

I roll my shoulders and shake out my arms. My dad and brothers are never going to see this. It's fine. All those men and women I hang out with at business receptions? They aren't going to see this, either. None of them spend their time watching YouTubers. This is purely for a demographic of people who are our target audience for our products. I'm speaking to them.

"You ready?"

I nod, so she nods to Enoch, and he starts filming.

"Hello, Bexlandians! We are back for our second interview with Roman Powell, the CEO of LivenUP. He has been playing racquetball for the past, what? Sixteen years? In the spirit of their new app that just released, Nudge Out, I decided we'd nudge Roman out of his comfort zone and try a completely new-to-him sport—pickleball!"

"Now, if you haven't heard of *Nudge Out* yet, I've got a link to our first interview below." She holds up her phone. "*Nudge Out* is an app that Roman put on my phone at the beginning of our previous interview. I put in the information it asked for, and it's just been sitting there, doing its thing, gathering data so it can suggest the best ways to nudge *me* out of *my* personal comfort zone. If you're curious about what that is, stay tuned for our fourth interview, because we are going to let the app decide where that will be."

Good. I'm glad she's talking up the app so much.

"We are going to start with Roman serving." She hands me the ball, and her fingers brush mine. It's like an electrical charge zips right up my arm just from the feel of her hand on mine, and it lights me up enough that I am suddenly more than ready to play. I serve the ball to Peyton, who is across the court from Bex. I have played enough sports to be able to hit a ball with a paddle just fine, but I am having trouble always using the right amount of force when I'm accustomed to playing a sport that requires so much more.

Luckily, Bex doesn't start off with interview questions so I can concentrate on not looking like a fool. Especially because simply being around Bex is occupying more and more of my attention, leaving less for paying attention to what I'm supposed to actually have my focus on.

I do pretty well for the first eight or ten times I hit the ball, but then I have to lunge for a ball, backhanding it as I do, and it doesn't even land in the court—it hits straight into the chain-link fence surrounding the court.

Bex laughs. "I can always tell when you revert to your racquetball roots because the sound of you hitting the ball is the same as that."

With as different as the racquets, the ball, and the court are, it surprises me that I catch that familiar sound, too. It makes me crave a game of racquetball, and suddenly, I'm picturing it with just Bex and me on the court. Getting in a good workout, competing, sweating together, and bumping up against each other. Then maybe leaning against the wall facing each other as we catch our breaths. And then kissing. A good amount of kissing.

The thought distracts me so much that when I pick up the ball I missed, I can't even remember whether it's my team's ball or Peyton's and Max's, let alone which one of them is supposed to serve it next. Thankfully, Max stands just behind the back line, looking like he's ready to serve, his eyes on me, so I toss it to him.

I've got to keep my head in the game, especially with that camera running. Besides, it doesn't matter how attracted I am to Bex—it only seems like it could work when I'm here with her in *Bexlandia World*. The real world is much more complicated, and just the thought of the two of us together in it and how much that would upend my world is all it takes to get me paying attention to that ball I just hit back to the other side.

"So…" Bex says, then pauses as Max calls out the score—seven, six, one—and then serves the ball, "*Nudge Out* isn't your company's first app." She hits the ball back. "You have some pretty remarkable ones. Which one would you suggest for the four of us?"

"*Group Eat*. It's kind of like Pandora, except instead of picking your music, it picks a restaurant, and instead of for one person, it can do it for a group." I hit the ball back. Maybe I *can* interview and play at the same time. It's definitely easier than thinking of Bex while trying to play.

"You can set it to automatically detect when you're at a restaurant by using location services, you can log whenever you go to a restaurant, or you can just put in your favorite restaurants."

Bex misses the ball, so she picks it up and uses her paddle to send it over the net to Max.

"Each time you go out, just log if anyone else is with you—your significant other, friends, family, co-workers—and rate how much each person liked the restaurant out of five stars. If anyone that you go with has the app on their phone, you can just add them as a friend, and they can log all their own information."

I hit the ball back, and it goes right to the back corner of Max's side, and he misses the ball. Nice. Even during an interview. So the serve goes to Peyton.

"Eight, six, two," Peyton calls out and then serves the ball.

"Let's say we're going out to dinner." I hit the ball back to their side of the court. "We could go into the app, tell it that the four of us are going, and tap *Where should we eat?* It'll look at where we've eaten and liked in the past, find commonalities in the types of food offered in our favorite restaurants, and suggest a restaurant that all four of us will like."

Bex hits the ball to Peyton, who hits it quickly back.

"So," I say as I return the ball, "it solves the all-too-common issue of one person asking 'Where do you want to eat?' and the other one saying, 'I don't know. Where do you want to eat?'" I motion to Peyton and Max. "You should get the app, and see how much more smoothly your next date together goes."

"Oh," both Max and Peyton stumble out. "No—" And then they motion back and forth to each other, making Max barely able to hit the ball back over the net toward me. Then Peyton manages to blurt, "We're just friends."

Wow, did I read that wrong. It throws me off just enough that I nearly miss the ball that has come clearly to me. I have to rush, lunge, and backhand the ball with all of my might to get it. It registers somewhere in the recesses of my brain that it not only makes that racquetball sound but also goes in the wrong direction. I barely turn back in time to see it head straight for Bex at the speed of a freight train and hit her right in the gut.

"Oof." Bex doubles over, clutching her stomach.

"Oh, sugar monkeys!" Peyton calls out, her hands flying to cover her mouth.

I rush to Bex. "Are you okay? I am so sorry." How bad did I hurt her? I can tell I hit the ball hard, but I have no idea how much damage it might have caused. "Is it going to leave a bruise?"

Bex stands up straight, a mischievous smile on her face, and holds up the ball. "Roman, these things weigh less than one ounce. I am *fine*." She laughs and presses the ball into my chest. My hand instinctively goes to it, landing right on top of hers.

"I see how it is," I say. "You helped me cover up one awkward moment by eclipsing it with another."

"I do what I can." She winks, and my heart might *flutter* just a bit. As she walks back to her position on the court, she asks, "Should we try again, and this time you hold back just a bit?"

"I *was* holding back." If only she knew how much I'm holding back with her.

"That was you *holding back*?" She looks straight at the camera. "Okay, then I want to see what it looks like when you *aren't* holding back. Toss me the ball and go to the other side of the court."

I do, and when I near Peyton, I say quietly, "I apologize for making a wrong assumption."

"Oh, my life, it's really no problem. But if you don't mind, I'm just going to..." Peyton points to the side of the court, and both she and Max head there.

Hit it like racquetball, I tell myself as Bex drops the ball and hits it with her paddle before ducking off to the side. It comes at me perfectly, and I take aim and swing like I'm playing hard with my buddy Kirk and I'm down by a handful of points. My racquet makes contact, the hit sounds completely unlike racquetball, and the ball hurtles straight for the chain-link wall surrounding the court. It hits one of the upright poles and falls to the ground.

Bex walks over to the ball, which now more closely resembles an orange peel that someone has managed to get off the orange in one piece. "Will you look at that," she says as she takes the evidence of my misjudgment over to the camera. "That is *thoroughly destroyed!* I think that signals the end of the game. This guy can definitely liven up a game of pickleball, so make sure you check out his apps."

Her chosen profession might not be my thing, but I have to admire how good she is at it. Just seeing how comfortable she is in front of the camera and how it feels like she is talking to actual people when she is looking at nothing more than the camera lens is impressive.

"And make sure you subscribe and hit the bell for notifications because you won't want to miss my next interview with Roman. It's going to be at a location he doesn't even know yet, and I can tell you right now that you won't want to miss it."

I notice that Peyton and Max have come right up behind me, and they wave to the camera as Bex says goodbye to her Bexlandians.

As soon as the camera is off, I say, "I didn't mean to end the game."

"We already got what we needed, and we were losing good light, anyway. Not to mention the fact that my sister is in the parking lot, waiting to take my cameraman to basketball practice." She turns to Enoch and accepts the camera equipment from him, giving him a fist bump. "Thanks for another awesome job."

"And thank *you* for an awesome job." He takes a few steps toward the gate to let himself out of the court, then he turns, walking backward. "Oh, can I get paid differently this time?"

"Sure. You finally want cash?"

"No." Enoch makes a face like that's ridiculous. "I was thinking bacon burgers."

Bex laughs. "You got it."

"We are going to head out, too," Peyton says, and she and Max start walking to the parking lot.

I know enough about cameras to know that their owner prefers to be the one carrying them, so I offer to take the tripod. She hands it over, and we walk toward the gate. "I'm sorry I ruined the ball."

"Don't be. That made for some great viewing—my subscribers are going to love it." She looks me up and down, and I try to hold back the involuntary flex several of my muscles try to do just from seeing her notice. I try to hold back the smile, too. "I think a lot of them have been hoping to see those muscles in action. The rest will see it as evidence of the passion you bring to the things you take on."

I nod. "Well, I am sorry I hit you in the stomach with it."

"I wasn't joking when I said it was nothing."

I sneak a glance over at her while we walk. Amazingly, it doesn't matter what she wears, or if her hair is down, in a ponytail, perfect, or messed up from playing hard in a pickle-ball game, she's beautiful. Confident. In control. Unstoppable.

She must feel my eyes on her because a smile lifts the corners of her mouth.

The sun has just set but it's still plenty light outside. She leads us to her car, which is parked next to a row of shrubs on the driver's side. She opens the door to the backseat and lays down the camera case, then accepts the tripod from me and lays it beside the camera before shutting the door. I probably should say goodbye and walk away, but instead, as she's opening the driver's door, I lean against the car and ask, "So when will the first interview air?"

She turns so she's facing me—just the two of us nestled in

the little space between her car and the shrubs, the open door behind her. "Next Tuesday. The same day your app releases."

"And you're going to show me before it airs, right?"

She gives me an amused smile that makes my chest tingle. "I always keep my word."

"So, are we talking five minutes before it airs, or with enough time to request changes?"

There's that same smile again, but she moves forward just a bit. Enough to make it feel like she wants the distance between us to close just as much as I do. "I will send it to you by Sunday evening so you'll have all day Monday to look at it."

I nod and turn so that I'm facing her fully, which puts me a little closer to her.

"We need to film the third one." Her eyes search mine. "When are you free?"

"Tomorrow," I say without thinking and instantly regret it. I don't want to tip my hand and show how much or how soon I want to see her again. So I add a quick, "Or next week," so it doesn't seem like I'm desperate.

"Tomorrow is perfect."

"Yeah?"

"Yeah." She moves a bit closer, and her eyes flick from mine to my lips. One slight little flick of her eyes, and suddenly all I can think about is her lips and how it would feel to kiss them. "Can you meet me at the inn?"

"Anywhere."

"Anywhere?"

I breathe out a chuckle and think, *As long as you're there.* Instead of answering, I just close the gap by a few more inches, and she's near enough that I can hear her soft breathing.

"I'm suddenly feeling drunk with the possibility of getting you to meet me anywhere."

I'm pretty sure she could talk me into anything right now. I reach out and run my fingers down her upper arm. She responds by touching her fingertips to my chest, and tingles spread up my spine as she starts to close the gap, her eyes on my lips.

"Bex!" Peyton yells as she runs around the bushes that separate where we are from the rest of the parking lot. "I'm so glad I caught you! Oh. *Oh!* My lands, I'm sorry. I didn't think I'd be interrupting… I just…" She opens the front passenger's door and tosses a bag inside. "I was afraid of leaving this in Max's car. I'll just…go now. Ignore me. Pretend I was never here."

Peyton races off, and we hear a car door shut and then the sound of Max's car driving off. Bex looks around like she's just come out of a daze. The moment is gone, though—I can see it in her eyes. I take a deep breath to pull myself out of the daze, too, and rub the back of my neck. "What time do you want me to meet you tomorrow night?"

"Oh, um, seven-thirty?"

I nod then turn and walk toward my car. It's probably a good thing we didn't actually kiss. What was I thinking? We're in a fairy tale world, not the real world. I'm reaching into my pocket to pull out my keys when Bex says, "Roman?"

I turn back toward her, not sure what, exactly, I'm hoping for, but knowing hope is very much alive and well.

"What was your favorite ice cream as a kid?"

That's not what I was expecting at all. "Uh, chocolate chip cookie dough."

She gives a nod and a wink, and then says, "See you tomorrow night."

Yep. Hope is definitely alive and well.

CHAPTER 11

Bex

THE TEXT COMES in from Ian's grandma, Shirley, next door. The woman has discovered the beauty of voice-to-text, but not how to edit what it thinks she said. Luckily, I'm practically a pro at translating voice-to-text. I have Vivian as a sister, after all. I type a quick response.

I get three eggs out of the fridge and head next door, breathing in the sweet afternoon air as I go. I started off the day by filming a *Hidden Inn Roomies* segment about the chaos of a morning when living in an inn full of entrepreneurs.

Peyton has been organizing bowls, mixers, food items, pots, pans, and containers to put the food in for a family she's making a week's worth of food. Timini has a play she's creating all the costumes for, and not only has she taken all six smaller tables in the dining area, but she's duking it out with Peyton over use of the dining table during the day, too. And all while Addison, Ian, and I are trying to grab something for breakfast before the three of us take half a dozen trips out to Addison's car to load up a ridiculous number of organization bins and other items for one of her clients.

Not long after Addison and Ian both leave, while Peyton and Timini are still discussing how to share the space, all of my sisters show up to film a *Sterling Sisters* segment. Then, once we finish, I figure I'll film my review of a stylish sports bag that a company sent me since Nikki can stay to film it. Enoch is my favorite cameraman, but since Nikki does most of the editing, she has a good feel for what, exactly, we need.

Filming always gives me a boost of energy. But now that it's late afternoon, all that extra energy is gone, and I'm crashing. The fresh air and time away from my computer help, though. I go straight to Shirley's kitchen door and knock twice before opening it.

"Oh, thank you," Shirley says as she turns from a bowl of something she's mixing on the counter and accepts the eggs from me. Her apron is covered in flour, and Carol, who is also wearing a flour-covered apron and stirring a bowl of something, sits at the kitchen table.

"What are you making?"

Shirley points at a muffin tin and a cake pan on the stove, the bowl in front of her, and the bowl in front of Carol. "Cookies, lemon tarts, and fudge jumbles. Our entire origami club district is getting together tonight."

"Wow! You guys really know how to party it up."

Carol stands, grabs a spoon from the drawer, and then scoops up a bit of the yellow substance in her bowl and hands it to me. "Here. Try this lemon curd."

I sit at the table, too, and put the spoon in my mouth. The curd is an explosion of flavor on my tongue—tart and sweet and so very lemony—and my eyes roll as I close them to savor every bit of it. "Oh, my, Carol." I lick the spoon. "This is divine. I can't speak for Addison, since she owns it, but if you two ever want to move into the inn, I'm sure we would all welcome you with open arms. And open mouths."

Both women laugh and go back to working on their sweet confections.

"So, tell me about who you're dating," Shirley says. "You know how much I love to live vicariously through your dating life."

"I actually haven't gone out with anyone in weeks."

"What? That isn't like you at all." Shirley grabs the bowl of dough she's mixing and brings it to the table, sitting down where she can face me. "What's going on?"

She's right. It isn't like me at all to not be dating. I always have at least one date a week. Quite often two or three. I love dating and am still convinced that if I date enough, I'll eventually find the right guy. How haven't I noticed that I'm not going on my usual number of dates?

"I guess I just haven't been looking lately."

Carol reaches a hand out and places it on my forehead. "Hmm. No fever. Strange. Are you feeling any other symptoms? Like maybe your mind just went for a walk without you?"

I laugh. "My mind and I are just fine." I think about it for a moment. "I guess maybe my mind has just been on Roman too much lately."

Shirley pushes the bowl she's been stirring to the side, like it's getting in the way of her listening to me, and leans forward, elbow on the table, chin in her palm. "This is the hottie you're interviewing for the Eddie Award judging thing, right? Are you thinking about dating him?"

"I'm not sure. I hadn't planned to at all, but maybe? All I

know is that we came *this* close to kissing last night, and let's just say I wouldn't have been upset if we had." In fact, I can directly attribute all of my over-scheduling for the day to my need to stop thinking about that moment next to my car with Roman. The expression on his face. The way it felt when he touched my arm and when I touched his chest. How unguarded he was. The way his eyes were alive and warm and definitely wanting the kiss. The way he smelled. How great it felt to be so close and how much I wanted to step into his arms.

Carol hoots.

A satisfied grin spreads across Shirley's face. "When do you see him next?"

"Tonight. We're filming the third interview at the inn."

"And is this kiss that almost was going to happen then?"

I let out a long breath and look down at my arms, which are crossed and resting on the table, pondering. "I don't know. He's just the wrong type of guy for me. Normally, I have no fears dating, because if it doesn't work out, there are more fish in the sea, you know?"

I look up at the wiser, more experienced eyes across the table from me. "But Roman is just…different. This is the first time I've felt afraid. Like part of me knows that if I fall for him and it doesn't work out—which it won't—then I'm going to get hurt. I'm not just going to be able to shrug it off and go for the next fish in the sea like usual."

Shirley nods. "He's special, that one."

"Yep."

"Are you sure he's the wrong type of guy?" Carol asks.

"Well, yeah. He's very much unlike the type of guy I always date."

"That doesn't mean he's the wrong guy."

"Well, no, but I date the types of guys that I do because I've learned by watching my sisters what happens when you do and what happens when you don't. And I don't ever want to have to go through what my sister, Nikki, did."

Carol stands and carries the lemon curd to the mini crusts on the stove. "Open yourself to possibilities, girl. I thought my Henry was the wrong guy, and so did every person in my family. Once I took a flamethrower to that thought so I could see what lay beyond my preconceived notions, I stepped right over its ashes and into a beautiful life with him. We got to spend fifty-five years together before he passed a few months ago."

"Sounds like you need to get a flamethrower, dear," Shirley says.

I chuckle. "I will definitely think about your advice, Carol." I stand. "I better get back, though. I've got a lot to do to prepare for our interview tonight."

And one of those might just be getting a metaphorical thought-scorching flamethrower.

———

I peek through the blinds on the gathering room window to the curved driveway in front of the inn. The moment I see Roman's car pull in, giddiness sweeps through me. "He's here!" I say to Enoch. He turns on the camera, and we both go to the front lobby.

As soon as Roman knocks, I open the door and say, "Hi."

His eyes immediately go to the camera. "Oh. We're starting off with the camera on, then?"

"I want to make sure I get on film your reaction to seeing where I am interviewing you."

He looks wary, so I open the door all the way, grab his hand, and pull him toward the gathering room, using my foot to shut the door behind us. Enoch moves from behind us to the side so he can film at a good angle.

The second Roman walks through the doorway and his eyes land on the gigantic blanket fort that Addison, Peyton, Timini, Ian, Enoch, and I built, they go wide, and it is worth every bit of struggle we had to get it to work. I don't remember the task being so difficult when I was a kid.

Of course, when I was a kid, our family room was less than one-third of the size of this huge room, and we were never as ambitious when it came to fort size as my roommates and I were tonight. Enoch had set up the camera back between the area with the couches at the front of the room and my desk at the back when we first started building the blanket fort. It will likely make for some great time-lapse footage, and if I want to post some bloopers at the end, we definitely had plenty of those.

"Oh, wow. You didn't. I can't believe—" Roman runs a hand down his face like he's wiping away any chance that this is a mirage. "It's been so long."

I look at the camera. "In our pre-interview, Roman said that one of his favorite things to do as a kid was to eat ice cream in blanket forts that he made with his brothers, so I figured it would be a great place to chat with him today."

I lead him to the opening and we crawl inside, Enoch right behind us. We used practically every blanket and sheet we collectively own, so surrounding us is quite the colorful tapestry. We put the cushions from all three couches on the floor, too, so we have soft places to sit. And, because I know how important it is, I have some great lighting set up that will allow my viewers to see everything yet still have that feel of being in a cave made of blankets. I added a few flashlights pointing at the blanket walls since that's the kind of lighting that completes the look.

I show Roman where to sit, then I take my seat on my mark and Enoch gets the camera into position.

Roman looks around at the area, which feels like one larger room and three smaller ones. One area is even like a hallway leading to another section. "The dress forms aren't bad, but those mannequins are really freaking me out."

I laugh as I look at the shiny white mannequins, standing like a mix between a pillar holding up our fort and a ghost wearing a blanket like a shawl. It doesn't help that their arms are positioned outward and up to help hold up the fort because now that I'm on the floor looking up at them, they appear more than a little menacing. "It's hard to come up with enough tall objects to hold up the blankets. Timini offered these, and I think they really add to the look of the place."

"Yep. They add to the look of it being haunted." He keeps glancing at the closest one like it can't be trusted, which makes me laugh out loud. And it makes Enoch keep taking his eyes off the video camera and looking at it like he's just as wary.

I start with an introduction of Roman, just in case people are watching who haven't seen either of the other two interviews, and I ask Roman a few questions about his company.

"Wow," I say after hearing him talk about it. "It sounds like you've put together a pretty stellar group of employees."

He smiles in a way that tells me he's really proud of them, and I can't help but just stare at his beautiful face for a moment. His beautiful, strong-jawed, perfectly-stubbled, melt-your-heart face. Then I realize that I'm just staring at that face for far too long to be a proper interview and clear my throat.

"You have an app that has been a fan favorite for quite a while now, right? I want to hear more about it."

"The one that made us famous is *Musicbound*. Think of the last movie you watched. Now imagine it without any music. No soundtrack at all."

I flinch, just thinking of how wrong that feels. And for some reason, it makes Enoch look at the mannequin closest to him like if he doesn't keep an eye on it, it's going to attack him or something.

"Music adds a lot to a movie. We thought book reading should be the same, so we created an app to provide music while you're reading an ebook or listening to an audiobook. The app will scan the book and look for subjects, themes, tone, and a couple dozen more metrics. Then it'll select music to play while you read that fits the feel and the plot of the book. In chapters where something sad happens, the music will be more somber. When it's an action-packed scene, the music will be upbeat and fast. Just like in the movies, it'll fit what you are reading."

"Shut the front door." I look at the camera, knowing that if my viewers aren't already using this app, they are going to be just as stunned by this as I am. "Are you kidding me right now? This is really a thing?"

Roman's smile is wide.

"If you re-read a book, will the music be the same the next time?"

"Not necessarily. If you read the same book a year later, there will be more songs that have been put out into the world, so it might choose one of those. And if you're a slower reader, you'll hear more songs than the faster readers."

I put my hands up and jerk back a bit, like I've been hit by a blast. "How do I not already have this in my life?" I take my phone out of my pocket and open the app store. "I need this right now. This purple one with the music note on a book is it, right?"

"Yep."

As it's downloading, I look out at my viewers. "Did you all already know about this? If so, why didn't you tell me? And if you haven't already told everyone you know about this, you should do it the second you finish watching this video." Then I turn back to Roman. "Does it work with nonfiction?"

He makes a motion with his head that is both a nod and a shake. "We designed it to work with fiction books only. I still use it with every nonfiction book I read, though. I've gotten some interesting results. It has made me double my nonfiction reading just to hear what kind of music it chooses for it."

"Give me an example."

"Let me think. Oh. Okay. I was reading B.J. Fogg's *Tiny Habits*, and one of the songs it played was *Hard Habit to Break* by Chicago. And while I was reading *Deep Work* by Cal Newport, it played a bunch of music that was scientifically proven to help with focus like classical music, nature sounds, and binaural beats."

"Impressive."

"I thought so, too. My favorite, though, was when I was reading *Year of Yes* by Shonda Rhimes. During one chapter, it played Kelly Clarkson's *What Doesn't Kill You Makes You Stronger*, and in another chapter, Katy Perry's *Roar*."

I laugh, feeling like they are some pretty appropriate choices, and Roman's eyes shine with a mix of pride, satisfaction, and enjoyment. I feel like I'm seeing through to the real him. And he read *Year of Yes*! My heart melts even more to know that he read a book by a woman who is all about creating shows that people can connect to. Maybe I've misjudged Roman and the way he feels about my job.

Instead of continuing to stare at him, my jaw still hanging at the revelations like I've lost all ability to control it, I look down at the app on my phone. "It feels like such a shame that this app has been out in the world and I haven't been using it."

"At least you have it now."

"Yes. This calls for a celebration." I twist to grab the mini cooler that I snuggled between a couch cushion and a blanket to my side and open it up. I pull out a couple of pints of Ben & Jerry's and two spoons and hand one to Roman. "Half-baked for the app genius, and Red, White, and Blueberry for the giddy new app owner."

We both take off our lids and scoop up a spoonful of ice cream. Roman closes his eyes and savors his bite, and I wonder how long it has been since he's eaten ice cream. Or at least a flavor of ice cream that reminds him of his childhood. He puts a hand behind him and leans back, stretching his legs forward.

The blanket fort is definitely much larger than a kid's version. But we aren't kids—we are two adults and a twelve-year-old who is as tall as I am and bigger or not, this place is still cozy. And Roman's legs are long. So when he stretches, they bump the base of the mannequin that Enoch has been most wary of.

Enoch flinches in surprise when he notices the movement from the corner of his eye, then jerks in fear as the mannequin wobbles, looking like it has come to life. In an instant, he is scuttling backward, the couch cushion he's sitting on and the blanket tucked under the edge of it going with him.

"No!" I shout as I instinctively lunge forward to grab hold of the mannequin that is now falling forward as the weight of the blanket resting on its head is being tugged, and Roman instinctively lunges over me to protect me from above. I grab the mannequin by its hard plastic ankles—not that it helps at all —just as it falls to the ground.

Then, like dominos, all of the mannequins and dress forms fall to the ground, all the blankets being pulled down on top of them.

And suddenly, I am in a very dark, very muffled, very small space, looking up at Roman, whose hands are on the floor, one next to each of my shoulders, the only space between us made by the length of his arms from wrist to shoulder as he hovers over me. He's currently the only thing holding up any part of the fort.

"Impressive save," I breathe.

He shifts his knees, and I let go of my grip on the mannequin's ankle that I realize my right hand is still clutching.

"This isn't quite how I remember blanket forts as a kid."

"What, you never had mannequins attack you in yours?"

He chuckles, and even though I can't see his face, I can sense exactly the way his mouth is tugged up on one side and how his eyes are twinkling. He is so close that I can feel his breath on my cheek, feel the warmth of his body emanating from him. "I don't suppose you know the best direction to head to find our way out?"

"Out?" I reach up and touch my fingertips to his cheek. I'm not sure I want to get out anytime soon.

CHAPTER 12
Roman

T HE FEEL of Bex's fingers on my cheek sends a thrill racing to every corner of my body. All I can think about is kissing her. She is right there, inches from me. I'd just have to bend my elbows a bit, and my lips could be on hers.

Is that what she wants? As her fingers run along my jawline and pause at my chin, her breath catching, her fingers tapping twice lightly, I think maybe so.

"I finally found you!" Enoch's face appears under the blanket next to us, a flashlight in one hand and the video camera in the other. He lets out a huge breath of air. "Whew. That wasn't easy. I swear the mannequin was still trying to attack me."

Now that I can see Bex's face, I see amusement. We both shift to where we are on our hands and knees and work our way to a spot where the blankets have pulled apart and we can see light. Once we make our way out, Bex runs her hands over her hair, which is looking rather staticy from all the blankets rubbing on it, and straightens her shirt. I do the same, figuring I probably need it as much as she does.

She surveys the damage as Enoch pans the camera around at the destruction. With her hands on her hips and the camera focused on her, she says, "Well, as is the eventual outcome of all blanket forts, this one has crumbled under the weight of its own greatness—just a little sooner than we had planned." She reminds her viewers about subscribing, getting notifications, and not missing our next interview, and then we both say goodbye.

I bend down, pick up a blanket, and start folding it. She gives me a strange look like she hadn't expected me to help, but then she grabs the other side of the blanket and starts folding it with me. I'm not about to leave this big mess to her, though. Even if my mom hadn't taught me to always show good manners, I'd want to stay and help just to be around her for longer.

She gasps. "The ice cream!"

"I've got this," Enoch says, dropping the blanket he's folding before making a show of diving into the pile of blankets. A minute later, he re-emerges holding two pints of ice cream and two spoons. "Only a little bit got on the hardwood floor—none on the cushions or the blanket." He looks at the pints in his hand. "Are you going to still eat these?"

Bex laughs. "Consider it your reward for rescuing them."

"Yes!"

Then the kid rushes over to Bex's desk and starts eating them at a speed that pretty much guarantees brain freeze. I shake my head. Enoch is impressively professional behind the camera, but he is still a twelve-year-old boy.

Once we get the blankets folded, the ice cream cleaned off the floor, and the furniture put back into place, Bex walks me out to my car.

"Thank you, Bex. Even with the fort crashing down on us, I quite enjoyed myself. That wasn't something I thought I would do again anytime soon." When she didn't tell me what we were going to do for this interview, my mind had been churning, trying to figure it out. It hadn't occurred to me that she would create an entire blanket fort. Climbing inside it brought back so much nostalgia.

"And thank you for being game for it. Now tell me, Roman Powell, when you were a kid, what was it about blanket forts that was so magical to you?"

It's dark outside yet the moon is bright enough that I can see the same look on her face that she gets whenever she is filming. Like she experiences her own kind of magic every time she has the camera on her.

We reach my car and I lean my backside against it, trying to remember back to what I loved so much about the forts we made. "I guess part of it was that we only made them when my dad was away on a business trip, which always meant that our schedules were less rigid. And the other part was the games my brothers and I would play in it. More often than not, we played business owner and employees."

"Was that really what you played?"

I chuckle and look down, shaking my head. "That's what we called it, even. I was always the business owner since I was the oldest, and I got to boss my brothers around."

"I see why it was your favorite game."

"My dad likes to control everything. So I guess a big part of why we loved it was that we could make all the decisions ourselves without our dad stepping in to tell us what to do." It has never occurred to me before that in my business, I walked right into a situation that, as a kid, I had worked to stay away from.

"Well, it looks like all that practice being a business owner as a kid really paid off."

She is so beautiful. And I really want to kiss her. But then a look crosses her face that makes me think that she's unsure about it. Or flat-out doesn't want to kiss me at all. I am, after all, just a stuffy businessman, which seems to be her least favorite type of person.

I need to convince her that I am right for her. She steps closer to me, and my chest lifts at the thought that maybe the moment we shared under the collapsed blanket fort hasn't been lost.

But then, just as I am thinking about how much I want to close the gap between us, a car pulls into the driveway, and I want to curse its driver. Its headlights shine on us, and Bex takes a step back, turning toward it with her hand shielding her eyes from its lights. "Oh. That's my sister, Kenna, here to pick up Enoch."

I hope that Enoch will see that she pulled up and run out to the car. But her sister pulls to a stop just in front of me on the curved drive and gets out. "Hey, Bex! Can I grab those frames you picked up for me?"

"Yeah. Just…" Bex meets my eyes and then turns back to her sister. "Go on in, and I'll be right there."

As soon as Kenna is inside the inn, Bex turns to me. "Sorry about the interruption. I believe you were about to tell me I'm pretty."

"And talented and a fairly solid blanket fort maker. And I believe you were about to tell me that I'm devilishly handsome."

"And a natural on camera—when you let your guard down—and an excellent kisser."

I quirk an eyebrow and drink in the brilliant smile on her face. "I know you have a rule of not endorsing products you haven't personally tried. I think I better help you to not break that rule."

"Don't let anyone ever tell you that you only look out for your own interests."

This time, I move toward her. We are standing so close. The air between us feels alive with electricity. A warmth. Like it's buzzing in anticipation. I feel the same buzz in me as I feel the warmth of her breath on my neck as she looks up at me.

We are only inches apart when I hear a meow and look down to see that a cat is rubbing up against Bex's leg, then forcing herself into the space between us.

"Skittles, go back home," Bex says. "I don't have any food for you, but I bet Carol does."

I shake my head. First her roommate, Peyton, interrupts us at the pickleball courts. Then Enoch in the blanket fort. Then her sister Kenna. And now the neighbor's cat. "Except it seems as though the universe is conspiring against us kissing."

Bex closes what's left of the distance between us and moves her hands up to either side of my face. "Then we need to show the universe who's boss," she breathes. She meets my eyes for a moment, then, like she's afraid something else will stop us if she doesn't hurry and seize the moment, she brings her lips to mine. They're firm and smooth, and they somehow feel like they're a perfect match to mine.

My spine tingles, and I wrap my arms around her waist, pulling her closer, loving the feel of her body against mine. I have never kissed someone so strong and decisive before, and her kiss is every bit as powerful as she is, seeming to shake me to my core. I break from the kiss just enough to whisper, "You are amazing," my lips brushing against hers with the words before they meet her lips again.

She moves her fingertips to just behind my neck, sending a new wave of tingles across my back. After a few blissful moments of her lips moving against mine, she pulls back slightly, a small moan escaping her lips. "Roman, that was… Wow. You really know how to kiss a girl."

I'm pretty sure the magic of that kiss is all from her. "Go on a date with me. No cameras, no interviews, just you and me."

"Just you and me?"

I nod.

She gives me one more slow kiss on the lips. "I would love that." She looks up, biting her lip like she's thinking through things, and it makes me want to kiss her again. "I have a pretty full schedule this weekend to prepare for the start of judging on Monday. Are you free next Thursday?"

I nod. "I'll pick you up at seven."

———

I get the last of the things I need for the day's meetings organized and into folders with a smile on my face and a lightness in my chest. I love the release day of a new app more than any other day—even more than the high we all get when we brainstorm a concept we know will be a winner. Even more than the day we work through the final issue and get it ready to go live. Release day is the day when we get to see what users think of the product we've poured everything into.

But that isn't the only thing giving me a bounce in my step. I wake up Monday morning realizing that I actually enjoy my interviews with Bex. Maybe because the first three were filmed with only a couple of days in between, but I have to wait a full eight days between the third and fourth. It gives me time to realize how much I want the next one to come.

My first interview with Bex goes live this morning, too. I never would've guessed I'd enjoy creating those videos with her, but there's something exhilarating about putting myself out there and having people respond. It oddly feels similar to putting a new app out there. I have given a part of myself to both, yet once either is released into the world, it feels separate from me. Almost like at that point, it's something that belongs to the viewers and app users, no longer to me, to Bex, or to my company.

Doing the interviews with Bex has also been oddly freeing. Opening myself up a bit and letting strangers get to know me comes with plenty of people who aren't bashful about criticizing. But more people respond positively. It makes me feel like there will always be people who will accept me no matter what. I don't need to be so guarded and careful. Maybe I'll have to say yes to interviews more often.

Another thing that surprises me is how much I enjoy the way Bex gets me to open up a bit more. It leaves me waking up each day more excited than I have possibly been, ever.

But maybe part of it is the creative ways I've been able to find to see and talk with Bex between our third interview on Thursday when we kissed and today.

I walk into my nine a.m. department heads meeting. Since it's release day for Nudge Out, it's Everly's meeting. I'm not surprised to see a giant cake in the middle of the conference table and several groups of balloons in the green and blue of the Nudge Out icon placed in groups around the room. My team has worked hard on this—they deserve to celebrate. We all do.

Everly opens the meeting by giving the release day numbers of app downloads—which are, by far, the best release numbers we've ever had, even though our advertising budget hasn't been much different from the last one. There's quite a bit of high-fiving and cheering all around the room.

"And I think a good part of those numbers came from the interview released early this morning that our illustrious leader did with Bex Sterling on *Bexlandia*." She meets my eyes. "Can I show it to them?"

It's nice of her to ask my permission, even though we both know there's no way the rest of my team is going to let me leave without it being shown. So I give the okay.

In all the time between when we filmed the hour-long interview and today, I've thought back through everything that happened. Sure, there were some exciting parts, but I worry the video will be slow and boring and no one will hang around for the exciting parts. But when Bex sent it to me on Sunday, just like she promised, and I watched it for the first time, I was surprised at how well-edited and well-paced it was.

The part with the deer staring us down right before it decides to charge makes me laugh, and now that I'm watching with my team, I smile at how much it makes them laugh, too.

If I were the one who'd fallen into the stream while being chased by the deer, though, I wouldn't have wanted it in the video. I'm impressed that Bex includes it. She was right—letting the viewers see all of that kind of stuff definitely makes the whole thing more interesting. And I get why it helps her audience connect with her more.

For so long, I had anticipated having multiple things in the video that I wasn't okay with including and possibly having to use threats to get Bex to edit them out. As it turned out, I didn't ask her to change a thing. I enjoy the email thread going back and forth to tell her that, though. I can't say I've ever flirted so much over email before.

As the video finishes and Everly takes it off the main screen, all my department heads cheer and it makes me feel a bit like a rock star. I'm enjoying this a bit too much.

"Now that's what I call good marketing," Wells says. "That's going to be giving us a boost for a while."

Daran chuckles. "Much like what that deer was trying to do to you."

"You guys don't plan on letting me live that down, do you?"

"Not anytime soon," Everly says, her eyebrows pulling together as she scrolls through something on her laptop. "So far, it looks like almost everything in the comments is positive. Lots of people are saying that they just downloaded the app, or coming back to say they got it and are so excited to use it."

"I bet those investors are going to love this," Melinda says.

I hope so. I'm having a meeting with them in a couple of weeks—long enough away that a few of the interviews will be out. I'll be surprised if this doesn't give them everything they need.

Everly gasps and puts a hand to her mouth. She stays silent, though, still reading. Finally, she looks up at me. "They're shipping you!"

I shake my head, having no clue what she's talking about.

"Shipping," she repeats, enunciating the word. "You and Bex."

"Everly, I heard you fine. I still don't know what you mean."

"Ship, as in relation*ship*. It means they want the two of you to start dating! Oh my gosh, that is so cute." She reads a little more. "Her viewers practically worship her. And whatever they saw during that video in her and whatever they saw in you made them think that the two of you should be together."

I don't know what I think about that. Part of me is completely unsettled that strangers are weighing in on who I should date. But as much as Bex has been on my mind lately, I like hearing that they can tell she's feeling it, too.

And it makes me want to win her over even more. Just two more days, and we're going on a date. I'm going to make sure it's perfect.

CHAPTER 13

Bex

I AM GOING to murder my sisters. All four of them. Starting with Vivian. Sure, Vivian says no to Asher getting a bird, but she doesn't say no to him signing up for *Forty Winks with Feathered Friends* camp. And then I am going to murder Kenna, Nikki, and Fiona for goading me, saying how good it will be for me to face my fears and maybe even overcome them. I am now quite convinced that science doesn't support that theory. Quite the opposite, in fact.

And while I'm at it, I'm going to murder the heart attack that killed Vivian's husband's great uncle Roger, because it makes it so Vivian can't take her own son to the mother-son event, and I have to step in.

"Just make a video for your channel of you overcoming your fears," they said. "It'll be inspiring to your viewers."

And I fell for it.

Even though I'm pretty sure that Nikki is just pushing for me to have this "opportunity" so that she can be the one at Vivian's house, sleeping over in a nice, soft bed, while watching the other three kids, instead of out here, under the stars, on a creaky cot with nothing more than a sleeping bag protecting me from the elements.

And by "elements," I mean the vile winged creatures.

I made it through the evening's events. I am proud of how strong I've been, actually. We studied the nests of birds and then built our own; watched a live show where they demonstrated the movement of birds as they dove, soared, waddled, strutted, and glided; learned enough facts about birds to make me even more wary of them; and went on a treasure hunt for the kinds of things birds like to eat. If nothing else, I did get some priceless footage.

But now it's after two in the morning, and even though I'm surrounded by a bunch of parents and bird-obsessed seven-to-ten-year-olds who are spread out across the pavilion, all in their own sleeping bags on cots, all sleeping, I haven't been able to close my eyes for more than a few seconds at a time. Birds are everywhere. Sure, some are behind a netted fence, but a lot of them are right here with us. Where they can just walk right up to us or land on our heads.

One, in particular, is as tall as a good-sized dog and apparently nocturnal, because it isn't tucked away sleeping somewhere—it's watching me. Not like, *Oh, she's something interesting to watch for a bit.* More like, *I'm going to wait for her to drop her guard long enough to fall asleep, and then I'm going to swoop in and peck her face.*

For the millionth time, I think about calling Nikki to see if we can switch places—her husband is easy-going enough that he'd be supportive. But sleeping on a cot is probably not the best thing for a pregnant belly. And, duh, neither of us can leave the sleeping kids in our care alone while we swap places.

I can't call any of my sisters, really. Not after how much grief they've given me about facing my fears. Besides, what I've filmed for my channel is great, and I know my audience will love it. So of course I want to air it. But if I don't see this through, I'll feel like I'm not being honest and authentic with them. Obviously, I can't do that. Besides, it's good to let my viewers know when I struggle with things and still overcome. So I will overcome.

Maybe.

Or maybe not.

All signs are pointing to *not*.

I suddenly feel hot, and like I can't breathe. And my legs won't stay still. I grab my phone and get out of my sleeping bag. I can't just lie here in such a vulnerable position any longer. If I'm going to get attacked, I want to be on my feet, ready to run, arms ready to flail. I shake out my hands—partly to shake away my fears, and partly to make sure they're ready for the imminent flailing. Then I fold my arms and rub them with my hands. It's a little chilly to be outside of my sleeping bag.

I have to stop thinking about the birds. I'm never going to sleep if I can't get them out of my mind. I just don't know how to accomplish that.

Oh! *Memes*. Nikki sent me a bunch made by viewers that are related to my first video interview with Roman that went live yesterday. I've been too busy to be online at all over the past day and a half, but Nikki assures me that she sent some good ones that are representative of what's out there. Maybe that will distract me. I open Messenger and start scrolling through Nikki's picks.

The first one is a zoomed-in screenshot of Roman's and my faces. By the terror in our expressions, I'm guessing it was the exact moment when we realized that the deer was going to charge, right before we turned to run. The words on the photo read:

When you write a cathartic email to your boss about his shortcomings and accidentally click send.

I chuckle and shake my head. The one right below it is the same picture of our panicked faces, only the words say:

When the teacher says one minute left to take the test, and you realize there's a back side.

The next one is an image of us running from the deer. I'm still impressed that Enoch managed to get ahead of us enough to video Roman and me running away. The picture is blurry in spots, but the look on our faces and the speed that we're obviously running tells a story all on its own. As does the look of determination on the deer's face. The word *Me* is placed over Roman and me, and the words *My problems* are placed on the deer.

There is another one of the same picture, but this one says, *I don't always run away, but when I do, I run through the least accommodating terrain possible.* I nearly laugh out loud, but then remember everyone sleeping around me. Looking back at our interview, it probably would've made a lot more sense if we'd just stayed on the path and kept running toward our cars.

Then a third with that same picture, which makes me wonder how many more are out there. It reads *I think she wants to nudge them out of their comfort zone.* A snort escapes my mouth on that one. Roman would probably even laugh at it.

Aww. And then one that makes me smile. It has two pictures, side by side. One is of me, looking at Roman like I adore everything about him. I hadn't noticed ever making that face when I was going through the edited video, but you can find pretty much any face on a person in a video if you press pause at just the right moment. The second picture is of Roman holding out a hand to pull me up when I'd fallen into the creek. The only words on the post are the hashtag *#RelationshipGoals*.

The last three are all the same animated gif—of me slipping

in the water and falling flat on my back, the two-second clip repeating over and over. The first has the caption *How my life is going.* The next says, *Me, any time I walk past my crush.* And then the last one—*When I'm trying to look like a skilled professional and my boss is watching.*

I can tell which posts come from fans because they all seem to have the hashtag *#BexVsDeer.* I click on the hashtag and start scrolling through the posts it brings up. There are dozens of memes. No, hundreds. All with videos, animated gifs, or screenshot images of something that happened during that interview. And that's just on one social media platform, with this one tag. I can't imagine how many more are on every other platform.

The last one I see before closing out of the app is a zoomed-in shot of the deer, with that murderous look in her eye. It says, *Say it to my face, bro. I deer you.*

Man, that deer really was creepy. Just looking into her eyes in a picture gives me a cold shiver.

And it very quickly reminds me of where I am and just as quickly alarms me. That had been one effective distraction to pull me from the danger of my surroundings. Now that I've been staring at my bright screen, my eyes are blind to the darkness, making it even more insidious. I aim the screen at the area in front of me, blinking to hopefully make myself focus more quickly.

The meager light shines on something in front of me, and I yelp and jump backward. The huge bird that had been watching me earlier has waddled over, quiet as a ninja, and is standing right at my feet, staring up at me. I suddenly find myself with my phone to my ear, listening to the ringing of my call to Roman.

Why am I calling him? I might not be willing to call one of

my sisters, but I could've called any one of my roommates. Or even my mom or dad. But no—I call Roman.

I keep my eyes on the bird, hearing my own heartbeat pumping in my ears like an overly excited aerobics instructor. My chest is getting tighter, which is unfortunate because it gives less room for the battle going on between the wildebeests in my stomach. I jump at the sound of a rustling behind me, then roll my shoulders, darting my eyes around at everything.

"Bex?" Roman answers the phone groggily, his voice thick with sleep.

"Please tell me you know how to talk someone down from a phobia attack," I whisper in a voice that is bordering on hysterical, clutching the phone with both hands. My breaths are coming fast and I keep glancing around, making sure no other birds are trying to flank me and attack from behind, all while keeping an eye on the one right in front of me.

"Phobia attack? What's going on?"

"There is a bird right in front of me that I swear has been around since the dinosaurs. That's how big he is. He's got black feathers and black legs and even a black beak that—I am not kidding you—is as long as a butcher knife. Around his eyes and cheeks and a giant neck thing, though. That part's not black—it's bright orange. Like it's there just to remind you that he's unpredictable. I saw him earlier on the tour, and I'm pretty sure he's been plotting my demise ever since. He was awake then, so I'm pretty sure that means he's not actually nocturnal —he just made an exception for me. And Roman! He is following me! Every time I take a step, he takes a step."

"Where are you?" His voice sounds a little more awake but also more baffled.

I try to get further from the sleeping people so I won't wake them. Every step I take is matched by the cursed bird and I can't slow my breathing. "The aviary."

"Why are you at the aviary if you have a phobia of birds? And why at nearly three in the morning?"

I let out a huff of air. "Because I'm stupid. And a sucker for helping out with my nieces and nephews."

"Ahh," he breathes. "You're at the *Forty Winks with Feathered Friends* camp. I did that when I was a kid, too."

"What? *Why?* Are you a secret bird lover? I might have to cancel our last interview. And our date."

"You're not a fan of birds or people who like birds. Got it. I assume your nephew is exempt from your ire?"

I take my eyes off the bird long enough to glance over to where Asher lies sleeping in the cot next to mine. "Yes. Because he's eight and adorable." Then my eyes are back on the bird's, and I swear he's moved closer during that second my focus was away. "Roman, what do I do? He just keeps staring at me with those beady eyes. I'm pretty sure he can see right into my soul."

"He probably likes what he sees. That's why he's following you."

"Roman!" I hiss.

"Okay," he says, and I hear some rustling, like maybe he's adjusting to a seated position in bed. "Tell me why you're so afraid of birds."

"Because they've got grabby, stabby feet. And grabby, stabby beaks. And since they can fly, they can attack you from any direction." I duck, looking all around, suddenly worried about how many birds are waiting on top of the posts and buildings and light poles. "They swarm. And they carry diseases."

"They do not."

"And they're smart—you've seen them fly in formations. They're capable of planning a coordinated attack to take over the world."

"No, they aren't."

"Remember how I said that they're smart?"

"Okay, they're smart, but they wouldn't. They aren't vindictive like that."

"Ducks are."

"Okay, ducks are. But not that bird in front of you."

"How do you know? He looks smart *and* vindictive! And birds can't be trusted!"

"These birds can be trusted. Bex, the aviary has been doing this activity for years. Since long before I was old enough to go. They wouldn't have started it and definitely wouldn't continue it if they were worried about that happening. Or if anything bad had happened in all the years they've done it."

"Maybe this is a new bird. He keeps cocking his head as he's staring at me. Like he's planning something."

"He's not sizing you up for a meal, Bex. He's just curious. Birds aren't mean—they're just inquisitive. He's watching you because you're the only one who's awake. There's no one else to watch."

I look out across the pavilion. Everyone else is all snuggled in their sleeping bags, snoozing. Is he really only interested in me because I'm giving him a show to watch? "Are you sure?"

"Positive. Birds are social creatures. This one got up in the middle of the night, scratched his head as he was wandering to the refrigerator, and noticed the TV was on. So he thought, 'Hey, that show looks interesting. Pretty girl, too. I think I'll just plop down on the couch and watch for a bit as I eat this slice of pizza.'"

I let out a quiet laugh and feel some of the tension leaving my shoulders.

"If you go climb into your sleeping bag and close your eyes, the bird's going to go, 'Looks like this show is over, and the next one is boring. I might as well go back to bed.' Then he'll stumble his way back to his nest and totally forget it even happened by morning. Unless he notices the missing piece of pizza, of course."

"And the pepperoni morning breath."

"Definitely that."

I take a deep breath as the war in my stomach calms down to a half-hearted disagreement. I hadn't expected Roman to be so patient. Nikki's ex-husband hadn't been, that was for sure. Maybe I've been wrong about Roman, and he isn't like my old brother-in-law. Maybe he isn't so rigid and overbearing. Not only does he pick up the phone in the middle of the night, but he's understanding. And, actually, helpful. I feel my heart rate returning to normal. I open and close my hand, trying to ease the cramp from my death grip on the phone.

"It surprises me that you have a phobia. I thought nothing could faze you."

"And I didn't think you'd be so patient after being woken up in the middle of the night."

He lets out a chuckling breath, and I can hear the smile in it. "For what it's worth, I'm impressed you were willing to go to this thing with your nephew. That took guts."

"And a lot of razzing from my sisters." I walk back over to my cot and sit down on it.

He chuckles. "That's what siblings are for."

"You really think it's safe for me to go to sleep?" I whisper. I hope so because I am so very exhausted.

"I do."

"Thank you, Roman, for answering in the middle of the night and for talking me down."

There's a long pause before he says, "Thank you for trusting me to."

"I'll see you tomorrow at seven?"

"Tomorrow at seven." I can hear the smile in his voice.

I hang up the phone, and I hear Asher's cot creak as he lifts his head. "Was that your boyfriend? I heard you talking." His voice is so groggy I can barely make out the words.

"I don't have a boyfriend, silly." I reach out and ruffle Asher's hair.

"Not usually, but Roman isn't usual. He's special." Then his head hits his pillow again, and his breaths turn to the rhythmic breathing of sleep.

"He is," I whisper, and then snuggle into my own sleeping bag.

CHAPTER 14
Roman

I PLACE my hand on the small of Bex's back as I guide her toward the restaurant. Kitchen Seven Twelve is my favorite in Gresham, and I'm excited to share it with Bex. I want every part of this date to go perfectly. "Have I told you that you look beautiful tonight?" She's wearing a sky-blue dress that looks amazing with her skin tone and heels that show off her incredible legs.

Even though it's only the third day since Nudge Out was released and the number of downloads is exceeding all our expectations, causing a buzz of energy to constantly run through the office, I still somehow think about Bex more than anything else.

I've especially been unable to stop thinking about her since the moment she called me in the middle of the night last night. Sure, she'd been unreasonably afraid of the birds, but in light of the fear she had, she showed remarkable fortitude. I like a woman who stands courageous in the face of opposition. And I really like the fact that I'm the one she called to calm her fears. More than ever, it makes me want this date to go perfectly.

As soon as the guy at the hostess counter walks over to join the rest of his group, Bex and I step up to it. The woman behind the counter gives a wide smile. "Welcome. Do you have a reservation?"

I nod. "For Roman Powell, in the summer room." The summer room is one of the main reasons why I wanted to bring her to this restaurant specifically. It's a room tucked away in the corner with just one single table. The room is modern, simple, and tastefully decorated. It's the perfect place for us to just go and quietly chat while eating great food, without the chaos of a busy restaurant.

"Oh," the hostess says, her brows pulling together as she looks down at the schedule. She flips to a different page in the folder and then checks something on a tablet. "I am so sorry, sir. It appears that the room was double-booked."

I rub my temple. "When will it be available?"

The woman winces. "Not for about two hours. If you don't mind sitting in the main lobby, though, I can bump you to the front of the wait list and get you seated within just a couple of minutes."

I look at Bex.

"That's totally fine," she says.

So I nod at the woman, and, true to her word, she has us seated in under three minutes. It's not even at a booth—it's a table right in the middle of the room. I'm irritated, but when Bex reaches across the table and places her hand on my arm, my irritation flees.

"Your face looks as beautiful as ever. So I'm guessing there weren't any bird attacks once you fell asleep? You *did* fall asleep, right?"

"I did. And nope, no attacks. You were right—the big bird wandered away as soon as there was nothing to see."

"Presumably to his nest, where he would wake up with pizza breath."

Bex laughs. "I can only assume." She meets my eyes. "Thank you, again, for answering your phone last night."

I smile at her, gazing at those alluring eyes with the rim of gold around the outer edge.

"Since you got to witness my biggest phobia last night, I think it's only fair for you to share yours with me."

"Is that how it works?"

"Yep. By answering the phone last night and not hanging up once you heard my panicked voice, you were thereby agreeing to share your biggest fear tonight. It's all but a legally binding contract."

I raise an eyebrow and try to hold back a smile.

"So spill it."

"Okay. I have automatonophobia."

Bex narrows her eyes at me for a moment, then, instead of asking me what it is, she pulls her phone from her purse and looks it up. I can tell the moment she finds it because she gives me a flat look. "'A fear of human-like figures.' Like, say, of mannequins that are holding up a blanket fort right before they come crashing down on you?"

This time I laugh. The name of that phobia is one of the useless bits of information floating around in my head that I never thought would come in handy. Like knowing the first twenty digits of pi or that a day on Venus is longer than a year on Venus. But today, I'm grateful that little tidbit is in there.

She puts her phone back in her purse. "Okay, now I want the real one."

My biggest fear is probably being judged by my peers as being not good enough. But I'm not about to tell her that. Instead, I go for a fear that makes me feel foolish for sharing but won't make me feel completely exposed. "I have a fear of needles. And, interestingly enough, I don't know what that phobia is called."

"Needles? Huh. So what happens when you need to get blood drawn?"

"Well, I'm not a fan of looking like a wimp, so I just focus on not freaking out. Usually, it works, but every once in a while I..." I glance around the room, embarrassed that someone might hear, "...pass out."

"Really! Here I thought you were invincible, but it turns out you are human."

"And now you know my Achilles heel."

"And you know mine."

The waiter comes over, and I realize we haven't so much as picked up our menus and have to ask her to come back. Once we order and she brings our salads, Bex stabs a forkful of hers and asks, "How is the launch of Nudge Out going?"

"Even better than we had hoped for. The reviews are coming in quite positive, as well. Everly thinks it has a lot to do with your interview, so thank you."

"Since this is the first week of the Eddie Award judging period, I've been slammed with work and haven't had time to even go in and look at the comments. But Nikki assures me that people love you. So thank *you*. It's been helping me out a lot, too."

Everly has told me that, too. That her viewers are loving both me and the product. I went to the comments myself yesterday, and there's a lot more to them than just that. There are haters, of course, but that's to be expected of anything. There are also enough people who are "shipping" us as a couple that it's making me uncomfortable.

I might have enjoyed being on camera and talking about my company and our products, and I might have agreed that sharing a few tidbits about myself was important. And it might boost my ego a bit knowing that Bex is drawn to me enough that other people can see it too. But so many commenters are discussing our relationship. Some are guessing at what point our relationship currently is at. Others are predicting where it might go. Some of them even fast-forward to marriage and kids. It's all too much.

What am I doing?

"So, we're filming our final interview tomorrow," Bex says as she pulls out her phone and gives it a little shake. "Are you ready to see what Nudge Out suggests we do?"

I nod. Honestly, I'm a little worried about what it will suggest. But Bex hadn't given me any notice on what the last two activities were going to be before I showed up to film, so at least with this one, I'll get a heads-up.

Her face lights up as she opens the app. She places the phone on the table between us and meets my eyes, a smile on her face. "Are you ready?"

I nod. "Tap it."

Bex touches the Nudge Me Out button, and the suggestion comes up on the screen. She reads it out loud. "'Are you ready to be nudged out of your comfort zone? Several factors were taken into consideration for this suggestion. Career factors: creative pursuits. Profile factors: a high tolerance for change. Location factors...' And then it lists a bunch of places I've gone since you installed the app on my phone that it saw as relevant."

She scrolls down.

"'Nudge Out suggests you should try... a painting class!' Wow. I hadn't even thought of that. Oh, and look—it brought up painting classes near me that I can sign up for. I am impressed. Very clever. I hope you're up for a painting class, because there's one tomorrow night at eight, and I'm signing us up right now."

That answers my question of what I'm doing and where. Plus, I'm spending time with a woman who is brave, daring, decisive, unpredictable, and who will stand her ground. She also just happens to be beautiful. "Let's do it."

She's putting in our information when I see from my periphery someone coming to our table. I assume it's our waitress or someone from the kitchen bringing the main course, but no—it's a tall, rather good-looking man who is clearly not an employee.

"Well, if it isn't Bex Sterling."

Bex looks up, flinching in surprise. "Derek."

He grabs an empty chair from the table beside us, swings it to where the back of the chair is against the table, and then sits down, resting his folded arms on the back of the chair. "I saw you sitting over here and thought I'd come by to say hi."

Bex looks at him, confusion on her face, but manages to pull her eyes off him and look back to me. "Roman, this is Derek Baylor. He and I went out a few times. Derek, this is my date, Roman Powell."

Derek holds out a hand and I shake it, wishing I could instead just give the guy a friendly shove back to his own table. "Nice to meet you, mate," the guy says. "I like wearing wild socks, too. It looks like our girl, here, has a type." Then he winks.

I really don't like the guy calling Bex "our girl," and I don't like that wink. Or the fact that he's read the *Business Success* article. I don't like the guy at all and wish he'd just walk away already.

"It's good seeing you again, Bex. We need to catch up." And

then the guy just sits there, like he wants us to catch up right now.

I pull at my collar, wishing a cool breeze would find its way through the restaurant and help me out. I'm just opening my mouth to tell the guy to get lost, but Bex beats me to it.

"Sure. Some other time. You'll have to excuse me right now, though. I need to get back to my date."

"Right, right. I wouldn't want to interrupt. Bex," he nods his head at her. "Roman." Another nod. "Enjoy your meal." And then he saunters back to his table.

"Well, if that wasn't strange, I don't know what was," Bex says. "I swear that wasn't even his real personality." She glances back in the direction the guy walked and then shakes her head. "Where were we? Oh yeah." She picks up her phone and taps a few things. "Okay, we are all set for tomorrow at eight. It's about fifteen minutes from here, just inside Portland—not too far from your work, actually. I could meet you at your offices and we could drive to it together. Do you want to grab a quick bite to eat from a deli or something before we go to the class?"

I love this take-charge side of her. How am I going to say no to that?

Our waitress brings our food a moment later and we start eating. About halfway through our meal, someone else walks up to our table.

"Hello, Bex."

Bex nearly chokes on the bite of cod she just took when she looks up. "Justin! Hi. What are you doing here?"

He turns around the chair that the last guy vacated and sits down. "Just visiting my sister. How have you been?"

"I'm good. Roman, Justin Tyler. Justin, Roman Powell. We have also gone on a few dates."

Either this is the strangest coincidence I've ever encountered, or Bex just dates a lot of people in Gresham. I smile and shake the guy's hand to be polite. As soon as the guy leaves, I'll have to ask the waitress if she'll take the extra chair far, far away, so no one else will get any bright ideas.

"My sister just had a baby. Jana—do you remember her? I think the two of you met that time we went to the concert in the park. Anyway, her baby is the cutest thing."

Justin pulls out his phone to show Bex pictures, and I hold in a growl. Can he not see that we're in the middle of a date? Bex glances in my direction and mouths *Sorry* as Justin shows his phone to her.

"Oh, she is adorable."

Then a guy walks up to the other side of the table, and before Bex even turns her attention to him, he grabs an empty chair from a table on that side and sits down. Bex hasn't looked over yet, so he holds out his hand to me. "Hi. My name's Darshan. I've gone on a couple of dates with Bex—thought I'd pop over and say hi."

"Roman," I say as I shake the guy's hand.

Bex looks over, baffled that Darshan is sitting at our table now. "Hi, Darshan. Wow, it's been a while. How are you?"

"I'm good! Living the dream. You're looking fantastic. I catch your show now and then—you're getting more and more popular all the time."

You'd think that Justin would leave when someone else pulls a seat up to the table, but he stays. Of course, having me here hasn't kept him away, so maybe I shouldn't have expected anything different.

Someone from the other side of the restaurant walks over, bringing a chair with him. He plunks it down right between Justin and Bex and takes a seat. "Mind if I join this party?"

Bex closes her eyes a small moment like she's hoping that when she opens them, all this craziness will be gone. It's what I'm wishing for, too. "Roman, everyone, this is Enzo Parks."

Justin holds out a hand. "Past flame of Bex's?"

The guy nods. "Went on three dates. You, too?" After Justin nods back, Enzo looks around the table. "What are we celebrating?"

"A first date between Bex and me," I say, hoping they all get the hint.

They don't. Enzo even flags down the waitress and orders a drink. I just happen to glance over at the hostess's table, where the hostess is looking at our table while a man points at it, and then waves at me. As smooth as can be, the man grabs an extra chair at a table along the way, then sets it down right between me and Darshan. "Hi," he says, tipping his head at me. "I'm Carlos. I used to date Bex."

"Roman. I'm currently dating Bex. As in right this moment."

The guy nods, and we both look at Bex, who hasn't even seemed to notice that Carlos has joined the table because she's talking to a guy who just grabbed the waitress's attention and asked for a chair. Then he asks Bex to scoot over to make room.

"Roman, this is Vaughan. Oh. Carlos. I didn't see you come in." She looks baffled at the seven people now crowding around our table for two. "You all just happened to be here eating at the same time I am here on a date?"

"Saul!"

I turn around to see who Bex's attention got pulled to, just as another man grabs a chair and carries it to our table, squeezing in between me and Justin. He says hello to Bex, then starts introducing himself to everyone else around the table, and each of them tells him their names. If all these guys want the table, they can have it. They can have the rest of the food, too. I just need to free Bex from her adoring ghosts of dates past and go find somewhere quiet to finish our date.

"Stop!" Bex says. "Okay, someone tell me what's going on here. This was definitely not a coincidence."

Everyone is silent for a few moments, and then Justin leans forward. "Check your X notifications."

She pulls out her phone and taps a few things. Her eyes scan the screen for a moment, and then her hand flies to her mouth. She turns to glance at all the people in the restaurant at the other tables, who all seem to be getting a kick out of watching this go down. Several even have phones out, video recording or taking pictures. Then she looks at me.

"Apparently someone—I don't recognize the name—saw Derek come over. The guy recognized us and posted about it."

"What did he say?"

She hesitates a moment before she passes me the phone, and I read the post.

At dinner w/gf & see @TheRealBexSterling eating with #Nudge-Out's Roman Powell. Her old bf pulls up a chair & the look on Roman's face is priceless! Please, X, send anyone Bex has dated to #Kitchen712 to do the same. Repost & tag or text anyone you know. I'll update w/results.

I scroll through the thread—the guy has posted a picture every time a new guy shows up, complete with some commentary on how I react. I look in the direction the guy must've been seated to get the pictures he did and see a man in his upper twenties sitting in a booth across from a woman I can only assume is his girlfriend. The man salutes me. I chuckle and give the guy a nod back. Not to thank him in any way. More as an acknowledgment of a game well-played.

"Well, guys," Darshan says, standing up, "I think that's our cue to leave. Bex, it truly was good to see you again."

Everyone else follows Darshan's lead and stands as well,

returning their chairs from where they got them. Another guy walks up and says, "Aww, am I too late? Did I miss the party?"

"Hi, Jack," Bex says. "And yes, you did."

"Bummer. Hey, anyone want to join me at the bar, since we're already here?"

About half the guys stay and join Jack at the bar, but at least they aren't around our table anymore. Bex still looks a bit flustered, though.

"What do you say we get dessert to go and get out of here?" I ask.

Bex smiles. "That sounds perfect. I'd love that."

Thirty minutes later, we are wrapped in a blanket I had in my trunk and sitting on a bench at my favorite place in the city —in the Tsuru Island part of Main City Park. Beautiful plants and pathways surround us, a creek is close by enough that we can hear its gurgling, the sky is clear so we can actually see the stars, and Bex is snuggled against me.

"You need to try one of the pears with the sauce," Bex says, holding her spoon out to me.

I eat the bite and am surprised at how great it tastes. I've never been a huge fan of pears, so I've never ordered the dessert before. It's good enough that I'll have to order it for myself next time.

"Okay, then you have to try a bite of mine." I get a forkful of my volcano cake, making sure to get some of the molten lava center and feed it to her. I smile when she closes her eyes in blissful contentment. This is definitely better than staying at the restaurant.

She sets her dessert on the bench beside her. "I had fun tonight."

"Even with the craziness?"

"Especially with the craziness."

I set my dessert aside and raise an eyebrow.

"I liked seeing you ruffled." She snuggles back into me. "You handled it well."

I like that she hasn't taken responsibility for them all showing up or felt like she needed to apologize for it happening since she had no control over it. She just sees it as a mutual issue to tackle together. It's refreshing.

Bex sits up straight and turns to me. "The Eddie Awards are coming up."

I brush a lock of hair back from her temple with my fingertips so I can see her beautiful eyes better. "And you are going to knock them dead."

"No, I'm talking about the ceremony itself, where they present the awards. It's in a different major city every year, and this year it's in Portland, so it isn't even far. Will you go with me? I probably won't win, but it'll be fun to get dressed up all fancy for it."

I was excited to be able to spend time with Bex tonight without cameras, but it seems like they follow her wherever she goes. I hate that people took pictures of our date and posted about it. So, the thought of a date where people will be taking pictures not so surreptitiously doesn't sound appealing at all. If it was anyone other than Bex, I would tell them no. But this is Bex. And I care about this award because she cares about it.

"I would love to go with you."

She smiles at me—a smile so brilliant that the stars above can't compete. Then she kisses me, and all my worries about our date becoming public knowledge fade away.

CHAPTER 15

Bex

I'VE BEEN SEEING Roman enough lately that I worry if I'm not careful, he's going to turn into a habit. Like my habit of starting each morning off with one square of fine dark chocolate. It's something I look forward to. Savor. And feel like the day just isn't right when I don't have it.

"Hi," I breathe as he gets into my car. I've dated plenty of guys who wear cologne. Some good-smelling and some not-so-good-smelling. Some wear just a hint, while others seem to take a shower in it. I've also dated plenty of guys who don't wear cologne. Actually, it's not something I normally notice unless it's a bad smell, or one that's too strong, or one that just really doesn't fit the guy.

But when Roman steps into the car, the scent of him comes in with him, and it's glorious. It doesn't even smell like cologne, exactly. It's more like it's just a part of him—a scent that is clean and fresh. Maybe birch? Bergamot? I don't know. Maybe it is cologne, and the guy is just ten levels beyond pro at picking out the right scent. I hope it stays in my car forever and ever. Then, whenever I need a pick-me-up and I can't be around Roman, I can just go sit in my car and breathe in the scent of him.

Wow, I am falling ridiculously hard for him.

"No Enoch today?"

I shake my head as I pull out into traffic. "He has a basketball tournament, and Nikki is at a weekend getaway. I have another backup videographer I sometimes use, but I thought this one could be easily filmed by my friend Tripod there in the back seat. Plus, I figured it might be a little less intimidating to everyone else in the class if there wasn't someone videoing it."

I looked up the address of the painting class earlier in the day. It's in a pedestrian mall with cute shops and plenty of places to eat, and the drive isn't long. Once I get parked, we find the shop where the painting class will be, then head two shops down to a cute little café with outdoor seating.

As soon as we finish ordering, a teenage girl walks up to us, doing a pretty good job of not acting nervous except for the way she fiddles with the keys in her hand. "You're Bex Sterling, aren't you?"

"I am. What's your name?"

"Lanie. I can't believe I'm actually meeting you. I love your show, and I want to start my own someday. I've been watching yours for like two years, obsessing over everything. Can I ask you for some advice about running a business?"

I'm pretty sure I hear Roman make a faint scoffing sound that he tries to hide. I ignore him and say to the girl, "Sure!"

"I start college in the fall, and I was thinking of doing a marketing major and entrepreneurship minor. Do you think that's good? Or would a different major be better? And should I wait until I'm all done with school and have everything ready to start? Or is it better to start now so I can get practice, and just build slowly?"

I answer her questions until the woman behind the counter says, "Excuse me—your order is ready."

The girl thanks me profusely and goes back to join her friends, while Roman and I take our tray outside and find an open table. As Roman takes our sandwiches off the tray and places one in front of each of us, I say, "Did I hear you scoff when she asked for business advice?"

"I just thought it was a strange question because it's not really a business." He hands us each a drink.

"I have a business license and incorporation papers that say otherwise. But I'm curious to know why you think it isn't."

He looks sheepish, like he knows he's in trouble. "I guess it was just because your only employees are your sister and your nephew."

"For a long time, it was just me. And it was still every bit as much of a business as it is now. We both make digital products, Roman. The only difference is that my business gets paid by companies showing ads and yours does by people buying apps." It bothers me that he doesn't seem to have the same respect for my business that he has for his own.

He rubs his hands over his face. "You're right. I apologize— that was very rude of me. Let me make it up to you."

"Ooo. I like the sound of that. Will it involve kissing?"

A smile lifts the corners of his mouth. "There can definitely be kissing. And how about I surprise you at the inn some random evening by showing up with dessert?"

"If it can be pie, then you're on."

In between taking bites of our sandwiches, I tell him a little more about what to expect tonight. We've been working on such short notice, not only to give the Nudge Out app time to collect enough data about me but also because all of the inter- views with Roman have been in addition to my normal produc- tion schedule.

"I called the owner of the shop where we'll have the painting class. There are eight people registered, so we won't be able to interview while the class is going on. But she said that if we can get there a few minutes early, we can film an introduction before it starts, and then film the rest of the interview at the end."

"That sounds great."

The weather is beautiful, and I wish I could just hang out at the diner, chatting and watching the cars and pedestrians go by for hours while I sit close to Roman, leaning my head on his shoulder. But this interview isn't going to film itself.

So the moment we finish, we stand up, collect our trash, and head toward the garbage receptacle. As I'm dumping the tray, the lid of the garbage can catches on the tray, causing me to dump all the crumbs from our sandwiches down my front. I'm just brushing it off and checking to make sure no sauce has jumped ship and is catching a ride on my shirt right before filming when I notice Roman stiffen beside me.

"Dad."

His tone is full of surprise and guilt, like a kid getting caught watching TV when he's supposed to be doing homework. I look up to see a man who, by the strong shoulders and jawline, is very much Roman's dad. The resemblance between the two is uncanny. Except his dad has gray in his sideburns, wrinkles around his eyes, and the aged skin of someone twenty-five or thirty years older, and has clearly spent a much larger percentage of his life not being in touch with his more calm, peaceful side. He is dressed in a suit, and so are the two men and one woman with him.

"Roman! What a surprise to see you here. What brings you to Portland? And with this lovely young lady?"

I stop brushing the crumbs off my blouse and jeans and hope I haven't missed any.

"Dad, this is Bex Sterling." Roman pauses a long moment, like he isn't quite sure what to introduce me as, then goes with, "She is a targeting specialist that we are using to make sure we are reaching the right audience. We just had a dinner meeting to go over some things. Bex, this is my dad, Doctor Richmond Powell the fourth."

"Nice to meet you, Bex Sterling." He reaches out and shakes my hand, then motions to the people standing with him on the sidewalk. "And these are some of my board members—we were just meeting to discuss strategy, as well. Are you an employee of Roman's, or are you freelance?"

I eye Roman. "Freelance."

"Well, then, I might have to see about having you do some work at our company as well. Now if you'll excuse us, we've got a reservation at Grill House." He motions at a restaurant three buildings down, gives us a nod, and then the four of them keep walking while Roman and I head to my car to get my tripod and video camera.

As soon as his dad is out of earshot, I stop next to my car, hands on my hips. "Why didn't you tell him my real job? Or what we were here doing?"

He stops too, turning to me as he lets out a big breath. "Because my dad isn't a nice person. And it's none of his business."

"He seemed nice enough. Are you saying he would've been rude if he knew that I'm a YouTuber?"

"It's more complicated than that."

I look out at nothing in the distance, feeling ruffled about the conversation. I don't know much about his dad at all, and I recognize that there's a lot of history and father/son dynamics between the two that I don't know about yet. But after his scoff when the teenager asked about my business earlier, his hesitation when talking about me to his dad bothers me and makes me feel like Roman doesn't respect my job very much. I look back at him. "Does he know that we've been shooting these interviews?"

"No. And hopefully, he never will. Like I said, he's not a nice guy."

I start walking toward the shop again, arms crossed. I'm not upset because he wants to protect me. It's that it doesn't seem like it's mostly about him protecting me. It seemed more like he'd been embarrassed to tell his dad the truth about me—about my job and about the fact that we aren't here for an audience-targeting meeting.

I need to know how he feels. From the start, I have been worried that he isn't the right guy for me. And then, because of all the ways in which he *is* perfect, I've let down my defenses. But I can't start a relationship with a guy who doesn't value me or my chosen career. So, if those defenses need to go back up, I want to know now—not later, when I'm even more invested. I don't want to experience what happened to my sister.

"Roman, do you respect me, as a YouTuber?"

He stops walking and the look on his face is softer. "I do, Bex. I think you are amazing at it, and I can see why you have so many subscribers and fans everywhere we go. I didn't mean to come off sounding like I didn't." I search his eyes and see truth there. Then he reaches out and pulls me close, like he doesn't care who sees, and kisses my temple.

"Thank you. But…camera…in my ribs."

"Oh!" Roman pulls back, and I adjust the camera strap so it rests in a more comfortable spot.

When we arrive at the shop, I set up my equipment right between our two easels, so our faces will be in frame. Then I shake out my arms and try to clear my head of leftover annoyance before I start to film. Not everyone has a great relationship with their parents. That's all it was.

Both Roman and I put on aprons with the *Paint Date* logos on them and sit down at the spots where we will be painting. Before starting the camera, I look over at Roman, and he gives me that smile that melts my insides, his eyes scanning my face like he really loves what he sees there.

I turn on the camera with my remote and start filming the introduction. I take out my phone and show them what the app suggested when I tapped *Nudge Me Out*, and how it even found a place near me with openings.

"So here we are," Roman says, holding up a paintbrush, "ready to paint. Even though I've never done this before in my life."

"What about art class in school when you were a kid? You never painted then?"

"No, I did. I just didn't paint actual things. Here, we are painting"—he glances at the front where the painting we will be duplicating is placed—"a starry night sky with a couple kissing in front of a full moon.

"I knew how awful my drawing skills were, so in school, instead of painting whatever we were supposed to paint, I just painted 'abstract art.' I found that if I could tell my teachers a good story about the meaning behind the painting or about the choices I made, they always accepted it. I was either really good at convincing them that I knew what I was doing, or they just knew that there was no help for me and were glad I was at least picking up the brush. Based on the art history classes I took later on, where we discussed actual abstract art, I think it was the latter."

I laugh, shaking my head. I'm grateful that he is willing to share personal things in our interviews now, and I'm impressed that he does it without much prodding at all. He is giving me exactly what I need for this interview, just like he has for the three others. And he is still here doing them with me—he didn't quit after the first one like I worried he would. He must trust that my final edited video will be something he's proud of. Surely that means that he respects my job and that the incidents today were just a fluke.

Right?

"How about you?" he asks. "Is this new for you?"

"Not completely new, but it has been a good long while since I last picked up a brush."

We chat for a minute about the Nudge Out app and the things it is doing for people who have been using it. Roman even tells a few stories of people who have contacted them to let them know the new things they have tried and how it has boosted their confidence in doing hard things.

People who are taking the class with us start trickling in, so I stop the recording and move the tripod behind us so viewers can see our paintings as we work and see the instructor as she teaches. It will all be edited down to just the highlights.

Roman rolls his shoulders. He sits on the stool that is placed in front of his easel, one foot resting on the bottom rung, his knee bouncing.

"Oh my goodness, you're nervous."

"About having your viewers see what I'm painting? No. What gave you that idea?" Roman keeps his eyes on the painting at the front.

A smile plays on my lips. Normally, Roman shows only confidence, whether he has to fake it or not. Seeing this anxious side of him is endearing. Maybe because he is actually letting me see that side. It wasn't so long ago that he wouldn't have. "Getting nudged a little too far out of your comfort zone, huh?"

He turns on his stool so he is facing me and leans forward before whispering, "What do you say we keep that our little secret?" And then he kisses me. It's a lingering peck on the lips, but it's enough to make me feel lightheaded.

That bouncing of his knee, though, continues to tell me how nervous he is. This interview isn't going to go well if the guy I'm interviewing is so distracted by his thoughts of messing up something he isn't familiar with.

"What about the painting are you least looking forward to?"

He nods toward the front. "The people."

I look at the painting at the front that we will be recreating. The focal point is definitely the moon. In front of it is a woman and a man facing each other, both standing with their hands behind their backs and bent at the waist, leaning forward to kiss. "Even though they're just silhouettes and not very big?"

He nods. "I paint abstract art when drawing is involved, remember?"

"How about this." I push our easels a little closer together and turn my canvas so it is taller up and down instead of sideways, then do the same for Roman's. "We'll each paint half. Since the couple is right in the middle, you'll only have to paint the girl, and I'll paint the guy."

"Okay. But my girl is going to look like a stick figure still. I hope you're okay with that."

The instructor has given us each a big circle that's sticky, like tape, and she demonstrates by putting the circle in the middle of her canvas where the moon will be. Then she puts paint right onto the canvas—black in the top corners, then purple, then a deep blue, then a lighter blue. She shows how to first spread the paint and blend the colors slightly, and then use a stippling brush to make the paint look like the night sky.

Roman and I start by trying to each put our half of the moon in the right place on our canvases and have it line up correctly so it'll still look like an actual circle. As we struggle, the instructor comes around to see how everyone is doing. When she sees we are each doing half, she pushes our easels together so that our canvases are touching. "You must have them touching if you want them to look right."

If this were a date, I'd be all for that. But this is an interview where I am interviewing the CEO of a company, not interviewing a date for my viewers to weigh in on. Not that the interview is supposed to be stuffy and professional—I want it to be fun. I'll just have to work extra hard to not show how attracted I am to the man.

The painting is going pretty well. The night sky is kind of like abstract art, so Roman actually appears to be enjoying himself. And so am I. We're both working on getting the top middle part to look right, and we are only a few inches apart. "You smell so amazing," I breathe. Then I suck in a breath and look back at the camera. "Nikki's going to have to edit that out."

A smile tugs at his lips, and then he closes the last couple of inches between us and gives me a peck on the lips. "While she's at it, she should probably edit that out, too."

I look at this man's beautiful face before I go back to work. I love the feeling of both of us being side by side, working together on the same project, helping each other to figure out what parts need to change and what parts are perfect like they are. This painting is definitely turning out a lot better with both of us working together than it would be if either of us were working apart.

And there are definitely a lot of parts Nikki is going to have to edit out so I don't totally give away how I feel about this man.

Our instructor has us remove the tape circle, revealing the huge, white moon in the night sky. Seriously, we could be done right now and I would call our painting a job well done. But apparently, the moon has to be painted, and the instructor shows us how to make it look like the moon. Then we paint black along the bottom for the ground, with little blades of grass coming up from it.

I am painting the grass at the edge near Roman's. I move my brush back to get more paint right as he leans in to paint the fine blades, and my paintbrush goes right across his cheek.

He turns to me, a giant black streak on his cheek, like a cat's whisker, and I gasp. "I am so sorry."

He doesn't say a word—he just reaches out and paints what I am pretty sure looks like a cat's nose on my nose. Then he goes back to work like nothing has happened.

I turn to the camera. "I guess that evens the score."

We watch as the instructor shows us how to paint the silhouettes of the couple about to kiss.

"Well," I say, "remember how the part of painting that you hated most as a kid was drawing the picture on it before painting? You don't have to draw on this one."

"I'm not sure 'can't draw it first' is any better than 'can't draw at all.'" He motions at the instructor. "How did she even know where to use the black paint to make it look like a person without drawing it first?"

I study our beautiful moon and night sky. "Maybe we should paint something other than people, then."

Forty-five minutes later, after finishing our paintings, using the handheld fans to dry them, and filming the end of our interview, we walk out to my car with our masterpieces.

Roman holds his up in the glow of the streetlight and studies it. "I can't believe you had us paint two cats instead of two people."

"Oh, come on. You know it was easier than painting a person."

"I painted a black avocado."

"But a black avocado with cat ears and a tail, so it counts as a cat."

I smile as he carefully places his painting in the back seat of my car. He might not admit it out loud, but he is proud of it. Just like I wouldn't admit out loud that even though this is an interview and not a date, I have still enjoyed myself more than I have on any date I've gone on with anyone else.

CHAPTER 16
Roman

I WALK OUT of my office building and immediately call Bex. Sometime over the past several weeks, calling Bex first whenever I have something I want to share has just become what I do.

"Well?" she asks, forgoing a hello, eager anticipation coloring the single word.

"They signed on the dotted line. It's official."

Her excited shout is loud enough that I have to pull the phone away from my ear for a moment. "Roman! I'm so thrilled for you!"

Adrenaline is coursing through my body, and it makes me want to run and leap over things. Like a fence. My car. My office building. The investors said they wanted to invest in my company around the time that the third interview with Bex aired, but I held back my own celebrations until the paperwork was done and everything was official. Now, though. Now I am letting myself be fully thrilled.

"I couldn't have done it without you, Bex." I unlock my car, start it, and let the car's Bluetooth take over the call.

"I know." I can hear the smile in her voice through the car's speakers.

"And not just because of the interviews. Although that did make a big difference with them. But I couldn't have done it without you staying up to brainstorm with me and pushing me to try things with my business that I hadn't tried before. I owe you."

"You agreed to put on a monkey suit and spend hours at an awards gala with me on Saturday. I think that is enough to call us even."

As I pull onto the road and head toward Interstate 84 to make the thirty-minute drive to my parents', I chuckle softly. I am equal parts dreading the gala and excited about it. Bex assumes that the parts I am dreading are the suit and the small talk. But I like dressing nice, and I like talking to people.

I'm not about to correct her because then I'd have to tell her the real reason—that I'm worried about what my peers and my family will think if they know Bex and I are dating. Not because she isn't the most amazing person on the planet. But because I know that they think like I used to, so not only will they see her job as not being legit, but they'll see it as frivolous. Unimportant. I realize now how wrong I was in thinking that way. But they haven't had those same realizations, and they just happen to be an extremely judgmental group of people.

Not that they won't find out eventually, but I want to keep it our little secret for as long as possible. As long as I can see Bex often. I need her in my life like I need food, business projects, and sleep. Actually, I could do without sleep if it meant seeing her more often.

"Is it weird that I kind of miss filming the interviews?" I ask her.

I can almost hear that brilliant smile of hers through the phone as she says, "I think you just miss me."

"True. Are you sure I can't see you tomorrow?"

"Not unless you want to crash the female entrepreneur's social."

"And I've got this business reception at my parents' tonight."

"Saturday it is, then. But on the plus side, you'll get to tell your dad about the investors tonight. He's going to be pretty proud of you for that."

I smile just thinking about it.

———

I arrive at my parents' early enough that no guests have arrived yet, but not so early that they don't already have April, the college student they always hire whenever they host a function, on staff to answer the door.

As soon as I say hello to April, I hear the quick clacking of my mom's heels on the hardwood floor.

"Roman," she says, arms outstretched. I give her a hug, and then she pushes back on my shoulders to meet my eyes. "You're here early. Is something up?"

"I just wanted to share some news before everyone got here. Is Dad busy?"

"He's in his office."

We both walk down the hall and step through the doorway onto the plush carpet. My dad looks up at us from where he sits behind a mahogany desk, shelves full of books and business awards framing him.

"I had my final meeting with the investors today." I try to play it cool, but I can't stop the smile that forms on my face.

Dr. Richmond Powell IV, D.B.A. stands. "And?"

"We exceeded the requirements they had set forth by so much that they decided to invest fifty percent more than they had originally offered. We signed the papers less than an hour ago."

"That is fantastic news!" He comes around the table to shake my hand. Then, he actually pulls me into a hug—something that happens so infrequently I can't remember when the last time was. "Good work, son."

My mom gives me a hug and tells me congratulations as well, and then my dad motions to one of the padded chairs in front of the desk. "Sit, sit. I want to hear all about it."

Then my dad actually sits in the other chair instead of going around his desk to sit behind it. He never sits beside me like this—he always takes the spot where he has the advantage of more power. So I tell him all about the presentation I gave them last week, conveniently leaving out the part about how the investors wanted me to do more things like the interviews with Bex.

"I am so proud of you."

It feels amazing to hear my dad say those words after having gone so long since I last heard them.

My dad turns to my mom. "It looks like I have a river rafting trip to plan!"

Seeing the excitement on my dad's face is going to fuel me for a very long time. I'd been thinking I wouldn't ever be able to earn the trip, but I finally have.

More than a dozen of my peers are at the reception—mostly CEOs, business partners, and other business moguls my dad knows—and every single one of them has brought their significant other. Even my brother, Legend, who broke up with Briza a week and a half ago, has brought a woman he's dating. Not only do I feel very alone and miss Bex terribly, but I also feel very guilty about not having invited her. Especially since I knew she was free and wanted to see me.

But I am so worried that people will start asking questions

and things won't go well. And I certainly don't want Bex to have to experience it.

Everyone is standing in clusters in my parents' back gardens and patio, drinks in hand, chatting with each other. I make a point to go from group to group, being friendly and chatting, so I never appear to be alone. It might help appearances, but it doesn't help my longing for a partner by my side.

I wasn't even aware of how much I wanted a partner until I started dating Bex. Before, I just thought I needed a date—and an eventual wife. I've dated plenty, but never anyone who I could see as a partner. Clearly, I've been dating the wrong people.

I pull out my phone when I hear the ding and see another email notification from Tarak about being on his social media panel. I really need to stop procrastinating the inevitable and tell the guy no.

I slide the phone back into my pocket and join in on a conversation with my brother, Drake, Drake's wife, Claire, Lucia, a friend who is the CEO of another app company, and her husband, along with one of my dad's board members and the guy's wife. When the conversation lulls, I say to Drake, "How did things go with that company you've been creating the business strategy for?"

"And…" Drake says, dragging out the word, "new topic! Let's talk about memes that have made you laugh lately. Did you all see the one with Roman and Bex Sterling from *Bexlandia* staring at the deer, and she leans over to him and says, 'I'm pretty sure people have been feeding this one.'"

I wince as everyone in our little group laughs. My brother was frustrated with that company the last time we talked, so I should've known not to ask. But throwing me under the bus to get the conversation off him is a low blow.

The sentence Drake had said by itself didn't warrant such a

hearty laugh from everyone, which means they have all seen the meme. Great. I shoot my brother a look.

"My favorite, though," Lucia says, "was the one that read *The moment I learned Santa wasn't real*, above an animated gif of the blanket fort coming down on you two."

The six of them are laughing enough that it's drawing people from other little groups to join the conversation. I glance at my dad, who is deep in conversation over by the camellias. Good. I just need him to stay there.

"I liked the one with the mannequin," Lucia's husband, Mateo, says. "Did you guys see it? It was a still shot of Roman looking at the mannequin like it was one of those stone angels from *Dr. Who* and it was going to attack him if he looked away. At the bottom, it said, *My reaction when my friend who just joined a multi-level marketing company says he wants to come over and chat.*"

Heat has been slowly building in my face and I'm sure it's to the point where it's visible to everyone.

"Have you seen the one with him smashing the pickleball?" someone asks from behind me. I don't even have a chance to turn to see who it is before my buddy, Shreedhar, says, "I liked the one even more that just loops his reaction when he aimed wrong and sent the ball right at Bex."

"How do you even have time to do interviews like that?" a fellow CEO, Archer, says. "My business keeps me so busy that I don't think I could ever pull that off."

I grind my teeth. Archer doesn't actually want to know the answer—it's an underhanded dig at the way I run my business, insinuating that I'm letting my CEO duties slip.

"I like the ones where people are shipping them as a couple," Legend's new girlfriend says. We haven't even been officially introduced yet, so I don't even know her name, nor had I noticed my brother join the crowd around me. "Like the one where someone Photoshopped them into a boat on Mirror Lake with a blanket as the sail."

Someone starts telling about one that has something to do with painting and cats, but I don't hear it because my dad has noticed that most of the people have gathered into one group and are laughing, so now he is on his way over. This cannot be good.

He is all smiles, but just under the surface, I can tell he doesn't like not being in on whatever is happening. "It sounds like all the fun is over here."

Several people nod, all while a chorus of "Did you see the one where…" continues around us.

"What am I missing?"

One of the guys my dad golfs with claps Richmond on the shoulder. "Didn't you know? Your boy here is an internet sensation!"

I wish they would all stop. Or better yet, that they would've never started. I wish that my dream of none of them ever seeing a single thing about my interviews had come true. I wish for a lot of things, including the ability to teleport so I could get myself out of here instantly.

Instead, everyone fills in my dad, and with as much as everyone is laughing, you'd think this is a college frat party instead of a respectable business reception.

"Richmond," Mom says, "could I get you to help me bring out some more refreshments for our guests?"

Dad nods, and then he leans close to me. "As soon as you can slip away, I want to talk to you in my office."

Then he heads into the house. Not to help bring out refreshments—they've hired servers for the evening. Mom has probably noticed the look on his face that says he's about to make a scene in front of everyone, so she's getting him away from the crowd. I give him seven minutes to cool down, knowing that's about the length of his patience before he starts fuming that I haven't come in.

When I walk in through the patio door, Mom gives my shoulders a quick squeeze. "Good luck, honey." Then she slips back outside to our guests.

When I enter Dad's office, he's sitting behind the desk. No more sitting side by side—this time, he wants to intimidate. And great—he's looking at his laptop. I don't even need to guess what he's been watching.

Why do I feel like a kid again, about to get into trouble for bad grades or for toilet-papering the boys' restroom that one time in third grade?

Dad just keeps looking at whatever he's watching for several excruciatingly long minutes, not even acknowledging that I've walked into the room. Eventually, he pushes the laptop aside. Which, honestly, isn't any better, because now his eyes are piercing into me. And he still isn't talking—just studying me. He has always been the master at getting the upper hand and making anyone else in the room feel like an ant. A little tiny ant who just spilled milk on the floor.

Finally, he speaks. "I thought you had learned a hard lesson with that *Business Success* interview. But then you went and made a fool of yourself on a stage with two million viewers. A stage that can be accessed anywhere in the world, no less. And that's not even counting the number of people who saw the memes once they went viral. I can't say I've ever been more disappointed in you."

He wants me to respond. But I have no idea what kind of response he could possibly want. So I go for the truth, to see how that goes. "Those investors who just gave LivenUP a pile of money? They liked the *Business Success* interview. They said they would only invest if they could see more of that. Of me showing the spark that told them LivenUP was going places and that I was going to lead them there. Those interviews I did showed them that. That was why they invested."

Dad pounds his fist on the desk, making everything on it—and my heart—jump. "You carry the Powell name, Roman! That means something. People hear that name and they know they are going to get someone who is a professional through and through. That name is a gift, and you need to treat it as such."

He clenches his jaw, giving me a look of disgust that he has perfected over the years. "Instead, you're trying to bring down the family. You don't change who you are just because a group of investors wants to give you a pile of money to do so."

All I can think of is how I haven't changed who I am—I've let the real me come forward in those interviews. *That* was a gift. One I hadn't been expecting that Bex had given to me.

Dad turns his attention back to the laptop, clicking a few things. Then he turns back to me. "That audience targeting specialist I saw you with a few weeks ago—that was her, wasn't it? She's the woman behind all of this."

"She is the producer of *Bexlandia*, yes." I ignore the flinch on his face when I mention *Bexlandia*. "She wasn't 'behind' it—we went to her to ask for the interview when my head of social media and marketing identified her audience as our target audience for Nudge Out."

"Then you need to fire your head of social media and marketing and do what you need to do to get those interviews taken down."

Yeah, like I'm going to do either of those things.

He studies me for an uncomfortably long moment. "You're dating this woman." It's a statement, not a question, but it's clear he doesn't know the answer. He's fishing. But I'm done hiding our relationship.

"Yes."

Richmond lets out a long, slow breath. "Is it a fling?"

"No."

"Roman, I don't think I need to remind you about the kind of woman you are expected to marry. She needs to be respectable and have a respectable career—not name her company something like *Bexlandia* and post simpleton content to a simpleton site. She needs to be someone who will respect the Powell name and the kind of public image we need to maintain."

"Dad, I—"

Richmond stands up. "I don't want to hear it, son." He walks to the door but pauses before he steps out. "Oh, and the Columbia River trip is off. You can see yourself out."

CHAPTER 17

Bex

"OH MY EXCLAMATION POINTS, I can't believe how beautiful you look!" Peyton says. She is working on my hair for the awards ceremony, and my sister, Nikki, is putting the finishing touches on my makeup while I sit at the vanity in my bedroom.

Nikki nods. "I hope you win. But, girl, you are going to leave a trail of scorch marks all the way up to the stage if you do."

I look down at my silky, red, form-fitting, full-length dress. It isn't too low in the front, but the back does dip down quite a bit. "Do you think it's too much?"

"I think it's exactly enough," Nikki says. "Your entire female audience is going to be going insane experiencing this vicariously through you—living the dream, getting dressed up all fancy, looking incredible, and having everyone talking about how awesome the thing you created is. I know I am."

"Yep," Peyton says as she twists one of my curls to lay just right. "Especially since they know you well enough to know how down-to-earth you really are. I mean, they've been with you at the drugstore as you were getting Tylenol and socks. Your viewers know you are practically them."

I laugh. The drugstore thing wasn't some calculated move or part of some bigger-picture video I was posting. I had just remembered I needed to tell them about an event coming up where viewers could join me, and I happened to be in the drugstore when I remembered, so that's where I did the Facebook live video. "That's me. Tylenol and sock girl. Oh, hey, speaking of drugstores, guess who I saw when I was in Hillsboro on Monday? Brant. He looked awful, in case you were wondering."

Peyton looks at Nikki. "Is that your ex-husband?"

"The one and only."

"Oh," Peyton says. "I bet he looked awful. He lost you, after all."

Nikki just shakes her head as she awkwardly leans around Peyton to brush some bronzing powder on me while trying not to let her pregnant belly get in the way. "Stop. You all don't have to say that anymore. I am married to Dylan now, so what Brant looks like is completely irrelevant. I don't need his life to be awful for mine to be amazing."

I hold perfectly still while they work on me. "Although it probably is awful because the guy is a jerk. I'm so glad you found Dylan."

"Me, too. I just wish I hadn't thrown away all those years dating Brant and being engaged and married to him. I should've listened to you all when you warned me that he was a jerk or paid more attention to the warning signs. I wasted a lot of my life on him."

Is that what I'm doing with Roman? I had been convinced that he was a jerk from the beginning and had told myself to stay away. But then he thoroughly swept me off my feet. Am I being just like Nikki had been back when she was dating Brant and ignoring all the warning signs?

Well, I haven't been ignoring them, exactly. I've been calling him on them. Like when he'd scoffed when the girl had asked for business advice. Then I ignored them. Kind of like how I've ignored how distant and clipped his responses have been ever since he called to say the deal with the investors had been finalized a couple of days ago.

"Stand up, sis. Let's take a look at you."

I look in my full-length mirror. This dress really is incredible, and I still can't believe I found it. Especially because the red is the perfect tone for my skin color. Peyton has worked miracles with my hair—it has big chunky curls pulled up beautifully, making my neck look pretty awesome if I do say so myself.

And my makeup makes me look like I'm practically glowing. Not in a shiny "use me as a beacon to guide in lost ships" way. In an "I have so much awesome inside me, it's bursting out the only way it knows how—by making my skin glow" way. Which I will take any day of the week.

"You two are miracle workers, and I am so lucky to have you!"

Peyton squeals. "Oh, my stars and stripes, you are so pretty! Let's go show you to Addison and Ian and Timini!"

Nikki and Peyton run out of the room and race down the stairs to get the others, so by the time I make it to the top of the stairs, all five of them are standing in a half-circle at the bottom, looking up at me.

I'm wearing four-inch heels, so I walk down the stairs a little slower than normal. With how dressed up I am and descending at this speed, I feel like it's either prom or a debutante thing, not just a prestigious web show award thing.

They all start *ooh*-ing and *ahh*-ing, so I stop for a dramatic pose. Timini snaps a picture on her phone.

"Okay, stop, guys. This is weird." I make it the rest of the way down the stairs.

"Seriously, Bex," Addison says, "you look absolutely beautiful."

Timini nods. "Stunning."

"You look ready to go on stage and win an award," Ian says.

"I still think you should've gotten a limo to drive you there." Peyton goes to the window by the door and moves the curtain aside. She claps her hands. "Oh, he's here!"

I turn to face the door as Peyton opens it wide. Roman had just been lifting his arm to knock and freezes when he sees me. Which seems appropriate, since I'm doing the same. He just looks so amazing in his suit! It's perfectly fitted and shows off those strong shoulders and arms, and his trim physique. He is one very beautiful man. I'm not going to be able to take my eyes off him all night.

I take a few steps toward him.

"Wow," he breathes. "You look incredible."

I come one step closer, to where we are only inches apart. "Right back atcha."

"You made my heart skip a beat."

I smile as I put my arms around his neck. "That sounds dangerous. You should probably get that looked into."

"Oh, I did. And I have a diagnosis."

"Yeah?"

He wisely bypasses my lipstick and places a soft kiss on my neck, right next to my ear, and whispers, "That I am very lucky to be on your arm tonight."

"Alright, alright, go already," Nikki says.

"Break a leg!" Peyton yells. "Do you say 'break a leg' for

this? Probably not, because you have to climb stairs to get on the awards stage. Um…go win and don't trip!"

I laugh. "Thanks, Pey."

We walk out of the inn to the sounds of everyone wishing me luck. Roman opens my car door for me and once I'm seated, he makes sure the end of my dress is all inside before he shuts my door and goes around to his side to get in.

On the way to Portland, we talk about random things, but something is off with Roman. Instead of our chatting being easy, like it usually is, his answers are short, and my back hurts from carrying the conversation. So I eventually stop trying. Because, truthfully, I'm feeling a bit off, too. I've had a nagging feeling for weeks that I'm making a mistake by dating Roman. Until now, I've been ignoring it. But since Nikki put it into words, I can't stop thinking that there might be warning signs I'm ignoring.

Once we pull onto Morrison Bridge and cross the Willamette River, though, the excitement for the evening really starts to build. We go around the loop and onto Pacific Highway, and moments later, we're pulling up to the Portland Marriott Downtown Waterfront hotel.

We follow the signs posted for the Eddie Awards to a valet who is waiting to take the car. Roman once again opens my door, then holds my hand and helps me out. I've never been to the awards ceremony before, but I've always pored over the pictures, imagining what it would be like to be here.

My imagination hadn't quite captured what it would actually feel like. So, although I know there will be a red carpet lined with photographers, it feels so surreal to walk down it, hand-in-hand with Roman. My goal with *Bexlandia* hasn't ever been to win an Eddie—it's always been to connect with my audience authentically and to encourage them to seek out the awesome in their own lives. But winning an Eddie Award is still on my bucket list, and I'm going to savor every second here.

When we get to the spot where we pose for pictures, Roman gives my hand a squeeze and then lets go. He brings his lips close to my ear and breathes, "Knock 'em dead."

I walk to the mark and pose, cameras flashing all around. After adjusting my pose a few times, each time waiting for pictures to be taken, I wave Roman over to join me. I definitely want pictures of him beside me, looking so fine in his tux. He shakes his head, though, and calls out, "This is your moment to shine."

So I motion a bigger *get-over-here* arm gesture, and he heaves out a breath before straightening and walking to me. When he gets to me, I ask in a quiet voice, "Do you not want to be in pictures?"

Roman shakes his head. "No, it's fine."

We smile and pose, and then I thank the photographers and head toward the door leading into the hotel.

Once inside, we make our way into the Oregon Ballroom, and I immediately gasp, a tingling sensation spreading through my whole body. "My goodness, it's gorgeous."

Round tables fill the room, with floor-length silver table-cloths and blue napkins. The centerpieces are beautiful white and silver flowers with a miniature Eddie Award trophy rising from the center. The back of the stage is an impressive structure with tall, textured plexiglass windows with blue and purple lights behind. An attendant leads us to our seats, which are perfect. Close to the stage and facing it so we won't have to turn our chairs around when the ceremony starts.

Once I set my handbag at my seat, Roman and I go around the room, chatting with all the other attendees—many of whom are YouTubers I know who create many different genres of video content—until everyone arrives and it's time for the meal to be served.

I lean in close to Roman as we sit at our table. "Is everything okay? You've been seeming really distant and hesitant all evening."

"Everything is fine." He gives me a full, beautiful smile. "Enjoy your evening! You've worked hard for this."

By the time our waiter clears away our salads, it becomes even more clear that something is up with Roman. He still isn't being himself, and I can't seem to think of anything else. Did he get bad news? Did something go wrong with the investors? Is this the shield he had up when we first met about the interviews, or is this something else?

"For the lady," the waiter says as he places the entrée I chose in front of me, "wild-caught northwest salmon with roasted yellow beets, foraged mushrooms, and fried Brussel sprouts. And for the gentleman," he places a plate in front of Roman, "Painted Hills Ranch grass-fed grilled ribeye steak with potato puree, winter squash, and a demi-glace."

I look up at the waiter. "Thank you. This looks delicious."

During the meal, Roman and I chat with our table mates, one of whom is also up for an award but in a different category than I am. We mostly talk about the awards, our shows, and the roles the others at the table play.

Roman takes a sip of his drink. "So, what kinds of perks come from winning an Eddie?"

His question is aimed at Tatum, the woman at our table who also has a YouTube channel, so she answers. "I've seen Eddie winners get more than a million new subscribers. These awards can give you so much exposure that it leads to interviews, guest spots on other big channels, and sometimes even book deals."

I glance at Roman. Why does it seem like he isn't okay with that?

When all of the entrées have been cleared from the tables and all of the desserts—cheesecake with a blackberry sauce drizzled over it—are served, the ceremony starts with the organizers giving a few speeches. Then it's time for the awards themselves.

I've been thrilled to be a finalist. It has already given me a significant boost in subscribers and views of all of my videos. That, in itself, has been amazing. I haven't even let myself dream that I might win because I don't want my hopes dashed. This is my first year as a finalist, and creators are rarely bestowed with the award their first year.

I totally and completely think I'll be cool as a tall glass of milk when they start announcing the finalists in my category. With zero expectation of winning, that's how it's supposed to be, right? I know and admire all four of the other finalists, so my plan is just to cheer on whichever of my peers is announced as the winner.

Yet my heart is pounding and my breathing is shallow, making me feel lightheaded. Roman gives my hand a squeeze, so I look over at him. His confident smile is just what I need to convince my body to take a few normal breaths.

"And the winner is…" One of the two presenters behind the podium opens an envelope and pulls out the card inside. She leans in close to the microphone. "Bex Sterling with *Bexlandia!*"

Did I really just hear my name? Is it a fluke? Did they say the wrong name? Everyone at my table is motioning for me to stand up or go to the front, so I stand in a daze. Roman gives my hand one last squeeze, and I make my way to the stage to give an acceptance speech I didn't even begin to plan.

CHAPTER 18
Roman

For as surprised as Bex was when they called out her name as the winner, she sure seems prepared when she walks to the podium to give her acceptance speech. Maybe she's just that good at public speaking without preparing.

As I watch her on the stage, talking about why she started *Bexlandia* and about all the people who support her in her dream, I start to grasp what a monumental feat she has accomplished. My heart swells with pride. What she has achieved is rather incredible, and I am so impressed with everything that she is and everything she's done. I'm glad I've gotten this glimpse into a business I hadn't known much about at all until I met Bex.

She thanks the people who were instrumental in her getting the award—like her sisters and her roommates, who are regularly a part of her show, and especially Nikki, who makes magic out of what Bex hands her. And, of course, her nephew videographer, Enoch.

"And I need to thank Roman Powell, who is with me here tonight. Against his better judgment, he said yes to a series of four interviews and a whole lot of things neither of us expected. Like being chased down by a murderous deer who felt the need to protect his territory, being attacked by a blanket-shrouded mannequin, and being here together tonight."

The audience all chuckles before she goes on to finish her speech.

How am I simultaneously feeling win-the-Powerball lucky to be Bex's plus one for such an important award and so uneasy that she is making our relationship public? With how far the memes of people "shipping" us have spread, I can't imagine how much the news of us actually dating will spread.

———

I walk arm-in-arm with Bex into the Columbia Room, where the after-party is being held. The room is smaller but still grand, less elegant but more festive, and the lights are lower but flashing more. Like a nightclub, but although I can feel the bass in my chest, it isn't so loud that conversation is obliterated. A bar and refreshments table sits at the back of the room, with small standing-height tables dotting the outer edge of the room.

I enjoy going around with Bex to talk to creators she has met at conferences or conventions, ones she has chatted with online but not in person, as well as those she has just admired from afar. This is so different from the business receptions and parties I go to. The mood here is more light and fun. I'm guessing that the people here are more in direct competition with each other than I am with the business friends I get together with, yet there doesn't seem to be an air of competition here. It's filled with people who are all trying to build one another up. I've never seen anything like it.

"Jules!" Bex says as she moves around a crowd to hug someone she is obviously friends with. I feel like I should know her, too, and not knowing her exposes a huge hole in my pop culture knowledge.

Bex introduces me to her.

"So good to meet you," Jules says as she shakes my hand. "I have a racquetball background, too, and I've also been accused of hitting a pickleball a little too hard."

"You watched my show?" Bex asks.

"Of course I did! I love your show. And I've been a fan of Roman's ever since his *Business Success* interview, so I doubly couldn't miss it."

The three of us chat for a few minutes. I'm really starting to enjoy myself and forget about all the worries that have been creeping in.

Until I see the two photographers taking pictures. I turn my back toward them, hoping I can just use that tactic all night.

"Anyway, I am thrilled you won," Jules says. "You are going to be amazed at how much more visible you'll be. I nearly doubled my subscriber count the year I won."

"Doubled!"

"Yeah. It was insane."

One of the cameramen has made it to our section of the room, so I move around to Bex's other side to still have my back to the man. Bex shoots me a confused look but keeps the conversation going.

Then, she looks out to the people dancing in the middle of the room and turns to me. "Come dance with me."

I join her, but I definitely don't feel at home on the dance floor, dancing to the fast music. Sure, I was great at the choreographed dance routines of my youth, but it doesn't really translate into real-world fast dancing. The business get-togethers I go to never involve dancing to fast music, and it always makes me feel like a remote control toy robot whose controller is in the hands of a toddler.

The thought of the people I normally hang out with being someplace like this is laughable. They're all a bunch of hard-working CEOs and business consultants and strategists. They all seem to think that the only way to be successful is to work all the time. If they see pictures of me here, dancing like I've lost the ability to control my own arms and legs in a place that looks more like a club than a respectable business gathering, half of them are never going to let me live it down. The other half are going to quietly lose all respect for me and make underhanded comments about it.

It's not that my friends never have fun—they do. When they schedule it, and always in more respectable ways. Like playing golf. Or going yachting. Or having donuts brought into the office on National Donut Day.

Having pictures of me, trying to dance, out there for everyone to see is not an option. So I try to subtly move us toward the end of the room away from the photographer.

Is this going to be my life if I keep dating Bex, especially now that she's won? Am I going to have to constantly try to keep our relationship and everything we do together from being a big thing online?

Guiding Bex toward the other end of the room, though, is a bad idea, because it leads us right down to the area where the second photographer is. And now that I'm closer, I see that this one is the photographer who took my pictures that they placed alongside my interview and on the cover of *Business Success* magazine. And not too far away is Tarak, the man who interviewed me, talking with one of the winners in a different category. I quickly move to where a crowd of about five people blocks us from the interviewer's line of sight.

Of course, Tarak and his cameraman are here for this—all of the finalists are business owners, after all. Even though I hadn't expected them to be here, even a little bit, it makes sense.

I definitely need to stay away from them. From the email I got from Tarak a month after that issue came out, I know that the issue with me on the cover had their second biggest circulation numbers. If they see me, they will want to talk to me, and they might want to mention something about me being here with Bex. Even if they only mention it on their social media and not in their magazine, it will get back to my dad. Anything related to *Business Success* will get back to him.

The words my dad said to me two nights ago are so fresh they're still running in a constant loop in my head. How I made a fool of myself in Bex's interviews, and how he has never been more disappointed in me. How I'm not living up to the professionalism required of someone with the last name of Powell, and how any serious relationship needs to be with someone who has a respectable career, someone who will not bring down the Powell name.

Yet, here I am, two days later, at a ceremony where they give out awards for placing "simpleton content on a simpleton site." And the channel that won in her category is the channel where I "made a fool of myself" for all the world to see.

Tarak spots us and heads in our direction. So I do a spin move that takes us out of his line of sight.

Bex sees the interviewer, though, and apparently isn't fooled at all by what I've done. She stops right where she is, a hand on her hip. "What is up with you tonight?"

I try to act like my mind isn't full of everything I heard from my peers and my dad on Thursday night, but she isn't buying it. Instead, she grabs hold of my hand and leads me to the doors, out of the party, and into the triangular space just beyond.

"Why have you been such a jerk tonight? I wouldn't have pegged you as someone who would get jealous of another person's success, but maybe I was wrong."

"What? No. It's not that at all. I am so proud of you, and I'm so thrilled you won." I do not want to have this conversation with her tonight. Or ever. This is her night, and all of my frustrations about what everyone I know thinks about me dating Bex are irrelevant. So instead of bringing up any of that, I say, "I just don't want to be in a bunch of pictures that people are going to be posting online."

"You're embarrassed to be seen with me?"

"No." I say the word emphatically, and I think I mean it without any hesitation, but even I can hear the lie in that one single word. If I'm worried about what my business friends, my brothers, and my dad think about the two of us together, and what they will think of me because I'm here and dating her, then embarrassed to be seen with her is exactly what I am. "Let's just go back inside."

"No," she drags the word out, irritation clouding her features, "there's something you want to say but aren't saying. Spill it."

Why is she pushing a conversation that shouldn't be happening tonight?

"Now."

Frustration that has been building all night bursts free. "I am so happy and excited that you won the Eddie! I am. But, come on, Bex. Your job is about creating content that helps people procrastinate doing the more important things they should be doing."

I know it's a mistake the moment I say it and instantly regret it. "I'm sorry, Bex. That's not what I meant to say."

She is quiet for a long moment. Then, in an eerily calm voice, she says, "Maybe not, but I think it's the first honest thing you've said all night."

"No, I—" I reach a hand out to her, but she steps back.

"I know you don't want to be here, so you should just leave. I'll find my own ride home."

"No, Bex. This is your night. I'll stay."

She shakes her head. "I don't want you to."

Then she turns and walks away from me and back into the party. I stand in the hallway for several long moments, running my hand through my hair and trying to calm my breathing, cursing my own stupidity, and wishing I could redo this entire night.

CHAPTER 19

Bex

I HAVE both of my video cameras set up in the kitchen on tripods at different angles, both running. I'll use my cell phone video camera here and there, and then Nikki will piece everything together later. Standing in front of one of the cameras, I introduce the video.

"Hello, Bexlandians! Today on our *Hidden Inn Roomies* segment, we are going to tackle something that everyone with roommates has to tackle—cleaning! What's that? Boring, you say? Mundane? A game where you're on one team, your roommates are on the other, and penalties are getting called on everyone?

"Then you're not doing it right." I hold up my phone. "Step one to getting it right: set up a Spotify music list that you all agree on. Step two: gather everyone together for a cleaning party." I motion for my roommates to come into the video frame, and they all squeeze in, waving with elbow-length pink dish-scrubbing gloved hands and cleaning bottles. "Step three: blast music and clean!"

I start the music, and we all scatter to mostly different parts of the kitchen, dancing as we do. We haven't decided ahead of time who is going to clean what, so my audience gets to see all the negotiations on that, too. Addison and Ian pair up to clean out the fridge, and I'm glad that I have one of the cameras aimed at them. The looks on their faces are priceless as they open containers of food and smell them to see if they're still good.

I use my cell phone camera to catch the disagreement between Peyton and Timini on who should work on the counters, the big dining table, and the myriad smaller tables in the inn's big dining room, and who should tackle the big job of sweeping and mopping the expansive floors. Once they agree to split both, I turn off the camera on my phone and start on the dishes.

The music is energetic, everyone is dancing and singing along and having a great time as they work, and I really try to do the same. I dance a bit as I rinse off dishes and load the dishwasher, knowing I'm in the frame, but my mind wanders to Roman, and my having-a-blast expression slips.

Then, as I'm scrubbing the sink and the handle breaks right off the scrubber, I decide maybe I'm pouring a bit too much emotion into the job. I have to get my head back into the game. Addison and Ian have already grabbed both mops and have started mopping the big floor, even though Timini hasn't finished sweeping, so things are moving fast.

Within moments, Peyton finishes the last of the countertops, and Addison and Ian race into the space, seeing who can finish mopping first. It ends with all of us in the space between the back counter and the island, panting and grinning at the clean kitchen.

"And that's how it's done, folks," I say, and then turn off the camera. Then I chuck both pieces of the broken scrubber into the garbage can.

Addison's gaze goes from the garbage can to me. "Are you sure you should be filming segments right now?"

"Yes."

"I don't know, Bex," Peyton says. "It's only been three days, and you can't get over a relationship like yours and Roman's in three days."

I shake my head. "There's only so much administrative work I can do before my head explodes. And I need to keep busy to keep my mind off him."

Because if I don't, all I can do is think of him. About how much I enjoy being with him. How much I love brainstorming with him about our businesses. How much I enjoy laughing and doing fun things with him. The sweet look on his face right before he kisses me. The way he challenges and pushes me and is never, ever boring.

But being in the spotlight as much as I am isn't for everyone. Especially now that I've won the Eddie. I know that. I don't know why I haven't been cutting Roman more slack about it all along. Sure, he was super resistant to the interviews at the beginning, but he was so good at it and he seemed to deal with all the attention they brought just fine. So I assumed he was okay with it and never really talked with him about it.

Maybe I handled things wrong at the awards party and overreacted. And maybe I under-reacted. I'm still so mad at him for the words he said. And not just for saying it, but for *thinking* it! For *believing* it. I need someone who will support me in my career, and not think it's trivial.

Maybe ending things with Roman is for the best. I remember very clearly all that Nikki went through after marrying a guy who was driven, opinionated, and stubborn, and I don't want to have to go through any of that. Maybe it's good we stopped dating before I got any more of my heart invested.

I *should* be relieved.

So why do I feel so awful?

"Whatever," I say as I remove one of the cameras from the tripod. "It's not like he's called, anyway."

When I turn back to my roommates/friends and see the looks of sorrow on their faces, I feel the tears welling up inside. I haven't cried in front of them at all. But as they surround me in a hug, the tears start falling freely, and I let myself cry.

CHAPTER 20

Roman

I COLLAPSE into the chair at the desk in my office at the end of a really long day. The end of a really long week, actually. I run my hands through my hair and then just sit, elbows on the table, hands holding my head.

I just *cannot* stop thinking about Bex. How have I managed to mess up the best thing I've ever had in my life?

I pull my laptop toward me, open a browser, and find her on YouTube. I got a notification earlier today that a new video was posted, so I push play on it. She has posted three new ones this week, along with two Facebook Live videos. I've watched them all. Each one is torture, but I can't seem to stay away. I miss her smile. Her personality. Her voice. Her determination, spunk, and drive. I miss *all* of it.

I startle when Everly pokes her head in. "Whatcha doing here still, Boss?"

I lift a shoulder in a shrug. "You?"

"I forgot my lunch bag and didn't want to leave it here getting gross all weekend." She sits down in the chair across from me and sighs. "Are you watching one of her videos again?"

I turn the laptop toward Everly. "Look how happy she is."

She looks at the screen for a moment, which is paused on Bex's face, then looks back at me. "And you're wondering why she's so happy when you aren't? You want to know why it isn't wrecking her the way it's wrecking you?"

I am. I'm too ashamed to admit it out loud, though. I *should* be happy that she's happy. I don't want her to be as miserable as I am.

"I don't know, Roman. Maybe she isn't. I mean, I've seen you fake it pretty well this week, too. And she probably filmed this before the awards ceremony." We both stay silent for a few moments and then she says, "Have you called her yet?"

I shake my head. "Those words I said to her—I would've only expected them to have come out of my dad's mouth. But they didn't—*I* said them, and it was bad. Some things just aren't forgivable."

"I don't believe that."

"Bex doesn't have any reason to forgive me for it. Or to believe that I didn't actually mean them."

"Well, then it sounds like you need to first make sure you don't actually believe the words you said, and second, find a way to convince Bex that she should forgive you." Everly stands up. "And when you get to the part of convincing Bex, if you need any help, I will gladly do whatever you need. Anything to get my old boss back."

I chuckle. "Thanks, Everly. Have a good weekend."

She nods, then turns and leaves. I pull the laptop to me again and start scrolling through the comments section, like I've been doing ever since I was such a jerk last Saturday. And like with every video, I quickly find comments from people who've been helped by Bex. *Many, many* comments. Like the one that's just five comments down on this video.

> *Thank you so much for your videos, Bex! Not long ago, I was stuck in an awful job with an awful boss, working for an awful company. Your videos taught me how to be brave and convinced me that I could be. I took some huge steps that I would've never dared to take if it weren't for your channel, and my life is so much better now than I ever thought possible. You changed my life, and I will be forever grateful.*

And plenty of ones like the comment just after it.

> *I have a very high-stress job, and if I want to stay healthy, when I come home, I need something to help me unwind. Your videos always do that for me, so thank you! I'm pretty sure my doctor would thank you for saving a life, haha. I know I do.*

I don't know if I ever would've thought that Bex's career choice was frivolous or unimportant or nothing more than a way to make people procrastinate important things on my own. I like to think that I wouldn't have.

But between having my business peers razz me about the wisdom in doing the interviews and my dad's lecture about what's expected of a Powell and how thoroughly Bex doesn't fit that requirement, I definitely thought it. And I feel like a jerk for having done so.

But now, on my sixth night of watching her videos and reading the comments from the people whose lives she has changed, I realize how very, *very* wrong I was that night almost a week ago. The night when she was being professionally celebrated for the contributions she had made, no less.

I want to be with Bex. More than anything. But I don't deserve her. Before last Saturday, I saw myself as my own man.

It isn't until I look back on everything now that I realize how much I've been letting other people in my life drive how I react to things, and even how I think about things.

And as long as I'm doing that, I am never going to deserve her.

CHAPTER 21

Bex

I DON'T HAVE any grandparents, and that's what I really need right now. A grandma who will feed me something sugary and fattening, rub my back in a circle, and spout wisdom. So I'm going to have to borrow Ian's grandma. I text Shirley, and she responds with a quick *Yes! Come ear. We want to see you!*

I open the kitchen door to Ian's house—the one his grandma and her friend, Carol, now live in—to the smell of brownies and the hellos of five women. All of whom get out of their seats and come to give me a hug.

"Wow!" I say, hugging each of them back. "I didn't know I'd be getting the entire origami club. Or this many hugs."

"Well, dear," Shirley says, offering me a seat and a bowl with a brownie and a scoop of vanilla ice cream, "a breakup on the level of yours and Roman's requires lots of hugs. Every single one of us has been there."

Meera nods. "Frances has been there three times."

"That's why I gave you the extra-long hug, honey," Frances says.

"I set her up with two of those," Brenda says. "Want me to set you up with someone? I have a grandson—"

Ian's grandma, Shirley, starts rubbing circles on my back. "She doesn't want to be set up on a date. She's still working on this one. How's the recovery coming, sweetheart?"

I sigh and take a bite of the brownie. The heat of the brownie next to the cold of the ice cream, all of it so sweet and so delicious, is just what I need. Then I look up at the women seated around the table, each of them showing enough wrinkles to prove how experienced in life they are, each with a pile of colored papers and half-folded creations in front of them.

"It's been a week, and it's just not getting any better. He was the only guy I never got bored of. I think I could be with him my entire life and not ever get bored of him. And now he's gone. And I just feel like…" I swirl my spoon in the part of the ice cream that's melting. "I feel like I lost something truly great, you know? How do I get over someone like that?"

"How long have you known him?" Carol asks.

"If you count since Ian's and Addison's wedding, then about three months. But we did our first interview two-and-a-half months ago. We've dated for about two." Which is about a month and a week longer than any other relationship I've ever had. Two months might not feel like a long relationship to some people, but it's an eternity for me.

"Well," Carol says, "I've seen you both enough that I'm going to tell you right now you're asking the wrong question. You shouldn't be asking how to get over him—you should be asking how you can get him back."

I give a humorless breath of a laugh. "No—that train has left the station." Then I take another bite of the brownie because it's really good and it feels like a warm hug in itself.

"Why has the train left?" Brenda asks.

"Because I already made the decision. And if you heard

what he said that night, you would've made the same decision, too. Just like with every decision I make, I go with my gut and stick with it. It has served me well so far."

Carol snorts. "Just because you're decisive doesn't mean you're always right."

"True," Shirley says. "Remember how we planned that backyard barbecue with all of us and we were trying to decide if we should cancel because it looked like rain? You decided we should keep it and wouldn't turn back, even when it was obvious that you should. Remember where that got you? In a soaking wet outfit with soaking wet hamburger buns. Sticking to that decision didn't help you then, and it isn't going to help you now."

My cell phone buzzes, so I take it out of my pocket. It's a text from my sister.

Nikki: Where are you?

I send a quick response back.

Bex: At Ian's grandma's, having brownies and ice cream.

The moment I tap send, I remember we were supposed to meet to go over some business items. So I send a second text.

Bex: So sorry! Are you at the inn looking for me? I'll be right over.

Nikki's response comes just as quickly.

Nikki: NO. STAY THERE. I'm coming where the brownies are.

"Shirley filled us in on what happened between you two," Meera says as soon as I slip the phone back into my pocket. "Men do stupid things sometimes. It's a fact of life. So does everyone. The point is that people do stupid things and you forgive them. You let them learn and grow and become better. If you didn't, no relationship would ever survive."

I could forgive Roman. In fact, I'm pretty sure that I already have. It doesn't mean I'm not still hurt, but I sometimes say rude things without really meaning to, too. I can let him learn and grow and become better, no problem. But does that mean I should continue to date him? I'm not sure.

Nikki knocks twice on the kitchen door before coming inside and moaning as she accepts the bowl with a brownie and ice cream from Shirley. She immediately sits down and eats a big spoonful of the dessert, mumbling "Thanks" and "*Mmm*, so good" around her mouthful.

And, even if she doesn't realize it, her presence reminds me *exactly* why I can't continue to date Roman.

"What was that expression?" Frances asks.

I look at her in confusion.

"You looked at Nikki like she has something to do with this."

"What?" Nikki says with a mouthful of ice cream. "I didn't have anything to do with it."

"No, I saw it, too," Meera says.

Nikki swallows. "Tell them I didn't."

I let out a huge breath of air. "All my sisters are driven and have strong opinions and even stronger wills."

"That's so true," Nikki says. "You should see what it's like just trying to decide where to go to lunch. And by the way, Bex is the most driven of us all. Oh, but did you notice? She said *all* our sisters. See? So whatever she's talking about, it isn't my fault."

I laugh. "It isn't her fault. It's just that all my sisters figured out that they couldn't marry a guy who was also driven with strong opinions and a strong will, except for Nikki. The guy she married was as strong-willed and driven as they come, and it was awful."

"Okay, that part's true. Between dating, engagement, marriage, and divorce, four years of my life: down the crapper. Wait. What does this have to do with you?"

"Well, obviously," I say, "it doesn't work for people like us to be with a guy like that. You married someone kind and sweet and easygoing and everything is rainbows and lollipops for you. Roman is totally driven and strong-willed and has strong opinions. So we would never work out. We'd just end up like you and Brant and waste years of our lives."

"*That's* what you think?" Nikki asks. "Wow, so it really *is* my fault. I would've never guessed."

"No, it's the opposite of your fault. I'm learning from your mistakes so I don't have to make the same ones."

Nikki turns in her seat to face me. "Bex. Brant and I didn't work out because he is a Class A—" she glances at the women in the room and amends whatever she was going to say "—Jerk. *Not* because he's driven and opinionated. Sure, Dylan and I are pretty much the best couple on the planet, but that's got nothing to do with how accommodating and flexible he is and everything to do with him *not* being a jerk. Do you know who else is *not* a jerk? Roman. Well, except at that party where he definitely was a jerk. But the rest of the time? Not so much."

Could it be possible that Roman *isn't* the wrong kind of guy for me? I feel a strange flutter of hope that I haven't felt in the week since the Eddie Awards.

But that doesn't change the fact that he showed that he didn't respect my job, and therefore didn't respect me.

Nikki takes another bite of brownie and ice cream, and then mumbles. "Sorry—I'm really pregnant and this is really good." She swallows her bite before pointing her spoon at me. "Maybe the reason you never stay interested in a guy longer than two or three dates is because the kind of guy that we all married isn't the kind of guy you need. You've stayed interested—*extremely* interested—in Roman for longer than I thought you'd ever stay interested in a guy, and based on the way you're dealing"—she clears her throat—"or *not* dealing with the breakup tells me that you'll likely be interested for the long haul."

"Besides, sweetie," Shirley says, placing a hand on my arm, "you've always struck me as someone who's going to be a formidable half of a power couple. You don't become a power couple with someone who bends like a willow tree. You do it with someone who's an oak."

I really have never thought about it like that before. But looking back, I realize how much Roman has pushed and challenged me over the past couple of months. We have pushed and challenged each other, actually. So many times over the past several weeks, we've brainstormed about each of our businesses, coming up with new ideas. Some, I've been nervous about trying, but he encouraged me, and I've accomplished things I didn't think I could. It has exhilarated me.

I've been more productive and have been willing to take bigger risks than ever before. I've dreamed bigger dreams and I'm going for them. I won an Eddie, and I know with all my heart that I couldn't have done it without him.

Maybe I need to dial back my commitment to sticking with a decision once I've made it. At least when it comes to Roman. But only if I feel like he truly does respect my job and isn't embarrassed to be with me.

And I'm not sure those things are true. If he does respect my job and isn't embarrassed to be with me, will I ever even know? And is he interested in a relationship with me? Because he hasn't called in a week, and that's not really what a guy who's interested does.

CHAPTER 22
Roman

I'm on my way to my dad's office when my phone rings. I was hoping to catch him at home, even though it's a longer drive than his office is, but of course, he has to go in to work on a Saturday. He's probably even wearing a suit.

I glance at my phone—it's my friend, Ian. If it was anyone else, I might ignore the call. I press to answer through my car's Bluetooth. "Hello?"

"Hey, buddy. How are you?"

"Feeling good for the first time in a week, actually."

"That's... not what I was expecting."

"Me neither. Especially because I'm on my way to talk to my dad."

"When is that *ever* a good thing?"

"When I've decided that I'm going to go tell him off. I am a twenty-nine-year-old man. Not only have I lived with zero support from him since college, but I am the CEO of a company I built from the ground up. He doesn't get a say in what I do or who I date."

"I so wish I could be there when you tell him that."

I chuckle. "I wish you could, too." I pause a moment, wondering if I should ask, then decide I want to know too badly to care if I should ask or not. "How's Bex?"

"Miserable. She's a million times better with you, and you're a million times better with her. Addi and I both hate seeing her so miserable. Please tell me you're going to do something about it."

"I am," I say as I pull into the parking lot of my dad's office building. "I'm going to do absolutely everything within my power. I have to convince her to give me another chance."

"Oh, good. Because I care about you both way too much for you to not work this out."

I take a deep breath. "Well, when you mess up as badly as I did, I think it's going to take a *lot* to work this out. And I may need your help."

"You've got it. Anything."

I look up at the building in front of me. "I need to go talk to my dad first, and then I'll call you back."

Normally, I would spend the entire walk into the building, the ride on the elevator, the walk down the hallway of the executive suite, and waiting outside his office dreading whatever talk we were about to have. Even if I have good news, talks with my dad are rarely all good.

But this time, I walk with confidence. Sure, I'm uncertain how my dad will react, and I know it won't be well, but I also feel the power that comes from making a decision so fully and gaining the knowledge that nothing can sway me from that decision. And that power fuels me.

Because over the past week, I've realized that I'm the most myself when I'm around Bex. I've been showing a modified, filtered and concealed, scrubbed and polished, masked version of myself that I've hidden behind for so long that I had forgotten what it's like to truly be me. The time we spent filming the videos and dating afterward has been the most *me* I've felt in a long time. And as it turns out, I like who I am.

And Bex is the one who has managed to pull me out from behind that front and make me feel like I don't have to pretend. I don't know how she managed to do it while filming for an audience of two million, but she did.

As grateful as I am for that, it's only a small fraction of why I love her. I want to be able to tell her all the reasons and keep telling her throughout our lives. Before I do, though, I need to set some clear, strong boundaries with my father.

It's been a while since I've been in my father's office on a Saturday, and everything feels so empty. His assistant, Susan, isn't here, of course, so my dad answers the knock on his door himself.

"Roman. This is a surprise."

"Do you have a minute? I want to talk."

He glances at the laptop on his desk, then must decide whatever he's working on can wait. "Sure. Come on in. But if this is about the trip, don't bother."

I close the door and stand in front of my dad. "It's not about the trip, Dad."

"Oh?"

"It's about me. And Bex Sterling. And about LivenUP."

Instead of sitting down behind his desk, my dad just leans against the front of it, crossing his arms.

"You and Mom raised me to be a good person"—okay, that part was mostly my mom, but I'm trying to start the conversation in a way that won't make my dad defensive—"and to be respectable. I am grateful for that. And I'm grateful that you've built the Powell name to be what it is.

"But through it all, I need to be who I am. And it will not always be in a way that you approve."

My dad just stands there, arms crossed, not interrupting. So I continue.

"I am going to run my business my way. I am going to make the decisions I feel are right for it and the ones I feel good about making. I am not going to let your approval in the form of words or a trip you've been hanging over my head influence my decisions. I am the CEO, and that means I make the calls."

His face is stoic, giving nothing away. I can't tell if he's agreeing with anything or getting more furious as I go on. But it doesn't matter, because I'm not going to stop until I'm finished.

"Next, you are wrong about Bex. *So very wrong.* She does not post 'simpleton content on a simpleton site.' And even if she did, there's a need for that, too. What she does is produce well-thought-out and well-planned segments that draw in millions. I have run into countless people who she has helped in one way or another through her channel. But even if you don't respect what she creates, you would respect the grace, skill, prowess, and professionalism with which she runs her business.

"But Bex as a businessperson is only a small part of who she is, and who she is as a person blows all that out of the water. She is generous in sharing her time, talents, knowledge, and money. She cares about people and will do anything needed to help. She can organize anything from big crowds to a rowdy bunch of kids to a successful business built on her image alone. She is kind and fun and thoughtful and strong, and she is deserving of your awe and respect in all facets of her life. If the Powell family is lucky enough to have her join our ranks, *she would bring us up.* Not the other way around.

"Now, I don't know if I can win her back, but I definitely know I can't if I only put forth the face I feel like I'm supposed to show. I can only do it if my true self is unapologetically coming through. So that's what I'm going to do.

"Now you can disagree with all of that, but it doesn't matter, because it's not going to influence me anymore. I am still going to go forward living my life the way I think I should, and I am still going to move heaven and earth to get Bex back in my life. And I'm going to spend my life being the kind of man who is worthy of her. The kind she'll want to have in her life always."

A smile plays at the corner of my dad's mouth, and I wonder if it's because he's thought of a retort that he's about to blast me with. But then he gives a single nod. "I won't stand in your way."

Is that genuine or passive-aggressive? It seems genuine, which makes no sense.

He stands up straight and walks around to the back of his desk, then meets my eyes. "If you were willing to walk away from someone you were interested in because I—or anyone else —said you should, or because someone cast doubts on your relationship, then either she wasn't the right one or you weren't ready for her. If you're willing to storm in here and stand up to me to fight for her, then I think you probably both have what it takes to last."

I just stare at him, dumbfounded.

Richmond Powell IV, D.B.A., takes a seat and picks up the pen he was probably using before I came into his office. "But I'm still going to tell you every time I see you making a decision that I think is an idiot move."

Fair enough. I give him a nod. "And I will listen and follow your advice if it rings true and ignore it completely if it doesn't." I'm not about to let him bully me into a decision ever again. "Now, if you'll excuse me, I need to go set something into motion that you are definitely not going to approve of."

I don't wait for his response. I walk out of his office with my chin up and shoulders back, ready to thrust a fist into the air.

This is the first time I've stood up to him and he's backed down. I hadn't even imagined that was possible.

It makes me feel freer to make my own decisions than I've ever been before.

That's one thing down, but I'm far from finished. I still have several people I need to meet with, including Tarak from *Business Success* magazine, to begin to undo the damage I've caused and make things right.

When I think back to the man I was a week ago when I ruined everything, it amazes me how different I feel now. I sent a clear message to Bex a week ago that I didn't respect her job and that I didn't want to be seen with her. It's time to show her how I really feel, and that I want the world—but most importantly, her—to know it.

CHAPTER 23

Bex

"I CAN'T BELIEVE I let you all talk me into coming here," I say to my roommates as we put our lanyards on over our heads that hold our name badges and the *PNW Open for Business* convention logo. I look around at the massive lobby of the Oregon Convention Center. Normally, I like being around this many people. Right now, though, I don't want to socialize.

I don't even want to talk shop in all the lectures or with the business product owners, which has never happened before. But everyone said that coming would be good "roommate bonding" and would "get my mind off of things." I'm pretty sure they're wrong.

"Should we go check out the exhibit hall?" Timini asks, eyeing the big doors leading into the vendor area.

Addison glances at her watch. "As long as we don't stay too long. I want to catch some of the programming."

The five of us start going up and down the aisles in the exhibit hall, checking out all the displays from companies selling products that help business owners. Everything I see reminds me of Roman. The business planning software reminds me of our brainstorming sessions. The breakroom furniture reminds me of sitting on the bench in Tsuru Island at the park together, eating dessert. The phone system reminds me of him being so sweet and helping me get past the panic of an imminent bird attack. It all makes my heart hurt.

"Anyone want to catch a panel or lecture? I need to…" I point toward the exit, but can't find a way to end the sentence. They all seem to get it, though.

"I want to!" Peyton says. "Ooh. There's one starting in ten minutes." She pulls out her convention schedule, and we all crowd in to look at it.

"That one," Ian says, pointing at the one on social media marketing. "I am terrible at that. Anyone else?"

Four minutes later, we're all filing into the big room numbered *A105-106* and finding seats. I sit down between Peyton and Timini and pull out my notebook. Instead of being a panel discussion, it's actually Tarak, the interviewer from *Business Success* who I spoke with at the awards ceremony, pulling in one panelist at a time and asking them questions.

Which hurts in its own way, since Tarak and *Business Success* played a big hand in Roman and me getting together in the first place. My viewers wouldn't have even known who Roman was if it weren't for that article.

It's probably a really interesting conversation. I just can't seem to focus. Instead, I start doodling. At first, it's just in the margins of the notebook. Before long, my doodles cover the entire page, and I have no idea what the speakers have been saying. I thought my mind was just blank—not thinking about Roman at all—but then I notice that most of my doodles resemble Roman's company logo, one of his app's logos, or something from one of our interviews together. Oh, look—that one is like the avocado-shaped cats we painted in our class.

I've been blindsided by how much I miss him. I have never

in my life missed a guy before. There have always been plenty of interesting things to move on to. But I miss just being in the same room as Roman so much it physically hurts.

I hear the name "Roman Powell" over the microphone, and my head jerks up. Roman is walking right onto the stage and taking the seat next to Tarak.

I look at my friends surrounding me so we can all share in the shock at seeing him on stage, but none of them look nearly as surprised as I am. I lean over to Timini. "Did you know he was on this panel?"

"Shh," she says. "I'm listening."

So I listen, too.

"A lot of you might recognize our next panelist. Roman Powell became much more of a household name when he made the cover of our magazine and it became our second best-selling issue of all time."

"It's good to see you again, Tarak."

I cannot believe how much I miss hearing that voice. Seeing him and hearing him again grabs at my throat.

"You, too. I'm glad you finally responded to my email to join me on the stage here."

Roman chuckles and rubs the back of his neck. "Better late than never, right?"

I miss running my own fingers on the back of his neck. I miss touching that spot where his hair curls just slightly right in front of his ear. And seeing the way his mouth curls up on one side when he's amused, kind of like it is right now.

"Now, your company was rocking before the *Business Success* issue with you on it. Which is why, of course, you were on it in the first place. But your business has exploded since then. You've had a new product release, Nudge Out." Tarak turns to the audience. "Which you should all get right now.

Roman told me about it in our interview, and the second it went live, I downloaded it. It got me to try synchronized swimming which, I've got to say, was much more difficult and more fun than I ever would have guessed. I'd like you to tell us, Roman, what you did to capitalize on the success of that issue."

"You know the old saying that the three most important things in a business are location, location, location? When you have a digital offering, I think it's more along the lines of excellent employees, luck, and finding your target audience. Thanks in part to a very persistent and very skilled social media and marketing manager at my company, and in large part to a lot of different pieces falling into place, I managed to get an interview with the amazing Bex Sterling of *Bexlandia*. A four-part interview, actually. She has a massive fan base that just happened to be my target audience, and those interviews helped so much to get the word out about our new product."

There's something about the way he says things. They're just more charming when they come out of Roman's mouth. He's so confident and relaxed up there, connecting with the audience so well. I never would have guessed that from our first couple of meetings before the interviews, but he has gotten more and more at home with it every time. It makes me long for the time when we were bantering together in front of the camera.

I can't leave. I want to see him again so badly that I can't pass up this chance to see him shine on stage. But I know that watching him and being reminded about all the things I love about him is going to wreck me later.

"Oh, that's a great show," Tarak says. "I was there nearly two weeks ago when she won an Eddie for it. Everyone, if you're not already watching *Bexlandia* on YouTube, you really should check it out because she is a savant at social media. I actually interviewed Bex that night. We're having a special issue with creators of digital content come out in about two months that she'll be in, and we're pretty excited about that."

He turns back to Roman. "But I saw you, too, that night, and it didn't look like things were going so well for you."

"No, Tarak, they were not."

Oh, how awkward. I can't believe Tarak is asking him about that. Especially since Roman didn't want anyone to know that we'd been dating. He probably wants to exit the stage pretty quickly right about now.

I want to exit the room, too, because I don't want to relive the moment when things went so downhill for us. I look to the left and the right. How did I manage to get stuck in the middle of the row? We're toward the back of the room, but there are several hundred people in it, so there's no way I can escape without making a scene.

Roman looks down for a few moments before he looks out at the audience. "You know how it is when you're running your business and things are going decently well but you still don't have everything figured out yet, and suddenly everyone is giving you advice?"

The audience is chuckling and nodding. They've probably all been exactly there. I know I have.

"And some of it is actually incredibly terrible advice, but you don't know that yet, so you follow it and everything goes wrong?"

More nodding from the audience, this time a little more emphatically.

"It was kind of like that, only so much worse. And instead of a business, it was a woman I'm in love with. And instead of just being clueless, I was also a jerk."

My eyes go wide, and I turn to Peyton and then to Timini,

Addison, and Ian. Did Roman really just say he's in love with me?

"I assume this woman we are talking about is Bex Sterling?"

Roman nods. "It is."

"And did I hear you right? You love her."

Roman lets out a breath and shakes his head like he's still in disbelief over it all. "It's pretty impossible not to fall in love with someone like Bex."

I gasp, and my hand flies to my mouth. My eyes start to water, and I blink fast, trying to clear my vision so I don't miss one second of seeing Roman.

"I'm impressed—it takes a lot of bravery to get up here and announce something like that to everyone."

"Actually, it doesn't. I want the whole world to know. I want my peers to know. I want my family, my employees, my friends, and all the Bexlandians to know that I am in love with Bex Sterling. It isn't brave of me to say it now; it was cowardly of me to not say it before."

Tears spill onto my face. He loves me. And not only that, he wants everyone to know.

"When you say 'before,' were you talking about that night at the awards?" When Roman nods, Tarak asks, "So what changed?"

"Me. Like I said, I was a jerk, and I was rude, and most importantly, I was wrong. It took a lot of intense soul-searching, setting boundaries with certain people, choosing which voices I'm going to listen to, coming to some realizations, and making a plan going forward."

Tarak nods. "Sometimes when we mess up badly, that's what it takes. Tell me: if Bex were here now, what would you say to her?"

Roman looks right out into the audience. "I would tell her

that she's the most amazing woman I've ever known and that I admire everything about her. She's organized, patient, dreams big, sets goals, works hard, and does everything she can to reach those goals. I have now watched nearly every video she has ever posted, and I can say without a doubt that she has created an amazing channel with incredible content, and I have so much respect for what she does.

"No matter how busy she is, she'll drop everything to help out someone in need. Whether it's someone wanting advice while she's waiting in line, someone needing a shoulder to cry on, an email asking for help, or her nephew, who needed an adult to attend a sleepover at the aviary with him when his mom was out of town. Bex stepped in even though she's terrified of birds. She's willing to help out regardless.

"She's got strong opinions and she isn't afraid to share them. Even when her opinion is the unpopular one. She fights for what she thinks is right. She stands up for the little guy. She pushes people to be better and brings out the best in them. She has definitely brought out the best in me." He chuckles, shaking his head. "I mean, before her, my personality only came out in my choice of socks."

Tarak and the rest of the audience laugh, and so do I as I wipe away the tears spilling onto my cheeks.

"I love her completely. I want the whole world to know it. And I am hoping that it's not too late to fully apologize and make up for the mistakes I've made."

The audience lets out a collective "Awww!"

I can't stay seated any longer. There's too much space separating me and Roman, and I need there to not be space. Tarak looks out into the audience and makes eye contact with me. He doesn't look at all surprised that I'm here—almost like he'd known I was here and where I was sitting all along. He gives me a single nod, like he agrees that it's time for me to come up.

I start trying to get to the center aisle as Tarak says to Roman, "Do you wonder what she would say if she were here?" Then he turns to the crowd. "Audience, what do you think?"

They all cheer and clap as each person between me and the aisle moves bags, shifts their knees to the side, or stands up to let me pass. I'm pretty sure I step on a toe or two, and even hit my arm against the back of a guy's head at some point, but I finally make it to the center aisle.

I rush toward the stage, wondering how I'm going to get up on it when one of the event center ushers holds both arms out in the direction of the stairs. I don't even have time to step into the front aisle, let alone head for the stairs, before Roman jumps off the stage and meets me, front and center.

His face is so full of love and apology and hope that I reach for it, putting a hand on each side of his face, and then crushing my lips against his. I'm vaguely aware of a roar of approval coming from the crowd, but it falls away. Off in the distance. All I can focus on is Roman's arms around me, his lips against mine, a confirmation that everything he said is true, along with a promise of the future.

When we finally break for air, we keep our foreheads together, breathing hard. A smile spreads across Roman's face, and I can't help the one that spreads across mine. Besides the cameras that are filming all sessions of the conference, I'm sure that there are more than a few cell phones out, recording our reunion.

"You just kissed me in front of a very large crowd."

"I hope it goes even more viral than the memes. I want everyone to know I love you."

"And I want them all to know that I love you just as much."

The smile on his face is so beautiful. I want to stare at it for hours.

Roman glances at the doors at the other end of the center aisle. "What do you say we go find someplace else to be?"

I nod and we both turn to give Tarak a thank you. Then I put my hand in Roman's, threading my fingers through his, and we walk to the doors together.

CHAPTER 24

Roman

I STEP out into the lobby with Bex before the current sessions end, so the area has a lot fewer people in it now than it will in just a few minutes. I lead her down the wide halls to an ice cream kiosk I found earlier. In hopes that everything would work out in my interview, I'd stopped by before and already ordered and paid, asking the two people working the kiosk to have them ready at about this time.

When Bex and I step up to the kiosk, the young man working grins as he hands the ice creams to us. They didn't have Ben & Jerry's flavors, but they do have blueberry, raspberry, and vanilla, so I'd asked them to put the three flavors together in a bowl for Bex and to make a chocolate chip cookie dough bowl for me. I slip the guy an extra $10 tip to say thanks.

A few minutes later, we're sitting on a bench in a secluded little spot I'd found earlier where we can talk. It overlooks a patch of grass, a few shrubs, and is shaded by a giant tree. We're both quiet for a moment as we take our first bites of ice cream, and then I turn to her.

"What I said in there was just a start in my plan to make

things up to you. I really am sorry for the way I behaved and the things I said. I would also like to apologize for taking nearly two weeks to say that. There were so many things I was wrong about, and I wanted to make sure I got them right first. I didn't want to give an apology that wasn't one hundred percent genuine, and I didn't want to make hollow promises. I love you and I respect you, Bex. And I promise to always try to show you and anyone watching exactly how much I do."

Bex smiles that smile of hers that I love. "And I promise to always let you."

I laugh, and then just take in the look of joy on her face.

Bex licks some of the ice cream on her spoon, then studies the half that's left. "You know, you didn't have to go that public to show you want to be with me. Especially in front of *Business Success* magazine, or at an event that will be streaming to such a large audience of your fellow CEOs." She puts the spoon in her mouth, her eyes on me.

"No, that's exactly what I needed to do. I want them all to know. Bexlandians, too. I don't know if you noticed or not, but Nikki and Enoch were also there."

Her head jerks in surprise. "They were? Where?"

"Enoch was at the front, filming me, and Nikki was at the side, very discreetly filming you. So if you want to use any of the footage in a *Bexlandia* segment, it's all yours. I even give you my express permission to play me saying 'I was wrong' on a loop."

Bex laughs. "I might just have to do that."

"Wait. You lined this all up with my roommates so they would get me here and in that room, didn't you?"

I grin and take a bite of my ice cream. Then I set it aside and scoot in closer. She sets hers on the bench beside her, too, and turns to me. "And, Roman, I just want you to know that I am truly, madly, deeply, forever in love with every single part of you. From everything in here," she says, placing a hand on the side of my head, "right down to your fun socks."

"And you're okay with letting everyone know?"

She smiles and nods, grabbing hold of my shirt and pulling me in closer.

"Good. Because otherwise, that whole thing in there would be rather awkward."

"Uh-huh," she breathes against my lips. Then she kisses me, and nothing in my life has ever felt so right.

PEYTON

"OH, my life, don't you just want that?" I motion from where I sit at the big table in the dining room to Bex and Roman, who are standing behind the island, making Rice Krispies treats with Bex's five-year-old nephew and three-year-old niece.

Timini looks up from the costume she's sketching a design for. "A Rice Krispies treat shaped like a stegosaurus? Sure."

"No, silly," I say. "The domestic bliss. Being a cute little family, hanging out in the kitchen together, making treats."

"Yeah," Addison says, glancing up from her computer, where she's probably online shopping for storage solutions for a client. "That looks nice."

Ian nods, too. Not in a *let's have a baby right now* way, but he is wearing an *I'd like that before long* expression.

I sigh as the five-year-old bumps into the three-year-old, and she pushes back with her marshmallowy hand, sticking both her hand and some of her hair to her brother's shirt. Bex frees the hand and then helps the girl wash it before scooting their stools further apart and setting her on it again. All while Roman helps the five-year-old free a dinosaur from the cookie cutter he pressed into the treats. "Aren't they going to make the most adorable parents someday?"

"Totally," Timini says.

"Oh my lands, Bex, you could do a pregnancy segment on your channel! You could let your viewers go on the journey with you and talk about all the funny and weird and wild things that happen when you're pregnant."

"Whoa," Roman says, only taking his eyes off what his future nephew is doing for a small second to glance at me. "Let's not jump so far ahead yet. Right now, the wedding planning and the impossible task of finding a home is taking up every bit of time we have. Let's conquer those mountains first."

"Oh, speaking of which," Bex says, "your mom needs you to call her. Something about a long-lost uncle or someone who needs to be on the boutonnière list."

"But the wedding planning is going well?" I ask. I should be working on my schedule right now, planning out meals and grocery lists for my clients, but I have a hard time focusing on my notebook while all my roommates are in the same room as me.

"Yep!" Bex says as she helps her niece press little candy balls into the treats for the dinosaur's eyes. "Well, I mean, as well as they can go when you're planning a wedding big enough for my entire extended family and Roman's and his parents' considerable list of business associates."

"Go big or go home, right?" Roman smiles at Bex, and she grins back before they lean behind the kids and kiss.

The two of them are so freaking adorable, I can hardly stand it. I want someone to love as much as Bex and Roman or Ian and Addison love each other. I turn to Timini. "You're bringing someone to movie night, right?"

Timini lifts a shoulder in a shrug but doesn't stop sketching. "I think so. It's a first date with a guy named Jake…Jack…

something like that. I mean, *if* he shows up. He seems a little flaky."

"If you, of all people, are calling someone flaky," Bex says, "I'm thinking the chance he'll show up isn't great."

Timini laughs, and then leans forward to grab an apple out of the bowl in the middle of the table and acts like she's going to throw it at Bex.

Bex's niece has a very concerned look on her face. "Does Timini not like you, Aunt Bex?"

"No, sweetie. Timini loves me."

"I do," Timini says to the little girl. "Even when she's probably right."

I don't have a date for movie night, so I asked my best friend, Max, to come. I glance at my watch. He planned to come a little early, which should be any minute. No sooner do I think it than I hear the unique sound his car makes as it pulls into the rounded driveway in front of the inn.

"Max is here!" I jump up and go to the front door, a skip in my step. I make it to the wrap-around porch just as he pulls to a stop, and I'm at the bottom of the three stairs just as he gets out of the car.

"I brought caramel popcorn," he says, holding the bag up.

"My favorite."

"I thought about getting a vegetable tray, but then I saw the popcorn and couldn't resist."

"You did not almost get a veggie tray."

He holds up a hand in surrender as we walk up the steps. "All right, you got me. I had a flashback to that one movie night when you tried to toss a carrot into my mouth and missed and hit me in the eye. I figured the popcorn was safer."

I give him a playful shove and then notice that the mailbox just beside the door has mail sticking up. Being the first person to notice always feels like I've won a scavenger hunt. I lift the flap, pull out the contents, and then scream.

Running into the house, Max right behind me—probably wondering what's happening—I shout, "Oh my stars, Bex! Roman! Everyone! It came!"

I race into the kitchen where everyone is standing, looking my way in alarm. There's no helping it, though—this is so exciting! I make a beeline to the table, and Bex and Roman quickly wash the sticky off their hands and rush around the island to crowd around the dining room table with everyone else.

I ceremoniously place the magazine right in the middle of the table so everyone can see. The glossy cover of *Business Success* magazine shows both Bex and Roman, both in business attire, giving each other the cutest *there's more to this story than you're seeing* looks on their faces. Bex's hand is on Roman's arm, and her engagement ring is absolutely shimmering in the studio lighting. The headline reads *These Two Executives Are Planning a Different Kind of Merger.*

"I think that's the prettiest magazine cover I've ever seen," Addison says.

Roman wraps an arm around Bex. She snuggles in close, then tips her head up and gives him a kiss on the lips.

I open the magazine to their article and read the subheading at the top out loud. "'After Roman Powell made the cover of our *Top 10 Young (and Single) CEOs* issue and, four months later, Bex Sterling was on our cover for the *Digital Content Creators to Keep Your Eye On* issue, we wanted to give you an update on these two executives, their rapidly growing businesses, and the joint venture they are about to embark on as they "tie the knot" on a merger that promises much future prosperity.' Aww! You two! This is so perfect!"

"We have to celebrate," Max says.

Bex looks at Roman, grinning. "Mandatory dance party in the family room?"

He grins back, and Bex gets out her phone to pull up her dance playlist as all of us head into the big gathering room. Within seconds, the music is on and booming and everyone is laughing and moving to the beat. Max is facing me, and we're both dancing like no one is watching. I love that he'll do things like have a spontaneous dance party without shying away. Everything Max does, he does with his full heart in it.

I add that to my mental list of what the perfect guy would be like. Really, what I want is someone exactly like Max. (Minus the part of him that sees me like a sister, of course! Or the part where he doesn't seem to be interested in ever getting married and having kids, even though I think he'd be great at both.) But where do I even look to find someone that perfect? I've been searching for a while and just haven't found him.

My heart is full to bursting just being in this room with so many people I love, yet there's still something missing. I want that domestic bliss, and time cooking with kids, and sneaking kisses with the man I love so badly that my heart aches for it.

Do you know what? I've made up my mind. I'm going to come up with an out-of-the-box plan to find my perfect guy— no matter how ridiculous the plan has to be to work—and I'm going to find him soon.

———

VOLUME

Three

HOW TO NOT FALL for YOUR BEST FRIEND

CHAPTER 1

Peyton

I HEFT my insulated bag of cold food items onto my dad's kitchen table. He bends to grab the bag of pantry items, but I slap his hand away. "Daddy. Your heart attack was barely two weeks ago. Obey your doctors."

"So I can't even lift a heavy bag for my little girl anymore?"

"Soon. Be patient."

I start unloading the ingredients in my bag onto the kitchen counter, and my dad helps. He pulls out the two small spaghetti squashes and a head of broccoli and then peeks into the bag at the rest of the produce. "Are you really going to make me eat this many vegetables?"

I smile. He complained a week ago, too, when I made him a bunch of heart-healthy meals right after he got out of the hospital. He never seems to complain after eating them, though. "You'll like what I do to them. Are you doing your exercises?"

He heaves a sigh once the bags are unloaded and sits down at the table. "Yes, but I need to get back to work. I think my doctor is being overly cautious. I've spent more time 'taking it easy' over the past two weeks than I have in the past ten years."

"Which is why you had the heart attack in the first place," I say as I start organizing the items on the counter.

My dad has always been a force. But since his heart attack, he sits less tall and doesn't seem larger than life quite as much.

"The firm needs me."

"They are handling things just fine on their own."

He lets out a long, slow breath. I can't see his legs under the table, but I can feel the slight tremor in the hardwood floor enough to know that his leg is bouncing. "I hate that people have to come to the house and help me. Flora shouldn't have to come. And I should be taking care of you, not the other way around."

When my dad went to the hospital and during those first few days after his surgery, my fear and worry were at the level of jumping out of an airplane. Now? I'm only at a bungee-jumping level.

"Your nurse will only have to come for another week or so. And if it helps, don't think of me coming to take care of you. Think of it as me just coming over for a regular old daddy-daughter chat."

He leans back in his chair, arms folded, a smile on his face. "Okay, then, Sugar Bug. Let's chat. How is work? Are you dating anyone new?"

I roll my eyes as I get out the pans I need. My dad takes any opportunity he can to ask about my dating life. "Not dating anyone, but I do have a story about work." Since being home all day with not enough tasks to fill his time, he has turned into the best listener. And since I figure the term "laughter is the best medicine" hasn't been around so long for no reason, I save my most embarrassing stories for him.

Well, not *all* of my most embarrassing stories. I'm not going to tell him about how I tried on a fitted shirt at Sloan's a couple of days ago and forgot there was a back clasp when it came time to take it off. I got the shirt halfway up, and, arms above my head, I got stuck. The shirt trapped my arms tight against my head, leaving me unable to get the shirt up or down.

Seriously, I was as stuck as a flip-flop in wet sand. I had to leave the dressing room to search for someone to help free me. Which wasn't easy, since I had a shirt covering my face. So I bumped into an embarrassingly large number of things, including a carousel of bracelets that crashed to the ground, all while showing off my bra, before someone came running to find the source of the destruction and saved me.

I'll keep that story to myself.

As I wash the spaghetti squash, cut it in half, and then scoop out all the seeds, I say, "I got a brand new client this past week. Her name is Lavender, like the plant. Or the color, I guess. Anyway, she was a referral from another client, and we talked over the phone quite a bit and I created a menu for her."

I turn the heat on a cast iron skillet and start peeling and slivering enough garlic for the marinara sauce and the Thai turkey lettuce wraps I'm going to make next. "So I arrive at the woman's apartment building with all my stuff, get in the elevator, and push the button for the fourth floor.

"Right before the doors close, this good-looking guy, who was probably about my age, got in and smiled at me. Of course, I smiled back. He was all trim muscles and dressed nicely. Smelled great, too. It was a small elevator, so we were standing pretty close. Okay, actually, he was *really* good-looking."

My dad is smiling like he is expecting this story to involve flirty banter and the exchanging of phone numbers.

I pour some olive oil into the pan and then add the garlic, the whole tomatoes I crushed, and seasonings. "We were just passing the third floor, and the guy said, 'I'm going to miss you.'"

My dad's eyebrows shoot up.

"Right? But hey, who am I to judge if someone feels affection toward other people quickly? And it's not like I'm going to be rude."

"Obviously."

"So I said back, 'I'm going to miss you, too.' Because it was the polite thing to do, right? Then, the guy turned to face me fully with a weird expression on his face and pointed at his Bluetooth headphones. He was on a phone call! Which, he probably should've let his elevator mate know if he was going to be saying words that would make things uncomfortable if I responded. Then he said to the person on the phone, 'I love you, too. See you in a week.'"

"So at this point, I was sure my cheeks were flaming red because they felt like they were on fire. And that was when I noticed the wedding ring."

My dad is shaking his head and chuckling now.

"I probably should've noticed that earlier. But once I did notice, I thought, *Aww*! He and his wife are so sweet to each other! And I felt bad that they weren't going to see each other for a full week."

As I mix together the Romano cheese, cottage cheese, salt, pepper, and broccoli florets, I continue my story. "Then the doors opened for the fourth floor, we got off, and we both started walking down the hall in the same direction, which was kind of awkward. But not as awkward as when we both stopped in front of the *same apartment*!

"He pulled out his keys to unlock his door and gave me this look like I was some kind of crazy stalker who followed him home and was about to announce that I lived there now, too. But he still opened the door. And then he just looked at me as if he was about to pop some popcorn as he watched whatever shocking thing I was going to do next."

"I can't blame the guy," my dad says. "I'm wishing for a bowl of it in front of me right now just listening."

As the marinara simmers and the squash continues to cook in the microwave, I start adding the cilantro sauce ingredients to the blender for the lettuce wraps. "I was about to pull out my phone to verify that I got the right apartment when Lavender came to the door and said, 'Oh, you must be Peyton! Come in! And I see you've met my husband already.'

"At that point, the guy hadn't said one single word to me—not even 'Hi.' And all I'd said to him was 'I'll miss you, too.' But we both knew that he'd just told a woman that he loved her and would see her in a week. A woman who I now knew wasn't his wife! And then he wrapped his arms around Lavender and kissed her and told her he loved her."

My dad's eyes narrow. "What a dirt bag."

"That's what I was thinking, too. Lavender sat down at the table in front of her laptop because she was on a huge deadline. The guy gave me a nod and headed to some rooms behind the kitchen."

I put the blender on its base and turn it on, then pull the spaghetti squash halves out of the microwave. Once the blender finishes, I turn it off so we can talk again, and I start the ground turkey browning in a pan for the lettuce wraps. I use a fork to scrape up most of the squash strands before layering the cheeses and marinara sauce in them.

"So I get out my supplies and start preparing their meals. A few minutes later, the guy comes out wearing lounge pants and a t-shirt, goes over to Lavender, and starts massaging her shoulders. She closes her eyes and leans back into it. The whole time, all I could think about was how this guy was cheating on his wife and she didn't even know! And he was totally giving her a guilt massage. Because he was a dirty rotten cheater!"

"So, did you say something?"

"Not until I finished preparing the *I'm Sorry Your Husband Is Cheating on You* spinach rice to go with the honey mustard pork and made an *It's Too Bad He's Such a Jerk* spring minestrone soup and had it on the stove cooking.

"Then, when I was about to start the next meal, the guy left to go to the restroom. I gathered up my nerves, went around the kitchen island, sat down at the table next to Lavender, and told her that her husband was cheating on her. I was in such a cooking rush, probably because I was fueled by my indignation at the husband, that I might have just spit it out instead of easing her into the news. Of course, she was pretty alarmed and wanted to know how I knew. So I told her everything."

I stop telling my dad the story for a minute while I add the jalapeno, ginger, and lime juice and measure out the soy sauce —low sodium, of course. My dad just had a heart attack, after all—and add it to the Thai turkey lettuce wrap filling.

"And? I'm pretty sure my doctor would tell you not to keep me in suspense. I'm recovering from a heart attack, you know."

I smile at my dad's eagerness. It's why I like telling him stories so much. But I also like to make him good food, too, so sometimes that takes precedence. I start grilling tomatillo halves and some tilapia and then get out the cabbage for the fish tacos I'm making for our dinner tonight and start slicing it.

"Okay, so Lavender got up, grabbed her husband's phone, and opened the app to show the recent calls. Then she held it out for me to see and said, 'He was talking to his twin sister who's moving to Philadelphia. He's going on a business trip nearby next week and is going to help her get settled.'

"Dad, I was so embarrassed. I was entirely convinced he was cheating on her! And what kind of person would I be if I didn't tell her? The guy came out of the bathroom or wherever he was, caught the end of the conversation, and finally said his first words to me, which were, 'Maybe you shouldn't be so quick to assume things.' Which, okay, is totally true. But he did not say it in a nice way at all."

"Uh, oh. Did they fire you?"

I sigh and I shake my head. "No. That didn't happen until the spring minestrone soup on the stove started boiling over while we were talking. I had totally forgotten about it.

"In my rush from the table and around the island to get to it to pull it off the burner, I tripped over their dog, who apparently was also a ninja, because I didn't even know they had a dog and definitely hadn't heard him come into the room. He wasn't a very big dog, and in my attempt not to injure him—or me—I got way off balance and grabbed the only thing nearby, which just happened to be the edge of a decorative lacy doily-type thing on a lower counter, which brought her great-great-grandma's china bowl crashing to the tile floor."

"I'm so sorry, Sugar Bug."

"Yeah, I felt bad. But don't worry. When I left, the honey mustard pork was still in the crock pot and the spinach rice I made was still on the counter. After they ate it, they called me back and asked if I could please be their personal chef again."

"That's my girl."

"I just won't be cooking at their apartment because, apparently, the husband likes me about as much as a flat tire in a downpour, which is totally fine with me. About half of my clients have me cook at the inn because their house is chaotic, they feel like they have to super clean if I go to their house, or their kitchen is small. So it's no big deal. There's so much more space at the inn anyway."

As the two meals I made for him to eat later in the week cool, I cut up the softened tomatillos and toss them in a bowl with lime juice, red onion, pineapple, jalapeño, and pepper.

"Oh, I got something for you." My dad gets up and rifles through some papers he has on the counter. He smiles when he finds what he is looking for and holds a business card out to me.

I take the card and look closely at it, smiling. This one is for Pete and June's Dry Cleaning. I started collecting business cards when I was ten, and I have an entire wall in my childhood bedroom covered in them. Someday, when I have my own office, I hope to have enough to wallpaper the entire room with them. Business cards are the best because they're filled to the top with people's hopes and dreams, and I swear that looking at them powers my own hopes and dreams. "Thank you, Daddy." I give him a kiss on the cheek.

As the tortillas warm, my dad sets the table, and I move all of the dinner items to it.

After we sit, my dad holds my hand as he says grace, like he always does. And, like always, he blesses the food and the hands that prepared it. He always, always ends the prayer after saying that part. But this time, he pauses and then adds, "And please help Peyton to find a husband."

After we say amen, I just look at my dad. I don't know if I want to roll my eyes, chuckle, give him a gold star for practically doubling his normal length of prayer, or worry that he's more concerned about his health than he's letting on.

"What?" he says, trying to make his voice come out innocent but failing miserably. He pulls the tortillas toward him, then lifts the cloth and holds the container out to me. "I just don't want you to be alone."

A hand flies to my mouth. "Oh, exclamation points. You think you're going to die!"

He lets out a long breath. Then, apparently giving up on waiting for me to grab a tortilla, puts one on my plate for me and then takes one for himself. "I'm not going to die, Sugar Bug. Not until I'm too old to make it to the bathroom on my own. I just want you to have someone in your life."

I finally breathe again in relief, then put some cabbage on my tortilla and pass the dish to my dad. "I have people in my life. I have you, I have three amazing roommates, I have great clients, and I have Max."

"A best friend is not the same as a partner in life."

"I do date, Daddy. I just haven't found anyone recently that I'm interested in."

"If this heart attack has taught me anything, it's the importance of your relationships with the people in your life. And the most important relationship you can have is with a spouse. The person who will be there for you in thick and thin, through the good times and the bad, in times of health or heart attack. I want that for you."

"*Aww.*" I reach out and give my dad's hand a squeeze. "I want that for me, too." I grab the pineapple and tomatillo salsa and put some on my taco, then hand it to my dad and grab the fish.

He doesn't put the salsa on his taco, though—he just stares at me intently enough that I look up from where I am placing the fish chunks all perfectly on my taco.

"I'm serious about this."

"I know." My mom died eight years ago when I was eighteen, and since then, my dad has been married twice more. Neither of the two marriages lasted more than two years, and he isn't currently married. I like how happy my dad is when he's dating someone seriously or getting married to them. "Do you know what? You should date someone again, too! It's been four months since you and Meleah divorced. Maybe it's time."

"We're talking about you, Sugar Bug."

"You know, you're not exactly walking your talk." I wink to let him know that I'm not being rude—I'm just directing the conversation away from my non-existent dating life.

"I did walk my talk. With your mom. She was my everything, and I relished every moment we had together. I want that kind of relationship for you."

"Don't worry, Daddy. The right person for me will come along eventually. I'm sure of it."

"I only got nineteen-and-a-half years with your mom. If I'd known I'd only get that long, I wouldn't have waited until after law school and getting settled in my practice to find her. I would've dropped everything and searched five years sooner so I could've had that much longer with her."

I just stare into my dad's eyes, seeing in them the love he had for my mom, soaking in the feeling of her being in the room with us for a small moment. The truth is I want exactly what he wants for me. I want what my parents had. I want a man who will have that look in his eyes when he talks about me. I always have.

"Don't just sit around and wait—get out there and find him. Don't waste any of the years you could have together."

I don't sit around, waiting, so much as I stand around, waiting. I am always standing in the middle of the metaphorical dating street where I can be seen, willing to talk to anyone who comes out of their metaphorical houses and walks up to me.

But maybe he's right, and it's time to start going door-to-door, knocking. I've never done that. Do I even know how?

"Like I said, I don't plan on dying anytime soon. But the chances of having a second, larger, much more devastating heart attack after the first are pretty high. I want to see my little girl married before I go."

The thought of him not being around forever feels like a skewer to my stomach, so I drop the thought faster than a hot pan. His doctor already told me the statistics about second heart attacks. My dad is granite, though. It doesn't seem like anything will be able to take him down. He's been assuring me all along that he still has a lot to do on this planet and isn't anywhere close to leaving it.

But the fact that he actually said, out loud, that the chances of a second heart attack are there means he's worried. That, or he's just plenty serious about wanting me to find true love. Whatever the reason, I can tell by the look in his eyes that it's important to him.

I should take his advice. If it's something that's worrying him so much, maybe if I start seriously trying to find the perfect guy, it'll make him less likely to have a second heart attack. And I will do anything to lessen those odds.

It's not easy, but I work to replace the worried feeling in my gut with a determination to do all I can to help move along the process of finding my true love. I have absolutely no clue how I will accomplish that daunting task, but I suddenly find myself with oodles of willpower and hope that'll be enough.

"Don't you worry, Daddy. I'm going to go out and I'm going to find Mr. Perfectly Right, and then we're going to live happily ever after. You'll see. It'll pretty much be the best fairy tale ending ever."

He smiles, gives my hand a squeeze, then grabs the pineapple and tomatillo salsa and puts it on his taco. "That's my girl."

CHAPTER 2
Max

I walk along the packed dirt of the McKenzie River trail in the Willamette National Forest, massive trees rising on both sides of me, my friends and co-workers Emilio and Leo right behind me. Ferns and bushes and various plants grow thick in the most vivid emerald greens, and down an incline at our right, the clear water of the McKenzie River moves around moss-covered rocks.

We've only seen two other hikers on the trail, both hiking in the opposite direction, so all we can hear are the sounds of insects buzzing and chirping, the breeze rustling the leaves and winding between the towering trees, and the river gurgling.

That and Leo swatting at every flying insect that nears him, cursing their very existence. It's as if the bugs know how much Leo hates them so they come near just to antagonize him.

"I don't think camping or hiking will ever feel right without hearing you wishing death upon all the insects," I say.

Leo squawks and slaps his arm. Then he says, "I can't help it if I'm naturally the tastiest option here. I'm like a succulent prime rib dinner." He swats at his leg. "Is this why you guys brought me?"

"Yep," Emilio says, looking at a bridge that crosses the McKenzie River up ahead. "We know that Max and I are basically chopped liver, so they've got no reason to come after us when they've got you as an option."

Leo gives Emilio a friendly shove that nearly knocks him off the trail. But then the guy takes off his backpack, unzips one of his four trillion compartments, and pulls out a neon bracelet. He tosses it to Leo and says, "Put that on your wrist. Then they'll think you're about as tasty as apple cider vinegar and garlic."

Leo looks between the pink bracelet and me and Emilio like he's trying to decide if we're pranking him.

Leo was the last to join our camping product testing group, but he's been on enough campouts that he should know to trust Emilio. I clap him on the back. "Come on. You know Emilio is the king of helpful gadgets. He wouldn't haul something out here as a joke. Besides, that was made by us."

Leo turns the bracelet, probably trying to find the Blue Mountain Gear logo, before he looks satisfied.

We are coming up to a log bridge that spans the McKenzie River, but I gesture to a fallen tree trunk sitting in the water, green with moss, that covers nearly the entire distance. "What do you say we cross there? It'll give us a chance to try out the tread on these boots. If it fails, it'll give us a chance to see exactly how water-resistant they are." Besides, the log looks way more interesting than the bridge.

We make our way down to the river and start crossing on the fallen log, Emilio in front of me and Leo behind. And because Emilio is Emilio and Leo is Leo—and, to be honest, because I am me—we start trying to push each other off balance as we cross.

We've all developed pretty good balance, but Emilio bumps me hard and Leo follows it up with his own forceful nudge. I come close to giving the river a kiss. But I keep my balance (score one in the "good traction" column for the boots I'm testing) and even manage to put an arm in front and behind myself to give both men a simultaneous shove.

"How do you never go down?" Leo asks, giving me another shove.

Probably because the only time I ever really got to spend with my dad when I was a kid was on adventuring trips in the mountains. I'd wanted to impress him so badly back then that I tried to be good at every aspect of camping. Even walking across logs. "Because I was a pro long before you guys decided to give me so much practice at it."

Emilio nods at Leo. "You, me, let's make a goal to knock this guy off balance before the weekend is over."

They make the mistake, though, of reaching across me to give each other a fist bump to seal the deal. So I shove both of their arms toward the river and both men lose their balance. We are right at the edge of the river, so they only step into water that is a couple of inches deep, but hearing the splash as I step onto dry ground is rather satisfying.

I lead us the rest of the way up the trail until it opens to the view of Tamolitch Blue Pool. As we reach the edge of the cliff that stands seventy feet above the water, I hear Leo's low whistle. "Wow. That's...Wow. You guys said the water was super blue, but wow. That's blue."

"We have the best job in the world," I say, and the men on either side of me just nod in agreement. Scenes like this lake never cease to grab hold of me and make me feel like I've somehow won the Powerball of life. How I got lucky enough to be out here, testing outdoor products—many that I've had a hand in designing—and getting paid for it is unreal. My life is nearly perfect. I hope I never lose the sense of awe that comes from it.

"Are those the rocks at the bottom of the pond that we're seeing?"

I nod. "Pretty incredible, isn't it?" As far as payoffs at the end of a hike go, this one is a good one.

"What makes it so blue?"

"Hunter could tell you if he were here since he's the expert—"

"—on pretty much everything—" Emilio interrupts.

"—but it has something to do with the McKenzie River coming up out of the ground here after finding its way through volcanic layers."

Now that we aren't in the dense forest, I wonder if I can get enough of a cell signal to send a text to Peyton. She would love this view. If I have more than a bar of signal strength, I might even be able to send a picture. I pull out my phone, but there isn't so much as a hint of a shadow of a bar.

Leo steps a little closer and looks down. "It's so clear it kind of makes you want to jump in, doesn't it?"

"Don't jump," Emilio and I say at the same time.

"The pool is thirty feet deep," Emilio says, "but we're seventy feet above it. And that water is only thirty-seven degrees, so even if nothing went wrong with the jump, you'd enjoy plunging into that water about as much as Max, here, would like a life without camping. Or going a week without talking to Peyton."

I try to surreptitiously slide the phone back into my pocket, but the guys still notice. So I redirect their attention to the trail that is a steep decline down the left that leads to the other side of the pond, right near the surface of the water.

Like always, Leo gets out his camera and starts taking pictures—ones he will later send to us and will become the wallpaper on our computers and cell phones. The guy has an eye for art. It's nice to have our trips documented and to be able to relive the beauty of our surroundings later when we're all sitting in cubicles.

Leo motions with his camera to a boulder at the water's edge, just a couple of feet above the clear surface of the water. "Hop up there and give me your best 'King of the Mountain' pose."

So I leap onto it and stand with my feet apart, fists on my hips, looking up and off into the distance.

"I just got cell service," Emilio says, "and there's a text from Peyton. Catch."

Shock, elation, and worry as to what emergency made Peyton text Emilio when she couldn't reach me hits me at almost the same time Emilio's phone does. It smacks against my hand and I fumble it before it smacks my chest and bounces off. I juggle it some more, scrambling to grab it before it falls to the rock or into the water. It takes a leap toward the water, and I lunge for it and lose my balance.

I barely have time to register that fact before my whole body, backside first, plunges fully into the near-freezing water. As my head resurfaces, I gasp at the shock of it and try to get my limbs to kick into gear and get me out of there.

The faces of both Leo and Emilio appear over the boulder I was standing on a moment ago, and both men hold out a hand toward me. I wipe the water from my face and then reach for their hands.

"Okay, for the record," Emilio says, "I did not think that would actually work."

Leo shakes his head. "Me neither. You're a pro at not getting knocked off balance, after all."

As the two of them help to pull me out of the water and I manage to get both feet on the rock, my whole body shivers, and I try to keep my teeth from chattering. "I'm sorry I dropped your phone in the water."

Emilio chuckles, shaking his head as he leans down to grab something from the water. He holds it up. "I'm not stupid enough to chuck my phone at you like that. It's my tin of shower wipes. I didn't think you'd actually fall for it."

Not that I had enough time to see what the object was before reacting. I shiver again. When I came here last time with Hunter and Emilio, I washed my hands in the McKenzie, so I knew how cold it was. But it's nothing compared to my whole body experiencing it at the same time.

"Dude," Leo says, his focus on messing with his camera. "That was classic. I think I even got it on film."

"Send it to me," I say before turning my attention to Emilio. "Wait, so did Peyton actually text?"

Emilio shakes his head as he takes off his backpack and pulls a shirt from one of the compartments. "No. Man, you are so gone for this woman." He tosses me the shirt. "Change into that so you don't freeze. And ask her out already."

I take off my backpack, which is thankfully waterproof, and then remove my wet shirt before putting on Emilio's. Luckily the guy is always prepared because I hadn't brought an extra. Although if I'd known I was going for a swim, I'd have brought dry pants, too. "I'm not going to ask her out. We're just friends."

Both guys give me a look as we head back toward the trail.

"And do you *want* to just be friends?" Leo asks. "Because that look on your face every time you text her, or talk on the phone with her, or talk about her says otherwise."

I take a deep breath, grateful for the steepness of the trail and all the rocks and weeds slowing us down so I can think about how to answer. There are more than enough reasons why I want to take our relationship beyond being best friends.

But there are also many reasons that make it seem like the worst idea ever. Just one is that Peyton is looking for a husband, and I don't trust marriage even a little bit after growing up with my parents' dysfunctional marriage. Not that I'm going to share all of my reasons with the guys. To keep it simple, I just say, "She wants things out of a relationship that I can't give her."

I can't see Emilio's or Leo's faces to tell if they're rolling their eyes or nodding in understanding, and neither man says a word. So I add, "Besides, look what getting married did to Hunter. He only comes with us about a fourth of the time now, and I don't think I could survive conditions like that."

"Whatever, dude," Leo says. "It's your life."

———

Back at camp, once I'm dry and have spent enough time in front of the fire to feel like my bones are the temperature of a human instead of an ice pop, I get dinner on cooking. We're testing a grill basket that's replacing the one we've been selling. We tested it back at work, but this is the first time we're using it in the wild. From what I can tell, the clasp and handle we designed are far superior.

I give the veggies roasting in it a shake and then feel a buzz in my pocket. I pull out my phone to see a text from Peyton and smile.

Peyton: How is camping?

It looks like she sent it a couple of hours ago, so I don't know if she's still by her phone or not. I don't dare move an inch for fear I'll step out of whatever window of cell reception I happened to step into. Then I type my response.

Max: We haven't gotten attacked by any bears or had our food stolen by enterprising raccoons, so I'd say it's going pretty well.

Peyton: Raccoons don't steal food from Snow White. If they wanted your food, they would come right up to you and ask for it.

I smile, and not because my best friend just called me the name of a character who is a woman. I smile because she remembers I told her the guys gave me that nickname when they noticed how animals seemed to instinctively trust me. It was *months* ago when I told her.

I'm also smiling because I caught her when she can respond. It makes it feel like she's nearby. Like in the next camp over. I type my response.

Max: I'm already regretting telling you that piece of information.

The dots showing she's typing a response come up but then they disappear, and I glance at the top of my phone. Whatever wispy fog of cell service had graced our campsite has drifted away so I'm going to have to wait for that response.

"Catch!" Leo shouts while I'm still looking at my phone.

I don't even look up—I just let the pine cone Leo threw hit me in the shoulder and fall to the ground before I slide my phone back into my pocket. "You didn't think you could catch me off guard twice in the same day, did you?"

Leo shrugs. "No. Only Peyton can do that. I figured since you were texting her, I'd have my chance."

"You didn't know I was texting her."

Leo rolls his eyes like the notion of him not recognizing when I'm texting Peyton is ridiculous. I'm going to have to get better at not showing whatever is on my face when I text, talk to, or talk about her.

"You're off guard any time you're thinking of her. It's pretty much the only time you are, so it's easy to see."

I pick up the basket by the handle to turn the veggies over. As I lift it, the clasp opens, and all the vegetables I've been cooking spill into the fire. I grind my teeth as I watch half our dinner go up in flames, and then take a long, slow breath. "Looks like we've got some work to do on this clasp."

"Yeah…" Leo says, dragging out the word. "It was totally the clasp's fault. It had nothing to do with you being distracted by thoughts of Peyton."

CHAPTER 3

Peyton

I TURN from the road onto the curved drive of Hidden Inn after a really long day at a client's home where I cooked a week's worth of meals for a blended family of eight with very specific likes and dislikes and a handful of food allergies between them. They have two four-year-old boys—one from each parent's previous marriages—and they decided that the best place to have an all-out battle between teeny cars and plastic dinosaurs was around my feet and on my calves. But the pair were just so adorable that I couldn't bring myself to ask them to play elsewhere.

I'd been pouring all of my focus into creating the perfect roasted butternut squash risotto and somehow missed that they were quiet and no longer playing at my feet. That is until I turned around to grab the red pepper flakes and saw that the boys had gotten hold of my bag of gluten-free flour, dumped it out, and were using it as their car and dinosaur terrain. The two of them managed to get themselves covered in the white powder and look more like ghosts than preschoolers.

Luckily, my client knows her sons well enough that it didn't surprise her or make her blame me. What she didn't anticipate was how much they and I bonded, so as she was shepherding them off to the bath, she didn't manage to intercept them before they each gave me bear hugs.

I thought I'd done a decent job of getting the bulk of the flour off my jeans, but as I'm getting out of my seat, I can see that I'll have to take a trip to the car wash and vacuum it out soon.

Roman, my roommate Bex's fiancé, pulls into the curving driveway, parks behind me, and gets out as I walk up to the porch that wraps around the inn. I'm opening my mouth to ask how he's doing when the front door bursts open.

"I'm so glad you're both here," my roommate, Timini, says as she grabs our hands and pulls us inside.

"We don't have our roommate dinner tonight, do we?" I ask.

Timini shakes her head as she gestures for us to follow her into the kitchen and dining room area. "No, but Bex ordered pizza. And she has something to tell us that she's been keeping all buttoned-up about while we waited for you two."

I walk past all the smaller tables in the big space that guests used to eat breakfast at back when the place was run as an inn, but they are all covered in stacks of fabric, fabric cuts, scissors, pins, measuring tapes, patterns, and everything else Timini uses to create the pretty costumes she makes.

My roommate Addison and her husband, Ian, are seated at the big dining table just in front of the island counter. Bex stands beside the table, next to a stack of pizza boxes. Her face lights up when she sees Roman, and they meet each other halfway into the room and give each other the softest kiss. I can't wait for their wedding—the two of them are just as sweet as strawberry ice cream. They both walk to the table as Timini and I sit down.

Bex and Roman don't sit, though—they just stand looking at all of us and each other with excited faces.

"Holy guacamole," I say. "You finally found a house, didn't you?"

"Sort of," Bex says, looking at Roman.

Roman nods, not taking his eyes off Bex. "It's more of an 'on paper' kind of thing."

"I don't know what that means," Timini says.

"Well," Bex says, looking at all of us spread around the table, "we found the perfect piece of land about a mile down the road. We've decided to build."

I clap. "That's so exciting! I was worried you would end up moving far away since you weren't finding anything close, but that's the best news!"

"The only problem," Roman says, "is that the builder told us it'll be six to nine months before we can move in."

Bex nods. "Which brings us to what we wanted to talk to you all about. After the wedding, we are hoping to have Roman move in here with me while the house is being built. We already talked to Addison and Ian, since they own the inn, but Peyton and Timini, we want to know how you would feel about that. It's adding another person to the mix, and if you're not comfortable with that, we can move into Roman's apartment in Gresham, but we like it here and—"

Bex stops talking when the force of my hug hits her. I don't mean to throw so much energy into it, but I am just so excited that all of us are going to be staying together for longer. I am thrilled that Bex and Roman are getting married in just under four weeks. But that happy day also marked the end of an era. And now that era is going to keep going on.

"It looks like Peyton's vote is 'yes,'" Roman says.

"Of course it is," I say, and then give Roman a welcome hug.

"Timini?" Bex asks, and then bites her lip, waiting for the last roommate's response.

"My vote's a no."

My heart sinks. "Really?"

Timini snorts. "Of course, it's a yes. Who wouldn't want more love invading us at Hidden Inn?"

That is the best news I could've imagined hearing today. My roommates at Hidden Inn feel like family, and now it feels like our family is growing.

Halfway through eating the pizza, I say, "I want even more love invading us at Hidden Inn." Everyone looks at me like they aren't quite sure what I mean, so I explain. "You know how a health scare can make you reevaluate your life? Well, my dad's heart attack did that, and he told me how much he wanted me to get married soon. And do you know what? I want that, too."

Addison smiles wide. "I'm excited for you."

"You can't be excited about it yet because I don't know how to go about doing that."

Roman looks at everyone around the table. "So just propose to Max. *Bam*. Done."

"Ha ha," I say. "No—I need to find someone to date who is as perfect as Max is, and they need to be someone who would actually want to get married. I'm a planner, but I can't exactly plan my way into a happily ever after. I don't know what to do because my current plan isn't working."

"That plan where you wait until you stumble across someone while doing the normal things you do?" Bex says.

"Yep, that one. And then I date them for just long enough to tell if they're the one and start the process all over again when they aren't. And I don't happen across people often because single guys rarely hire personal chefs. If I keep doing what I've been doing, I'll be forty before I find someone. I want someone soon."

"So you need to speed things up," Timini confirms.

"Yes."

"Well," Addison says, "we could probably all set you up on dates with people we know."

Ian shakes his head. "If she goes on a few dates with each one, it'll take weeks before she gets to the next one. I bet we can think of a way to speed up the process."

"Like speed-dating?" Addison asks.

"No," I say. "I've gone to those things before. You can't tell enough about a person in a few minutes. You need at least a full date."

"And," Timini says, reaching to the middle of the table to grab a second slice of pizza, "if you go on a few dates in a row, it's easier to see what you like and don't like about the guys. What? That's not weird. Just ask Bex."

"The girl's got a point," Bex says. "In a strange way, it led me to Roman."

Addison taps a finger on her lips. "So, you need a lot of dates in a short amount of time."

"Yes," Timini says, "but you can't just *say* you'll go on a lot of dates. You need incentive or you'll give up when things don't go well. And it *will* get to a point when things don't go well. That's just the way it works."

"I already have incentive. I want a husband."

Timini shakes her head. "It's too far out. You need something more immediate."

"Oh!" Bex's eyes grow wide and she grins. "Maybe you can take those planning skills of yours and plan your way to a happily ever after. A *Find Peyton a Husband* plan. Make it a contest with someone else. Keep it short, like..." She looks around, her hands moving like she's trying to grab hold of something. "A week. See who can date the highest number of different people in seven days."

I sit up a little straighter. That might do it. Then, even if things don't go so well, it's not too long of a time frame. I can handle anything for a week.

"And then, at the end of the week," Addison says, "you can ask the one you liked the best to be your date at Roman's and Bex's wedding."

"Oh, this is perfect!" I say. Then I turn to Timini. "Do it with me. We can be in competition with each other, and it'll be fun. Plus, we'll each get a date for the wedding."

Timini snorts. "No. No way am I going up against the Queen of Enthusiasm in a contest."

I look at my roommates for help talking Timini into it, but Bex and Addison both hold up their hands.

"If I were single," Addison says, "I wouldn't have gone up against you, either."

"Same," Bex says.

Roman and Ian share a look that I can't quite interpret, and then a smile spreads slowly across Roman's face and he says, "Ask Max."

Max? I'm not so sure about asking him. I kind of sort of fell for him about a year ago, before I found out that he wasn't interested in me that way. It was tough, but I found a way to stomp out my feelings for him. If the two of us are competing, that might make me think about him dating more, which could make those feelings resurface.

But Max really does love any kind of competition. He will likely not only agree but push me to get so many more dates than I would on my own. He could be the key to the *Find Peyton a Husband* plan actually succeeding.

All I have to do is not fall for my best friend. That's it.

Succeed, and I will be well on my way to getting a date for the wedding, finding a husband, and making my dad happy.

————

We are all still in the kitchen when I hear the sound of Max's car, and I go to the front door to greet him. I open it right as he reaches it, looking all manly in his snug jeans, hiking boots, and a t-shirt that hugs his chest perfectly. "You're back!"

"I just wanted to stop by on my way home and say hi."

I sniff as he steps past me into the lobby of the inn. "I smell campfire, but you look way too clean to not have been home to shower yet."

He gets the cutest look on his face. He ducks his head and his brows come together just a bit, almost like he's embarrassed about something, but one corner of his mouth curls up like he thinks something is humorous. "That's because I took a bath in the cleanest spring water there is."

"Are you hungry? We have some pizza, and I have a plan."

"A pizza plan?"

"No. Something even better."

I lead him into the kitchen and let him eat first because he's probably starving, even though I am dying to talk to him about the competition. About halfway through his second piece, he turns to me. "So what's this plan?"

I clap my hands together. "I was talking with my dad while you were gone, and I realized just how badly I want love in my life. You know, like Addison and Ian or Bex and Roman have. And I've decided I am done waiting for it to come along—I'm ready to go out and grab it myself."

Max is giving me a look, but I don't know what it means. "So this is where your plan comes in?" he asks.

"Yes. Well, we all came up with it together, and it's a competition. I know how much you like challenges, so I'm hoping you'll be my competition buddy. Anyway, the contest is about which of us can go on the most dates in a single week, and each date has to be with a different person.

"Date nights don't have to just be Fridays or Saturdays—we could go on dates every single night of the week. Lunch dates, even, if we wanted. And I figured we could fit a lot of dates in on the weekends. Like a breakfast date, a lunch one, an afternoon one, an evening one—we can even do a dessert date on the same night as a dinner date. Or a breakfast date before work. It doesn't have to be expensive dates, either. They can be walks in the park, or watching the sunset, or whatever."

Max just leans back in his chair, his pizza sitting on his plate like he's forgotten about it.

"So we were thinking," I continue, "you and I could find the dates this week, go on the dates next week, and then whichever date we liked the best, we'll ask them to be our dates for Bex and Roman's wedding two weeks after that. Because we can both bring a plus one."

"That's…a lot of dating," Max says.

"Doesn't it sound so fun? We can even help each other get dates! And we can ask everyone we know to set us up with people. And we can ask people out that we already know, or get a dating app this week and meet some new people. So what do you think? By the end of next week, maybe I'll actually find someone to marry, and I know you don't want to get married but you like to date and you might find someone you really want to keep dating."

"Did you say that all with a single breath?" Roman asks, looking impressed.

He shouldn't be so impressed, though. I shake my head and hold up two fingers, but keep my eyes on Max. He seems like he's really thinking strongly about it, which probably means he's going to say yes. "I know you're used to winning, like, every single thing always, but don't just assume this is going to be easy. I plan to win. I'm going to be the toughest competitor that you've ever competed against."

"I don't know, Peyton."

I'm confused. Max lives for competitions. Normally, he would be smack-talking right now about how he's going to win by a mile. And he seems to like dating. "Oh! Of course! We need a prize for the winner." That must be why he isn't fully on board. "Um…" I look around at my roommates and soon-to-be roommate.

"I know," Bex says. "How about whoever loses has to sing karaoke?"

My face falls. I'm not good at that at all, so I'm going to have to make sure I don't lose.

Max looks at the others for a long moment, then his eyes find mine. "You seem really excited about this. Okay, I'm in."

"Yes!" Now that I have a competitor, I'm going to stick to this. The excitement for the next week is building up inside me to higher and higher levels the more I talk about it. "It is going to be the greatest week ever. You'll see. By the time Bex and Roman's wedding comes around, you're going to be so happy you agreed to do this competition with me."

"I'm sure I will."

He seems…unsure of himself, maybe? Almost nervous. Not his always-confident self. I've never won a single challenge against him before, so this face on him is new. Maybe he knows I'm going to win. Probably because *I* know I will win. "Don't worry. I'll be your wingman and help you find as many dates as you'd like."

"Thanks."

"Aww," Timini says. "Look at you two. You're going to go

on a million dates and find the perfect one, and then all of you will have love."

"You're going to find love, too," I say. "We can help."

"Maybe you should get a dating app," Addison tells her.

Timini shakes her head. "I'm terrible at those things. You've all seen some of the guys I've dated—I always pick the pretty ones that turn out to be the wrong ones. I need a way to find someone to date without seeing their face. Like a blind date, only we find each other and talk a lot and find out if we're compatible before looks ever enter the picture. Then maybe I wouldn't always choose so poorly."

Bex's hand finds Roman's. "Your company should make an app like that."

"We should. Everyone deserves to find love." And then he gives Bex a kiss.

And it reminds me of what my dad said about relationships and how the most important relationship is with a spouse. I gasp and my hands fly to my mouth as the most wonderful, perfect idea flies into my mind. "Oh my life, Max. We should set our parents up with each other. My dad deserves love again and heaven knows that your mom deserves the love she never really got to have ever. It would be so perfect if they started dating each other."

"Set up our parents? Really?"

"Wouldn't it be so great?"

Max looks as uncomfortable as a cat wearing a bulldog costume.

"Max, it's not like I'm saying you should go on a double date with them. But think of how great it would be if they dated and things did work out between them. Then we wouldn't be just best friends—we would practically be brother and sister. I know you said you love me like a sister, but wouldn't it be so fun to actually be siblings?"

He stands up, and I search his face, trying to see if he's in a hurry, or upset, or just plain bored, but it doesn't give me any clues. "We have enough dates we need to set each other up on. I think we should just focus on that instead of setting up our parents right now."

"True," I say. "You're right—it can wait. Right now, we need to focus on this competition that I'm going to win."

I know enough about Max's competitive nature to know that the more I smack talk, the more committed he becomes to winning. Not that I'm good at smack talk. I wonder if there's some class or online course or YouTube video that could help me. In the meantime, I'm not going to let the fact that I'm bad at it stop me from doing it. Because this competition is a little bit scary and feels kind of huge if I'm being honest. And if Max is all-in on trying to win, it's going to make it that much easier for me to be all-in, too.

He gives me a smile but it looks tired, and it reminds me that he's on his way home from a camping trip. "I don't know, Abernathy. You're going to have to find a way to go on a lot of dates if you're going to beat me."

Max always uses my last name when he smack-talks. Which is fine, but then it makes me feel like I should use his last name, too. But since his last name is the same as my first name, it really just makes me feel like I'm talking about myself in the third person. So, instead, I always go for his middle name. "Bring it on, Augustus. I'm not afraid of a little competition." There. That sounded like decent smack talk. Score one for Peyton.

"I will definitely bring my A-game." Max glances at all of my roommates and then hitches his thumb over his shoulder. "Okay, I should probably go home to shower and unpack."

He says goodbye to me, and as he walks out of the kitchen and I hear the front door close, I feel the excitement for what lies ahead bubbling up inside me. I turn back to my roommates who are all looking at me with such a varied mix of expressions that I can't take it all in. "You guys will help set me up with dates, too, right?"

They all nod, and Timini says, "Of course. What are friends for?"

CHAPTER 4
Max

HUNTER TURNS the shoe dryer around in his hand. "It worked well, then, huh?"

The two of us are in the design cave, the area that is part computer lab and part showcase of some of the great items our team has designed.

I nod. "Like a charm. The inside of my boots were dry in no time after I fell into the lake. I'm sure we can make it smaller, though. I don't think it should have to be this bulky."

The two of us switch between physically picking up the piece of equipment we designed and turning to the big design computer screen in front of us, studying it, brainstorming ways to make it even better.

Hunter spent Monday through Thursday in our Hillsboro office working with the marketing team, so today is the first time I've seen my best guy friend since the camping trip that he missed. Emilio and Leo are great, but not the ones I'd ever go to for relationship advice. Hunter and I have been friends since before I even knew Peyton, so he knows our entire history. I've been dying to talk to him about her, but it's more of an in-person thing than a phone call thing.

"What if we make the length adjustable," Hunter says, then draws a circle around the middle of the shoe dryer on the screen, "and have this part collapse in and pull out? We'd have to make a little more space around the fan, but the overall bulk would be less."

"Good idea. And I was thinking we could alter the angle of the fan—" I use the mouse to move that element of the design "—and it might cut down on the space it takes. It would probably be enough to compensate for the collapsible section."

Hunter takes the mouse to make some changes, and I let him. I've got too much on my mind to focus on details. "So, um, Peyton decided that she wants to get married."

Hunter's attention jerks to me. "To you?"

"Okay, you don't have to look so shocked. But no, genius, not to me. Just, in general, she's ready to get married."

"You kind of knew that already."

"True. But she's ready to speed up the process." Peyton's my best friend—I want her to be happy. That doesn't mean I'm in love with the idea of her finding someone to spend her life with who isn't me. Imagining her married and moving forward with her life and leaving me behind has been playing over and over in my mind ever since she dropped that bomb on Sunday, and it's all making me a little crazy.

Hunter turns back to the screen, making adjustments to our design. "How is she planning to speed it up?"

I turn and lean against the design table, my arms folded. "A competition with me, actually. She wants us to see who can go on the highest number of dates—with a different person each time—in one week, and then we each take our favorite date to our friends Bex and Roman's wedding."

Hunter's still looking at the screen, but I can see the smile spreading across his face. "Stakes?"

"Karaoke for the loser."

This time, Hunter laughs. He even lets go of the mouse and turns in my direction so all his focus can be on me.

"And she wants us to be each other's wingman. So not only am I going to have to be hearing about her dates, but I'll actually be setting her up on dates with guys I know."

"Oh, man. I don't think you could get much more friend-zoned than that. Not that you haven't spent the last year pretty solidly in the friend zone."

"Thanks. I'm feeling better already."

Hunter chuckles. "Is she setting you up on dates as well?"

I nod.

"Well, at least you'll get a lot of dates out of the deal."

I let out a grunt of frustration and turn to the design screen. Getting a few dates isn't worth nearly as much as it's costing me.

"Why don't you just tell her how you feel about her already?"

I stay focused on the design, tweaking and re-tweaking the angle of the fan but making no progress. "Because that's not fair to her. I can't tell her, knowing how important getting married and starting a family is to her, if I'm not willing to get married or start a family."

Besides, even if marriage is something I could ever even fathom being okay with, based on the genes I got from both of my parents, I'm not going to be good at it—the being a husband part or the being a dad part. Both of which are important to Peyton.

"Oh," I say, "and I almost forgot the other twist in the story. She wants to set my mom up on a date with her dad."

This time, Hunter's laughter is so loud that the clothing

design team on the first floor probably hears him. I turn away from the screen and wait patiently as Hunter finishes laughing.

"So, wait," Hunter says. "You're telling me that she's hoping to make you two officially brother and sister? That time when she almost kissed you and you said you love her like a sister is just going to keep coming back to bite you over and over, isn't it?"

Worst mistake ever. Someday, when I die, they're going to engrave on my headstone *Here lies the guy who told the woman he loved that he loved her...like a sister.*

I had sensed a shift in our relationship a year ago but was still caught off guard when we found ourselves face-to-face on a porch swing, whispering to each other just inches apart. Then Peyton glanced at my lips and began to close the considerably short gap between us.

I had been so panicked at the thought of not being enough if our relationship morphed from platonic to romantic, and therefore possibly losing a relationship with the person in the world who was most important to me that I had turned into an idiot and uttered the words that would follow me everywhere like a lost puppy.

"Hunter, I don't need to tell you how much my mom and her dad cannot date each other."

"Yeah, you've definitely got to squash those plans. Does your mom even want to get married again? I don't know her well but I didn't get the vibe that she was the marrying type."

"She isn't."

"Okay, the way I see it, you've got three choices. One: get over your issues and decide to be the man Peyton wants."

I roll my eyes. Like that's something you can just do.

"Two: keep things the way they've been. You go on your dates, she goes on hers, and you just keep acting like you've been acting for the past year—or really, the past four—and hope that Peyton never moves on and stays single forever so she'll always be your best friend and the woman you wish you could share a life with but know you never will."

I grab my chest, jerking back like Hunter just stabbed me with a sword. "Ouch."

"Or three: try to win the challenge. Go on as many dates as you can next week. Give them your all. Who knows? Maybe you'll find someone to date who will help you get over Peyton once and for all."

I nod. I haven't really put enough into dating lately. Partly because I'm not dating to find happily ever after like most people are, and partly because a big chunk of my heart has a *Reserved for Peyton Abernathy* sign on it.

But maybe Hunter is right. Pouring my focus into dating could help me change that. I don't want to think about Peyton dating other guys and have actually loved that she's been too busy lately to date much. If she starts dating a ton next week, it will be easier to keep my mind off her if I'm going on dates as well. It could help me keep her in the friend zone as effectively as she keeps me in the friend zone.

Then, as long as whatever guy Peyton finds is worthy of her, I can be all-in happy for her.

"Good plan," I say.

"Yeah?"

"Yeah. I think it's just what I need. So if you have anyone you want to line me up with, next week is the time."

Based on the smile that spreads across Hunter's face, he already has some ideas of people I could date who would be perfect for me. Fantastic.

CHAPTER 5

Peyton

MY FINAL DISH for the family I'm preparing meals for, lemon chicken and rice, is simmering on the stove in Hidden Inn's kitchen, and the rest is finishing cooling as I clean up the last of the pots, pans, mixing bowls, utensils, and other dishes I've dirtied.

"And your dinner date tonight," Timini says as she cuts a pattern out of a large swath of fabric that covers our big dining table, "that's the one who is Bex's friend?"

I shake my head. "The dinner date is with a guy one of my clients set me up with. His name is Tyler, and I'm headed straight there after I drop off these meals. After that, I'm having dessert and a walk in the park with Bex's friend. Cohen, I think."

I hurry to dry my hands, then pull up my calendar app on my phone to make sure. How embarrassing would it be to get the guy's name wrong? "No! Cohen is dessert tomorrow! Grant is tonight. He seems as nice as summer sunshine. I don't know much about Tyler. I'm going in pretty blind for that one."

I put my phone down and start drying and putting away the dishes.

All of my roommates own their own small businesses. Addison and Ian are gone most days at clients' homes or Ian is in his shop. Bex spends probably half of her workday here in the inn, and when she's home, she usually works in the gathering room. But Timini does most of her work in the big room that holds the kitchen, our big dining table, and the half-a-dozen round tables. So the two of us have shared a lot of heart-to-heart talks over the past several months.

Bex must've finished her workday because she comes into the kitchen, searching for food.

"The pasta salad in that bowl is extra if you want some."

"Oh, Peyton! You are seriously the best." She must be really hungry or really in the mood for pasta salad because she's eating her bowl of it like she has just been found after being stranded in the desert for days. Between bites, she says, "Your week of dates starts today, right?"

"Yep! I meet the first guy in an hour."

"Bex," Timini says, "help me convince Peyton that one of her dates this week should be Max."

"Totally." Bex takes another bite, then adds, "You two get along great. You should try dating."

"Are we talking about Max?" Addison says as she walks into the room. She must've just gotten home. "Because if we are, I agree."

I start putting the lids on each of the dishes I've made, adding labels with reheating instructions along with which side dishes go with which main dishes. "Right. We should date and then get married and live happily ever after." My roommates are so funny.

"Exactly!" Timini says with a big exhale, like she's glad I

finally understand. But really, it's Timini who doesn't understand.

"It's not going to happen, Timini. You know that." I grab the insulated bags I carry food in and start adding the ice packs to their linings.

"Name an objection if it did happen," Bex says.

I push the bag to the side. "Okay, here's one. Max's last name is Peyton. So if we got married, my name would be Peyton Peyton. *Peyton Peyton!* My name cannot be Peyton Peyton."

Bex grins. "Oh, but then we could call you PeyPey."

"No," I say. "Not allowed." I pull the first stack of containers toward me and start placing them in the insulated bag.

"You don't have to take his last name," Timini says. "You can each keep your own."

Addison sinks into a seat at the dining table, looking like her day has been exhausting. "Or have him take yours. Max Abernathy has a great ring to it."

I shake my head. "I'm a traditionalist. I'm taking my husband's name no matter what."

"Peyton Peyton aside," Bex says, "you can't tell me you've never thought about dating him. Because I don't buy in a million years that you've never thought of him as more than just a friend."

"Oh, I've thought about it, alright," I say as I put the last of the cooled meals into the bag and zip it up. "About a year ago, I kid you not that it was all I could think about. Then, one night, in the middle of me thinking how much I wanted to date Max, there were eight of us at a friend's house, playing games. Between having that many people in a smallish space and using the oven nonstop for appetizers, it got hot. So I went outside to cool down, and Max came out, too.

"You know how when you're super-hot and you go into cooler weather, it feels great at first but then you start to shiver even though you're not all the way cooled off yet? Well, Max and I were sitting on our friend's porch swing, and when I shivered, he put his arm around me and pulled me in close.

"We were whisper-talking so near to each other, and then suddenly we were having a moment. I swear to you, he looked at my lips. Which made me look at his, of course, because that's what you do when someone looks at your lips. And then I realized just how badly I wanted to kiss him right then and there.

"So, I started leaning in close, waiting to see what he'd do, and he leaned in close, too. We were maybe an inch away from each other when he pulled back and said, 'You know I love you, right?' Which really was exactly what I wanted to hear in that moment. But then, right after, he added, 'I always will. You're like a sister to me.' He loves me *like a sister*. So obviously that was the end of that, because *ew*."

Bex takes the last bite of her pasta salad, then goes to the sink and starts washing the bowl and fork. "Maybe he doesn't still feel that way. Or maybe it was a smokescreen. Maybe he wasn't ready for a relationship at that time and his brain just dumped that out as a way to stop its progression without ruining the friendship."

I put the lid on the shallow pot on the stove and flip up the locks that will hold it in place before nestling it into the insulated bag that will keep the meal warm for my client's family to eat for dinner tonight. "If that was the case, he wouldn't have spent the past year acting like it was exactly what he meant." I zip up the bag. "Plus, he's gone a lot. Which isn't a huge deal, but sometimes I just really miss him."

"See?" Addison says. "That's proof that maybe there's something between you."

"I really missed Timini when she went to visit her family for a week a couple of months ago." Missing someone is proof that you like hanging out with them. Not that you want to marry them. "Why are you all pushing this so much?"

Timini stacks her cut fabric pieces on top of each other. "Because, hello, we've seen the two of you together."

"I do think he's pretty perfect," I say because Max totally is. He's such a great friend, he's so much fun to talk to, we get along so well, and we're good at looking out for each other. "And I love being around him. But," I add, before they can comment too much on it, "it just wouldn't work out. I already came to terms with that." Of course, accepting that something is never going to happen and still pining for him are two different things.

I look at all the food I just prepared. "I like cooking for people, and I love that I can make a living doing it. But I don't have huge aspirations like you all do. I don't have dreams of owning my own restaurant someday or of having a big catering business. I really just want to get married and have kids and have them stand on stools beside me in the kitchen, wearing cute little aprons, and teach them how to cook, too. I might want to make a kids' cookbook or have a cooking with kids blog or something like that, but mostly I just want to make meals for people so they can be happy and healthy and have time to eat it with their loved ones.

"The part about my future that makes me so excited is being a wife and a mom, and I want to do it in time for my dad to meet his grandkids. Being good at both is my greatest aspiration. But Max has told me so many times over the years how much he doesn't want to get married. Not just that he's not ready yet—that he doesn't want to get married *ever*. Or be a dad. Which is just crazy, because I think he'd be great at both."

"Do you know why he doesn't?" Addison asks.

"Yeah." I look around to make sure I've packed up everything I need, then let out a big breath, resting my arms on the cooler. "Mostly because his parents were Mr. and Mrs. Bicker McBickerson. So he grew up thinking marriage was a horrible thing that constantly annoyed people.

"He must've gotten over it a teeny bit, though, because at some point he met Laurel. This was before he and I became friends. Apparently, they had a lot of chemistry and things got pretty serious between the two of them. Like, I think Max might have actually been considering marriage.

"But I guess chemistry didn't really matter, because they got along about as great as Max's parents had, and, I don't know. I think that kind of broke whatever thread of desire for marriage Max had left, and no one could convince him otherwise now. Plus, Max's dad was absent pretty much all of his childhood, so he never had a good example of a dad, either. I think he worries he might be the same.

"Anyway, I'm not going to give up my biggest dream in life, so it doesn't matter how great Max is. Not wanting marriage and a family is a deal-breaker for me."

A year ago, I had wanted to have my cake and eat it, too. Since then, I've come to accept that I can't have both and that Max and I will only ever be friends who love each other like siblings.

Or possibly actual siblings, if I can get our parents to fall in love.

"I get it," Bex says. "I couldn't imagine being as in love with Roman as I am and not being able to marry him."

Addison nods. "I agree. I want you to have it all. The falling in love, the marriage, the family—all of it."

"Me, too," Timini says. "So go out there and find the one already!"

I smile and then gather them all into a hug. I glance at the clock on the wall. "Oh! I better get going, or I'm going to be late for my date!"

I put a strap for each bag over my shoulders, then heft both out to my car. All I have to do is drop them off at my client's house and head over to the restaurant to meet my first date of the week. It's Monday. By Sunday night, just over six days from now, I will hopefully have gone on enough dates to have found the man who will be my future. Someone who will be open to marriage. Who knows? Maybe I'll even find him tonight.

CHAPTER 6

Max

THROWING myself into dating is the perfect way to get my mind off Peyton. I'm ready for this. Excited, even. It has been a while since I've gotten myself this psyched up for a date. I'm even wearing my favorite button-down and the cologne that always gets me compliments.

Caroline, the woman I'm going on a date with tonight, is someone Leo set me up with. Leo started out in hiking equipment design, and he and Caroline worked together before she left to work for a rival company. So at least we'll have something in common to talk about right off the bat.

Traffic on the I-205 is worse than I anticipated, and it's putting me a little behind. I left myself a cushion of time for something like this—I hope it'll be enough.

As I turn down the street the restaurant is on, I think about how Peyton is going on her first date of the week right now, too. Actually, she planned two dates for tonight. I'll have to step up my game if I'm going to fit in enough dates this week to win our contest. I wonder if she's going to have as easy of a time talking with her dates as she does talking to me. It's a given that the guy is going to fall for her. Peyton is an easy woman to fall for. But is she going to fall for any of them?

I need to get my mind off her dates and back on my own. Am I going to have as easy of a time talking to my dates as I do talking to Peyton?

I'm hopeless. I can't even stop thinking about her when I'm purposely thinking about my own date. *Come on, Max. You can do better than this.*

Okay, what do I know about Caroline? She worked at Blue Mountain Gear, so she's probably a fan of the outdoors. That could be fun. And Leo seemed really enthusiastic about setting the two of us up because he thought we'd be a great fit. The more I think about the date, the more possibilities it feels like it holds.

I've managed to get myself excited enough about it that when the traffic light turns yellow, I actually consider speeding up and racing through the intersection. But I'm far enough back that it'll be red by the time I reach it, so I ease on the brake to slow down. As soon as my car slows, I hear screeching then a crunch right as I'm thrown forward. It takes my brain a second to process that I've actually been hit in the rear by another car.

A quick glance in my rearview mirror tells me that a woman drives the car behind me, and other than experiencing a bit of shock, she looks okay. The light is red, so I quickly call 9-1-1 through my car's Bluetooth and report the crash. As soon as the light turns green, I drive through the intersection and pull off to the side. Great. Not only is this going to be a huge inconvenience, but it's really going to make me late for my date.

We both get out of our cars to check out the damage. We weren't driving fast, but it still did a good amount of damage to her front end and my back end—a little more than just replacing a bumper for both of us.

The woman whirls on me. "What were you thinking, stopping in the middle of the road like that?" She motions at our damaged cars. "This is exactly why it's against traffic laws. When it's a straight road in a thirty-five mile-per-hour zone, people expect you to go at least thirty-five, not just stop!"

My eyebrows come together. "There was a traffic light. It had turned yellow."

"Which means you speed up!"

"No, it means you slow down, which I did." I want to laugh at the ridiculousness of it.

The woman looks at me like I'm stupid, then puts her hands on her hips and shifts her focus to the road ahead for a moment. "Listen, I'm running late for an appointment." She turns and walks back to her car. "Let's just exchange information and get on our way."

I stay right where I am. "No, we need to file a police report."

"That'll just take longer. We don't need one."

If this woman is going to claim she isn't at fault for the wreck, I definitely want a police report saying in writing that she is. There must be an officer in the area because she pulls up behind the woman with her lights on before the lady who wrecked into me even gets a paper and pen from her car. The woman lets out a defeated sigh and stands with one hand on her hip, tapping her foot impatiently for the officer to get out of her car.

The woman argues with the officer, too, about who is at fault. Seriously, does she think that'll work? Based on how long she pushes her point, she must.

"Ducks are yellow, right?" the officer says. "Next time you're driving and you're wondering what a yellow light means, imagine a mama duck and her little ducklings crossing the road. They go slow, not fast, just like you should do when you see yellow." She marks something down on her clipboard.

"Oh, and remember to follow at a safe distance so you've got time to stop when needed."

When she asks for our information, the woman steps forward to give hers first. I'm in a hurry, too, but this woman seems extra stressed, so I'm fine letting her go first. She still has to wait until the officer finishes the paperwork, so it's not like it really matters.

I stand back to give her some space while she gives her information, and I just watch, wondering what she's so stressed out about getting to. She's wearing a red dress. Not a business-like dress—more casual and fun, which really doesn't fit with what is obviously her current state of mind.

The moment the officer finishes getting our information and gives each of us a copy, the woman grabs it out of the officer's hand, gets into her car, and speeds off.

I toss the accident report into my front seat, then walk to the back of my car. I run my hands over my face and look at my ruined bumper and dented trunk. I haven't been on a date in nearly three months, and this week is supposed to get me back into dating again and get my mind off Peyton. This is not how I want to start it all off. I pull out my phone and open the message from Leo with Caroline's phone number, then send her a quick text.

> Max: I apologize for being late. I'll be at the restaurant in 5 minutes.

Then I take a picture of the damage and include it in a text to Peyton.

> Max: I hope your first date is going better than mine.

She responds quickly.

Peyton: Max! Are you okay? What happened?

Max: Just a fender bender. It's all good. I actually haven't met my date yet. Wish me luck!

She responds with three four-leaf clover emojis. Then one with a grinning face with fingers crossed on both sides of it. I smile and put the phone into my pocket, get into my car, drive the last few blocks, and then find a parking space. As I get out of my car and walk up to the front doors of the restaurant, I take a deep breath and hold my shoulders back.

This week of dates might be Peyton's *Find a Husband* plan, but it's my *Stop Thinking of Peyton as More than a Friend* plan. Today is the first day of it, and I'm going to crush it.

My date has already checked in with the hostess, which is no big surprise since I'm so late. What *is* a surprise is who the hostess leads me to.

The woman in the not-business-like but casual and fun red dress looks up at me as we near, a look of hope and anticipation on her face—until she realizes who I am and the expression immediately changes to a scowl. "Are you following me?"

I turn to the hostess and give her a "thank you" nod.

"Giving the officer my contact information because of the wreck doesn't give you permission to stalk me."

I hold out my hand. "Hi. I'm Max Peyton. You must be Caroline. Leo has spoken very highly of you." I speak formally as if we haven't just met in unfortunate circumstances. Knowing her last name for my introduction would've made it that much better—I wish I had at least glanced at the police report to see it before I came in.

"No," Caroline says. "No, no, no. This cannot be happening."

I take a seat. "The night is young, and we really haven't gotten a chance to know each other yet. What do you say we pretend we are meeting for the first time and go from there? We can consider the wreck a memorable meet-cute. Who knows? Maybe someday we'll tell this story at a party and everyone will be roaring with laughter, including us."

"I have a dented front end to my car. I'll have to spend time working with the insurance adjuster, find a reputable shop, and then be without my car while they repair it. My insurance won't even cover a rental car while it's in the shop. Oh, and my insurance rates will probably rise, and it's all because of you."

"Wait. You still think it was my fault?"

"So, no. I don't think we'll be at a party someday, telling people about our 'memorable meet-cute.'"

"Even after the officer told you I wasn't at fault?"

Caroline stands and puts her purse strap on her shoulder. "You are the most inconsiderate man I've ever met, and I hope I never have the displeasure of meeting you again."

"Well," I say, even though she is already storming out of the restaurant and won't hear, "I guess this date is over, then." I pick up the menu and start looking it over.

My start to a week of dating hasn't gone nearly as smoothly as I had hoped. If nothing else, I should at least get good food out of it.

As I wait for the waiter to come, I can't help but wonder how Peyton's date is going.

CHAPTER 7

Peyton

As I STAND in line at the host's podium, I glance at the dining area of The Stone Slab. It's a fun, trendy restaurant that I've never been to before. I'll have to compliment Tyler on choosing a good one.

For a moment, nerves bubble up inside me. I've texted Tyler a few times as we ironed out the details of the date but we haven't chatted much, so I really don't know him at all. I can somewhat guess what he looks like simply because he's the brother of my client who set the two of us up, but I haven't even seen a picture of him. It's okay, though, because I trust my client and she thinks we'd be a good match. This isn't nerves. This is excitement about the possibilities of what this week will bring.

When the couple in front of me walks away to take a seat in the lobby, I step up to the host. "Hello. I'm meeting someone—Tyler. Has he checked in yet?"

The host runs his pen down his list. "I have a Ty."

"That's him."

The guy nods and picks up a menu and a set of silverware wrapped in a napkin. "I'll take you to him."

My date is seated at a table with his back to the room, so I don't get a chance to see his face until I get close. He's cute. A little younger than I was expecting—he doesn't look like he could be over twenty-four. But he has a sweet face and pretty eyes. "Hi," I say, sitting down across from him. "I'm Peyton."

The look on his face surprises me. If I had to name it, I'd say alarm or confusion, and it makes me wonder what my client told him about me. But then his expression seems to morph into curiosity, so maybe I'm not what he expected but he's okay with it.

He gives a nod, still with that curious look on his face, and says, "Ty."

I look down at the plate of food in front of him. "You already ordered?" If I was late, it was by one minute, tops. How early did he arrive? And why would he order just because he got there early?

Ty crinkles his brow. "That's what I always do when I sit down at a restaurant and the waitress comes to take my order."

I don't say that it's customary to wait for all members of your party before you do. But it's fine. It's not like everyone has the same customs. And maybe he's just an awkward type of guy and felt weird not giving his order when the waitress came. Awkwardness is fine. It's kind of cute on him. I pick up the menu that the host placed in my spot.

"So," I say as I glance at my choices, "would you recommend I get the same dish that you chose? Or should I try my luck at something else?"

Ty looks down at his plate, fork hovering just above it. "I got the Pan-Seared Salmon Rice Bowl. It's good, but if you get it, I'd recommend asking for it without the green beans. They make it taste weird."

I find it on the menu. It also has carrots, zucchini, squash, and a roasted red pepper sauce. It actually sounds really good, and Ty's looks tasty. So when the waitress comes by to take my order, I say, "I'd like the Pan-Seared Salmon Rice Bowl without green beans, please."

Ty smiles and takes another bite of his.

Honestly, it's kind of weird sitting across from him while he's eating when I won't have my food for a while. But he seems content to just sit there and eat. "So, Ty, what do you do for a living?"

"I'm an advertising copywriter."

"Does that mean you have jingles stuck in your head all day long?"

"Hah. No. I mostly write product descriptions for gardening supplies and fertilizer."

"You sound really passionate about that." He doesn't, actually. He sounds a little like he loves it about as much as a trip to the eye doctor, but I'm hoping that asking will prompt him to say what he's passionate about.

Instead, he just shrugs. "How about you?"

I tell him about being a personal chef, which he hasn't heard of before, so I tell him I have clients who want home-cooked meals but can't fit cooking into their schedule, so I cook for them regularly. And I tell him about how some clients have busy times because of various things and use my services only as needed. If nothing else, it fills the awkward time while I'm waiting for my food since he doesn't seem interested in filling it with anything else.

Eventually, my food comes—thank heavens—and I have something to do other than try to carry the conversation.

My cell phone text alert sounds—the text sound that I've set for Max. "I apologize—I have my phone on 'Do not disturb,' so that's an emergency bypass number." I pull the phone out of my purse and scrunch my brows at what little I see on the screen. I swipe to go into the text fully.

"Is everything okay?" Ty asks.

I shake my head. "My friend just got in a car accident."

"How bad?"

I pause a moment as I wait for Max's response to come in, then let out a relieved breath. "Just a fender bender. Everyone is okay." I quickly type a response back to him, and then put my phone back in my purse.

I'm only about four bites into eating my meal when Ty sets his fork down, apparently finished. Maybe he'll be chattier now. "So, Ty, where did you grow up?"

He eyes me. "You aren't trying to get password recovery information out of me, are you?"

I laugh. "If you could include your mother's maiden name in your story, that would be great. Oh, and your first pet's name, please." Then I take my fifth bite of dinner.

I'm glad when Ty laughs because, honestly, I wasn't sure if my comment would make him more at ease or convince him that I'm a spy trying to infiltrate his life.

"I grew up along the southern Oregon coast, then went to Portland State. I got a job as an intern my senior year at the company I work at now and then just stayed after I graduated because there was really no reason to leave, you know? Well, except for the fact that it's boring, but I guess most jobs are."

"I don't know about most…"

The waitress comes by just then and sets the bill down next to Ty. The woman is about to walk off, but then Ty says, "Hang on a second." He gets out his wallet, pulls out a few bills, puts them in the folder, and hands it to the woman.

Then, to my utter bafflement, he turns to me and says, "It was really nice meeting you. Enjoy the rest of your meal." He then stands up, dabs at his mouth with his napkin, sets it on his plate, and walks away.

I notice a few moments later that I've been staring with my mouth open at the spot where I last saw him before he rounded the corner to the lobby. What just happened?

The waitress comes to my table and starts clearing away Ty's dishes because she doesn't want them to be in my way. So now I'm just sitting in the restaurant, all alone, looking like I'm here by myself. At least if the waitress had left Ty's plate and glass, it would've looked like my date had gone to the restroom or something.

I don't want to bug Max during his date, but I have to send him a text about this. Hopefully, he won't actually look at it until his date is over. I pull out my phone and slide open the camera first, adjusting it until I get my hardly touched meal and the empty spot across from me in the shot. When I open my phone, I'm still in the text with Max, so I attach the picture and type, *This is how my date is going. How's yours?*

His response comes less than a minute later. It's a picture of his meal at a different restaurant with a different background, but one thing is the same: the spot across from him is empty. His text reads, *About the same as yours,* with the zany face emoji next to it.

Peyton: Oh, no! Did she never show up?

Max: She showed up. I'm pretty sure she wished she hadn't, though.

Peyton: [frowny face emoji] Want to talk?

As I wait for his response, I notice that I missed other texts while my phone was in *Do Not Disturb* mode. A few from my roommate chat… one from my dad… Oh! And one from Tyler. I tap that one first.

> Tyler: Hi, Peyton.

> Tyler: My boss dropped a huge project on me right as I was heading out the door and said it was important enough that none of us could leave if we valued our jobs. (Great boss, right? HA HA.) I am so sorry to cancel on you. I hope I caught you before you got to the restaurant. Can we reschedule for later in the week?

I stare at the text for a full minute, trying to make sense of what I'm reading before I stare at the spot across from me, eyes wide. Who have I been eating with? I grab the waitress as she walks by.

"Excuse me, what can you tell me about the guy I was having dinner with?"

The waitress shrugs. "Nice enough guy. Good tipper. I've seen him in here a few times—always alone, always orders the same thing. He didn't say he was expecting anyone today, or I would've had a glass of water waiting for you."

As the waitress walks away, I bury my face in my hands where I can feel exactly how hot my cheeks are. So I walked into a restaurant, sat down with a stranger who was very much not expecting me, and tried to make small talk with him while he ate?

I take my hands off my face and fan myself with my cloth napkin. But my level of scorching embarrassment is at a fire-alarm level, and the napkin is a water-pressure-challenged garden hose.

Seriously, what are the chances of a guy named Ty sitting in this restaurant, eating alone, at exactly the same time that I'm supposed to meet a Tyler? The chances are about as good as Bex going a week without using a single sticky note or Timini not leaving dirty dishes in the sink.

A business coach I worked with when I first started *Home-Cooked Heaven* told me, "Start as you mean to go." I really, *really* hope that this start doesn't have anything to do with the way my week is going to go.

No, I decide, it's *not* how it's going to go. I'm going to stay focused on finding the perfect guy, so I'm going to attract the perfect guy. That's all there is to it.

CHAPTER 8
Max

After Peyton and I pick up our sandwiches—mine a pulled pork and hers a roasted chicken salad—I head out to the café's large outdoor patio with her to find a seat. Thankfully, it's a sunny day and not looking like it's going to rain anytime soon. After having dates every night for the past four days, it feels so right to just be with Peyton again.

As we sit down at our favorite table at this restaurant—one that's a bit away from the other tables so no one else can hear us—Peyton puts a hand on my forearm, which always causes a buzzing in my chest. She gives a slight nod toward a young couple sitting on the far side of the patio. "Let's voice-over that couple."

One of our favorite pastimes when we're somewhere good for people-watching is to make up fake conversations that couples are having when they're too far away for us to hear what their conversations actually are.

This couple is probably discussing how work has been so far today or what their weekend plans are going to be. But the guy reaches his arm up to scratch his back, his elbow sticking out above his head. So I pretend to be the guy's voice, making sure to keep my voice low enough that only Peyton will hear. "How about I wear a harness and we attach a rope right here. Then we could just lower me down through the skylight and I could grab the key. It seems easier than just breaking into the back door of the place. And, added bonus, we wouldn't have to rely on your ninja skills."

The woman says something next that we can't hear, and Peyton pretends to be the woman's voice. She gasps, sounding offended. "How dare you dis that! I have incredible ninja skills."

The guy looks down just then, which is perfect. "Not with those shoes, you don't."

The woman looks down, too. They probably just saw an ant or something crawling across the outdoor patio, but it fits. "True," Peyton says for the woman. "And these are pretty fabulous shoes, so I wouldn't exactly want to go in without them."

Then the woman must've gotten something on her hands, because she looks at them, palms up, rubbing her thumbs across her fingers. "Maybe we should lower *me* through the skylight, though. I'm the one with sticky fingers—you've got fumble fingers. You might just drop the key into a vent or someplace equally irretrievable."

The guy looks at his hands, too, so I say, "Yeah, I do drop things a lot. Okay, we'll lower you in through the skylight."

When the woman says something else, Peyton says, "But how, exactly, do we sneak onto the roof of the building without getting the cops called on us?"

Neither of the two says anything for a moment, so I use my narrator voice and say, "They both sit in silence for a moment, taking bites of their food, clearly thinking things through."

The woman is the next to speak, so Peyton says, "I know it'd be embarrassing, honey, but it might make everything easier if we just called the locksmith and admitted that neither of us grabbed the house key when we left for work this morning."

I laugh out loud. I love playing this game with Peyton. It's been five days since I last saw her. Plus, it's been a very taxing week, so it seems as if it's been even longer than that. After going without seeing her, my whole mind and body are soaking her in, making me feel more grounded and alive.

She bites her sandwich and I take a bite of mine while I take in how beautiful she looks in the sunshine. Her curls are soft and look like spun gold. She's going to find someone to date and probably get married to this week. How can she not? She's amazing, and she attracts amazing people to her. Am I going to forever lose my chance with her? The thought causes sharp pains in my stomach, right along with a yearning to be the kind of man that Peyton would want to be with—the kind of man I very much am not. "How many dates have you gone on?"

She's chewing, so she holds up her fingers in answer.

"Nine? You've gone on *nine dates*?! We've only been doing this for four days!"

She swallows and dabs her mouth with her napkin. "Well, I've gone on two each night—Monday, Tuesday, Wednesday, and Thursday. I've been telling the first guy that I'm free from six to nine or so and the second that I'm free from nine until midnight. Then none of them expect the date to go longer. And I went on one lunch date. Why? How many have you gone on?"

"Four, if you don't count the one that first night where she left. One each night since then, plus a dessert date." I thought I was doing pretty good with four. It felt like a lot.

"I can see you are really dying to sing karaoke."

I rub my hands on my face. I completely forgot about the stakes.

"Max, why didn't you have me set you up with people? I know single women who I think you would like."

I haven't let her because it's weird to have the woman I've been in love with for the past year and a half set me up on blind dates. I don't want to say that, though, so I shrug. "The guys at work have been way too zealous on their own."

"Well, you better tell them to step it up, or I'm going to win."

I really want to win. It doesn't matter the contest—I have a drive to win. But winning this contest kind of seems pointless because my plan is failing epically. None of my dates are actually taking my mind off Peyton. In fact, dating like this is practically guaranteeing she'll be on my mind all the time. If I'm not comparing one of my dates to her, I'm wondering how hers are going and hoping any dates that go well aren't going to impact my relationship with her.

She seems so excited about this competition when all I want to do is stop competing. Stop dating anyone who isn't her. Wish she would stop dating anyone who isn't me. I imagine how her face would fall if I backed out, and I know I can't do it. I need to stop thinking about it so much and just play to win.

"I have a present for you," I say, pulling my wallet out of my jeans. I open it and remove the three business cards I've collected since I last saw her and place them, one at a time, into her open palms.

The look of wonder on her face is probably what makes me always keep an eye out for any she might not already have. That, and the fact that whenever she gets a business card to add to her collection, she says she knows it's going to be a great day. And I kind of want her to associate good days with me in the same way I associate good days with her.

She smiles. "You really are the best, Max."

The look she's giving me makes my heart race and my pulse

pound. Then she reaches out and runs her thumb just beside my lips, soft and caressing. It's all I can do not to lean into her touch. I'm not sure what expression I have on my face, but the expression on hers feels like it mirrors my feelings toward her. I want to reach up and cradle her soft hand in mine. I want to touch her face, to run my finger along her cheek. To skim a finger along her lips.

"Mustard," Peyton whispers as she wipes the thumb she's run alongside my mouth on her napkin.

I clear my throat, forcing myself out of the trance I've fallen under, then nod toward another table, hoping that my voice doesn't come out as husky as I fear it will. "Voice-over that mom and three kids."

She seems to have been in a bit of a trance herself because her eyes stay on mine for a long moment before she turns to look in the direction I nodded.

The family is at a picnic-style table, with two young brothers on one side and the mom and a little girl on the other. The two boys are bumping shoulders and pushing each other for sport.

Peyton carefully puts the business cards I've given her into her purse and then says in a voice meant to mimic that of the little girl, who's probably five, "Can I have some of your fries?"

"Mom, tell him to stop touching me," I say.

The older boy starts putting his hands in his brother's face at the perfect timing, so Peyton says in a boy's voice that, honestly, is kind of hilarious, "I'm not touching you. I'm not touching you."

"Stop it," I say, as the younger brother, "or I'll tell Mom about the moldy cake under your bed."

Peyton, in that funny older brother's voice again, says, "No you won't, or I'll tell her how all your socks actually got holes." Then, in the little girl's voice, she says, "Can I have your fries?"

"Kids," I say in my best impression of a mom, which isn't going to win any awards, "stop tattling."

The older boy flicks the younger brother's hair, messing it up. "Hey," Peyton says.

"I was just making it look better," I say as the hair-flicker.

When the older boy tries to flick the younger one's hair too, the boy slides off the bench and maneuvers out of his brother's reach. The older one keeps trying to mess up the younger one's hair, but the younger brother is fast. Peyton says, "How will you know I love you if I don't 'fix' your hair?"

While the two boys are bobbing and weaving in the small space next to their table, the little sister quietly slides off her bench, goes around to the boys' side of the table, and sits with her legs across the bench, taking up both spots. "You didn't call seats back," Peyton says, as the little girl, "so that means I get to eat all of your fries."

When the little girl actually starts eating her brothers' fries, both Peyton and I laugh.

She gives me a smile that could power the sun. "I think we did pretty good on that one, especially considering the fact that neither of us have siblings."

I drink in the look on her face. I could stare at it all day. But as much as I don't want to know how her dates have been going this week, a part of me has to know. So I proceed cautiously. "Tell me about one of your dates that was just kind of *meh*." Then I take a bite of my sandwich so my face won't give anything away.

"Well," Peyton says as she swirls the straw in her ice water, "I went out with this guy on Tuesday, I think, and we met at a game center. I got there first and just waited for him in the lobby. When he came in, he got a little excited to meet me and decided to go for a hug. But then his foot caught on the rug at the door, tripped, fell into me, and we both went all the way down.

"So then, this guy who I've only known for about four seconds is on top of me and trying to see if I'm okay while trying to hurry and get up and act like it wasn't awkward while apologizing and still trying to make a good impression."

I'm smiling on the outside and laughing on the inside. Man, that would've been embarrassing.

"All of that would've been fine. I mean, I've had my share of unfortunate tripping. I don't know if it was just because of how things started out or if this was his normal, but for us being at a place that had 'fun' in its name, it was a pretty boring date. We played arcade games, bowled, played ping pong—he somehow even made laser tag boring."

"That takes some skill. You've got to give him that."

"Okay, tell me about one of yours."

"All right. I'll tell you my most boring one. I with with a woman to a restaurant. She was fairly interesting, and the conversation during dinner went pretty well, which kind of made me not expect the rest of the date. She said her roommates were watching TV at their apartment and asked if I wanted to join them. So I did.

"We got to her place about eight-thirty, and her roommates were all watching some show they all watch together about health insurance problems that I'm pretty sure wins awards for its ability to help insomniacs fall asleep. So I'm trying to act interested and marvel at how different this woman was when it was just the two of us versus how she was with her roommates.

"Then, at nine on the dot, an alarm on her phone sounded, and right in the middle of the show, she said it was her bedtime, thanks for the lovely evening, I'll see you later."

"Why didn't she just end the date after the dinner?"

"I have no idea. But that was definitely one where I should've planned a second date for the evening."

"Seriously, Max, it's like you're not even trying to win."

Okay, I can't have her thinking that. I need to redirect. "Maybe I'll win for the most awkward date. Tell me yours."

"Only if we don't count the ones where you got in a wreck and I had dinner with an unsuspecting stranger."

"Deal."

"Mine would probably be… Oh. Got one. I went out with this guy on Monday night, right after my dinner with a stranger. He wanted to go bowling, so we went to the bowling alley, and I found out that we were actually bowling with seven —*seven!*—of his guy friends. Apparently, they're a tight-knit group, and the guy was terrible about knowing if he should go on a second date with a woman, so he relied on them to make the decision for him."

"And? Do you pass their test?"

"I don't know—they didn't loop me into that conversation. But when my date went up to the snack counter to get us sodas, one of the friends started hitting on me, so, well, I guess that meant his vote could've gone either way."

I laugh. "Okay, that one's pretty good. I still think I've got you beat, though, from my date yesterday. We went to play tennis at some courts near her home. Another couple—friends of hers—were supposed to go with us so we could play doubles. When I got to her house to pick her up, she said that her friends had to cancel. But she insists that we can only play tennis as doubles, so we double—I kid you not—with her parents."

Peyton laughs, and, suddenly, the whole awkward date was worth it just to hear that laugh. "Tell me you have at least one good one, though."

I nod. "One was." She's the one who's most like Peyton,

though, which just makes all the ways she isn't Peyton stand out. And that pretty much does the opposite of helping me get over wanting a romantic relationship with Peyton. "How about you?"

I asked the question, and now it's too late to take it back. Every part of me does not want to hear about a date that went well. I hope she'll be as vague with her answer as I was with mine.

"A couple went pretty well. I'll probably date them both again. One was Wednesday night. My date and I went to dinner and couldn't find a single thing in common. The chitchat was epically awful. I'm talking 'bringing up foot fungus during dinner' awful."

"This was your good date?"

"Shh. I'm not done. So we were getting close to finishing our meal when the waiter came over to refill my date's water, and he spilled it all down the guy's front. My date gasped, called the waiter an idiot, and then said he needed to leave, obviously. Then he left before even paying for his half of the meal."

"That's awful."

"Wait, it gets better. So, after the guy left, the waiter came over and apologized. Then he told me that when my date got up earlier to go to the restroom, he actually went to the waiter and paid him twenty dollars to spill the water on him so he could make an early exit."

Why anyone would ever want to get out of a date with Peyton early is beyond my comprehension.

"So my waiter said he took the twenty bucks because if the guy was that big of a jerk, then not only should he be out of the money and have water spilled on him, but that I should know he's a jerk."

"I still don't get how this was a good date. Other than the fact that you get to end it early."

"Because the waiter used the twenty bucks to pay for the guy's meal, comped my meal, and then said he was getting off in ten minutes and took me for ice cream. His name is David, and he's pretty great, actually."

I really don't want to keep hearing about any dates that go well because imagining another guy with her makes me realize exactly how much I'm not okay with that. I have to get the subject moved off of dates. "Voice-over that older couple over there."

As Peyton starts talking in a voice that's supposed to be the older woman's, telling the guy about how he's a superhero for fixing her broken lamp, one thought keeps going through my mind. Why can't things just stay the way they are?

Because right now, with Peyton in my life, everything is perfect.

CHAPTER 9

Peyton

EVERYTHING IS ALMOST ready for our big roommate date night. I just slid a spinach artichoke dip into the oven, Bex and Addison are putting together some cute little antipasti bites, Timini is scooping the filling into stuffed mushrooms, and I'm threading marinated tortellini onto skewers with bite-sized mozzarella, peppers, tomatoes, and basil. My date for the night is Noah, someone Bex lined me up with, and I've had a great time chatting with him over text all week.

I breathe in the scent of all the appetizers cooking. Tonight is going to be fun.

"I love *How Much Do You Know*," Timini says. "I'm excited we are going to play it again."

Bex lets out a long breath. "Oh, I so need this tonight! These last two weeks of preparation before the wedding are going to be brutal. And I swear all we've been doing lately is work and wedding prep. A night of fun is a godsend."

"When will Roman be here?" I ask.

"Soon. He had something he's finishing up at work, and then he'll be here. When's Ian coming?"

"He's just showering, and then he'll be down."

I turn to Timini. "You've got a date, right?"

"Yep." She sets down the scoop she's using and pulls out her phone. "His name is Mason. Isn't he basically a Greek god?" She holds out her phone so we can all ooh and ahh over him. "And look at this." She swipes to the next picture, which is a full-body image of him leaning his shoulder against a wall, legs crossed at the ankle, looking off into the distance like he's a model.

"He's definitely a pretty one," Addison says.

The guy is super pretty, but he really doesn't have anything on Max.

"Yeah," Timini says, sighing as she looks at the picture again before putting the phone back into her pocket. "So he's probably either a jerk or not so intelligent. I'm basically a pro at picking the beautiful man who's a jerk. I need to get over that."

"Well, you are an artist," Bex says. "So of course you're going to appreciate the beauty."

Timini laughs. "I just need to get better at recognizing the inner beauty, too."

"Oh," Addison says, "I forgot to tell you. I was next door at Ian's grandma's earlier and mentioned we were playing *How Much Do You Know*. She said they love that game. Apparently, Carol can cream anyone at it. Meera can't because she's the least observant person she knows. Although Meera did say that she might not actually be the least observant person because she isn't observant enough to notice if someone else is less observant. Anyway, they want to come. Is everyone okay with that?"

"Oh, of course," I say. Everyone else agrees, which of course they would—they all like our next-door grandmas. When Meera moved in with Shirley and Carol a month ago, I told them that we needed to get one more of their Origami Club ladies to move in so that my roommates and I would each have a grandma to ourselves.

I'd said it to be nice, but then immediately realized that the reason either of them moved in with Shirley was because their husband recently passed away and they didn't want to live alone. So I had basically accidentally wished someone else's husband would pass. Sometimes I shouldn't talk.

"Meera said she'll run the game and come up with questions," Addison says, "which works out perfectly because it'll keep the teams even. Oh, and Shirley and Carol said to come prepared to lose."

A text notification buzzes on my phone, so I wash and dry my hands, then pick up my phone and read the text.

"What is it?" Addison asks.

I sigh. "It's Noah. He says his sister just went into labor. Which is exciting! But she wasn't supposed to for a few more weeks, and he had already told her he'd watch her two other kids while she and his brother-in-law were at the hospital. So he's on his way to their house now."

I type a response to him, telling him not to worry about having to cancel, and that I hope everything goes well with the delivery. Then I put down the phone. "What am I supposed to do now? *How Much Do You Know* only works if you play it as couples."

"Text Max," Bex says.

"I just had lunch with him today—it sounded like he had a date already planned for tonight."

Bex keeps her eyes on the antipasti she's working on, probably so I won't see the smile she's trying to hide. "It wouldn't hurt to ask."

Do you know what? It wouldn't. I open Max's name in my texting app and ask if he has a date for tonight. Part of me is crossing my fingers that he'll be unexpectedly free, and part of me is actually kind of worried he will be. Especially after our lunch today. We shared a moment where I'm pretty sure my feelings for him were on full display.

Going on so many dates this week has made my old crush on him not only resurface but come back with extra force behind it, which I hadn't expected to happen at all. This week was supposed to be about finding a partner who *wasn't* Max.

For so long, I've done amazingly well at only seeing him as a friend. Like seriously, someone should put me on a stage and hand me a really heavy crystal trophy with *Managed to not have romantic feelings for her very incredible BFF* engraved on it because that has been a monumental feat.

This week has been filled with so many guys. Tonight would make number ten. True, some of them have been disaster dates, but some of the guys have actually been pretty fantastic. There are four so far that I would go on a second date with. And I have a breakfast date, a lunch date, an afternoon date, and an evening date tomorrow. I even have a date to go to church with a guy on Sunday morning. So fifteen dates this week. Going out with that many guys and having the potential of going out with several again gives me so many choices.

So why does it make every part of me want to be with the one guy I can't have a future with? My heart races until his text comes in.

> Max: I did, but I canceled it.

> Peyton: Why?

> Max: We've been chatting over text and could both see there wasn't anything there, so a date was pointless.

Wow. With as competitive as Max is, I'm surprised he's

willing to have one fewer date. He's going to have to squeeze in so many dates a day just to catch up.

> Peyton: My date just canceled on me, and we were going to have a quad date with my roommates and play How Much Do You Know, which I need a partner for. Are you free? If you say yes, I'll even let you count it as one of your dates.

> Max: How can I say no to that? I'll be right over.

A smile spreads across my face, and I do a happy dance.

Timini raises an eyebrow. "Peyton, do you ever wonder if the fact that you get so happy whenever you find out you're going to get to see Max might be a sign?"

I pause a moment, then decide to tell the truth. "Lately? Yes."

"What?" The word practically explodes out of Bex.

All three women close in.

"Are you saying you have feelings for Max?" Addison asks, looking at Bex and Timini before her eyes find mine again. "Like, outside-of-friendship feelings?"

"It's terrible, isn't it? Because my life goals and Max's life goals can't co-exist. So I shouldn't be doing a happy dance because he's coming. Having feelings for him just makes finding the right person to spend my life with so much more difficult. And I really want to find that someone soon because what if something happens to my dad? I want him to get to know his future son-in-law."

"Do you know if Max has feelings for you?"

I shake my head. "I don't know. Sometimes I wonder if he might. But do you know what? It's irrelevant because we already know that the two of us would never work as a couple."

It isn't long before everyone's dates arrive and we all move into the giant gathering room and start snacking on the appetizers. The chairs are in two straight lines facing each other, five on each side, and we all find our way over and sit down across from our partners for the game. I grin at Max as Meera hands each of us a stack of note cards and a Sharpie.

"Anyone want to predict who will win?" Meera asks.

"We will," Carol says with as much conviction as she'd use when saying the grass is green.

"I don't know," Addison says. "Ian and I are pretty in sync. We plan to win."

"You might want to change your plans," I say, "because Max and I have known each other longer than everyone but Carol and Shirley." Look at that! I just smack-talked. I'm so proud of myself.

"Okay," Meera says, standing at the head of the rows of chairs, right in the middle of the two rows. Then, motioning to my side, she says, "Ladies, write down your biggest pet peeve, but don't show it to anyone. Gentlemen and Carol, write down what you think your partner's biggest pet peeve is. You've got sixty seconds. And…go!"

Pet peeves aren't the easiest thing to think of, but I immediately come up with an answer and write it down. I wonder if Max will even think of it.

"Addison," Meera says, "what did you put?"

Addison holds up her card. "Unorganized office supplies."

"Oh, man!" Ian says, holding his card. "I thought for sure you would say bead collections!"

We've all heard Addison complain about beads enough that it's probably what I would've guessed, too.

"Bex?" Meera prompts.

"Road construction when I'm in a hurry," she says, holding up her card.

Roman holds up his. "I went with 'People who are impatient with waiters at your favorite restaurant.'"

They chuckle and share a smile that tells me there's more to the story.

"Peyton."

I hold my card out for everyone to see and say, "When people say, 'I don't mean to be rude, but...' Because they *do* mean to be rude. What they should be saying is 'I'm about to say something rude, but I don't want you to judge me harshly for it.'"

"And Max?"

His grin spreads all the way across his face as he holds up his card. "Also 'I don't mean to be rude, but...'"

I reach across the space between the two rows and give Max a high five.

"Next up, Timini," Meera says. "What have you got?"

"Too many rules," Timini says, holding up her card.

"Well, I didn't have a ton to go on," Mason says, "but I wrote *high heels* because women hate high heels."

Everyone laughs and nods. But in our heads, we're probably only laughing and not nodding, because Timini is currently wearing high heels and had been showing them off earlier, talking about how much she loves them.

Meera gestures to the end of the row. "Shirley?"

"I put 'unclear instructions on origami or recipes.'"

"Yes!" Carol shouts. "I wrote 'when a recipe doesn't say all the instructions.'"

As we play each round, I keep watching Max, trying to guess if he knows the answer to one of mine or trying to guess his answer when it's one of his. His face is the cutest when he's trying to guess my answer. He looks at me like he's trying to see right into my brain. His eyes squint a bit, and his mouth does this little twitch-up at the corner that makes me want to kiss it.

Oh my goodness. I can't be thinking like that!

An hour later, Meera announces, "And that's the end of round ten!" The older woman is happier and more alive than I've seen her since her husband passed away. I'm so glad Addison asked them to come. "Max and Peyton are tied with Shirley and Carol at nine points each."

Carol raises her hand. "Only because one of the questions was 'What is your favorite number,' and who talks about their favorite number, anyway? Well, other than Timini."

Timini laughs. She had a giant number one on hers, which all of us could have guessed. Except for Mason, obviously. Every other couple got theirs wrong.

"Hey, don't blame the game. Now you know what to talk to each other about. Okay, Addison and Ian have seven points. Bex and Roman have six. Timini and Mason are bringing up the rear with one point."

Timini and Mason got that point because the question was "What was the last song you heard," and we were all listening to the same music. Mason was somehow still surprised that Timini guessed correctly. With as off-the-wall as the rest of Mason's answers have been, I'm kind of surprised that he didn't put a different song down on his card.

"Addison has a prize for the winner," Meera says, "so I say we do a lightning round with Max and Peyton and Shirley and Carol to determine the winner. Five rounds, and whoever has the most points at the end is the winner. Max and Carol, write down a food you won't eat." She pauses until we have our answers written down. "Max?"

"Apricots, kiwis, peaches, or anything like that."

I grin. "I wrote, 'Anything furry. Animals are furry. Fruit shouldn't be.'"

"Point for the whipper-snappers! Carol?"

"Oatmeal, because what I thought was a raisin in mine when I was seven was actually a curled-up spider." She shudders.

"Shirley."

She holds up her card with pride. "Oatmeal, because of childhood trauma."

"Point for the oldie-locks!"

For the next three questions, Max and I stare hard at each other, trying to make sure we get them right. The tension is mounting, and I really want us to win. First thing I'd buy if I won the lottery? A blast chiller and I'd make near-instant ice cream. I've dreamed about it in Max's presence enough that it's a quick answer for him. His worst habit? Biting pens. Easy. First thing I'd save in a fire? My business card collection.

It hits me how remarkably in sync with each other we are. I know more about him than anyone else in the world, and he knows more about me than anyone does. We know the best and worst of each other, have lived through our highs and lows, and have been there for each other through the good and the bad. Our relationship is stronger for it. It had been a teeny little shelter made of a rope and a tarp when we first became friends, and because of how much we know and care for each other, it has grown into basically a fortress.

"And we still have a tie!" Meera calls out. "Okay, last question. You'll both write down your answer and what you think your partner's answer is. I beg one of you to get it wrong or we might have to rock, paper, scissors the winner. Okay, all four of you, write down what your biggest fear is on one card, then write what you think your partner's biggest fear is on the other one. Go!"

Mine is easy. It's making the wrong decision, especially when it's something big. That has always been my biggest fear, ever since I was little. Well, that and bugs. But mostly choosing wrong.

Max's biggest fear, though… He's the most fearless person I know. He climbs mountains, jumps off cliffs, paraglides, takes off on camping trips with only the supplies he can carry on his back, and goes white-water rafting, skiing, and mountain biking. He doesn't even flinch a tiny bit when there are bugs. I study his expression as I try to decide.

Time is almost out, so I quickly write down what I see the most in his face. *Missing out on an adventure.*

Although that doesn't feel quite right. Missing out on… on what? Meera calls time, so I can't change it now. Besides, it has to be an adventure. He lives for it.

"Okay, let's get your answers. Peyton, show your biggest fear first."

I hold up my card and say, "Making a wrong choice."

The expression on Max's face is disappointment, and he bites his lip. Then he grins and holds his card up. "Making a bad decision, or having a big decision to make."

"Yes!" I hold my breath as Meera asks Carol what her answer is.

Carol holds up a card that reads *Bunnies.*

Then Shirley holds up her card, which has *Bunnies* written on it.

"Bunnies?" I ask. "For real? Floppy, hoppy bunnies?"

Carol shudders. "I can't even look at a picture of them."

I've heard some strange things tonight. Like the fact that Mason's dream job is to be the person who designs the little round metal rivets that are at the edges of front pockets on jeans. But *bunnies*?

"Okay, Max," Meera says, "show us your biggest fear."

I bite my lip. We're still tied, so we have to win this one. I finally exhale when Max holds up a card that reads, *Missing a chance at something*.

I look at Meera, and she says, "Point for the younglings!"

That was close. Especially because when I look at Max, I can tell that there's more to his answer than what he wrote.

"Okay, Shirley, it all comes down to this. What's your biggest fear?"

Shirley holds up a card that reads *Not moving forward*. "I know that you can't keep things the way that they are—things can't ever remain the same. My biggest fear is not moving forward because that means I'm moving backward."

That is such a great sentiment! I look over at Max and see the strangest look on his face. I don't have enough time to figure out what it means before Carol says, "*That* was your answer? How can that be your answer?"

"What did you guess?" Shirley asks.

Carol holds up the card. "Being alone."

"That used to be my biggest fear back when Henry first got sick. But I have all of you now, so I don't even worry about it anymore."

"Well, I hope you know that getting over your fear cost us the game." Carol puts a hand on her hip, trying to look judgmental.

"Max!" I say, "We actually won!" I jump out of my seat and he jumps out of his, and we hug. I'm so excited I have trouble keeping my feet on the ground.

Suddenly, I realize how very close our faces are. How I can feel the tickle of his breath on my lips. See up close how beautiful his eyes look as he gazes into mine. How amazing it feels to have his arms wrapped around my waist, his hands warm and strong against my lower back. How perfect it feels to have my arms around his neck.

He's your friend, not a date, I remind myself. *And definitely not a boyfriend. Back away.* I pull back a friend-sized distance. Or what I guess that would be. It's as if I suddenly lost all sense of how far that actually is. I've spent the whole night ogling him and thinking about how great he is, and it's as if it has made me forget how to act around him.

A flash of confusion crosses Max's face, and I don't know if it's because I've gotten the distance wrong and am sending an unintended message, or if he just can't guess what's going through my mind. Honestly, I'm not so sure myself anymore.

CHAPTER 10
Max

I SHOULD'VE GONE on a date last night. And another this morning, especially since today is the last day of Peyton's challenge.

But on Friday night, things just felt different with Peyton. Possibly because we spent so much time being so focused on each other and on how deeply we know each other. But I kind of think that maybe it was something more. That Peyton was feeling it, too.

I keep my Saturday morning breakfast and bike ride date with the woman Hunter set me up with. The date goes fine. The woman is fun to talk to, and we're pretty evenly matched when it comes to bike riding. She just isn't Peyton.

And going along with Peyton's week of dating hasn't helped me keep my mind off her at all.

Is it even fair to the last two women I have dates lined up with to take their time when my heart isn't in it? Probably not. So when Emilio calls and says they're doing a last-minute overnight camping trip in the Mount Hood National Forest with everyone, including Hunter, and that we're going to hike to Ramona Falls, I don't turn it down—I just cancel my dates. I think what I need is a night of camping to clear my head. It always does the trick.

———

Okay, it did the trick a little too well. Last night, as I lay in my tent listening to the sounds of nature, my mind did clear. But a clear, open, uncluttered mind leaves a lot of space available to really think about things, and I really thought about things. This morning, I still am.

We adjust backpacks at the trailhead, make sure boot laces are tied, and take last-minute drinks of water.

"Are you sure you remember how to do this?" Emilio says, bumping his shoulder into Hunter. "We could help you out and give you some tips."

Hunter, the guy who probably spends two hours a day reading about outdoor activities.

"I'm sure Max could give you some tips on how to not fall into freezing lakes," Leo says.

"Actually," Hunter says, giving Emilio a playful shove, "the thing I've forgotten the most from my long absence is how to carry a backpack. You could help out by carrying it for me."

As we head down the dirt path, surrounded by firs and pines whose trunks tower ten, twenty, or even thirty feet toward the sky before their lowest branches spread out, I ask Hunter, "So, do you miss coming out here as often?"

Hunter looks at the trail in the distance. "Yes and no. I've gone camping with Tami a few times on the weekends that I haven't come with you guys, so I haven't been nearly as camping-starved as you think I have been. I'm just waiting for you all to get spouses so we can go on couples' camping trips."

"Yeah, I wouldn't hold your breath waiting for me on that,"

Leo says. He's by far the youngest of us. He's also the most impulsive, so I wouldn't put it past the guy to be the first to surprise everyone and get married.

As much as I plan to never get married, Hunter's statement plants an image of being married to Peyton and going camping with her. Is that irrational? An impossibility?

The trail is only a slight incline through this part, and Emilio and Leo run ahead like they're brothers who are racing to get to the end. This time, I don't even care about winning. My mind is full and I have questions for Hunter.

"Can I ask you something personal? You don't have to answer, but if you do, I need your answer to be real."

"Shoot."

"I've hung out with you and Tami plenty of times, and you two always seem to get along decently well. Is it always like that? You know, even when you're not around other people?"

"A lot of the time, yeah. I mean, we don't get along one hundred percent of the time, of course. We have disagreements and we can get on each other's nerves pretty well, but we work through that stuff. Our marriage is not at all like what your parents' marriage was like if that's what you're asking—we don't just pretend to get along when we're in public. I know it's a weird concept, Max, but we actually, truly, enjoy being around each other. We are each other's favorite person."

For a long time, I thought my parents' marriage was normal. It was pretty much the same as all my friends' parents' marriages, so it seemed like that was just the way things were. I'm coming to realize that a big part of me still believes that. I wasn't married or even engaged to Laurel, but that was how things were with her from the moment things started getting serious between us. Our relationship dragged me down so low.

But that kind of relationship isn't universal—some people's marriages are great. I get that now. But could *mine* be, if I ever decided to get married? Or, since I have my parents' genes, am I destined to have a marriage full of bickering up until the day it dissolves?

"Does Tami like camping?"

"Not as much as I do, but she likes it well enough to go with me once a month or so. It helps that I go to farmers' markets and antique stores with her just as often."

I wonder if Peyton would like camping or if my two passions would be forever separated. "You ever think about having kids?"

Hunter nods. And then, in a quieter voice that tells me he isn't willing to share the information with anyone else, even though Emilio and Leo are too far ahead to hear, he says, "We are trying right now, actually."

My eyebrows shoot up. I hadn't even guessed that Hunter and Tami were to that point yet. After a long moment, I ask, "Do you think you'll still be able to go adventuring once you have kids?"

Hunter shrugs a shoulder. "I don't know. I mean, yeah, when they're older. For those first handful of years, though, I have no idea. I don't think we'll really know until we experience it. But I do worry about that. Especially because I won't be as effective at my job if I don't go out and test things.

"And you worry that you might lose a part of yourself if you just quit going."

"Yeah."

We both walk in silence for several long minutes. It's possibly the most honest, raw thing I've ever said to Hunter, and I'm kind of surprised that I actually have. It's not something I would've been willing to say to any other male on the planet, but I've known Hunter for long enough and trust him enough that my fears found a voice.

Because the truth is, my fears of marriage go further than

worrying how my own marriage might turn out anything like my parents', strong as that fear is. I love my life. I had gotten a pretty clear picture of what I wanted my life to be like by the time I was a sophomore in college, and then I made it happen. It's even better as a twenty-seven-year-old than I imagined it would be as a nineteen-year-old.

But I worry that with all the concessions I'd have to make if I got a partner in life, the life I created would disappear. And that life is so intricately tied to who I am. I would feel lost and adrift without it.

Emilio and Leo are far enough ahead that I can no longer see them on the winding trail. Or anyone else. As the trail takes a sharp turn to the right, though, I hear another group coming toward us, and within minutes, they come around the bend. It's a husband and wife, and they're each wearing a child-carrying hiking backpack. In the wife's backpack is a baby that's probably less than a year old, and the dad has a bigger child-carrying backpack, probably for the preschooler who's running alongside him.

The trail is narrow in this section, so Hunter and I move off into the undergrowth as the little family passes, and we both stare at them the whole time. There's something about seeing a married couple—with kids!—doing the exact same thing we're doing that strikes me pretty hard.

I don't know why it hasn't occurred to me before that following my dream might be possible with little kids. The logo on their backpacks is a Blue Mountain Gear one, after all. I know my company creates them—I've just never been in on those projects.

I look at Hunter and can see that the same realization has hit him. That it's possible to involve a family in his passion. As we hike around the same bend the family just came from, we see

Emilio and Leo at the river crossing, trying to push each other off a log that runs across it.

"Date Peyton."

My attention flies to Hunter. "What?"

"Is Peyton everything you want?"

"Yes."

"She seems to like being around you pretty well, and with as much of a pain as you are to be around, that's impressive."

I laugh and give my friend a shove down the path toward the river.

"There is no world in which I can imagine the two of you getting along as poorly as your parents did. The only thing stopping you is your own stupid issues, right? So just…get over them."

"Oh, is that all?"

As I step over a fallen tree in the path, Hunter says, "Your job is basically getting over obstacles. So you're literally a pro at it."

Could I overcome my obstacles? Could a future with her be possible?

The four of us hike the rest of the way to the falls more or less together. Except for the last bit, where Leo runs ahead to be the first one there. When I reach the falls, I take a moment to soak in the feeling of standing near the base of the waterfall. The water isn't as deep here—or as cold—as the one at Tamolitch Blue Pool, but I still make sure not to stand on any rocks at the edge, especially since my mind is even more full of Peyton than it was on our last trip.

The trail to the side that leads to the top of the falls is steep and narrow, so of course we take it.

"Hey," Hunter says as we ascend the trail, grabbing hold of weeds, brush, and logs as we make our way up the steep incline, "what do you all think of Max inviting Peyton to one of our trips?"

I shoot a look back at Hunter, wondering what he's up to.

"Think about it, Max. She could come with friends so she won't feel like she's just going with a bunch of guys. We have plenty of tent options. Then she could see what she thinks of camping."

"I like it," Emilio says. Then, throwing me a look, adds, "It would give us a reason to make better food."

"Hey. Blame it on the cookware," I say. "That meal would've been a lot better if half of it hadn't fallen into the fire."

Maybe inviting Peyton to go camping is a good idea. It might help me to know if camping together might be something in our future. Maybe it would help calm my worries that my life as I know it would cease to exist, making me lose myself, if I got into a serious relationship.

Leo makes it to the top first and disappears behind some small trees. Emilio is right in front of me, I'm a few steps away from reaching the level area at the top when Leo comes back around the corner, screaming, "Bobcat!"

My eyes widen in shock. I barely have a moment to react before Leo and Emilio are both half-running, half-sliding down the path, and crash right into me. I manage to pitch to the side so the three of us won't go bowling into Hunter, and then I'm tumbling through the undergrowth at the side of the path.

The upside to descending so quickly down a non-path is there are more things to grab hold of on the way down than there are on the path. The downside is, that the non-trail is every bit as steep as the trail and has quite a few more obstacles. Like half-buried fallen tree trunks. Big rocks. Bushes.

I bump and bounce and tumble my way down and, when I finally come to a stop at the bottom of the hill that seems to go on forever, I land in a patch of poison oak, their three-leaved vines beneath me, beside me, and stretching over me like they want to pull me down and bury me in the world's itchiest hug.

Between the fall and the poison oak landing, I am definitely going to be feeling this later. I lie on the ground for a couple of seconds, trying to catch my breath, as I hear my friends scrambling down the mountainside toward me.

My body aches—dull in some places, sharp pains in others—and the poison oak already burns. Yet, still, the thought pops into my head that maybe I should wait for my rash to clear before asking Peyton to go camping.

CHAPTER 11

Peyton

"So," Max's mom says, "I gave him a look that told him, 'If you steal this parking space from me, this face is going to haunt your dreams for the next seven years.' Then the guy motions that the parking space is all mine, and he drives off to find a different one."

"Eleanor, you are so funny!" I remove the chicken I've been browning in a pan on Max's mom's stove and put in the veggies for the chicken cacciatore I'm making for her.

"I tell you. You've got to know when to be fierce to make it in this world. And by 'when,' I mean 'all the time.'"

We both laugh, and I say, "I love hanging out with you. I wish we could do it more often." Max's mom is just so different from me and always gives the most impossible-to-pull-off advice. It's fun and gives me a glimpse into a world I've never experienced. Really, the woman does everything fiercely, including loving people. It's nice.

"Oh, you know you're welcome here anytime you want. Especially if you're going to make something as divine as what you've got going in that pan."

My phone rings, so I put down the spatula and pick it up. Seeing Max's name on the phone causes my heart rate to quicken. I answer with, "Are you on your way back?" I miss him. Sure, he's only been gone a day, but it's been two since I last saw him. Should I really be missing him this much? That's probably a warning sign that I should focus more on relationships that might be destined for more than just friendship.

"Yep. Do you want to hang out tonight, or do you have other plans?"

"I'm at your mom's right now—you should stop by. I'm making chicken cacciatore."

"I, uh, haven't showered yet."

I mouth to Eleanor, *Can Max shower here?* She nods, so I say, "Your mom says to just shower here. That way you don't have to go home and then come all the way back."

"Okay, then. I'm actually only five minutes away."

And he really does show up in about five minutes. When I hear the front door open, I go to the foyer to say hi and then stop in my tracks. "Whoa. Max! I've never seen you this dirty before!" From his head to his toes, he's covered in dirt. Like every square inch of him.

He looks at his mom. "You're having second thoughts about saying yes to me showering here, aren't you?"

"I'm just trying to decide if I should have you go in the backyard so I can turn the sprinklers on you first."

He holds up an empty garbage bag. "Don't worry. I'll put my clothes straight into here, and I'll leave the bathroom as clean as I found it. I'm going to have to wear one of my spare sets of clothes I left here, though. Nothing in my pack is clean enough."

The meal is simmering on the stove, so I just sit at the table, talking and laughing with Max's mom about my dates. Then I take a deep breath and bring up something I've been worrying about. "I've gone out with fifteen guys, so that's fifteen times I had to decide if I should continue to date them or not. I'm afraid I'm making all the wrong choices. I'm just not good at decision-making."

"You decided to come over here today, didn't you? I'd say you're pretty good at making decisions."

I laugh.

"In all seriousness, though, I think you *are* good at decision-making. I've never seen anyone more suited to being a personal chef than you are. I see the joy it brings you, so that's proof you can make good decisions."

"But I didn't make that decision—my mom did." Eleanor looks confused, so I explain. "When I was seven, I was helping my mom cook dinner and told her how much I liked helping her. She said I would be a great personal chef someday. So, I started watching cooking shows and she put me in cooking classes.

"When I was eighteen and just starting culinary school, she passed away. Before she died, she told me not to give up on my dream. It's the one decision I've always been totally confident about because it's the one she made for me. And now she's gone, so she can't tell me what the right decision is on anything. Like who to date."

"Peyton, I think you're better at it than you realize. Just listen to your gut."

"But what if I think everything is exactly right with a guy, and then later I find out it isn't and it's too late to change my mind? I mean we are talking about a decision that has lifetime implications! It's kind of an important thing to get right. How are people supposed to choose a partner for life based on such limited information?"

Eleanor looks like she's going to say something, but then Max walks in. It must have been a while since he last checked his spare clothes inventory because he's wearing a pair of teal gym shorts with a blue shirt that looks about as wrong next to the teal as peanut butter and grapefruit.

He's also limping and walking like everything hurts. And now that he's clean, I can see that there's a red, bumpy rash on his neck, hands, and one ankle, and several bruises on his legs and arms that are just starting to form.

"Max!" I say, hurrying to him. "What happened to you?"

"Well, a bobcat attacked. Except it wasn't really a bobcat so much as it was a cute little furry yellow-bellied marmot. So mostly Leo attacked, and I got to take the scenic route down the hill and got up close and personal with some poison oak. There were good times to be had by all."

I help Max to a chair. By the way he sits down, it looks like he has injured everything possible to injure. "What can I do? What do you need?"

"I'm good. I just need to sit for a minute. By tomorrow, I'll be one hundred percent."

His mom snorts.

"Okay, not a hundred percent, but better."

I look him up and down. "That rash'll take a week or two to go away, and bruises like the one I can see by your knee are going to take more than a day."

Max raises a shoulder in a shrug. He's trying to be tough, but I can tell it hurts. I want to wrap him up in, well, something that will make him feel better. I don't even dare hug him for fear it will make things worse.

As I sit back down at the table, his mom says, "Peyton was just telling me about some of the crazy dates she's gone on this week. Did she tell you about the one where the guy fell asleep?"

Max looks rather amused. "She did not." He leans forward, putting an arm on the table, resting his chin on his fist to show he's interested in the story. But it must hurt because he immediately puts his hand back down. "Tell me to distract me from the pain."

So, even though it's getting weirder to tell Max about my dates, I tell the story again. "Well, to start off, he didn't tell me that they had a huge deadline at his work and that he'd only slept an hour or two each night all week. He did tell me that they had worked all through the night and that he'd been up for thirty-six hours straight, but that he hadn't wanted to cancel the date. He didn't tell me that, though, until we were in the middle of a walk in a park. We saw a bench and he veered toward it. I don't think he'd even fully sat down before he fell asleep. Right there on the bench with people all around and kids laughing and yelling."

"That sounds like the most interesting date ever," Max jokes.

"Oh, it was," his mom says. "Keep listening."

"Max, I'm telling you that I tried hard to wake this guy up, and he just wouldn't. So I tried calling Addison, since she was the one who set me up with him, hoping that she knew someone I could call. But she was in the middle of organizing someone's cinder block garage and had no cell reception at all. So then I tried again to get the guy to wake up so he could tell me who to call, but, as I found out, when your body shuts itself down from lack of sleep, it shuts it down very effectively.

"So, I pulled the guy's phone from of his pocket and was trying to get his face to unlock it so I see if one of his contacts said 'Mom' or something, but did you know that you can't unlock your phone if your eyes aren't open? Anyway, I was kind of panicking by that point because I didn't even know if the guy was okay or if he was having some kind of medical emergency, and there was no way I could haul him back to the car to drive him home. And believe me, I tried.

"Then the police showed up, which was pretty handy—I wish I would've thought to call them. So I heaved a big sigh of relief that I was going to have help, and then the officer said to me, 'We got reports that you killed a guy and are trying to break into his phone and haul the body off to hide it.'"

Max starts laughing. And I do, too, because looking back now, it *is* funny. At the time, it was more embarrassing and exhausting than funny.

"But then I explained everything, and did you know that on an iPhone, from the password screen, you can tap Medical ID and it will show you who their emergency contact is? Because I didn't. Anyway, the police were going to take me to the station because even though the guy was clearly alive, they worried that I poisoned him or something, since he would not wake up.

"But then the guy's emergency contact, who was his roommate, told the police that the guy had only slept something like ten hours total in the past week, and the officers decided that I wasn't a criminal mastermind—I was just the victim of an unfortunate blind date. Which, if you ask me, was pretty obvious. If I were a criminal mastermind, would I really put the guy to sleep in the middle of a park with people all around?"

Max is laughing in earnest now. "Your date makes mine seem like a walk in the park. You know, the kind of walk in the park where your date doesn't fall asleep halfway through."

"Since Peyton told hers," his mom says, "you have to tell one of yours."

"Okay, then. Mine was lined up by a friend of a friend, so we both went in blind. Her brothers decided they needed to make sure their sister wasn't going out with a creeper, so they went to the same movie and snuck into the seats right behind us.

"The whole time, they were kicking our chairs, throwing popcorn, shouting at the decisions the characters made—all of it. I found out that it was a test to see how I'd react. I guess I passed the test because they started leaning forward and whispering advice on how I could subtly put my arm around their sister and when. All with her right there, listening."

My cheeks heat up just hearing about it. "Was she so embarrassed?"

Max shakes his head. "She high-fived her brothers on the way out."

"So who won your contest?" Eleanor asks. "And what does the winner get?"

We haven't actually discussed the final numbers, so I look at Max.

He sighs. "Peyton won."

I clap my hands, I'm so happy. A win against Max is nearly impossible, but I've done it. "How many dates did you go on?"

"Not important. Mom, to answer your question, the loser has to sing karaoke."

Eleanor covers her mouth with her hand like she's trying to hold in a laugh. "In public?"

Max's eyes shoot to mine before going back to his mom's. "Either, I guess. We never said."

"Well," Eleanor says, "then I suggest you not do it at home or your neighbor will be knocking on your door, asking if you have a cat in need of medical attention."

I chuckle. Max never sings for me—or anyone. I can't wait.

"So did either of you find a date for Bex and Roman's wedding? That was the goal, right?"

"Well, part of the goal," I say. "My ultimate goal is to find a husband. Or at least to hurry along the process." I glance at Max because apparently I'm now thinking of him as more than a friend, and it's weird to talk about stuff like that around him. The look on his face is unreadable. "I think I've narrowed it down to three. I might go with David."

"The waiter?"

"Yeah. He's a software tester during the day, and he's waiting tables a few nights a week to help pay for his niece's heart surgery." I turn to Max. "Have you decided who you're going with?"

Max immediately fumbles, and it makes me wonder if he hasn't already figured out who. "Um, yeah. I went on a bike ride with a girl named Clara. She seemed nice, so I thought I'd ask her."

"It's hard to choose, isn't it?"

I thought the date thing was a great idea, that I would sail blissfully through it, find someone incredible, and sometime soon, I'd be engaged, then we'd get married and live blissfully ever after. But I'm at the very end of my week of dating, and I'm more confused than I ever was. Especially whenever I look at Max. And especially when I think of Max going to the wedding with Clara.

Eleanor gives a rare sweet smile. Not a teasing one or a patronizing one or a conspiratorial one. It's one full of love. "I'll just say that I think both of you will find who you're supposed to be with, and you'll know that person is right."

By the look on Eleanor's face, I can't tell if she's just wishing me good fortune in general or if she's thinking of Max and me together when she says it. I'm going to assume good fortune in general because the other is too big to wrap my head around.

"Aw, thank you," I say. "Speaking of finding who you're supposed to be with, I was talking to my dad the other day, and I think he's ready to start dating again."

Max kicks my shoe with his under the table. I glance at him, expecting his expression to be apologetic for straightening his legs right into mine, but he's just looking at me with an intense face that I can't read.

"Anyway, so then I got thinking that you—"

Max hits his leg right into the table this time, shaking it, and causing him to wince in pain at the bruise that must be on whatever part of his leg hit the table. As he's wincing, he reaches up and starts scratching at the rash on his neck.

"I'll go get the calamine lotion," Eleanor says. "With a son like Max, I know to always keep it on hand. Oh, and I finished putting together a scrapbook for you, Max. I'll grab that, too."

As soon as she leaves the room, Max says, "Peyton! I thought we agreed not to set them up!"

Why did I even bring it up? Maybe because I'm having trouble shoving my feelings for Max down, and him being my brother seems like an effective way. I hadn't even realized that was what I was doing.

Sneaky subconscious.

Max lets out a big exhale. "My parents' marriage wasn't like your parents'. Unless they were performing for an audience of friends, mine bickered nonstop. I think the reason they went on so many vacations when I was a kid was because the only way they could almost get along was if they were somewhere exotic. They didn't like each other like your parents did. Do you really want your dad to be with someone who will bicker with him all the time?"

"You don't know they will bicker. Your parents probably did just because they weren't a good fit for each other. My dad was so happy when my mom was alive. I want that for him again."

"Peyton, your parents' marriage was a unicorn. Something rare that can't be duplicated. That's not how it works for other people."

"It *is* how it works for other people." I wish he understood that. "It just didn't for your parents. My dad is a nice guy, and your mom has been nice to him the few times they've met. I think she'll like him. Don't you want her to experience a marriage that is better than the one she had with your dad?"

And now I'm fighting for it. *What is wrong with me?*

Max runs his hands over his face, frustrated. "Can you— Will you at least just wait a while, like a month or two, before doing anything?"

Give in, Peyton. Just back away. You don't want to win this one. "Okay. I won't set them up."

I'm just going to have to come up with another way to keep my thoughts under control about having a romantic relationship with Max. Preferably before my subconscious brain starts making plans again without my consent.

CHAPTER 12
Max

I'M SITTING with Clara in the audience for Bex and Roman's wedding ceremony. Everything looks so nice. And Roman looks like the happiest man who has ever lived. It makes me actually imagine myself standing at the front of a crowd of my closest family and friends, about to be married to Peyton, looking every bit as thrilled. It surprises me how much the thought doesn't freak me out.

I turn as Peyton comes up the aisle with the other bridesmaids and groomsmen, arm-in-arm with one of Roman's friends, and then goes to stand at the front, facing the guests.

All seven of the bridesmaids are wearing dresses with the same slate blue fabric, but each in a style all their own. None of them stand out the way Peyton does, though, or look as amazing in that color. Hers is fitted to just past her hips before it flares, the silky fabric falling in perfect waves, showing off her incredible legs. I'm having the hardest time keeping my eyes off her.

The music changes, and then Bex comes in, escorted by her dad, and I go on imagining what it would be like if it was

Peyton walking up that aisle, looking just as thrilled about our future together as Bex is looking about hers.

Bex and Roman have written their own vows, and I'm not ashamed to admit that I tear up a little. Peyton's eyes find mine, and the look she gives me makes my heart race and swell and maybe even melt a bit. I try to read her expression to guess if she is possibly picturing this happening with us like I am. It occupies all my attention.

Once the ceremony is over and it's time to head into the reception, I walk in with Clara. Peyton is right in front of me, practically floating. I know from watching her during the ceremony that she has loved every minute of it.

Clara reaches for my hand and gives it a squeeze, reminding me that Peyton and I aren't here with each other and that I shouldn't be imagining a life with Peyton when I have a date by my side. I shouldn't be thinking of her at all. Peyton's eyes immediately shift to David's, who she's walking hand-in-hand with, and she gives him a smile.

It's a clear reminder that things are the way they always are. I'm in love with Peyton, and she doesn't know. I'm just moving through life with her as a best friend and not as a partner.

"Look how beautiful everything is," Peyton says as she motions to all the fancy tables and place settings and chairs with bows tied around them. The big long table where Bex and Roman will sit, along with her four sisters, his two brothers, two groomsmen, and both of their parents, is long and at the top of the room, facing everyone. The rest of the tables are circular and go along the other three sides of the room, leaving the middle open for dancing. All of us find our way to the tables we're assigned to.

My table is at the top of the U, closest to the long bride and groom table. I find my and Clara's names at two of the place settings, pull Clara's chair out, and then tuck it in as she sits.

Peyton is seated at the same table, directly across from me, which makes her the easiest to look at and the most difficult to speak to, especially in a room with the noise from so many people talking. And, of course, David is by her side.

Addison and Ian are seated to the left of my date, and Timini and a guy named Orion are to my right. I've only known the guy for an hour, but already he doesn't seem like Timini's type at all. Other than the fact that he is pretty and she seems to like the pretty ones.

I scratch the back of my neck, the very last of the poison oak rash looking like it's gone, thankfully, but not all the way over its itching. Especially when I'm wearing a collared shirt. I'm glad that the bruises and aching bones didn't take as long to heal.

As soon as we are all seated, Bex and Roman come into the room, waving to everyone and smiling like they aren't freaked out at all about having just gotten married.

"You know when I tie the knot," Orion says as the wait staff places salads in front of each of us, "I'm not going to worry about all this traditional stuff. In fact, I think I want to purposely do the opposite of tradition."

Kind of curious, but mostly looking to make conversation that will keep my mind off Peyton, I ask, "So, in regards to the meal, does 'opposite of tradition' mean something along the lines of serving breakfast instead of dinner, serving dessert first, or having the guests be the servers and the servers eat the meal?"

"Well," Orion says as he picks up his dessert fork and stabs a piece of lettuce in his salad, "I was thinking more like having it on the beach, and instead of tables, everyone just sitting on beach towels in the sand to eat, but I like the way you think."

Timini tries to hide her smile. Orion might not make it to

another date after this one, but she is clearly fascinated by him. Actually, everyone seems to be a little bit.

"I want a flash mob at my wedding," Clara says. "But since those are usually a surprise to the bride and groom, it's the one thing you can't plan, which is too bad."

"Invite me," Orion says, "and I'll make sure you have one."

"Thank you," Clara says, seeming very touched by his offer, especially since they only met minutes ago. Then her expression turns unsure. Probably because she's imagining what kind of song for the flash mom he might consider the "opposite of tradition."

Movement from the dance floor catches my attention, and I look over to see three of Bex's young nieces, each smiling and carrying something in their hands, and it looks like their focus is on my table. While chatting with my tablemates, I keep glancing back at the girls, who are making their way closer, but only because they are doing a lot of nudging each other.

I'm surprised when they come straight over to me, and each of them places the things they have been holding—which turn out to be rose petals—in a pile next to my plate. I've seen all three girls at the inn before, but I don't know their names.

"She thinks you're cute," one who looks about five years old blurts out, giving a little shove to a girl who is probably around seven.

"No, she does," the seven-year-old says, pointing to someone barely older than her.

The oldest smiles at me and says, "Actually, we all think you're cute."

The other two nod.

"And I think all three of you are beautiful," I say. "I like your matching dresses. Thank you so much for the rose petals."

The three girls giggle, and then flat-out run their way across the dance floor and back to their parents' tables.

"Aww," Peyton says, watching the little girls run. "Wasn't that the sweetest thing?"

"It was." Addison shifts her attention to the table where Bex and Roman are sitting, making moon eyes at each other. "I can't believe our little girl is all grown up."

Ian chuckles. "I can't believe Roman finally stopped caring what his dad thought."

"I can't believe two of us are married now," Peyton says.

"I can't believe more of you aren't," David says, which really just kind of irks me.

"I can't believe that's how you'd measure a woman's worth." I'm not sure David hears me, and I'm not sure I want him to.

"I can't believe they put cream in the dressing," Clara says next to me.

Orion looks over at the tables where Bex's sisters' husbands and kids are seated. "I can't believe they let all these kids come to the reception and run around everywhere."

"I can believe it," Timini says. "Bex wouldn't have had it any other way. Plus, they're sweet."

"Excuse me a moment," Clara says, and then gets up and walks away.

I give her a nod and then look back at Peyton and David. I know that what I'm feeling when I look at David is jealousy— I'm not so oblivious of my own emotions to not recognize it. What I've wished a million times over during the past two weeks is that I'd been willing to tell Peyton I wanted to come with her to the wedding before she asked David.

Actually, I wish that I'd confessed my feelings for her anytime in the past year. Or, if I'm going to go back in time with my wishing, I wish I'd been open to the possibility four years ago when we first met and became friends.

But now I'm here with Clara, on a second date after the first hasn't even been great, and she's here with David on a date that *does* seem to be going great.

After a few minutes of trying to focus on eating the grilled beef tenderloin with lobster risotto, mushrooms, and carrots that a server has placed in front of me, Clara sits back down and leans in close to me. "I'm…not doing so well. Do you think you can take me home?"

One look at her could've told me she isn't feeling well. Which is crazy, because she looked fine just a few minutes ago. I hurry and put my napkin on the table. "Yeah, of course."

"Clara!" Timini says when she looks over. "Are you okay?"

"I just ate something I'm allergic to." She waves her hand. "I'll be fine."

My eyes meet Peyton's as I stand, and I see a sadness in them that I'm leaving. A longing for me to stay. My face probably mirrors hers. I give her a small smile and escort Clara out of the building, then run ahead to get my car which is finally back from the auto body shop, good as new, and drive it back to her.

"Do you need me to take you to the hospital? Or to an urgent care clinic?"

"No. I just need to go home."

I know I wouldn't be the most pleasant person to be around if I were sick, and I don't expect Clara to be, either. But I also don't expect her to be so mad at me for bringing her. And I think it's a bit much when she starts shouting curses at the chefs, the wait staff, the people who purchased the ingredients, Bex and Roman for choosing the menu, the dairy farmers who sold the cream, the cows who produced the milk, and everyone who attended the wedding for supporting such an atrocity.

She was such a calm, even person for our first date and the first half of this one. I never would've guessed she'd turn into someone capable of coming up with the vocabulary needed to swear up the storm she just unleashed.

Once we pull up to her apartment, I open the door for her and help her out of the car. She looks miserable. "Can I come in and help? Or go get medicine? What do you need?" I feel helpless and am not quite sure what to even offer.

"I just want to suffer alone." She turns and puts a hand on my shoulder. I'm not proud of the fact that it makes me flinch like she might slap me. "You are a lovely man, Max, and I appreciate you for leaving your friend's wedding to get me home. But obviously, we can never go out again after this."

She turns and walks away, and I'm left feeling bad that she's so miserable from the date I've taken her on.

As I get back in my car and drive away, though, I glance at the clock. The night is still young—it isn't too late to go back to the wedding. Sure, Peyton will be with her date all night. But she's Peyton, so I feel pulled back to the event, anyway.

CHAPTER 13
Peyton

Bex's wedding is magical and the most beautiful ceremony I've ever witnessed. Bex and Roman look amazing and so happy. Both the room with the ceremony and the reception room are fancy and pretty. The dinner is delicious. And now I'm dancing with David, having fun and feeling so elegant in my perfect dress.

So why has my mind spent so much of the night thinking about Max?

Probably because I don't get to see him so dressed up very often, and he looks so good in his suit. And probably because I'm having a harder and harder time viewing him as just a friend. Which is probably why I'm having such a difficult time watching him with Clara. Max and I haven't ever doubled on dates, so I'm not used to it. I might be a little bit jealous.

And I'm probably thinking about him so much simply because he's Max. Max just pulls people to him.

But Max left, the music is great, everyone is on their feet on the dance floor, and I'm dancing with a guy who has been a model of a perfect date all night long. So I put all of my focus on him and on enjoying the moment and not thinking about Max. And mostly succeeding.

Well, succeeding a good half of the time.

We are dancing to a song that is great for the swing, and David is an excellent dance partner. He twirls me out, and right before he twirls me back in, I swear the feel of the reception hall changes. As we dance, I try to look around to see what's different.

And then I see it. Max has come back to the reception. My heart feels like a balloon being blown up to bursting that he came back. Bex's little nieces must feel the shift in the room, too, because they immediately run over to him. And then he starts dancing with them and my heart melts into a big pile of goo.

David and I continue to do the swing—arms extended and then back together—and I do a pretty decent job of having all of my attention on him. Well, except for when I'm facing Max's direction and catch another glimpse of him doing the random silly dance moves the little girls are doing. He's such a good sport. At the end of the song, David drops me into a dip, and I smile up at him.

When he pulls me back up to standing, he meets my eyes and says, "Thank you for the dance." Then he glances toward the doors. "I think I'm going to go."

"What?" I study his face. "Already? But it's not over."

He gives me the sweetest smile and then touches a lock of hair that is resting on my shoulder. "I know. And I've had a wonderful time with you, but I pride myself on being a gentleman." I look at him, not making the connection between that and him leaving, so he nods at something behind me. "Your friend Max is now dateless, and he is in love with you, so I'm going to take a step back."

I jerk my head back in confusion. "What? Max? No—we're just friends."

David shakes his head. "Not to him. And by the way you light up whenever he's in the room, I think the feeling is mutual. I've been watching all night, and I think you should go explore that."

I turn to glance at Max, who must sense we are talking about him from across the dance floor because even though he has three little girls pulling on his hands, his eyes are on mine.

When I look back at David, I say, "I'm sorry I've been a terrible date." Because if I've been focusing on Max enough for David to notice, I very much have been.

He shakes his head. "You've been a phenomenal date. I like you, Peyton. If things between the two of us went somewhere, I'd be thrilled. But not while you're in love with your best friend."

Am I in love with Max? A voice in my head counters with *Was there ever a time when you weren't?*

"If things with him don't work out, give me a call. If they do, then I wish you two all the best."

I study David for a few moments, trying to take in everything he's said. "You're a good guy, David."

He gives me a smile and I give him a thank-you hug. Then David gives Max a nod and walks out of the reception hall.

I don't quite know what to do. I haven't ever let myself think about what I would do in a situation like this. Actually, I haven't even had to stop myself from thinking about this scenario, because I've never imagined it. Yet the moment David says that I am in love with my best friend, I feel the truth of it burning in my heart. Like I've always known it was there, but haven't acknowledged it.

Plus, I don't know how Max feels about me. Sure, I know that he likes spending time with me and that we get along well.

We wouldn't be best friends otherwise. But what about beyond that? He has definitely given me looks lately that I swear mean he sees me as more than a sister, but he hasn't acted any differently.

I've only been standing on the dance floor alone for a few seconds, as the band is playing a slower song, before Max says something to Bex's nieces and then crosses the floor in long strides to meet me. He puts his hands in his pockets before glancing at the door David just exited.

"He left?"

I nod.

"But he likes you."

I nod again but I didn't need to—there must've been an entire wordless conversation between David and Max as David gave him that nod because Max seems to understand what has happened.

"Are you okay?"

I meet his gaze and nod. My mind is a jumbled mess like it hasn't yet processed everything that has just happened. But as I look into Max's hazel eyes, I feel like everything is okay. Max is here, and everything is good.

"Do you want to go sit down? Or do you want to dance?"

We are standing in the midst of a lot of couples dancing, and I realize that we are the only ones not moving. I don't know what I want yet—I just know that I want to keep Max close, so I put my wrists on his shoulders, my hands meeting at the back of his neck. His hands find my hips, and we dance to the slow music.

My mind is racing so much faster than my body is moving, though. It's as if years of romantic feelings toward Max have been in my brain, back in some hidden reserve I hadn't known about. And then David's parting words flung the gate wide open and everything is spilling out, flooding my mind with thoughts and feelings and possibilities. And images of the way Max has been looking at me. It's all more than I can take in.

And this music is way too slow for the speed at which my brain is moving. "Actually, do you mind if we go outside for some fresh air?"

"Not at all." He guides me through the crowd with his hand on the small of my back, and I soak in the touch. David's hand has been on my back a good portion of the time we'd been dancing, yet having Max's hand there feels so new. Like something I haven't experienced before. Like it's the first time feeling the sun shine on my face.

We walk through the door at the back of the reception hall and onto a balcony that runs the full length of the back of the venue, overlooking the lawns and gardens below, lights illuminating all the beauty in the darkness. The fresh air is cool, and as I breathe it in, it helps to calm my body.

My brain is still running too fast, though. I can't stand still, just looking out over the railing. I need to move. So I head toward the stairs leading down to the gardens. Max doesn't say anything—he just walks beside me like he's unsure what I'm feeling or what he should be doing right now.

I'm pretty unsure myself. All I know is that my feelings for him are so intense. How has this massive amount of feelings been trapped behind that gate? It seems impossible.

We walk, neither of us talking, until we reach a secluded alcove where the ground rises up on three sides. At the back, an impressive twelve-foot rock structure has water tumbling down it, like a waterfall. A koi pond is nearby, and the most beautiful flowers and greenery are all around, and everything is lit by lights at our feet.

Normally, I would love to just sit on the nearby bench and immerse myself in the peaceful surroundings until the moment they kick us out. Right now, though, I'm not feeling peaceful. I am full of questions that I need the answers to.

The main one is whether Max will ever see me as more than a friend. Or a sister.

I'm not sure what his answer will be. I face him, searching his eyes through the glow of the moon and the landscape lighting, trying to guess. Once before, I allowed thoughts of a romantic relationship with Max to invade my senses. Not to the extent of what has just been released in me now, but enough that I knew I wanted to pursue it. I waited weeks to act on it.

When I finally did, he pulled back just slightly enough to stop the kiss, but with an effort not to make me feel rejected. I still felt it, though. It hadn't been easy to switch back to just seeing him as a friend, but eventually, I did it.

Now, though, the thought of ever going back to just being friends seems impossible. What has been released at the opening of that gate now fills every space in my mind, expanding to fill every corner. And the longer it roams free, the more it's going to wreck me. I have to know how he feels now.

But I'm so scared. What if he still just thinks of me as a sister? If I can't trap these feelings back inside again, what will it do to me? To our friendship? What if he tells me he isn't interested? Can I handle that news? Or will it crush me?

It very well could. But I decide that not knowing is worse. I have to ask.

How, though? My mind keeps cycling through questions I could ask, but each sounds awful. Maybe instead of talking, I just need to act.

Heart pumping faster than a hummingbird's, hands shaking, breaths coming in small little puffs, I step closer to Max, searching his eyes. I don't find the answers there, but he also doesn't back away like he did a year ago. I move in closer, so we are only the smallest breath apart. He still doesn't pull away.

Feeling exposed and vulnerable and open to the worst pain imaginable, I make the decision to risk it all. I rise up on my toes and close the remaining distance, crushing my lips against Max's.

His arms immediately wrap around my back, pulling me tight to him, that one motion wrapping a protective barrier around everything vulnerable, keeping me safe from harm.

I start the kiss as a desperate plea to know how he feels and he answers with the same desperate need. But then his kiss turns cautious and hesitant. Almost like he's just as afraid as I am of something happening that will break the magic spell we seem to be under.

Eventually, I pull away from the kiss just a couple of inches, but almost of their own accord, my arms around his shoulders still hold him tight like they're afraid that if I let go, he'll be gone forever. He keeps his arms just as tight around me.

"Max?" I whisper.

"Yeah?" he says, his voice low and gruff.

"Do you still think of me as a sister?"

He lets out a humorless chuckle enclosed in a single breath of an exhale. "No, Peyton. I never did."

CHAPTER 14

Max

I REPLAY Peyton's kiss next to the waterfall in my mind as I drive to Hidden Inn. Even though we've kissed quite a few times in the two weeks since that night, I still replay it several times a day. Every kiss with her feels significant, perfect, extraordinary. But none of them have the same raw, terrifying, exposed emotions that our first kiss had, where we laid everything on the line. Every kiss with her feels exactly right, and I wonder how I ever lived without them.

I pull into the long, curving driveway of the inn and park near the porch. I've made it up the stairs and almost to the front door when it flies open and Peyton steps out, her hands immediately finding my face, her lips pressing against mine. I put a hand on the small of her back and cradle her head with my other hand. Her lips move against mine, sending electricity flying in every direction.

When she pulls back, we stay close, smiling at each other, her breath tickling my cheek. I move my hand slightly so my thumb can caress the skin of her cheek. "I missed you, too."

She smiles and drops her hand from my face, wrapping it in

mine as we turn to walk into the inn. Can something this great possibly last?

This is my very first "Roommate plus significant others" dinner, and I've actually been slightly nervous, which I know doesn't make sense. I hang out with these same people all the time. Here. While eating food. I just never have at an official roommate dinner.

But it turns out it isn't that different from having pizza here —except there's better homemade food and everyone sits in the chairs the way they're meant to be sat in. It somehow feels like I belong. Like I've always been a part of this group.

Addison has made chicken piccata, which is apparently one of her specialties, and we mostly listen to stories about Bex and Roman's honeymoon in the Seychelles Islands, since they just got back yesterday.

"It's good to have you here, Max," Bex says as she reaches for a dinner roll from the middle of the table. "Are you in town for a while?"

I grin at Peyton. "It's good to be here. And, actually, I wanted to bring that up."

I hope Peyton will be interested in the plan I'm about to propose. I asked her once if she had much camping experience, and she said she'd wanted to go as a kid but that it wasn't in her dad's wheelhouse. Not wanting her to miss the chance entirely, I set up a tent in their backyard, made food on the barbeque, and we toasted marshmallows in the metal fire pit I bought. I so badly want her to experience real camping and see what she thinks of it.

"I'm heading into the mountains this weekend with three buddies from work that I camp with a lot, and I am hoping that you all might want to join us. We've got a big tent that everyone could fit in or smaller tents if you'd like to stay as couples, and as far as equipment goes, we have access to everything we could possibly need." I hold my breath as I wait for everyone's responses.

"I've always wanted to go," Peyton says. "Not that I have any clue how to camp."

Timini grins. "Neither do I, and I'm all for doing things I have no clue how to do. Count me in."

Addison and Bex both look at their husbands, a question on their faces.

"I can't," Ian says to Addison. "Roman and I are heading to Eugene Friday night to help my brother move, remember?"

Addison's face falls. "I forgot that was this Friday."

"And by the time we finish on Saturday and make the two-hour drive back, it might be after midnight before we get home. Depending on how much work there is to do, it might be Sunday morning. But you should still go if you want to. Camping here is pretty amazing."

Roman turns to me. "Your friends are experts, too, right?"

I nod. "A little too expert sometimes. Hunter knows practically everything there is to know about the outdoors. Emilio will make sure we have every gadget we could possibly need, and Leo—well, Leo keeps it real. And he whittles. They're all good guys. We'll keep everyone safe."

Roman looks at Bex, whose face clearly shows she's interested. "I think you should go, too."

Bex's eyebrows draw together. "Without you?"

He nods. "I think the four of you would have fun being in a tent together. A girls' trip, roughing it and braving the wild."

Bex looks at him for a long moment.

"Do you want to go?" Roman asks.

"I do. But I don't want you to miss out. Are you sure you don't mind me going when you can't?"

Roman nods. "I'll be here to see you off on Friday night, and then I'll be back by the time you're home on Sunday."

She turns back to me. "Can I film a *Bexlandia* episode while we are there?"

I'm so thrilled they want to come that I'd probably agree to anything. "Yes."

Peyton turns to her roommates. "We are going to go on an adventure!"

Seeing her get so excited about something so important to me is thrilling. I can't wait to show her firsthand all the things I love about camping, hiking, and spending time in nature. I so badly want her to love it. It feels like everything hinges on that.

Now I just need to plan the perfect trip so everything will go well and she will want to keep going with me forever. I'm a pro at this—it's practically in my job title. I'll have no problem at all making sure things go just right.

CHAPTER 15

Peyton

IT FEELS wrong to pack a suitcase for a camping trip, so I pack all the stuff I think I'll need into a big beach bag and a gym bag and heft them out onto the wrap-around porch.

Since Ian is driving his truck to Eugene and none of the rest of us drive vehicles meant to handle possibly rougher terrain, Bex swaps her car with her sister's Yukon. Bex's and Addison's husbands help to get everything loaded, then the guys head west on Highway 26 and my roommates and I head east. "It has been so long since I last went camping," Addison says. "I can't wait to get there!"

"And I can't wait to see what Max's other world is like." I pick up my phone and call him. When my call goes to Max's voicemail, I say, "It's five-thirteen, and we're just pulling out. See you at about six!"

Max went to our campsite a few hours ago because he wanted to get everything set up for us. There isn't cell service there, but there is a half mile down the road, so he asked me to leave him a message. He'll go check every half hour or so for a message from me so he'll know what time to expect us. How sweet is that? He really is the greatest guy.

I'm a little nervous about camping because I've never done it before. Not for real. But Max will help me through everything, and I'm glad that I'm going to experience something so important to him.

About a mile down the road from the inn, Bex slows and pulls the Yukon off to the side. "Look! They've started framing the walls!"

"Oh my stars," I say from the passenger seat, "you're going to have a real house soon." I let myself dream for a minute about what it might be like when I'm in Bex's shoes and have a husband and a house in the works. But lately, that feeling makes my guts get all tangled in knots.

It only takes about twenty-five minutes before we turn off the main road and head onto the tree-lined one leading into Mount Hood National Forest. Max camps all over Oregon and Washington and sometimes into California. I like that he chose a site so close to home for our first excursion.

"So," Timini says from where she and Addison share the backseat, "how are you and Max getting along now that you are dating?"

"Great! I mean, he's Max, so it's easy to get along great with him. That's why he's always been such a good friend."

The pause of voices in the SUV feels like a physical thing. A weight in the space.

"But?" Addison finally asks.

I look out the window at the mix of evergreens and maple trees we pass by and take a deep breath. "I don't know. I guess I'm just worried." Then, I turn in my seat a bit so I can see all three of my roomies. "Okay, so that night at the wedding when David pointed out that Max and I were in love but weren't acknowledging it, there was so much swirling around in my head. Like a tornado hitting a cotton factory. But something changed for me that night.

"To find out that Max felt the same way about me was so exciting! The last couple of weeks have been a whirlwind of new things. And it's a different kind of new than I've ever experienced with other guys I've dated because it's Max. I mean, we've been friends forever. And now with the dating and the kissing and the cuddling up to him on the couch, it feels so incredible, you know?"

All three women sigh audibly.

"Turn right here?" Bex asks.

I look down at my paper with Max's instructions. "Zigzag, left, left, left, right. Yes." As Bex turns the vehicle onto the dirt road, I continue. "And in so many ways, it feels so right. Like things are finally the way they were always supposed to be.

"But I realized that even though so much changed for me that night at the wedding, nothing really changed for Max. Well, I mean, our whole relationship changed, but nothing changed *in* him if that makes sense. I don't know if it was just seeing him with your nieces, Bex, and thinking about how great of a dad he would be, or seeing the expressions that were crossing his face during your wedding ceremony that threw me off, or what.

"But, I've known him for four years, and he has always said he'll never get married. He's convinced that most marriages are bad and almost none are good, and he's not willing to take the chance. Same with being a father. And he hasn't said that he feels any differently about it now."

"Have you talked to him about it?" Addison asks.

The SUV bumps around on the rock and dirt road that seems to have ruts going in every direction. I shake my head. "I think I'm afraid to hear the answer. He'll probably say he never wants to get married, and then what? I don't think I can just go back to the way things were—too much has changed between us. So will things just end? Am I supposed to go without Max for the rest of my life? I don't know if I can do that!"

I turn to look out the window again. "I am the worst at making important decisions. I need my mom." I've been aching for her lately as much as I did back when she first passed away. She probably would've helped me figure things out ahead of time so I wouldn't have found myself in this mess.

"What about—" Timini is cut off by a loud, deep popping sound, right before the Yukon tips to the right a bit.

Bex's attention flies from mirror to mirror. "Oh, no. What just happened?"

She brings the vehicle to a stop, and all four of us get out to see that the back passenger tire is completely flat.

"How?" Bex says. "The tread on these tires is way too thick for one of these rocks to pop it!"

Addison crouches down by the tire and sticks her head underneath to check out the backside. She emerges holding a little ancient screwdriver that's only about three or four inches long, including the handle. "This," she says, getting to her feet. "We must've run over it or something flipped it into the tire. It was stuck into the tire up to its handle."

I immediately try to call Max. "I don't have service. Do any of you?"

They pull out their phones, too, but nothing. I wasn't checking my phone during the drive, so I have no idea when we last had service.

"Don't worry," Bex says, heading around to the back of the vehicle. "One of my dad's requirements for me and my siblings to get a driver's license was to first show that we could change a flat tire. And I changed one on my car about a year ago, so

I've got recent experience, too. We've got this, ladies. We just need to…"

She reaches the back of the vehicle as a collective, "Oh" sounds from all of us. All of our gear is blocking access to the tire.

It doesn't take long before all of our bags and bedding are in a pile on top of the dirt and rock road, the back of the Yukon is empty, and we're all looking for something on the floor of the vehicle to lift to get to the tire. I haven't exactly changed a flat tire before, but I'm pretty sure that's where they're kept.

"Where is it?" Bex says, baffled. Then, seeing a little hatch on the side panel, she opens it to check if the jack is inside. All it contains, though, is a stash of Bex's nieces' and nephews' stuffed animals.

Addison gets back down on the dirt road and looks under the vehicle. "It's mounted underneath."

I look over at all the stuff we already unloaded from the back and try to think of something positive that came from it. More exercise?

Timini leans down to look. "Umm…how are we supposed to get it down?"

"Changing a tire is like baking a cake," I say. "We just have to follow the recipe." I go back to my seat and start looking through the glove box until I find the recipe—a.k.a. the owner's manual—and flip to the section about the spare tire. I walk back around to the back of the vehicle, shaking my head.

"Okay, so see that cup holder? The jack and tools are hiding under that."

Timini climbs into the back of the Yukon and pulls out the cup holder, then I point at the objects that are shown in a drawing in the owner's manual. "See those two spinny things? You unscrew one to get to some tools that look like rods and you unscrew the other to get to the jack.

"Then we connect the rods and stick them into a hole…" I look between the picture in the manual and the bumper. "Oh! It's behind that two-inch square on the bumper that just blends right in—we have to first pry it off or something—then we twist the rods to lower the tire. My stars, it's like they made it a scavenger hunt to see if people are smart enough to find everything."

Luckily for us, we're all smart. But that doesn't mean figuring it all out is easy. Also, jacks aren't designed to be put on super lumpy, bumpy, rocky, packed dirt roads. We know that now.

Another lesson learned: lug nuts are hard to loosen. And though it may sound like a good idea to put your entire weight on the big X-shaped tool to help get them not so tightly on, it's not actually wise to jump to land on the rod because when it does loosen, it might just send you flying off, landing you in a heap, half on the dirt road and half in the underbrush.

So now, I'm all hot and dirty, especially on my backside, and I've freed more than a few twigs from my hair.

I'm also really getting concerned about what has been keeping Max from coming to look for us. We should've arrived at camp about forty-five minutes ago, and we haven't even seen a single vehicle pass by.

It takes all four of us to heft the massive wheel off the SUV and then to get the holes in the rim of the spare tire lined up with the screw things sticking out. But we do it, and then take turns getting the lug nuts screwed onto the part sticking out through the wheel and tightened.

When we finally let the jack down, we all collapse against the side of the vehicle, exhausted, looking at the flat tire lying on the dirt road, hoping for some of our energy to return so we can get the heavy thing back underneath the vehicle and to get our gear loaded up again.

"I feel like I just wrestled a bear," Timini says. "And lost."

"This was way more difficult than changing the tire on my car," Bex says.

In a voice so weak it hardly sounds like Addison, she says, "We should take a victory photo."

I nod. "We should, because yay us." I was going to raise my arm in some kind of show of muscles or triumph but decide it's going to take all I've got just to pull out my phone.

Before I even open the camera app, I see the time. It's almost seven now and the sun is getting low in the sky. Surely Max knows by now that we've run into a problem. Why hasn't he come? Did something happen to him? Did something happen to all of them? Did bears attack the camp? Is he in trouble? Did he get his own flat tire? Does he need us to come to rescue him?

We really need to get going. I snap a picture of us all being exhausted first.

I've just pushed myself off the side of the SUV when I hear a vehicle's tires on the rocky dirt. My heart soars and excitement fills me at the hope of seeing Max and gives me enough energy to run a little way down the road to where I can look past the bend. Sure enough, Max is in the passenger's seat of his friend's truck. I let out the hugest breath of relief that he's okay and race to him as they come to a stop and he gets out.

He looks every bit as relieved to see me. He wraps his arms around me and pulls me in tight, then backs up, putting distance between us, looking me up and down. "Are you okay? I was so worried, especially when we couldn't find you."

"I'm fine. And you're fine?"

He nods and places a kiss on my forehead. Then he pulls another twig from my ponytail.

"Yeah," I say, "I took one for the team. I swear I'm a twig magnet. Which is okay—I'll take twigs over bugs any day."

"About time, slowpokes," Bex calls out.

Max's friend, Emilio, laughs. "You know, it'd be a lot easier to find you if you stayed on the main road instead of turning onto some cabin's driveway."

I look up and down at the long road we're on. "This is a *driveway*?"

Bex groans. "Please tell me there isn't a cabin like twenty feet in that direction."

Emilio rises up on his toes. "I think I see one through the trees."

"Are you kidding or being real right now?" Timini asks. "Because if there is one, I'm just saying that they might have a hot tub and we deserve a good soak about now." Then she stands taller. "Or snacks. Did you bring snacks?"

"Even better," Emilio says. "We have dinner waiting back at camp."

Max chuckles but then turns all of his attention to me. He reaches a hand up and skims his fingertips down my cheek, along my jaw, and across my lips, all with an expression on his face like I'm adored and cherished and the most beautiful person he's ever seen. Even though I'm covered in dust, I'm sweaty, and there's probably more hair outside of my ponytail than in it at this point. I know that no matter what kind of pickle I manage to get myself into, he'll be there, helping or supporting me in any way that he can. He loves me that much.

Then he breathes, "I'm sorry we didn't find you sooner so we could've helped with all this." He pulls me in for a dusty hug before giving me the sweetest quick kiss and a squeeze of my hand and then heading to the Yukon.

He and Emilio get the popped tire mounted under the Yukon and heft our gear back inside the vehicle.

For our entire friendship, I've always noticed how good-looking Max is. But because we were just friends, I never let myself notice *too* much. Kind of like how you don't let yourself stare directly at the sun. So now that we're dating, watching him lift heavy things is different. It's suddenly okay for me to notice just how beautiful those shoulder and back and arm muscles are. I can't even believe it's okay for me to look now.

Once we're back in our vehicles, Max and Emilio lead the way to the camp, which ends up only being about an eight-minute drive. I can't believe we got so close before I led us off course. We pull to a stop first, and then Max directs Bex where to park the Yukon.

"Wow!" Addison says as she steps out. "I wish camping as a kid had been like this!"

I am speechless. The guys have set up two big tents at the far end of the camp. Right in the middle is a campfire surrounded by camp chairs, with a nearby picnic table and food tables. The entire area is enclosed by tall hemlocks and cedars and Douglas firs, their branches reaching out over the camp like they're protecting us, a ferny woodland at their base.

Mosses grow at the feet of the trees and up the sides and branches of the trees. And it smells incredible. Fresh and clean and earthy. It's as if we've stepped into another world that I hadn't fully known existed.

Emilio and Max's other friends, Hunter and Leo, go to work emptying all our gear from the SUV and transporting it to our tent. But Max grabs my hand and says, "Come on. I want to show you everything."

All four of us follow as Max points out our tent, how there's an extra tarp in case it rains, that there are restrooms down the road a ways, but that they've set up a portable latrine and shower, all of the gear they brought to make the trip more enjoyable, and which items he helped design. I look around, realizing all that he has done for me just so I can experience what he loves in as amazing a way as possible.

"And look," he says, "just over here we even have a stream!

This is one of my favorite camp spots because it has everything."

The stream is only about twenty feet away from camp, the water in it looks cool and crisp, and the sounds it makes are musical and perfect. The way Max grins is so adorable that I just want to hold his face in my hands and admire it for ages.

CHAPTER 16

Peyton

I SNUGGLE down into my sleeping bag, trying to get warm now that we're no longer in front of the fire. Except for my dinner roll falling into the ashes from the fire (covering it in what Leo calls "nature's pepper"), dinner tasted amazing.

And except for a giant moth landing right on Max's face when he was giving me a goodnight kiss under the stars and causing me to scream before smacking him on the cheek to scare it off, it was the most amazing kiss ever.

And except for the fact that I left my pillow at home on the check-in desk of the lobby and am now using my gym bag stuffed with the clothes I was wearing earlier as a pillow, sleeping in a tent is a lot more comfortable than I thought it would be.

As Addison, Timini, and I are getting all situated, Bex comes in with a big mischievous grin and a bag of Chips Ahoy she found in the food bins. So we all sit up in our sleeping bags, eat cookies, and talk like we're at a sleepover. We even film part of it for an episode on Bex's YouTube channel.

So after such a full day and such a late night, I have no

problem drifting off to sleep to the sounds of the crickets and the gurgling stream.

————

My eyes fly open. What did I just hear? I have no idea what time it is, just that it's somewhere in the middle of the night.

There it is again. *Inside* the tent.

A crinkling sound. A scraping. Then nothing.

I'm sure I heard it this time. I hold my breath, straining to hear what it is. After a few moments of nothing, I figure it must be Bex shifting in her sleeping bag. I close my eyes and start to breathe normally.

Then the crinkling is louder, and I can tell it's not coming from Bex. I sit up, scrambling for my cell phone, and turn on the flashlight as quickly as I can.

A raccoon inside my tent freezes, his eyes shining in the light, his arm deep in the Chips Ahoy bag. And there's another raccoon just inside the tent opening. No, two! And three more just outside the tent door!

I scream. And not just any scream, but a horror movie bloodcurdling scream that could probably be heard three states away. I'm pretty sure the raccoons will be telling their grandkids about it someday. "Ah, yes cubs. We almost got away clean, but then she screamed, and we all knew just how badly we'd messed up."

Quick as a flash, all six raccoons scatter like a perfectly executed heist gone wrong. I swear one does a backflip out of the tent and another disappears so quickly I'm convinced he teleported. The one with his hand in the bag, though, gives me a death glare before he skedaddles. Left in their wake is a mostly empty bag of cookies, three more people awake, and my racing, thumping, crashing heart.

About one second later, Max is at our tent door, barefoot, in sweatpants and a hoodie, his hair a mess, wielding a marshmallow roasting stick in his hands like a bat, and a wild and confused *I-was-sound-asleep-and-now-I'm-alarmed* look on his face. "What is it? What happened? Is there a bear?"

"Raccoons." I duck my head. "I didn't mean to wake everyone." Embarrassment at having screamed so loudly mixes in my chest with immense gratitude that Max would come to my rescue so quickly. And that marshmallow roasting stick? That thing means business, and he's gripping it like he'd actually be willing to take on a grizzly. Man, can he pull off *knight in shining armor* well, even when he's ripped from sleep in the middle of the night.

"But you're all okay?"

"Our heart rates are a little faster than they have a right to be in the middle of the night, but otherwise, we're right as rain." Which, I'm realizing, isn't a good metaphor now that I'm picturing how *not* right rain would be while camping. Of course, if Max was with me, anything would be right.

And now I'm wondering if I'm breathless because of the raccoons or because Max showed up in a hoodie, hair a mess, being all protective and heroic.

As he lowers the marshmallow stick, I can't help but think he's the most attractive human I have ever seen. How can he look so good at this hour? He should come with a warning label: May cause swooning and dizziness. I have to stop myself from fanning my face. My heart dances the salsa whenever I'm around him. How in the world am I ever going to live without him?

He says he's going to get something to help, disappears into the darkness for a moment, and then comes back holding a single twist tie from a bread bag. I half expected him to return with a dagger, or at least a bungee cord or something. Instead,

I'm supposed to defeat the raccoon hordes with a teeny little twist tie?

He kneels down just inside our tent, then crawls to me and places the tie in my hand. "When I leave, pull the vertical and both side zippers together tight. Then put this through the little hole in all three zipper pulls and twist it. Then nothing will be able to unzip it from the outside."

He gives me the sweetest kiss, and then he backs out of the tent. Right before he zips it closed again, he grabs the cookie bag. "Oh, and keeping food away from your tent is a good idea, too."

"So… did the raccoons win?" Bex asks before collapsing back, making asleep breathing sounds before her head even hits her pillow. I have no doubt she'll have no memory of this in the morning.

Unlike me. I lie back down on my makeshift pillow, close my eyes, and try to calm my racing heart. But I can't help but replay over and over the moment when Max showed up instantly to defend my honor against raccoons. And how attractive he looked doing it. And how sweet he still was when he found out it was just raccoons in our tent and not a giant bear.

He's such a beautiful man. A beautiful man I know I can't have in my life for very long.

CHAPTER 17

Max

I WANT everything to go perfectly for Peyton's first camping trip. The guys have been completely on board with this plan, which is why they were willing to take off work three hours early to get camp set up. Yesterday didn't quite go as perfectly as I'd hoped, but with all I have planned today, it is sure to.

Well, okay, the morning hasn't been without its own issues. Leo slept the latest, like usual. When Emilio, our resident early-riser left the tent, he "accidentally" left it unzipped. The jury is still out on whether or not he lured an extended family of squirrels into the tent, knowing how much Leo fears anything with legs that isn't human, or if the squirrels sensed it on their own and thought terrorizing him might be fun.

Admittedly, seeing the horde of squirrels literally bouncing off the tent walls, all while Leo was in the middle of the chaos doing his squirrels-are-attacking dance, was kind of funny. But it probably didn't help me be convincing in my morning conversation with Peyton about how animals rarely get into tents.

"Need some help?" Peyton asks as she snuggles up next to me at the portable griddle where I'm making omelets.

I have spent so many hours daydreaming about moments exactly like this. Waking up to see her beautiful face. Having her snuggle up to me as I make breakfast. Sharing all of my life with Peyton.

Yet it all feels temporary, like this can't be real life, and real life is going to swoop in and change things before long. Unless I can make this weekend—or at least the rest of this weekend—perfect. If Peyton loves everything about being out in nature and wants to go with me on more camping trips, then maybe I wouldn't have to worry about losing who I am at my core.

"Nope. You always make food for everyone. This weekend is about you sitting back, relaxing, and enjoying nature while I make food for you."

She looks up at me with eyes that are so sweet and perfect that I could stare into them forever. I've enjoyed being friends with her over the past four years. During that time, I've daydreamed about a romantic relationship with her almost daily. Just imagining that has gotten me through some exceptionally tough days.

Actually living my daydreams has been beyond incredible. So much better than I ever imagined. Peyton is everything I want in a friend and everything I want in a partner. She makes me feel capable of reaching for my loftiest goals, desire to be the best man I can be, and so hopeful about everything. She sees the absolute best in me and helps me to see it in myself.

She gives me a quick peck on the cheek and joins the others standing around the campfire, trying to shake off the morning chill. That is good, too, because with her over there, I can admire how incredible she looks in jeans, a flannel shirt, hiking boots, and a ponytail.

Or maybe admiring her is a bad idea. I quickly flip the omelet I'm burning.

When I finish the last omelet, I join everyone else around the campfire and we all eat breakfast.

"You think I *lured* the squirrels into our tent?" Emilio asks, wearing a grin that doesn't do much to hide his guilt.

Leo shrugs. "I left the toy snake in your sleeping bag, so you're the most likely culprit."

Even if Leo doesn't see Emilio's guilt, it's obvious that Hunter does. But Hunter is smiling like stirring the pot is the game we're playing, so he says, "Not Max? You saw how easily he got them to follow him out of the tent."

"True," Leo says, dragging out the word as he turns on me. "You *did* seem to instantly know to cut up pieces of an apple to get their attention. And who else can lure squirrels with apple chunks in their hand? Only Snow White." Leo looks at the four women around the campfire. "This is why we are always trying to scare him or knock him into streams or lakes. The guy has nature on his side, so we have to do something to keep things even."

Then the three guys—my friends and camping buddies—go on to share a bunch of stories about me in the wilderness that I would've preferred not be shared. Maybe bringing them all along was a mistake after all. Especially because Bex is filming a lot of it, so it will likely make it into one of her episodes. There is so much laughing going on, though, especially from Peyton, that it can't be anything other than good.

Hunter tells a story from a few years ago about me being away from camp and looking for tinder for a fire. I had accidentally slipped a foot into an animal hole that had been buried by leaves and got a bit stuck. Then Hunter swears that a chipmunk came into camp and started chattering urgently like it was trying to tell them something. So they went out looking for me in the direction they'd seen me leave and rescued me.

The truth is, I hadn't even seen a chipmunk while I'd been searching for tinder. I don't tell them it was a coincidence, though, because no one seems to want to hear that part of the story. So instead, I just stand up and take a bow.

"All right. You've all had your morning coffee. I need to go get mine." I head over to the stream to free one of the cans of Mountain Dew that have been chilling with five of their friends in the cool water in the river. I've never liked the taste—or the smell, actually—of coffee. So even on the really chilly mornings in the mountains, I still go for my Mountain Dew.

I have to take a few steps onto rocks in the water to get to where the six-pack lies nestled. I'm almost to them when I hear some rustling in the bushes behind me. Of *course* they would come and try to get me to take a misstep and fall into the water. I call over my shoulder, "I know it's you, Leo, and Emilio. You're not going to get me that easily."

I do make sure I'm balanced a little more than normal, just in case they jump out or throw something at me. Then I bend down and free one of the cans from the plastic ring that holds it to the others.

More rustling.

I turn around but don't see either of them. I know better than to let my guard down, though—they're both pretty good at hiding. So I step onto the rocks in the water carefully the rest of the way back to the shore, keeping my eyes toward the area with the rustling.

Then, to get the upper hand and keep them from knocking me off my game, as I leap onto the shore from the last rock, I scream, my arms raised high in the air, knowing it will make Leo yelp.

It's not Leo in the bushes, though.

It's a skunk.

I know the warning signs that skunks give before spraying —tail raised and shaking, stamping feet—but that's when the skunk sees you first and wants to warn you. We have both been so surprised by the appearance of each other that the skunk skips the formalities and goes straight to offensive mode. The animal shifts into a U-shape with both its face and hind end aimed toward me so quickly that I barely have time to turn, covering my face and head with my arms, before the animal sprays. And then we both run.

I hear the sounds of everyone reacting to the smell—and probably my scream that preceded it by about one second— before I even come around the edge of the bushes and trees to see them. And I get it. I'm barely keeping myself from gagging from the smell.

"Max, is that…you?" Emilio plugs his nose.

And that is the moment that everyone's faces go from scrunched at the bad smell to horrified. Especially Peyton's. I want to shout to the universe, *Didn't you know I needed this weekend to go perfectly?!*

"Did it get you in the face?" Hunter asks. When I shake my head, he says, "Good. Because that stuff's like pepper spray. Okay, we need to deal with this quickly."

Hunter is up, heading over to the supply bins.

"Tomato sauce!" Leo shouts, rushing to join Hunter at the bins. "I heard that helps."

Hunter shakes his head. "That's a myth. It just masks the scent for a bit. Skunk spray contains sulfur-based compounds called thiols. We have to break those down to get the scent to go away. The quicker the better."

"Should he go wash off in the river?" Addison asks.

"No. We need hydrogen peroxide, baking soda, and dish soap, and since Emilio is always prepared for everything, I'm sure we have some. Ahh," Hunter says, pulling the items from the bins and then grabbing the dishwashing tub. "Emilio, grab the shovel and go dig a shallow hole off in that little area surrounded by trees. We're going to have to use dish detergent, and we'll need to bury it. Leo, go grab a pair of Max's gym shorts from his bag. Does anyone have shampoo for greasy hair?"

"I've got some," Leo says from inside our tent.

Hunter throws a black garbage bag at me. "You go—" he waves his hand in the general direction he sent Emilio to dig the hole—"far away. Get your clothes in that bag and close it tightly, then put on the shorts."

When I planned our perfect camping trip, getting sprayed by a skunk wasn't on the docket. Neither was having to strip down not far from where seven of my friends are, including the woman I've been dreaming about for years.

"You're totally going to have PTSD after this, aren't you?" Emilio asks as he finishes digging the hole I'll be standing in soon. "Post Traumatic Skunk Disorder. Hey, do you think this will affect your standing as Snow White?"

I give my friend a little shove, and Emilio laughs. "Hey, now. Don't get your stink too close to me."

A moment later, Leo sets down a jug of water and the shampoo, then tosses me my shorts, and I put them on. I have barely pulled them up when Hunter rounds the corner, lugging the dishwashing tub full of liquid, with Peyton beside him. Great. Couldn't she be far away and not be witnessing this scene?

Hunter sets down the tub and then stands. "I know this stuff works because I've used it before. And since we're doing it so quickly, I can pretty much guarantee it'll get rid of the smell completely." He hesitates for a moment. "You know if it was just us guys up here, I'd literally have your back, right?"

I nod.

"But, well, since Peyton is here and your back took the brunt of it, we thought it might be better if she was the one to wash it off."

Better? I know my face must be red because of how hot it is. *Better* would be Peyton not being within a hundred miles of this happening and no one who witnessed it ever speaking of it again.

Then Hunter gives a nod, like everything is decided, and leaves me standing in a hole and Peyton holding her fingers just under her nose in our little cove surrounded by trees and bushes.

"Okay," Peyton says, nudging the tub closer to me and bending down to get the washcloth from it. "We can do this. I've seen you shirtless before. I mean, not since we started dating, but this is no big deal."

The blush on her face says otherwise and kind of makes me just a bit more okay with her being here. And, okay, it may make me suck in my gut a bit.

She stands behind me and starts running the washcloth wet with Hunter's concoction over my back with one hand. I may be covered in stench and in a situation I hoped to never be in, yet I can't help but marvel at how amazing this feels, knowing the cloth is in Peyton's hand.

After a few times dipping it back into the solution, she starts washing with a little more pressure, reaching around me to put her other hand on my chest as a counter-pressure, and my heart rate and breathing kick up several notches. I close my eyes just to more fully take in the feel of it. Peyton makes a little *eep* sound that tells me having her hands on me is affecting her, too.

"Oh, my goodness. That little guy sure packed a punch, didn't he?" A moment later, probably when she realizes she has to take a breath, even if she doesn't want to, she says, "Wow. That was some impressive work. He deserves a medal. Maybe if he sees you're bringing him a medal and you turn on that fabled Snow White charm, he'll let you get close without retaliating."

I laugh along with her. No one can find something positive in a situation like Peyton can.

I'm all too keenly aware that she is rubbing her hands all over my back, shoulders, chest, and arms. Of course, if I'm going to have Peyton's hands all over my torso, I really would've chosen other circumstances. I know that when I look back at this skunky situation, what I'm going to remember is this moment, with Peyton's hand on my chest while she washes my backside. I'm hoping that the memory that sticks with Peyton is similar and that she doesn't just take away from this a strong association between me and this stench. I'm hoping that part doesn't stick with her for long at all.

I'll give her something better to associate with me tomorrow morning. Before we break camp, we are going to head to French's Dome to do some rock climbing and rappelling. I know that for most people, watching a climber is impressive. I really hope she'll think so, too, so I can earn back whatever masculine points I've lost by my unfortunate skunk encounter.

"Okay, I think the back and your sides are done. Do you want me…" She motions at my chest. "Or would you rather…"

She has rested her hand on my chest plenty of times over the past few weeks—I remember each time rather vividly. She has laid her head there, too. In fact, she has fallen asleep during movies leaning against my chest plenty of times before that. It's different here, though, with me facing her as I stand barechested in the woods, covered in skunk.

If I wasn't worried I might get some of the thiols, or whatever Hunter called the stink molecules, on Peyton, I would pull her in close and drop her into a dip or something, just to ease the awkwardness.

"How about I wash my chest and legs and shampoo my hair, and then you rinse me and give me a good smell test to make sure we got it all." Skunks aim for the eyes. Since I turned quickly enough and ducked my head, my back and arms have taken most of it, anyway.

Once I get myself washed and Peyton rinses me, I try to not let my pecs, biceps, or any other muscles twitch or involuntarily flex as she gets super close and smells my back, chest, and arms. I am successful a good seventy percent of the time. Those last two twitches were beyond my control.

And then she smiles, smacks me on the rear, pronounces me skunk-free, and walks back to join the others in camp.

As I watch this woman I've been in love with for so long walk back, her flannel shirt wet and pushed up to her elbows, water splotches all over her jeans, a few small locks of hair falling out of her ponytail, I can't help but smile, too.

CHAPTER 18

Peyton

As we get to the end of the short walk between the parking lot at the trailhead and French's Dome, the tall canopy of evergreen trees opens up to show a massive hunk of rock that shoots up from the ground like someone planted a little rock seed, watered it, and then a few hundred years later, it grew to the size of a skyscraper.

"You're going to climb that thing?" I ask Max. I probably shouldn't let my voice tremble at all—I don't want to psych him out. But man, that is tall. And straight up. And pretty impossible-looking.

Max doesn't look psyched out, though. He looks more than a little confident.

"Wait, you've climbed this one before?"

"This will be time number five."

I just look up at the massive structure in awe. "How did this thing even get here?" It's not part of a mountain. It's simply here, acting like it's not strange to be right in the middle of the Oregon forest.

As I tear my eyes from it to look at Max, he says, "It's a

volcanic neck core. Whatever else used to be around this eroded away over who knows how long, leaving this beauty as a gift to climbers."

I've heard Max talk about climbing plenty of times, and I've always pictured it like an indoor climbing wall, except outdoors. The scale of it is so far beyond anything I've imagined.

As all four of the guys get their harnesses on, check all their gear, and inspect the rope for any damage, I take plenty of pictures. And when it gets to be Max's turn to climb up, I take about a billion more. The man just looks so incredible as he makes his way up the side of the rock. As each arm reaches up, his hand searching for a handhold, I watch those arm and shoulder and back muscles and can't help but think about yesterday when I was washing them.

"I think I'd be passing out at that spot right there," Addison says. "How can they convince themselves to climb so high?"

"That's just straight-up impressive," Bex says, aiming her video camera at them. "It looks fun, but I don't know if I could do it."

"Me neither," I say. "I've always wished I could be as brave as Max. I swear he can accomplish anything, no matter how impossible it seems. He just always finds a way."

Timini chuckles. "Girl, you are so gone for this boy."

I really am. But how could I not be? He is just so inspiring! So comfortable and confident. Daring and adventurous. I grew up having so many things done for me that when I decided I was going to be independent, not get any financial help from my dad, and start my own business, a lot of things were really hard. And there were so many times when I wasn't sure if I could even do it. But Max was so good at encouraging me when I wanted to give up and inspiring me to find ways of doing things that I hadn't ever thought of.

He feels like peace and acceptance and home. And how can a girl not be gone for that?

Somewhere around the halfway-up mark, though, my feelings switch from admiring everything about him that brought him to the point where he can accomplish a feat like this, to fear.

He's just so high up! I know he has a rope connected to his harness, and that the rope is going through some kind of bolts in the rock itself. But it just looks so dangerous.

I've known that he does things all the time like paragliding, cliff-jumping, mountain biking over rough, steep terrain, and sleeping in places where bears could probably wander, but I haven't imagined any of it being as dangerous as how things appear right now. He looks so teeny being so high up, and he still has so far to go! What if his arms get tired before he gets to the top and he just can't keep going?

And before I know it, the injuries he had when he showed up to his mom's house while I was cooking dinner—from falling down the mountainside on their hike—come to mind. And all the others I've seen over the years. Sore muscles. Stitches. A broken finger. Bruises all over. So many bruises.

Now that I'm seeing how scary his adventures are in person, I suddenly wonder if I can handle knowing how badly he could get hurt every time he goes on a trip. As I hold my breath when he gets to a really difficult spot where he can't seem to find a foothold, I'm not sure.

CHAPTER 19
Max

IF ONE OF the guys is holding a stopwatch, I'm sure I've just gotten a record time climbing French's Dome. This might be my fifth time climbing the monolith-like rock formation hidden in the evergreens, but it's the first time I've pushed myself so hard. If it was just the guys with me, I would've paused more on my way up, letting my legs hold my weight for a few moments whenever they were on steady footholds.

But this time, Peyton is watching and taking pictures, and I really want to impress her. So even though my legs and arms burn and my fingers ache from holding on to the tiniest handholds, I push on.

This is one of my favorite places to climb, and it attracts crowds of climbers. The rock is practically straight up and, at one hundred twenty feet tall on the part I'm climbing, it's an impressive height without being massive. And it's full of hand and footholds that are marked with chalk by plenty of other enthusiasts who have climbed the route before us. Two or three climbers are making their way up each route around the dome right now, and people are even waiting below for a turn.

Leo crests the top first, hooking the lead rope into the bolts in the rock. Emilio goes up next, and he offers me a hand once he gets to the top. As Hunter makes his way up the rock face last, I, along with half a dozen other climbers who also stand at the top, look out at the view. For as hidden as this place is from the roads around it, this vantage point allows me to see everything—Mount Hood, the mountains beside it, the wilderness surrounding it—and it seeps into my soul. Scenes like this are my fuel. My stress-reliever. The thing that keeps me going.

I offer a hand to Hunter as he gets to the top, and the four of us stand, side by side, looking out over the edge at Peyton and her roommates, who are waving, whooping, and taking pictures. My chest swells with pride.

Then Hunter's phone dings with a text, and all of our attention goes to him. There wasn't reception down below—I hadn't imagined there would be up here. Hunter pulls his phone from a side pocket on his climbing pants and looks at the screen, brows drawing together, before he looks at us, alarm and worry all over his face.

"Tami's having a miscarriage. She's been trying to get hold of me—she's at the hospital now. I've got to go."

Hunter immediately goes to the edge and picks up the rope, but I put a hand on his shoulder. "We've all got to get down before we can leave. Let your body rest for a minute and let your heart rate calm down so you don't make a fatal rappelling mistake. Let Leo and Emilio go first."

Hunter nods, and I stand next to my friend, my arm around his shoulder, as Emilio connects his harness to the lead rope and makes his way down while Hunter texts his wife to let her know he'll be there soon.

"I shouldn't be here," Hunter says. "What was I thinking? I should've been home with her. Or I should have been somewhere with cell reception. What if she's not okay? She shouldn't have to face this alone."

Over and over, Hunter's worries travel in circles, coming back around to the same thing—that being out here, pursuing our passion, kept him from being a good husband. I try to calm my friend so he'll be going into the descent with as clear a head as possible. But the truth is, all of Hunter's fears and concerns mirror my own fears and concerns.

Once both Leo and Emilio are on the ground, I help check Hunter's gear, making sure he has redundancies and that everything is safe and good to go before rappelling down. I know that most accidents happen during the descent and how important it is to have your head in the game, so I find myself holding my breath nearly the entire time that Hunter is climbing down. Once he finally steps foot on the ground, I let out a massive breath of relief.

Peyton blows me a kiss from one hundred twenty feet below, so I pretend to catch it and put it in my pocket. Then I hook up my own gear, making sure everything is hooked through both loops in my harness, that the lead rope is connected correctly in the chain in the rock, and that I have redundancies and everything is safe, too. My own head is full of too many worries, and I'm not about to make a mistake.

As I rappel down, my feet landing against the same stones I used as hand and footholds on the way up, I force my focus to stay on tending the friction hitch with one hand and feeding the rope through with the other.

It mostly works, until thoughts and worries about whether I'm going to be able to be everything Peyton deserves keep creeping in. *Focus. Focus on the rope.*

About halfway down, things are going well, and I've fallen into the familiar rhythm, letting the joy of the height and my surroundings push everything else out. Then, a climber who is ascending with a lead rope to my left and a good eight feet higher up the dome loses his grip and falls. He's almost to the next bolt, which means that he's falling the biggest distance possible—probably ten feet.

It's nothing. It happens all the time. Except this climber somehow gets his foot stuck in the crevice he planted it in, throwing him upside down as he falls. As the man swings wildly, trying to right himself, he bounces against the rock and swings back, heading straight toward me.

All of my training tells me that if something is ever coming at me from above or from the side, I should cling to the rock face and keep myself as flat against it as possible. If my head was in the game instead of on the beautiful woman watching from below and how to keep her in my life, I know I would've done just that. Instead, I let my normal, human reactions through. The one that says to reach out and try to catch the person coming at me, to cushion them.

The force of the climber plowing into me is enough to knock the breath out of me a micro-second before my shoulder is wrenched back and smacks against the rock. I nearly lose my grip on the rope and fall a few feet before instinct makes me grab tight with my uninjured arm. I swing wildly back and forth, the pain in my shoulder so sharp and unrelenting I have trouble thinking of anything other than it.

Eventually, with sharp intakes of breath sucked through my clenched teeth, I start to hear the shouts of the people below. Not enough to tell what they're saying, but enough to know they're there. With one good arm and the small amount I manage to force my injured arm to do, I continue my descent, much more jerkily than the first half.

By the time my feet touch solid ground, I collapse from the pain, a swirl of activity around me, a bevy of questions I can't make out or answer.

Once using my arm is no longer a life-or-death necessity, the mind-numbing pain slowly lessens just enough that it's not the only thing I can focus on. I manage to get to my feet and into Hunter's truck with Hunter's and Peyton's help. Then the three of us head to the hospital while the others go back to pack up camp.

Every bump in the road jerks my arm enough to send a new wave of sharp pain, but Peyton is here, trying to hold me so the bumps are lessened. With her at my side, I can handle this just fine. Her presence tempers the pain and clears my mind.

CHAPTER 20

Peyton

WATCHING the doctor put Max's shoulder back into its socket is the most painful thing I've ever witnessed. And that's just for me! I can't imagine how bad it is for Max. Thankfully, they give him something for the pain before they set it. I'm not sure it has actually started working yet, though, based on how much pain Max seems to be in while they do it.

I just keep reliving that moment in my mind when the other climber fell and smacked into Max. The way that I can tell, even from sixty feet below, that his shoulder bent unnaturally. The way his body bounced back after hitting the rocks so forcefully. That bit of a drop that seized my heart and made me worry he was about to fall all the way. I hope the horror of it isn't still showing on my face. I'm trying to be strong for Max.

"Okay, we got it set," the doctor says. "My guess is that you won't need surgery, but we're going to send you in for an MRI to see what damage was done. You'll need to follow up with an orthopedic surgeon in the next couple of days, and you'll need their clearance before climbing again.

"And don't drive with that pain medicine we've got you on.

But we'll get you into a sling before you go. Keep it on—it'll help you heal and remind you not to use it." The man gives him a sympathetic smile. "It was a bad one. You're going to be feeling it for a while. Be careful with it."

Then the doctor turns and gives me a sympathetic smile, too. Like he can tell that Max is an adventurer and it's going to be hard to get him to not use his arm, and there won't be much I can do about it.

Once everyone else is out of the room and we're just waiting for someone to come take Max to the MRI machine, I sit on the side of his bed, careful not to bump him, and hold his hand. "I'm sorry you got so injured."

He lifts my hand and brushes his lips across my knuckles. "I'm sorry the camping trip was such a bust."

"What are you talking about? I got great food, prepared and handed to me by the most gorgeous server ever. And I got to hang out in the most amazing scenery and fall asleep to the sound of crickets. And I got to witness Leo freak out more about acrobatic squirrels than I did about thieving raccoons, which was pretty satisfying. Actually, I think he would freak out about spiders more than me, too, which is saying something."

Max gives a weak but amused smile. "I've seen you both happen upon a spider, and I can confirm that he freaks out more."

"See? And that's good to know. I like not being the one with the most extreme reactions. Plus, I got to wash skunk off you, and that was pretty great." I can feel the blush on my cheeks. That part had been pretty great. Even if I had to turn away from him every few moments to get a breath of fresh air.

It makes me smile that he blushes a bit, too.

My phone lights up with a text—Timini is asking for an

update. So I quickly type that Max had a dislocated shoulder and that we should be leaving in the next hour or so.

> Timini: Oh, I'm so glad it wasn't worse!

> Timini: We got camp all packed up, and Addison and I are here at the hospital—we brought your car. They wouldn't let us come and give you the keys (probably because we smell like campfire and are covered in dirt from head to toe), but they are with the check-in nurse. We'll be home making food.

When they take Max to get an MRI, I call my dad.

"Hi, Daddy!"

"Hi, Sugar Bug."

"Do you mind if I cancel coming over for dinner tonight? I'm in the hospital with Max."

"Oh no!"

"He dislocated his shoulder while he was mountain climbing. He'll be okay, but I think I should help take care of him tonight. Is that alright with you?"

"Of course it is."

"Daddy, are you okay?"

"I'm fine."

I'm not sure I believe him. "You're sounding...off."

"I'm fine. Really. You take care of Max—don't worry about me."

I glance at the hallway they took Max down. I really hope he'll be okay soon. It doesn't look like the kind of injury he'll recover from as quickly as he usually does. "Are you sure?"

"Very. Want to reschedule for tomorrow?"

I tell him yes, we work out a time, and then hang up. And I immediately go back to worrying about Max.

————

It takes a lot longer than I think it will to leave the hospital and get Max to his apartment. I get him settled in his bed with the big fluffy couch pillow from the living room that I gave him last Christmas propping him up, his regular pillow just under his elbow helping to support the weight of his arm. I get him water, his laptop so he can watch a show, and am about to make him some soup when I get a call from a local number and answer it.

"Is this Peyton Abernathy?"

"It is."

"This is Sue from Kaiser Sunnyside Medical Center."

Kaiser Sunnyside? That's not the hospital I was just at with Max. I look over at him, dread already filling me.

"Your dad wanted me to let you know that an ambulance just brought him in for a possible heart attack. The doctors are checking him out right now."

Fear clutches at my heart just like it had weeks ago when he had his first one. "I'll be right there."

As soon as I hang up the phone, I stand, frozen, my mind and heart racing, my body not knowing which direction to go.

"Peyton," Max says, reaching his good arm out toward me. "What happened?"

"My dad. They think he might've had another heart attack."

Max's eyes grow wide. "Go. I'm fine."

"Max, you're not! Your shoulder wasn't even connected to your body a couple of hours ago. You have bruises everywhere, you're on pain medicine, and you nearly died!" My breathing is so fast I worry I'll pass out, but my heart is so afraid for the two men I love most in the world.

I let Max pull me to sitting on the edge of his bed, and he runs a hand down my arm. "Shh. Breathe with me."

I match my breathing to his. Slow and steady. In and out. It doesn't take long before my nerves don't feel quite so much like a train that has left the tracks and is barreling down a mountainside.

"Look at my eyes."

I do, and those green eyes capture me, holding me up, keeping me strong.

"I am okay," he says, stressing each word. "You have me set up like royalty in here. I'm banged up all over, sure, but my legs still work. I've been injured pretty bad before and have been just fine. I will be this time, too. Go to your dad, stay calm while you're driving, and keep me updated."

I stand but give him one last long gaze before my legs pull me away and to the front door. He is strong. He is always so strong.

———

My dad looks so weak as he lies in the hospital bed in the thin gown, wires coming out from the neck and arm openings, all hooked to beeping machines that surround him like a silent army protecting their king.

"Hey, Sugar Bug. I didn't mean to alarm you."

A nurse is on one side of the bed, checking something with the machines, and the doctor is on the other side, looking tall and in charge in her white coat. So I stand at the bottom of the bed, wishing I could just hurry to my dad's side and wrap my arms around him.

The doctor reaches her arm out toward me, her dark skin such a contrast against her coat. "You must be Peyton," she says as she shakes my hand. "I'm Doctor Lewis. Your dad gave us a bit of a scare. But we've had the heart monitors hooked up to him for a good forty-five minutes now, and things are looking good. It doesn't appear to be a second heart attack."

"It doesn't?" Relief whooshes out of me.

"A lot of things can feel like a heart attack, especially in the first few months after a major one, like your dad had before. Even indigestion can feel like it's a legitimate problem. I'm glad he came in."

"The doc told me I was being a wimp." My dad may look weak, but that doesn't stop the teasing glint in his eye. It makes me happy to see it.

"No." The doctor shakes her head and chuckles. "I told him it's sometimes hard to tell, and it's a lot better to be overly cautious than under. We still aren't ready to give him a clean bill of health, either. We'd like to keep him overnight for observation."

Once the doctor and the nurse leave, I give my dad that hug. But it's a slow, careful hug that doesn't bump any of those wires. Then I pull a chair up close to his bedside and hold his hand.

"I'm sorry to make you go from one hospital to the next, Sugar Bug. I should've waited until they decided what was going on with me before calling you."

"No, it was good to call me at the beginning. Or to have told me you were worried when I called earlier."

He shrugs. "I was still convincing myself it was nothing when I talked to you. Plus, you've had quite the day, I'm sure."

I feel like I've run two back-to-back emotional marathons today. I can't believe it was just this morning that I woke up from my second night in a row of actual camping in the actual forest, and my second time waking up to Max making me breakfast.

Since then, I have experienced two separate moments where I feared for the lives of the two men most important to me and have sat in two different hospital rooms, holding each of their hands. And twice, I have felt torn about where I should be.

When I called my dad, I already knew that Max likely wasn't going to need surgery and that he would be going home soon. It felt like an easy choice to make at the time to stay with him instead of going to my dad's for dinner. But I'd felt in my gut that something was wrong with my dad, and I chose to ignore it. I should've recognized that it was something more serious. I should've chosen to go be with him. What if he hadn't called 911 quickly enough? What if he had really needed me there and I wasn't?

Sure, today worked out fine. But what if it hadn't? I glance at the screens of all the machines just to assure myself that he is actually, really okay.

"I wish Mom was here."

My dad squeezes my hand. "I miss her too."

"I need her to make my decisions for me." I need it desperately.

"What kind of decisions?"

Well, all of my decisions today, for one. And all of my dating decisions. Whether I should've started dating Max. All of my Max decisions, actually. Whether or not I should have bought those uncomfortable but super adorable heels last week. But mostly everything to do with Max. I wave my hand around, trying to encompass everything. "All of them."

He chuckles softly. "You know your mom wouldn't have made them for you."

"Yeah, she would have. She always did. I trusted her to make the right choice for me so much more than I trusted myself." No, that should be present tense. It's not like I trust myself any more now than I did as a kid.

My dad shakes his head. "Even when you were a little girl, you struggled to take risks, regardless of how badly you wanted the payoff. On the playground, if you brought your little plastic dump truck and you saw a group of kids playing with their trucks in the wood chips, you'd be afraid they might not want you to join and so you'd sit and play by yourself. If you saw a puddle that you weren't sure you could jump all the way over, you'd take the really long way around to avoid it.

"Your mom never told you to go play with the kids or try to make the jump. Your mom was just really good at seeing what your passions were. Or really good about getting you to talk about them. Then she would give you a boost of encouragement to take the risks. She never made the decisions. That was all you."

Yes, my mom saw my passions and was great at getting me to talk about them. But she also told me if pursuing something was a good idea or not. So if my passion was to run across the street to smell a pretty flower and a car was coming, my mom helped me make the right decision then, too. It's my dad who gives me boosts of courage to take risks but doesn't make decisions for me.

And right now, I really need someone by my side to tell me when I'm running out into traffic where Max is concerned.

CHAPTER 21

Max

THERE IS nothing like the call of nature to remind me that, although my shoulder took the brunt of that hit, the entire left side of my body smacked into the uneven rock. And to let me know exactly how difficult everything is with one arm in a sling. Or how much the tiniest jostling makes everything hurt.

After washing one hand without the aid of the other, I head back into my room and take one long look at my bed. I don't want to be here. I just need to get better already. Being this injured is ridiculous.

I have thought through my rappelling accident several times, each time trying to figure out what I should've done differently, but the nature of a freak accident is that you can't really plan for it. Yes, I could've hugged the wall, like I'd been taught, but the other climber and I still would've collided, and I still would've taken the worst of it. And since, as a climber, you can't plan for freak accidents, you just have to expect that you'll get blindsided by one at some point.

But did it have to happen during my camping trip with Peyton?

Instead of getting back into bed, I shuffle into my living room and look long and hard at the couch. I know that moving from standing to sitting will hurt, so instead, I choose to just flop down on it. Okay, so that might not have been the best choice.

I had so badly wanted everything to go well at the campout. I wanted Peyton to love the experience. I wanted to know that if we can handle a camping trip together—something that one of us loves and one of us is inexperienced at—then we can handle any experience either of us has. A trip gone well would also confirm that I can, in fact, do what I love most and get married to the person I love most. I know how important marriage and family are to Peyton, and I will never ask her to give those up just so she can be with me.

But instead, more things went wrong on the trip than I've ever had go wrong in one single trip before.

Which reminds me that I don't actually know where my bag of skunk-scented clothes currently is.

Not only was the trip a disaster, but it made Peyton not be with her dad when he needed her. Because if we hadn't been on that trip, I wouldn't have gotten injured, and she'd have gone to his house for dinner. And now, because I'm on some stupid medication, I can't even drive to join her at the hospital and support her while she's waiting for news about her dad.

How can I make sure things between us work out if I can't get one weekend to work out?

I think about Peyton being at her dad's side at the hospital and about how she grew up with the perfect example of a marriage right in her own home. Then I glance at the scrapbook that my mom gave me. It still lies, unopened, on my coffee table, and I have no intention of opening it anytime soon. I don't need the reminder that my genes come from a couple of people who couldn't stand to be married and made absolutely terrible spouses.

And that I might never be able to be everything Peyton needs me to be.

CHAPTER 22

Peyton

As I WALK through the hospital hallways, I try to convince myself that it's better to drag my tired body out to my car and not lie on the floor right here and just stay unconscious for about two years in an attempt to recover from today. My dad is finally sleeping and I want to do the same, but I am too worried about Max for sleep.

So, even though it is nearing eleven, I gather all my extra energy reserves and drive to his apartment instead of driving to Quicksand. Well, I do after I find a soup and sandwiches shop that is still open and get him some chicken noodle soup. It is as close to homemade as I can get, and I am convinced that it helps heal a body, not just a cold.

When I pull into Max's apartment's parking lot, I text to see if he is still awake. If he isn't, I plan to use my key to leave the soup and check on him to make sure he is okay. Because if I don't, I won't be able to sleep no matter how tired I am.

He texts back that he is, so I order him not to get up and tell him I will unlock the door myself. I am surprised to find him on his couch instead of in his bedroom.

"Max!" I set down my things and rush over to him. He looks so much worse than when I left. I shouldn't have stayed at the hospital with my dad for so long. "Are you okay? What's wrong?"

He shrugs with his good shoulder like he doesn't have the energy to do anything more. "I didn't know you'd be back tonight. How's your dad?"

"They don't think it was a heart attack. He's okay, but they are keeping him overnight. Let me help you get into bed. You must be so tired. Oh! Food! It's probably been way too many hours since you had anything to eat." I turn and grab the container of soup I set on the coffee table and hand it to him. "Your body needs fuel to heal. Let me get you a spoon."

When I come back from the kitchen and hand it to him, he says, "You don't need to take care of me."

I scoff. "Obviously I do. Look at how much worse you've been doing without me here."

He gives me a sad smile. There is more to it than sadness at getting injured, though. I study him for a long moment, trying to figure it out. Finally, he puts the spoon and soup down on the coffee table, the lid still on it. "I'm not good enough for you."

"That's the pain medicine talking. You know you're perfect."

"It's not the pain medicine talking."

"Oh no—did it wear off? I haven't paid attention to the time." I grab the medicine bottle to see how often he should take it.

"Peyton."

He grabs hold of my hand and gives it a tug, so I sit down on the couch next to him.

"I can't get married. I can't be a dad."

I stare at him, confused. The words coming out of his mouth

don't seem to be related to anything going on, so I wonder what has been beating around inside his head while I've been gone. "Max, you'll be fine. Before you know it, you'll be back to doing the same things you used to do. This injury isn't going to stop you. Just wait for your follow-up appointment with the orthopedic surgeon. He'll look at the MRI and make a game plan, and everything will be okay."

"Everything won't be okay. Not with us."

"Oh." I feel like my heart is collapsing down into itself at the words, trying to protect itself from what is coming.

"You deserve the perfect husband. Kids. The perfect family, the white picket fence, all of it. I really want you to have all of it. But I can't give it to you."

No, no, no. I cannot be getting the "You're the perfect girl… for someone else" speech. Especially not from Max. I stand and pace back and forth in the three feet beside his coffee table, trying to get my heart to stop racing like it is determined to take home the gold. "You're injured. This is just because of that accident. We should talk about this later."

"This isn't because of the accident."

"Are you saying we should stop dating? Because I don't know how to do that, Max!" I've been worrying about this moment coming ever since I made the foolish decision to kiss him at Bex and Roman's wedding. But I am so very tired, and the words I am hearing don't feel real. Like they are happening in a dream and I am watching from afar.

"I don't, either. But we are going to have to figure it out."

His face is full of so much pain. It is etched in every line, in the curve of his mouth, the shape of his eyes. I want to hug him and hold him and lay my head on his strong chest and tell him everything is okay and make all the pain go away. I step closer and reach an arm toward him. "Let me help you get into bed."

"I don't need help."

His words feel like a slap, and my eyes fall to my arm that is still stretched toward him before I drop it to my side.

"Peyton—"

I meet his eyes.

"I'm sorry."

———

I drive away from Max's apartment, too mentally exhausted to process what has just happened. My eyes are blurry from tears, my breath is hitching, and the inn is too far away to drive to in my current state. So I choose the closer option and drive to my childhood home.

Even though I've known that Max never wants to get married, I haven't realized how much of me has been holding out hope that I'm going to be the one to make him feel differently. I've seen the pain in his eyes. We've been such good friends for so long that I know it couldn't have been easy for him to end things. I don't question how much he cares for me— we wouldn't have been such good friends for so long if he didn't. So it's stupid to feel like I haven't been enough for him when I went into it knowing that he doesn't want to get married.

Yet I feel that way anyway.

With my dad in the hospital, the house feels empty and alone. Fitting. The darkness is pressing down on me, though, so I flip on every light as I make my way from the front door to my old bathroom to take a shower. Then I put on some fluffy Hello Kitty pajamas that I haven't worn since probably my sophomore year of college and thank my lucky stars that my dad has left my bedroom the same as the day I moved out. With the bedroom light still on, I crawl into my old bed that I haven't slept in for years and stare at the wall covered in business cards.

I stared at this same wall for hours as a kid and a teen, letting the power of so many fulfilled dreams fuel me. Inspire me. Make me feel like anything is possible. Now I look at them and wonder something I haven't ever wondered before. All of the people on the business cards obviously had a dream that they brought to life. Did any of them then have to walk away from it?

If so, how did they survive it?

I started off my week of fifteen dates hoping to find a date for the wedding and a future husband, and not only ended with neither, but ended minus one best friend. One best friend who, for a glorious moment, was also my boyfriend.

I need my mom.

CHAPTER 23
Max

My mind is a tumultuous mess. The kind of mess best fixed by a hike up a mountainside or a good long jog. But with the way my body feels, both are out of the question, so I instead take a slow, careful walk along the Quicksand River trail.

Like I have since the moment last night when I basically told Peyton that I don't want any of the things that she wants, I've been replaying that conversation in my head. What was I thinking?

Okay, I know exactly what I was thinking—that I'm afraid. Scared to death, more like. Why do I have no fear when it comes to jumping off a cliff into the water down below, soaring through the air on a paraglider, climbing a sheer face with nothing but a bolt and a rope keeping me from falling, or eating food that Leo cooks over a campfire, but I run away screaming from a life spent with the woman I love?

Why does the big M-word cause me to quake in my well-designed hiking boots? I love Peyton. I love being with her. The thought of *not* having her in my life is actually even more terrifying than marriage. So why did I tell her I wanted to stop dating her?

It hasn't even been a full day, and already I have to stop myself from texting her out of habit. I want to find out how her dad is doing. Give her an update on how I am feeling this morning. I want to text her a picture of how the sun is glinting off the river as it goes over two boulders in one area. I want to ask how she slept last night. When I can see her next. What she has on the docket for today. I want to see her smile, hear her voice, wrap my arms around her, and tell her I love her.

Instead, I am hiking alone, doing none of that, and wondering how I can make it through today without her, let alone a lifetime. In one single fear-filled night, I lost the love of my life and my best friend all at once.

CHAPTER 24

Peyton

AFTER THE WEEKEND I've had, it would be as good as finding a twenty-dollar bill in a jacket I haven't worn for months if I had a day with no clients so I could recover. Instead, I drag myself, puffy-eyed and exhausted, to my first client's at eight a.m. sharp to make a week's worth of meals for a family who is usually three but who currently has a married son with a wife and two kids staying with them for the week, so it became a family of seven.

Then I go straight to another client's home who always insists I cook at her house, even though her kitchen is the size of a child's play set. Then I stop and check on my dad, who is back home again and doing great. His nurse is staying until he goes to bed, which makes me feel a ton better, even if it agitates him. Then I shop for the groceries I need for the first client I'll be cooking for tomorrow because I'm not about to go to the grocery store at six in the morning just to get out of going today.

On the positive side, if I'd stayed home like I wanted to, my eyes would be much puffier and redder from all the extra time being sad about Max. My busyness has also been keeping me from having to deal with what is by now surely two very stinky bags from camping. They're probably sitting in my bedroom, making the whole place smell like dirt and campfire. And possibly skunk.

When I finally pull into the parking lot at the inn late Monday afternoon, relief washes through me to finally be home.

I step into the lobby, my arms laden with bags of groceries and my equipment like I'm a pack mule, and I hear Addison and Bex talking in the gathering room to my left and Timini's sewing machine in the kitchen and dining room to my right. So Addison must've finished up with clients early.

I texted the three of them to give updates on Max's injuries, but I haven't given updates on my relationship with Max. Which is good, because if I had shared the news about me and Max at any time earlier today, things wouldn't have been pretty for my clients.

And by "things," I mean my face.

But it's good they're all here now because I don't want to tell the story three times. They all hear me come in and help to lighten my load by taking some of the bags into the kitchen. As I start putting the cold groceries into the fridge and the others into my zippered bags, Addison asks, "How is Max doing today?"

"I don't know, actually." My voice comes out quieter than I mean it to.

"Pey?" Bex says, prompting me for more information.

I put the cheese into the drawer, and then turn around to my friends and roommates. "Max says that he can't be a husband or a dad, so things can't work out between us. I already knew he felt that way, but it still hurts to hear it. So he thinks we should stop dating."

"Oh, Peyton," Addison says, and all three women come in for a group hug.

With my arms around them, I lay my head on Timini's shoulder. The flowing tears finally stopped sometime during the middle of the night, but my body still manages to produce ugly hiccuping breath-hitches that sound suspiciously like sobs.

"Why did I have to kiss him at the wedding?" I ask them, not really expecting an answer. "Everything was just fine before, and then I went and ruined it all. I knew he didn't want a marriage and kids. See? This is why I shouldn't be trusted to make my own decisions! An eight-ball would be better at this than I am. In fact, I should go out and buy an eight-ball and start letting it do all my deciding. Then maybe I wouldn't be in messes like this."

"Well," Timini says as she tries to brush a tear off my cheek along with the lock of hair that was stuck to it from the tears and the hugging, "on the positive side, at least you won't have to worry about being Peyton Peyton. Or about Bex calling you Pey Pey."

I let out a sobbing chuckle. I don't see the looks on Addison's or Bex's face, but they must've shot Timini a look, because she very defensively says, "What? Peyton always looks on the positive side."

"Peyton," Addison says, and I lift my head from Timini's shoulder to look at her. "You're obviously good at decision-making."

I lift a skeptical eyebrow. Just because she says it doesn't make it true.

"Well, obviously you're good at it," Timini says. "Look at where you are. Look at who you are. Look at what you're doing. It was a lot of good decisions that got you to this point."

"No. I'm here because of luck and good advice."

Bex starts opening drawers, searching for something.

"Where are sticky notes when you need them?" She finds a pad of them, then a pen, and motions all of us over to the dining table. "Okay, we're going to come up with a list of decisions you've made in your adult life."

I let out a breath and sit down. Bex looks like she's a woman on a mission, and it's pointless to try to stop her. "Okay, like what?"

Bex writes on the first piece of paper, "College," and then pulls it off the stack and sticks it to the table.

Ten minutes later, there's a huge pile of sticky notes that include everything from starting my own business to buying the cute floral blouse I'm wearing, to becoming friends with Max, to that time I cut my own bangs after my boyfriend broke up with me during my junior year of college, to moving into the inn, and everything in between. A good three dozen sticky notes are stuck in a cluster on the table.

Then Bex stands up and motions to her seat. "Sit. Look at each decision. If it turned out to be a good one, put it on the right. Bad ones go on the left."

As I go through the list, I'm surprised at how many sticky notes go on the right. In fact, the only ones on the left are relatively inconsequential. Like forgetting to make sure my back windows weren't down a crack before going through the car wash. (The inside of my car needed a good washing, anyway.)

And choosing not to check to make sure the quart of olive oil in my trunk has the lid screwed on tightly before I bring it in the house, along with armfuls of other supplies, because I was in a hurry. (For months, my old apartment looked better with shiny tile.)

And watching an infomercial that time I tried to skip an entire night's worth of sleep, just to see if I could do it. (Who doesn't want a supply of Snuggies, the wearable blanket, in every color ever made?)

By the time I'm done, I'm in shock at how many are on the "Good choices" side. Probably more than three-fourths.

"See?" Addison says, motioning at the sticky notes like she's Vanna White. "You always listen to your gut and think things through. You should trust your ability to make good decisions more."

"And you've stayed friends with Max for four years," Timini says. "You listened to your gut in becoming friends with him, and you've loved that decision."

I look from my friends to the sticky notes on the table. "Becoming friends was a good decision. But deciding to turn it into a romantic relationship wasn't."

"Listen up, Pey." Bex grabs hold of my hands like she wants to be able to just zoom the info from her head to me through our hands. "You said that when everything changed at the wedding, it was because David had opened the floodgates, right?"

I nod. "That was the problem. That was why I made the bad choice."

"Nope. Not a bad choice. Your gut had been feeding you information on the right decision for years, and you'd just been shoving it all behind those gates. So when he opened the gates, all those thoughts and feelings that spilled out were your gut helping you to decide. It told you to go for that relationship. It wasn't a spur-of-the-moment thing. That answer had been percolating for years."

"Think back to the wedding," Timini says. "Imagine you never kissed Max. You never did anything to start that relationship moving forward. How would you feel now?"

I imagine that scenario, and wow. I had not expected that *not* kissing him would feel so wrong. Not for a second would I have skipped these past few weeks with Max as a boyfriend instead of just a best friend.

"This," Addison says, motioning to the little yellow notes, "proves that you listen to your gut and make good decisions, even when someone isn't making them for you. And since you are a good decision-maker, then the fact that you opened yourself to a relationship with Max means that in your gut, you have hope that things will work out. You need to trust that."

I realize that I do have hope that things with Max will still work out. And that maybe my dad and my roomies have been right about my ability to make my own decisions. I do trust my own gut. And that causes a bubble of excitement to build up in my chest that makes me want to take action. I just need to figure out what that action should be.

CHAPTER 25
Max

WHEN I HEAR the knock on my apartment door, I hurry to it as quickly as a body that recently got slammed into a rock face can, hoping it might be Peyton, here to call me on my poor choices and make everything better. Not that she can fix any of my issues other than the ache I feel for her. When I open it, though, Hunter is standing there instead.

As my friend walks in, I ask, "How's Tami?"

"She's home. Physically, she's doing as well as could be expected. Emotionally?" Hunter shrugs. "It's hard. She's resting now. She told me I should come and check on you, and it looks like a good thing I am. Are you sure you shouldn't still be in the hospital? You look awful."

I sit in the padded chair that I've discovered has armrests at the perfect height for my sling, and Hunter sits on my couch. "I ended things with Peyton last night. Well, I ended the dating part. I'm hoping the friendship part can survive, but I don't know. I don't know if we can go back to the way things were before now that we know what it's like…"

I can't even finish the sentence. What it's like to date each other finally? What it's like to hold her in my arms? To kiss her? To be so much more than we ever were as friends?

Hunter's eyebrows rise, but then he looks down, like the fact that I ended things doesn't surprise him yet it explains why I look so awful. "Because the camping trip didn't go well and so now you think you can't get married?"

It sounds so stupid when he lays it out like that. "You've got to admit: it went bad." I tick off the items on my fingers. "Flat tire, skunk, raccoons, squirrels, my injury, Tami's miscarriage. That many things going wrong during one trip, the only one I've ever done with Peyton, is a pretty convincing sign that it's not going to work out." I feel bad, wallowing in my own struggles when Hunter is hurting, too.

Hunter is quiet for a long moment. Then he says, "You know it's not about the camping, right? It was never about camping. It's about your relationship with your dad and your thoughts about your parents' relationship."

I look at where the scrapbook my mom gave me is sitting on the coffee table.

"Maybe it's even about your relationship with Laurel." Hunter lets out a long breath. "I don't think I need to say anything about how great you and Peyton are together. I think every single cell in your body knows that. What I do think you need to do is realize that you are responsible for everything in your life. And not just responsible for it, but capable of changing it. Want a life with Peyton? Figure out your issues. Change your situation."

Ouch.

It's not like Hunter is telling me anything I don't already know at some level. It's not even the first time Hunter has told me that. It hurts worse this time, though.

After Hunter leaves, I pick up the scrapbook my mom gave

me. She made it for me to relive happy memories, so how bad can it be?

As I flip through the pages and pages of pictures, I do come across a lot of happy memories. Birthday parties, racing down the street on bikes with my friends, school awards, scout pins earned, looking proud in my first suit, lots of different sports activities, my first time riding a horse, building a bonfire in my backyard, standing next to the hole I dug in my backyard that I'd thought was big enough to be a swimming pool.

But flipping through them also makes me realize how many of those pictures were taken by babysitters, neighbors, a friend's parent, teachers, scout leaders, or friends. There are hardly any pictures with either of my parents in them. It's not just because one of them was behind the camera, either. They simply weren't present at any of those picture-worthy moments.

And in the pictures where they are present, it's always both of them, and they always have the same smiles. The ones that aren't real—they're the "See? We can pull off the happy family image long enough to snap a picture" smiles that my parents were famous for.

I knew my dad had been absent most of my life. Somehow, I'd forgotten how absent my mom had been. Maybe because after the divorce when I was in junior high, she was around more but my dad was around even less, which was saying something.

And just like that, all the sadness and loneliness I had as a kid comes back, full force. I don't think any parent should ever be as absent in their child's life as mine were. I vowed back when I was in fifth grade that I would never be a dad like my dad was. And that I'd never have a marriage like my parents'. But seeing all of these pictures doesn't help. They all feel like proof that I came from two people who weren't good at being parents or spouses.

The pictures continue after my high school graduation, which surprises me. When I come across some of my father's viewing and burial, instead of pushing my emotions away like I usually do, I let myself feel them. All of the regrets, all the pain of my dad abandoning me permanently, all the sadness at missed opportunities, all the anger about not feeling like I had a dad.

Then I come across two pictures I've never seen. One is of Peyton hugging my mom at the burial, and one is her holding my hand as I stand in front of the casket, giving my dad a final goodbye. I had only been friends with Peyton for a few months at that point, but she helped me get through those first weeks after my dad passed. It was the thing that strengthened our friendship so quickly.

As I look at the picture of her hugging my mom, I realize how much she has done to help me improve my relationship with my mom. We hadn't been close at all before Peyton came along, and if it wasn't for her, I probably still wouldn't have much of a relationship with her.

It makes me wish I'd known Peyton for longer. Long enough that she could've helped me improve my relationship with my dad because even though I never trusted him to be around, I realize that I wish I'd spent more time with him. Because now, I can't go talk to him. I can't ask him what I need to know.

Before I even have time to think about it, my phone is in my hand and I'm calling my mom. She answers and starts in with the small talk, but my mind is too full for that. I need my questions answered. "Mom. Why was Dad absent so much of the time?"

As my mom takes a deep breath, I hold mine. I expect her to

say, "He just wasn't dad material. Not everyone is," because that's my biggest fear about myself.

Instead, she says, "I ran into Judy about a year ago."

"Dad's ex-wife?" I don't know her well at all. I haven't thought about her in a long time.

"Yeah. We talked for quite a while. It was nice, actually. And we talked about your dad, so I know exactly what your dad would say if you asked him that question. He would say, 'Every single day, you choose to put your focus on what is most important to you. It's a conscious choice.' And he would also tell you that he made the wrong choice."

The words hit me with a physical force that makes me fall back into my chair, reminding me of just how injured I am. "You think he wished he would've been around more?"

"I think it was his biggest regret that he constantly made the wrong choice." She's quiet for a long moment and then says, almost in a whisper, "I *know* he wished he would have been around more because I wish I would've been, too. I have those same regrets, those same wishes that I would've spent more time with you.

"Then Peyton came along. She got me to recognize my mistakes. She helped me to turn things around while I still have the chance, and I'll be forever grateful for that girl."I sit, too stunned to talk.

"She taught me that it's never too late to make different choices. I'm betting she's taught you the same thing."

"Why didn't you tell me this before?"

"You haven't always been in a place where you could handle hearing how your dad felt. I was waiting for you to be ready."

"I know I don't tell you this often, but you're a good mom. Thank you."

My mom sucks in a quick breath. After several long

moments, her next words come out filled with emotion. "I love you, son."

"I love you, too," I say, and I do.

I hang up the phone, feeling a mix of sadness and heaviness about a past I wish I could change and a lightness greater than I can ever remember experiencing about a future that I *can* change. I haven't allowed myself to believe before this moment that being a good husband and eventually a good dad doesn't have anything to do with my genes. It's all a choice and not something outside of my control.

Even the way my relationship with Laurel went was a choice. I bickered right back, and I chose to stay in that relationship for so long because I thought it was exactly what was to be expected.

Peyton helped me realize long ago that I don't want to be that person, and it's been a long time since I have been. And I decided long before I knew her what kind of dad and husband I wanted to be. I just need to let go of those past fears that I've been holding onto so tightly.

Now is the time to be the man I've always wanted to be.

CHAPTER 26

Peyton

"CAKE!" I say as I open the cupboard where we keep the mixing bowls. "I should make a fortress cake. Because it feels like our relationship grew into a fortress. Then I could take it to Max and say something about how our fortress can't be toppled so easily and that we need to defend it. Except cake isn't really very fortress-like. Hmm." I try thinking of a dessert that is more dense. Like stone.

"Or," Timini says, "you could just text him."

I think for a minute and decide texting would probably work just as well. Besides, no dessert that's dense like stone sounds good. So I pull out my phone and type out a text. *Hi. Are you home? I want to come over and talk.* I backspace over the *and talk* part because I don't want to sound scary. Then I imagine him reading it and thinking it sounds like I'm trying to pretend like our breakup didn't happen, so I delete all of it. After hesitating a few moments, trying to think of what to say, I just type *Can I come over?* and then press send before I can second-guess it.

There. Done. It's vague, so he can interpret it however he

wants to. Except I'm suddenly unsure if that's a good thing. I hold my breath, waiting for his response, my heart beating a million miles an hour.

A minute later, his response comes in.

> Max: Instead, can you meet me at Pioneer Park at nine? In that clearing on the north side of the pond. I need to pay up for losing our competition.

Tonight? While he's still recovering? I type *Max, you don't have to do it so soon* and press send.

> Max: Yes, I do. Will you meet me there?

Really, I would meet him anywhere.

> Peyton: Yes.

It's fully dark when I pull into the lot at Pioneer Park. From there, I can see the playground at the right, but trees hide the pond. I follow the winding trail off to the left that leads through the trees. Butterflies are having a party in my stomach, and the skin on my arms feels like it's on high alert, noticing even the slightest breeze. Even though it's not cold outside, I rub my arms to get them to calm down.

I know that the pond is small and there are a few lights around it, but I still worry that I won't be able to see where Max is.

Once I'm past all the trees that have been blocking my view, I see the clearing at the north end of the pond and two strings of lights leading into the woods at the end of the clearing. I head toward them, and when I get closer, I see that a lamp sits on a little table. An envelope with *Peyton* written on it in Max's handwriting is tucked just under the edge of the lantern.

I open the envelope, and inside, a card reads *Follow the lights*. So I pick up the lantern and do just that. They lead down a natural pathway between the trees, the strings of lights guiding me. I've been to the pond plenty of times, but this is the first time I've headed off into the woods here. The cedars and Douglas firs towering over me remind me of going camping with Max. This place even has that same fresh, earthy smell. That feeling and that smell are so intrinsically tied to Max—I've missed it.

Eventually, the trail and the strings of lights through the woods open up into a dark clearing. I hold up my lantern but it doesn't shine enough light for me to see further than a few feet in front of me. I want to walk forward, into the unknown, but nerves flutter in my stomach. "Max?" I call out.

Another set of lights turns on, bathing the clearing in golden light and showing that the space contains an actual couch. Just like one in a regular house, but sitting on the pine needle-covered ground. A little table is nestled in front of it, and across from it in the clearing sits a big outdoor movie screen. "Oh my lands," I say out loud. Is Max going to sing his karaoke song to a video? Maybe it will be the music video for whatever song he chooses.

Whatever it is, I love the idea. I love the couch, the screen, and the woods that are right in town but feel exactly like camping. He's gone to a lot of work to set this up. Maybe it's because even though he doesn't want to date anymore, he wants to try to make sure our friendship can stay intact. I like that it means this much to him.

And I want the friendship, too. But I also want more. I want it all, and I want it with Max. I know it to my core now, and no matter where that leads us—even if it leads me to heartbreak—I trust myself in making that decision more than any I've made in my life.

I walk over to the couch and sit down. That's when I notice a remote control on the table with a sign on it that reads *Press play*. So I do.

The projector on the table hums to life, and the big outdoor screen lights up with a photo—a selfie Max took of the two of us eating cotton candy at the Quicksand Carnival a couple of years ago. Music plays in the background of the video as it switches to a five-second clip of the two of us at a get-together with friends at Christmastime. Then a picture of us in a theater before the movie starts.

The video shows pictures and video clips one after another of so many things we've done together over the past four years. Some make me laugh, some bring a tear to my eye, and some have me grinning like it's my birthday. Some of the pictures are of things I haven't thought about in years. Some I've seen before and some are new. Seeing the past four years of our life together in one place like this makes all the emotions I feel about Max swell up and overflow. I wipe away a tear that has escaped.

Then a picture comes up in the video and it stays on the screen. It was taken just over a week ago as Max and I walked down the sidewalk in front of the shops on Settler's Boulevard, heading nowhere in particular, just enjoying being together. I had stopped to take a selfie with him, but a stranger had offered to take the picture for us.

I have stared at it several times since then just to relive the feelings of that moment. Max's arm is around my back, and we're both looking at each other like we couldn't be more in love. Max's face is especially adorable in the picture, and I stare at it now.

Then the song on the video changes to *Marry You*, and I gasp.

No. That can't be the reason why he chose that song. He just chose it because it has a great tune. This isn't about that.

Then Max steps out from behind the big screen and starts to sing. The lyrics aren't the same as they are in the song, though. He sings about how we have been friends for so long and how great that has been. He doesn't have perfect pitch, or anything close to it. But he has confidence, and that is even more attractive. The man looks like a dream.

He may have an arm in a sling, but he is moving as though he doesn't hurt, unlike the last time I saw him. And the words he is singing are just so sweet.

"Hey, Peyton," Max sings, "I think I am in love with you."

Max and I love each other. We have for a long time—this isn't new information. Max and I couldn't have been as good of friends as we are without loving each other. Being *in love*, though, is something completely different, and his words make my heart blow up like a balloon.

Then Bex, Addison, and Timini all step out from behind the screen and start being Max's backup singers, dancing to the music, and I scream and clap. How are they in on this without me having a clue?

Max sings the next verse, matching the music pretty impressively, but changing the lyrics to be about how I tried to kiss him a year ago and how he'd been in love with me even back then. *He had?* And about how he'd been so scared at the time and said something he had regretted so many times. He makes a face that has me laughing out loud.

Then his friends, Hunter, Emilio, and Leo, all come out from behind the screen and join Addison, Bex, and Timini as the backup singers. I find myself grinning until my cheeks hurt as I sway to the music.

When Max starts singing about when I kissed him in the moonlight, I blush and goosebumps run down my arms. I had been so nervous that night. Now I realize it was one of the bravest things I've ever done, and I am so glad I did.

Ian and Roman join the others in front of the screen that shows Max and me being in love, and I shake my head. He has lined up all of this for me. I want to jump out of my seat and hug him. But I also want this moment to never end, so I am not about to do anything to cut it short.

"Guess what, Peyton," Max sings, his eyes on mine, making me feel like I am the most important person in his universe. "I know I am in love with you."

My heart starts sprinting. And then it keeps on sprinting when my dad and Max's mom also appear and join everyone singing. How have all of them been back there without me suspecting it? Or hearing them? I haven't fully recovered from Max's words before he goes on, singing about how we started dating and that since then, everything in the world has felt the most right. It is like he is singing exactly what my heart is feeling.

Everyone—Max, my five roommates, his three friends, my dad, and his mom—sings the next part of the song together, belting it out in the woods. When it gets to the part of the song that gives it its title, everyone stops singing and silently takes a few steps back toward the screen as the music fades to a soft sound.

Except Max. Max steps forward, coming right up to where I sit on the couch, and I want to leap up and wrap my arms around him. He pulls a ring box out of his pocket and then gets down on one knee. "Peyton..."

My hand flies to my mouth and before I know it, I am kneeling on the ground in front of him. "Max, yes! The answer is yes!"

He smiles, then reaches out and runs a knuckle along my cheek. "I haven't even asked the question yet."

My whole body is acting as if he has, though, including the tears that are falling. "It doesn't matter—the answer is yes. No, never mind. Ask. I need to hear the words or I'm not going to believe it. And if they aren't the ones you're making me think they are, Max, I will personally go out and find a startled skunk to bring back to you."

He laughs, and the sound is magical.

"Peyton. I'm not sure when the moment was that I first fell in love with you, but I can tell you it was nearly four years ago. I'm sorry it took me so long to figure everything out that I needed to."

He gives me a smile that is sweet and so full of love and everything Max is, wrapped up into one little package. "We've been through practically everything together. When I think about the rest of my life, I know I want to experience every-thing it has to offer alongside you. And not only as my best friend but also as my wife." His voice is not shaky or unsure. It comes out with the confidence of someone who knows with exact certainty what he wants.

My breath hitches, and the tears are falling in earnest now.

"Peyton Abernathy, will you marry me?"

This time, I don't hold back. I wrap my arms around his neck and squeeze him tight, planting kisses all over his cheeks, saying "Yes" in between each one. The ten people watching—who I managed to forget all about the moment Max got on one knee—start cheering. Max and I are both smiling so wide we can barely kiss.

He stands and pulls me to my feet, then he wraps those strong, protective arms around me and pulls me close, and it feels like a promise that he will always protect my heart. He kisses my neck and then the space just under my ear, and then whispers, "I am in love with you, Peyton. And I want nothing more than to spend forever with you."

CHAPTER 27
Max

I love that all our friends and family came to participate in my proposal. I also love that they know to leave not long after. Peyton has said yes, and I want to soak that in for as long as I can.

The two of us, alone in the clearing, sit on the couch. A part of me wants her to sit snuggled up into me so I can put an arm around her and she can lay her head on my shoulder. But the bigger part wants exactly what happens—Peyton sits facing me, her feet curled up under her, the strings of lights bathing her face in a golden glow. I sit with one leg bent in front of me, facing her, too, and I just take in how beautiful her eyes are. Her soft pink cheeks. Her perfect lips. Her golden curls.

"I'm really glad you're the one who lost our competition."

I laugh a hearty laugh. "Oh yeah?"

"Yep," she says, her lips curving into a smile. "I think you might have a future in karaoke."

"Maybe, but I am only going on tour with the show if we can sing as a couple. Oh! We can get business cards made up with our faces on them, holding microphones. Maybe even have a neighbor on it, too, knocking on the door to see if our cat is ill. And then it can go up on your office wall along with the rest of your business card collection in whatever house we live in."

This time Peyton laughs. Then her face turns more serious, and she runs a finger along one of the swirly designs on the sofa, biting her lip. "Max," she starts and then pauses. She opens her mouth to speak again and then closes it.

So I reach out with my good arm and hold her hand in mine, giving it an encouraging squeeze.

Peyton takes a breath, and then says, "Did you propose because you *want* to get married? Or only because you know it's what I want?"

"I *thought* I didn't want marriage. Or a family. It turns out I had an emptiness right here—" I reach up and touch my chest, right over my heart "—that was trying to tell me I was wrong. I had just lived with it for so long that I didn't fully know it was there. If it weren't for you, I would still be thinking it was normal—a flaw in the way I was made." I can't believe I am actually admitting this stuff out loud. If it was anyone other than Peyton, I wouldn't.

"The thought of living a life without you is probably the only thing that could've made me search out the source of that hole and work my way through it."

Peyton gives me that smile of hers that feels like it can power the sun. "And you did work through it?"

I nod. "That's how I knew that you fit perfectly into the space like it was made for you."

She reaches out and puts her hand over my heart. "I like being here."

I put my hand over hers, holding it there. "There's nothing I want more than to be able to spend the rest of my life married to you, Peyton. I wish I would've figured things out sooner because I don't want to waste a moment."

"That's just what my dad said." When I raise an eyebrow in question, she adds, "After his heart attack—the real one—he told me that he wanted me to get out and find the person I was supposed to spend my life with. And he said, 'Don't waste any of the years you could have together.'"

"That might have been why his smile was so big when I told him I wanted to propose to you."

Peyton chuckles.

"I wish you could've seen the smile on my mom's face, too, when I told her."

Peyton grins like everything in the world is perfect, and then she snuggles into me. I wrap the arm not in a sling around her, knowing she is exactly right.

Epilogue

TIMINI

I PUT a tablespoon of sesame oil in the pan on the stove, just like the recipe says, and then spread it around with the spatula before dumping the cut-up veggies in. It's my turn to cook for the roommate dinner, and I found a recipe online for 15-minute Lo Mein that looked easy.

Except the recipe lies. It took me thirty minutes just to cut up all of the carrots and green onions and cabbage and mushrooms and red peppers, especially since I keep getting distracted by thoughts of a pirate costume I'm designing. And then it takes a few minutes longer because I don't think to cook the lo mein noodles while I'm cutting up vegetables.

But I already have the soy sauce, sesame oil, and sugar for the sauce whisked up in a bowl, and am feeling pretty proud of myself for getting all the ingredients ready to go into the pan before I put the first ones in. I'm getting better at this cooking thing.

But suddenly, I'm wondering how frequent the "stir" is supposed to be in "stir fry."

At least this is an original roommates' dinner instead of the one with significant others. Cooking for four is less pressure than cooking for seven.

Peyton comes running into the kitchen, her curls bouncing, and her face flushed. "Guess what?"

Addison and Bex both stop setting the table and look up.

I give the vegetables another stir. "Um…You found a venue, set a wedding date, and it's only three months away."

"How did you know?"

"Wait." I look around. "I was right?"

"We decided that since we both have small families, we could totally do a wedding on the beach. We found the most beautiful spot with the most adorable place for the wedding dinner—and the ceremony, if it rains that day. It's perfect." She places some brochures down on the table. "And they had a cancellation, so a date was available. We just really don't want to waste any time in getting to our together life, you know? And three months—well, two and a half, actually—to plan a wedding isn't crazy. Right?"

All three of us join Peyton in a group hug, squealing.

"That's plenty of time to plan a wedding," I say.

Bex looks like she isn't so sure, but she still smiles and says, "Right. And we'll help."

Peyton lets out another squeal. "Two and a half months and I'll be Peyton Peyton!"

As we all gather around the brochures to look at the venue, Peyton says, "We were going to look for places to live, but, well, I wanted to talk to you all. Addison, since Ian lives here, and Bex, since you and Roman are going to be here for another four or five months—"

"Six months," Bex cuts in. "The builder ran into some problems and had to delay our move-in date."

"Oh. I'm sorry."

Bex waves her off. "It's fine."

"Well, and since Bex and Roman will be here for six months, Max and I kind of want to join in on the fun for as long as we can. You know, keep us all together for a bit longer. How would you all feel about Max moving in after the wedding?"

"Oh, whew," I say. "Now I don't have to enact my elaborate plan to keep you here longer."

Peyton laughs, but the truth is, I've actually been coming up with plans. I'm used to spending a good half of my workdays in the same room as Peyton, and I'm going to miss her terribly when she moves out.

"I think him moving in is perfect," Addison says. Then she sniffs. "What's that smell?"

The smell hits my nose at about the same time. Panicked, I rush around to the stove on the island counter and grab the spatula. The more I "stir" the stir fry, the more I see how many of the bottom parts of the vegetables are burned black.

The recipe says to put in a couple tablespoons of mirin—a mysterious clear liquid that is who knows what—to loosen the browned bits in the pan. So I splash the liquid in the pan and stir some more. It does help to loosen the browned—black, actually—bits, but it just spreads the black bits to the few parts of the veggies that aren't already blackened.

Bex looks into the pan and then at her wrist, even though she isn't wearing a watch. "Time of death: seven-thirteen."

I move the pan off the heat and pull out my phone. "And, we're having take-out for dinner! It's my specialty, anyway."

"No need," Bex says, opening the fridge and pulling open a drawer. "I'm sure we have enough random veggies in here. We can cut some up in no time. It'd be a shame to waste those noodles and that sauce."

As Bex and I cut up more vegetables and Peyton talks more about her upcoming wedding, my mind starts wandering in the direction of dating. I don't need a man to complete me. I never have. I've always been just fine on my own.

Except lately, I've been thinking about how nice it would be to have someone. Someone serious. It's been a while since I've been in a committed relationship. And it's definitely not because lately I've been surrounded by couples in love who've completely ignored our pact not to fall in love. It has nothing to do with that at all.

In fact, you know what? I'm fine. I don't need someone serious. There is nothing wrong with dating guys who are beautiful but shallow and having things end after a date or two. They are the ones I always seem to pick, and who doesn't like going with their default choice? There's a reason why established patterns hang around for so long. They're classic. They have staying power.

Well, okay, and they're boring and predictable and produce the same results.

"Oh, Timini," Bex says. "I forgot to tell you. Remember how you told Roman that his company should make a dating app where you can't see each other's pictures, so you have to rely solely on the conversation the two of you strike up to see if you're a good fit? They are making it!"

I perk up. "For real?" I've always thought I might make better decisions on who to date if I couldn't just choose the ones with the prettiest faces.

"Yep," Bex says, grinning. "It'll be ready for beta testers soon, and Roman is hoping you'll be one of the first to try it out and see how you like it."

I smile. Maybe it's time to toss away boring and predictable after all. New and different? That is exactly what I need.

———

VOLUME

Four

HOW TO NOT FALL for YOUR EX

CHAPTER 1

Timini

I STRETCH after a good night's sleep.

Wait. Why am I so well-rested? And why is it so light outside? I fumble for my phone, knocking a bottle of lotion off my nightstand, and manage to light up the screen to see the time.

"No!" It's eight-oh-six, and I have a nine o'clock meeting with the director of an upcoming show at the Williams Theater in Hamilton Hall, and it's a good forty-minute drive to get there. I throw off my covers and leap out of bed. I can do this. I stand in the middle of my room, being pulled in a million directions at once until my head clears enough to think.

"Clothes," I say out loud, heading to my closet. Then I remember I already planned my interview outfit—a fabulous blouse and the perfect jeans. I even planned ahead enough to throw them into the washer. Then I got sucked into a Hallmark movie and hadn't remembered to put them in the dryer, so they're probably still damp, crumpled wads of fabric sitting in the washer.

I can find something else, no problem. I throw open my closet doors and look at what I have to work with. Which isn't much, because last night I had been feeling particularly proactive and I'd thrown most of what I own into the wash.

An oversized sweater with big, bold burnt umber and gold stripes calls to me, so I pull it out. I normally wear it with jeans, but every pair I own is currently residing with its friends in the bottom of the washing machine. Leggings with subtle geometric shapes are peeking out from one of my drawers, so I grab them. None of the colors on the leggings go with the sweater, but maybe I can pull one of the greens through to the top with a scarf. I scan the closet, and my eyes land on a vest whose green will work great.

I throw off my pajamas, swipe on deodorant, and pull on the outfit in about two seconds flat. It's not a pairing I would've ever picked under normal circumstances, but these aren't normal times. I glance in my full-length mirror. Surprisingly, it's actually an okay look. I grab a pair of light tan strappy wedges from my closet that can turn any outfit into something incredible and put them on. There. With these wedges and a confident stride, I can totally pull this outfit off.

As I race to the bathroom, I look at the time. Eight twelve. I brush my teeth (definitely not getting through the Happy Birthday song twice), then run a brush through my hair. At least I had the foresight to shower last night instead of this morning. It means that I have some hairs that bend at weird angles, though, so I just pull it into a messy bun.

After splashing water on my face, I put moisturizer on using both hands, then swipe on some mascara and force myself to slow down long enough to put lip gloss on without accidentally drawing a smile worthy of an emoji.

I race down the stairs and into the large dining area of the inn-turned-apartment where I live with my roommates. The bulk of my work is spread across the half-dozen round tables in the space meant for guests to eat breakfast. I grab my portfolio and the concept drawings I made for this particular play from a shelf along the back wall.

Then I start lifting piles of fabric and half-finished projects as I look for the pirate costume I'm so proud of designing and an eighteenth-century ball gown I just finished for a private school's sixth-grade play. It isn't adult-sized, but it's well made and I love it.

"I take it you're meeting with a client this morning?" my roommate, Addison, says as she cuts up a banana for her oatmeal in the kitchen end of the room.

"Potential client." I lift a stack of pattern pieces for a design I'm working on.

"Oh. Need help?"

I remember that I took the costumes upstairs to the closet in one of the extra bedrooms we have. "No, but I'll take one of those bananas to eat along the way." Addison tosses one across the room to me. I catch it and then race back up the stairs to grab the outfits.

Once I get everything shoved into my car and am on the road, the song on the radio ends, and a commercial plays that is probably for a gym or a life or relationship coach. Or maybe a pizza place. "If you don't figure out what you want in life, you'll never get it. So slow down and—"

I switch to a station with music. Whatever. No one has time for that. I take a bite of the banana and focus on getting to my destination.

My clients usually include directors for school plays— elementary through high school—and community theaters. My dream, though, is to have my own design studio and design the costumes for professional plays, just like the ones in the theaters at Hamilton Hall. If this interview goes well today, it could mean big things for my career.

By the time I drive through Gresham and pull onto Interstate 84 toward Portland, my heart rate has calmed, I take slow breaths and think only about the meeting I'm about to have. I will be pitching myself as the costumer to the director of the show *An American in Paris*.

Then a light on my dash catches my attention, and I glance down at my gas gauge. "No. No, no, no!" I've already driven a full day after the light came on. I forgot that I was going to wake up early and stop at the gas station before leaving Quicksand.

I wish my past self would quit having so much faith in my ability to get things done. Because there is definitely no time to stop and get gas now. The numbers on my dash say I will run out of gas in fourteen miles. I glance at the GPS on my phone that is leading me to Hamilton Hall—my destination is still fifteen miles away.

It's only a one-mile difference. All I have to do is a little more coasting than normal and not pull into a different lane and speed up to go around another driver. I pat the dash. "We can do this."

Twenty minutes later, I'm stopped at a red light. My fingers drum the steering wheel as I look at the dashboard that shows my range based on the gas in my tank is at zero miles. I murmur over and over, "Change to green, change to green." Finally, it does, and I press the gas slowly, trying to use as little of what fumes are still in the tank as possible.

I have just three blocks left to go when I pass a gas station. If only I had time to stop! But that is a problem for Future Timini. Present Timini is already late. Besides, two of the numbers in the gas price are ones, so that has to be a sign that I will make it.

A block from my destination, the gas—and my luck—runs dry. I hurriedly shift into neutral, flip on my right turn signal, and crank the suddenly hard-to-turn steering wheel to get my car off to the side of the road. It isn't the best parking spot, and it's still a block away from the building, but at least my car isn't blocking traffic at all.

But I am in a sixty-minute parking zone, so I pull a napkin from the stash in my glove box, a pen from my purse, and scrawl on the napkin, *Out of gas. Be back soon!* and then put it on my dash. Hopefully, that will be good enough. Then I get out, grab my portfolio with one hand and the two costumes with the other, and take off running toward the building.

My wedges hit the sidewalk with light clunks, in the graceless way wedges tend to do when running, the costumes swinging back and forth. I try not to think about what the bouncing motion is doing to my messy bun and whether it can still be called a bun at this point.

Halfway through the crosswalk, with the beautiful glass and brick building that shines in the sunlight just a hundred yards away, one of the straps on one of my shoes breaks free from where it connects to the sole, and my foot twists. Luckily, I catch myself and don't go down with my adorable shoe. I limp the rest of the way across the street. Not because my ankle is hurt, but because I can't walk normally and still cross the street while keeping the shoe on my foot.

Once I have made it to the sidewalk, I stop to check out the damage. Really, if I don't move, my shoe looks just fine. I test it a bit. It is the part by the toes that has broken free. If I kind of shuffle-walk, it will stay in place. Which is going to have to be good enough, because this is a really important meeting, and my wedges have a five-inch heel, so I can't exactly just take one of them off.

So I shuffle-walk my way right up to the front doors of the

building and shuffle-walk my way to the receptionist. I take a quick glance at the clock on the wall behind her. Nine-eleven. Honestly, I'm impressed at how quickly I got here, all things considered. "Hello. My name is Timini Jensen, and I am here to meet with Aftyn Flint."

The receptionist opens her mouth to say something, but before she can get it out, a woman with a stern expression and an even sterner bun—the kind that doesn't have a single hair out of place—walks into the foyer. I immediately recognize her as the director. "You're late."

"I know," I say. "I am so sorry."

"Follow me," the woman says and starts walking down the hall.

Even with my additional five inches, courtesy of my struggling shoes, the woman still has me beat by a few inches. That isn't abnormal—at five-foot-one on a well-rested day, I am used to most people being taller than me. But those long legs of Ms. Flint's don't make it easy for me to keep up, especially when shuffle-walking. When the woman reaches the elevator and stops to see that I am still a dozen feet away, she glances at my footwear.

"I swear I know how to walk in these. The strap just broke as I was crossing the street and…" I trail off. I can tell that Aftyn Flint is not the type of woman who cares about excuses, so I speed up my shuffle-walk to something resembling a four-year-old pretending to be a choo-choo train and hurry into the elevator.

I finally take a breath in relief when we make it to the woman's office and I get to sit down. Ms. Flint stands behind her desk for a long moment, considering me, as if she is cataloging the strikes against me. Then she sits, and instead of easing in with small talk before heading into a conversational interview, the director says, "You've already wasted enough of my time, so let's just skip past the pleasantries. Pitch to me."

"Oh, um, okay." I pass my portfolio to Ms. Flint, but the woman doesn't even glance at it. She just keeps her steely eyes on me. So I talk. I tell about how a neighbor taught me to sew so I could help in her Etsy store when I was eleven, but shift to first talking about college, then to an amazing internship I had, and then to starting my own business, quickly shifting to the next item once it's apparent that each is irrelevant to the woman.

I've heard that giving some background helps the interviewer to see you as a real person, but I drop all background information pretty quickly and instead focus on telling what kinds of costumes I've made most recently.

As I am talking, the woman opens my portfolio and starts looking at the pictures of things I've made and my concept drawings for *An American in Paris*. She seems to be slightly more interested, so I stop talking and let her look. Maybe I should've just started with that.

It isn't long after, though, that the woman's eyes glance for the smallest second to the door. There is an invisible timer counting down to her exit through that door—I can feel it. So I grab one of the costumes I brought and unzip its bag while I talk as fast as I can.

"This is a pirate costume I designed." I pull the stylish costume out and hold it by its hanger. I start to give details about the piece but stop when Ms. Flint immediately stands and hurries around her desk to it. The woman fingers the details around the collar and then opens the jacket to better look at the poet's shirt underneath, inspecting the jacket lining and seams and buttons. This time, I know that silence is the best course of action.

"This is exquisite workmanship. What's in that bag?"

I unzip it and pull out the ball gown, holding it up. "I know that every director has their own spin they like to put on a play or show, and I incorporate whatever that is into the pieces that I design. For this one, the director wanted it to feel more modern and trendy, so I added the strong angular layers and the bead-work spray to help fit her vision."

"Stay here. I want to grab a colleague."

At least the woman seems impressed with my pieces. It probably won't undo the first impression she has formed of me, but it's something. Hopefully, it will be enough—I really want to be chosen to make the costumes for the show they are plan-ning. Getting my costumes into a place like the Williams Theater could open so many more doors.

As I wait, I notice the stapler on the woman's desk. Oh, that is perfect! I grab it, open it up flat, and then maneuver myself and my leg so that I can get to the part of my shoe that has broken. I hold the strap against the sole of the wedge, then press the stapler against it and staple. With a whoosh of grati-tude that it works, I put a second staple into it, just to make sure it holds tight.

And, of course, that's when Ms. Flint opens the door again. I hurry to right myself in the chair, bend the stapler into its orig-inal shape, and sneak it back onto the desk. The director narrows her eyes at me but then acts like she hasn't seen anything as she turns to her colleague.

"Naya, I'd like you to meet Timini Jensen. Timini, this is Naya Mallick."

The two of us shake hands, and then Ms. Flint goes to work showing Naya my costumes. Which is fine by me, because I really don't want to start my disastrous pitch over again. Both women ask me several questions, and then they both look at my portfolio.

"Thank you for meeting with me," Ms. Flint says. "We will make a decision in a few days, and then we'll get in touch with you to let you know one way or another."

Well, based on how emotionless the director's parting words are, I'm not so sure I impressed them after all. I gather my things and head back to the elevator and then out to my car.

I put my portfolio and my sample pieces into the back seat then shut the door and sigh, wishing the meeting had gone better. Then I sigh at my car. I hate running out of gas. Not enough to have chosen to go to the gas station last night, apparently, but enough to not be happy with my decision not to. At least I keep an empty gas can in my trunk for situations like this.

There will be no hurrying to the station with my shoes in their current condition. As I trudge down the street, the gas can swinging in one hand, I'm grateful that I can at least trudge instead of shuffle-walk. Or worse, walk barefoot. Because at least this way, I still look fabulous.

But there is the cutest little girl ahead of me, maybe five years old, walking hand-in-hand with her dad. She has the same dark hair that I have, and it makes me wish I had grown up with a dad because the two of them are adorable.

And wow, that gas station is so much further away than I remember. About halfway there, one of the staples on my shoe pops loose, and I groan. I look up and down the street. I wish I were in a Hallmark movie right now. Wouldn't this be the perfect time for a meet-cute? A knight in shining armor would pull up to the curb next to me, his window down, his tanned arm resting across the door of his truck, and ask if I wanted a ride to the gas station. And I would say no, that I could do it myself, and then I'd keep walking.

Then my shoe would break the rest of the way, and I would turn to see that he's still there, a half-smile on his face, complete with an adorable dimple, and I would accept his help.

Instead, it is only me. No knight, no shining armor.

Although, with my next step, my shoe does break the rest of the way, so at least that part of the story comes true. I sigh and shuffle-walk like I'm a choo-choo train the rest of the way to the gas station.

CHAPTER 2

Jackson

MY EYES OPEN. It is still dark outside, but I can tell it is morning. About five seconds later, my alarm goes off, and I give myself a mental high-five as I turn it off. I always feel like I've just won a *Get Exactly the Right Amount of Sleep* award whenever that happens. It's probably just because my body is so used to waking up at six a.m. that it does it on its own, but I prefer to think it is because I'm disciplined enough to go to bed at the right time.

I stretch my arms wide before getting out of bed and dropping to the floor for fifty push-ups, just like I have every morning for the past eighteen years. When I was eleven, my favorite college basketball player came to speak at my school, and he said that he did fifty push-ups every single morning, first thing, no excuses. And then, anytime he needed to tackle a big project, or start a new habit, or get better at something, he could tell himself that he did that one thing consistently, so he could do anything consistently. He told us about what a difference it had made in his life.

It didn't hurt that the guy also had some seriously impressive arm muscles, and mine had been, well, the arm muscles of a sixth-grader who had grown two inches in the two months since school had started but hadn't gained a pound. So I decided right then that I was going to do the same. I no longer even have to think about it—it is just what I do.

After drinking a tall glass of water, brushing my teeth, and throwing on my gym clothes, I head down three floors to the gym for my section of apartments in this building. There are six treadmills, and three of them are filled by the same people who are with me every morning at six-fifteen—strangers I don't know outside of standing next to them in a row, running toward something none of us can see.

I give them each my customary nod and they give their customary nod back, a quick jerk for so little a motion, like they aren't willing to be pulled out of wherever they currently are in their mind. The woman always looks fierce and determined. She is probably running a marathon in her head. The older guy looks like he is imagining running on a sandy beach. The third one, though, usually looks like he is Rocky in that training montage where, at the end, he runs up the steps of the Philadelphia Museum of Art. Today, though, he looks more like he is running from zombies and they are about to win.

Me? I don't really picture myself running somewhere so much as I picture myself doing something other than running. That's why I never listen to music while I run. Sure, it is helpful to have the rhythm, but then it keeps the focus on the running, which makes forty-five minutes seem like hours. I run because it serves a purpose—to stay in shape. I don't run because I enjoy it.

I put in my earbuds, get on my treadmill, and go into my podcast app. All the daily business reports from the East Coast are posted by six. I find that if I turn the speed to double, not only can I get in all the ones I want to listen to in exactly forty-five minutes, but their fast, chipmunk-y voices are actually the perfect beat to run to. I get all my news listened to, and I have to focus to understand what they are saying at that speed, so it keeps my mind off the running and on their words.

Bam. Two birds, one stone.

When the last podcast sounds like it is getting close to wrapping up, I set the speed to a walk to cool down. At their final words, I stop the treadmill and go over to the weights. I spend fifteen minutes there, and for that, I *do* listen to music. Then I head back upstairs to shower.

At seven forty-two, exactly on schedule, I walk out of my room wearing slacks and a white button-down shirt. I use the remote to open the curtains covering my floor-to-ceiling windows along the wall of my living room and stand in front of them to look out over the Portland skyline from the twenty-first floor. I've been in this apartment for a year and a half now and never tire of the view.

I head to the kitchen, get out my bowl, spoon, cereal, and milk, and sit down at the bar to eat and watch cartoons. I'm not ashamed that cereal and cartoons are part of my morning routine. I decided long ago that it's important.

By eight-thirty, exactly, I've cleaned up breakfast, gone down to my car, driven the twelve minutes to Oliver Innovations—the business my family owns—parked, and made it up to the eighth floor. As I walk down the hall, I stop to poke my head into my sister Naomi's office. I know to not do anything more than wave hello. She has a fierce work ethic and swears that she gets more done between seven-thirty and eight-forty-five—before anyone is there to bug her—than most people get done by noon.

I pass right by my brother Ethan's office—Ethan doesn't believe any work worth doing should be done before ten, so it'll still be a while before he's in. Luckily, his job in sales seems to agree with his schedule. I do stop at the next door and say, "Good morning," to my sister, Emma, who's also Ethan's twin.

"Good morning!" she says, stopping organizing whatever papers are on her desk and coming over to give me a hug. She is the hugger of the family and would've seen it as a crime if I walked past her office without stopping for one.

"I've got a meeting at nine that I'm not ready for yet, but Dad wanted me to tell you that he needs to talk to you. I think he's in the break room."

I find both of my parents in the break room, along with one of my co-workers, Ramesh, all getting their morning coffee.

"Morning, sweetie," my mom says. "I've got an early stand-up meeting with my team in a few minutes, so I'll see you later." She gives my shoulder a squeeze as she passes me.

"Jackson!" my dad says. "Did you hear? Ethan got the final retail chain we were hoping for in Delhi to agree to meet with you next week."

My eyebrows shoot up as a grin spreads across my face. I hadn't heard—it was probably something Ethan set up late last night. That is great news. My trip is going to be full of successes, I am sure of it.

"And Kim found another manufacturing possibility, so we've added that to your schedule, too. It looks like it'll be a full one."

"Just the way I like it."

Back when I decided to get my degree in International Business, I mostly had my family's business in mind. Or at least I hoped I would be able to use it there. I never imagined back then that all of my siblings and I would be working for Oliver Innovations, that we all would find our niches, or that I would love all the aspects of getting our products sold in international markets so much.

"And we should talk about some last-minute strategy," Ramesh says. "Do you have time in your schedule today to meet?"

I know my day is already packed, so I pull out my phone to check my schedule for any free windows of time. Ramesh steps up next to me to look. As soon as I unlock my screen, though, it goes straight to the classic *Phineas and Ferb* episode I ended on. I try to swipe it away quickly, but Ramesh has seen. Just because I'm not ashamed to watch cartoons with breakfast every morning doesn't mean I want my co-workers to know.

"Oh, hey! My kid loves that show, too!" Then Ramesh gives me a look, probably remembering that I don't have kids so it was me who was watching.

I don't respond to Ramesh's comment like the man will simply forget if I forge on with enough force. "I've got twenty minutes at two fifteen."

"Two fifteen it is."

By the smile on Ramesh's face as he walks away, my forging on didn't make him forget.

Most of my day is spent lining everything up that I need to have in place before I leave for my trip on Friday. My trip requires coordination with sales and marketing, advertising, manufacturing, acquisitions, finance, and our law department, as well as more than two dozen contacts in India.

Since most of my day was spent in meetings, by the time six o'clock rolls around, I am a strange mix of exhausted and on fire, ready to start my trip right now. I loosen my tie and unbutton my top button. I'm organizing the papers on my desk that have been collecting on it all day when Ethan walks in and leans against my desk.

"You leave Friday morning, right?"

I nod.

"I'm going with Tricia to that business reception at the Burgesses on Thursday night. Want to double? I can set you up with Bronwyn. She's been asking about you."

"No."

"Are you not going at all?"

"I might go." I lean against the desk next to my brother. "I'm just kind of sick of dating people in our social circles. They're all..." I try to think about how to explain. "Like the people we went to school with when we moved my senior year, you know?"

"I think the words you're looking for are 'pretentious snobs.'"

"Actually, I'm kind of sick of dating people outside our social circles, too. I'll date a woman who seems great, and then suddenly everything will change, and I know she's Googled and found our family."

"It's like you can no longer tell if they like you for you, or if they like you for your income or status or job."

"Exactly."

"I get it," Ethan says. "So what are you going to do? Just not date anymore? Because bro, you're twenty-nine. Mom's only going to get on your back more and more about giving her grandkids."

"I know." I twist to look back at the pile of papers I haven't organized yet, trying to decide if I'm ready to make this decision. Because once I tell Ethan, I have to be ready. I take a breath. "You know Roman Powell, right?"

"Yeah. The CEO of LivenUP, right? I've met him a few times."

"A few weeks ago, we had lunch to catch up. He said that his company is coming out with a dating app, and they're doing a soft launch just in this area so they can see if there are any bugs before they release it nationwide. He asked me if I'd help him by trying it out, and I told him yes. The app opens for us today."

"A dating app? Really?"

I shrug. "It might be a way to meet someone who doesn't know me. Everyone's bios only have first names, so they can't exactly Google me."

Ethan nods slowly. "True...so that might work. When are you going to do it?"

I walk around to the other side of my desk and start arranging my papers. "I was thinking of creating a profile tonight."

"Tonight?" Ethan stands up from my desk and turns to face me. "Dude, in two days, you are leaving the country for three weeks. Do you really think now is the best time?"

A smile spreads across my face. "It's exactly the best time. Hopefully, I'll find a few women who are interesting. We won't be able to meet in person because I'm out of town, so we'll get plenty of chances to talk and get to know each other before they find out who I am."

"Huh. Sometimes I don't give you nearly enough credit for being brilliant."

I laugh. "So does this mean you want to try it with me?"

"Nope." Ethan shakes his head. "I like dating pretentious snobs and gold diggers. I figure it'll keep Mom from coming to me for grandkids for a little longer. I mean, I am the younger twin, and I'm nearly three years younger than you, but it doesn't hurt to have redundancies in place."

"You keep your redundancies," I say as I file the papers and turn off my laptop. "I'm going to find someone I want to go on more than one date with."

"Just promise me one thing," Ethan says as we walk out of the room.

I turn off the light and pull the door closed behind me. "What's that?"

"Don't...overthink it. Just have fun. Don't make any charts or plan things out in detail."

I'm not going to promise my brother anything, but I sure will try.

CHAPTER 3
Timini

MY MORNING MIGHT NOT HAVE BEEN optimal, but at least it waited to start raining until I was on my drive home. And something about the drive home makes the solution for the Cheshire cat costume I need to make suddenly pop into my head. By the time I get home, my mind is flooded with ideas that need to be sketched, planned, and created.

My roommate, Peyton, is a personal chef and often cooks for her clients in the kitchen at the other end of the dining room from where I work. Peyton is at the home of a client today, though, so I have the entire room to myself.

The more I work, the more the project comes together. I start with sketching, but before I have even sketched out the full thing, I'm sketching close-ups of different parts and scribbling notes into the margins. I never manage to get a project fully sketched before it calls me to start working with paper and fabric on a dress form.

For the more difficult parts, I start with cheap muslin before using the actual fabric, and for some parts, I just throw caution to the wind and start with the fabric for the finished product.

As I work, more and more details come to mind to make it even more fabulous.

I hear the front door open and voices chatting. Then, Bex and Roman walk into the kitchen and Roman says, "Cool costume. Is this for *Alice in Wonderland*?"

I look at him in confusion. "Why are you home so early?"

"It's after six."

What? It can't be. I glance at the clock on the wall. Just in case I'm inclined to not believe it, my stomach growls loudly just to prove that so much time has passed since I ate that banana. I stand and stretch my muscles that have been sitting, crouching, and standing in way too many places in this room for way too long.

"Remember that dating app you suggested my company make?" Roman says.

I look over at him. "It's finished?"

Roman nods, looking like a proud parent. "It went live for beta testers in this area today. Once we get any kinks worked out that we find by having real people use it, we'll release it nationally. Are you willing to be one of our testers?"

I like to date, but just like my mom and my sister, I'm usually better off when I'm not dating anyone. So even though I like it, I don't always take the time to do it. And when I do, I am terrible at it. Ridiculously terrible.

Actually, I'm really good at finding guys who are pretty—on the outside. It's the pretty on-the-inside guys that I am terrible at finding. There must be some kind of look about a guy that I'm drawn to that just also happens to make for a not-great dating experience. The guys always tend to be not bright, not nice, or not a good fit.

Which was why I'd suggested to Roman that his company make a dating app that doesn't show people's pictures. That way, people like me won't make bad choices based on what their options look like—they would get to know them first.

It sounded like a great idea at the time. Obviously, it had to Roman, too, or he wouldn't have had his company invest months into developing and testing the app. As perfect as it is in concept, now that it's actually here, I am a little afraid that I'll mess things up completely if I don't have anything to go on when choosing guys.

"So, what do you say?" Bex asks. "Roman was showing it to me—it has some pretty cool features."

"I don't know. I'm not sure I want to date right now." Life is going pretty good lately. Well, okay, maybe not good, *exactly*. But it's going well enough. Do I want to mess it up by dating?

Peyton and Addison must have gotten home from clients' houses, because they both walk into the kitchen, laughing about the awkwardness of using the restroom at a client's home and realizing the toilet paper is out.

Bex turns to them. "I need your help talking Timini into using Roman's dating app."

"You don't want to use it?" Peyton asks. "But you were the one who suggested the app in the first place."

"I know. It's just…" How can I even explain? They've all found guys who are perfect for them. And with each of my room-mate couples, they are better together than they are separate. But that isn't the way it is for me. Once upon a time, Bex was in my corner about this. Now, I'm the only one in an inn full of love who is walking around loveless and not unhappy about it.

"I've always been bad at choosing who to date. I thought that not seeing their pictures might make it better, but who says that's actually what my problem is? What if I'm just bad at interpreting the facts I have, and I'll be even worse at it when there's less information to go on?"

"I think we did a good job of giving you more to go on," Roman says. "Can I show it to you and then you decide?"

Of course, I am going to say yes to that. Roman took my suggestion to create the app, after all. I am excited to see what it's all about, even if I never use it. I unlock my phone and hand it to Roman. His finger flies over it for a moment, and then he hands it back to me, the icon with two text bubbles—each with a heart—showing on my screen. I tap on it, and then put in my name.

"Why is it asking to take my picture? I thought this was a picture-free dating app."

"That's so no one will hack your account," Roman says. "It'll compare it to your face each time you log in. It'll ask for your driver's license, too. We want to make sure we keep all hackers, catfishers, and creepers away. The guys you'll see in the app will only be verified accounts."

"Nice." I snap a picture of myself, then glance at the table currently covered in fabric scraps where I'm fairly certain I sat down my purse earlier. I go over and start digging through it, but it isn't there. Halfway through checking under all the fabric detritus at half of the other round tables, I remember that I left it on a half-height bookshelf I use for folded fabric.

After putting in all the required information to get an account, it brings me to a screen to create my profile. Then I look at Roman. "It's all yours. Sell me on it."

"Okay," Roman says, and it is clear by the way his face lights up that he is proud of this app. "Your profile has four parts: your bio, your personality traits, personality traits you're looking for, and how serious a relationship you want."

I nod. That sounds like good info.

"The bio is pretty standard. This is the relationship scale. You can slide it all the way to the left if you are just looking for friendship or all the way to the right if you're looking for marriage. Or anywhere in between. That way, you can find someone who is looking for the same thing in a relationship that you are."

That's good. If I decide to do this, I can just choose an option that shows I don't want anything too serious.

"For personality traits, you can just tap on the buttons on the screen that fit you. Then you tap the ones you're looking for in a match. Later, when you are flipping through the guys in the app to find potential matches, little icons will show at the top if they match what you're looking for."

Okay, that is actually pretty cool. Maybe with that, I can make better choices on whom to even start chatting with.

"There are a lot of safety features built-in. Other people on the app will only ever see your first name, and they won't have any of your contact information. So if you only communicate through the app and then decide you aren't really a good match with someone, you can un-match them and they won't have any way to contact you.

"And if you do like them and decide you want to meet in person but are a little nervous about that, just click right there on the 'Track My Date' button. It'll turn on GPS tracking and let you put in the number of a friend. If you go somewhere unplanned or if you are out longer than expected, it'll notify the friend to check on you. If they can't get in touch with you, they'll have a link they can press that will notify the police and give them your date's contact info. It'll keep you and your date safe, even if you don't have each other's contact information."

I hadn't realized that was an obstacle to my wanting to use the app. Maybe this app *is* just what I need to find someone. It doesn't mean I'm not still hesitant, though. I look into the faces of my roommates. "I don't know. Do I even want to date someone right now?"

Addison shrugs. "You're always saying that you can't get

serious with a guy because you always seem to choose those who aren't your type on the inside. Maybe this will help you to find someone more serious."

"But do I want to find someone more serious?" Sometimes I like living in a fantasy world and totally do want what my roommates have. Other times, I am a realist and don't want to even try. When I was growing up, my sister and I learned to dread hearing our mom say the words, "Things are getting serious with the man I'm dating," because it never turned out well.

"You don't have to find someone to be in a serious relationship with," Bex says. "How about just finding someone for group date nights?"

"Ooh. That sounds good. I like group dates." It doesn't have to go beyond that at all. No long-term relationship needed. "Okay, but if I do this" —I meet each of my roommates' eyes— "you have to promise not to push things between me and anyone I date to be more serious. Even though you're all head-over-heels in love and want the same for me. I'm just looking for someone for date nights with you all. Deal?"

Peyton squeals and gives me a hug. "I promise. We all do. Right?"

They all nod. They seem like they'd agree with anything to get me to try the app, so I add, "And I should get crème brûlée since I'm the only one who has stuck to our 'No falling in love' pact."

Bex laughs loudly. "Girl, you've earned it."

I sit at the dining table and they all gather around to help me make my dating profile, and I bring up the first thing. "Ugh. The bio." That's always the hardest part. "What kinds of things should I even put on this?"

"Say that you're a burst of energy in a little tiny package."

Bex makes her hands into fists and then opens them wide, fingers splayed. "Like a firecracker."

"Or an energy drink," Addison says.

Peyton sits down next to me. "Say that you're beautiful and sassy and will never get mad at him for being late."

I laugh. "Only if he never got mad at me for the same."

"I know," Addison says. "Put that you are spilling over with talent and creativity."

"Oh," Peyton says, sitting up straighter. "Maybe you could have quotes from us. You know, like some guys put *'Such a sweet boy'—my grandma* in theirs. We could tout all your good qualities."

I shake my head. I do not like where this is going at all.

"Guys don't want to read a list of everything awesome about a woman," Roman says. "They want to discover that as they get to know you. On a dating profile, they just want you to be real. Genuine. Someone they feel they could relate to."

"Thank you," I say. It's helpful to get some advice from my target audience. I tap my finger against my lips. What is most real and genuine about me? "Hmm. Okay, so how do I say that I'm a hot mess without actually using those words? Authenticity is one thing. Scaring them away is another."

Roman just chuckles and shakes his head.

"Well," Bex says, "you focus on the thing that needs the most immediate attention. Maybe something with that."

"True. *That* I am good at. Okay." I type part of it into my phone.

"Don't forget to put what your job is," Addison says. "I think that tells a lot about a person in just a few words."

I nod and type that in.

"Hobbies, too," Addison says.

Hobbies... Do I have hobbies? Creating wearable masterpieces has been my hobby practically my whole life, and then it became my career. I don't think I can still count it as a hobby, even though it still feels like it. "Do impromptu dance parties count as a hobby? Because I'm a fan. And I really don't want to say something like 'I collect buttons,' or 'When most people people-watch, I outfit-watch,' because then he'll think I'll be judging his."

"Which you totally will," Bex says, "since you notice what people are wearing more than most."

I point a finger at Bex. "But I don't judge. I just study them, because they tell so much about the person."

"What about your love of high heels?" Peyton asks. "Then it gets the fashion thing in there without making it sound like you'll be judgy."

"Oh, good one." I type more into the app. "Okay, tell me how this sounds. 'Costume designer by day, cookie connoisseur by night. Hater of to-do lists. Skilled at putting out the nearest fire. Lover of high heels and the number one.'"

"That's really good," Addison says. "Now add a part about what you're looking for in a guy."

"But I don't know what I'm looking for in a guy. Besides 'pretty on the inside.' But I don't think I can put that."

Bex shakes her head. "Girl, you need to spend some time figuring that out. You can't find what you want if you don't know what you're looking for."

Yeah, I probably should. Maybe that is why my dating life has never gone anywhere. "No, do you know what? I've got this." I read it out loud as I type it in. "Looking for a guy who doesn't judge a girl by her inability to cook food that shouldn't be blackened, can reach objects on high shelves, and can handle going on group dates with my roommates who are all ridiculously in love."

"I love it!" Peyton says. "Now just add a call to action."

When my eyebrows draw together, Peyton explains. "If you

give them something to chat with you about, they'll be more likely to start up a conversation."

"Ahh. Gotcha." Peyton did seem to find a lot of dates very quickly when she was trying to fit fifteen dates into a single week, so she knows what she's talking about. I bite my lip as I type things in, backspace, try again, delete it all, try again, and then fix the errors.

"Like this? 'Need a taco recommendation? As a starving artist, I can suggest the tastiest and most inexpensive tacos in Portland and all surrounding cities. Or, tell me your favorite place to get a taco, and I'll rate it like I'm a food critic.'"

"Yes!" Peyton says, clapping.

"Okay, now I pick twelve of my traits." Luckily, the list seems to have mostly positive traits so I don't have to feel guilty about not choosing the negative ones I have but would rather not mention. I scroll through quickly, tapping any that sound like me. Active, adventurous, curious, daring, determined, empathetic, flexible, free-thinking, imaginative, observant, and playful. I count, and when I get to eleven, I tap on sentimental for the twelfth.

"And five traits I would like in a man. That list is long! How do I choose?"

"Well," Addison says, "there will probably be some traits you'll want in a man that matches yours. But the best kind of partnerships are ones where you balance each other's strengths and weaknesses. So pick some that would balance you."

"Okay..." I scan the list. "Then I definitely need to add Clean, Focused, and Organized, since I am none of those. Hmm. And I think I'm going to choose Adventurous and Flexible or I don't think things would work out so well with us."

Which leaves me with one thing: the sliding scale of how serious I want to be. I move the little indicator from left to right along the options, reading each one.

Seeking friends
Down for coffee
Keeping it casual
Looking for romance
Seeking something serious
Ready for a ring

I select *Keeping it casual*. Once I tap *Submit*, a message comes up on the screen that reads, *Success! Your profile will be approved within the next twenty-four hours, then get ready to start matching!*

I look up at Roman. "I have to wait twenty-four hours to actually use this?"

He shrugs. "It's the price of having verified accounts."

When I decide to do something, I want to do it now. None of this waiting-for-twenty-four-hours business. I need to find something else to do for the next twenty-four hours to get my mind off it, or I'm going to go crazy.

CHAPTER 4

Jackson

I'VE JUST PARKED in my reserved spot in the parking garage for my building and am heading to the lobby when my little sister, Emma, calls.

"Are you home?"

"In the building."

"Great. I'm coming over to help you with your dating profile."

"Wait!" I head toward the mailboxes, where several other residents are picking up theirs, too. "Don't come. I'm having second thoughts."

"Not allowed. You already made this decision."

"Is now really the time, though? I'm leaving in a day and a half, and I'm going to be gone for three weeks." Sure, I just told Ethan that leaving for three weeks makes it the perfect time. And I still believe that—if I'm going to do it at all. But it feels like a good stalling tactic as far as Emma is concerned.

"That's not the reason you're stalling."

I curse under my breath. Emma and Ethan have the whole *I'm your twin so I can read your mind* thing going on. But I swear that Emma can use it on everyone, not just Ethan. Or at least everyone in our family. It makes it hard to do things like lie about the true reason I'm getting cold feet in regards to a dating app.

I put my key into my box, open it, and pull out the half a dozen envelopes inside. "It sounded like a good idea when I was talking with Roman about it. I was even on board earlier today. But, I don't know. Now I'm not so sure."

"Why." It is not a question—it is a demand. For most of my life, I have fought Emma on her demands. She is the youngest and I am the oldest, so if anyone is the boss of anyone, she isn't the boss of me. But she is relentless on some things, and it sounds like this is one of them. It is always easier and faster to give in. Sometimes easier and faster wins, and sometimes it doesn't. Today, I need to get to my apartment and get some last-minute things done before my trip.

I heave out a long breath and head toward the cleaners at the back of the lobby so I can pick up my shirts. "Because it feels like admitting defeat."

"Explain."

"Dating apps are for people who can't get dates on their own." I'm not about to admit that not being able to get dates on my own means I have lost the ability. I'm kind of worried that maybe I have, but I'm nowhere close to being ready to full-on admit it.

"No," Emma says, dragging out the word, "they're for people who aren't meeting people to date in their normal routines. You aren't meeting the types of people you want to date doing what you're doing, so you need to do something different."

"Maybe." The types of people I do meet are very much not the type I want to be in a relationship with. "But it's also a lot of work setting everything up, chatting with a ton of people to narrow it down to who I should date, and going on lots of dates to find someone with relationship potential."

"And you're afraid that if you fail using a method of finding dates that you already see as second-class, it'll make you feel like a loser."

"What? No, I'm not afraid."

"Then do it."

She is goading me. Earlier, it was worth it to give in to her need to be the boss. Now it isn't. "Not going to happen."

"You'd rather die alone, after a life spent in unfulfilling relationships."

Of course, I wouldn't. "Sounds good. Sign me up for the unfulfilling life."

"You are impossible."

"Hang on." I lower the phone and hand my ticket to the clerk behind the counter, an older man who runs the kiosk with his wife. As the man shuffles off to find my shirts, I turn to lean against the counter. I am just lifting the phone back to my ear when a mom holding the hand of a little boy, probably about three years old, walks toward the kiosk.

When they are within a dozen feet, the little boy holds his arm out, his finger pointing at me. "Look, Momma!"

The boy's mom pushes his hand down and says, "Sweetie, we don't point at people, remember?"

The little boy puts his arm out again, but this time, his hand is in a fist. "Momma, look. See the direction that my arm is pointing? Is that my daddy?"

The woman's face immediately goes red. She pushes her son's arm down again, opens her mouth like she is going to say something to her son, but then gives up and just looks at me. She puts her fingers on her forehead, possibly because she is trying to see how hot her face has gotten in a span of five seconds, or possibly because she is trying to hide her face. "I'm so sorry. It's just your suit. His dad wears one to work, so he was really just asking if you and his dad work at the same place. You know—if you're the same as his dad."

I can't keep the smile off my face. "It's fine."

She glances back at her son, and then puts her hand back on one side of her face, covering one cheek and eye as she looks back at me. "I swear he knows who his dad is but he still says that to everyone. And, um" —she glances toward the elevators — "we're just going to go now. Bye."

I'm still grinning as I put the phone back to my ear. "I'm ordering Thai food. Be here in twenty minutes if you want to eat while it's warm."

"You're going to do the dating app?" Emma's excitement is so loud that I probably didn't even need to lift the phone to my ear.

"I am." I want my own little kid who is going to embarrass me in public, and the only way I'm going to get that is if I meet someone worth marrying. And this app sounds like a possible way to do that.

"Then I'm going to run—okay, jog—and be there in ten."

Fifteen minutes later, I'm sitting on the couch in my apartment, staring at my phone. So far, all I've managed to do after ordering the food is enter my name and take a picture of myself and my driver's license. The rest is intimidating.

My front door opens and my sister walks in. "Okay, I know I'm later than I said, but it had started to rain, and running while holding an umbrella is weird. But I did meet the delivery guy in the lobby with the food. He said you already paid but had me sign your credit card receipt. I decided that you're feeling generous today, so I tipped him fifty bucks for you."

I shake my head, chuckling. I have no doubt she did.

Once we get out the food and I have a few bites of yellow

curry and rice in me, I pick up the phone again, as if inspiration has struck while it has been sitting on my coffee table.

It hasn't. The bio is still as blank as before.

Emma takes a big bite of stir-fried rice noodles. Before she even finishes chewing, she says, "You know…" She swallows. "You don't have to tell your life story. You just have to give a little something that will make someone want to know more."

No pressure. Piece of cake.

She sets her box of Pad Thai on the coffee table. "You don't want to attract the same type of women that we see at all the functions we go to, right? So let's start with what you don't want women on the app to know."

That part is easy. "My last name, who I work for, probably my job title."

She nods. "That's easy enough. The app won't even show your last name. Okay, so what's something you do want them to know?"

That's the hard part. Everything I think of sounds too dumb to utter, let alone type.

After a moment of me staring at the screen again, Emma says, "Okay, type this: *The first thing people notice about me:* and then press enter."

I do. I wait for her to tell me what to type next, but by her exasperated huff, I guess I'm supposed to come up with that. Okay, so something about my looks. Women I've dated in the past have told me a few things they liked about my looks, but I'm pretty sure they were just telling me what they thought I wanted to hear. Nothing about them, though, was genuine, so I doubt any of those things were, either. So I try to think of what I've heard from complete strangers. "I've been told I have nice ears."

She raises an eyebrow. I figure it might be enough for her to take pity on me and tell me what to put. But then she just shrugs. "You know what? Put it."

"For real?"

"Sure. It's different. A little intriguing. Besides, I know I judge a guy based on how cute his ears are."

I grab a couch cushion and toss it at her.

She picks up her noodles again. "Now write *Three things I can't live without,* and then come up with three things."

Okay, things. This shouldn't be too hard. I run through a typical day in my mind, thinking about what things are important to me and weeding through anything that hints at my family having money or me having a very well-paying job.

Things like the view from my apartment (my day definitely goes better when I take the time to admire and appreciate it before heading to work).

Or my favorite restaurant (which serves a Japanese Wagyu ribeye that makes me think that is exactly the food they are going to be serving in heaven, but which also costs roughly the same amount as a month of my entire food budget in college).

Or my office chair that is so perfect I could sit in it all day long if needed, and my back wouldn't even hint at being upset about it. (Yeah, that one cost more than the car I drove all through college.)

Or anything about my car.

I do include in my bio one extravagance, though. *The cleaner who irons my shirts so I don't have to.* I ironed my own dress shirts from the time my mom started making me iron my church shirt when I was eight until the end of my first year working at my current position at Oliver Innovations, and I've always hated it. The moment I was making enough to have someone else do it, I celebrated.

Then I type *The day planner in my phone.* Emma is waiting patiently, but her eyes never leave me as she eats bite after bite, so I force myself to think just so she will eventually stop star-ing. I add *Cold cereal and morning cartoons*. I don't have to put the reason. People who see it will probably assume I'm a kid at heart, or nostalgic, or that I'm lazy. I don't care if they think any of those things. I haven't ever told anyone the real reason, but it is definitely on my personal *Things I can't live without* list.

The moment I finish, she says, "Okay, now put *What I love the most.*"

"Easy. Family." As Emma throws her hands over her heart in an exaggerated motion of being touched, I say as I pretend to type, "Well, not all of them equally," and she throws the pillow right back at me.

"Okay, now put…" She looks up, thinking. "I don't know. Something like *Extras* or *More about me.*" When I do, she says, "Now list stuff like your job. I mean, obviously, you don't want to put 'I'm the VP of International Business.' Just give a clue. Say you work in business or that you travel a lot for work."

I nod and start typing.

"And say what you like to do in your spare time."

Honestly, I work in my spare time. If it's not at work, it's at one of my family's charities. Whatever look I have on my face must tell Emma I'm going to struggle. "Just say what you most like to do when you go out with friends or go on dates. It'll help women know what kinds of dates you'll likely want to go on."

Okay, that makes it a little easier.

"And you can say that you enjoy helping kids learn to read without mentioning our family's charities."

"True. Okay, I will."

"Now lighten it up a bit. Tell something random and incon-sequential."

There is no way I could have ever done this on my own. How does Emma even know what my bio needs? If I had done this myself, it would have been organized, thorough, and probably would have put anyone to sleep who made it all the way to the end. I add *I can shower in seven minutes flat.*

I look at Emma. She reads over my shoulder, nods, and then says, "Now just give them something that'll make an initial conversation with you easy. Give them something to talk to you about."

Nothing comes to mind. Emma breathes that exasperated breath she perfected years ago and says, "Write 'If you like movies, cheese, or traveling, we should chat. If you like all three, we should definitely meet in person at some point.'"

That is good. Once I type it in, I say, "Okay, now it wants me to pick twelve personality traits."

"Hand it over." Emma holds her hand out to me, palm up.

I pause, trying to decide if that's a good idea. She holds her hand out a little more insistently, so I put it in her palm.

"Just so you know, I'm choosing your twelve *and* the five for her."

When she hands it back, I glance through the list she's chosen. *Active, adventurous, appreciative, ambitious, clean, confident, decisive, disciplined, focused, innovative, leader, organized.* All right. That isn't too bad. At least she didn't put embarrassing things on the list like I thought she was going to.

"Obviously," she says as I look at the list, "'confident' is based on everything except writing your own bio for a dating app."

"Obviously. Now defend your choices for what I'm looking for in a woman." I actually think that it's a pretty great list, too, but I have to give my sister a hard time.

"Okay, adventurous and active, because you'll want to do things together that you both enjoy. Playful, because you need to get out of your shell and your routine more often. Flexible, because she'd need to be to balance your rigidity." She shoots me a look. "And focused, because it fits with who you are. Down-to-earth wasn't one of them, so you'll just have to keep an eye out for that one on your own. Now don't question my choices—just move onto the seriousness slider."

I read through the list. Honestly, I want to choose *Ready for a ring*, but I don't want to scare anyone. So instead, I choose *Seeking something serious*.

"Should I press Submit?"

"Yes!" she shouts. "Submit!" Like she's afraid if I don't press it in the next one-point-two seconds, I will delete the app instead. Her excitement makes me stop for a moment just to question if that might be the best option.

Instead of letting my mind go in that direction, though, I think of the little kid downstairs and how much I want my own someday. I tap *Submit* with conviction. When the message comes up saying that my profile will be approved within twenty-four hours, I am relieved. I don't want Emma looking over my shoulder as I scroll through potential matches.

CHAPTER 5
Timini

I AM WORKING on designing a Revolutionary War-era costume that comes to me in the shower. It isn't even for a job—it's just an idea that is too amazing not to start right now. I am a little (okay, a lot) focused on it when my phone starts blaring my ringtone.

"Timini!" Peyton says from behind the kitchen island where she is making something that smells divine. "That about gave me a heart attack!"

"Sorry!" I have to have it loud, though, if I want any chance of finding it when it rings. The song I use as my ringtone keeps playing at full volume as I go from table to table to find the one that holds the phone, then search under each layer to find it.

"Hello?" I say as I answer, out of breath from my frantic search and worry that I haven't caught it in time.

"Timini Jensen?"

"This is her."

"Hello, this is Aftyn Flint."

My mind is so deep in what I am working on that it takes me about a second and a half to recognize the name as the woman I interviewed with yesterday. Then I listen in disbelief and shock as Ms. Flint tells me that they were so impressed with my work that they decided they want to use me for two separate projects, and she gives a little information about what the scope of each will be.

When she says she'd like me to come in to discuss everything further and to make it official, I can barely find my voice enough to agree to the date and time.

I hang up the phone and drop into a chair at the dining table, stunned.

"Is this good news or bad news?" Peyton asks.

"The best," I say as what has just happened starts to sink in. "I get to design costumes for *An American in Paris*, so lots of period clothing, and another director isn't happy with the Prince Charming costume their costumer made for *Cinderella*, so they want me to do that, too. Costumes for two shows, and both are at Hamilton Hall! I know that one of them is in the Williams Theater. I don't know about the other. *Hamilton Hall!*"

Peyton doesn't know a ton about my industry, but she gets excited for me anyway and comes around the kitchen counter to hug me and squeal and congratulate me.

I want my own design shop. And not just someday, like when I'm fifty, but soon. Like by the time I turn thirty. That is only two years away, and I have felt like the path I need to take to reach my goal is by first designing for a show at Hamilton Hall. I am still in shock that they said yes. Especially after how disastrously my interview went.

After the initial shock lessens a bit, I start thinking about the implications of all of it. It's going to be so much work. What if they want to start right away? They probably do. And I still have so many other jobs waiting in line. What have I been thinking, working all day on a project that isn't for a client? It hasn't been the nearest fire to put out at all.

"Oh my goodness," I say in a new type of daze brought on by realizing all this entails. "I'm going to have to hire an assistant."

Peyton's eyebrows shoot up as she whisks something cooking in a pot. "It's that big of a job? That's exciting!"

It is. I know I can't work out of the dining room of the inn forever, and this isn't exactly going to be what I need to open my own shop, but it is a very big stride toward my goal. I need to start planning.

I pick up my phone to type in some notes about all the things that are coming at my brain, rapid-fire, but stop when I see all of the notifications. How long has it been since I last looked at my phone?

I scroll down the long list. Some are just from social media. Quite a few are texts. Several are from stores telling me about a sale or that I can get $2 off a lunch entree. Some calendar items. Oh. A reminder to pay my credit card bill. I cannot forget that again. Ooh! And a notification from Chat Match.

"My profile has been approved!" I say and go right into it. Peyton takes the pot off the stove and hurries around the island to join me at the table. "Okay, it says to swipe up to read more about each person. I double-tap if I like them and swipe down if I want to dump them out of my list of potential matches. All right. Let's do this."

I click *Okay* on the message, and the first profile pops up. I have used dating apps before, and I am so used to seeing a picture of the guy as the first thing that this feels weird. A row of five icons is at the top, and each one represents the five personality traits I am hoping for in a match. For any where he also lists that he has those personality traits, they light up green. Then right below that is the guy's bio, and below that is how serious a relationship he is looking for. I can even see a full list of his personality traits at the bottom.

Still, though, it doesn't feel like enough. I usually look at the full package before making any decisions and then focus on his face to see if he looks kind and easygoing. Not having that makes me feel like I'm trying to shower and get ready for the day with my eyes closed.

"That guy has three of your things," Peyton says, then reads the man's bio out loud. "'Love dogs? Me, too. We just might be soul mates. Message me to discuss.'"

"That's it? That's the entire bio?" I scroll down, but it really is it. The guy doesn't even choose all twelve of his personality traits. This is impossible. I swipe down.

Brevity isn't a problem for the next guy, though. It looks like a bullet-pointed resume of his skills, accomplishments, and talents. Curious about how long it is, I scroll all the way down. Apparently, the app has a limit on the size of the bio, because it cuts off mid-sentence. I swipe down again.

Then I read the next one out loud. "'Reasons you should date me: One, I can quote at least one line from pretty much any movie ever. Two, I don't have a criminal record. Three, I can make minute rice in fifty-eight seconds.'" I laugh and double-tap on his.

"Really?" Peyton says. "Why?"

I shrug. "He made me laugh."

One of the first things the next guy talks about is his Bentley. I can't swipe down fast enough.

"Okay, why did you swipe down on that one?"

"He was bragging about being rich. Rich guys are jerks."

"All of them? Or just the ones who brag about it?"

"All of them. Maybe I should've put that in my bio. 'If you're rich, save us both some heartache and just swipe down on me immediately.'"

Peyton is quiet for several moments as I go through each

profile as they come up. I can feel her eyes on me, though. Finally, Peyton says, "Who hurt you?"

The question is so earnest and blunt that, for some reason, it makes me laugh. "Well, I can tell you that the guy I swiped down on won't!"

Peyton is still looking at me with those sweet, caring eyes, though, so I answer her question for real. "My first real boyfriend, Jack. I knew the Jack he was before his family had money and the Jack he was after, and it was a night-and-day difference. After his family's business took off, he did everything he could to make me feel inferior about my own family's humble situation. Plus," I shrug, "a couple of my mom's boyfriends when I was growing up. I mean, they were all jerks, really, but the two with money were the biggest jerks of all."

Peyton nods like she understands, so I go through a couple dozen more profiles. Some are awful. Some are good. Some are boring. But at least I get used to the format after a while. In fact, I am starting to get a lot more out of each of the men's bios than I have with any other dating app. Maybe it isn't as hard to go without a picture as I thought.

"Ooh, here's one," I say, seeing a guy who has four of the five icons in green at the top. "'The first thing people notice about me: My nice ears.' Weird, but I like it. 'Four things I can't live without: The cleaner who irons my shirts so I don't have to, the day planner in my phone, my morning routine, and cold cereal with cartoons.' Organized and fun. That's good. 'What I love the most: My family (parents, two sisters, and a brother).'"

"Aww, that's sweet!" Peyton says.

I nod. "'More about me: I'm in international business, love helping kids learn to read, and I can shower in seven minutes flat. If you like movies, cheese, or traveling, we should chat. If you like all three, we should definitely meet in person at some point.'" I immediately double-tap on the guy and cross my fingers that he will double-tap on me so we can start chatting. I really want to ask about those ears. Oh! It is even 4:11. So that is a great sign.

As I scroll through more profiles, Peyton goes back around to the stove and starts cooking something else. "So, how are you going to find an assistant? Do you already have someone in mind?"

"I can't believe I got so distracted I forgot about that!" I close out of the app and go into my notes app—the thing I opened my phone for in the first place. I don't have any idea who to hire. All I know is that it is going to take a lot of focus to pull everything off, and if I don't start making lists, then I'll likely get distracted again and forget half of the vitally important things.

So, even though a Chat Match notification pops up on my screen, I clear it off without even looking to see what it is.

CHAPTER 6

Jackson

I GET the notification that my Chat Match profile is live during one of the final planning meetings for my trip to Delhi, and my phone has been burning a hole in my pocket ever since. The meeting lasts over two hours, and I am barely making it back to my office for the first time since lunch.

I glance at the clock on my computer screen as I sit down. 4:13, so I have seventeen minutes until my last meeting of the day. Seventeen minutes to go through some profiles and hopefully find someone to at least chat with, maybe date, and preferably be in a long-term relationship with. Like until-death-do-you-part kind of long.

But, really, I'll settle for someone to chat with while I'm halfway around the world. As I read the screen explaining how to go through the profiles, I amend my lower goal to settling for someone I double-tap on to double-tap on me as well.

I double-tap on a few that make me smile and a few that sound like I would get along with them. I roll my eyes at a few that are over-the-top or so generic that they could've been anyone. And I scratch my head at a few really short bios that I guess might be a quote from a TV show or a song or something that I don't get.

Then I come across one that catches my attention. *Hater of to-do lists.* Why do I find that so attractive? I love them, so being attracted to a self-proclaimed hater of them surprises me. She has to be creative if she is a costume designer. I chuckle at her comment about burning everything she cooks.

It sounds like she is short, which for some reason reminds me of my high school girlfriend, Minnie. I really liked her, and the nostalgic feelings spill over to this woman's profile. Plus, this woman loves tacos. That is definitely a good sign. And the number one, apparently.

I find myself cradling the phone as I scour her profile. The personality traits icons at the top are mostly lit up green. That is also a good sign. The relationship meter isn't over as far as mine is, but she is at least open to casual dating.

I scroll down like I will be able to find more information about her if I just try scrolling past the end, but, of course, there is nothing else.

"Knock, knock. Are you ready for the team meeting? They're all waiting for us to share what we discussed yesterday."

The sound of Ramesh's voice startles me out of a focus on this other world that apparently has been so deep I've forgotten where I am. As my attention jerks up to Ramesh, I fumble my phone. It tumbles and I grab for it, managing to catch it before it clatters to the floor.

But just as I do, my thumb runs across my screen, swiping down on the profile of the woman that I've found so intriguing, and it disappears.

I want to shout, "Nooooooo!" to the sky. But instead, I look at Ramesh and force a smile. "Sorry, yeah. Um, conference room, right?" I glance at the clock. Am I really already late?

"Yeah. But hey, I understand that you've probably got a lot on your mind before you leave tomorrow. If you'd rather cancel…"

"No," I say, placing my phone to the side like it isn't the source of every thought on my mind at the moment. "The meeting's fine. We've got last-minute stuff we need to discuss. Can you give me five minutes and I'll be in?"

Ramesh nods and leaves, and I grab my phone again, trying to see if there is some way to get the woman's profile to come back. But I can't find anything.

And it's not like I can Google to see if there is a way—it is a brand-new app that isn't even available outside the test group in the Portland area.

But Roman has let me know that he wants me to tell him if I find any issues with the app. And this is definitely an issue. An issue that is going to sound really stupid when I tell him, but an issue nonetheless.

I call Roman and nearly hang up while it's ringing. He and I don't know each other super well—we have never socialized outside of business functions. And Roman has given me a way to submit issues I find to the developers, so I shouldn't be taking this issue directly to the CEO of the company. But before I fully decide to hang up, Roman answers. I say, "Please tell me there's a way to get back to a profile that I accidentally swiped down on."

Roman chuckles. "Got in the habit of swiping down and then noticed something promising in one just as you swiped down?"

"Nope. Noticed *lots* of promising things in one, but my co-worker startled me and I dropped the phone. The act of catching it swiped down."

Roman chuckles again. "There's some bad luck for you. The free version doesn't allow you to go back to previous profiles—

only the premium one does."

"Please tell me the premium one is available."

"It's still a little too glitchy for beta testers."

My heart sinks—until I hear the next words that come out of Roman's mouth.

"But if you're willing to test a product not ready for the public, I can give you access. You just have to let my developers know about any issues you find."

"No problem. Anything you need."

"I'll send you an access code right now. You'll find a place in the app settings to enter it." He pauses for a moment and then says, "That must be an amazing woman you found."

"I think she might be."

I put in the access code as I am hurrying down the hall toward my meeting. The moment it's in, I feel a release of tension. I will be able to find her again.

The moment I walk into my apartment after work, I pull my phone out and go into the Chat Match app. I hesitate a moment, though. What if I find her profile again but she never double-taps on me, so I never get to know more about her?

I'll just have to keep my fingers crossed.

The app now has left and right arrows at the bottom—I can scroll through profiles without double-tapping or swiping down. I press the back button. As much as her bio has been burned into my brain, I can't believe that I didn't pay as much attention to her name. It's something different. It starts with a T and has a lot of i's in it.

I find it within seconds. *Timini.* I like it. I double-tap quickly before anything else can go wrong. Immediately, a message pops up that reads, *You matched! Send a message?*

A grin spreads all the way across my face. She *did* double-tap on me. I tap the *Send message* button and immediately wish I had spent the drive home thinking about what to say to her instead of mentally going through my list of things to pack, trying to think of anything I've forgotten and planning exactly what time I will get each of my trip preparations done.

I decide to go for the obvious.

> Jackson: So you're a taco savant. I had Taco Sabroso for lunch. Any guess on how my afternoon went, based solely on that?

I don't want to stare at my phone, hoping she will respond soon, so I turn my sound on, volume up, set it on the counter, and walk away. I am leaving the country bright and early in the morning and I need to pack, after all.

I make it as far as my bedroom door when I hear the ding from a notification and run back to my phone.

> Timini: It depends. What kind did you get?

> Jackson: One carnitas and one al pastor.

> Timini: Then you walked away with a smile on your face and a bounce in your step. That little feeling of longing in the pit of your stomach that slowed you down about three o'clock was because you didn't also get a fish taco. The combination of all three at Taco Sabroso basically gives you superpowers.

> Jackson: So I take it you've had the combination before?

> Timini: Just once. I was able to leap over tall buildings in a single jump. But I'm not going to lie—trying to stick the landing while wearing heels wasn't pretty.

Jackson: I see now that eating all three takes advance planning.

Timini: I was there with my sister and two of her kids once when she ate all three. It really freaked them out when she turned invisible, so you definitely want to warn whoever you go with.

I find myself grinning through the conversation and just wanting it to continue.

Jackson: I see that you're a cookie connoisseur. Have you found any of those that also grant superpowers?

Timini: There's a restaurant on Belmont that has cookies with smoked almond, salted caramel, and chocolate chips. They make you good at math. I get one every time I have to pay my bills.

Jackson: That's handy. How long does the math skill last?

Timini: About as long as it takes to feel the sugar crash, so you've got to be ready to use it.

I message back and forth with Timini for hours, throwing my entire planned schedule out the window. The funny thing is, I'm not even sad about that. Even though normally, it would drive me nuts not to be keeping up with my schedule down to the minute. *Especially* on the night before such an important and long trip.

I love that she is so playful. That isn't a trait I have seen in a woman I've met in my own circles since college, probably. It is awakening a playful part of myself that has lain dormant for far too long.

At eleven p.m., I finally decide we need to say goodnight—I have to be at the airport at five a.m., and I got almost no packing done while we chatted.

It has been worth it, though. Even though Timini and I haven't talked about anything of substance yet. We've just had fun chatting. I have learned a few things about her, though. That she is five foot one inch (if she is currently "thinking really tall thoughts"), which is a full ten inches shorter than me. Unless, she points out, she is wearing heels. Then it is more like a six-inch difference.

I also learned that her favorite food is anything someone else cooked, which I could have guessed from her bio. When I pressed for something more specific, she mentioned Mexican food. Then Thai. Then Chinese. Then pizza. Then cheesecake. Then Italian. Eventually, she said she just really liked food, to which I replied that—surprise!—I really did too. So she said it was such a coincidence that we must be soul mates, and I laughed so hard that every neighbor of mine on this floor probably heard me.

By the end of our chat, I am dying to ask for her number, or her last name, or to follow her on social media, but I force the thought away. If I ask it of her, she will want the same from me, and that will ruin everything.

No. Now is the time to just enjoy communicating with someone I am really connecting to. I need a chance to really get to know her before introducing things like who my family is into the mix.

CHAPTER 7

Timini

I PUT a bag of popcorn in the microwave, push the popcorn button, and then look up at the cupboard above the microwave where we keep the big popcorn bowl. Sure, near the microwave makes sense for a popcorn bowl, but does it have to be up so high? I am currently barefoot and literally can't even reach the knob to open the door, let alone reach anything inside.

I turn to where my roommates are all chatting and snacking on the cheese and vegetable trays before we move into the family room to watch a movie. "Ian, can you help me?"

He comes around the island, opens the door, and gets out the bowl with no problem at all before handing it to me. "How can you handle being so short? Does it drive you nuts?"

"Hey," I say. "There are benefits to being short."

Addison just smiles, like she knows what's coming, but Ian looks like he doesn't believe that I am actually going to be able to come up with a list. So I start laying it out for him, ticking each one off on my fingers. "I always have all the legroom I need. I can wear high heels all I want. I get to be in the front of group pictures. I never hit my head on things. I can move through a crowd like no one's business. Short people have less of a risk of cancer."

"You're making that one up," Roman says.

I shake my head. "I'm not—look it up. We also live longer and get fewer blood clots. Oh, and I totally killed it at hide-and-seek when I was a kid."

"So you've always been short?" Ian asks. "You didn't hit five feet—"

"Five feet one inch," I correct.

"My apologies. You didn't hit five foot one in third grade and just decided to stop growing right then and there?"

I shake my head and grab a carrot stick. "I've been the shortest kid in every single school class I've been in. I hadn't even hit the five-foot mark when I started high school. In fact, I didn't even go by 'Timini' back then."

At everyone's confused faces, I explain. "Even though the last part of my name is said 'muh-nee,' it's spelled 'mini,' and, because I am short and kids are kids, that's what everyone started calling me. But by fourth grade, it was clear 'mini' wasn't going away anytime soon, so instead of fighting it, I embraced it and just became 'Minnie,' and spelled it M-I-N-N-I-E. It was my dad who chose my unusual name, and I'd been mad at the fact that I'd never even met him, so I had no problem changing it. I even got my mom and sister to call me that."

Well, I didn't exactly get my mom to call me "Minnie" as much as she called me "Mini Me." It annoyed me, but at least it was close to Minnie. Eventually, my mom dropped the "Me" part of it and just called me Minnie when I was an adult and finally caught up to her (also short) height. She never switched back to calling me Timini, though, once I did. Maybe because she was still mad at my dad, too.

"And then, I made my mom go to the school and have them

add the 'goes by' name to their rolls so that at the beginning of each new year, I wouldn't have to have the teacher call roll and say 'Timini' just for me to correct them and say, 'Actually, I go by Minnie.' It was the only name I went by until I got to college and decided it was time to take 'Timini' back." I stick the carrot in my mouth and take a bite.

"How did we not know this?" Bex asks. "Seriously, girl, you went by a different name for, what? Nine years?"

I shrug and take another bite. "I also had braces for four excruciatingly long years, and I've never told you that, either."

"True," Peyton says, "but your beautiful teeth told that story for you."

"It was a long time ago. I've been Timini again for ten years."

The smell of something burning hits my nose. How have I missed the microwave beeping? I run to it, throw the door wide, and open the top of the bag as I'm pulling it out so the heat can escape and quit trying to burn the beautiful popcorn inside. I dump it in the bowl to let it cool even more quickly.

"Well, at least it was only a little part that burnt instead of the whole bag," I say as I pick the blackened pieces out of the bowl.

"So," Roman says, "not to talk shop at a friend get-together or anything, but how is Chat Match going? Any issues or suggestions?"

I can actually feel my cheeks warm as I pick the last few blackened kernels out of the bowl. I never blush. "It's going well," I say to the bowl, just to give my cheeks a chance to return to normal.

"Have you met any good guys?" I can hear the grin in Peyton's voice.

Okay, I am probably in the clear with the cheeks now, so I turn around and put the bowl of popcorn next to the other snack foods. "I've been chatting with a handful of guys, actually."

"Oh yeah?" Addison asks. "And what did you think?"

"One guy was pretty chatty. I felt like he was super honest and authentic, which was nice. He even shared his feelings. He was an open book."

"All good stuff," Ian says. "Is it looking like it will go anywhere?"

I shake my head. "He is an open book, but the book just isn't very thick. It's more like a pamphlet."

Bex laughs loudly.

"There is one guy I matched with, so I sent him a message but he never responded."

"Well," Peyton says, "obviously he was so excited to hear from you that he fainted."

This time, I'm the one who laughs. "Yeah, I'm sure that's it. There was another guy yesterday who asked me to go on a date with him within five minutes of saying, 'Hi,' and I responded with, 'I'm excited to meet you in a busy, well-lit area.' Because we hadn't gotten to know each other well enough to *not* make that part clear. Things fizzled out with him pretty quickly."

"Any good ones you've been talking with?" Bex asks, and I swear she is doing it because she saw the blush and is trying to bring it back. She might just succeed.

"One." And there's the blush again that apparently that has only ever been absent in my life when we're not talking about Jackson. "His name is Jackson, and he's so much fun to talk to. We chatted for more than four hours last night."

"Four hours!" Peyton says.

I just smile. It was long enough that going all day without talking to him has actually been hard. I'm fairly certain that I can't miss someone I've only known for four hours, but I do a little bit. Oh, and look at that—it's seven-oh-one. It's about the tenth number one I have seen today, and I'd been thinking of Jackson when seeing each of them. That has to mean something.

Peyton cocks her ear toward the doorway, hearing a sound that I swear only her ears are tuned to hear. "Oh! Max is here!" She runs toward the front of the inn to greet him.

"And?" Bex says. "How much have you talked to him today?"

"Not at all." I try to not show how sad that makes me. "He hopped on a plane to Delhi early this morning, and it's a twenty-four-hour flight."

"Ouch," Max says as he and Peyton join us, hand-in-hand, looking like adorable little lovebirds. "Long flight."

It is long for me, too.

"Okay," Addison says, picking up the cheese tray, "let's get this party started!"

We all head out of the kitchen and into the lobby, walking under part of the paper chain that goes over the doorway and has one link representing each day until Peyton and Max get married—fifty-one left!—toward the family room.

Then, I hear the notification sound that only comes from Chat Match. I race back into the room, looking around at all the tables I've been moving between as I worked today. Where did I leave my phone? I knew Jackson couldn't message me, so I haven't been keeping track of it. Logic tells me that it isn't him now, either—he still has many hours to go before his plane lands—but I can't bring myself to ignore that notification.

I lift up so much fabric, and soon Bex and Peyton are helping me. Roman must've recognized the sound the notification made, because he just stands, leaning against the door frame, grinning. Probably because his company made the thing that is causing me to lose my mind.

I tell myself that it is probably just one of the other guys messaging. Which is totally fine. I am having fun chatting with them, too. Not as much fun as with Jackson, of course.

"Got it!" Bex shouts, holding it up in triumph.

I run to the phone and look at the screen. "Aww! It's from Jackson!" With as much as I've thought about him today, I shouldn't be surprised at how thrilled it makes me to see his name. It especially thrills me because I thought I wouldn't for many hours. I swipe to open it. Maybe he is on a layover, waiting.

> Jackson: I've got a riddle for you. What do you call a guy who has spent the day working 35,000 feet in the air, doing it all without in-flight WiFi, then breaks down and buys it at the end of the day just to send a message to a girl he met twenty-four hours ago and has never laid eyes on?

> Timini: I'd call him a smart man with very good timing.

> Jackson: Ooh. Tell me more about this "good timing" I have.

I make my way to the family room and hurry to claim the comfiest chair. It only fits one person, so it's not like anyone else is going to claim it, but still. It feels like a victory when I act like I have to race for it. I tuck my feet up under me on the chair, and then I respond to Jackson.

> Timini: We are having TV night with my 3 best friends and their 2 husbands and 1 fiancé.

> Jackson: Ahh. So I'm the virtual date so that you won't be a 7th wheel.

Jackson: Wait. You don't have a date there, do you? Am I crashing the date, making me… what? The 9th wheel? Does that metaphor even make sense after about the number five?

Timini: I don't have a date already. Want to be mine for the next little bit? Or is it too soon to move from chatting to dating? And semis have 18 wheels, so I'm pretty sure you can use the metaphor up to 19.

Jackson: I'd love to be your date for the evening.

Jackson: And if this feels too fast, we can just promise not to kiss at the end of the date. Heck, let's say no arm around the shoulder, no holding hands, nothing. Hands and lips to ourselves. Deal?

Timini: You drive a hard bargain, but I promise not to kiss you or try to hold your hand.

Jackson: I might be a little underdressed—I'm wearing worn jeans and a T-shirt. What are we doing for said date?

Timini: You're not underdressed. In fact, if you're on a twenty-four-hour flight, you're clearly overdressed. This is the kind of situation where you wear sweats. And it's "Unsolicited Advice Night" over here. It's where we watch the show "Flip My House, Not My Life," and shout out what we think they should do and not do. Have you seen it?

> Jackson: That's the show where they completely renovate a house while the owners are still living in it, right? I haven't seen it, but I've heard about it.

> Timini: That's the one. Oh, and we place "bragging rights" bets on whether or not the couple will still be married by the recap.

> Jackson: Ouch. The remodels are that rough?

> Timini: Yes. This is the show where you learn how to do home improvements, and also learn to NEVER do them if you value your relationship with the people in your home.

> Jackson: That should be their slogan, right there. Which episode are we watching?

I look up to find all six of my roommates—well, five plus one who will be a roommate soon enough—watching me. Like I'm the entertainment for the night.

"What? Did I miss something?"

Ian says, "Nah," at the same time Roman says, "We were just asking if you were ready to start," and Peyton says, "We were just enjoying watching you fall for a guy on the dating app."

"I'm not falling for him!" But if I think about it for two seconds, I know it's a lie. My stomach gets all fluttery with every message from him that comes in. "Okay, maybe I am a little. But he's out of the country for three weeks. And it's not like you can really tell if you're falling for someone before you see them in real life. He's just fun to chat with, and he's going to be my date for the evening. And it's not like he's the only guy I'm chatting with. What episode are we on?"

Okay, normally when I go on an occasional date, I only get excited about their looks and never the conversations I have with them. So maybe this is something different than my usual. It explains why my roommates are all giving me looks of barely concealed glee that I am thoroughly ignoring right now.

"Season two, episode four," Addison says, and I let Jackson know.

> Jackson: I'm pulling it up right now.

> Timini: Right now. While you're on a plane.

> Jackson: Yep. Flying over the Atlantic. Tell me when to press play.

We start the show, and everyone immediately begins giving their unsolicited advice. The couple has only been married for six months, so from the start, we all think it's a bad idea and are vocal about it. The wife is open to half the house being remodeled—the kitchen and bathrooms. The husband wants it all done. Every square inch.

Both spouses make their share of bad choices that even the contractor gives them unsolicited advice on. (I can understand the wife wanting double sinks in the master bathroom. But double toilets? In the same room? And I can't understand even a little why the husband wants built-in shelf-like padded seats going all the way around all four walls in their family room instead of having furniture that they can move.)

It is a great episode. All of my roommates give the funniest advice to the couple. I type a lot of it in messages to Jackson, along with my own advice, and he types back plenty of his own funny advice.

I've brought dates to group things before. Never, though, has my date joined in with the group so seamlessly. It's nice.

I'm so used to feeling like the odd man out on group dates, but I don't feel like that at all tonight.

Jackson: Thank you for the enjoyable date. I can't say I've ever gone on one while on a plane, with someone I've never met in person, especially not a group date with six of her roommates.

Timini: I'm guessing you thought all your first dates with women from this app were going to be predictable.

Jackson: That's some pro-level mind-reading right there. Wait. You didn't get the super-power-granting trio of tacos without me, did you?

Timini: It was the cheese tray that granted me mind-reading capabilities, actually.

Jackson: What am I thinking right now?

Timini: That they turned down the lights in the cabin, so they clearly want you all to go to sleep. And you're feeling a little guilty that you have a bright screen that's probably annoying your seatmate. So you should go, but you'd really rather stay up for hours, chatting with me.

Timini: But also, part of you just wants to fall unconscious right now, since we stayed up so late last night, chatting, and you had to get up so early. And you're landing in a country that's already half a day ahead of you, so sleeping sounds like the responsible thing to do.

Jackson: It's astounding how correct you are.

Timini: #Pro

Jackson: You're going to have to introduce me to this cheese when I get back.

Timini: I wouldn't miss the chance. Have a safe flight! Get good sleep.

Jackson: Will do. Goodnight, Timini.

I close out of the app and sink back into my comfy chair, happiness filling me. Never did I imagine that a virtual date with someone who is practically a stranger would leave me feeling so amazing.

CHAPTER 8

Jackson

AFTER AN EXTREMELY LONG DAY—MY first full day in Delhi—I finally get back to my room. I got a few messages earlier in the day from people I matched with, but I didn't even have a small moment to respond until now.

Responding, though, doesn't give me a fraction of the high I get from talking with Timini. I glance at the clock on my phone. It's nearly nine p.m. for me, but that puts Oregon at almost seven-thirty a.m., and I suddenly realize that I have no idea what time Timini normally wakes up.

I send her a good morning message through the app, hoping that the notification won't wake her up if she isn't ready to be awake yet. But also really hoping she is already up because, after such a long day, I really just want to see words with her name next to them.

Timini: Good morning!

Timini: Oh. It's probably not morning for you, is it? It isn't the middle of the night, is it?

Jackson: Nope. I'm thirteen and a half hours ahead.

Timini: "And a half." Interesting. I'm guessing what you've gotten done today has to be way more impressive than what I've gotten done. Especially since all I've done is wander into the bathroom to see how messy my hair is.

I suddenly want to know exactly what Timini looks like with messy hair. Or with any kind of hair.

Timini: How was your first full day there?

Jackson: I went to half a dozen meetings at three different locations. I got to ride their train (the metro), a rickshaw (which is a vehicle that comfortably seats a person and a half and only has one wheel in the front), and a taxi. And today I learned that you're supposed to negotiate a fare with the driver BEFORE driving an inch. I know that now.

Timini: Uh oh.

Jackson: It's all good. And this place is amazing. It just bombards you with all the sights, sounds, smells, people, culture, art, and food. Oh, and the heat.

Timini: That sounds INCREDIBLE.

Jackson: Were you referring to the heat or the rest of it?

Timini: All of it.

Jackson: You're a fan of hot weather, huh?

Timini: The hotter the better.

Jackson: This place resembles an oven. You would love it.

Timini: Clearly, I'll have to go there sometime. Now tell me about the food you've eaten.

Jackson: I tried Thali, which is a flatbread that you use to scoop up chickpeas in a sauce. And also Chat, which the guy told me will pretty much give me superpowers that rival the taco combo at Taco Sabroso. And I managed to get out of eating the goat brain, so I'm calling it a win.

Timini: Now I'm hungry. I think I'll wander downstairs and find some food.

I picture her making her way down to the kitchen and opening the fridge door, and I really want to see her. To know what she looks like.

But I also really want to spend time finding out more about her.

Timini: Do you travel out of the country often?

Jackson: Only 2-3 times a year. And then a handful of times in the country a year.

Timini: What's the most memorable place you've been?

Jackson: Guatemala. It wasn't for business, though. It was the summer after high school, and I was building houses for struggling villages. It was literally a life-changing experience.

Timini sends the emoji with heart eyes, and I suddenly want to know everything I can about her.

Jackson: I feel like we've gotten to know each other's personality pretty well but I don't feel like I really know who you are. What do you say to us asking each other questions? You know, to dive in deeper.

Timini: Oh. Like whether or not I put my toothbrush under the water before I put toothpaste on it? Because I'm going to tell you right now that putting toothpaste on a dry toothbrush is just plain weird. We're talking deal-breaker territory.

I laugh out loud. Then I leap onto my bed, landing stretched out on my side and propped up on one elbow.

Jackson: See? I already feel like I know you more deeply.

I look up at the ceiling, trying to think of what I want to ask. With more than half a day time difference between the two of us for the next eighteen days, I realize I want to know when she might be awake.

Jackson: Are you a morning person or a night owl?

> Timini: A night owl, FOR SURE. I start working at an okay time in the mornings. Usually. I mean, depending on your opinion, I guess. I went to bed at a decent time last night. But night is when all my best ideas come. Sometimes, I get working on a project and suddenly realize it's 3 a.m. You?

> Jackson: I can't say I have that same issue. Like, ever. I'm an early bird. Up at exactly six. I have a morning routine. It feels like a game that I've already figured out my high score on, so I try to reach that same high score daily.

> Timini: That sounds like a SUPER fun game.

Then she sends a text with the emoji of the yellow circle-faced guy raising one eyebrow, probably so I won't take her comment seriously.

> Timini: You sound like you're very consistent with your bedtimes. How is the time difference treating you?

> Jackson: Ask me tomorrow. That's when the crash usually hits. Right now I'm doing just fine.

Although I shouldn't be just lounging around like I am. I met with several investors, potential manufacturers, and a potential retailer today. I should be typing up my notes and sending them back to the office because they probably want to discuss them today. And I should be preparing for my meetings tomorrow.

It isn't like me to just blow it all off so that I can message a woman on a dating app. But nothing about Timini is making me want to do what I normally do.

> Jackson: What is the one thing you most regret?

> Timini: Oh, wow. You're really going straight for the vulnerability topics, aren't you?

> Jackson: Go big or go home, right?

> Timini: It couldn't be just something I regret? It has to be what I MOST regret? Because I regret not having donuts waiting in the kitchen for me for breakfast.

> Jackson: Well, I guess it depends on how deep of an answer you want from me.

> Timini: You do know how to sweeten the deal. Okay, fine. What I most regret. But I'm swearing you to secrecy because this isn't something I share with people.

I send her the emoji of the little yellow face with the zipped lips.

Timini: My biggest regret is not finishing college. I went for two years and fully planned to go for four. But then I got the opportunity to intern for a year with a giant in the field of costume design, and I couldn't pass it up. She let me work with her full-time, and I at least doubled everything I had learned about costume-making from my entire life up until that point. She helped me get going on my own, helped me make connections, and recommended me to several people in the industry.

Timini: Doing this on my own—with running my own shop on the horizon—is only possible because of that internship. But when it finished, I had to make a choice. Instead of going back to college, I chose to run with the momentum I gained in that internship and started out on my own.

Jackson: And you regret that?

Timini: Yeah. It feels unfinished. But if it was only that, it would be okay, because I feel like I made the decision with my eyes open. It's whenever "What college did you graduate from?" comes up in conversation that I most regret it. Not being able to say that I graduated makes me feel inconsequential. Not capable of finishing things. Like I wasn't smart enough to do it. I avoid the conversation at all costs because it always makes me feel like a loser.

Jackson: From everything I know of you, I can certify that you're not a loser. You just finished your education in a different way. If you'd like, I can make you a very official-looking graduation certificate. You can have it framed and hang it on the wall of your future design shop.

Timini: I'll take it! Okay, your turn, Mister.

Jackson: Mine happened in middle school, the class right after lunch. Our teacher was late getting back so we were all just waiting in the hallway outside the classroom for the door to be unlocked. There was a kid in my class who was brilliant but socially awkward. A few of the other kids stood right in front of him, making fun of everything about his appearance from his hair to his freckles to his too-short pants and "not cool" shoes.

Jackson: My biggest regret is not stepping in to defend him. I could've asked them to stop. Physically stepped between the kid and his attackers. Put my arm around the kid and led him away. Turned their attention on me. Anything. But I didn't—I just stood there. I felt bad about it for weeks. I still do, actually. I think about that often. I made a promise to myself from that point on to always step in and defend someone whenever they needed me to.

Timini sends me the emoji that has hearts for eyes, but it doesn't feel earned when I just shared something I don't like that I did. Or, in this case, didn't do. A few moments later, she sends a message that catches me off guard.

> Timini: So…do you think we should exchange pictures so we have a face to go with the names and winning personalities?

> Timini: Or should we not and keep the magic going?

It makes me smile that she wants to know more about me just like I want to know more about her. Part of me wants to type a quick YES! A big enough part that I have to try hard to stop myself and truly think about it first. I want to see Timini.

The entire reason I agreed to use this app, though—especially at a time when I literally can't see any matches in person—is because I want to know if there is someone out there with relationship potential. Someone who won't just like me because of what they can Google about me or my family. I want a relationship that goes beyond the superficial things.

> Jackson: As much as I want to see you, I kind of like the magic.

> Timini: OH GOOD. As soon as I asked, I wished I hadn't. I like it, too.

> Timini: Do you make your bed in the morning?

I laugh. When I picture us getting to know each other further, I haven't been sure what questions to ask that won't lead to asking about each other's families. I haven't imagined us talking about bedmaking or teeth brushing or sleeping patterns. But this is perfect.

> Jackson: Always. Before I leave my room. There's an admiral who says that if you do that first thing, the momentum created by getting that task done will help you accomplish more in a day.

> Timini: Yeah, I never really got that. There are lots of things you can do in the morning to feel accomplished. I would never choose the one that made the least sense.

> Jackson: How does making your bed not make sense? If you do it, then your sheets and blankets are all straight and ready for you when you go to bed.

> Timini: Nah. Made beds look off-limits and intimidating. Unmade beds look comfy. I don't want to get to my room at the end of a tiring day and feel like I can't even get under the covers.

The thought of crawling into an unmade bed isn't a pleasant one. Yet I love how unapologetically herself Timini is, and it helps me at least understand her perspective.

For the next week, every evening when I get home from a packed, exhausting day, I message Timini as she's waking up. And in her evenings, she messages me as I'm waking up. Sometimes we tell each other about our days. Sometimes we banter about inconsequential things. Sometimes we ask each other questions. Funny, serious, shallow, deep, insightful, blunt—I love them all.

I especially love hearing about her job and the new project she's taking on. It's bigger than anything she's done before, and she even hired an assistant to help her. It's exciting to see her business in the beginning stages of it really taking off. I remember hearing my parents talk about their business taking off when I was in elementary school, and it's fun to watch it happen now with Timini.

I end the chats on the app with other women I matched with and push the pause button on my profile. Timini and I haven't even come close to talking about being exclusive, but the only thing I use the app for now is talking to her. It feels like it has always been only about her.

One night as I'm waiting for food in a restaurant, I imagine going on a date with Timini when I return to Oregon and send her a question, hoping to get some ideas on where to take her.

> Jackson: What was your favorite date you've ever gone on and why?

The second I tap *Send*, I wish I could call it back. It's a stupid question to ask—I really don't want to hear about a date she had with another guy. So I just wait for her answer, turning my phone over and over in my hand, wishing my food would arrive more quickly so I could do something other than wait.

The second I feel the buzz of the notification, I go in to see what she has written.

> Timini: Oh, gosh. I'm going to have to go all the way back to high school for that one. I was going with a guy and a group of friends to a school dance—a casual one at the end of my sophomore year. We went on a "day date" before the dance. Did your school do day dates on the day of dances, too?

> Jackson: We totally did. Dances were an all-day thing.

> Timini: So, like probably half the nation's high school students that year, we decided to do a photo scavenger hunt.

> Jackson: Ahh, yes. The photo scavenger hunt. We did that, too. We thought we were so original back then.

> Timini: The reason the date made it to the top of my list wasn't even because of the scavenger hunt, exactly. It was more of the way we connected, I guess. My date just made me feel loved and cared for.

After chatting with Timini for so many hours over the past nine days, hearing that just makes me want to be the person who makes her feel loved and cared for.

> Timini: Your turn. What was your favorite date and why?

Her answer about a high school dance takes me back to high school, too, and suddenly I can't think of any date other than those. I dated my girlfriend, Minnie, all of my junior year. We were apparently as original as Timini's group and also decided to go on a photo scavenger hunt. Then we went to dinner, the dance, and then we all went back to my house for a movie on an outdoor screen that my buddies and I set up before the date.

My favorite part, though, was after the movie. All the other couples left, but Minnie and I stayed in the backyard, lying on a blanket in the grass, holding hands in the dark, staring up at the millions of stars overhead.

We talked for the longest time. Minnie told me about her mom's current boyfriend and how terribly he treated her mom yet somehow always made her mom believe that she was the one treating him terribly.

And I told her about how my parents' business was starting to grow so much in such a small amount of time, and how it felt like everything was on the brink of changing. How scared it made me. I talked about how worried I was that my parents might want our family to move soon, and Minnie said she was worried that her mom would never move on. We shared our hopes and dreams and plans for college, and I had never felt closer to another person before.

> Jackson: My favorite date was in high school, too (junior year for me, though), and it isn't really about what we did for the date, either. We went stargazing (also a super popular date activity in my high school), and what made the date memorable was the conversation, not the stars.

> Jackson: Although the stars did add some great ambiance.

> Timini: So true. Do you have any stars there yet?

I duck in my seat to see under the awning that covers the outdoor seating area. I got through an exhausting day of travel and meetings later than normal, so I'm eating in the dark tonight.

> Jackson: There's a lot of activity going on in this market—too many lights. I'm not sure I've seen any while I've been here. I'll have to check when I get back to my hotel.

> Timini: How much longer are you gone?

I smile at her question. Maybe she wants to see me as badly as I want to see her.

> Jackson: 11 more days.

When I left home for this trip, three weeks didn't seem too long to be gone at all. And, really, for all I have to accomplish, it isn't long at all. But the more I chat with Timini, the more I want to meet her in person and the longer it feels like it will be until my trip comes to an end.

CHAPTER 9

Timini

I'm still feeling the euphoria from an incredible date as my high school boyfriend, Jack, walks me up the steps to my front porch. I am still me, but I am also the sixteen-year-old me. A very distinct mix of the Timini I am now and the Minnie I was back then. Jack is still Jack, too, but he somehow feels older.

When we get to my door, we face each other, less than a foot apart. Close enough that I can smell the wintergreen scent of his gum. We talk, but the words are wispy and intangible, drifting away in the wind on ephemeral clouds. Then Jack reaches out, cupping my head with one hand and with the other, brushing the hair away from my face with his fingertips as they skim ever so slightly across my cheek.

The date has been so magical that every nerve tingles in anticipation of his lips against mine. I lean closer to him, letting my eyes drift closed. The moment his lips touch mine, sparkling lights fill my mind. As he so gently, carefully, moves his lips against mine, like I am precious, fragile, of great worth, my knees literally weaken and nearly buckle. He just holds me closer, using his strength to add to mine.

Then he pulls back from the kiss and looks me straight in the eyes, and I sit up in bed with a jolt, gasping. It takes a few minutes of panting before I get my bearings and realize where I am and that I have been dreaming. The dream has been so intense and has felt so real! I fall back onto my pillow, still trying to reclaim my breath and calm my heart rate.

Why in the world am I dreaming about a boyfriend I had a dozen years ago?

It's probably because of that question Jackson asked last night about my favorite date. And I probably only went all the way back to high school for my answer simply because Jackson's name is similar to my high school boyfriend Jack's.

That's all it is. I hadn't thought of that night for so many years that the dream had to have been triggered because of our conversation.

It was a pretty great date. And an even more incredible kiss at the end. We had been dating for most of the school year at that point.

For the photo scavenger hunt, we'd split into teams of two. One of the things we had to get a picture of was a Dumpster. We both thought of the same one—one in an alley between a restaurant and a hair salon. At least one of us had to be in the picture with the object we were searching for, and it was my turn. I crouched down, like I was hiding, just beyond the corner, waiting for someone to come so I could jump out and scare them or something. Jack took the picture, and as I turned to stand, I realized that I had been crouching next to a nest of very large spiders.

I was so freaked out. I screamed, batting at my clothes and hair, worried that they were all over me. Jack was to me in a second, pulling me away from the danger, checking to make sure no spiders were on me, batting away the one that was with his bare hands, and then pulling me to safety and into his chest.

His shoulders were strong, and he wrapped his arms around me, holding me tight, whispering promises that I was okay and that no spiders were on me. He didn't rush the moment even though it meant losing the competition.

I felt so loved and cared for. The experience was so different from any of the guys who moved in with my mom, and I knew at that moment what I wanted—a guy who would care for me just like Jack did.

After dinner and the dance, our whole group went to Jack's house for an outdoor movie. We planned to watch a scary one about a cabin in the woods, but the scare from earlier was too fresh, and I worried there might be spiders in the movie. I didn't even have to say a thing; Jack just announced to the group that we were going to watch a different movie. A happier one.

After the movie, when everyone else had gone home, we held hands as we looked up at the stars and talked. I remember thinking how perfect the date was and how much I yearned for a life exactly like that night.

I shake my head as I force myself to a sitting position on my bed. Jack told me that night so long ago that he was worried about everything in his family changing. But it only took a couple of months before *he* changed the most, and that ruined everything. Suddenly I—and my not-so-affluent upbringing—was no longer good enough. My image no longer fit with his new image. I no longer belonged in the world he was suddenly entitled to because of his family's wealth.

The worst part was, the day after I broke up with him, I saw him at Jumping Trolley, a place we all liked to hang out. I was with my friends, and he was with his. My group had to pass by his on the way to our seats, and when we passed, he acted like he was in the middle of a conversation with his friends, but his words were clearly directed at me. "So then the doctor asked her, where does it hurt? And she unlocked her phone and showed him her bank account." And then all his friends laugh.

I shake off the bitter memory and the happy dream. Then I pick up my phone to look at the time and congratulate myself for waking up a full thirty minutes before my alarm is set to go off. So there's something good that came from the dream. It's like a gift of thirty minutes just plopped into my lap, and I smile big.

Then I notice a calendar notification.

"No, no, no!" I say out loud as I go into it. "That can't be today!"

But there, on my calendar, is the appointment I listed for a final fitting for a series of costumes I've been working on. How have I not realized that we are already this far into the month? I need an extra six hours this morning, not an extra thirty minutes.

A week ago, I met with Aftyn Flint, the director I interviewed with at Hamilton Hall. The meeting went well, but I also found out the scope of what I will be doing. Naya, the other director, joined the meeting for a bit, too, and she talked about what she was looking for in the Prince Charming costume. It's an intricate one that will take quite a while just by itself to concept and create.

Over the past week, I've gotten the measurements for all the cast members, got my initial ideas for the costumes approved, posted a job opening for an assistant, interviewed applicants, and hired someone. I am still impressed at all I've gotten done.

What I haven't gotten finished, though, is a set of *Beauty and the Beast* costumes for a middle school play. I've already finished the most difficult pieces with the exception of one dress. It's mostly the costumes for the townspeople that I have left. None are intricate, original, or detailed like the ones for the

Williams Theater at Hamilton Hall, but they are still a lot of work.

At least now I have Evie. She is twenty-five. She dropped out of college after her third year of business school, took a few years off, and then figured out that clothing design was her true passion and went back. So I only have her part-time, and she just started yesterday, but already she is a godsend and is keeping me on track.

If only I had thought to tell my new employee about the *Beauty and the Beast* client. Yesterday, when we made a list of all the things that needed to get done for my existing projects and the new ones I just took on, the deadlines for each project, decided how long each one would take, and then plugged it into a calendar, taking both of our work schedules into consideration, I completely forgot about it. I have no idea how. Sure, my processes (until yesterday) have been lacking, but I have never completely forgotten about a project before. Especially a half-finished one.

Well, except that one teeny one last year.

This isn't a huge project, but it also isn't a finish-in-one-day project. We are seriously going to be scrambling to get them ready to try on today, and it's going to throw our entire schedule out of whack.

I send a quick text to Evie, hoping that six thirty-seven isn't too early to text.

Timini: I forgot about a set of costumes that is due today! If you have any spare time and are willing to work more hours, I will make it up to you somehow. You name it.

Evie: My 2:00 class just got canceled, so I can work until 4:00 now. I'll be over ASAP!

I breathe a huge sigh of relief as I race into the bathroom. My hair is still in the crazy bun I put it in after showering last night, and it's still a little damp. That is going to have to be good enough—the only thing I have time for today is teeth brushing.

I take the stairs two at a time and race into the kitchen. It doesn't sound like anyone else is even up yet. Hopefully, they are either sleeping deeply or are close to waking up anyway, because I am about to tear through the contents of the six round tables in this dining room and my shelves like a tornado. All of the costumes are started—some just have the pattern made, some are cut out, and some are at least partially sewn. And I need to find them all.

Six hours later, Evie and I are both slowing down from the marathon we've been running, even though we aren't close to being finished. Jackson sent me a few messages earlier, just checking in to see how my day was going, and I quickly filled him in on the chaos that is my day. He wished me luck. As much as I would've loved to chat with him, I'm glad he hasn't sent me any other messages because I wouldn't have had a chance to respond.

I just finished sewing a very puffy, multi-layered skirt to a corset—the most difficult part in the costumes we are making today—and hand it off to Evie to pin the fabric that goes from the bust up over the shoulders. Then I move on to doing the finish details on a dress for one of the townspeople.

"This doesn't fit," Evie says. "The top part's too big for the corset."

I look over at Evie's bewildered expression, rather bewildered myself. I go over to the table where she is working with her own sewing machine.

"How? I checked it right before sewing the skirts on!" But I look at the partially sewn top, and it is indeed too big. So I gather up the dress and take it to the same dress form with all the actress's measurements that I tried the corset on before starting on the skirts. I pull the dress onto the form and then try zipping the corset. It only goes halfway up and stops.

I adjust the dress, in case it isn't sitting just right anywhere, but it still won't zip. Then I notice that the base of the corset is looser than it should be.

"Oh, no. Oh, no, oh no." I take the dress off and put it on upside down, with the skirts going up over the lack of a head on the dress form. The corset fits perfectly. "I just sewed that entire skirt on the wrong side of the corset!"

"So what do we do?" Evie glances from the dress to the clock on the wall.

I put a hand on my forehead. It's 2:11, and the cast is coming for the fitting at three. Two ones in the time—that has to mean something good, but nothing here looks good. We are behind more than we can possibly make up at this point. "I have no idea. It'll take an hour to unstitch this and another thirty minutes to sew it back on correctly. We don't have that kind of time."

Not to mention that we are both fading fast. Probably because we haven't eaten anything all day. Evie's stomach is growling as loudly as mine is.

At the sound of a notification on my phone, I go back to my table to look at it, hoping for some kind of miracle. Like the school saying they can't actually come for the fitting until tomorrow.

Instead, it's a message from Jackson.

Jackson: Has the chaos died down at all?
How are things going?

Timini: They are going SO BAD.

Jackson: Have you eaten?

Timini: No.

Jackson: You'll work more quickly if you do.

Timini: I know. But there's no time to make anything. No time to even order anything.

Jackson: Do you have time to answer the door?

I've barely read the message when the doorbell rings. My brows come together, and I walk out of the dining room to the lobby, my phone still in my hand, the dating app still open. I reach out and pull the door open, and standing on my porch, under cover from the rain that is drizzling, is a guy in a Taco Sabroso shirt, holding a bag.

"Are you Timini?"

I nod.

"Someone really, *really* wanted you to have these tacos today. Enjoy."

I take the bag from the man and try to pay him, but he says that the bill—and a sizeable tip—are already covered.

As I take the bag into the kitchen, a sense of wonder fills my entire body. Has Jackson seriously ordered me food from Taco Sabroso and arranged to have it delivered, all the way from Delhi, India?

After setting the bag on the big dining table, I take out the first food container—the one with my name on it—and open it. It contains three tacos: one carnitas, one al pastor, and one fish. I suddenly realize how famished I am, and a tear nearly escapes my eye as I think about how sweet Jackson is to do this.

The second box has *Timini's Assistant* written on top of it, and it contains the same three tacos. He's even thought of my assistant! I hand Evie the one for her and then send a message to Jackson.

Timini: I can't believe you did this for me! How did you even know where to have it delivered?

Jackson: That was a gamble. You told me you lived in an inn that was no longer an inn in Quicksand, so I did some research and some finger-crossing. I figured if there was a day when you needed superpowers, it was today.

Jackson: And here's hoping that they give you super speed or time travel, and not one of the ones that wouldn't be so useful in this situation, like the ability to speak any language or fly or indestructibility or animal transformation.

Jackson: Telekinesis or object manipulation might even be good.

Timini: I know we haven't met in person, but if you were here right now, I would kiss you.

Jackson: And if I were there, I would probably let you.

Timini: Only probably? ;)

Jackson: I wouldn't want to keep you or your forthcoming superpowers from pulling off a fourth-quarter miracle.

Timini: For right now, then, I'll just have to give you a giant THANK YOU.

The tacos might have given me superpowers.

As soon as Evie and I eat them, I get the idea to give the dress a more open back. We use some of the flowing fabric that goes over the chest and into the sleeves and continue it down along the deep V of the back of the dress. It turns out so much more beautiful than the original design had been.

And somehow, we get most of the costumes finished before the dozen castmates with the biggest parts show up for their fittings. Evie finishes up the last few ensemble costumes while I do the fittings, and everything works out. The actress playing Belle loves the dress so much she begs to wear it home.

Those superpowers from the tacos really are quite impressive.

Or maybe it's all Jackson, delivering food at a time when we couldn't function well any longer without it. Either way, I am grateful.

CHAPTER 10

Jackson

I DISCONNECT the conference call with the executive team and the international expansion team at Oliver Innovations, which includes both my parents and all three of my siblings as well as a handful of others, and shut my laptop. It's the beginning of their workday and the very end of mine on my last night in India.

During my three weeks here, I have not only managed to get a deal in the works for a manufacturing plant to start producing our mattresses and cushions, get contracts for distribution in the works, and get retailers on board to carry our product, but I've also made more connections than I ever imagined I'd be able to that will pave the way for future successes in this country.

By all accounts, everything about this trip has been more successful than I hoped for. Yet the thing that excites me the most at this moment is, strangely, not those successes. It's the fact that I will be able to meet Timini in person soon. I have never been so thrilled about a new relationship before. In fact, I've suspected I never would be. Yet here I am.

I grab all the shirts from the hotel's closet except for the one I will wear on the plane in the morning and start folding them, then drop each one into my suitcase.

Thinking back to every single person I've dated since college—or since high school, even—I am sure I haven't known any of them as well as I feel like I know Timini. Apparently, three weeks of nothing but talking has been rather effective. I can thank this trip for that. If I'd been home, I'd have given in and asked to see her in person a couple of weeks ago if being half a world apart hadn't stood in my way.

As effective as all the chatting has been in helping us to get to know each other, I am so glad that my flight leaves for home in the morning.

Over the past three weeks, we have discussed many things. Trivial things and soul-baring things. I have learned a lot about her, yet there is still so much I want to know. I've found out that she has a sister and several nieces and nephews. I've wanted to ask more, but I've been too worried that she will ask more about my family, and I haven't wanted to share that yet. Soon, though. Once we meet in person and have that connection outside of words typed on a screen, then we can cross that bridge. And that time is soon.

Now that meeting her in person is a very real and present thing, though, doubts and worries have started creeping in. Getting to know someone over a messaging app is one thing. Getting to know someone in person is entirely different. So much doesn't come through when it's just text. Will we connect the same way in person that we have through messages?

Timini does seem to genuinely like me. Will she still feel the same once she meets me in real life? And will everything still go as smoothly as it has been going?

My familiar habit of questioning the motives of anyone who seems to like me has popped up quite a few times, but I've mostly managed to push those away. The thing about having a lot of money and having an influential family is that it brings people close who are looking for something they think I can get them.

Which is fine. I don't mind helping people out in ways that I can. Except it means that I can never really trust whether the reason I seem to get along well with someone is because we are genuinely forming a friendship or if the person is just using me to get what they want.

But Timini doesn't know my last name. Or who my family is. Or who our company is. So I push those thoughts out whenever they surface. Well, I mostly do. Old fears and past relationships still try to haunt me, but I am aware of that fact, which helps. Still, though, money changes things. I have seen it up close and a little too personal in my life. I don't want it to touch my relationship with Timini.

I pick up my phone. It's getting late and I really need to pack, but it's only nine a.m. for Timini. I open the Chat Match app, tap on her name, and send her a good morning. After a couple of messages back and forth, I find out that she has already been working but has stopped for breakfast.

Jackson: Do you have a breakfast food you eat every morning?

Timini: Nope. It depends on how busy I am or how focused on a project I am. If I have tons of time, I'll always go for an omelet chock full of veggies. If I don't, then toast, a protein bar, an apple, or whatever is quick.

Timini: I just remembered from your bio that you can't live without cold cereal and cartoons in the morning. Is there a specific cartoon or cereal?

Jackson: Nope. That doesn't matter, as long as both are present.

It takes her a bit longer than normal to respond. I busy myself with packing so I won't feel quite as vulnerable and exposed.

Timini: So the guy who is about the most responsible, self-disciplined, organized person I know eats breakfast like he's an eleven-year-old? Interesting. Tell me more.

I knew the question was coming—I set it up myself, after all. I just hadn't really thought through telling her. Maybe I brought up the question because I've wanted to share it with someone. Or maybe because I haven't exactly had my usual breakfast since I've been in India and I've missed the way it grounds me. I take a deep breath and then just spill all of it. The stuff I haven't told anyone before now.

Jackson: I feel like I had a strong sense of who I was when I was a kid. All through middle school and halfway through high school, even. Then I kind of lost sight of who I was for a while. Once I figured it out again, I started back with the daily cold cereal and cartoons of my childhood. It took me back to that time when everything was simple and I liked who I was. Even now, it still keeps me grounded.

It sounds stupid when I write it out like that. I wish I could take it back the moment I press send. But then her response comes in.

Timini: That's beautiful.

I wish I could see the expression on her face right now.

Timini: And it makes me want to toss this toast and boiled egg and eat Froot Loops.

Jackson: It might not give you superpowers, exactly, but who doesn't want to start off the day with a food whose box also includes such brain-stimulating games as "See how many Froot Loops you can stack on top of each other," and "Help Toucan Sam find his way through the maze."

Timini: Haha!

Timini: With as busy as my day is going to be today, I don't need brain stimulation as much as I need mental calmness. Tell me: what's the most relaxing situation you can imagine? Maybe it'll get me there.

Jackson: Being outside, preferably after sunset, walking in a slight rain.

Timini: Rain?! How can that be your most relaxing situation? A good half the time, the rain is freezing! You are no help at all.

Jackson: A slight freezing rain at night is the best time to go on a long walk. You live in Oregon but don't like the rain? How do you survive?

Timini: By soaking in the sunshine every chance I get.

Jackson: I forgot that you would prefer living in an oven. I'm going to call you Sunshine from now on.

Timini: You know it. Okay, it looks like I'm going to have to rely on my own most relaxing situation. It's on a beach with plenty of sunshine. Or in a canoe on a lake. Anywhere with a big body of water and a bright sun. Or even a skinnier body of water, like a rushing river. You're welcome to join me when you change your mind. ;)

Jackson: I'm not really a "body of water" kind of guy. I prefer it falling from the sky.

Timini: Like from a waterfall? Into a body of water?

Jackson: Haha. Okay, I'm going to have to call you the winner of this conversation. And for now, I'll acquiesce on the body of water thing in the best interests of your need for brain relaxation.

Then I send her an animated gif of a sunny beach with the waves lapping at the sand.

Jackson: Just to make sure we're still compatible, though, even with the body of water revelations… Let's say you go to Voodoo Doughnut. What kind do you choose?

Timini: Apple Crumble, because it's like a pie in a doughnut. Plus: ginger snaps. Or the Portland Cream. You?

Jackson: Solid choices there. I usually get Chuckles, because of the mix of chocolate, peanuts, and caramel, or the classic Bacon Maple Bar. Some days, though, it's more of a Grape Ape kind of day.

> Timini: A man who's got his priorities straight. Now I see why we matched.

I glance at my room, which currently looks like it could be declared a national disaster area. I really haven't made much progress since I disconnected from that conference call, and I have to be at the airport long before the sun rises.

> Jackson: I'm traveling all day tomorrow, but I'll be home the day after. Want to meet for dinner?

I normally have no problem at all asking a woman out. Why does waiting for her answer make me feel like a nervous high school kid again?

> Timini: I would love to.

I let out a huge breath of relief and start thinking of places where I can get a reservation this late and pull up a couple of restaurant's sites on my phone.

> Jackson: How does Chef's Star at 7 sound?

> Timini: Never been there. Sounds great! And so you'll recognize me when I come in, I have dark brown hair halfway down my back. Wavy. And there's a 99% chance I'll be wearing heels.

> Timini: Who am I kidding? There's a 100% chance.

I smile and imagine how it's going to feel to finally see what she looks like. To be with her in person. My thumbs hover over my phone screen as I think about how to describe myself. Is there even anything about me I can mention that isn't average?

Jackson: I'll be wearing a dark gray suit with a light blue shirt.

Timini: I can't wait!

Nerves or not, neither can I.

CHAPTER 11
Timini

I RUN my hands down the length of my dress, smoothing everything out. Then I turn from one side to the other in the full-length mirror. Since Jackson said he's going to be wearing a suit and a light blue shirt, I decide I should wear a dress that goes with it. Mine is a deeper blue, bordering on navy, and is one of my favorites. The top is fitted yet still somewhat flowy, and the skirt ruffles above my knees just the right amount.

"You look beautiful!" Peyton says from where she, Bex, Addison, and Evie all sit on my unmade bed, watching me like I'm the most interesting TV show ever. "Do you think he's good-looking?"

I freeze. "I don't know. I mean, I assume so, but I guess I could be wrong." I realize that I have been picturing him based on how much I like chatting with him, and I have no idea if the guy in my head is anything like he is in real life.

Evie grins. "Here's hoping he's not a fifty-year-old couch potato."

A moment of panic hits before I remember that I already know his age—twenty-nine. And couch potatoes aren't the kind of people that companies send to put together huge business deals halfway around the world, or who get up at six a.m. to try to "match their high score" on getting ready for the day.

"I don't think I've ever seen you this nervous about a date before," Addison says.

I adjust my necklace and smooth my hair around my ear. "Well, I've never gone on a date with a guy I like this much before. Do I look too dressed up? I've never been to the restaurant, but he said he'll be wearing a suit."

"You look amazing," Evie says.

Bex nods. "You do. And I'm so proud of you for not self-sabotaging this time."

My attention whips to Bex. "What? I do not self-sabotage."

"You totally do. The whole time I've known you, you've always chosen guys where it's obvious that things won't work out, almost as if you're ensuring that things won't work out. But, from everything you've told us, Jackson sounds like a really good guy."

Peyton shoots Bex a look and then hops off my bed. She gives me a quick squeeze. "He does sound like a great guy. Now stop being nervous because this date is going to go better than hugs on a bunny."

I turn to look once more in the mirror. "Are you sure I look okay?"

"Yes!" all four women shout at the same time. So I take a deep breath and head down the stairs, all of them following close behind.

Both Ian and Roman are standing in the doorway to the family room, bonding over making it to the end of Thursday after rough work weeks while some kind of sporting event plays behind them on the TV. Both look over as I get to the lobby.

"Your Chat Match date, right?" Roman's smile is wide like a parent watching a kid learn to walk.

"Am I the first one to date someone from the app?"

He shakes his head. "We have a couple thousand people beta testing in the Portland area, so I doubt it. You're just the first one I know personally."

"Have fun," Ian says.

"And turn on your tracker!" Roman adds as I near the door.

I turn and give him a look.

"What? Do you know the guy's last name? Contact information?"

I don't. I actually haven't even thought about it since about the third day. I had been dying to ask him his last name so I could look him up on social media and get a glimpse of what he looked like. But then I thought about how I'd had a long line of poorly chosen dates based on looks, so I managed to convince myself that I most definitely didn't want that information. It would've just led to more bad choices.

"Safety first," Ian says and puts his arm around Addison as she snuggles up next to him.

Roman nods. "It's why we have the feature."

I take a deep breath and pointedly get out my phone, tapping the button that says I am going on a date with Jackson, where we are going to be, how long I anticipate us being there, and to automatically contact Peyton if I go somewhere unexpected. Then I hold up the phone as evidence that I did it.

Roman wears that smile again like he is so proud of his app that maybe his bad week was worth it. And I am glad—Jackson and I wouldn't have met if Roman hadn't decided to have his company make the app.

Thirty minutes later, I am still just as nervous as I pull up to the front of Chef's Star. I crane my neck, trying to see the parking lot, but I can't see it on either side of the building. I don't even notice that a man has been standing there in a valet's uniform until he steps forward. I roll down my passenger's window. "Could you direct me to the parking lot?"

"I'll take it for you."

I try to tell the man no thank you, that I can park and walk in just fine but he is already coming around to my side of the car. I let out a breath and look around. A few stray paper napkins are scattered around, a few random bags of things I meant to take into the inn, my running shoes lay on the floor in the back, and little fabric snips and strings are everywhere. Besides the fact that my little car is nowhere near fancy enough to be driven by a valet.

But he opens my door for me, so I grab my purse, pull the car's key off my key ring, and then hand it to the man. He gives me a ticket stub in exchange, and I thank him.

My nerves double and then triple as I walk up to the door. And then they shoot up exponentially when I walk into the lobby. I press a hand to my stomach. This place is way too expensive. I would've thought that Jackson knew me well enough to know that he didn't need to impress me by going to an expensive restaurant. But I really hope that is the reason why we are here—because he has a misguided need to impress and thinks a nice restaurant will do it, instead of places like this just being normal for him. It is probably because this is our first date. Maybe he is as nervous as I am to finally meet after getting to know each other so well. I step up to the host's table, a shiny polished mahogany, and tell him that I am meeting someone named Jackson.

He gives a quick nod. "Follow me, please."

The man leads me from the lobby, around a few dividers that look like light-covered trees growing up from the floor and disappearing into the ceiling, and into a cozy section of the restaurant. On the other side of the room, a man in a dark gray suit with a light blue shirt stands, and he is definitely a very fine man. Not a couch potato. Maybe a couch model. In fact, he could model anything—a gym membership, car repair tools, deodorant—and I would buy it whether I needed it or not.

I hope I am not blushing. I am probably blushing. So much heat has risen to my face that I must be. It's the Jackson blush I only get for him. And by the expression I am already able to make out on his face, he is looking at me much in the same way.

The man motions to the table as we near, says, "Your waiter will be by shortly," and then turns and walks back to the lobby.

As I close the last few steps between us, things start looking familiar about the man. The way his eyebrows—thicker now than they were—seem to exist to perfectly frame his eyes. And those brown eyes have so much golden in them that they shine and make it feel like he can understand what I'm thinking without me saying a word.

The perfect dip just under his bottom lip that is now covered with a short scruff. Those ears that are the most symmetrical of anyone I've ever seen. The cheekbones that go up at the most perfect angle. The ones that were once soft and entirely kissable but are now strong and are still every bit as—

No! I am not thinking about planting kisses on those cheeks! I am furious that I am thinking of any nice things at all. This is the man who changed, after all. The man who got rich and broke my heart. And then stomped on it.

"Jack Oliver?" My words come out as a curse. A bomb whose explosion is barely contained.

His expression turns baffled. "Minnie?"

"*You're* who I've been chatting with?" A different kind of heat rises up in me. A kind that fills every last bit of me. I feel deceived by every traitorous feeling I've had while messaging him during the past three weeks.

"No wonder… Wow… I guess that makes…Wow." Jackson —or Jack, apparently—just keeps muttering in an awed voice.

I am not in awe. I am in shock. An angry, disbelieving, furious shock. A couple thousand people are beta-testing Chat Match. Over three million people live in Portland and the surrounding areas. And I match with Jack Oliver.

The one guy I have connected with—the *only* guy I have connected with in years—and it has to be the one who so thoroughly broke my heart years ago.

I turn to walk away, but Jack reaches out and puts his hand on my arm. "Minnie. Timini. Wait."

I don't meet his eyes. I just shake my head. "This was a mistake." And then I stride out of the restaurant, my heels pounding on the ground with each step. I don't even slow down when my heel hits the floor a little harder than it is designed for and snaps right off. I just keep walking like my shoes are meant to be at two different heights, my right toes pointing up at the sky.

As the valet brings my car around, I glance at my broken, very recently adorable shoes. My luck with men is about as impressive as my luck with heels.

When I get back home and walk into the inn, I don't see a single one of my roommates, and Evie would've left long ago. Good—I'll have an unimpeded path up to my room. They must've all heard me get home, though, because within a minute, Addison, Bex, and Peyton have all made their way into my room. I unzip my dress, grab my fluffiest pajama bottoms and a tank top, and head into my bathroom to change.

When I come back out, I toss the dress over the back of my chair and point at Bex. "This was not self-sabotage. This was *the universe* coming together to sabotage *me*."

"What happened?" Peyton asks.

I pull my fancy barrette out of my updo, toss it on my bed,

and run my fingers through my hair in frustration. "It turns out that Jackson is Jack. My high school boyfriend."

"Oh," Bex says.

Addison looks from Peyton to Bex, then to me. "Isn't it sweet that you found each other after all this time? Wait. Why do you look like you want to stab something?"

I plop down on my bed and soon my roommates are all on the bed around me. I haven't told them much about Jack. It was so long ago that it hadn't seemed relevant. "I dated him all through my sophomore year in high school. He was a year older and he played a few different sports and he was so popular and I just felt so special that he liked me. Out of everyone.

"And he really was the sweetest boyfriend. *So* sweet. Whenever I had a rough day, he would slide a dozen notes telling me how awesome he thought I was into the slats at the top of my locker. Whenever things got crazy at home with my mom's boyfriend, he immediately planned something at his house that he wanted me to come to."

A chorus of "*Awws*" comes from my roommates.

"But his family owned a business. Oliver Innovations, actually."

Peyton's eyes open comically wide. "Wait. His last name is *Oliver*? He's one of those Olivers? The ones who make those beds with the stuff that's not memory foam or a gel but a squishy white stuff? I have one of those beds! And the shoe inserts. Oh my goodness."

"And I have their seat cushion on my office chair." Bex shakes her head. "I've actually met him. A couple of times. Roman knows him, too. I can't believe you've been chatting with Jackson Oliver all this time!"

"Yeah, well, me neither." I am mad that I wasted so much time getting to know him. No... That isn't it at all. It isn't that I didn't enjoy our chatting. I am mad that I let my heart get invested when it was all just going to end and it was going to hurt.

"I'm sorry," Addison says. "I still don't get why this is a problem? I mean if he was a sweet boyfriend, and he's been great to chat with…"

"Because he didn't stay being that way!" I say. The emotions are strong and exhausting, and I turn to lie flat on my back. "I knew him all through middle school. We became friends my freshman year and started dating just before my sophomore year. Back in middle school, his family's business was small and struggling. Then, almost overnight in high school, it took off big time. And just as quickly, sweet Jack was gone and was replaced with a version who thought he was better than everyone. And I mean *everyone*. Seriously, I'd never met a more arrogant, entitled, awful jerk."

"And then he broke up with you?" Peyton asks.

I shake my head. "I mean, he probably would have, because he thought he was better than me, too. I was no longer good enough to even be in his house. And he definitely thought he was way too good to get anywhere near mine. But I beat him to the breakup. My heart was still just as broken either way. Mostly because of all that I had lost. I had known what it was like to date the amazing version of him."

For quite a while, all my roommates stay silent, and I just play with the frayed edge of my favorite blanket, twisting it over and over in my fingers.

Then another thought emerges that I hadn't even realized I'd had until the words escape from my mouth in a whisper. "My mom went through a lot of boyfriends in my life up until that point, and every single one of them made her life worse. I loved Jack. He was supposed to be proof that it was only the guys my mom chose who were like that. Jack was supposed to show that love made things better. Instead, he proved that money ruins everything."

"You've gotten along pretty well now, though," Bex says. "Do you think you might be judging him solely off who he was twelve years ago?"

Peyton nods. "Does he feel like he's the same as he was back in high school?"

I let out a slow breath. "I don't know. People can put forth whatever persona they want to when all the communication is done over messaging."

"True," Addison says. "So how will you ever know if the guy you've been messaging with is like that if you don't get to know him in real life?"

I don't know. And I'm not sure I dare to find out.

CHAPTER 12

Jackson

I MAKE my way through the office, chatting with everyone extra after having been gone for so long. As happy as I am to be back, I just really want to get to my office before the delivery guy checks in.

I am still blown away that the Timini I've been talking to is Minnie. I've been wracking my brain ever since meeting for the dinner that didn't happen, trying to remember if I ever heard that her real name was Timini during any of the time I had known her in middle school and high school. I don't think I did.

But I desperately want to keep seeing her. I had been a world-class jerk back in high school when we broke up. Actually, I had been a jerk both before we broke up and after. My face burns just thinking about how I acted back then. I'm not sure I can convince her to take a chance on me again, but I am sure going to try.

I know she wouldn't appreciate flowers if I sent them to her —I remember that from when we were teens. But who knows? A lot has probably changed in the past twelve years. But I don't want to chance it. Instead, I go with my sister, Emma, to Voodoo Doughnuts and get all of her favorites plus a couple of mine. Then she helps me stick an eighteen-inch long small wooden dowel into each donut, and we arrange them in a vase like they're flowers. We even use tissue paper as the green stuff that is usually behind flowers.

I get a card and one of the plastic poker sticks that go in floral arrangements to hold it. On the card, I write out "I donut want things with us to end." It's cheesy, but it reminds me of the myriad of ways we had asked each other to school dances back in the day, and I hope it will make her smile.

And not at all remind her of the days when I had truly been a jerk to her.

Then I find a delivery driver who will take it to her place and is willing to contact me as soon as it has been delivered.

Emma sneaks into my office, seeming as if she's supposed to be in a meeting somewhere and is skipping so she can find out the results. I glance at the clock. In eleven minutes, I have to head to a meeting I can't skip. We both sit in silence, watching my phone—me trying not to bounce my leg incessantly and her trying not to bite her lip.

Finally, my phone lights up with a text from the delivery driver: *Just dropped it off. Thanks again for the big tip!*

I thank the man and then go back to staring at my phone.

"What now?" Emma asks.

I lift a shoulder in a shrug. "I know she's received them, so it's not like I need to check in with her to see if they were delivered or anything like that. If she is willing to message me, she will. If she isn't, she won't." I try to act like it is no big deal, but it is a huge deal. I really like her and really want to get to know her in person again.

A full eight minutes go by. I finally convince myself to stop staring for a response that might never come in and am gathering my things for my meeting when my screen lights up. I nearly knock my phone off my desk in an attempt to grab it and swipe it open. Emma immediately jumps up and scoots in next to me so she can read, too.

> Timini: You were wise waiting until this morning to contact me.

> Timini: And you were wise to send donuts instead of flowers.

> Timini: The card was a nice touch.

> Jackson: Does this mean you'd be willing to meet in person again? I would love to talk face-to-face.

I hold my breath as I wait for her response.

> Timini: If I get to choose the place this time, and if it's tonight.

> Timini: Also, I'm not sure if I'm okay with this. No guarantee things with us will go past tonight.

> Jackson: Fair enough. Let me know the time and place, and I'll be there.

I put the phone on my desk, take a deep breath, and grin at my sister. "I got a second chance. I just have to make sure I impress her enough that she'll want more than that."

———

I pull into the parking lot of the Jumping Trolley in Gresham. I've never been to this particular Jumping Trolley, but Minnie and I went plenty of times to the one in Forest Grove when we were in high school. It was one of the few places to hang out that was both cool and inexpensive enough for our teenage wallets.

I smile. It could not be a more different place than the restaurant where I tried to have dinner with her last night. It is loud, not intimate. Cheap, not elegant. Passable food, not award-winning. Just like the one in Forest Grove, a cover band of forty-somethings plays on the raised stage on the weekends. I suspect we aren't here because of the nostalgia or even because it's a place that Timini likes. The reason we are here is precisely because it is the opposite of where I picked. She is trying to see how I will do outside of what she thinks is my element.

Chef's Star is definitely in my element. But so is Jumping Trolley. Mostly.

As soon as I walk into the restaurant, my eyes immediately find Timini. She is sitting at a table toward the side of the room, but not in a booth, and she takes my breath away. Her smile is bright even if it does have a hint of trepidation behind it. Her hair is loose and curly, and she is wearing jeans and heels, and that is now my favorite combination of clothing items ever.

As I walk over to her, a strange buzzing fills my insides. I don't know what it is, exactly—all I know is that I am so glad that she agreed to see me again.

"Is this okay?" she asks as I near.

I grin and take the other seat at the table. I want to say that I would've gone anywhere, even if it had been to get hot dogs from that one convenience store we went to that one time when we both got food poisoning. That would've been too much, though. Instead, I say, "It's great."

We order our food, and just like when we were teens, Timini orders dessert along with her meal, so I do, too. As we get our food and start eating, our small talk is awkward and stilted. Not at all easy, like our conversations over the app have been.

But it does give me a chance to fully take her in and see how much she has changed since we were teens. She has the same mischievous gleam in her fiercely blue eyes. Those long lashes still frame them just as beautifully. They contain a strength that is new, but they have that warmth that I've always loved.

Her face is still as stunning and is even more refined. It is as if the last dozen years have taken everything amazing about her and made it impossibly better. I can't take enough of it in, no matter how long I sit across from her.

When she purses her lips just on one side, it reminds me of every time she did exactly that when we were teens and she was thinking through something.

I set my napkin on the table. "I think it's time to address the elephant in the room. I was not a good person at the end of my junior year and that summer before I moved. Actually, I was still not a good person for a bit longer than that. And I definitely didn't treat you the way I should've treated you. That is a part of my life that I'm not proud of, and I hope that I'm nothing like the guy I was back then. I should've found out where you lived a long time ago and apologized for everything, and I'm very sorry I didn't."

She picks up a fry and eats it, studying me as she chews. Then she gets a forkful of her layered chocolate cake and pauses right before the bite reaches her mouth. "And you're sorry about standing me up for that date when you went and hung out with your friends? And then took a page out of my mom's boyfriend's playbook and made me feel like I was over-reacting when I brought up the fact that you hadn't even let me know? Or about humiliating me in front of both my friends and yours?"

My face burns with shame and embarrassment. "I'm especially sorry about that." That hadn't been the worst of it, either. Thoughts of how I acted back then feel like a brick in my stomach.

She eats her bite of cake, so I take a bite of my cheesecake, too. Mostly because it makes things slightly less awkward and not at all because my stomach wants me to add anything to the brick that's already there.

Timini reaches a hand out and places it on my forearm. My eyes are immediately drawn to it and the electricity that buzzes through me at her touch. When my eyes go to hers, she says, "I forgive you."

I had no idea how badly I needed to hear that until she says it. I exhale, and my whole body seems to fill with light, making my heart feel like it is floating, my throat feeling like it is closing off. I swallow hard. My eyebrows draw together, and I look down at my cheesecake. "Was that almond extract?" I ask, my voice scratchy.

"Oh! You're allergic, aren't you?"

I'm not epi-pen allergic. I'm just uncomfortable-squeezing allergic. Raspy-voice allergic. That is all. Nothing catastrophic. "I'll be fine. I just..." I stand up. "Give me a minute."

I hurry toward the restroom on the opposite side of the building. Once inside, I turn on the cold water and splash some on my face. Then I splash some more, hoping it'll somehow mimic going outside on a chilly night. It isn't, exactly, but it helps a little. I lean in close to the mirror to see how awful I look and immediately jerk back when I realize I've leaned against a very wet counter, soaking my shirt.

Great. That is just what I need—a shirt that now looks like I don't know how to make it through an uncared-for restroom unscathed. I turn to grab paper towels for my face, my hands, and my shirt, but the dispenser is empty.

Of course, it is.

I shake off my hands, wipe them on my pants, and then pull my shirt up enough to wipe off my face. Not that it needs any more water on it. Then I head out to the restaurant to find someone who can give me some paper towels.

I go to a little alcove where the wait staff works, tell them about the restroom, and they say they will get some paper towels for me. Sounds of cheering grab my attention, so I look as the lead singer makes his way down into the audience, chatting and making jokes with the people sitting at the nearest tables, looking for someone to come up on stage with him.

My eyes immediately go to Timini. She is easily the most beautiful woman in the room, and she is sitting all alone—there is no way the lead singer isn't going to ask her to go up on stage. I don't know if she'd like that or not. I turn to the waitress in the alcove and ask if I can just grab a couple of napkins from her so I can head back to Timini more quickly.

As soon as they are in my hand, I turn and nearly knock into the lead singer of the band.

"You look like someone who's ready to perform," the man says, his band playing a repeating tune from the stage. "What's your name?"

"Um, Jackson." My voice is still just as scratchy as it was when I first took the bite of cheesecake. I can breathe okay enough to get by, but I won't be running anytime in the next few minutes.

"Patrick up there needs to take a song off. Why don't you come up on stage and be our backup singer for one?"

I shake my head. "I can't sing." Forget the allergic reaction —I can't on a good day.

The man—a guy with a goatee, fancy jeans, and graying hair by his temples—leans in close and whispers like he's trying to tell me a secret, except he's whispering into the microphone for all to hear. "Want to know a secret? It doesn't matter if you can or not, as long as you do it with enough confidence."

I glance at Timini. She's watching me, a curious, interested expression on her face.

Then, one of the guys up on stage—Patrick, probably—starts chanting into his microphone, "Go on stage, go on stage," and within seconds, everyone in the restaurant is chanting the same.

What am I supposed to do—tell him no? If Timini chose this location as a test to see if I can feel as comfortable in a place like this as I used to be, I think saying no would mean failing that test. So I do like the man suggests. I walk up to the front of the room and get on stage with as much confidence as a guy can whose throat is closed off and whose shirt is soaked, clearly from a poor choice at the bathroom sink. The man hands me a tambourine, of all instruments, and clips a mic to my shirt.

Then the band starts playing "Livin' On a Prayer" by Bon Jovi, which I'm grateful for. My scratchy voice matches that much better than it would have with a song from, say, Mariah Carey. I bang the tambourine against my hand until the chorus comes along. Then I take a deep breath and sing, my voice rough and ragged from my current situation, and also so very off-tune from my all-the-time situation.

Eventually, I manage to stop caring what I look and sound like, which is rather impressive considering how very badly I want to impress Timini. But I'm pretty sure that impressing her definitely dropped off the menu a while ago.

When the song finally ends, I bow to the applause, then jump off the stage and walk back to the table where Timini is clapping along with the rest of the room. She stands to greet me and moves in so close that I can feel her warmth and smell her citrus perfume. My senses are on high alert, trying to catch it all.

Then she leans in even closer, bringing her lips near to my ear. Her breath tickles my skin, sending waves of voltage plowing through me. I don't know if she's going to kiss my cheek or tell me I did a good job or something I haven't even imagined yet, but I'm going crazy waiting to find out.

Then she whispers, ever so gently into my ear, "Your fly is down."

I close my eyes, trying to block out everything in this entire building as I sit down and attempt to surreptitiously zip my pants.

Maybe this date was doomed from the start. As our waitress passes by, I ask for the check. I just need to pay and get out of here as soon as possible. Then Timini and I can each drive our separate ways, and I can start working on what is sure to be a very long, painful process of forgetting that this night ever happened.

Timini puts her elbow on the table, her chin resting in her palm, studying me. I'm not even sure what happened to the napkins the waitress handed me before I went up on stage, but for a moment, I think about using my napkin at the table on my shirt. Then I decide that it doesn't really matter at this point.

I meet Timini's eyes again. Mostly because hers haven't left mine, and it's awkward to keep avoiding them.

But then the waitress sets down the check, the spine of its folder ripped so far up that it barely holds together. I slip in cash to cover the bill and a tip good enough to make the teenage waitress's night and hand it back.

When we head outside, I walk Timini to her car. Instead of getting in and driving away as fast as she can, like I've assumed she will, she leans against it, studying me again. Finally, she speaks. "I think we should go out again."

"I…what?" There is no way I heard that correctly.

"You aren't the same guy you were just before you moved.

Tonight, you weren't protecting your image or your ego—you were thinking about people. Tonight, I saw the man I've been chatting with for weeks, not the teenager who broke my heart."

That's what she got out of this night? I no longer care about all the things that went wrong if it brought her to that conclusion.

She takes a step closer to me, her eyes flicking from mine to my lips and back to my eyes. She's back. We're back. We're suddenly back to the point we'd been when it was all just messages sent over a dating app.

Except now, I'm seeing her in person. Talking to her. Feeling her hand as she places it on my chest, right over my heart. Fireworks and cannons erupt in me, and I reach out and cradle the side of her face with one hand and wrap the other around her waist. She immediately closes the remaining space between us, and I press my lips to hers.

I know my lips are moving with hers to fill a desperate need to have her in my life. To fill a longing for her that I hadn't known was so strong until this moment. Then she lets out a small moan that tells me that maybe she wants this relationship to work out just as desperately as I do.

And that makes my whole body relax into the kiss. I soak in the softness of her lips, the warmth of her breath, and the smoothness of her cheek as I run my thumb along it. Then I bring my other hand up to cup her face as well, feeling like I'm holding something precious. Beyond worth. I break the kiss and rest my forehead against hers as we both breathe heavily.

"Woah," she breathes. "And I thought you were a good kisser back in high school. But that... Wow. That was incredible."

I have to agree—she definitely is incredible.

CHAPTER 13

Timini

I LOOK up from the suit coat I'm sewing when my older neighbors, Carol and Meera, walk into the dining room. Peyton hurries out from behind the kitchen island, where she's cooking food for a client, to give the women hugs, and my assistant, Evie, waves at them.

"Thank you for being willing to do this," Meera says as she hands me a skirt. "Normally, I would ask Shirley for help, but since she's off visiting her newest great-grandchild, I had to go to Carol, and…let's just say that wearing it unfixed would've been better."

Carol shrugs. "In my defense, I warned her about my lack of skill before I touched it."

"Well, I figured you'd at least be better at it than me!" Meera turns to me. "And I haven't sewn a stitch in my life. Are you sure you have time to fix it?"

"Yep," I say, moving some of the items from one of the round tables to another so I can spread the skirt out to see what it needs, "because I have Evie. She has kept us on track and aimed in the right direction. We just met with the directors of both shows yesterday, and they both approved the direction we are going with all of the pieces. We even did an impromptu fitting with a couple of the actors who were in the building. We should have no problem meeting our deadline in two weeks. Oh wow, what happened here?"

It looks like the skirt had ripped at the seam. But instead of turning it inside out and sewing the seam so the raw edges would be on the inside of the garment, it appears that Carol placed the two sides one on top of another and then just stitched across it all. And it's not even a straight line.

Carol shrugs, palms up. "Hey, I never said I was an expert."

I grab my seam ripper and go to work undoing the stitching.

"So," Meera says, "how are things with your new man?"

I miss a stitch and poke the end of the seam ripper into the fabric. Luckily, I wasn't pressing hard enough to do any damage. But the question apparently has the ability to make my mind stop working as it simultaneously turns me to goo.

"Addison told us that he's your ex," Carol says.

I smile and go back to work, focusing more this time. "Yeah, and that made it really awkward for a bit, but we got past it. Things are actually going pretty great."

More than great, actually. We've seen each other nearly every night for the past couple of weeks, and we've been texting during the day, too. I've been surprised to find out that he's like the version of Jack I dated in high school before he turned into a jerk, not the guy he became after. Except he's had twelve years to become even more incredible. I never thought I'd enjoy dating someone so much.

"They're adorable together, too," Evie says as I finish removing Carol's stitching and take it to my sewing machine. "He knows that Timini thinks things are going to turn out well if she sees the number one in random places. Well, Jackson's company's offices are in Portland, and they just happen to be pretty close to Hamilton Hall. So yesterday, he snuck over there before our meeting with the directors, guessed where we would likely park, and placed a bunch of sticky notes with the number one written on them in random places all along our path from there to the front door."

A smile spreads across my face just thinking of it. I snip off the stray strings on the part I've sewn, then turn around to my serger to reinforce the seam and keep it from fraying.

"He's come over for a couple of roommate dinners," Peyton says to the sound of chopping vegetables. "You should see the two of them together. It makes you feel like you're wrapped in a warm, fuzzy blanket. I made lasagna and homemade bread-sticks for dinner last time. Everyone was already seated when I took them out of the oven. As I brought it to the table, every-one's eyes were on the food with that look you get when you're really excited about what you're about to eat and just can't wait until it's right there in front of you. Except Jackson. He still had that same look on his face but his eyes were on Timini, not on the food."

Carol whips around to face me, pointing a bent finger at me. "You marry that man!"

I laugh. I'm not actually looking to get married, but I do love Carol's enthusiasm.

"Aww," Evie says, "I want a boyfriend like that."

"Are you single?" Carol asks. "Because I have a grandson."

Evie lifts the presser foot on her sewing machine and pulls out the piece she's working on, snipping the threads. "No, I have a boyfriend. He's just...not like that."

"Well," Meera says, "maybe it's time you dropped him like a wad of cash at Costco and get yourself someone who is." Evie nods, but even Meera picks up on the fact that Evie's expres-sion says she doesn't want to keep discussing her love life. So she turns to Peyton. "And what about you? How much longer do you have until you tie the knot?"

Peyton sighs happily. "Thirteen days. In less than two weeks, I'll be Peyton Peyton and I'll get to wake up every morning next to Max."

We all sigh just as happily. Really, it's hard not to when it's Peyton. She just makes everything seem heavenly. At least I don't have to stress about who to take to the small event. Jackson has already agreed to join me.

"Then Max is going to move in here until Bex's new house is finished and she and Roman move out. Then we'll get our own place. So we'll be here for about three and a half months."

"It's five now," I say. "The builder ran into more problems."

"Aw, poor Bex and Roman!" Peyton makes a sad face, and then it instantly goes back to happy. "But hey, more time with all of us together!"

"Ask Meera why she's so interested in everyone's love life," Carol says.

Meera wears an expression that is much too innocent-looking to actually be innocent. "What? I'm just interested in our neighbors. I'm being neighborly."

Carol crosses her arms and raises an eyebrow. "Okay, then, ask her what she needs the skirt for." When Meera doesn't respond quickly enough, she says, "She's going dancing with a boy tonight!"

Peyton, Evie, and I all cheer and whoop while Meera blushes. Then she playfully slaps Carol's shoulder. "My goodness. With *a boy*. You make it sound like I'm in eighth grade again. I won't ever get over my Faris, but some companionship would be nice. Jerry is a widower, and he's been asking me to go dancing with him for weeks. I woke up one day and went, 'Do you know what? I want to go dancing.'"

"We should celebrate," I say as I toss the repaired skirt to

Meera. Then I hurry out of the kitchen and head across the lobby to the big family room. Bex is working on something on her laptop that she seems pretty focused on but Bex is always up for a distraction. "Want to join us for an impromptu dance party?"

Bex immediately perks up, grabs her phone, and starts scrolling through something. Music, probably.

"Is Addison home?"

Bex looks up from her phone. "She came home to get some organizational supplies for a client, and I don't think I've heard her come back down."

I go to the base of the stairs and yell up, "Addison! Dance party in the kitchen!"

Addison comes bounding down the stairs just as Bex's phone connects with the inn's speakers, and dance music floods the inn.

The three of us join Peyton, Evie, Carol, and Meera in the kitchen, and we all dance to the music, not caring how uncoordinated any of us look, weaving in and out of the six small tables that are covered in fabric, costumes, machines, notions, and patterns. Impromptu dance parties are what get me through any challenge, and I love that my roommates feel the same way about them.

None of the guys are home, but Ian, Roman, and Max have all joined in before. We haven't done an impromptu dance party with Jackson around, so I don't know how he would react to knowing how much of a necessity they are. But the man got up on stage to play the tambourine and be a backup singer when he had a water mishap in the bathroom and a voice that could barely squeak out words. My guess is he would join in.

I'm surprised at how much I want him to be around all the time just so he'll happen to be here for the next one.

My phone blares, even louder than the music, and I find it

under a folded costume. I look at the number on the screen and then answer the call. "Hi, Mom." I press my hand against my other ear and head out to the front porch so I can hear her above the music.

"Hi, Minnie."

Two short words, and I can already hear the stress in her voice.

"Is everything okay?"

"You said you were going to come help me organize the storage room yesterday, but then you never came."

"Oh! Mom, I'm sorry—I completely forgot about that." Maybe I should see if Evie would be willing to organize my personal schedule as masterfully as she organizes my work one. "Why didn't you call me when I didn't show up?"

"I figured you had more important things to do than to help me. Keala, too. I wasn't going to call at all, but it's too big of a job for me, and Neal just keeps complaining about it, and—"

Whenever my mom gets a new boyfriend, it always starts off with euphoria. Then, as their relationship gets more serious, each one makes her react a little differently, and always in a bad way. This one makes her stressed out and unsure of people's motivations. I don't know the guy super well; he had only dated my mom for a couple of weeks before he moved in, and that was only a month ago.

"Mom. I don't mind helping. I just got focused on something and forgot." I can't even remember what stole my focus at the time I was supposed to leave. Maybe a project. Or the Hallmark movie I convinced Jackson to watch with me. Or anything, really. Forgetting things is too often a state of being for me. "Can I come tonight instead?"

"Yes," she squeaks out.

"I'll be there. Mom?"

"Yeah?"

"We'll get it done tonight. No worries."

She lets out a long breath and then takes in a few slow breaths. Her next words come out calmer. "Okay. Thanks, kiddo."

I disconnect the call and then call my sister, Keala. Her two older kids are in school but the chaos of the younger three can still be heard. "We forgot to go help Mom organize her storage room last night."

"Oh, shoot! Is she a ball of stress?"

"You know it."

Keala lets out a long sigh. "I really can't wait until she breaks up with this one."

"Me neither."

I make plans with my sister to help that night and then hang up just in time to see a text from Jackson pop up. It's a picture he has sneakily taken while in a meeting that shows nothing, really, except part of one of his legs and one foot, saying he is thinking of me, and it makes my heart beat double-time.

Like euphoria.

A pang of worry stabs me in my heart. But then I push it away. I am not going to let my relationship with Jackson turn out like every single one of my mom's relationships always do.

CHAPTER 14

Jackson

I KNOW that Timini's day has been busy, but she somehow still looks amazing when I pick her up. Her hair is in a low, loose bun at the nape of her neck, with pieces of hair that haven't stayed in the bun curling by her face and neck. One part, in particular, touches her neck right at the spot where it curves into her shoulder, and all I can think of is how much I want to kiss that spot.

Something seems off, though, and I can't quite tell what it is. Maybe I can get her to say what it is if I ask the right questions. "How did things go at your mom's last night?"

Her brows pull together for a quick second like my question is so far from what is on her mind that it takes a moment for her to pull back. "It went great. It actually wasn't as huge of a job as my mom had imagined it was, and with all three of us working together and having fun doing it, we were finished in no time."

So it's not that, then. I glance over again as I stop at a traffic light before getting on the interstate. She runs her hands down the fitted skirt she's wearing and then looks out the window at nothing in particular.

"Oh!" I say. "You're nervous about tonight. Why are you nervous?"

She looks over at me, and I take a glance back at her before I pull the car forward and maneuver into the lane that will merge onto the freeway.

"Oh, I'm just meeting your family tonight, along with your business friends. Why would you think I'd be nervous?"

I reach out, find her hand, and give it a squeeze. "Okay, first off, it's just my family. You've already met them. They're not scary."

"It's been twelve years since I've seen them, Jackson. It's not like I know them anymore. A lot has changed since I saw them last."

"Fair enough. But they like you."

"Not Naomi. She's never liked me."

"Naomi's just intense. People think she doesn't like them all the time, but I swear that's just her thinking face. And she thinks a lot. Besides, she'll be in a good mood because we're going to be having cake for her birthday."

"It's her birthday, and you didn't tell me?" Timini sounds even more stressed than she was before.

"It's not a big deal. It's not a big birthday celebration or anything. I went with my parents and siblings to her house last night to give her presents while you were at your mom's. Her building doesn't allow candles, though—long story—so we are just blowing out the candles tonight. That's all. I promise it will be fine.

"And as far as the business thing after, it's just a small reception. Not more than a dozen people. And since it's at my parents' house, you'll basically have the home-field advantage by that point. Not a big deal at all."

For the rest of the drive from Quicksand to my parents' place in Lake Oswego, I banter with Timini, like we do over text and over the app's message system while I was in Delhi. I think it's really helped her nerves to relax.

When we get to my parents' front door, before I open it, I turn to her and cup her face in my hands. I give her a look that I hope will make the feeling that everything will be okay sink into her. She smiles up at me, and I just want to drink every bit of her in. And then I kiss those beautiful lips of hers. She melts into me, so she must've gotten the message.

She seems content to stay outside, kissing, all night long. And I'm tempted to do just that. But my family is just on the other side of the door, so I finally pull my lips away. "Come on. I want you to meet my family."

My mom welcomes Timini the moment we walk through the door, complimenting her and trying to make her feel at home. My dad is right behind her, introducing himself. Naomi, Ethan, and Emma are already here, and none of them have brought dates. I introduce them all, and they are kind and welcoming, too. Emma even manages to keep her excitement that Timini is here from bursting over too much. We make our way past the foyer and into the family room.

"Your home is beautiful," Timini tells my mom.

She thanks Timini, but I look at her curiously. There's something behind the words that I can't quite guess. Not enough for my mom to notice, but I've known her well enough to see it hiding.

The more I try to figure it out, the more I realize that she is uncomfortable—she's just very good at hiding it. I look around at the large family room through her eyes. The vaulted ceilings, the ornate trim, the nice furniture, the family picture over the mantel, the art on the walls, the big dining room and kitchen off to the side, and the patio that can be seen beyond the floor-to-ceiling windows. I love my parents' house. It's nice, but also feels warm and homey. I can't guess what about it is making her uncomfortable.

We all chat, and Timini seems to get along with my family so well. I haven't realized how much I've yearned for this until I feel the weight of it lift from my shoulders.

"Well," my mom says, putting her hands on her knees, "we are going to have guests showing up in thirty minutes or less, so we better get to lighting those candles!"

I offer a hand to Timini and pull her to standing. For a moment, we are only inches apart, and she leans into me and whispers, "I like your family. They're more down-to-earth than I was expecting."

I put a hand on the small of her back, guiding her to the dining room table, grinning the whole time. I pull out a chair for Timini and then sit down next to her, and Naomi takes a seat on the opposite side of the table, across from me. She keeps giving Timini odd looks like she wants to say something, but she never does.

Ethan cuts the cake and puts it onto plates, and Emma practically skips around the table as she puts one in each spot. Then my mom follows behind Emma, putting a candle in each person's piece.

Timini's forehead crinkles. "You do candles in everyone's cake?"

I'm surprised to realize I never had her over for a family birthday celebration in high school.

"You can thank me for that," Ethan says before licking the frosting off the knife and setting it aside.

My mom smiles at Timini. "Since Ethan and Emma are twins, they both had candles in their cakes. When Ethan was little, he couldn't understand why everyone wouldn't have candles if they did, so we just went with it. Once he was old enough to understand, he said that since they were the only ones getting presents, everyone else should at least get wishes. It spilled over into everyone's birthdays, and it just kind of became a tradition."

"That's sweet," Timini says. "I like it."

My dad goes around the table and lights each candle. He only has two left when Naomi bursts out, "I'm sorry I hated you in high school!"

My eyes fly to my sister as Timini tenses beside me. *Everyone* seems to be frozen in place, actually. Timini was right about Naomi not liking her? And why hadn't Naomi liked her? Naomi looks embarrassed. And then, like she has been holding her evidence in for far too long, it all seems to spill out of her in a rush.

"Even though we were in the same grade, I hadn't known you too well before you started dating Jackson. And then we were in a history class together. The teacher split us into groups and each group was supposed to make a diorama of a Revolutionary Era town. I was a group leader and you were, too, remember?

"Anyway, I practically had to bribe my group to meet together, and even so, I only got them to come over three times, so I had to do hours and hours of work on it by myself. And then in class, Mr. Zabinski reminded us that it was due in two days and I saw the look on your face—you had completely forgotten about it. So I thought your group's was going to be awful. Especially because after class, you gathered your group together and said to bring ideas and supplies the next day and you were just going to meet at a table in the lunchroom and put it together during lunch.

"And then I watched you guys do it the next day and there was no organizing of the ideas—everyone just started making things and throwing them in and I knew my group's was going to be the best, especially since we spent so much more time on it, but then your group's was the crowd favorite. So, I'm sorry I was mad about that.

"And then you broke up with Jackson. And I know he was being an"—her eyes shoot to our mom for a second— "sorry, Mom—a pack mule's hind end, but I would hear him crying about it at night in his room when he didn't think anyone could hear. And that just really made me not like you even more. And then we moved away for that year, and I didn't really see you when we moved back. And then I just kind of forgot all about you. Anyway, you're actually very lovely. Jackson has told us so many great things about you, and you're everything he said, and it just makes me feel even worse for not liking you back then. Will you forgive me?"

Naomi reaches a hand across the table toward Timini. I am in shock at all my sister has just spilled, and I don't manage to take my eyes off her until I see movement out of the corner of my eye and turn to see Timini reaching out for Naomi's hand.

"I forgive you."

Our table is wide, though, so she really has to stretch to reach Naomi's hand.

And that's when I smell burning hair, and everyone lets out some kind of sound between a startled shriek and a guttural shout as Timini jerks back. I'm not sure who starts smacking at her hair to get it to stop burning first. All I know is that one of our hands manages to catch her plate on the way to her hair, and it lands with the frosting side of the cake pressed into her shirt.

Everyone in the room freezes in stunned silence, our eyes on the lock of hair that apparently burnt through right in the middle because a perfect curl lies on the table. The perfect curl that had rested on the curved part of Timini's neck earlier—the spot I'd wanted to kiss.

Timini tries to peel the cake off her shirt. Half of the frosting stays put and the other half, including the candle, is still stuck to the smashed piece. Big crumbles of it fall to the table as she puts it back on the plate.

"Please tell me you at least made a wish before that candle went out," Ethan says, picking up his fork.

My shock only grows that my brother would joke about that.

But then Timini lets out a sound that is a mix between an exhale and a laugh. "I did—I wished that I'd make tonight more memorable."

And just like that, the tension in the room deflates and everyone starts chuckling. How quickly Timini can recover from something like that and how easily she forgives is astounding to me. I can tell that she's holding some tension that she is trying to keep hidden, though.

"Come on," my mom tells her. "Let's get you in a new blouse."

Timini throws her a grateful look and then gives me a smile and a shoulder squeeze before getting up and leaving the room with my mom.

"I like her," Emma says before taking a bite of her cake.

My dad turns to me. "Listen, son. I know you're not going to like this, but I just got a message and wanted to warn you. Remember how we invited Robin to the get-together tonight?"

I nod. Her family owns a company that we partner with on a few things, so we make sure to keep things cordial with them. My attention is still on Timini's retreating back, though. I am warring between following her to see if there is anything I can do and forcing myself to stay in my seat because helping right now would probably be the opposite of helpful.

"She is dating someone new, and she's bringing him tonight."

I don't get why my dad thinks I'd have a problem with that.

Robin isn't someone I've ever wanted to date. The fact that she is dating someone is great news.

When I don't react, my dad continues. "The guy she's dating is Harper."

Oh.

Harper and I were actually good friends. Or, at least, I thought we were. I hadn't found out that the guy had been using me and hadn't had any interest in actually being friends until a year later when he used some sensitive company information he got from me to buy his way into a position at a rival company.

The betrayal hurt Oliver Innovations. Probably not as badly as Harper thought it would, but I am still feeling the damage the guy did to me personally. His betrayal made me question the motives of everyone who wanted to get close to me a good ten times more than I had before. And now I am going to have to spend the evening in the same room with the guy.

I meet my dad's eyes. "I thought we agreed that Harper was never going to step foot in this house again."

"And he doesn't have to," my dad says. "Robin didn't send the email until they were almost here, but I can email back and say they aren't welcome. Or, I can stand at the door, tell them to leave, and physically stop him from coming in."

I shake my head. That would damage relations with Robin and her company, and I don't want that. "No, it's okay. I can handle Harper for one night."

I take a deep breath. At least I'll have Timini by my side. I can get through this.

CHAPTER 15

Timini

THERE'S a reason all the kids in school called me "Mini." I was petite back then, and not much has changed.

Mrs. Oliver, however, is not. She's plenty thin, but she's also tall and graceful and could pretty much walk around with a crown and the title of "Empress" and no one would question it.

So, grateful as I am that Jackson's mom has taken pity on me and has brought me to her own closet (which is big enough to park my car in) to help me out, wearing one of Jaclyn Oliver's blouses makes me feel like a kid playing dress-up.

I walk down the winding staircase into the family room and Jackson's eyes find mine immediately, a tentative smile on his face. Good golly, he is one beautiful man. How did I ever think I could stay away when I first found out he was Jack in that restaurant? I return his smile and take his proffered hand in mine.

"Is everything okay?"

"Totally. It's cool to have your boyfriend's mom dress you so you'll look good at their business event."

He grimaces.

"Really, though, I'm super grateful. I would much rather be wearing this than a cake-and-frosting-covered blouse."

The doorbell rings and Emma says, "I'll be on door duty!" and practically skips her way to the door. I draw in a slow, deep breath and try to get the Zumba party in my stomach to calm down as Jackson turns to greet the first of the night's guests.

Something I learn very quickly is that business people are on time. That, or they all arrive on a bus together. I'm guessing it's the former, though, because I really can't picture them all on a bus together. All I know is that "a dozen people" means "a dozen plus dates, if they brought someone, so more like twenty." Twenty people—plus Jackson's family—to make small talk with, memorize the names of, and try not to embarrass myself in front of.

I remind myself that I'm here, in Jackson's family room, milling around with a couple dozen people because it means a lot to Jackson. And because "you can't experience new lands from the confines of your comfort zone" and all that. But this is so far out of my comfort zone that I need a map.

Sure, I run my own business, and I'm in a room full of business people. But these aren't people like my roommates, who I met at the Creative Women Entrepreneurs seminar. These are people who help run big, multinational corporations, and I don't think I could feel more out of place.

Well, actually, I do feel more out of place than just that. I sneak a hand up and tuck the lock of hair that is now only an inch and a half long into the part that is pulled back. Jaclyn got me a pair of scissors to trim the singed ends, but that lock doesn't exactly look natural or like it's meant to be that short.

Then I adjust my shirt again. Not that I need to—the thing goes halfway to my knees. Why didn't I ask for a scarf to tie around my waist? Or simply tucked it in?

I can do this. Jackson leads me to a group of three people

who are talking and introduces me to them. I've learned that I can remember people's names more easily if I tie them with something else as soon as I hear it. So when Jackson introduces me to a guy named "Drew," I think of the word drew, like he drew a picture. I imagine him drawing a picture and me getting out a big black marker and writing his name on his breast pocket.

Which is great, except before I even finished tying Drew's name to him, I had two more names thrown at me in quick succession, followed just as quickly by a need to follow the conversation. And the small talk for this group is always about business, never about the weather or how the Trail Blazers are going to play this year. We aren't even two minutes into the conversation when I have to use the guy's name and call him Mark. *Mark.* Because my brain somehow remembers that I marked his name on his shirt, not drew it on.

At the guy's expression, which hovers somewhere between confused and offended, I try to explain that it's because the two names are similar and I wrote it down wrong. When his expression drops "offended," keeps "confused," and adds "judging my lack of an IQ," I stop talking. With how this night is going, I would probably prove him right if I continued.

This place is making me itchy. Everything about this home is rich and elegant and everything I've learned to dislike about money. So are all the people in the room. I've had enough experience around rich people to know that they are not super likely to be nice people regardless of how nice they are acting.

I like dressing up and looking nice. But that is only part of who I am. Being here makes me feel like I'm a messy bun and yoga pants kind of girl in a coiffed hair and pencil skirt world.

I make it through meeting and chatting with the next half dozen people without an incident. I put little check marks in my head for each one because they make me feel rather accomplished right now.

As Jackson leads me across the room toward some other people he wants to socialize with, he puts an arm around my waist and I tuck myself into his side, loving the small moment to just soak him in. I turn my face to him. "You've got a lot of friends here. They're nice, and they seem to really love you."

There's an uncomfortable look on Jackson's face, and I think I know why. "Well, except for that one guy. Harper, right? He tries to come across as a good guy but he's not."

Jackson stops our path toward a small group of our guests and gives me a curious look. After a pause, he says, "Then you are better at sensing authenticity than I am. It took me a year of becoming really good friends with him before I figured that out. If I'd had your help back then, it would've saved me a sizeable number of struggles."

I look at him, hoping he will tell me more. He lets out a quick breath. "Let's just say that the experience left me questioning everyone's motives and wondering what they were looking to gain."

So that was the source of the uncomfortable look I saw on his face when I said that people here loved him. How does he manage to enjoy this world? It seems like he feels the same way about it that I do.

He looks away at a random spot on the wall and says in a low voice, like he's embarrassed to admit it, "It has just left me wondering if people only like me for outside reasons."

I reach a hand up and turn his face toward mine, then place my hand on his chest. "I like you for inside reasons."

The smile he gives me is wide and beautiful and very genuine. And it makes me want to just stare at his face all night. Well, except for the times when I'm kissing those beautiful lips of his.

But preferably not in this place that makes me so itchy.

Getting through the next handful of introductions and small talk with guests is exhausting. Way more exhausting than the first ones were.

And it's not just because of the elbow bump mishap, although that's part of it. I've heard that some people bump elbows instead of shaking hands, but I've never actually seen it happen before. How was I supposed to know that the awkward way the guy held his arm meant he was trying to elbow-bump me? And how could I have guessed that someone had turned in my direction with their drink so close to me, yet completely out of my line of sight, when I went in for a (in hindsight, too enthusiastic) elbow bump? So now I have to feel bad about the carpet, too.

And my feeling exhausted is not just because my compliment to a woman backfired, although that's certainly part of it, too. If I'd stopped to think for two seconds about the type of people I'm currently occupying a room with, I'd have known better than to burst out with, "I love your shoes! I have some in blue. Did you get yours at Target, too?" So I also add feeling bad for being the cause of the hurt look that crosses the woman's face.

It's also because I unknowingly offend someone's grandma. (May she rest in peace.) And because I make a comment about preferring one product over another, only to find out that I'm speaking to the head of product development for the company that makes the product I don't like.

Although the heels I'm wearing are not from Target and are to die for, I really am not looking to put my foot in my mouth again. Before I even have a chance to, Jaclyn steps up to me, linking her arm in mine, and says to Jackson, "Do you mind if I steal her away from you for a moment?"

She heads toward the kitchen, and without meaning to, I let out a massively relieved breath.

Jaclyn chuckles and leads us behind the long island counter. "I find the need to get away from the crowd now and then, too. I figured you might want to help me refresh the cheese tray."

"That's twice you've saved me tonight."

"Well, this is twice that you've dated my son and given him a glow that only exists when you are in his life, so it only seems fair."

From where we stand, I can see across the dining room and into the room with all the people. Jackson is talking to a couple. His eyes shift just enough to meet mine, and he winks. That tiny little motion by him makes butterflies and hope spread throughout me. How can I like this man so much yet be so wary of the world that surrounds him?

I glance at Jaclyn as we work side by side, putting cheese slices and cubes on the tray. "Is this the house you moved to back when we were in high school?"

Jaclyn shakes her head. "This same city, but no. It was several miles away. Did Jackson ever tell you what happened?"

"He didn't." I am so curious to hear the answer now that it's unfathomable I haven't thought to ask the question before.

"I don't know if you remember, but when Jackson was a junior, our company started making a lot of money. I don't know why, but for some reason, we thought that meant we had to buy an expensive house in an expensive neighborhood. Maybe we thought our kids needed to start associating with other wealthy kids or to be in wealthier schools. I don't know. Why we ever thought that was a good idea for our kids at that point in their lives is beyond me. Maybe we just got too wrapped up in everything."

My eyes find Jackson, Naomi, Emma, Ethan, and then Jackson's dad in the crowd, watching them as Jaclyn talks.

"I'm sure you saw some of it before we moved. In fact, I'm guessing that's why you broke up with Jackson. Anyway, it got a lot worse for all four of them once we moved. And it kept getting worse. We absolutely loved our new home. But one night, close to a year after we moved, Grant and I were sitting up in bed after everyone was asleep, and we came to the realization that if we stayed there, we would be ruining our kids. And we were willing to do whatever it took to save them.

"So that summer, we canceled the trip to Rome we had planned and instead took all the kids to Guatemala for six weeks to build homes in poor villages. They resisted the trip so much that we knew it must be the right decision. And it was. Living among some truly impoverished people changed us all."

That was the trip Jackson mentioned as his favorite. I find him in the crowd and can see the difference it made in him. Then I turn back to Jaclyn. "You were able to leave your business for that long?"

"That was very tough for Grant and me, for sure. Our company had been on quite the upward trajectory at that point, and there was the fear that if we took that break, we'd lose all momentum and the company wouldn't recover. But I think we needed that experience away from it as much as the kids needed the experience they got.

"We also decided that our kids' experience in Guatemala and the changes it made in them would just be forgotten if we didn't also get away from the situation that had caused it. So, we went to the people who we'd sold our home in Forest Grove to and offered to buy it back for a sizeable amount over what they had paid us for it.

"They jumped at the offer, so we moved back home just in time for Naomi to start her senior year and the twins to start their junior year. Jackson went away to college, so we didn't get him back home until that next summer. It took a lot of work—

much more than simply moving back into our old house—but I think we managed to undo the damage. We didn't move here until they were all graduated and off to college."

I look at Jackson and his siblings, then again at his dad. "It sounds like you and Grant made quite the sacrifice for your kids."

Jaclyn lifts a shoulder as she arranges the cheese. "'Sacrifice' means giving up something good for something even better, right?" She looks out at her family. "And raising kids who grow to be wonderful adults who we love spending time with is definitely something better."

I smile. "I think you did a good job." I pause a moment, and then a realization dawns on me. "That's why Jackson eats cereal for breakfast while watching cartoons even still."

Jaclyn's perfect eyebrows draw together. "Cereal and cartoons?"

Maybe she doesn't know. I like that it's something Jackson has shared with me.

His dad walks over to us and asks if Jaclyn would like him to take the tray to the party.

"No, I've got it." She picks up the tray. "You take a moment to escape."

Grant smiles at me. "I take it you're escaping, too?"

I nod, and he chuckles. "It can be a lot, can't it?"

We stand in silence for a few moments, Grant on one side of the island and me on the other, both enjoying the get-together from a distance. Then, Grant says, "Jackson tells me that you are designing costumes for a couple of plays at the Williams Theater. How is that going?"

I've forgotten how much Jackson's dad cared about what was going on in my life. He always made me wish I'd had a dad myself.

Work has been so far from my mind all night that his question jolts me back to it. "Really well. We've got a bigger budget for the materials than I usually have, and we've been able to do some really cool things with it. I can't wait to see my designs in action."

Jackson looks like he's ending a conversation with a trio of people and meets my eyes, a smile tugging at his lips. He starts making his way to me, walking with a grace that I now realize he gets from his mom.

"Did Jackson tell you that our family donates heavily to the theaters at Hamilton Hall? So, I've gotten to know a few of the directors."

My eyebrows shoot up. "He hasn't." Long before we started dating again, I knew that his family donated to a lot of causes and charities. They have a lot of art hanging on the walls of their home; it makes sense that they would donate to the arts because it's obviously important to them.

Jackson walks around to my side of the counter and wraps his arm around me.

"I better be getting back," Jackson's dad says. "But, Timini, I'll have to introduce you to the directors you haven't met sometime and see if they might want to send some more work your way."

I feel Jackson tense beside me. But by the time I finish thanking his dad for his offer, Jackson's posture has relaxed, and he meets my lips with his in a quick peck. "I have one more person I'd like you to meet. And then what do you say we get out of here?"

"I would have to say, Jackson Oliver, that you have brilliant ideas."

CHAPTER 16

Jackson

I PULL into the gravel driveway of the house that Timini grew up in. Except for the tree out front that looks twice as big, the house is surprisingly similar to what I remember. Small, with reddish-orange brick, sparse grass in the yard, flowerbeds that are mostly weeds or dirt but always have a flower or two that seem determined to stand proud regardless of what any of their flower buddies want to do, and several wind chimes hanging around the house, their music tinkling in the slight breeze.

Timini told me that we didn't need to leave so early to come here today and that it was okay to be a little late. I pushed her to leave on time, though—I want to make a good impression. I grab the flowers I got for her mom, then get out of the car and go around to Timini's side to open her door.

I was excited to reintroduce Timini to my family. It took a lot longer for Timini to want to bring me to meet her mom again. I don't know if it's because she doesn't want our relationship to move to that level or if it's because she doesn't think her mom will be happy to see me again after all these years. As she steps out of the car, I decide to ask, even though I'm not sure I'll like either answer.

"Do you think your mom won't approve of me?"

Her eyebrows fly up and her head twitches back in surprise. "What? Why would you think she wouldn't? I don't know if you've had very many past girlfriends who've introduced you to their parents, but you're pretty much a parent's dream." She tips her head toward the flowers I hold. "Those are just frosting on the cake. She's going to love you."

I have to admit, that makes my chest puff out a little. But it doesn't help my confusion as we walk up the sidewalk toward the front door. "Then why were you so hesitant to bring me here?"

She shrugs as we go up the stairs to the porch and then she turns toward me as she pulls open the screen door. "You didn't exactly think my family situation was something to be proud of in high school. Things aren't much different now, so..."

My mouth falls open. Back when we were in high school, I didn't come to her house much—we mostly hung out at my place. Was that why? Did I really make her feel like her family or her home was something to be ashamed of? Sometimes I really wish I could have a talk with my high school self. "Timini, I—"

I'm cut off by her mom opening the front door, even though we haven't knocked or rung a doorbell. She must've heard us pull into the driveway. "Oh, goodness. You two are exactly on time. I wasn't expecting you to be here yet. Come in, come in."

Timini's mom isn't a single hair taller than Timini. Unless you count her actual hair—it's about the color of Timini's except for a few streaks of gray, but it's teased enough that it gives her a couple of inches over her daughter. Her face is bright and welcoming, and even though it's a dozen years older than the last time I saw her, it's obvious who Timini got her looks and her ever-present smile from.

"Mom, I'm sure you remember Jackson Oliver. Jackson, this is my mom, Flora."

I shake her hand, thank her for having us over, and present her with the flowers. She beams down at them. I look around at the living room that I haven't seen in so long. It holds a lot of stuff for such a small space, but it isn't messy.

"I am thrilled to have you and Minnie here," she says over her shoulder as we follow her into the kitchen. "Dinner isn't ready yet, of course, but maybe it will be by the time Keala and my grandkids get here."

A marinara sauce simmers on the stove, and Timini and I cut up vegetables for a green salad and chat with her mom while she prepares garlic bread. The kitchen is small and the table pushed against the wall is much too big for the space, but Timini seems so relaxed here. Until each time she meets my eyes. When she does, I can tell that she is suddenly seeing the space through my eyes and is worried about what I think of it. I make sure to keep my expression non-judgmental in any way.

Flora is just putting the garlic bread into the oven to broil when the front door opens and a mass of kids spill inside, an explosion of sound spilling in with them. The oldest looks about seven or eight and the youngest is a toddler. Then a woman hurries in behind them that I'm pretty sure is Timini's sister, Keala. If I remember correctly, she is about three years older and had already moved out when I started dating Timini in high school.

All the kids race to Timini or their grandma, and Timini scoops them into hugs as they come to her. Then she picks up the toddler girl and holds her on her hip. The sight strikes me in a way I haven't expected—there's a warmth in my chest but also a buzzing. I can't spend time trying to figure out what the emotion is because I want to take in Timini with her niece. There's something about her that just causes a…yearning. That's it. Huh.

Timini gives her sister a hug as the other four kids run around the legs of everyone in the cramped kitchen, and then she turns to me. "I don't know if you two remember each other, but Keala, this is Jackson, and Jackson, my sister, Keala."

Keala shakes my hand. "Of course! I totally remember you. You're the one who tore out Timini's heart, threw it on the ground, and then tap danced on it."

I grimace and scratch the back of my neck. "Yeah, I'm that one."

"Keala!" Flora says.

Keala gives me a big smile. "I'm the big sister—it's my job to give you a hard time. For what it's worth, I've heard nothing but good stuff about you lately."

Timini blushes and I have a hard time hiding a smile.

We all start sniffing the air at the same time, and a second later, Flora shouts, "The bread!" She grabs an oven mitt, and when she opens the oven door, thick smoke rolls out of it. A moment later, the high-pitched deafening beep of the smoke detector sounds.

"That means dinner's ready," the oldest boy calls out. All the kids laugh like this might be a joke they tell often.

To the sounds of four adults and five kids coughing in between laughing, Flora tosses me a hand towel and says, "Alarm's in the hall. Timini, grab that door."

Timini opens the door to the patio just off the kitchen, and Flora takes the sheet of garlic bread outside as I head to the hall and hold the towel like it's a flag I'm waving, trying to clear the smoke away from the alarm. I grin the whole time, remembering that Timini's dating profile said something about her needing a guy who wouldn't judge her by her inability to make food that wasn't supposed to be blackened. Apparently, it isn't just height and looks that she got from her mom.

Keala opens a window in the living room and turns on a box fan that is nearby, maybe kept there for this very purpose, and the smoke clears. Before long, we're pulling the table away from the wall, dishing up the food, and all crowding around the kitchen table. The ends of the table have chairs, but the two long sides have benches, which makes the squishing together easier. I somehow end up across the table from Timini, with her four-year-old niece and six-year-old nephew sharing a bench with me.

The pasta and marinara are actually quite good, so she can cook just fine when she isn't distracted by a handful of kids. The conversation around the table moves quickly, gets interrupted frequently, and is often several conversations at the same time. Although there's so much going on with the kids that I'm not sure most of it can count as conversation.

Then the six-year-old boy on the other side of the little girl next to me turns and says, "Do you like kids?"

I smile and distinctly hear Timini stop talking in the middle of a sentence to hear my answer. "I do. I hope to have my own someday."

"How about today?" The boy pushes on his sister, sliding her down the bench closer to me. "Because we have an extra one. It'll only cost you five bucks."

The little girl turns to her brother and returns his shove. "I told you I can't be bought, so quit trying to sell me to random people!" Then she turns back to me, and in a much calmer voice, says, "But if you want to give me presents or candy, that would be okay."

I chuckle right along with Timini and her sister, but her mom gives a loud laugh that's contagious enough that all the kids start laughing, too.

When it dies down, Timini looks at her mom, studying her. "You seem so calm and happy today, Mom. Are you…" She looks around the room like she's noticing something for the first time. "Wait. Where's Neal? Why isn't he here?"

"Well," Flora says, straightening out her crumpled paper napkin and then folding it, "after the two of you came and helped me clean out the storage room, I just kept thinking how nice it felt to have all that old, worthless stuff out of the house and how great it was to free up so much space. It made me want to get rid of other dead weight, which got me thinking about other projects I wanted to take on. I realized that the dead weight I wanted to get rid of most was Neal. So I broke up with him."

"Finally!" Timini shouts and then reaches toward the end of the table to give her sister a high five.

The kids all pump fists and shout, "Yes!"

All I can do is look around the room at everyone's reactions, tilting my head to the side as I try to figure out why everyone is reacting the way they are to their mom and grandma breaking up with…her boyfriend, I guess, since none of the kids seem to view him as a grandparent. Still, it's kind of disturbing.

"You didn't like Neal?" Flora seems just as confused as I am, at least. So I'm not crazy.

"I just…" Timini seems to be choosing her words carefully. "…didn't like how much he made you constantly worry that no one cared about you anymore."

"You're supposed to tell me when a guy is no good for me!"

"Tell you?" Keala asks. "When you were as stressed out as you were with Neal living here? You wanted us to add to that?"

Flora draws in a deep breath and then blows it out slowly. "You're right. I probably couldn't have handled it. Although I did figure this one out and got him to leave on my own."

"And we are proud of you," Timini says, beaming at her mom.

We stay and play games with her family (including one that seems to be called "All the kids huddle together to come up with a plan to tackle and then wrestle Jackson to the ground"). And even though we've been here for another couple of hours, the moment they all cheered to find out that Flora broke up with her boyfriend keeps unsettling me.

It takes half the car ride home before I figure out how to bring it up in a nonchalant way. Finally, I settle on, "I remember from high school that you said your mom went through boyfriends pretty frequently. I was surprised to see that she was still living in the same house. She never moved into a boyfriend's place?"

Timini shakes her head. "Nope. I think she knows not to do anything too permanent since none of her relationships last very long."

"She goes into them thinking they won't last?"

"No, she always expects them to last. Weirdly, she never sees it herself because I got to the point where I knew they wouldn't last by about the time I was seven. And trust me; it's a good thing that they don't last. She's never been the best judge of who will be a good fit with her."

Timini's life growing up was so different from mine. I can't fathom how it must've been for her to have never had a father figure in her home for very long. And if I'm being honest, it worries me a bit that Timini might not see a relationship as something that should last a lifetime. I want to straight-up ask her what her thoughts are on it but I can't right now. She's already been worried that I'll be a harsh judge of her family, and a question like that would only confirm it.

So, instead, I just ask questions I'm curious about. "Were

there any where your hope that things would work out over-powered your thinking that it wouldn't?"

At her silence, I glance over to see that she's biting her lip, thinking. "One, I guess. I was probably nine, and even I could tell that money was tight and that my mom was really worried that we'd lose the house. But she always said that we never had any reason to worry because things always worked out in the end. And then she started dating someone with a lot of money, and she thought—we all thought—that everything would work out. But that one *really* didn't."

I'm not going to ask any more questions about her mom. The answers are just filling me with dread. Instead, I switch the conversation to the charity dinner she'll be joining me for and Peyton's wedding that I'll be joining her for. If agreeing to attend two functions like that together isn't a sign that this relationship is serious, I don't know what is.

CHAPTER 17

Timini

OKAY, so admittedly, I have been dreading this charity dinner with Jackson. But now that I'm walking into the ballroom of the Sentinel, arm-in-arm with him, I realize that there are actually three really great things about it.

One, the event is mostly for business people, but it isn't like they're here to discuss business or how to be pretentious or anything like that. It's actually a charity dinner—the kind where people pay an obscene amount for a meal and all proceeds go to a charity.

That charity is the arts in the Portland metro area, which is cool. Because the more people donate to the arts, the more places like the theaters in Hamilton Hall can produce shows. And I've seen firsthand how much theater alone can bring up a community and the people in it.

Plus, the more they can produce shows, the more costume designers are needed. So events like this are helping me get that much closer to one day having my own space for my own shop. Then I'd be able to hire more people like Evie.

Two, I get to wear a fancy dress. This is one I designed

myself months ago. Inspiration struck between projects, and I ran with it. I can't explain it, but with my height and build, wearing a full-length dress always makes me feel like a little kid. But this dress has the elegance of a long gown yet comes to just barely above my knees. The skirt is a little fuller but doesn't flow out like a princess's dress—it drapes beautifully, like a queen's. It's a deep purple and has a shimmer to it, and it makes me feel amazing.

Plus, my hair is up. Which means that it's easy to hide the lock that got burned off and still looks weird if I don't do my hair right.

And three, Jackson is wearing a tux. And oh boy, is the man on fire in a tux. He looks tall and lean, and his face is just so beautiful that I want to pull him into an alcove and make out with him for several long minutes. Or hours.

I must be sending those thoughts out there pretty loudly and Jackson must be catching them because he gives me a look that nearly turns my knees to jelly. Then he leans in close to my ear and breathes, "Have I mentioned how beautiful you are?" His breath is warm and tickles my ear, sending little zings of electricity down my neck and across my shoulders.

I turn to him, although I can't exactly get my lips as close to his ear even with these heels, and say, "Only a couple dozen times tonight. But don't worry—you aren't in danger of hitting the maximum number anytime soon."

He chuckles and then leads us along a pathway toward the table we've been assigned to but by way of a few dozen people who we stop to say hello to.

I can tell that this dinner is geared toward people who support the arts because of how beautifully decorated it is and how expensive the place settings look. Everything is in Kelly green and white, and the table centerpieces include the most unusual live plants I've ever seen. They look like a cross between a bonsai tree and a succulent.

Someone steps up to the podium on a stage at one end that I hadn't even noticed and asks everyone to find their seats so that dinner can begin. When I sit in my seat and Jackson tucks it in, I take a moment to run my hands over the soft fabric of the chair. Even it is elegant.

All of Jackson's family is present, but I'm dismayed to find out that none of them will be sharing a table with us. So that means our table includes six other people that I don't know.

The salad has the most vibrant, beautiful vegetables I've seen in a long time. The cherry tomatoes on it are especially huge. Like more-than-one-bite huge. I'm not about to bite into the tomato and have the insides squirt out onto the people sitting on either side of me. I cringe in embarrassment just thinking about it.

Instead, like a perfect lady, I decide to spear the tomato with my fork, gently slice it in half, and then eat half at a time. Except when I attempt to stab it, it instead flies from my plate to the middle of the table and lands on the bonsai-succulent like a too-big Christmas bulb.

My immediate instinct is to awkwardly stand, since my knees will have to stay bent—this tucked-in chair's legs aren't going anywhere on this carpet—and reach for it. Although, logically, I know that these tables are big and I can't reach it, I somehow still decide to try. Of course, the awkward standing just calls more attention to myself and what I've done. And it makes me come alarmingly close to knocking over the wine glass of the man to my left.

I sit back down, deciding that my tomato is just part of the centerpiece now, and glance at Jackson. He's just hiding a smile, gives me a wink, and leans in close to whisper, "I think it looks good there."

Okay, Timini, pull it together.

You'd think getting past the tomato-flinging incident would've calmed my nerves. Apparently, though, all the small talk is keeping my nerves on edge because those nerves, which have taken up residence in my hands, show themselves again not long after the wait staff serves the main course. In a move that I couldn't replicate if I tried, I pick up my fork and it flies out of my hand and lands somewhere under the table by my feet.

I make a move to reach for it, but Jackson puts a hand on my arm, stopping me. Instead, he looks over to the nearest waiter and holds up a finger. Within seconds, the man is at his side, and Jackson asks if he can bring a new fork. Yeah, in hindsight, that really is a better option than what had been my plan.

I swear I can act normal in social situations. Why does everything go wrong when I'm around people who care even more than usual that I act normal?

The waiter nods but instead of stepping away from the table, he bends down close enough to whisper in my ear. "Ma'am, you might want to check the back of your dress. It seems it got caught in one of the rungs of the chair."

My eyes grow wide and I suck in a breath as my hand flies to my backside. Sure enough, the skirt is elegantly draped upward, very un-queenlike, resting on one of the four rungs of the chair, lifting it enough that I'm sure I'm giving the tables behind me a perfect peek at my underwear in the space between the bottom rung and the seat.

My face burns red hot as I smooth down the fabric and tuck it under me as it should be. I dare a quick peek behind me to see just how many people might likely have caught the view, and several immediately drop their smiles and light chuckles right along with their gaze.

My mind scrambles back through the dinner, trying to

figure out how and when I managed to get my skirt up there. Probably when I reached forward to grab the tomato, which still sits in its place of honor on the plant. How did I not notice it, though? Probably because the fabric of the seat doesn't feel so different from the fabric of my dress.

Moments later, the waiter places a fork next to my plate and gives me a small nod.

The dinner and the speeches can't end fast enough. It says volumes about my flubs since first sitting at this table that I am looking more forward to the "gather in clusters and socialize" portion of the evening than to the "eat delicious food" portion.

I briefly think of my mom and how she never seems to know when she is dating a guy who is completely wrong for her. She just seems blind to all the clues. And then, for a moment, I wonder if maybe my clues are all the things that are going wrong that don't usually go wrong for me.

No. I stop myself. I am *not* going to think that way.

We make our way to several groups of people that we hadn't said hello to on the way in and are currently standing with two couples and a single guy who are giving me looks like they definitely think I don't belong here. Okay, so I might agree with them, but they don't have to try so hard to make sure I am even more uncomfortable about it. Then, someone walks up to Jackson and says, "Can I pull you away for two minutes?"

The man doesn't need to apologize—I want to thank him for getting me away from this group! But then Jackson turns to me, gives my hand a squeeze, and says, "I'll be right back."

Oh. I'm not going with him. I'm staying with this group. I try not to panic and really wish I had Googled how to be better at small talk before I left home. Maybe I should just excuse myself to go to the restroom and Google it while I'm there.

I am opening my mouth to do just that when someone steps into the space where Jackson had been. I glance over to see it's

Harper. The guy from the reception at Jackson's parents' home who Jackson really doesn't like. The one who had used him. Harper shakes everyone's hands, going around the circle, shaking mine last.

"It's good to see you again, Timini." He clasps his second hand on the outside, trapping my hand between his, his brows drawn down in concern. "I know how uncomfortable it can feel to be a fish out of water." He sucks in air through his teeth, grimacing. "I mean, you didn't grow up with any of this, right? It can be a lot to get used to. You have to deal with so many obstacles—everything from slippery silverware to wardrobe malfunctions. Tough stuff. Anyway, I've got to get back to Robin, but I wish you all the best in surviving the night."

I'm so in shock from his words that I don't even have time to form a thought before he walks away, leaving me with a burning face and a spinning head. I would escape straight to the restroom without even excusing myself from the other five people in this group, except that my eyes are still on Harper when he walks right over to where Jackson is talking with the man who pulled him away.

Harper's back is to me, so I can't see his facial expression, but he only has time to say a sentence or two before Jackson's eyes flash to mine, and they don't look happy. Almost accusatory.

I am still reeling from Harper's words and Jackson's expression when Jackson comes back over to join me. He doesn't slip an arm around my waist like I expect him to or ask if I'm okay. He just stands next to me, arms folded, like he is coming back to fill his hole in the group but isn't happy about it.

The other five have apparently switched the conversation from where Harper left it to education quite seamlessly because they've gotten pretty deep into the discussion while I haven't been paying attention.

"I mean, really, a Master's degree is the new Bachelor's," one of the men is saying, "and for most people, that isn't enough. If you only have a Bachelor's nowadays, you're no one."

The more he talks, the more I seethe. I am here to support Jackson, so I need to get out of here before I say some things that would be very unprofessional.

"And if you don't have a Bachelor's?" the single guy asks.

"Well, that's why they have jobs like flipping burgers and cleaning out sewage systems, am I right?" He claps a hand on the other guy's shoulder and they both guffaw.

I can't believe that Jackson is staying quiet through this.

The men haven't even finished laughing before the woman who is with the first guy turns to me and says, "Where did you graduate from, dear?"

I look at Jackson for a long moment, giving him plenty of time to say something before turning back to the woman. My pulse is racing, and heat rushes through me. I take a calming breath and then say, "I didn't. Now, if you'll please excuse me."

I walk out of the ballroom as fast as my five-foot-one height plus four-inch heels can take me. So, Jackson can manage to not let money turn him into a jerk when it's just the two of us, but he can't when he's around groups of people with money. And dinners like this are a big part of his life.

Which means that I can't be part of his.

"Timini, wait." I hear Jackson's footsteps behind me as I near the doors leading outside.

I turn to face him.

"I—" He starts like maybe an apology is coming, but it doesn't come.

I give him a small moment, and then say, "So much for your promise." Then I walk out of the hotel, already bringing up the app to request an Uber.

CHAPTER 18

Jackson

I SIT with my laptop in an empty conference room, trying to get through my emails. Not that I have to be in the conference room for this, but I haven't been able to focus at all in my office.

So far, the conference room isn't working, either.

I spot movement from the corner of my eye and glance at the door in time to see my entire family filing into the room. Naomi and my parents take seats around the conference table, Emma stays standing, and Ethan half-stands and half-sits on the conference table, all of them facing me.

"What the h—" Ethan glances at Mom. "Sorry, Mom. What in the world happened last night? The one time I saw you after the dinner finished was when you were by the wall, talking to Mitch. Then I saw Harper go over to you for, like, two seconds. I was wondering what he possibly could have to say to you and was on my way over to tell him to leave when you walked over to Timini. You were there for under a minute before she was fleeing toward the door like she never wanted to see you again."

My eyes drop to the table. "That's a fair assessment. I'm sure she doesn't."

"So what happened?" Ethan asks, spreading his arms wide.

"What happened was, I turned into an idiot." I run my hands through my hair, frustrated. "Just being around Harper always makes me question everyone's motives and wonder if people are getting close to me because of who I actually am or because of something stupid like money or influence or something.

"Timini was talking with the Chesworths and Finn McKee. After Harper joined them, he came over to me and said, 'Just a bit of friendly advice: you might want to keep a close eye on your girl. She found out how influential the people she was talking to are in the theater world, and she's name-dropping you like crazy to get what she wants.' And then I glanced at Timini, and she had this look on her face like she was appalled that he told me."

Emma had been pacing while I talked, but she stops and turns to me. "And you believed him?! *Harper*. The least trustworthy person you know. And you were like 'Oh, tell me anything about Timini and it doesn't matter how much I actually know her and you don't, I'll believe you.'"

Also a fair assessment. I can't believe my own stupidity.

Naomi shakes her head. "Harper probably has some plan. Like 'warning' you will get him back in your good graces so he can use you again. Or maybe he's just being petty. Why would you ever listen to him?"

"I don't know! Things have just been messing with my head lately. Like at that reception at our house—Dad, you and Timini were talking in the kitchen, and I came over just in time to hear you tell Timini that you were going to introduce her to people at Hamilton Hall."

Dad gives me a stern look. "She wasn't the one who brought it up. *I* did, because I know how serious you are about her, so of course, I would offer to do something that helps her."

I probably knew that. Of course, that is something Dad would do. And if I wasn't sure, I should've just asked him instead of letting it seep into my head like poison. No, I realize. I shouldn't have asked Dad. I should've just trusted Timini from the start.

"And now I've ruined everything. She broke up with me a dozen years ago because I was a jerk. I somehow got her to forgive me and trust that I am a different person now. And then I went and repeated history all over again. I was a jerk again last night, so she's got no reason to trust me."

Mom reaches across the table, squeezes my hand, and speaks for the first time. "You don't know that. Don't give up so easily, and don't take away her chance to choose that herself. But right now, go home, dear. It's clear just by looking at you that you didn't get any sleep last night. Sleep first, and then you'll be able to get things figured out when you wake."

I shake my head. "No, because then it'll be all I can think about. I need to be here so I can keep my mind busy."

Ethan leans forward so he can peek at my computer screen. "How's that working out for you?"

I let out a humorless chuckle. "Maybe not so well."

"I agree with your mom," my dad says. "You were supposed to be driving to the coast for Timini's roommate's wedding today, so no one was planning on you being here. You don't have any meetings. Go home."

———

I do go home, but I don't go to sleep. Instead, I flop down on my couch with the curtains open, facing the city but not really seeing it. Then I pull out my phone and open Chat Match for the first time since Timini and I switched to texting after meeting in person.

Then I start scrolling through our conversations from the beginning. It makes me long for her so deeply that it hurts.

It's strange reading everything now, knowing that it was Timini I was chatting with. And especially after getting to know her so much better over the last couple of months. Some parts make me laugh all over again. Some parts make me miss her even more. And some parts remind me of things I've already forgotten.

I get to the part where I asked what her biggest regret was, and I feel a physical pain in my heart when I read her words about not finishing college.

> Timini: It's whenever the subject comes up in conversation that I most regret it. Not being able to say that I graduated makes me feel inconsequential. Not capable of finishing things. Like I wasn't smart enough to do it. I avoid the conversation at all costs because it always makes me feel like a loser.

And then I feel a second stab when I read my own words, not too much further down in the conversation.

> Jackson: So I made a promise to myself from that point on to always step in and defend someone whenever they needed me to.

I didn't step in to defend her last night when she needed me to. Especially when it was regarding something painful to her. I've broken a promise to myself, and I've broken an unspoken promise to Timini. She knows it, too. I hadn't understood what she'd been referring to when she said, "So much for your promise" right before she left the hotel. But now I know for certain that she was talking about that promise.

I lie down on the couch, grab one of the couch pillows, and bury my head under it.

CHAPTER 19
Timini

It is easier to keep my mind off Jackson now that we are in the bride's room at the cute little reception area on the coast, helping Peyton get ready for her big day, than it was during our caravan from Quicksand to the coast. At least in this room, it is just the girls—me and my roommates. No couples.

Peyton is just so beautiful and so happy and so excited to become Peyton Peyton. Now that she has her wedding dress on —a fitted white one that flares just past her hips and is so very Peyton it should be named after her—we all stand around her, making sure her hair and makeup and veil and shoes and dress look perfect. Peyton is practically glowing, and the three of us are just basking in it.

"I can't believe the day is finally here," Peyton says.

Bex nods. "This was a long time coming. Emphasis on the 'long.'"

Peyton playfully smacks Bex's arm with the back of her hand. "Hey, now. Not all of us can figure things out as quickly as you did."

"Well," Addison says, "I think it's sweet that you're

marrying your best friend. I bet it'll be nice to have that friend-ship foundation in your marriage."

I reach out and twist a curl of Peyton's that isn't exactly right. "That, and the fact that you two are perfect for each other."

"We are, aren't we?" She gives a happy sigh, smooths down the front of her dress, and then turns toward us to wrap us all in a hug. "And I'm so glad that you are all here with me."

There's a knock on the door, and then Peyton's dad pokes his head in. "Hi, Sugar Bear. It looks like they're ready for us. Are you ready?"

"I am so ready!"

As the rest of us file out of the room, Peyton slips on her white, sparkly sandals and then hooks her arm in her dad's. The two of them are so sweet together. I try not to let thoughts enter my mind about how, if I ever get married, I won't have a dad to walk me down the aisle.

I follow Bex and Addison out to the beach where everything is set up for the ceremony. Just behind the minister stands a simple arch with gauzy sea foam green fabric draped along it. A carpet of the same color leads from the edge of the wooden patio down the center aisle to where Max stands in a light gray tux, looking like he is as happy standing in the sand as he would be standing on a cloud in heaven.

Which is practically the case—the waves coming into the shore in the background, the ocean sounds, the shades of blues and greens that are only found on the shore, the sandy beach—all of it is pretty heavenly.

Two rows of four seats sit on either side of the carpet, keeping things small and intimate, just like Peyton wanted, and I know almost all of the people sitting in them. Ian and Roman are already seated on the front row on the left-hand side, with empty seats next to them for Addison and Bex. Max's friends

Hunter, Emilio, and Leo—the three we all went camping with back when Max was trying to convince Peyton that they should be more than friends—are all seated on one side along with Hunter's wife and Emilio's and Leo's dates. Max's mom sits on that side, too, with an empty seat beside her that is probably for Peyton's dad.

On the row behind my roommates are the grandmas next door, Shirley, Carol, and Meera. Which leaves one seat next to them for me. As I slide into my seat, it strikes me how badly I wanted Jackson sitting here, an empty seat beside him, waiting for me. And how badly I miss him.

No matter what, though, I am going to keep my emotions in check. This is Peyton's day.

Meera leans over Carol to give me a fist bump and whispers, "Welcome to the single ladies' row!"

This is the first of my roommates' weddings where I hadn't needed to go find someone to be my date for the evening. It's the first one where I had a date set up and assured for weeks. It is also the first one I've shown up to without a date at all.

Carol leans toward me and says, "I always wanted a beach wedding."

"Oh, yeah?"

Carol nods. "I mean, who wouldn't? This is gorgeous!"

"I wouldn't." Usually, I never think about my own wedding or if it will ever happen. I find myself actually thinking about it, now, though. "When I get married, it isn't going to be someplace where I can't wear heels."

Carol chuckles and pats my knee. "Your time will come. And when it does, you wear the most fabulous heels you can find."

The soft music coming from the speakers changes to the wedding march and we all turn in our seats. Peyton and her dad are nearing the end of the wooden patio. Her dad looks like he's going to burst some buttons on that tux shirt with how proud he is, and Peyton looks like the universe has come together to turn this one moment in time into perfection, and she's wearing a smile to match.

I turn to see Max's reaction just as he brushes under his eye with his knuckle. As long as he waited for Peyton to view him as more than a friend, I can see why getting to this moment would bring a tear.

We all swivel in our seats as Peyton and her dad walk up the aisle. Then he gives her a kiss on the cheek, squeezes both her hands, and takes his seat next to Max's mom.

Back when I first signed up for Chat Match, I had zero plans of finding someone to have a serious relationship with and definitely wasn't looking for a future husband. But seeing how happy and in love Peyton and Max are as they hold hands and smile at each other while the minister speaks, and seeing my blissfully wedded roommates sitting on the row in front of me makes me actually yearn for it.

And it makes me miss Jackson horribly. Most of my dating experiences with guys have only lasted one or two or three dates. I have had a few relationships that have lasted over a month, though. Each time I ended things with one of them, I actually felt a huge sense of relief. Ending things with Jackson brought me no relief—only heartache as I've never known before.

Peyton and Max have written their own vows, and as they recite them, almost everyone is reaching a knuckle up to dry a tear.

Once they finish promising to always be there for each other, the minister pronounces them husband and wife. They kiss the sweetest kiss, and cheers erupt from all of us before they break the kiss and turn to us, grinning. Peyton motions to have all sixteen of us come in for a group hug. Then she goes around and gives us all hugs individually.

When Peyton gets to me, she holds out her bouquet. "This is for you."

My eyebrows draw together. "What? Why?"

"You know—the bride tosses the flowers to the single ladies and one of them catches it. But I wanted to give it straight to you since you're the only one of us still single."

"I am not the only single lady! There's Shirley, Carol, and Meera. And Max's mom. They're all single."

Shirley places a wrinkled hand on my arm. "But we've all been married before."

I motion to where Emilio and Leo stand with their dates. "And there are two more single ladies over there." I hold my hands out like a shield between the flowers and me. "Really, you should toss it. It's tradition, and I know how much you want a traditional wedding."

"Are you sure?"

I nod with complete conviction. "Yes. Please." That bouquet represents hope, and hope is dangerous. Sure, I ache for Jackson. But something has changed for him, and I'm not sure he still feels the same way.

Peyton nods once. "Okay. I'll toss it." She gathers the three grandmas from next door, Emilio's and Leo's dates, and even manages to get Max's mom to join in.

But I don't stand with the others. Instead, I take a seat in one of the vacated chairs to watch. Peyton turns her back to the group and then tosses the bouquet high into the air. And I guess she doesn't know her own strength because it goes sailing over the heads of all of the single ladies gathered to catch it.

But to everyone's delight (based on how much they are cheering), Carol, Meera, and Shirley are the ones who go running for it. Then, in a move that surprises everyone, Meera leaps for it. She jumps high enough, but instead of her hand grabbing onto the bouquet, she just bats it, sending it hurling at a much faster speed straight at me. I don't even have time to fully get my arms up to protect myself before the bouquet smacks me right on the forehead.

And then it falls into my arms that were going up to protect my head.

Honestly, I didn't know that seventeen people could cheer so loudly. I let out a breath of a chuckle at the absurdity of it all. Then, as I gaze at the flowers in my hands, the full force of how much I want a life with Jackson—dinner parties and business receptions and all—comes crashing down on me. The emotions that I have been working so hard to keep inside all day long spill out and run down my cheeks.

Within seconds, Peyton, Bex, and Addison are wrapping me in a group hug. A second or two after that, Shirley, Carol, and Meera add themselves to the hug.

They hold me for a long moment as silent tears run down my face. Then Peyton, who is the closest to me, tips my chin up, brushes away my tears with her fingers, and tucks some of my hair that has fallen into my face (including the short piece that was burned) behind my ear. "Things will work out," she says in a voice that is so sure and so confident that I believe her. "You will get everything you never knew you wanted—because you never did make that list of what you wanted in a man—and you will get your happily ever after."

"You will," Bex says. "And then we'll have a group date where we eat amazing food, watch *Flip My House, Not My Life*, give unsolicited advice, and have a dance party with all of us."

I hug all the wonderful ladies in my life and let myself hope that they might be right.

CHAPTER 20

Jackson

I WAKE up from a very rough night at the sound of my doorbell. I'm still in the same spot on the couch where I crashed last night, still in yesterday's clothes. All I managed to do was eventually close the curtains. I ignore the bell.

Then I hear a weird knocking on the door like it's from an elbow instead of knuckles.

"It's Naomi. Let me in, Jackson."

My head throbs. Whether it's from dehydration or from the terrible nightmares I had all night, it's hard to tell. "Go away."

"Remember how you let the front desk know that I could have a key to your apartment so I could come in and water your plants when you were on long trips? I'm betting you never revoked that. Don't make me go all the way back down to get a key from them. Because I will, but I will drop the açaí bowl I brought you in the trash on the way down if you don't let me in. And it has all your favorite toppings. Even dragon fruit."

I sigh and get up. If my sister is one thing, it's persistent, so there's no sense fighting it. Of all the people I might have expected to show up on my doorstep, though, I would've guessed Emma, not Naomi. I open the door, and Naomi comes in, a container in each of her hands.

"Thanks for not making me go back down. I wasn't about to toss the bowl I brought for me even if I did toss yours, and I planned to eat it in front of you and make you totally jealous." She sets them down on the bar counter, motions to one of the bar stools, and says, "Sit." Then she goes around to the kitchen side and gets out two spoons before making a detour to the living room, grabbing the remote, and pressing to open the curtains covering the floor-to-ceiling windows.

Sunlight spills into my apartment as she comes back to the bar and hands me a spoon. "Dude." She wrinkles her nose as she takes in my disheveled state. "Don't you have a morning routine that you never stray from? You should've stuck with it today."

I'm not sure I want to do anything today. "Is that why you came over? To tell me to shower, shave, and put on clean clothes?"

She takes a bite of her açaí bowl. It looks good, but I'm not sure my stomach can handle eating mine.

"I hadn't planned on that. But now that you mention it, let's add it to the list. No, I came over to get you out of your funk and kick you into action."

I just look at Naomi, not quite understanding what she means. It's Saturday. It's not like she needs to get me off to work or anything.

Naomi lets out a long sigh and then sets her spoon down, turning to face me. "I want Timini as a sister-in-law. So I'm here to help you figure out how to win her back."

My head jerks up in surprise.

"I like her. And I think you really do, too."

I nod.

"Do you love her?"

I loved her a lot back in high school. Enough that it took a very long time to get over her and move on. It really didn't take long into our relationship this time around before I fell for her just as deeply. And I've been falling even more in love with her daily since then. "Yeah, I do."

Naomi nods like I'm confirming what she already knows, and then picks up her spoon and takes a bite of her fruit. "She's the most down-to-earth person I know, and I know that's important to you. She's also fun and kind, and I've actually seen some of her work as I've helped out with the arts side of our charity. She's pretty incredible."

She is. All of it.

"I wish you could see yourself from our point of view. Ever since you started dating Timini again, you've been happier. Calmer. More…self-assured. Confident. Focused. Hopeful. You come up with more creative solutions to issues at work. And, to the shock of everyone, you've been more flexible. You no longer stress so much about little things not going according to your schedule."

A few of those things I have noticed in myself. Most I hadn't before Naomi pointed them out. All I know is that I'm happy and I like who I am when I'm dating Timini.

"But most of all, I've seen the way she looks at you. She loves you, Jackson. You. Not your job, not your money, not your influence. *You.* And as a sister, I can't see my brother get someone like that in his life and then stand by and let him just mess it up. This needs fixing."

I realize that both times I dated Timini, she always liked me for me. The outside things that people in my circles always seem to like me for are actually repellents to Timini. She doesn't like fancy dinners or networking events, yet she still goes to support me.

She has looked beyond all the biggest, loudest, most obvious things in my life and saw through to the core of who I am. It is a gift I haven't experienced in my life for a long time.

"*How*, though? I'm not sure it is fixable. I put her in a situation I knew she was uncomfortable with. I'd been trying to get a quick meeting with Mitch for weeks, and I knew he wouldn't talk about his company possibly helping ours with this Delhi thing if Timini was present.

"But I never should've left her in the presence of three people I knew were arrogant, pompous jerks. Well, four, once Harper showed up. But then, when I came back, I just stood there while they attacked, knowing that they were attacking her Achilles heel."

My stomach roils just thinking about it again. How could I have done that?

Naomi smacks my shoulder with the back of her hand. "Honestly, I sometimes wonder how we can even be siblings." She stares at her açaí bowl for a long time and then pushes it away. "Well, I think you need to prove to her that you can be trusted. And however you do it, make it meaningful."

I nod.

"And then don't *ever* be someone she can't trust again."

I let out a humorless breath of a laugh. This is one lesson that is burned so deeply into me that I don't think I'll have to learn it twice.

"Ever."

"I know."

"I'm serious, Jackson. You've got to have her back, always. No matter what."

"I promise," I say with a more firm conviction than I've ever made a promise before.

"Okay," Naomi says. "Go shower. Take longer than seven minutes, and while you're in there, figure out how you're going to win her back."

CHAPTER 21
Timini

AFTER WE ALL make the drive back to Quicksand the day after Peyton's wedding and Peyton and Max head off on their honeymoon, I go straight to my room and think about unpacking the overnight bag I took. Then I decide I don't care and just drop it on the floor by my closet.

I turn around to see Bex and Addison at my door, a bowl of peanut M&M's in Addison's hands.

"Can we come in?" Bex asks.

"If you're bringing peanut M&M's, then always."

The three of us sit on my bed in a circle, the bowl of candy in the middle of us. Rain is pouring down outside, so it's dark and gloomy, just like I'm feeling. But it also makes me think of how Jackson actually likes being in the rain, which makes me miss him even more.

Bex told me a few weeks ago that I self-sabotage relationships. I was defensive about it at the time, but I spent the whole drive home from the coast thinking about it. "Do you guys know why I self-sabotage?"

"Timini," Addison says, "I don't think that what happened was your fault—"

"No. I don't need you to…" I let out a frustrated breath, not knowing how to explain. "Listen. This is important. I need to figure it out."

Addison nods. "Okay, then, we'll help you. Uh, I'm guessing it probably has something to do with your mom and how her boyfriends are always bad for her."

"I know that I grew up thinking that things were always worse when you were with a guy, and I kind of internalized that. It was probably the reason why I always chose to date the kind of guys I did because then I knew I wouldn't be with them for long." I shake my head. "But I don't think that's my issue with Jackson. I just don't know what is."

"Oh," Bex says. "I've got an idea. Addison and I will list, rapid-fire, every reason we can think of that might be the issue, based on what we know of your situation growing up. When one hits you differently, stop us."

"Okay." I sit up straighter, ready to figure this out. I try to get in tune with whatever part of me is at my core so I will recognize when one of the things they say is it. The thing I need to know. "Let's do this."

"Guys don't stick around for long," Bex says.

No.

"Love isn't worth the struggle it causes," Addison says.

No.

"Guys don't make you a better person."

No. Jackson totally makes me a better person.

"You aren't attracted to the right guys."

No, because I am attracted to Jackson, and he feels like the right guy.

"Love doesn't last."

Nothing. This isn't heading in the right direction.

"You don't believe relationships can work."

"It's easier to quit than work things out."

"You don't need a guy in your life."

"No," I burst out, frustrated that none of it was right. "It's because my dad left, so I'm afraid to give my heart to a guy." I gasp, my eyes wide as my hands fly over my mouth. I stare in shock at my friends for a long moment as my own words sink in. "It's because of *my dad*? I did not know that!"

Bex and Addison both reach out a hand and hold mine as I work through things out loud. "I didn't know my dad. He was like all of my mom's other boyfriends—there for a bit and then gone. I wasn't born yet when he left. I don't even remember wondering about him much as a kid—I haven't thought about him in ages."

My brow crinkles. "That's really my issue? I didn't know my dad had ever had a part of my heart—let alone that it made me afraid to give it to anyone else for fear they would leave like he did." Somehow, knowing that makes it easier. It makes me realize how illogical it is. And that means I have the ability to set my mind and emotions straight about it.

"Remember when you were setting up your profile for Chat Match," Bex says, "and you told us you didn't know what you wanted in a guy? Maybe that was the reason why you never stopped to figure it out. You were afraid of a relationship getting to the point where it would matter." I'm quiet for a long moment before I say, "I did figure out what I want in a guy, though."

"You did?" Addison asks. "When?"

"When I was sixteen. I'd just forgotten that I had. Before I found out that Jackson was Jack, I had a dream that I was on a date with Jack and we kissed. Oh, stop giving me those looks. Anyway, when I woke up, I thought back to the date I'd dreamed about that Jack and I actually had. We'd been stargazing after an amazing date, and at that moment, I knew I wanted a guy who would care for me and love me just like Jack did. I wanted a life like the one I'd experienced with him that evening." I take a long, slow breath and then bite my lip. "Do you think I overreacted at that charity dinner?"

Bex looks thoughtful. "I've been to a lot of events like that. Most of the people there are great. There are always a few who are exactly like the ones you experienced that night. I wish I could've gone to that one! I would've stuck by your side the whole time and kept all the awful ones away. Knowing what those kinds of people can be like, do I think you overreacted by leaving that night? No, I don't."

I look down.

"Do I think you overreacted about Jackson's part in it? I don't know. Tell us about the other times Jackson has been a jerk."

"Like back when we were in high school?"

"No," Bex says. "From dating him now."

I blink as I scour my memory. "Just that one time."

"Do you think there was something more going on that night?" Addison asks.

"Harper, this guy who already burned Jackson a while ago, did go over and say something to him."

"Any guesses what he said?"

I shake my head. "Right before going to Jackson, Harper was telling me how I wasn't nearly good enough to be there. If he'd gone over and said anything like that to Jackson, though, Jackson probably would've punched him and then come to my rescue."

And I suddenly know to my core that's the kind of man Jackson is. The kind who would come to my rescue, not the kind who would stand by while people poked at my insecurities. I don't know why he did something so out of character that night, but I know that's not who he is. I want to give him a chance to explain.

And I desperately want a chance to fully move past all my own relationship fears and have the life with Jackson that I knew I wanted clear back when I was sixteen.

CHAPTER 22

Jackson

I ALWAYS MARVEL when I'm thinking about someone and then I get a text or an email or a phone call from that person soon after. I've been thinking about Timini nonstop for quite a while now, so maybe it's not the same thing, but I'm about to send her a text to see if we can talk when one comes in from her.

> Timini: I miss you. Do you think we can get together and talk?

Relief whooshes out of me. She's willing. And she misses me. I just stare at the text for a moment, letting the hope it contains wash over me. Then I respond. I want to type yes in all caps, with several exclamation points. And maybe add the heart balloon expanding. But I hold back.

> Jackson: I miss you, too. Any chance you could meet me here tonight at 7:00 at Mocha Falls? It's an outdoor café by my building.

I feel bad asking her to come to me—I should be moving heaven and earth to get to her. But I can't actually move my building, and it's kind of key to my plan. Well, it is if things go okay at Mocha Falls.

———

At ten minutes to seven, I'm sitting with two dark mochas at a small outdoor table right next to an eight-foot-high water feature that mimics Proxy Falls. When I chose a seat, I thought that maybe the water cascading down over moss-covered rocks would calm my nerves, but I still have twitchy muscles and a rolling feeling in my stomach. Hopefully, though, the falls will make Timini smile.

From knowing her, I doubt I'll see her until about seven-fifteen, so I tell my bouncing leg to calm down. But it's barely seven-oh-one when I see her rounding the corner to the open café. She's wearing those jeans and heels again that I love, along with a jacket, which I'm glad about. The night is warm currently, but I'm not sure it will stay that way.

And she's wearing a smile. It's a nervous smile, full of trepidation, but a smile nonetheless. There's not a lot in this world I wouldn't do to see that smile.

I stand and wave, and her eyes immediately fly to me as she walks over.

She glances at the waterfall next to our table, and her mouth twitches like she's fighting a smile. "I see you took my offer to heart to join me when you changed your mind about bodies of water."

I had hoped her mind would immediately go to our conversation through the app about bodies of water and how she prefers them to water falling from the sky. We both sit down, and I say, "Well, I'm not afraid to admit when I'm wrong."

I hadn't even planned to say that and didn't mean for it to

be a segue into what I want to say. Maybe it just came out because it's been on my mind so much.

"I talked to Roman," I say, and her eyes flash to mine. "I hope that was okay. He told me what happened with the Chesworths and Finn McKee. But mostly about what Harper said to you while I was gone."

Hearing from Roman what Harper had said to Timini makes my heart ache for her. "I am so sorry I left you open to that. I wish I never would've gone to talk to Mitch."

She nods but stays quiet.

"But that doesn't explain my part that night. Not that it excuses what I did at all. After Harper poked at your fears and doubts, he came over and poked at mine, too." I let out a humorless laugh. "And, obviously, you handled it about a million times better than I did. I reacted by being the worst kind of jerk at that party. You deserve to have someone who has your back no matter what. Someone who will stand up for you in any situation." I pause for a moment and then add, "And I want to be that guy."

She studies me, and I hold my breath, waiting for her response as a slight breeze blows past us, bringing the scent of coffee from the outdoor café.

Finally, she nods and smiles. "I really want you to, too." Then she reaches forward and takes my hand in hers.

I look down at our hands, marveling at her. "Based on your background and all you've been through, I am baffled at how forgiving you are. I think you might be the most forgiving person I have ever met."

Timini shakes her head. "I'm not, though. I don't do it often. I think that *with my background,* I've learned to really trust my gut and to act based on that. When it comes to forgiveness, well, that's when I've learned to trust it the most. My gut seems to like you." She smiles. "And your family."

I swallow hard, as the understanding of what a gift she's giving me fully hits me. "I want to be the one person in your life who doesn't need your forgiveness. I can't promise I'll never stumble, but that's what I will always be striving for."

Her eyes go back and forth, scanning mine for a long moment. Then she stands, grabs hold of the fabric of both sides of my jacket, and pulls me to my feet. Then she tugs me to her and presses her lips against mine. Her kiss is soft yet fierce, and through it, I can feel that she's missed me and has worried that she was losing me every bit as fully and achingly as I have worried I was losing her.

I wind my fingers in her hair, holding her close, and her grip on my jacket tightens. My body seems to melt, and I move my hands to the sides of her neck and slide them to her shoulders. Then I pull back from the kiss just enough to whisper against her lips, "So, does this mean you want to stay together?"

"Yes, it does."

I smile against her lips and then whisper, "Will you come with me? I want to show you something."

In answer, she tucks her hand into mine, and I lead the way to my building.

CHAPTER 23
Timini

I walk with Jackson, tucking myself into his side and reveling in how great it feels to be with him again as he leads me around the corner to his building.

When I left that charity dinner without Jackson, I thought it was because I couldn't trust him. I studied him intensely as he apologized, and I was blown away by how much I knew, deep in my gut, that I trust him. Probably more than I trust anyone. People make mistakes. I do all the time. Pretty much daily. I can forgive Jackson for making a mistake, especially when he fully owns it and has such a desire to not make the same mistake again. I want him to do the same for me.

And at the top of the list of things I know that I can trust without a doubt is this man's love for me. And mine for him. Even when we were teenagers and had so little experience with relationships, I knew what we had was something special. I'm not saying that we didn't both need to go off and figure ourselves out, but I am very glad that we found our way back to each other after all this time.

And this time, I think we truly understand exactly what we have.

As we walk past the front desk attendant in his building's lobby, the man smiles at us and winks. Then Jackson leads me to the elevator bank. I know that he lives on the twenty-first floor, so I'm surprised when he presses the option for the roof and then slides an access card into the scanner. I give him a questioning look, but he just looks at the digital sign above the doors that shows which floor we're on.

That's okay. I can be patient and wait to see why we're going to the roof.

Or maybe not. Patience isn't exactly my strong suit.

To keep from asking, I focus on the screen that shows the floor numbers we're passing and counting how many ones I see as we ascend. Thirteen of them. That's a lot of ones—that has to be a good sign. And in between glancing at the floor indicator, I distract myself by noticing how amazing Jackson looks in that casual button-down, those jeans, and that jacket. He is just so very handsome.

The elevator doors open to a roof that is very different from the one I've been picturing. Instead of being covered with gravel, it's tiled with big slate tiles. Glass goes up from the edge all the way around, forming a safety barrier between the roof and the ground below, and, I realize, making it look from the ground like the roof area is just another floor. And everything is so clean.

A man wearing a hotel uniform stands ten feet in front of us. When we step off the elevator, he smiles at the two of us, then says to Jackson, "Everything is ready for you."

Jackson thanks the man and shakes his hand, doing the sneakiest job I've ever seen of passing along a tip. The guy gives a curt nod and then also gives Jackson a wink before stepping into the elevator.

Once the doors close, we're alone on the roof. It's a rare cloudless night, and the moon and a few of the brightest stars shine above us.

"What do you think?" Jackson asks, and I manage to pull my gaze away from the beautiful man in front of me to look out over the city.

The view is incredible. All the lights from a city with over half a million residents shine around us in every direction. It's breathtaking.

He grabs hold of both of my hands and says, "I read back through our messages in Chat Match from the beginning, back before I knew you were you and you knew I was me. And I realized that when we were both talking about our favorite dates, we were talking about the same date. The one we went on at the end of your sophomore and my junior year. Since it was a date we both loved, I thought maybe we could do something similar tonight. With a few modifications."

My pulse races, and there's a lightness in my chest that makes me feel like I'm floating. Although part of that could come from being on, essentially, the twenty-ninth floor.

He reaches his hands up to my shoulders and turns me in a direction I haven't looked yet. A blanket is spread out on the tile, a picnic basket on it, and a tall lamp spills golden light down onto the blanket. A large outdoor movie screen is set up, too, along with a projector. Jackson walks over to the blanket as he talks. "The 'day date' part of that date we had for the dance —the photo scavenger hunt—didn't really fit into the plan, especially since it isn't exactly 'day' right now. So that means dinner is first."

He sits down on the blanket, and I sit beside him. It's fluffier than I expected. He must've put some kind of padding under the blanket to make the tile floor feel more like soft grass.

"When I asked you in a message what your favorite foods

were," he says, pulling container after container from the basket, "you mentioned quite a few."

"Oh my goodness," I say, putting a hand over my mouth. "Did you really get them all?"

Jackson grins. "I've got Mexican, Thai, Chinese, pizza, Italian, and"—he pulls one last container out of the basket—"cheesecake."

"*Without* almond extract?" I ask.

He chuckles. "I even double-checked. And don't worry—I didn't get full meals at any one place."

We each eat a taco from Taco Sabroso, some red curry, an egg roll, a mini pizza, and some ravioli. And in between them all, bites of cheesecake.

"So," Jackson says as he finishes a bite of curry, "if the combination of a carnitas taco, an al pastor taco, and a fish taco give superpowers, do you think a carnitas taco combined with this many types of food will grant us anything?"

I savor a bite of cheesecake as I consider the combo. Then I nod. "It'll definitely grant us a superpower. Possibly accidental time travel. Or we might start glowing."

"Or the ability to speak squirrel."

"Or to find the perfect parking spot anywhere in Portland. Or maybe levitation."

"So, what you're saying is, if my feet leave the ground, I shouldn't panic."

I smile. "That's not from the food. The feeling of soaring is just from being with me."

Jackson laughs, and I soak in the joyful sound. It's just so good to talk with him. To be near him. To spend time with him. To eat a meal with him. To know that there will be more of this in my future.

Just like the date we went on in high school, we go to "the dance" after dinner. Instead of being in the high school gym, though, it's on a rooftop overlooking the Portland skyline. And, just like at our high school dance, we dance to *All of Me* by John Legend, *A Thousand Years* by Christina Perri, and *I Won't Give Up* by Jason Mraz.

For each of the three songs, I relish being in Jackson's arms as we dance even more than we did back in high school. He's different now. I'm different. Both things make our relationship even better. Stronger. I look up at him. "Please tell me we will do this often."

"Every night, if you'd like."

Once the third song ends, Jackson pulls back a bit. The grin on his face is so wide it makes me smile, too.

"Okay, during that date, the movie was next. You told me once that you loved Hallmark movies, so I did a lot of Googling to find the one that people liked more than any other. I figure that we could watch that one."

"Be still my heart," I say, putting a hand over my heart. "Did I really find a man who will watch Hallmark movies with me?"

"You did. But, I propose we do things out of order tonight and go straight to stargazing first." He takes my hand and leads me to the glass wall that surrounds the roof. "You might have noticed, though, that, unobstructed view or not, downtown Portland isn't exactly the best place to stargaze. So we are going to have to light gaze instead."

The glass wall rises almost to my shoulders, and I rest my elbows on the top of it, looking out over the lights of the city. It really is incredibly beautiful and mesmerizing.

After several minutes of "light gazing," Jackson turns toward me, a more serious expression on his face. "Timini, I really want you in my life."

"Oh, thank heavens. Because this was going to get awkward really quickly if you didn't."

Jackson chuckles. "I promise to be *by* your side and to always be *on* your side. Even still, I know that if you are in my life, it would often put you in an environment that you wouldn't necessarily appreciate. Would you be okay with that?"

"Well, you've seen the state of the round tables in the dining room at the inn. I figure if you are in my life, you will just as often be subjected to environments you don't necessarily appreciate, either. If you can handle it, I can, too."

He brushes his knuckles along my jawline, sending shivers across my neck and back. "You are one incredible human, you know that?"

"I'm pretty sure that's why you love me." It's a bold response, but I'm feeling bold tonight.

"That, and a lot of other reasons."

"Oh, yeah? Tell me more about these reasons."

"I am pretty sure I love everything about you. Your kindness. Your willingness to try new things. Your strength. Your creativity. Your ability to find a solution to anything. Your ability to not feel guilty about being late."

I playfully smack him on the arm. He chuckles and says, "The way you keep me from sticking so strictly to a schedule and being inflexible. I love that you stay up late, that your preferred outside temperature resembles an oven, and that you see the beauty in a messy bed."

"You do not love those things about me."

"Oh, now, see? That's where you're wrong. I love them all because they're all part of you. And I love all of you."

"Okay. Then I'll say that I love your morning routine. That you eat cereal and watch cartoons, wake up early, like the freezing rain, look out for others, look out for me, volunteer so much, and are pretty much to die for in a suit."

The corner of his mouth twitches up in a smile.

"Oh, and I can't forget your ears. You do actually have really great ears."

He laughs a loud, happy laugh.

"Which is great, because here I thought it was just one of those things a guy would say in a dating profile that wasn't true. So I'm feeling pretty lucky that it turned out to be one hundred percent real."

He gives me a look then, so pure and genuine and sweet, and I want to put my hands on his face just to feel it, too. But before I get the chance, he drops to one knee, and my hands fly to my mouth.

"Timini. I want nothing more than to have you in my life always. Please say you'll marry me, and I'll promise to always have your back, no matter what, in everything that you do. And I'll make sure your car always has gas in it. And I'll bring you cookies from that restaurant on Belmont every time you're doing bills or business accounting. And I'll bring you the magical trio of tacos from Taco Sabroso every time you have a deadline. And I'll love you more every day forever and ever, and I'll never stop doing everything I can to show that to you."

I'm laughing and crying so much I can barely breathe or see. I wipe the tears from my eyes, then pull Jackson to standing, take his face in my hands, and kiss him. "Yes," I say, and kiss him again. "Yes, I will." I kiss him again. "Of course, I will marry you." I kiss him some more. "Yes, yes, yes."

And then I give up talking and kiss him until I'm breathless.

Epilogue

MEERA

I HOLD Bex's phone up to where it shows my face at a flattering angle instead of at the double-chin angle that so many people my age use, and then I press the record button. Then I say, "Hello, Bexlandians! I don't know about you, but I am thrilled that Bex let me take over the camera to film a Hidden Inn Roomies Segment for her show and to give you one final update. I am here with my own roomies, Shirley and Carol."

Shirley and Carol both crowd into the frame and wave.

"These two oldie-locks and I have been friends longer than most of you whipper-snappers have even been alive. But I'm here to update you about Addison, Bex, Peyton, and Timini, not us."

"No," Carol says, "you've got to press that button to flip the screen."

"Oh, get your hands off. I know which thing to press." I tap the correct button, and the screen shows everything else, so the three of us make our way through the maze of boxes in the kitchen where Addison, Bex, Peyton, and Timini are all talking as they stand at the kitchen island, eating veggies and dip.

"This room is feeling so vacant and echo-y right now. And can you even believe it took this many boxes to pack up this room? Actually, I think it was even more because some have been hauled out already.

"Anyway, the update! Let's start with Timini because tomorrow is her big day! Yep, folks, you heard it right—the last of these gals to break the 'No falling in love' pact they all made when they first moved in is getting married tomorrow!"

Addison, Bex, and Peyton all cheer and scream, and Timini smiles widely.

"Look at her face glow. I hope you can see it through the camera. Tell us all about it, Timini."

Timini sighs. "Jackson is just the most amazing guy ever. And we're getting married! I still can't believe it's true. And oh my goodness, y'all, he is tears-in-your-eyes beautiful in a suit. And tomorrow he'll be in *a tux*. Which I know will bring tears to everyone's eyes. I'm sorry you can't all be there to witness it. You'll just have to take my word for it that there will not be a dry eye in the place just from looking at him."

I flip the camera so it's back on me. "I am going to second that statement. Not that I've seen Jackson in a tux. Or a suit, really. But I've seen him in a dress shirt and slacks and I had to pretend that I got dust in my eye. Tell us about the wedding." I flip the camera back to Timini.

"Okay," Timini says. "Well, Jackson and I grew up in very different worlds. I mean, we went to the same high school and all, but still very different. Our engagement was probably twice as long as my family thought it should be, but only about half as long as his family thought it should be. In the end, we chose the date that was how long *we* thought it should be.

"Well, actually, I would've married him soon after he proposed, so I guess the date we chose was kind of a compromise, too. Which is what marriage is all about, right? So it seemed fitting. And because we've only been engaged for four months, it limited where we could have it, which actually worked out well, because it meant we couldn't have it at any pretentious venues. I mean, don't get me wrong, the place is still crazy nice and all the guests are going to love it. And Jackson and I do, too. But it won't be an uncomfortably nice place, you know?"

"And where are the two of you going to live?" I ask. You know, I really should be a professional interviewer. I'll have to ask Bex if I can get into something like that at age seventy-two.

Timini's smile widens. "At his apartment in downtown Portland. Mostly because it's so very pretty! I mean, it comes in second to the man himself, but it's nice. And it has floor-to-ceiling windows overlooking Portland. Plus, it's where he's lived while we've been falling in love, so..." Timini lifts a shoulder in a shrug, her cheeks reddening. It's so cute, and I'm pretty sure the viewers at home will be able to see that just fine.

"And after the wedding tomorrow, they're going to soar off to their honeymoon! In Italy, right?"

Timini grins. "I've always wanted to go there."

"Okay, Bex! You're up. Bex and Roman have been living here while their house was being built, and it took quite a bit longer than they thought it would, didn't it?"

"If you've watched my other videos, then you've probably heard some of the story. Basically, everything went wrong every step of the way, but now everything is right. It's just three months later than we thought it would be. But the house is perfect. So perfect. We had the final walk-through and closed on it just a little over a week ago. Roman and I have both had crazy busy work weeks, so we've just been moving things over slowly. The day after Timini's wedding, though, we plan to move everything else in and then happy dance for a good week straight."

I turn to Peyton. "Peyton, your home-buying experience hasn't quite been the same, has it?"

Peyton giggles. "No, thank the stars. We found the cutest little house ever! And I'm not even joking, it has a white picket fence out front. It's right here in Quicksand, and the backyard butts up to the woods. So someday when we have little kids, Max will practically be able to take them camping in our own backyard. And the inside of the house is adorable."

"And when did you close on the house?" I already know the answer, but I think Bex's listeners might get a kick out of Peyton's answer.

"Six weeks ago. We tried to have the closing day later, but the people selling it had to move for work and couldn't wait any longer."

"But you haven't moved in yet?"

Peyton shakes her head. "Why in the world would we move when everyone else is still living here? We didn't want to miss out on this kind of fun!"

I chuckle and aim the camera at Shirley, who is just shaking her head.

"Okay, Addison. You're up. So, you've got your three best friends and their husbands—or in Timini's case, very soon-to-be husband—moving out within the next few days. What are your plans?" I am so excited just asking the question that I can barely get it all out.

"Well," Addison says, "Ian owns the house next door."

I turn the camera back to myself. "That would be the house that me, Shirley, and Carol live in, for those of you following along at home." Then I switch it back to Addison.

"Ian and I decided that we would like to start a family in the next year or so, so we chose to move into his house."

I switch the camera back to myself. "And that means that the oldie-locks are moving into Hidden Inn!"

I press the phone into Bex's hands, and Bex aims the camera at me, Shirley, and Carol as we dance like music is playing and everyone is watching. Which is pretty much the same as dancing like no one is watching only with more gusto. We dance in place and move and jive and even do a TikTok dance that my granddaughter taught me once.

"Did you hear that, folks?" Carol says. "It's going to be out with the new and in with the old!"

"What do you think, ladies?" I say to Carol and Shirley. "Should we make our own pact to not fall in love, just like these ladies did? You saw what it did for them."

Shirley does a dance move that looks like she's stomping on invisible bugs. "I say we do it! I'm single and ready to get nervous around anyone I find attractive."

I nod. "Aren't we all. Addison, there's one thing you and Ian are going to need to know before we become neighbors again by switching homes. You're going to be hearing a lot of loud music at all times of the night because we are going to be partying it up over here!"

Carol nods. "Very loud music. Our hearing isn't what it used to be, you know."

Bex laughs loudly and turns the camera back on herself. "And there's your update, Bexlandians! Wish the soon-to-be new residents of Hidden Inn the best of luck in the comments. While you're at it, you might want to wish Addison and Ian the best of luck living next to such noisy neighbors. And give the biggest congratulations to Timini and Jackson! Remember to like this video and tap the subscribe button. Until next time, goodbye from all of us!" She pans the camera around to all of us and then shuts it off.

"Aww, you guys," Timini says. "I can't believe this is our last night with all of us together!"

"Don't," Peyton says. "You're going to make me cry again."

Addison motions for her roommates to come in for a hug. "I just want to soak in every last minute we have together." She wraps her arms around Timini, Peyton, and Bex. "There are great things on the horizon for all of us, and being here together made so much of it happen. I love you, ladies."

There is a chorus of "Aww, I love you, too!" coming from all of them.

"Make room," Carol says. "We want in on this hug."

I squish in with my roomies, and I wrap my arms around everyone I can reach in our seven-person hug and squeeze tightly. It isn't going to be the same without them all living here. Which, as far as I'm concerned, means that we are going to have to have game nights frequently and invite them all.

"I think we need to do one last dance party," Timini says. "With music."

"On it," Bex says, tapping her phone.

Within moments, music sounds through the Inn's speakers, and all seven of us are dancing around the half-dozen round tables in the dining room, giving them a send-off to remember.

———

Author's Note:

I hope you enjoyed this final book in the *How to Not Fall* Series! If you have read all four books, you've read the epilogues for each of the four couples. Even after I finished writing this final epilogue, though, I still couldn't stop thinking about these characters and where their lives led them after Timini and Jackson's wedding. They are a hard group of people to let go of!

I decided to write a series epilogue that takes place one year after the series finishes, and Addison, Bex, Peyton, and Timini each get to narrate a chapter in this scene with all of them present. (With plenty of commentary from the grandmas next door!)

If you'd like to join my VIP newsletter subscribers, you can get the *How to Not Fall Series Epilogue* FREE.

—Meg

Get your copy

Romancing the Spy

WANT TO READ MORE OF MEG'S ROMANTIC COMEDIES?

Need more adventure and humor in your life?

In a family where the spy business is the family business, falling in love is the real mission impossible. Follow the six Lancaster siblings—each uniquely trained, fiercely loyal, and more than a bit protective—as they navigate top-secret missions, unexpected romance, laugh-out-loud situations, witty banter, an abundance of chemistry, and lots of adventure.

Spies Don't Fall for Their Asset
Spies Don't Fall for Their Rival
Spies Don't Fall for Their Neighbor

Meg Easton is the *USA Today* bestselling author of contemporary romances and romantic comedies with fun, memorable, swoon-worthy characters, and settings you'll want to pack up and move to. She lives at the foot of a mountain with her name on it (or at least one letter of her name) in Utah. She loves gardening, bike riding, baking, swimming before the sun rises, and spending time with her husband and three kids.

She can be found online at www.megeaston.com

Sign up to receive her newsletter and stay up to date with new releases, get exclusive bonus content, and more.

If you liked this book please leave a review. Your review can help other readers find books they might fall in love with.

youtube.com/@megeastonauthor
bookbub.com/authors/meg-easton
instagram.com/megeaston_author
facebook.com/MegEastonBooks
tiktok.com/@megeaston_author

www.ingramcontent.com/pod-product-compliance
Lightning Source LLC
Chambersburg PA
CBHW061528190726
48289CB00004B/962